NINETOES 2

REAPER'S SORROW

TIM ANDREWS

Published by Level Up in the United Kingdom in 2022

Cover illustration by Sippakorn Upama
Cover by Claire Wood

ISBN: 978-1-83919-395-8

www.levelup.pub

Without my wife, I'd never have had the courage to write this book and so to her I am eternally grateful. Without my daughter, I wouldn't be the story teller I've become. And without my friends, I wouldn't have created the world of Adrenon. This is for all of you.

PRoLoGUE

Arthur unlocked his front door and stepped in from the damp and grey weather. It was 10:30 and he'd already been to uni, suffering through one of Wilkins' lectures. Jesus wept but the man could go on! Worse still he only ever had morning lectures; 8:30 in the morning! Seriously, what was the world coming to? Arthur had only gone to uni to avoid working for a few more years. And to shut up his bell-end father of course.

Well, he was home now and just in time for his mid-morning cereal. He'd saved the last of the coco pops from the variety pack for a special treat. After that, he'd have a nice cup of tea and, if he was still hungry, some toast. Then maybe, just maybe he'd feel up to working on his dissertation.

He was right. The special chocolatey milk only found in a bowl of coco pops, had sorted him out and now he felt ready to start doing some work. As he passed through the lounge with his tea and toast he noticed Jack, one of his housemates and cringed. He hated the pillock.

Climbing to the attic bedroom of his shared house, Arthur closed the door with his bottom and settled to his desk. A stack of books was waiting to be read for his dissertation, 'Fantasy novels of the 20th century: A retreat from modern life?' but lying next to them was Arthur's notebook.

He tried, he really did, to pick up a textbook, but, he reasoned, there were still two days left due until the deadline, so it couldn't hurt to spend a little time making some notes.

Arthur's father had given him an ultimatum, go to university and get a degree first or take his place in the family firm as soon as he finished 6th

Form. He'd been a tosser like that ever since Arthur's mum had died. Always berating him for reading too much and not having any friends. Arthur didn't see the problem. Most of the kids at school were twats. They never left him be, calling him minger, throwing food at him or laughing at his briefcase. Why, on earth, would he want to spend any more time with them?

He supposed his dad had been alright once, in fact he'd bought Arthur his copy of the Lord of the Rings. But, after mum had died, dad had thrown himself into work. By the time he was 11 Arthur could use the hob and would make his own dinner. His father seemed to live off of crackers, cheese and scotch and not a night had gone by where he didn't fall asleep in front of the TV. Arthur simply learned to avoid him and so avoid his temper.

For Arthur, going to uni was a relief... for both of them really. A cheque arrived once a month in an envelope addressed by his father's secretary, Mrs Goggins. Apart from that the old fool could be dead.

As a child, Arthur had loved going into his father's office. Mrs Goggins, who Arthur was always sure had been the inspiration for the elderly postmistress, always had a bowl of boiled sweets on her desk. When Arthur first came to uni, Mrs Goggins would slip a couple of sweets into the envelope, but when his father had commented to her at the staff Christmas party that Arthur was getting "tubby" she'd stopped.

Well, his dad could go fuck himself if he thought Arthur was going anywhere near those bloody offices. He'd get a job as far away as possible, like Portsmouth or Reading, that'd piss off the old man.

He did still have the same copy of the Lord of the Rings of course. The spine so cracked and creased from where he'd read it so many times. That was when he'd first fallen in love with fantasy and where he'd drawn his first ideas for his own world. Or, at least he thought he did.

He'd woken up one night during 6th Form covered in sweat, which was a unique experience for someone who considered wanking exercise, bursting with ideas. He'd grabbed the first thing to hand and started writing. Since then he'd filled half a dozen exercise books with notes, details, pictures and maps. His imagination never seemed to leave him alone.

Opening his notebook to where he'd left off yesterday night, he read through his last few notes. He'd had an idea for a city within his world. It was called Ffestyn and it was a city of men, halflings and orcs. The men ruled, keeping the orcs as slaves and using the halflings as traders and artisans. He'd had the most vivid of dreams the night before and wanted to add in some details for a character he'd invented, a villain perhaps, called Xavier Clemons. As he wrote, time seemed to pass by like his childhood had; in a confusing blur of actions and reactions.

His stomach grumbled and, looking at his clock, he realised it was early evening. He decided to stick a pizza in the oven and then watch some tellie. While he waited for the pizza to cook, he let his mind wander to thoughts of Adrenon, the world of his creation. He could see the ancient walls of Ffestyn, hear the seagulls drifting on the warm breeze off of the Sweetsea and feel its waves lapping at his feet. Reaching down he cupped some water and drank it down, sure enough it tasted of sugar. Looking along the beach he could see a beautiful maiden, cooling her feet in the surf while collecting sea shells.

Looking up she notices him. Her face takes on a look of confusion, "From where do you hail, to be wearing such strange garments?"

Looking down, Arthur noted that the same Transformers t-shirt was stretched over the curve of his belly. *Nice one imagination!* He thought. Even in my dreams I'm a fat bastard!

Looking up into her eyes "Hail lady, my name is…"

BEEP, BEEP, BEEP, BEEP, BEEP!

Shaken out of his daydreaming Arthur coughed through black smoke and he grabbed a tea towel and opened the oven. His pizza was now a black charcoaled mess.

"What the fuck Forsythe? Can't you even make pizza without burning the fucking house down?" Jack came bustling into the kitchen. Although not out of any concern for him, Arthur reasoned

7

Arthur cringed. "Sorry Jack, I'll clear it up."

"You'd fucking better! I'm sick of this fucking shit!" he raged.

"Calm down Jack, it was an accident, wasn't it Arthur?" His saviour had arrived, as she always did. Arthur had met Beth on his first day and at the end of the first year they'd moved into a house with Jack and Dave. She was, in Arthur's mind, perfect. Like him, she studied Literature. She'd read all of Tolkien's books and loads of other greats. And, she was so pretty.

"Every day it's something else," Jack continued. He was, in Arthur's humble opinion, a wanker. He studied Colouring-In, or Geography as he called it, and was in the running club, so clearly, he was a Neanderthal.

"If his dad didn't pay double rent we'd never have let him move in with us." Arthur recognised that Jack was working himself up into a fall on meltdown. He seemed to enjoy getting worked up, especially with Arthur.

"That's enough Jack. He made a mistake and he's cleaning it up, so there's no need to be a dick about it. Miami Vice is about to start, so why don't you go watch that and I'll put the kettle on while Arthur clears up?" said Beth as she opened the backdoor and wafted smoke out with a tea towel. She was always doing stuff like this for Arthur, although he had no idea why. Every day something Arthur did something to piss Jack off and yet every day Beth came to his rescue.

"What was it this time Arthur? Day dreaming about Adrenon? Or picturing today's page three model?" said Beth, grinning as she filled the kettle from the sink.

"Adrenon again. It's so real, I feel like I'm there." Arthur responded, almost pleading with her to believe him.

"I assume you still haven't finished your dissertation?" She gave him her older sister-tone. He hated this tone even more than getting shouted at by Jack. He didn't want her to be his sister, he wanted her to... well, not to be his sister anyway.

"No but I've got everything I need, just gotta settle down to it. I'll make some beans on toast and then I'll go and get out of everyone's hair.

I'll finish it tonight, I promise," he said placatingly. It was so important to him that she didn't think he was a complete fuck up.

"Look, between you and me, I think Miami Vice is for nobheads. So why don't I come upstairs and help you finish?" Arthur nearly turned her down but then she gave him that smile and he said,

"That'd be great, thanks."

CHAPTER 1
QUESTIONS

RAVESLAN, SWEETSEA REGION, 2301 AC

Somewhere far away, but also just next door, was another world. One connected and, in some ways, beholden to our own. In this world of fantasy, a hobgoblin wizard sits and ponders: *What the fuck?*

***

Ninetoes stared aghast at his character sheet. Confusion was flooding his system and for a time, he simply sat with his mouth agape. When his faculties returned, he scanned through the document more closely, looking firstly for what had changed, hoping that he'd find answers.

CHARACTER NAME: NINETOES	RACE: HOBGOBLIN (+1 END, +1 INT)
LEVEL: 12TH	EXPERIENCE POINTS: 75,565/88,000
CLASS: WIZARD	SPECIALISM: NECROMANCER
HIT POINTS: 252/252	MANA POINTS: 380/380
STAMINA POINTS: 190/190	

BASE STATS:	VARIED STATS:
STRENGTH - 15 (9)	
AGILITY - 19 (16)	FITNESS - 21
ENDURANCE - 25	
INTELLIGENCE - 38 (33)	WILL - 24
WISDOM - 18	
CHARISMA - 12 (7)	

LANGUAGES:	ARMOUR CLASS: ARMOUR 17+ WIZARD ARMOUR 10.
COMMON - FLUENT	
GOBLINOID - NATIVE	TOTAL: 27
ARCANE - POOR	
KAVRALARIAN - FLUENT	

SKILLS

BASIC FIRST AID: LEVEL 5 - BEGINNER CAN USE BASIC BANDAGES AND SIMPLE OINTMENTS TO HEAL MINOR WOUNDS.	ONE-HANDED BLADES: LEVEL 13 - POOR +13% DAMAGE. +13% CHANCE OF CRITICAL HIT. FIGHTING STANCE - YOUR FOOTWORK IS NOW MORE EFFICIENT, ALLOWING YOU TO SWING WITH MORE POWER, INCREASING DAMAGE BY 5%.
TRAP BUILDING: LEVEL 4 - BEGINNER CAN USE MUNDANE ITEMS TO CREATE POOR QUALITY TRAPS.	SNEAK AND HIDE: LEVEL 7 - BEGINNER +14% CHANCE OF SUCCESS TO ATTEMPTS AT CONCEALING YOURSELF.
LONGBOW: LEVEL 13 - POOR +13% DAMAGE. +13% CHANCE OF CRITICAL HIT.	LIGHT ARMOUR: LEVEL 12 - POOR 12% DAMAGE REDUCTION WHILE WEARING LIGHT ARMOUR.

QUICK SHOT - CAN FIRE AT TWICE THE SPEED, LOSING 50% ACCURACY.	
MEDIUM ARMOUR: LEVEL 13 - POOR 3% DAMAGE REDUCTION WHILE WEARING MEDIUM ARMOUR.	ARCANA: LEVEL 10 - POOR CAN UNDERSTAND BASIC AND DEVELOPED SPELL CONCEPTS AND LANGUAGE
CHANNELLING: LEVEL 13 - POOR CAN CHANNEL 12 MANA POINTS INTO OR OUT OF AN OBJECT, SPELL OR CREATURE PER SECOND	SKINNING & BUTCHERING: LEVEL 3 - BEGINNER +3% CHANCE TO DISCOVER AN ITEM/COMPONENT/INGREDIENT/MATERIAL OF ONE LEVEL OF RARITY ABOVE THE CREATURE'S BASE LEVEL.
RITUAL CASTING: LEVEL 2 - BEGINNER -2% COST OF MANA REQUIRED TO CAST A RITUAL SPELL.	
SPELL SCHOOLS	
EVOCATION - LEVEL 8 BEGINNER +8% DAMAGE FOR EVOCATION SPELLS	CONJURATION - LEVEL 4 BEGINNER -4% CASTING TIME FOR CONJURATION SPELLS
TRANSMUTATION - LEVEL 4 BEGINNER +4% DURATION FOR TRANSMUTATION SPELLS	DIVINATION - LEVEL 5 BEGINNER -5% TIME FOR DIVINATION CASTING TIMES.

ABJURATION - LEVEL 8 BEGINNER +8% DURATION FOR ABJURATION SPELLS	ILLUSION - LEVEL 5 BEGINNER +5 DURATION OF ILLUSION SPELLS
ENCHANTMENT - LEVEL 2 BEGINNER +2 DURATION OF ENCHANTMENT SPELLS	NECROMANCY- LEVEL 41 PRACTITIONER +50% POTENCY OF NECROMANCY SPELLS DEATH'S TOUCH I - YOUR FAMILIARITY WITH THE ENERGY OF UNLIFE HAS GIVEN YOU +10% RESISTANCE TO NECROTIC DAMAGE. KNOWLEDGE ARCANE I - ALLOWS THE CASTER TO CHOOSE ONE APPRENTICE RANKED SPELL. NECROMANCY SAVANT I - NECROMANCY SPELLS COST YOU 25% LESS TO CAST. CONTROL UNDEAD - DOUBLES THE NUMBER OF UNDEAD THE CASTER CAN CONTROL.
SPELLS	
BURNING HANDS - LEVEL 4 EVOCATION CASTING TIME - INSTANTANEOUS MANA COST - 30 POINTS DURATION - CHANNELLING LVL 1. SHOOTS A 10FT CONE OF FIRE, DEALING 5 POINTS OF FIRE DAMAGE PER SECOND.	FIND FAMILIAR - LEVEL 10 CONJURATION CASTING TIME - ONE MINUTE MANA COST - 80 POINTS DURATION - CONSTANT RANGE - BOUNDLESS LVL 1. CONJURES A SPIRIT FAMILIAR, BONDED TO THE CASTER THROUGH AN EMPATHIC LINK. LVL 3. ALLOWS THE CASTER TO EXPEND THEIR OWN ENDURANCE POINTS TO ENHANCE THEIR FAMILIAR'S.

LVL 4. INCREASES TO A 15 FT CONE.	LVL 4. LINK WITH BONDED CREATURE CAN NOW ALLOW SIMPLE IMAGES TO BE COMMUNICATED. LVL 5. ENHANCED BOND - SEE FAMILIAR STATS.
MENDING - LEVEL 3 TRANSMUTATION CASTING TIME - 15 SECONDS MANA COST - 5 POINTS LVL 1. REPAIRS MINOR, NON-MAGICAL DAMAGE OR SHARPENS NON-MAGICAL ITEMS. LVL 2. ALLOWS CASTER TO REPAIR/SHARPEN TWO SIMILAR ITEMS WITHIN THE DURATION OF THE CASTING.	SHOCKING STRIKE - LEVEL 6 EVOCATION CASTING TIME - 2 SECONDS MANA COST - 5 POINTS DURATION - 5 SECONDS OR UNTIL USED LVL 1. DEALS 4-7 POINTS OF LIGHTNING DAMAGE LVL 2. 5% CHANCE OF STUNNING A TARGET FOR 5-10 SECONDS. LVL 5. DAMAGE INCREASE TO 6-12 POINTS OF LIGHTNING DAMAGE.
ARCANE BOLT - LEVEL 6 EVOCATION CASTING TIME - 1 SECOND MANA COST - 25 POINTS DURATION - INSTANTANEOUS LVL 1. SHOOTS A BOLT OF MAGICAL FORCE UP TO 100FT. DEALING 5-30 POINTS OF FORCE DAMAGE LVL 4. INCREASES RANGE TO 120 FT.	WIZARD ARMOUR - LEVEL 5 ABJURATION CASTING TIME - 1 MINUTE MANA COST - 20 POINTS DURATION - 5 HOURS LVL 1. REDUCES 10% OF MUNDANE DAMAGE RECEIVED. LVL 3. ALLOWS CASTER TO INCREASE DAMAGE REDUCTION BY CHANNELLING MORE MANA INTO THE ARMOUR. DAMAGE WILL THEN DRAIN MANA POINTS, INSTEAD OF HIT POINTS.
MINOR ILLUSION - LEVEL 5	CHARISMA - LEVEL 1 ENCHANTMENT

ILLUSION CASTING TIME - 10 SECONDS MANA COST - 25 POINTS DURATION - CONCENTRATION LVL 1. CREATES AN ILLUSORY OBJECT OF THE CASTERS DESIGN. CAN BE NO LARGER THAN 1 FOOT BY 1 FOOT BY 1 FOOT. LVL 5. INCREASES SIZE OF ILLUSION TO 5 FOOT BY FIVE FOOT BY FIVE FOOT.	CASTING TIME - 1 MINUTE MANA COST - 75 POINTS DURATION - 1 MINUTE LVL 1. MAKES YOU MORE APPEALING TO PEOPLE, MAKING THEM MORE FRIENDLY TOWARDS YOU.
IDENTIFY - LEVEL 6 DIVINATION CASTING TIME - 1 SECOND MANA COST - 10 POINTS DURATION - CONCENTRATION LVL 1. IDENTIFIES ANY SIMPLE OR UNCOMMON OBJECTS OR CREATURES OR THE UNCOMMON PROPERTIES OF AN OBJECT. LVL 6. IDENTIFIED RARE OBJECTS OR CREATURES OR THE RARE PROPERTIES OF AN OBJECT.	COMPREHEND LANGUAGES - LEVEL 3 DIVINATION CASTING TIME - INSTANT MANA COST - 20 POINTS DURATION - 1 HOUR LVL 1. EACH CASTING ALLOWS YOU TO READ AND UNDERSTAND ONE UNKNOWN LANGUAGE.
GRIM VOID - LEVEL 41 NECROMANCY	ARCANE STEP - LEVEL 5 CONJURATION CASTING TIME - 1 SECOND

CASTING TIME - 1 SECOND MANA COST - 50 POINTS DURATION - CONCENTRATION LVL 1. ALLOWS CASTER TO DRAIN THE LIFE FORCE FROM ONE CREATURE OR VEGETATION THAT IT TOUCHES AT A RATE OF 3 HP PER SECOND. LVL 4. INCREASES RATE OF DRAIN TO 6 HP PER SECOND. LVL 11. ALLOWS THE CASTER TO CHANNEL HEALING ENERGY INTO ANOTHER CREATURE AT A RATE OF 1:4 OF HP GAINED. REQUIRES TOUCH. LVL 18. INCREASES RATE OF DRAIN TO 12 HP PER SECOND. LVL 26. INCREASES RATE OF DRAIN TO 24 HP PER SECOND. LVL 36. GIVES THE CASTER A 5% CHANCE TO ABSORB KNOWLEDGE FROM THE HOST.	MANA COST - 60 POINTS DURATION - INSTANTANEOUS LVL 1. ALLOWS CASTER TO TELEPORT TO A LOCATION THEY CAN SEE WITHIN 50. LVL 4. CASTER CAN CARRY ADDITIONAL CREATURES OF A SIMILAR SIZE AT AN ADDED COST OF 240 MANA PER CREATURE.
BARRIER - LEVEL 4 ABJURATION CASTING TIME - 1 SECOND	CLOAKING SHADOW - LEVEL 4 ILLUSION CASTING TIME - 1 MINUTE MANA COST - 100 POINTS

Mana Cost - 50 points Duration - 5 seconds Lvl 1. Creates a magical shield that absorbs 100 points of ranged damage.	Duration - 1 hour Lvl 1. Cloaks the target in shadows, making them more difficult to detect, increases Sneak and Hide skill by a factor of 2.
Force Wave - Level 10 (Item) Evocation Casting time - 1 second Duration - Instantaneous Lvl 10. Creates a 15-foot radius wave of force that shoots out in 360 degrees from the caster. Deals 6-30 points of force damage of anything caught within the area of effect.	Create Undead - Level 21 Necromancy Casting time - 1 minute Mana Cost - 50 points per level of creature Duration - Until dispelled or the undead is destroyed. Lvl 1. Allows the caster to reanimate and control one corpse into an unintelligent undead. Lvl 3. Allows the caster to reassert control over up to two unintelligent undead. Lvl 9. Allows the caster to reanimate and control five corpses into unintelligent undead. Or to reassert control over four. Lvl 20. Allows the caster to reanimate and control ten unintelligent or one intelligent undead. Or to reassert control over sixteen.
Reaper's Sorrow - Level 15 Necromancy Casting time - 1 minute	

Mana Cost - 250 points Duration - 24 hours Lvl 1. Once cast, if the recipient of this spell is reduced to 0 HP, the spell triggers and saves them from death and restores a number of hit points equal to the caster's level of skill with the spell.	
Ritual Spells	
Dispel Magic Abjuration Casting time - 1 minute Mana Cost - Variable Duration - Instantaneous Allows the caster to cancel active magical effects within an object or creature.	Faseer Conjuration Casting time - Ten minutes Mana Cost - 150 points Duration - Concentration Allows the caster to control a floating eye. The caster can see through the eye as though it were their own but is blind to their own surroundings. The caster can also control the movement of the eye which moves at 5 foot per second in any direction.

Unspent ability points - 10, Unspent skill points - 17.

He really needed to work out what in the Nine Hells had happened and make a plan for what to do next. His body and mind were frazzled and he still sat on the roof of an ancient keep.

His Character Sheet had undergone a massive upgrade. The first and most obvious thing that he noted was his level; Level 12! How on Adrenon had he jumped six levels? He knew Bofar has been powerful, but to earn enough experience points to jump so high? Surely Bofar couldn't have been that powerful.

The question was so confusing because of a little piece of information that Ninetoes' mentor, Foresto, had shared during their training. At the time, he'd been blasting Ninetoes with a constant stream of pressurized water, forcing the hobgoblin to maintain his Wizard Armour while under attack. This seemed to be the wicked little creature's favourite method of tuition actually.

He'd explained something that few but the most learned understood, spelling out why it was so difficult to gain enough experience to become truly powerful.

He explained that the necessary experience needed each level was significantly more than the previous, almost double in most cases and that most people never gained more than a few levels as they never did anything particularly dangerous or out of the ordinary, like fighting monsters or discovering lost cities.

There was such an abundance of Adventurers, who so willingly threw themselves into such life or death situations, that there was never really a need for other folk to do so. Occasionally a person would have the means or interest to travel and so gain some experience, but even most of them never went beyond level 6 or 7.

Reaching level 10, he'd explained, required a cumulative experience gain of nearly twenty thousand experience points and the next level was nearly doubled again. What made this even worse, was that the greatest gains of experience came from fighting the most dangerous of monsters which was, in Foresto's opinion, just plain stupid. The old gnome had admitted that he was nearly two hundred years old and was just nearly level 11, which meant, in terms of raw experience, Ninetoes had more than double his greying mentor!

Even more odd was that he now had a Specialism, Necromancer. Now, while he'd found Grim Void incredibly useful, it was his only necromancy spell. Or, at least, it had been.

Apparently, he'd now gained two more necromancy spells, Create Undead and Reaper's Sorrow. How had he learned those? And, what's more, how had he reached a skill level of 41 in Necromancy? Before the battle he'd still been a mere beginner in the spell school, now he'd leapt dozens of levels in the skill and had gained some incredible bonuses too; not that he understood how to utilise any of them, of course. Except, as he thought about it, he realised that he did.

AAAAASARRRRRZZZGGGHHHHHHHHHHHHH!

***

Honestly, it was times like this that Libby seriously wondered why she felt so attached to the ugly, foolish hobgoblin. Furthermore, why in all Adrenon she called *him* Master was frankly beyond her, as clearly she was the clever one.

The slightly rotund squirrel had become Ninetoes' Familiar when the two of them had saved one another from an ettercap, a vile spider-like monster. Since then they had been inseparable.

As she looked down at his unconscious form, she wondered yet again how he'd lasted this long, even with her help.

Although, she had to admit, that on this occasion he only seemed to be reading his Character Sheet before he'd screamed his effeminate scream and collapsed.

For a moment she'd been worried, checking over his body for signs of a wound or perhaps some kind of leftover damage from his battle with the wizard. But, when her search turned up nothing of interest, apart from some leftover hardtack in her master's pocket, she instead decided to stand guard, while eating the morsel; one of them had to stay conscious and well-fed.

She might even drag out his spellbook and start trying to learn to read. After all, it couldn't be that hard if her Master could do it.

***

Some time later, Ninetoes awoke, his head still throbbing from the massive onslaught of information he'd absorbed in a matter of seconds. Groggily, he sat up, casting his gaze over the, now darkened, rooftop. Nearby, he found his familiar, preening her autumn-coloured fur while sitting atop the parapet. Once again, he noticed her expanding belly and considered telling her. But then, the brave Adventurer who had so recently bested a master mage and an army of goblinoids, decided that he'd had enough battle for one day.

"Hello Little One. I see you're well."

Indeed master, and you are... well?

"I am sweet one, I am. Just, tired? My mind feels crammed and stretched thin all at once."

Hmmm, that sounds uncomfortable. Perhaps some cheese would make you feel better? She suggested hopefully.

"Cheese? I'm not sure..."

Now now master, you're beginning to look thin, I can see your ribs. You really should eat more.

"Yes, yes perhaps you're right my little tea-leaf," he replied, placing his hand into his Bag of Holding. Libby's eyes gleamed with excitement, which turned onto sorrow as Ninetoes continued to speak.

"But, first..." he said, taking his hand away from the bag, "... I'd rather we relocated, the bodies are starting to smell."

So saying, he headed down the spiral staircase in search of more pleasant surroundings. Two floors down, he found what must have once been the dining room, a grand and beautifully rich space with velvet covered chairs and a gorgeous mahogany table running the length of the oblong-shaped room. For a moment he considered taking his ease here, he was after all now the lord of this castle.

But ultimately, the room seemed too empty and austere for his needs and so, heading through a plain wooden door at the back of the room, he found the kitchen. This room was still a massive space, but somehow felt cosier and more to his tastes.

The same magic that had protected so many of the treasures of this ancient kingdom were at play in the castle. He quickly found a large pile of wood that appeared to have been chopped only that morning and, within a few short minutes, he had a large fire burning in the main hearth.

At first, he'd only planned to use the fire's warmth to ward off the chills of the ever colder nights, but as he gazed across the homely space, he started to form a plan.

It had been weeks since his last home cooked meal, having survived on mainly trail rations and cheese. Certainly, his taste for the fungus had increased of late, but he wanted something... more. Thus it was that he found himself searching the kitchen for the vittles needed to make tomac pa. A taste of home would warm his soul, although for a moment his stomach felt even more empty at the thought of how much further he needed to travel and grow before he could actually return home.

It felt like years, although it had barely been weeks since a strange twist of fate had turned him into an Adventurer. His people, the hobgoblins of the Dakhec Druul, had looked on him as some kind of monster, and it was only the intervention of the village's Elder Brev that had stayed the executioner's blade.

Nonetheless, Ninetoes had been banished from his home and given a straightforward, if seemingly impossible, task. Grow stronger and find out what you are.

Brev sent him to find the wizard Foresto, with a promise that the mage could help. The gnomish wizard had taught him more about what he was and, most significantly, how to wield magic. He'd also given Ninetoes his first Quest.

Such thoughts and emotions churned within Ninetoes and his chest clenched with pain and the thought of his loss and that he might never return home. Rather than allow himself to give in to his pain however, Ninetoes set himself to his task.

Tomac pa was simple enough to make, but took a lifetime to master. Although he was definitely no master cook, Ninetoes could, like all his folk, make this one dish.

First, he searched for a cauldron to hang over the fire but his search turned up nothing to use and, he noticed, there was nothing in the hearth to hang it from anyway.

His search did, however, turn up a strange valve attached to a pipe that left the hearth and ran along the ceiling. Following its course, he found that it divided into four smaller pipes, each one leading to a quartet of stoves.

Turning the valve, he heard a sound like rushing water and, as he approached a stove, he found that it was already giving off immense heat. Checking over the vast contraption, he found yet more dials. One of which, he was pretty sure, would manipulate the heat of the stove.

Gingerly turning the others, he was surprised when a steady flame sprang forth from three circular vents on top of the stove. He realised that this must be how these ancient people had cooked, a mixture of magic and engineering that must have allowed even those without magic to benefit from it.

Emboldened by his discovery, he set to work chopping meat and vegetables from his Bag of Holding, which he then cooked in a skillet over the open flame. As the meat simmered, he boiled and mashed potatoes and once everything was piping hot and merrily crispy, he spread the potatoes over the top of the other ingredients and finally placed the whole lot into the oven to finish cooking.

***

Libby, meanwhile, has been beside herself throughout the entire process, at first asking, then demanding and finally begging for a little cheese or even some hardtack, rather than be tortured with his "cooking"! But, as the hobgoblin reached into the oven with a pair of blackened tongs and the smell of the hotpot was released, the cheeseboard mutineer quietened enough to climb onto her Master's shoulder and greedily take in the incredible smells.

As Ninetoes removed a block of cheese from his bag, her breathing quickened in anticipation and, when he removed his knife and began cutting small slivers of the wondrous buttery bliss.

She nearly bit him to end her torture. The anticipation was almost too much! Only hours before she and her Master had struggled with the strange and unknown power within the device on the Keep's roof. At the time it had felt monumental and certainly the most difficult thing she'd ever done. She'd nearly lost Ninetoes to it, its enthralling power had been so great. But even that struggle paled in comparison to the torment of awaiting cheese.

But then, her Master, the centre of her world, the most wonderful creature ever to walk on two legs, used a knife to cut into his creation and the smells it released were incredible. Libby had never smelt anything so divine, she was, after all, only a squirrel. Or, at least, she *had* only been a squirrel, now she was so much more. Now, she was alive.

Although, she couldn't promise the same would be true of her Master if she didn't get fed soon.

***

Pulling the skillet from the stove, an array of emotions crashed into Ninetoes, triggered by his olfactory sense. While his people had never added cheese, as it was a luxury to them, the tangy orange delicacy had melted and formed a slightly browning web of goodness.

Ninetoes took a moment to appreciate Libby's silence, before spooning a large helping of the tomac pa onto a plate and placing it in front of her.

"Be careful Little One, it'll be h...," he tried to warn his Familiar. But he needn't have bothered, as Libby was already wolfing down the meal.

Aaaaaaawwwwwwwwwwwwwhhhhhhhmmmmmmmmmmmmmm! Master! This is soooo good.

Not for the first time, Ninetoes thanked the gods that his connection to Libby meant that they could speak telepathically, because otherwise he'd hear little of what she had to say on a subject, so often was her mouth full of food.

Why have you never cooked this for me before? Have you been keeping this to yourself? she demanded, her tone accusatory. Ah yes, he reasoned, perhaps it would be better if, just sometimes, she couldn't talk.

I have not kept it from you, we have simply been too busy staying alive. Up until now. He replied, using his mind to speak, while he enjoyed his own meal. It wasn't perfect, not like it was made in his village, but it was excellent and while his stomach filled, his aches and pains and the empty feeling in his chest eased just a little.

Smiling, he dragged a chair over to the hearth and sat with his back to its warmth. Finishing his meal, he leaned back contentedly and closed his eyes, enjoying the feeling of warmth and a full stomach. Opening them, his eyes fell onto the imposing form of Bluzag, who stood in the doorway.

His half-ogre ally had followed the hobgoblin's every instruction since the battle on the rooftop without question. Ninetoes' first look over his character sheet had offered some answers to this strange behaviour and he thought perhaps he had some idea of what had happened. He thought that rather than save his ally's life, he had instead turned him into an unwavering and obedient undead servant.

As he considered this more deeply, his newfound knowledge filled in some of the gaps. Bluzag was not only a servant but a **Wight**, an undead that would serve Ninetoes in whatever means he demanded, even walking into harm's way, if he so commanded it.

Bluzag, however, was more than this. As a Wight, he was classed as an "intelligent" undead, meaning that he both maintained some of his knowledge and skills from his life before he'd died and, more thrillingly so, he could continue to learn and gain Skills and Abilities. Ninetoes had inadvertently created the perfect walking shield, someone that would stand as a towering bulwark between Ninetoes and his enemies, without ever faltering or even feeling pain.

While he grieved for his fallen friend and felt guilty for his part in turning him into this... creature, he was certainly glad that it had turned out so well... for him.

Still, what Ninetoes needed, more than anything, was more answers. The knowledge that spiralled through his mind told him much, but it didn't offer him any answers as to how he had become so strong or how he'd gained his Specialism of Necromancer. Some of those questions he realised would have to wait until he returned to Raveslan and spoke with Foresto. For now, he would have to content himself with learning all he could from his Character Sheet.

Reaching into his bag again, he pulled out the three sheaves of parchment; *Wait, three?*

The first two were his own and Libby's, much as they had been since he'd last looked, but now there was a third, this one apparently belonging to Bluzag.

UNDEAD NAME: BLUZAG	RACE: HALF-OGRE WIGHT (+1 STR, +1 END)
BOND LEVEL: 12TH	BONDED WIZARD: NINETOES
HIT POINTS: 594/594	MANA POINTS: NONE
STAMINA POINTS: 430/430	
CLASS: WARRIOR	SPECIALISM:

BASE STATS:
STRENGTH - 47
AGILITY - 16
ENDURANCE - 43
INTELLIGENCE - 9
WISDOM - 8
CHARISMA - 7

LANGUAGES: COMMON - BASIC UNDERSTANDING GOBLINOID - BASIC UNDERSTANDING GIANT - BASIC UNDERSTANDING	ARMOUR CLASS: ARMOUR 10 + SHIELD 20 TOTAL: 30

RACIAL ABILITIES

TOUGH:
THE HALF-OGRE IS TOUGHER AND HARDIER THAN MOST CREATURES. +10% HIT POINTS.

LEARNED ABILITIES

CHARGING BULL - LEVEL 4 COOL DOWN - 25 SECONDS STAMINA COST - 50 POINTS LVL 1. AFTER TRAVELLING AT LEAST 15 FEET IN A STRAIGHT LINE, THE USER ADDS 50% DAMAGE TO THE NEXT ATTACK AND HAS A 10% CHANCE TO KNOCK OVER THE TARGET.	WHIRLWIND STRIKE - LEVEL 3 COOL DOWN - 30 SECONDS STAMINA COST - 50 POINTS LVL 1. CREATES AN ATTACK THAT SPINS 360 DEGREES THAT HITS ALL ENEMIES WITHIN 5 FEET FOR 50% DAMAGE. LVL 3. INCREASES DAMAGE TO 60%.

LEARNED SKILLS

ONE-HANDED BLUDGEONING WEAPONS: LEVEL 4 - BEGINNER +4% DAMAGE. +4% CHANCE OF CRITICAL HIT.	
SPELL CASTING AFFINITIES - NONE	

Unspent upgrade points - 12

Bluzag's character sheet seemed to offer only more questions. It was infuriating!

No. Don't do that. Stop. Ninetoes reprimanded himself. He was clever, he could work this out.

Firstly, Bluzag's "Bonded Level" was twelve. Well, that riddle was easy enough to solve, as it was the same as Ninetoes' own Level, who was also noted as the "Bonded Wizard". Thus, it seemed reasonable to assume that Bluzag's bonded level would increase in line with his own level.

Checking over his stats, something seemed wrong with Bluzag's hit points. Even with the added ten per cent from the Tough racial ability, Bluzag still seemed to have too many. Ninetoes knew that his own hit points came from his Fitness rating multiplied by his level and that his Fitness rating came from an average of his Strength, Endurance and Agility scores. Bluzag's agility was pretty low however, which would pull the average down quite a bit.

Perhaps it was something to do with his class, Warrior. Ninetoes knew that when he'd chosen his own class of Wizard, it had changed how his mana was equated, no longer using an average of Wisdom, Intelligence and Charisma, but instead using only Intelligence. If Ninetoes' maths was correct, then Bluzag's hit points were coming from an average of just his Strength and Endurance scores. Well, for now at least, that was an acceptable answer for Ninetoes.

The rest of Bluzag's character sheet seemed to be skills that he'd learned in life, as none of them were skills Ninetoes had ever seen before. None of these skills were especially high, clearly due to Bluzag having spent most of his life as a pack mule for other Adventurers. Well, that would start to change, if he was going to be Ninetoes' meatshield.

To start with, Ninetoes wanted to spend some of the Upgrade Points the Wight had. He reasoned that, like Libby, these points could be spent on increasing Bluzag's stats, but he wondered if he could also increase Bluzag's Skills as well. As he considered this, his mind found the answers in the knowledge he'd recently received.

Indeed, Upgrade Points could be spent on Skills and Ability points and that because Bluzag was a servant to Ninetoes, he could spend the points for the Wight. He also understood that at each threshold of ten Ability points, new Abilities or Skills would become available.

With this in mind, Ninetoes started considering how best to spend the points. Looking first at the Wight's Ability points, Ninetoes noted that Strength, Intelligence, Wisdom and Charisma were all close to a threshold and so he wondered how these might affect his servan...- er, ally.

Certainly, Intelligence seemed a must. It was only a single point and increasing Libby's had given her the ability to communicate and later to cast magic of her own. Since the battle, Bluzag had not uttered a word, instead he simply continued to stare blankly at Ninetoes. Even when Ninetoes had commanded it to speak, nothing. Decision made, Ninetoes focussed and placed a point into Intelligence and, as he watched the Character Sheet, not only did the Intelligence score increase, but each of the languages on the parchment changed from Basic Understanding to Beginner.

"Bluzag, my friend? Can you understand me? Can you speak?"

"Yes Master," came a monotonic response.

"Phew, this is excellent news and how do you feel?" he asked.

"I do not understand the question Master," Bluzag drawled, his voice never changing in lilt or timbre.

"Hmmm, perhaps if I placed more points into Intelligence…" He seriously considered it. With eleven points left over, he could have crammed them all into Intelligence and maybe Bluzag would come back to himself

29

a little. He owed it to the half-ogre, didn't he? After all, the brute had given his life fighting alongside him.

But, no. He wouldn't do it. If Ninetoes was to grow strong enough to return to his people, he couldn't be wasting resources on such notions. Worse still, if his understanding was correct, then Bluzag would only get one point every time Ninetoes himself Levelled Up and, knowing what it had taken to reach level 12, he didn't see that happening anytime soon. So, he must be more deliberate.

Bluzag was now his bulwark, or 'tank' as master Foresto had described it. Ninetoes needed to make decisions based upon that. And so the next three points went into Strength, the score now reaching 50. Firstly, his hit points increased to six hundred and thirteen, which meant that Ninetoes' hypothesis about how they were equated was correct. But, more excitingly, Bluzag gained a new skill, Powerstrike.

POWER STRIKE - LEVEL 1
COOL DOWN - 10 SECONDS
STAMINA COST - 25 POINTS
LVL 1. ADDS 25% DAMAGE TO THE NEXT ATTACK.

This seemed pretty good and definitely something that he could use. With that in mind, he immediately used four points to upgrade the skill to level 5. To his joy, the skill gained an extra trait at level 4, increasing the additional damage to thirty per cent.

Curious, Ninetoes wanted to place an upgrade point into Charging Bull to see if it gained a trait, as most of the skills he'd seen gained at least one within every five levels. Deeming it worth it, Ninetoes did so. But, while the skill level increased, nothing else changed. A shame, but nothing worth losing sleep over.

With only three points left, Ninetoes looked over the other areas he could improve and pondered what gains might be earned from reaching the Wisdom and Charisma thresholds. As much as he debated it, he couldn't think of anything that would make the cost worth it and so, for the time being, he elected to keep hold of the points until he had more information.

Checking over Libby's Character Sheet, he noted that she had gained three levels herself and decided he'd take the time to help her level up. When he suggested it to her, she lazily explained how she'd already spent her Upgrade Points, two into Intelligence, to increase her mana pool and one into Agility. Scanning over her sheet he could see that she'd also reached a threshold on Agility and that her Zippy skill had been upgraded to include Quick-Witted.

It seemed that Libby's increased Agility had served an increased spell-casting ability. She could now, once per day, create an illusory copy of herself to help distract a foe. It was odd that the Agility skill had provided such a bonus and he made a mental note to ask Foresto about it. With Bluzag's and Libby's upgrade points spent, Ninetoes thought about his own, but as he did so his mouth stretched into a wide yawn.

"Ahhhhwww! Well, Little One perhaps we should rest through the night and in the morning, consider our next move," he called to the room at large. As he searched for his familiar however, he discovered that she was way ahead of him.

Curled up on the cushion he'd once stolen for her, which she'd evidently dragged from his bag to the fireplace, was his truest friend. Laying his own bedroll down next to her, Ninetoes quickly drifted into a long and peaceful sleep.

CHAPTER 2
ANSWERS

Ninetoes woke to the morning's bright welcome; yawning deeply and wincing from a crick in his neck, earned from sleeping on the hard floor. Magic had healed all of his wounds from the previous day's trials but his body had still, it appeared, required a good night's sleep to throw off all of the lingering effects.

Bluzag still stood inert at the door leading into the dining hall and a cursory glance showed him that his Familiar yet again filling her belly. Clearly every point of intelligence that the little rodent possessed had gone into cleverly solving the problem of how to gain access to more of the tomac pa's rich cheese-laden goodness, that Ninetoes had left inside the stove; with the dish's lid still on! Somehow, she'd fashioned a ramp of sorts and slid the entire dish to the floor, then levered off the lid with a knife. She was currently spooning what appeared to be a second helping of the pie into a bowl with a ladle. *Well, at least she's using her own crockery.*

Noting, as he watched her, her expanding belly, Ninetoes crossed the intervening space and grabbed up the pie dish and Libby's own bowl in a single assault manoeuvre, "One helping is enough; you're getting fat little one. No more for you until dinner."

Two helpings. She replied, managing to send her disapproval and ire at him with the same thought.

I was just getting myself some breakfast, seeing as you had elected to sleep in, yet again... Master She added, almost as an afterthought.

"Well, I am awake now and we have much to do today. I'd like to check over the castle for any more loot and then take our leave of this lifeless city by noon," he summarised.

His plans were simple enough. His Bag of Holding was almost totally full with books and food but he wanted to pick over the rest of the castle. He simply didn't have the means to carry much more and he'd need a solution to that, as he planned to leave nothing behind that might come in handy.

As far as he was concerned, the books were worth more than their weight in gold, but if what Bofar had told him was true, then this had once been the home of kings and thus, he hoped to find a king's hoard of treasures.

He was also, however, conscious of time. While he had plenty of food and water, Foresto had set him this Quest more than a week ago, presuming it to be a quick task to simply check in on an old colleague. He didn't want the gnome thinking he'd shirked in his task. Finally, he was keen to be back amongst the living. He could return to this place anytime, it's treasures safe from the average grave robbers, due to its seclusion deep within the Forest of Myrr.

While he broke his fast with an apple, he retrieved his Character Sheet, intending to spend his own Ability and Skill points. The parchment told him that he now had ten unspent Ability points and a whopping seventeen Skill points to spend. Considering this, he realised that the numbers were off. He'd previously been earning two Ability points and three Skill points per level, plus one in both Intelligence and Endurance because of his race.

Before the battle against Bofar and his goblinoids, he had been a seventh level wizard and had now increased by five levels to his current level of twelve. Based upon this, his Ability points were correct, but he seemed to have two too many Skill points. Focusing on his Character Sheet, the information provided itself and his Character Sheet changed slightly to elucidate the answer; after level ten, he received four Skill Points instead of three.

While he'd prepared the previous evening's meal, he'd thought long and hard about how to spend his points. After witnessing the benefits that Bluzag had gained from reaching his Intelligence threshold, Ninetoes was keen to experience some of the same gains. His closest two scores were Intelligence and Agility, but both were buffed by items, his own scores printed in red brackets next to the total score. He hypothesised that he would only gain the threshold benefits by crossing his personal scores, but he wanted to test the theory and so, concentrating, he placed a point into Agility. While both pairs of numbers increased, he gained no additional benefits. A shame to be sure, but not unexpected and it proved his hypothesis. Agility was still one of the closest Ability scores he had to a threshold and so, as he'd already decided to do the previous evening, he pumped three more points into the score.

As he'd hoped, as his base score reached twenty, a new skill became available as a benefit.

DODGING: LEVEL 1 - BEGINNER
+1% CHANCE TO COMPLETELY DODGE AN ATTACK TARGETED AT YOU.

He could certainly see the uses of such a skill, although he was surprised he hadn't learned the skill himself, simply through successfully dodging attacks in the past. Perhaps reaching the Ability score threshold was only one of the prerequisites of attaining certain skills?

Without the buff of his items, his next closest was Wisdom, at eighteen. As Foresto had told him many times, Wisdom and Intelligence were a Wizard's most important ability scores and, while Ninetoes wasn't sure that was completely true for him, he'd certainly felt the lack of mana more than once and the recharge simply took too long, he needed to increase the score as much as possible and so he dropped two points into it straight away. He had a mind to put all four of his remaining points in as well, but was curious to see if he gained a threshold benefit first. He was not disappointed.

> TRANCE: LEVEL 1 - BEGINNER
> BY CONCENTRATING YOU ENTER A MEDITATIVE
> TRANCE AND GAIN +1% MANA REGENERATION
> OUTSIDE OF COMBAT SITUATIONS.

The skill, while still weak at only one per cent, was brilliant and meant that, out of battle he could regain his mana more quickly, he would have to practice the skill as often as possible. It also helped make his decision and the other four points went straight into Wisdom as well.

The more difficult decision to make by far was how to spend his Skill Points. While seventeen was a huge boon, he'd likely be getting few more anytime soon and he had so many useful skills, two more including Dodging and Trance, since he'd considered this problem at length the previous evening.

His apple finished, he decided to try and kill two birds with one stone. Rising from his chair and with a mental command to Libby, he started his exploration of the keep. At the same time, he pondered his choices.

His massive boon in Necromancy and the information dump his brain was still trying to work through had given him some useful insight into the way that schools of magic levelled. It seemed that as each Skill ranked up they gained new facets and benefits, much like he gained from the thresholds of his ability points. Within the spell school of Necromancy he'd gained a number of benefits, which definitely gave him cause for excitement.

It also gave him a moment of pause. While he'd gained two new necromancy spells when he'd levelled up, he hadn't understood where they'd come from, now he understood. One, he guessed Create Undead, had come from levelling up his skill in necromancy to the Apprentice rank. But the other spell's origin was still a mystery. That was until, reading through his other necromancy spell, Grim Void.

He noticed the level 36 ability he gained that gave him a five per cent chance to absorb knowledge from the target of his spell. He must have inadvertently absorbed the knowledge of how to perform Reaper's Sorrow from Bofar!

It must have been the spell that had meant that the dwarven mage hadn't died from Bluzag's earth shattering surprise attack on the rooftop; a spell that had cost his ally his life and nearly Ninetoes' and Libby's own. He vowed then and there, never to let his arrogance or foolishness cost another friend their life.

With this vow in mind, he stopped deliberating and spent four skill points to increase Abjuration and a further four to increase Evocation to level 10, thus earning them both the rank of Poor. The writing on his Character Sheet morphed before his eyes and his new Rank Benefits showed clearly.

EVOCATION - LEVEL 10 POOR	ABJURATION - LEVEL 10 POOR
+10% DAMAGE FOR EVOCATION SPELLS	+10% DURATION FOR ABJURATION SPELLS
DAMAGE ARCANE 1 - +10% DAMAGE WITH CHOSEN DAMAGE TYPE (COLD, FIRE, LIGHTNING, FORCE). *	ABJURER'S CHOICE - CHOOSE ONE ABJURATION SPELL YOU ALREADY KNOW TO INCREASE TO SKILL LEVEL 10.*

Both Rank Benefits apparently came with a choice, something he'd never experienced and made him wonder about whether he'd had a choice of what Necromancy spell he'd earned at the Apprentice rank. His choice of which Abjuration spell he'd choose was simple enough; Wizard's Armour had kept him alive so far. Making his choice, he was emboldened by the added protection it provided.

WIZARD ARMOUR - LEVEL 10
ABJURATION
CASTING TIME - 1 MINUTE
MANA COST - 20 POINTS
DURATION - 5 HOURS

LVL 1. PROVIDES AN ARMOUR CLASS OF 10.
LVL 3. ALLOWS THE CASTER TO INCREASE DAMAGE REDUCTION BY CHANNELLING MORE MANA INTO THE ARMOUR AT A RATIO OF 20:1 (MANA TO AC).
LVL 8. INCREASES BASE AC CLASS BY +2.

His total armour class was now a whopping 29, almost as high as Bluzag's, who wore a heavy jacket and carried a massive tower shield, even if it did look like a dinner plate in his giant-sized hands. Moving onto his choice for Evocation, he found the decision more difficult. Currently he had no spells that caused cold damage, so that was out, although he made a mental note to try to find one as soon as possible.

No, the choice was between force, lightning and fire. He'd certainly found Shocking Strike to be incredibly useful, but if he was going to be a true Wizard, then he needed to stop relying on his martial and melee skills and focus on ranged attacks. So, Burning Hands or Arcane Bolt?

So far, his Arcane Bolt had been frankly a little lacklustre. Although, he admitted, that was because he'd been more inclined to close the distance and fight his foes head on. *No more!* He chose force damage and his Evocation skill description changed to accommodate his choice.

This left him with nine Skill Points left to spend. With all of the other choices he'd made, he'd been focussed on improving his magical prowess and these last nine points would be the same. It was only planning and a whole lot of luck that meant he'd survived his confrontation with the wizard Bofar. He needed to find a party to work with and so he must become a Wizard through and through. Concentrating on his area of greatest ability and the spell school that fate seemed to have chosen as his speciality, Ninetoes focussed on placing a couple of skill points into Necromancy, but unlike the other spell schools that he'd needed to place two points into to gain a single level, he met no such resistance. What's more, instead of increasing to level 42 as he'd intended, the skill jumped another level in 43.

Checking his Character Sheet, worried that he'd accidentally spent two more points he saw that he'd still only spent the two points that he'd intended. That's when it dawned on him, of course a Speciality would make it cheaper to level up the Spell School, and as he focussed on the word Specialism, Ninetoes mind absorbed a little more information.

Firstly, it seemed, he was correct, that skill points spent in Necromancy didn't suffer the 2:1 ratio that he needed for the other schools. But more than that, he understood that Necromancy spells would be easier to learn and eventually easier and cheaper to cast.

Well, he had seven Skill Points left and seven levels between him and the Competent rank in Necromancy. *Coincidence? I think not.* All seven remaining points went into his specialist school and the immediate gain was not to be sneezed at.

NECROMANCY- LEVEL 50 COMPETENT

+50% POTENCY OF NECROMANCY SPELLS

DEATH'S TOUCH I - YOUR FAMILIARITY FOR THE ENERGY OF UNLIFE HAS GIVEN YOU +10% RESISTANCE TO NECROTIC DAMAGE.

KNOWLEDGE ARCANE I - ALLOWS THE CASTER TO CHOOSE ONE APPRENTICE RANKED SPELL.

NECROMANCY SAVANT I - NECROMANCY SPELLS COST YOU 25% LESS TO CAST.

CONTROL UNDEAD - DOUBLES THE NUMBER OF UNDEAD THE CASTER CAN CONTROL.

KNOWLEDGE ARCANE II - ALLOWS THE CASTER TO CHOOSE ONE COMPETENT RANKED SPELL.*

Firstly, his Necromancy spells were now fifty per cent more powerful and cost less to cast, which meant that using Grim Void, he could drain and absorb thirty-six hit points of life a second from his enemies, making it by far his most efficient and dangerous spell. Perhaps he needed to find a style of fighting that allowed him to get a little closer?

More exciting however, was Knowledge Arcane II, he could choose a necromancy spell to learn and it would already be at the Competent level. *But how do I choose?*

At that very thought a rush of information filled his mind, showing him the three choices available.

CURSE

PREREQUISITES - NECROMANCY COMPETENT.

CASTING TIME - 10 SECONDS

MANA COST - 100 POINTS

DURATION - 1 MINUTE

LVL 50. ONCE CAST, THE TARGET OF THIS SPELL CANNOT REGAIN HIT POINTS FROM MAGICAL HEALING FOR 1 MINUTE. FURTHERMORE, THEY SUFFER A -5 TO THREE RANDOM ABILITY SCORES.

VOICE OF THE VOID

PREREQUISITES - NECROMANCY COMPETENT.

CASTING TIME - 10 SECONDS

MANA COST - 50 POINTS

DURATION - 1 MINUTE

LVL 50. CAST ON A CORPSE THAT HAS BEEN DEAD FOR NO MORE THAN 1 YEAR AND THE SPIRIT OF THE DECEASED WILL AWAKEN AND SPEAK WITH THE CASTER FOR THE DURATION.

GRIM BOLT

PREREQUISITES - NECROMANCY COMPETENT.

CASTING TIME - 1 SECOND

MANA COST - 25 POINTS

DURATION - INSTANTANEOUS

LVL 50. SHOOTS A BOLT OF MAGICAL DEATH UP

TO 150FT. DEALING 12-72 POINTS OF NE-
CROTIC DAMAGE. IF THE DAMAGE KILLS THE
TARGET, THERE IS A 1% CHANCE THAT THE
CREATURE BECOMES AN UNINTELLIGENT UN-
DEAD UNDER THE CASTER'S COMMAND.

The choices were all incredible and made his decision all the more difficult. *Alright, let's just be logical.* Firstly, as useful as it could be to speak with the dead, it didn't currently apply to anything the hobgoblin wanted to achieve, so Voice of the Void was discounted. Curse sounded brilliant and could clearly come in handy in a fight, but his mind kept coming back to the same issue, he needed more range and Grim Bolt did exactly that. On the surface, it appeared to be the necromancy version of the Arcane Bolt, which gave him another reason to choose it. Instead of gaining another spell that he'd need to level up, he could use Grim Bolt instead of its Arcane brother and so not worry about levelling up the weaker spell. Plus, with his Necromancy bonus, it would deal anywhere between eighteen and one hundred and eight damage, it was perfect.

While he was slightly annoyed that it made his choice of force damage less important, Ninetoes chose not to dwell on it. With his final choice made, Ninetoes smiled and focussed on the task of looting the keep.

***

An hour later and Ninetoes' search had revealed a number of items of jewellery and a bundle of ancient coins. He'd emptied a few pounds of food from his bag to accommodate the treasures, but as far as the hobgoblin was concerned, his search had been mostly fruitless.

Clearly, he realised, his perspective had changed, for the loot he'd collected was more wealth than most people would see in a lifetime. But, as far as he was concerned, it was not a king's hoard. He also hadn't found any more magic items.

Well, he admitted, that wasn't strictly true. The keep was full of other magical devices like the stoves in the kitchens. Magic that worked alongside engineering marvels the likes of which Ninetoes had never heard of, many of them serving simple purposes, like switches to illuminate rooms or moving cupboards that could travel up through the keep's floors. None of this, of course, held anything more than a passing interest to Ninetoes, as he could hardly take them with him.

He assumed that if he spent the time to pick over every inch of the city, he'd be bound to find a great deal more wealth, but that could take years. No, for now at least, he'd have to content himself with the treasures he'd already found. That was, he reminded himself, except the spoils of the battle on the rooftop.

Since he'd left the rooftop the previous day, he'd been reluctant to return there. The device, the Animator, had held Ninetoes in its sway and had it not been for Libby, it might have taken him completely. Thus it was, that rather than going himself, he sent Bluzag to collect the bodies of the fallen bugbears and of the wizard, Bofar.

In anticipation of leaving the best for last, Ninetoes checked over the bodies of the four bugbears first. There were two more, smashed on the cobblestones of the courtyard, but Ninetoes had already checked them over and found nothing of interest. Unsurprisingly, the bugbears had no weapons or armour that he could use, but between them they had enough pieces of armour to better equip Bluzag.

PLATE IRON GREAVES - NORMAL, COMMON
SKILL TYPE: HEAVY ARMOUR
ARMOUR CLASS: 3

FULL OAKEN SHIELD - NORMAL, COMMON
SKILL TYPE: BLOCKING
ARMOUR CLASS: 25

```
┌─────────────────────────────────────────────────┐
│ PLATE IRON HELM - NORMAL, COMMON                  │
│ SKILL TYPE: HEAVY ARMOUR                          │
│ ARMOUR CLASS: 5                                   │
└─────────────────────────────────────────────────┘
```

Sadly, Bofar's fatal attack on the half-ogre had also burned a hole clear through Bluzag's Iron Scale Jacket, cutting its armour rating in half, but none of the bugbear's chest armour was even half the size it needed to be to fit Ninetoes' monstrous ally, so it would have to do for now. What was more concerning, however, was that there was still a small, yet obvious, wound on the half-ogre's chest. He couldn't walk into Raveslan with his ally without scaring the townsfolk out of their wits.

So, using a tabard taken from one of the bugbears, Ninetoes covered the ghastly sight. Stepping back, he admired his handiwork, a smile stretching across his maroon-coloured face. *No one will ever notice.*

With that done, Ninetoes stepped up to the corpse of his enemy. In life, the dwarven evoker had seemed like an insurmountable foe and indeed, Ninetoes had nearly fallen to the mage. But now, laying there broken, he looked rather small. He'd been overweight and, now that Ninetoes thought about it, he'd realised that the dwarf had been puffing when they'd fought on the rooftop.

Leaning down, he cast his gaze over the body. The wizard's robes were still sodden and sticky with blood and, rather than dirty his own hands, Ninetoes instructed Bluzag to remove them.

Once removed, the dwarf seemed even smaller still, his arms thin and weak looking and his belly rotund and pale.

Screwing the robes into a ball, Ninetoes thrust them into his bag, deciding to deal with them later. Apart from this, the body had only two items left on it. A ring and a bracer. Strange that someone so powerful should have so few items. No weapons, not even a bag. Then Ninetoes remembered the pavilion tent still outside and reasoned that the dwarf must have travelled light in preparation for combat.

Casting Identify, Ninetoes inspected the two items. The ring was apparently mundane, simply more loot to add to his bag but the bracer shone with magical light.

> **BRACER OF FIRE RESISTANCE** - FINE, UNCOMMON
> PROPERTIES: PROVIDES WEARER WITH +30% RESISTANCE TO FIRE DAMAGE.

Wow! This item was strong. But he already had a pair of magical bracers. Slipping one off his wrist, he replaced it with the new bracer, hoping that he could gain the benefits of both items. But, while his Character Sheet now showed the fire resistance, it also showed that he'd lost the benefits of the Guardman's Bracers.

Ninetoes was loathe to lose the added Strength and Agility provided by the bracers, not to mention the slight bonus to his AC, but he had to start thinking and acting like a Wizard.

Beckoning Bluzag, he pulled a length of cord from his satchel, hoping to affix his old bracers to the wight's arms.

But, as he lifted them towards the half-ogre's wrists, something... well... magical, happened. The bracers enlarged, to fit perfectly around Bluzag's forearms. Ninetoes was ecstatic. Checking over Bluzag's sheet, it was clear that his Wight was becoming a bastion of defence for the hobgoblin.

UNDEAD NAME: BLUZAG	RACE: HALF-OGRE WIGHT (+1 STR, +1 END)
BOND LEVEL: 12TH	BONDED WIZARD: NINETOES
HIT POINTS: 627/627	MANA POINTS: NONE
STAMINA POINTS: 430/430	

CLASS: WARRIOR	SPECIALISM:

BASE STATS:
STRENGTH - 52 (50)
AGILITY - 19 (16)
ENDURANCE - 43
INTELLIGENCE - 10
WISDOM - 8
CHARISMA - 7

LANGUAGES: COMMON - BASIC UNDER-STANDING GOBLINOID - BASIC UNDER-STANDING GIANT - BASIC UNDERSTAND-ING	ARMOUR CLASS: ARMOUR 15 + SHIELD 25 TOTAL: 40

RACIAL ABILITIES

TOUGH:
THE HALF-OGRE IS TOUGHER AND HARDIER THAN MOST CREATURES. +10% MORE HIT POINTS.

LEARNED ABILITIES

CHARGING BULL - LEVEL 4 COOL DOWN - 25 SECONDS STAMINA COST - 50 POINTS LVL 1. AFTER TRAVELLING AT LEAST 15 FEET IN A STRAIGHT LINE, USER ADDS 50% DAMAGE TO THE NEXT ATTACK AND HAS A 10% CHANCE TO KNOCK OVER THE TARGET.	WHIRLWIND STRIKE - LEVEL 3 COOL DOWN - 30 SECONDS STAMINA COST - 50 POINTS LVL 1. CREATES AN ATTACK THAT SPINS 360 DEGREES THAT HITS ALL ENEMIES WITHIN 5 FEET FOR 50% DAMAGE. LVL 3. INCREASES DAMAGE TO 60%.
POWER STRIKE - LEVEL 5	

COOL DOWN - 10 SECONDS STAMINA COST - 25 POINTS LVL 1. ADDS 25% DAMAGE TO THE NEXT ATTACK.	
SPELL CASTING AFFINITIES - NONE	

With that done Ninetoes considered his next steps. In the short term he needed to return to Foresto in Raveslan and formally complete his Quest. Before he left the ancient and crumbling ruin however, Ninetoes intended to pick over the goblinoid camp, or at least Bofar's tent.

He knew there was loot to be had, perhaps it was even enough for him to return to his people. He might even be able to return with his people to this very castle and take it for his own. Could he help his people make a new home here? To grow strong once again?

Right now, however, he had to find his way safely through the magical field that surrounded the castle.

CHAPTER 3
LEAVING

As Ninetoes checked over his gear, making sure his potions and weapons were in easy reach, he found a suitable container for the leftover tomac pa. Meanwhile he sent Bluzag to carry the remains of his enemies and pile them in the courtyard.

Once Ninetoes had completed his preparations, he joined the Wight outside and, using oil he'd found in the kitchen, coated the pile of corpses. A quick Burning Hands spell and the remains were set ablaze.

His plan to return to this ancient city, Kavralach Bofar had called it, was a longer term goal. He hoped its treasure and knowledge would help to make him rich and powerful. He hoped this could even be a home for his people, something worthy of the Dakhec Druul, maybe even a replacement for Vawshak Nye.

Ninetoes had been born decades after the great fortress city had been lost, but his people's history was almost exclusively oral tradition and so every young hobgoblin had learned the stories of the stronghold.

Stories that told of massive stone walls, twenty feet deep and fifty feet high; of towers armed with all kinds of savage machines that could rain death as far as the horizon. They told of a tower at the fortress' core, so tall that it touched the sky. Well, this city was a ruin to be sure, but perhaps it would give his people a place to grow strong again, it certainly offered better protection than the wooden palisades of their hidden village.

Crossing the courtyard, Ninetoes searched the twin towers of the barbican, finding both spaces all but empty of weapons and arms. It seemed that someone had cleared them out and, seeing as he knew the goblinoids hadn't ventured this far, he reckoned that it must have been the previous residents. He did find one item of use, a leather baldric, made to carry a weapon across someone's back. With a little ingenuity, some spare leather and a liberal use of the Mending spell, Ninetoes managed to enlarge it to fit Bluzag and allow it to hold his javelins. The Wight had been carrying them in his shield hand up until this point and although the Wight never complained, it would clearly make him less effective at blocking.

Considering this, Ninetoes realised that the half-ogre's Character Sheet did not have the Blocking skill. He knew from his lectures with Foresto that Blocking was a learned skill, related to the Strength stat. With this in mind, he decided that he would start training with Bluzag a little each day to hone their skills and try to develop tactics and Skills for working together.

Before moving out, Ninetoes checked over the massive wood and iron gate, but even a cursory glance told him it was secure. Rather than make the structure insecure, he decided to leave the castle the way he'd come in and so headed up onto the curtain walls via one of two staircases in the barbican.

Reaching the top of the walls, Ninetoes sent Libby ahead to scout along the crenellations, as he still didn't know the fate of the goblins who had been outside of the walls. He was pretty sure they were dead, their lifeforce stolen by the Animator, but he had vowed to be more careful and thus he was the embodiment of caution.

Within moments his Familiar returned to report that the goblins were still at their stations but that something was... off? Ordering Bluzag to wait behind; the half-ogre not having a stealthy bone in his undead body, Ninetoes followed Libby back along the wall.

Ninetoes slunk along the wall top, ducking low behind the merlons. When he reached the corpse of the bugbear commander and the gap in the magical shield that he'd used to enter the castle he stopped. Slowly, inch by careful inch, Ninetoes raised his head between the defences and spied down on the goblins beneath.

As Libby had reported, they were all still on their feet and at their posts, four now standing guard on the palisade they'd erected between the castle walls and the townhouses beyond. More were standing beyond it, leading towards the centre of their camp. He could even see some bugbears, holding the reins of their worg mounts.

Ninetoes could quickly see what Libby had described as 'off'. Not a single one moved. Not a muscle flinched amongst them, they stood statue-still, not even breathing... and then it hit him, they were like Bluzag, they were Undead!

Oh no! This is not good! His panic made him express the thought in his mind.

Indeed Master. Those things are like Bluzag aren't they? If they're all like that, then an army stands between us and escaping this lifeless city. It appears that the wizard's plan succeeded, at least in part.

The same thoughts had been crossing his own mind. Never one to dally however, Ninetoes considered his options, but realising that it really didn't matter, they had no choice but to find a way past them.

Only, he had never fought anything undead before and so he had little knowledge of how to combat them, except... he did, he had mountains of knowledge about the undead, he was in fact the local expert on the subject.

He was still trying to get used to the hoard of information about necromancy that was swirling around in his mind and had yet to make total sense of, but it seemed that if he concentrated on a specific question, that he already knew the answer to, he could, know it... again? *Hmm, now all I need to do is ask **all** the right questions.*

For now, he focussed on what he knew about the undead. Based upon the fact that not a single one was moving or, doing anything really, he reasoned that they must be 'unintelligent' undead, meaning that they were simply animated husks that held little to none of the knowledge that their bodies had known in life, only maintaining the muscle memory to perform simple tasks and obey straight forward commands. These undead didn't need to sleep, eat or even breathe and while they were not particularly strong or combat effective, they would not cease from their last command until they were almost completely destroyed, thus making them the perfect form of infantry. Without commands, these undead would simply act towards their own self preservation, attacking anything that threatened them.

This meant, if Ninetoes was correct, that these undead would ignore him and his allies unless they were to attack one and then they might all attack his party, swamping them quickly. This might also mean, a greedy part of him pointed out, that as long as he was careful, there was nothing guarding the treasures in Bofar's tent.

But first, he'd need to test the idea. Gathering his focus, Ninetoes cast Minor Illusion, creating a simple copy of himself on the cobbled street below him, right in the centre of a group of undead. While one or two of the creatures turned their heads to look at the figure, but not a single one moved towards it and while Ninetoes' Beginner ability with the spell meant that he couldn't make the illusory copy move its limbs, he could still change the location of the figure.

Doing so, he hoped would allow him to test whether the undead were simply ignoring an immobile target. Still, not a single one moved to intercept his double and, once the illusion had moved from the cone of vision of those watching it, they simply turned their heads back, seemingly forgetting its existence.

What do you think Little One? Is it safe? He questioned his Familiar, not wanting to make any decision that risked their lives without checking with her first. Mostly because he didn't want her to blame and scold him, when it inevitably went poorly.

For a moment he questioned this. Little more than a week ago Libby had been nothing more than a simple animal. A clever one to be sure, but still just a beast. Within that short time however, she had grown much, in both intelligence and experience. Now, his small squirrel Familiar was his closest friend and he respected the wisdom of her words and opinion.

I think we must risk it Master. Based upon what we have already seen, they seem harmless. Perhaps if you were to teleport down to the palisade to test it? Then you could teleport back if they become aggressive? She responded. It was a well thought out and sound judgement and, while he wasn't keen upon the idea of risking himself in the attempt, he quickly accepted that he was the best choice and once again he smiled and how clever she had become.

Firstly, he recharged his mana by channelling some out of his Gem of Power, bringing himself back to full. Then, holding a deep breath and concentrating on the small gap between the forceshield and the wall, he 'stepped' to the palisade below. He'd had to step right next to one of the undead, but there had been no avoiding it, his spell was limited in the distance it could carry him.

Still holding onto his breath, he watched. As the first of the undead took notice of him something very odd happened.

As though he was a stone, dropped into a still pool, a wave rippled outwards and every single creature within sight turned to look directly at Ninetoes. Within a moment, roughly forty pairs of lifeless eyes were gazing straight at the hobgoblin.

To say that it was unnerving would be a massive understatement. Ninetoes was only glad he'd had nothing more than an apple for breakfast, as his stomach dropped into his feet.

For a moment, he nearly 'stepped' away, but then he overcame his initial fear and a logical thought crossed his mind, if they meant him harm, they'd have moved to attack.

Master? Are you alright? Came his familiar's worried voice in his mind.

I think so, Little One. They don't seem aggressive.

But, why do they all look at you so? Those distant ones cannot have heard you your 'step' is almost silent.

The same thought had occurred to Ninetoes and he definitely hadn't stopped considering plans for escaping the mob. He needed more information, however, and so he stepped forward, along the wooden palisade, heading for a ramp a few feet away. To reach it, he would need to pass by the closest undead goblin as the palisade was too narrow to permit him passage without the creature moving.

"Excuse me," he whispered, mostly just to break up the silence, than for any actual sense of courtesy and that's when things got even weirder.

Not only did the creature in front of him move to the side, so did every other animated corpse within earshot. Ninetoes froze.

What happened Master? Why did they all move? Libby's voice was anxious and, as Ninetoes glanced back, he could see the squirrel attempting to squeeze through the gap in the forceshield.

I… I think they moved, because I asked them to? Ninetoes responded. The end of his reply became more question than answer, but it stopped Libby in her tracks and she moved back behind the protective field and clambered onto the top of the crenellations so that she had a better view.

Well, then I suppose you try something else? Her response was also formed into a question and Ninetoes could certainly understand why. Why would they be responding to him?

Alright, he could do this, but what should he ask them to do? "Er…" he raised his voice to be heard by all those he could see, "…um, please sit down."

WHUMPH!

Every single undead creature that he could see, be it bugbear, goblin or worg, sat straight down with an audible slap of skin and leather behinds on the cobblestone floor.

Huh! I really need to come up with a new way of testing my undead.

***

And they really were… his undead. A veritable army of animated corpses, each one beholden to his every whim. Over the next hour, Ninetoes experimented.

He had the undead stand up, lie down, fetch things and run relays. The more he worked with them, the more he felt confident of his ability to command them and the stronger he felt the strand of magic that connected him to the many, many undead.

He also learned one of the limitations of this magic. These unintelligent creatures could perform only very simple tasks and, what's more, they would all attempt to perform the same task unless he directed his attention and will on one specifically. He could see how, in battle, this could be dangerous and time consuming. His untapped knowledge gave him further detail however, and he understood that he could, with practice, come to be able to control multiple undead with different tasks at once and, what's more, he could give them more difficult tasks as well.

With confidence came the assuredness that these creatures offered no threat to him or his companions and so he informed Libby that it was safe and so, cautiously at first, she joined him.

Soon, she too grew in security and became accustomed to their presence. Excited by his discovery, Ninetoes quickly 'stepped' back to the top of the wall and, taking Bluzag by the hand, 'stepped' down.

Even with his mana topped off, he felt the strain of mana depletion as he 'arrived' and checking his Character Sheet, he found that the one single trip had cost him three hundred and sixty mana, one hundred and twenty mana more than the lvl 4 version of his spell quoted. He reasoned that this must have to do with Bluzag's massive size. He had hoped that such a large undertaking would level up the skill, but alas it did not.

Before he'd gone to collect his ally, he'd shouted out, his voice breaking the stillness and instructed the undead to stand at the far end of the camp. He had the strangest feeling that there were more of them nearby. Many more.

While he waited to find out, he walked the short distance to the pavilion tent in the centre of the goblinoid camp, excited by the prospect of taking ownership of Bofar's treasure.

As he walked into the gloom beneath the canvas, his dark vision kicked in and he quickly scanned the interior. It was much as he'd left it, a small work station that held potion making equipment and a number of components kept in labelled jars, cases and small wooden boxes.

It also held a small collection of books and scrolls. Towards the back stood a cot bed, lavishly adorned with silk sheets and rich animal furs. Finally, standing proudly off to one side, were two chests, each one brimming with gold and platinum coins, colourful gems and jewellery. His underarms felt wet with perspiration as he took in the scene, it truly was a king's ransom! There must have been thousands of gold coins and the gems must be worth ten times as much; he was rich!

His only problem now was, how in all Adrenon would he carry it all. His Bag of Holding was reaching its limits already.

He'd have to empty out some books… *or food?* Yeah, he didn't need to carry so much food, he could hunt, or send Bluzag to do so.

Without realising it, he'd moved and Ninetoes found himself crouching before the treasure, his eyes gleaming with avarice. With this wealth and the castle behind him, his people would never want for anything. They could hire the best craftsman in the region to rebuild the homes around the city and he'd be able to live with them once again, surrounded by his people. All of whom would be protected by his power.

He reached out to pick up a handful of coins, the warm glow of the gold illuminating his callous hands and as they closed around the cool metal the coins clinked against one another. Turning his palm up to his face, he brought a coin closer to his mouth to bite down and test the metal.

His teeth met only a little resistance before he left the canine indentation of his sharpest teeth, *Gold! It's really gold!*

A small part of him had worried that fate would cheat him and that the gold had been an illusion. Now, the larger part of him told that part to bugger off.

Picking up a gem, he checked it over. He had little knowledge or experience but they seemed real enough. On a hunch, he cast Identify and sure enough, the spell confirmed what he'd hoped, the gem was real and, as he cast his gaze over the rest, so too were they all. His Identify spell had the added benefit of giving him the possible value for each gem. Even as his eyes swept over the hoard, the values on display were simply eye-watering and, he realised, his original estimation that the gems were worth ten times as much as the coins was a vast understatement. The wealth here wasn't only enough to give his people a home and protection, it was enough to make them a force to be reckoned with once again. The thought energised him and his body shook slightly with excitement. Could it really be that easy to return home?

The sweat under his arms was making him uncomfortable and so he removed his cloak, folding it and placing it in his pack. This was so much wealth, it was almost a little scary and, based upon the collection of coins just in his hands must be a mixture of wealth that Bofar had brought with him and loot his goblins had collected in the ancient city. In part, it had been this wealth and more importantly the power it could garner, that had drawn Bofar to find the lost stronghold.

Ninetoes feared that others would come and steal it all from him, and such a thought galvanised him into action.

Stepping out into the open space in front of the tent, Ninetoes removed his Bag of Holding and, turning it upside down he held a hand in front of the opening and clearly enunciated one word, "Everything."

A deluge of items tumbled out of the bag, quickly piling into the space beneath, so much so that Ninetoes was forced to move to the side and let the items spill into a line of loot instead of a large heap.

Some of the items he'd almost forgotten existed. There was food, books, trinkets, gold and weapons. He'd collected a goodly amount of his own treasure already, enough to consider himself rich, but his paltry findings were nothing in comparison to the wealth inside the tent.

This then, is where he started, shovelling the gold in large handfuls into the mouth of his bag. The weight was such that he quickly grew tired and so, passing the bag to Bluzag, instructed the Wight to complete the task.

Moving back outside, he shivered. The days were certainly growing colder and, if the heavy, dark clouds on the horizon were any indication, it would soon be the rainy season. While the loot he'd found here was exciting, he'd have to get moving soon. He had no desire to travel during the rain but more than that, if he was too slow, his people would have to wait until the Spring to journey here.

He would not leave a copper behind, however, and so he must choose carefully what he could take with him.

He considered for a moment using the undead to carry everything for him, but he knew that most people, certainly the folk that dwelt in Raveslan, feared such decaying creatures and realised that this was not a viable solution.

He could, however, use the undead to help him sort through the piles of items. It would also be a good test of his control and just how much the creatures understood and the limits of the jobs they could perform. He'd already worked out that he needed to concentrate on a single… um… unit? when giving an instruction or all those within earshot would perform the same task. A useful trait in the right circumstances but it clearly wouldn't do for now.

Since he'd been in the tent, a large number more of the undead had arrived and stood in a large gaggle in the space around the tent.

He mentally divided the group into quarters and then counted this group. He reached twenty-six and so reasoned that there must already be more than a hundred undead in the space and more were coming every minute.

He didn't want so many tripping over his stuff and so he concentrated on a group of five, giving each the task of finding a different type of item, instructing each to collect that type of item into a pile.

The one he instructed to collect food set straight to the task, as did the creature he'd told to stack the books. But the other three, who he'd told to divide the treasure, weapons and potions simply stood stock still with vacant expressions across their faces.

Indeed, all of the undead had the same empty look, but on these three the expression seemed even more devoid of sense. Clearly, this was their limit. *Their current limit.* He corrected himself. Necromancy was his Specialism now and he would learn to master it.

Instead, he began standing the undead in groups of ten. As he did so, he concentrated on his Identify spell and checked over a number of the creatures.

ZOMBIE GOBLIN - LEVEL 8
PRIME STAT - ENDURANCE
PRIME TRAIT - UNDEAD
22/22 HP
100XP

ZOMBIE BUGBEAR- LEVEL 10
PRIME STAT - ENDURANCE
PRIME TRAIT - UNDEAD
41/41 HP
450XP

ZOMBIE WORG - LEVEL 4
PRIME STAT - ENDURANCE
PRIME TRAIT - UNDEAD
36/36 HP
400XP

Alright, this was useful information. Now he had something more specific to call them and understood a little more about them.

Although he'd never seen the term 'Prime Stat' used before, it was fairly self-explanatory and now he had an idea of the relative strengths of his creatures.

The Zombie Worg was obviously more dangerous than the goblin. Despite the disparity between their levels, which made sense as the worg was much bigger and obviously stronger and faster than the goblin, even in its zombie form.

Finally, his knowledge of Necromancy told him that the 'Prime Trait' was the most powerful Skill, Ability or Racial trait that the creature had. While they might hold other traits, this trait was predominant. Ninetoes also knew that the 'undead' trait was as he'd previously understood, that undead didn't need sleep, sustenance or to breathe. It also revealed something else useful. Monster's also had Levels but they seemed to differ from those of Adventurers.

As he'd Identified these first three creatures, more undead had arrived, including a number of undead animals, including a small flock of ravens, two boars and an entire plague of rats. As he identified a member of each group, he found that they resembled their larger brethren, all of them now having the Undead trait and their Prime Stat was now Endurance. All, that was, except for the ravens, whose Prime Stat was Agility. This, Ninetoes assumed, was due to their ability to fly, but he made a note to research this further.

As the morning wore on, Ninetoes sorted through the piles for those things that he could absolutely not do without. He took enough food for himself and Libby to survive off for a journey of twice the length than the one back to Raveslan, reasoning that this would serve him even if he ran into difficulty.

His Adventurer's backpack carried all of his essentials, like a bedroll and mess kit, so he need not worry about those. He also began to pack all of the treasure that he'd found before today. This included a number of items of jewellery, some coins and a simple silver ring with a black gem. This ring was one of the first pieces of loot he'd ever found, taken from the corpse of a dark-elf, in the hollow of an ettercap. At the time, he'd considered the item worth selling, but now, with so much other wealth and with his new specialism of 'dark' magic, he decided that a small affectation was in order and so he placed the ring on his own pinky finger.

As he cast his gaze across the mounds of stuff, he considered how to be most efficient and thus take as much as possible.

Firstly, he planned to keep Bluzag with him. Although the Wight was undead, apart from his wound and the pallor of his skin, there was nothing that made Bluzag look undead. Unlike the zombies, Bluzag's eyes now showed a degree of thought behind them and he'd already proven himself capable of following more complex instructions.

Ninetoes had already solved the issue of the unsightly wound and his pale skin could be explained simply as a poor constitution, although, if he could find a cloak big enough or a helmet that covered more of his face, that would be even better.

With this in mind and due to Bluzag's prodigious Strength score, Ninetoes intended to use him as a bit of a pack mule.

"Bluzag my friend. Search these nearby buildings for a large backpack. Once you have found one, or once you've been through these five buildings," he said pointing at each building in turn, "return here to me."

"Yes Master," came his deep droning response. As Ninetoes considered it, he added.

"If you find any treasure, weapons or armour, bring that as well."

"Yes Master," the Wight said, before moving off. Ninetoes trusted that his servant understood his instructions, but to be sure, he turned to his Familiar, who was currently lazing on the furs of Bofar's cot.

Little One? Please go with him and ensure he does as I've told him. Libby didn't move and, if it hadn't been for their connection, he might have believed that she was actually asleep, but for once it worked against the cheeky little rodent.

Hurrmph. Ergh, you have no idea how hard it is to get comfortable with all these undead moving around and making noise. She sent back, stretching languorously, before skittering off to do as he bid.

Standing alone, well apart from the scores of undead, Ninetoes cast his gaze over the stack of books. He simply couldn't take them all and so he'd have to be more picky. Firstly, he packed the spellbooks he'd found, *Corvash's Monograph on Animation* and the three books that he'd chosen for Foresto. Next, he selected each of the books on the various schools of magic. He'd found some for Evocation, Abjuration, Transmutation and

Conjuration, he started packing these, but as he reached the second to last book, his Bag of Holding reached its limit and wouldn't allow him to place anymore within. He set those books aside and a couple more; one, a book on types of monster and the other a book about potions, with the intent of packing these with Bluzag.

Leftover was a sizable stack of books, hundreds of spell components and ingredients and, finally, Libby's cushion. Clearly, he couldn't leave the last item behind and so he stuffed this straight into his backpack. He also wanted to take all of the components, which created a problem.

While the weight of these items wasn't significant, there were so many of them and many of them were so tiny or delicate, having Bluzag carry them would be inefficient and would probably cause them to be ruined.

Ninetoes thought about it and hypothesised that his Bag of Holding worked on weight rather than size and shape and so, removing all of the books, he started placing all of the other items in. He found that while he could fit in a larger quantity of items, there simply wasn't room for everything. He would have to leave a sizable number of components and ingredients behind.

It was annoying, but he could always buy more with the wealth he carried and, if his plans worked out, he'd be returning soon enough with his people.

The cumbersome books, however, he did not want to leave behind, they would travel with Bluzag.

While he waited, Ninetoes continued to concentrate on his Identify spell, analysing each and every zombie that joined the massing horde.

As he stood before the ranks of zombies, it struck him just how powerful he'd become. Only a couple of weeks had passed since the council of his people had cast him out, since Elder Brev had sent him to seek out the wizard Foresto and yet, in those two weeks, look what he'd achieved. Surely there was no way that they could turn him away now, not with the treasures he had to offer them.

No. His goal was simple. Travel back to Foresto and complete his Quest. From there, his peoples' settlement was but a few short days hike.

By the time the half-ogre and his familiar had returned, Ninetoes had levelled up both the spell's level and his ability with Divination. Across Bluzag's shoulders was what appeared to be a large saddle bag, the pocket at the front bulging with a large dull, brown cloak.

This was all we could find of his size Master. But the cloak seems to fit him perfectly. What's more, I think the colour really matches the vacant expression he always wears. She quipped.

"Good work. Both of you, we can certainly make something out of the bag."

Due to his earlier successes, Ninetoes quickly set to work.

Using strips of leather from some old pieces of armour he'd found lying around in the camp, Ninetoes used his Mending spell to create a strap that went under Bluzag's weapon arm to connect the front and rear pouches of the saddle bags. He made sure that it sat over the shoulder opposite the one with the quiver of javelins.

Having Bluzag raise his shield and maul, he tested the bag and made a few adjustments to ensure that the Wight could still move freely. Within ten minutes it was finished and packed with all of the books. All of them fit snugly into the back pouch, leaving the front one mostly empty.

Looking up at the sky, Ninetoes searched for the sun. While it was mostly hidden behind the rain clouds, he could still reckon its location and judged the time to be around midday, *perfect!*

Turning around, Ninetoes took in the army of undead that had gathered to his call, there must be hundreds.

"Um.... all of you," he called, "stay here and, if the need arises, stop anyone or anything from entering the castle." He wouldn't risk anyone stealing his stronghold.

With that, he turned and began making his way out of the city and sent Libby ahead, to act as his scout, while Bluzag trailed a few steps behind. A grin stretched across his face. He was returning to complete his first Quest, already richer and more powerful than he could have possibly imagined.

CHAPTER 4

NECROMANCY

Somewhere else, in a different and yet connected world people play a game. This game, and the stories it tells affect the very lives of the people of Adrenon, not that the players know it of course. And not all such players are worthy of this power.

PORTSMOUTH, 2017

"When last we left our heroes, they had survived the dangers of-"

"Yeah, yeah, yeah, we get it, we're brilliant, come on Bruce, get on with it!" Tony seriously wondered where they'd found this numpty, he was always waxing lyrical and going on. Admittedly, he knew his stuff; had the monster's stats committed to memory and ran some great combat, but the man did not shut up!

"Look Tony, I am just trying to inject a little narrative into our games, you guys are turning into a bunch of murder hobos," Bruce explained. Tony seriously needed to head him off at the pass, before he started going on again. He needed to be careful though, it had taken him months to find a new group willing to take both him and Daph to play after that knobhead Mike had booted them from his wanky little game.

"Ok, ok. You're right, I'm just… excited is all," he said, attempting to mollify Bruce.

Argh! If he didn't like playing so much, he'd get rid.

Bruce was a weirdo and, staring across the table he almost met eyes with Felix. Man, if any of them was a murder hobo, it was that guy. Tony wasn't too much of a man to admit that the guy scared him... a little. Tony would bet good money that he was the type of kid that caught dragonflies, just to pull their wings off.

Instead, his eyes settled on Solveg. Now, here was something worth staring at, Solveg was gorgeous and she was completely out of place at this table of nerds. She probably felt the same as him, loved the game but hated having to play with weirdos. Perhaps he should invite her to a little one on one, ha!

Looking up he caught Solveg's eyes and he grinned his most wolfish smile. The girl looked away, her hands moving to zip up her hoody.

Whoops, she must have caught him ogling. No matter. The way he saw it, that just meant she knew what he was about.

"Righ' are we doin' this then?" asked Daphne in a snarky voice. Shit, it looked like she'd caught him too.

"Of course. As I was saying, 'Striding confidently, your party heads into the great port city of Pamor. When the bards sing tales of this metropolis they tell us its many wonders, the city filled equally with opportunities for rise... and or for ruin. Many stories are told about the city, but the one thing upon which they all agree; is that in Pamor, anything can be bought.'"

***

STONEBARROW REGION, 2301 AC

The journey back to Raveslan was going well. Ninetoes was well rested and his improved Endurance seemed to make the hike each day easy.

They had been travelling for three days now and Ninetoes was beginning to show signs of the extended travel. Libby however, despite having only been able to share his rations and spending all day on the move, seemed to be growing around the belly and had hours where she simply rode on his shoulder, so out of puff had she become. He hadn't dared point this out of course.

Each evening they'd set their camp and Ninetoes would leave Bluzag on watch.

With each passing day, he was becoming more and more accustomed to the Wight's presence. He wasn't, Ninetoes admitted, much of a conversationalist, but he was welcome company, the forest seeming less empty with him nearby. And besides, Ninetoes enjoyed Libby's company.

...and then it fell off! While she spoke only into his mind, her slightly strange tittering laugh bounced down from a branch above where the hobgoblin rested.

A wonderful result of Libby's increased intelligence was her ability to tell him stories. Ninetoes had never considered that the life of a squirrel would be very interesting, but the way his Familiar told it, her life had been one exciting adventure followed by the next, each one more amusing than the last.

So, then you have a family somewhere? He asked delicately.

Libby stopped laughing to consider this. *Hmmm, not in the way you'd mean it.*

This is the best part of their connection, while the odd the pair could visualise words to 'talk' at a measured pace, they could also share one another's meaning at the speed of thought. Indeed, the two were ultimately connected constantly. That's why Ninetoes instantly understood that for his Familiar, a family wasn't a unit of linked individuals, but rather just a community of squirrels that lived and survived together.

I suppose you could say I had a 'brother' of sorts.

An image and a feeling flashed into Ninetoes' mind of another squirrel that was younger and smaller than Libby. She had, in some sense, felt an obligation towards protecting him. As she dwelt on the thought, other images flashed through Ninetoes mind, and he saw how the other squirrel had been caught unawares by a massive spider and how, in an act of incredible bravery, Libby had shot in front of the monstrous creature to grab its attention.

The act had saved the other squirrel, but Libby had been caught herself. Within the same instant, Ninetoes realised that this was the very act that had meant that Libby was in the ettercap's hollow and the reason that they had first been thrown together, fighting to survive the spiderkin's clutches.

We could look for him Little One, once we're back. He offered.

Thank you Master, but I hold out little hope for him. He is much like you... a disaster waiting to happen. And...

And, Little One? Ignoring the snide remark, Ninetoes could sense there was more Libby was trying and failing to find the words to say.

And, I don't think I can go back. That small thought came with a flood of emotion from the small creature, much more than her tiny form should be able to hold. Libby was equal parts saddened by the realisation, as she was emboldened by it. She had, like him, become so much more in the last few weeks. What's more, she now recognised that there was no limit to how far she could grow in both power and experience.

Ninetoes knew, however, that no words could help her in this moment and, more so, that it was for her to deal with. So instead, he opened himself up to her and warm feelings of friendship spread between them.

Meanwhile, Ninetoes further assessed the progress they made over the last few days. They had spent every evening training for an hour or so. Ninetoes had divided this time into three equal sized parts. Firstly, they worked on Bluzag's ability to block incoming attacks. Ninetoes knew that Blocking was a skill and he hoped that it was one that the half-ogre could learn. On their second night of practicing, their hard work had paid off and the skill appeared on the Wight's Character Sheet. More excitingly, the skill had already improved to level 2.

```
BLOCKING - LEVEL 2
COOL DOWN - NONE
PREREQUISITES - A SHIELD LARGE ENOUGH TO
COVER AT LEAST 30% OF BODY
+2% CHANCE TO BLOCK
-2% DAMAGE REDUCTION
```

With their training the previous night, they had managed to increase its level again.

The next portion of their practice time was spent sparring. Ninetoes charged up his own Wizard Armour and, only using his ability to Dodge and his Barrier spell, defended against Bluzag's attacks. For the first couple of days, Bluzag had barely hit him, showing the disparity in their Skill levels. But on the third night, Bluzag had landed a bone-shaking blow to Ninetoes shoulder. The hobgoblin was eternally grateful for his magical armour, otherwise the attack would have done more than just shake his bones.

After that, Ninetoes was more careful, trying not to rely too heavily on his magical armour. He remembered how easily Bofar had gone down to a single strike from the brute and, by the end of last night's session, Ninetoes Dodging skill had levelled up to sixth and Bluzag's skill with bludgeoning weapons had almost reached tenth. Ninetoes was excited for their session in the coming evening, he looked forward to seeing what bonus skill the half-ogre gained from reaching the Poor rank.

The final segment of their training was spent practicing as a group.

Ninetoes knew that Bluzag was only really as useful as the instructions he gave to the Wight, his limited intelligence meaning that he couldn't really think for himself in combat.

Ninetoes needed to work out how best to utilise the brute and so they practiced with different methods. In the end, what seemed to work best was sending Bluzag forward at the beginning of the battle to harry their opponent while Ninetoes threw spells.

Of course, their 'opponent' was a static illusion created and maintained by Libby, so this was definitely the area where they needed the most work. Libby had, however, improved her own use of the Minor Illusion spell to allow her creations to move.

Libby's illusion's movements were spasmodic and lurching, but it was a level of mastery that he hadn't yet achieved and showed that the Familiar was already growing beyond him. Since her illusions began to move, their training sessions had improved.

Ninetoes had been worried, after he'd discovered his massive leap in experience points and Levels, that his growth would stagnate. It was why he trained so hard every night and why he was so happy that both he and his allies were improving so well.

It was these thoughts that carried him into a large and beautiful glade, the dappled light of the autumn sun suddenly replaced by a blinding light as he stepped out from under the browning, autumnal canopy.

The sudden change shook him out of his reverie and he finally took in the beautiful scene, and the sun's warmth breaking a smile across his deep-reddish skin. He took a deep breath of clean, fresh air.

The glade was idyllic. The whole space was covered in grass of the most vibrant green and was split in half by a sparkling stream that crashed down from a rocking outcropping and opened into a large pond, before disappearing off into the forest beyond.

Ninetoes' long legs quickly closed the distance as he made his way towards the pond, retrieving his water pouch from his pack as he did so. Kneeling, he began filling the pouch with one hand and dipped his hand in and splashed water onto his face and the back of his neck.

"It's normally polite to announce one's presence."

Thump!

Ninetoes fell back onto his bottom as the voice broke the pleasant silence and surprised the aspiring wizard.

"Uh, um, hello. My apologies," he responded, searching around for the voice's owner.

Some excellent scouting Little One. He sent to his familiar, lathering the thought with sarcasm.

She wasn't there a moment ago, I promise Master. Came the response, her own voice confused and concerned.

She? He questioned and then he saw her. Stepping out from behind the outcropping strode a tall and severe looking elven woman.

Her features were flawless, but to call her beautiful just seemed... wrong somehow.

Her skin was totally unblemished and her face absolutely symmetrical. She was just too perfect to be considered attractive, but there was something... otherworldly about her.

"Ah, hello. My apologies for not announcing our presence, I had thought the glade empty."

"No matter, and please drink deeply from the pool. Bathe in it if you like, you have clearly travelled far to... ah, how to put it? To have acquired such a treasure trove of flavours and scents."

Ninetoes untangled her words. *Do I smell Libby dearest?*

Horribly Master. I've been assuming that's why we'd made it this far without being attacked by any monsters, they simply didn't want to eat something so foul. She explained.

So saying, the squirrel leapt down from her perch at the edge of the clearing and moved closer to the pool. It didn't escape Ninetoes' notice, however, that she kept himself between her and the woman.

Humph, a simple 'yes' would have sufficed. Looking back at the women he smiled apologetically.

"You are correct, I have travelled far. Perhaps I should bathe."

Keep an eye on her Little One, there's something strange about all this.

Of course, Master.

"Please, go right ahead. I even have some soap here. I was coming to the glade to do the same."

She said, retrieving a small bar of blue soap from a small satchel and offering it to him. When he looked around for somewhere to disrobe, she laughed.

"Of course, I sometimes forget how prudish the other races are. Please go ahead," she said, turning her back and placing a long delicate finger over each of her eyes, "I will not watch." She promised.

A little embarrassed, Ninetoes turned his own back to the woman and began taking off his clothes and armour. With a brief command, he had Bluzag collect his belongings and watch over them. Stepping into the water he received a slight shock; the water was warm.

Libby meanwhile approached the water's edge and, after a cursory sniff, she lapped at it to quench her own thirst.

Shouldn't you bathe as well. Ninetoes asked his Familiar.

Squirrels do not smell like larger beasts and I had a dust bath this morning. She answered waspishly. Ninetoes simply grinned and waded deeper into the pool.

The climate of late had been growing colder and wetter each day and he'd expected the water to be freezing, but instead it was lukewarm. It was also crystal clear; he could see all the way to the silty bottom.

The pool was also deep enough for him to fully submerge himself if he knelt down and doing so felt instantly cleansing. Using the soap she'd provided, he quickly worked up a lather and scrubbed at the dirt and grime across his whole body.

Most of the humans and other folk of Adrenon considered his people to be filthy beasts like their bugbear and goblin cousins, but it couldn't be further from the truth. In his village his people bathed daily and it was only the constant travel and danger that had meant he had not done so more recently. It felt wonderful to be so clean, he couldn't remember ever being so spotless.

Enjoying himself now, Ninetoes dunked his head beneath the surface and then, resurfacing, worked the lather into his hair.

As a warrior of his people, the Dakhec Druull, Ninetoes had worn his hair in the topknot. But when he'd been banished from his people the leather cord he wore had been stripped from him as a sign of his dishonour. Since then he'd simply allowed his hair to hang loose over his ears.

Now, as he dragged his fingers through it, he noticed how long and matted with filth it had become. Without a comb, he could only use his fingers, trying to tease out the worst of the knots.

But it was no good, it was too tangled. Calling over Bluzag, he retrieved his elven dagger from his belt and began slicing off large clumps of his mop.

"Hmmm, that's an exquisite dagger you have there. Elven-made and ancient by the looks of it. How did you come by it?"

The woman was seated on a rock in the middle of the brook, her eyes locked onto Ninetoes's weapon. Ninetoes could see the interest in her eyes and suddenly felt exposed.

"An elder of my village gave it to me," he told her, purposefully vague on the details.

"Indeed, and how did he come upon it? Your people are known to have warlike tendencies, did he perhaps take it from a fallen enemy?"

"Alas, I do not know the details. But I think you are likely closer to the truth of it," he answered, as honestly as he could.

"Huh? May I see it?" she reached out her hand, as if her request was more of an expectation. Ninetoes was naked and waist deep in water, and it was a little late to be worried that she might attack him. So instead, he turned the knife so that he was holding the blade and offered her the hilt.

Taking it, she drew it closer to her eyes and muttered a spell.

It was in a language that Ninetoes didn't understand but by her actions he assumed that the spell was something akin to his own Identify spell.

"Mmmm," she murmured "perhaps not Arcturan after all... strange." She continued muttering to herself as she studied the blade, apparently forgetting that Ninetoes was even there.

"What do you know of this blade's powers hobgoblin?" she asked, her tone stricter than it had been before.

"Powers? I only know that it's magical somehow and that I can use it to channel my own magic."

"Ha!" she barked. "Oh my friend, it is so much more. Look," she said, climbing off of the rock and crouching by the pool's edge, "these runes are ancient magic and they would allow for much more than channelling, in fact if I'm not mistaken, they will **amplify** a spell cast through them." The word carried a degree of weight with it that made the hobgoblin's ears perk up.

"Really? Amplify how?" he asked, his interest growing. So much so that he'd stepped out of the pool to sit beside her, naked as a babe. The warmth of the sun began to dry him and his earlier priggish attitude dissolved in its comforting embrace.

"Well that, I think, would depend upon the spell. With a spell meant to attack for example, the dagger would increase the damage it caused, or perhaps add an extra effect. If used to focus a Conjuration spell, it would increase the range or definition. But really, I think you're missing the true purpose of this dagger."

"Really, how so?" His interest was now truly piqued.

"Well, while this dagger is clearly a dangerous weapon, especially in the hands of a magic user, it's actual purpose is not that of a weapon, but rather as a tool. Meant for extracting and inserting magic into an… object maybe?"

"Extracting? How?" Ninetoes' tone had reverted to that which he used when working with Foresto. A tone of wonder he'd used when the magician began lecturing. Sometimes he would use it to tap more information from the gnome because he was truly intrigued by a topic, but oftentimes he'd found that by keeping the old kook talking, he could rest. On this occasion he was enraptured by the elf's lecturing tone.

"As you should be aware, mana resides in all living things, it is the very essence of life and every living thing has a field or aura of this mana surrounding them. As I can tell, you already understand that magic users tap into this well of magic to cast spells and such. What you may not already know is that the mana or magic of a thing has a certain… flavour, taste or colour to it. A signature that makes it unique. What you also don't yet understand is that this mana can be drained out of a creature, sapping its life. Some wizards call this death magic, but they're missing the point." She paused for thought and Ninetoes considered what she'd said. She was talking about necromancy and spells like Grim Void.

"One of the reasons that so many mages fear this kind of magic is that by removing a thing's mana, you invariably take its life, hence the name, 'death' magic. But true practitioners of this field of magic are able to remove this mana **without** killing the host. What's more, they can extract the essence or flavour of the thing, taking with it its own unique properties without killing it. These runes here," she said, pointing out some etchings on the windward side of the blade, "are used to draw the mana out of the target and these," she said, turning the blade over, "are used to insert it."

"So, if I cut into something or stab it, I can draw out its mana?" Ninetoes asked.

"Ha! I pity your misunderstanding. To you and many others all you see is a blade, but look closer, use your Mind's Eye." The way she said the term, she clearly meant it in a more purposeful way than just as the common saying.

"My Mind's Eye?" he asked, hoping not to look foolish.

"Yes, your... wait, are you saying that you've reached level twelve as a wizard and you haven't yet learned the Mind's Eye skill?" Ninetoes shook his head, feeling the annoying sting of not knowing something. A look of shock crossed over his face as well; how did she know his Level and Class?

Her eyes softened and she took pity on him. "Fear not my friend, it is simple enough to learn. You have, I'm sure, already felt or 'tasted' magic, yes?"

He nodded, glad to be back on firmer ground.

"Well, the reason for this is that, as a spellcaster, you are mana-sensitive and, by focussing a little mana into your eyes, you can see the flows and traces of mana. Now, close your eyes,"

"But, they how will I—"

"See? With your Mind's Eye, haven't you been listening?"

"Sorry." He apologised, feeling stupid.

71

"Just so. Close your eyes … Thank you. And now channel a little of your mana into your eyes. It'll feel itchy at first but you'll get used to it quickly enough."

Ninetoes focussed his attention on the well of magical energy in his core and imagined himself pulling a strand from it and guiding this towards his eyes. As soon as the imagined tendril was level with his nose it divided in two and each smaller strand sought out one of his eyes.

Woah! It was like someone had turned on one of the magical lights he'd found in Kavralach, he could… See!

As the ability kicked in, he opened his eyes out of habit and the world he saw was an incredible array of colours and light. His vision blurred with so many new and strange sensations and at first he found it unnerving.

Master, your eyes! They're glowing! He could sense the concern in his Familiar's thoughts.

Calm yourself little one, I must concentrate.

"Good. You have done well to succeed so quickly and do not be alarmed, with practice you'll be able to see much more clearly with your Mind's Eye, eventually even more so than your normal vision. But for now, focus on the blade."

Her voice was reassuring and soft. She handed him the knife and, taking it, he stared at it and he was amazed.

The blade itself was sharp, this much he already knew, but looking at it with his enhanced vision, he could see that a whisper thin layer of mana extended out a few millimetres from the metal of the blade, this mana was like a thin, black light and he understood, inherently, that this was the magic she spoke of.

"Yes, you see it now. As I'm sure you've already discovered, this dagger is incredibly sharp, but its real edge is that which you see now and that is infinitely sharper. That edge could slice into a creature's aura, without cutting the skin, a cut so slight that the aura can easily repair itself."

"But, why would anyone want to cut the aura and not the skin?" he questioned.

"To take the essence of a thing, without killing it. I believe that the ancients created tools such as these to take, mix and change mana into incredible effects."

"Intriguing," he whispered, his voice displaying his awe.

"Intriguing? Oh, my dear Ninetoes, it is so much more. The other schools of magic are powerful to be sure, but they all have the same limitation. Each of them 'uses' magic, controls it. Necromancy has the power to 'create' new magic."

If what she's saying is true Master, then this is incredible. Libby's thoughts reflected his own and, searching the glade, he found her stretching out belly-up on a rock nearby. This could mean so much to him. Ninetoes simply stared into the middle distance. He'd been so uncertain about his unchosen Specialism. Foresto had been so negative about the school, telling him that only dark and evil wizards focussed on the discipline.

His own experience had taught him that it was a powerful and, most definitely, dangerous school, but he'd always felt that it was misunderstood. This proved it.

"But, then why don't more mages practice necromancy?" he asked.

But, as the silence lengthened he realised he was alone. He stood up and looked around.

Wait, where'd she go? She was right there. A chill fled down Ninetoes spine at Libby's question.

The glade was as it had been, although the sun was hidden behind some clouds and goosebumps stubbled his skin. It suddenly felt very different to how it had.

Crossing the glade to Bluzag, he reached down for his clothes. "Wait, how did she know my name?"

Worse still, now that the thought occurred to him; what in the Nine Hells had he been doing? He'd met a stranger in the woods and not only had he almost immediately taken his armour and clothes off and entered a strange pool, he'd even handed her a weapon. He was lucky to be alive.

Libby, what just happened?

I don't know Master. This place felt so warm and comforting.

The thought of how both of them let their guard down made him shiver once more and he quickly started to dress, his eyes darting about, suddenly and distinctly uncomfortable.

CHAPTER 5

NEW THREATS

By the time he was dressed, the memory of the elven women seemed like a dream and Ninetoes barely gave her another thought. The sun that had seemed warm enough to dry his crimson skin, now felt cold enough to freeze the last few specks and once he'd replaced his armour, he wrapped his traveller's cloak tight around his shoulders and wished for a pair of gloves.

Before he moved off, he checked over his Character Sheet and sure enough a new Skill had been added. And, while the cost in mana was comparatively high, the skill seemed to have already levelled twice and it looked as though the mana cost was reduced by five per cent per level.

> MIND'S EYE: LEVEL 3 - BEGINNER
>
> MANA COST - 10 POINTS/SECOND
>
> USING THIS SKILL ALLOWS ONE TO SEE THE FLOWS, COLOURS AND SOURCES OF MANA.
>
> -15% COST IN MANA.

Ninetoes decided that he would practice using the skill each day, as part of his training regimen. It also made him consider how he could practice more with his spells. He now kept both his Wizard's Armour active all the time and cast Reaper's Sorrow every morning. This had allowed him to see steady growth in his Abjuration skill, levelling once already.

But he'd realised that he needed to practice with his other spell schools as well. He couldn't practice them all, but he knew that he needed to improve his Conjuration and Divination schools if he could, these being his next most useful.

Arcane Step was one of his most useful spells and he wanted to see how far he could take it and his Identify spell could, potentially, save his life. Still, it would certainly make him more coin if he could level it to the point that it could provide more useful information. He also wanted to discover the rank bonuses by reaching Beginner level in each school.

With this in mind, Ninetoes started using these two spells as he hiked. He'd cast Identify and analysed everything he saw: trees, plants, animals, rocks, everything. Then, as he moved he'd 'step' a few times, back and forth, never draining more than half of his mana pool. Finally, he'd concentrate on his breathing and his emotions and Meditate until his mana was back to full and then repeat it all over again. Doing this was a bit of a grind, but had the added benefit of helping him get a sense of how 'full' his mana was, simply through the feel of it.

For the next three days, this is how his time went. During the day they'd march, Libby scouting ahead and Bluzag acting as rear-guard, while Ninetoes practiced his spells. In the evening, they'd set camp and train.

At times, doing so felt boring, but the more he practiced, the more he learned about his spells. He even spent some of his time after their evening meal, practicing on his Illusion magic with Libby. There was no question that she was becoming much more proficient in the spell school than he was, but he was making steady progress.

When he'd awoken this morning, he'd performed what had become his morning ritual. As he broke his fast, he checked over their Character Sheets and was pleased with the healthy gains they'd made.

Character name: Ninetoes	Race: Hobgoblin (+1 End, +1 Int)
Level: 12th	Experience points: 75,565/88,000
Class: Wizard	Specialism: Necromancer
Hit points: 240/240	Mana points: 380/380
Stamina points: 200/200	
Base stats: Strength - 13 (9) Agility - 20 Endurance - 27 Intelligence - 38 (33) Wisdom - 24 Charisma - 12 (7)	Varied stats: Fitness - 20 Will - 25
Languages: Common - Fluent Goblinoid - Native Arcane - Poor Kavralarian - Fluent	Armour Class: Armour 15+ Wizard Armour 12. Total: 27 +30% resistance to fire damage +25% resistance to necrotic damage
Skills	
Basic first aid: Level 5 - Beginner Can use basic bandages and simple ointments to heal minor wounds.	One-handed blades: Level 13 - Poor +13% damage. +13% chance of critical hit.

	FIGHTING STANCE - YOUR FOOTWORK IS NOW MORE EFFICIENT, ALLOWING YOU TO SWING WITH MORE POWER, INCREASING DAMAGE BY 5%.
TRAP BUILDING: LEVEL 4 - BEGINNER CAN USE MUNDANE ITEMS TO CREATE POOR QUALITY TRAPS.	SNEAK AND HIDE: LEVEL 7 - BEGINNER +14% CHANCE OF SUCCESS TO ATTEMPTS AT CONCEALING YOURSELF.
LONGBOW: LEVEL 13 - POOR +13% DAMAGE. +13% CHANCE OF CRITICAL HIT. QUICK SHOT - CAN FIRE AT TWICE THE SPEED, LOSING 50% ACCURACY.	LIGHT ARMOUR: LEVEL 12 - POOR 12% DAMAGE REDUCTION WHILE WEARING LIGHT ARMOUR.
MEDIUM ARMOUR: LEVEL 13 - BEGINNER 3% DAMAGE REDUCTION WHILE WEARING MEDIUM ARMOUR.	ARCANA: LEVEL 13 - POOR CAN UNDERSTAND BASIC AND DEVELOPED SPELL CONCEPTS AND LANGUAGE
CHANNELLING: LEVEL 14 - POOR CAN CHANNEL 14 MANA POINTS INTO OR OUT OF AN OBJECT, SPELL OR CREATURE PER SECOND	SKINNING & BUTCHERING: LEVEL 3 - BEGINNER +3% CHANCE TO DISCOVER AN ITEM/COMPONENT/INGREDIENT/MATERIAL OF ONE LEVEL OF RARITY ABOVE THE CREATURE'S BASE LEVEL.
RITUAL CASTING: LEVEL 2 - BEGINNER -2% COST OF MANA REQUIRED TO CAST A RITUAL SPELL.	DODGING: LEVEL 7 - BEGINNER +7% CHANCE TO COMPLETELY DODGE AN ATTACK TARGETED AT YOU.

MEDITATION: LEVEL 7 - BEGINNER +7% MANA REGENERATION OUTSIDE OF COMBAT SITUATIONS.	MIND'S EYE: LEVEL 5 - BEGINNER MANA COST - 10 POINTS/SECOND USING THIS SKILL ALLOWS ONE TO SEE THE FLOWS, COLOURS AND SOURCES OF MANA. -25% COST IN MANA.

SPELL SCHOOLS

EVOCATION - LEVEL 10 POOR +10% DAMAGE FOR EVOCATION SPELLS DAMAGE ARCANE I - +10% DAMAGE WITH FORCE DAMAGE.	CONJURATION - LEVEL 7 BEGINNER -7% CASTING TIME FOR CONJURATION SPELLS
TRANSMUTATION - LEVEL 4 BEGINNER +4% DURATION FOR TRANSMUTATION SPELLS	DIVINATION - LEVEL 9 BEGINNER -9% TIME FOR DIVINATION CASTING TIMES.
ABJURATION - LEVEL 14 POOR +14% DURATION FOR ABJURATION SPELLS ABJURER'S CHOICE - CHOOSE ONE ABJURATION SPELL YOU ALREADY KNOW TO INCREASE TO SKILL LEVEL 10.* WIZARD'S ARMOUR.	ILLUSION - LEVEL 6 BEGINNER +6% DURATION OF ILLUSION SPELLS
ENCHANTMENT - LEVEL 2 BEGINNER +2 DURATION OF ENCHANTMENT SPELLS	NECROMANCY- LEVEL 50 COMPETENT +50% POTENCY OF NECROMANCY SPELLS DEATH'S TOUCH I - YOUR FAMILIARITY FOR THE ENERGY OF

	UNLIFE HAS GIVEN YOU +10% RESISTANCE TO NECROTIC DAMAGE. KNOWLEDGE ARCANE I - ALLOWS THE CASTER TO CHOOSE ONE APPRENTICE RANKED SPELL. NECROMANCY SAVANT I - NECROMANCY SPELLS COST YOU 25% LESS TO CAST. CONTROL UNDEAD - DOUBLES THE NUMBER OF UNDEAD THE CASTER CAN CONTROL. KNOWLEDGE ARCANE II - ALLOWS THE CASTER TO CHOOSE ONE COMPETENT RANKED SPELL.*
SPELLS	
BURNING HANDS - LEVEL 4 EVOCATION CASTING TIME - INSTANTANEOUS MANA COST - 30 POINTS DURATION - CHANNELLING LVL 1. SHOOTS A 10FT CONE OF FIRE, DEALING 5 POINTS OF FIRE DAMAGE PER SECOND. LVL 4. INCREASES TO A 15 FT CONE.	FIND FAMILIAR - LEVEL 11 CONJURATION CASTING TIME - ONE MINUTE MANA COST - 80 POINTS DURATION - CONSTANT RANGE - BOUNDLESS LVL 1. CONJURES A SPIRIT FAMILIAR, BONDED TO THE CASTER THROUGH AN EMPATHIC LINK. LVL 3. ALLOWS THE CASTER TO EXPEND THEIR OWN ENDURANCE POINTS TO ENHANCE THEIR FAMILIAR'S. LVL 4. LINK WITH BONDED CREATURE CAN NOW ALLOW SIMPLE IMAGES TO BE COMMUNICATED.

	LVL 5. ENHANCED BOND - SEE FAMILIAR STATS.
MENDING - LEVEL 4 TRANSMUTATION CASTING TIME - 15 SECONDS MANA COST - 5 POINTS LVL 1. REPAIRS MINOR, NON-MAGICAL DAMAGE OR SHARPENS NON-MAGICAL ITEMS. LVL 2. ALLOWS CASTER TO REPAIR/SHARPEN TWO SIMILAR ITEMS WITHIN THE DURATION OF THE CASTING.	SHOCKING STRIKE - LEVEL 6 EVOCATION CASTING TIME - 2 SECONDS MANA COST - 5 POINTS DURATION - 5 SECONDS OR UNTIL USED LVL 1. DEALS 4-7 POINTS OF LIGHTNING DAMAGE LVL 2. 5% CHANCE OF STUNNING A TARGET FOR 5-10 SECONDS. LVL 5. DAMAGE INCREASE TO 6-12 POINTS OF LIGHTNING DAMAGE.
ARCANE BOLT - LEVEL 6 EVOCATION CASTING TIME - 1 SECOND MANA COST - 25 POINTS DURATION - INSTANTANEOUS LVL 1. SHOOTS A BOLT OF MAGICAL FORCE UP TO 100FT. DEALING 5-30 POINTS OF FORCE DAMAGE LVL 4. INCREASES RANGE TO 120 FT.	WIZARD ARMOUR - LEVEL 14 ABJURATION CASTING TIME - 1 MINUTE MANA COST - 20 POINTS DURATION - 5 HOURS LVL 1. PROVIDES AN ARMOUR CLASS OF 10. LVL 3. ALLOWS THE CASTER TO INCREASE DAMAGE REDUCTION BY CHANNELLING MORE MANA INTO THE ARMOUR AT A RATIO OF 20:1 (MANA TO AC). LVL 8. INCREASES BASE AC CLASS BY +2.
MINOR ILLUSION - LEVEL 6 ILLUSION CASTING TIME - 10 SECONDS MANA COST - 25 POINTS	CHARISMA - LEVEL 1 ENCHANTMENT CASTING TIME - 1 MINUTE MANA COST - 75 POINTS DURATION - 1 MINUTE

DURATION - CONCENTRATION LVL 1. CREATES AN ILLUSORY OBJECT OF THE CASTERS DESIGN. CAN BE NO LARGER THAN 1 FOOT BY 1 FOOT BY 1 FOOT. LVL 5. INCREASES SIZE OF ILLUSION TO 5 FOOT BY FIVE FOOT BY FIVE FOOT.	LVL 1. MAKES YOU MORE APPEALING TO PEOPLE, MAKING THEM MORE FRIENDLY TOWARDS YOU.
IDENTIFY - LEVEL 9 DIVINATION CASTING TIME - 1 SECOND MANA COST - 10 POINTS DURATION - CONCENTRATION LVL 1. IDENTIFIES ANY SIMPLE OR UNCOMMON OBJECTS OR CREATURES OR THE UNCOMMON PROPERTIES OF AN OBJECT. LVL 6. IDENTIFIED RARE OBJECTS OR CREATURES OR THE RARE PROPERTIES OF AN OBJECT.	COMPREHEND LANGUAGES - LEVEL 3 DIVINATION CASTING TIME - INSTANT MANA COST - 20 POINTS DURATION - 1 HOUR LVL 1. EACH CASTING ALLOWS YOU TO READ AND UNDERSTAND ONE UNKNOWN LANGUAGE.
GRIM VOID - LEVEL 41 NECROMANCY CASTING TIME - 1 SECOND MANA COST - 50 POINTS DURATION - CONCENTRATION LVL 1. ALLOWS CASTER TO DRAIN THE LIFE FORCE FROM ONE CREATURE OR VEGETATION THAT IT TOUCHES AT A RATE OF 3 HP PER SECOND.	ARCANE STEP - LEVEL 7 CONJURATION CASTING TIME - 1 SECOND MANA COST - 60 POINTS DURATION - INSTANTANEOUS LVL 1. ALLOWS CASTER TO TELEPORT TO A LOCATION THEY CAN SEE WITHIN 50. LVL 4. CASTER CAN CARRY ADDITIONAL CREATURES OF A SIMILAR SIZE AT AN ADDED

LVL 4. INCREASES RATE OF DRAIN TO 6 HP PER SECOND. LVL 11. ALLOWS THE CASTER TO CHANNEL HEALING ENERGY INTO ANOTHER CREATURE AT A RATE OF 1:4 OF HP GAINED. REQUIRES TOUCH. LVL 18. INCREASES RATE OF DRAIN TO 12 HP PER SECOND. LVL 26. INCREASES RATE OF DRAIN TO 24 HP PER SECOND. LVL 36. GIVES THE CASTER A 5% CHANCE TO ABSORB KNOWLEDGE FROM THE HOST.

COST OF 240 MANA PER CREATURE.

BARRIER - LEVEL 4
ABJURATION
CASTING TIME - 1 SECOND
MANA COST - 50 POINTS
DURATION - 5 SECONDS
LVL 1. CREATES A MAGICAL SHIELD THAT ABSORBS 100 POINTS OF RANGED DAMAGE.

CLOAKING SHADOW - LEVEL 5
ILLUSION
CASTING TIME - 1 MINUTE
MANA COST - 100 POINTS
DURATION - 1 HOUR
LVL 1. CLOAKS THE TARGET IN SHADOWS, MAKING THEM MORE DIFFICULT TO DETECT, INCREASES SNEAK AND HIDE SKILL BY A FACTOR OF 2.

FORCE WAVE - LEVEL 10 (ITEM)
EVOCATION
CASTING TIME - 1 SECOND
DURATION - INSTANTANEOUS
LVL 10. CREATES A 15-FOOT RADIUS WAVE OF FORCE THAT SHOOTS OUT IN 360 DEGREES FROM THE CASTER. DEALS 6-30 POINTS OF FORCE DAMAGE OF ANYTHING CAUGHT WITHIN THE AREA OF EFFECT.

CREATE UNDEAD - LEVEL 21
NECROMANCY
CASTING TIME - 1 MINUTE
MANA COST - 50 POINTS PER LEVEL OF CREATURE
DURATION - UNTIL DISPELLED OR THE UNDEAD IS DESTROYED.
LVL 1. ALLOWS THE CASTER TO REANIMATE AND CONTROL ONE CORPSE INTO AN UNINTELLIGENT UNDEAD.

	LVL 3. ALLOWS THE CASTER TO REASSERT CONTROL OVER UP TO TWO UNINTELLIGENT UNDEAD. LVL 9. ALLOWS THE CASTER TO REANIMATE AND CONTROL FIVE CORPSES INTO UNINTELLIGENT UNDEAD. OR TO REASSERT CONTROL OVER FOUR. LVL 20. ALLOWS THE CASTER TO REANIMATE AND CONTROL TEN UNINTELLIGENT OR ONE AN INTELLIGENT UNDEAD. OR TO REASSERT CONTROL OVER SIXTEEN.
REAPER'S SORROW - LEVEL 15 NECROMANCY CASTING TIME - 1 MINUTE MANA COST - 250 POINTS DURATION - 24 HOURS LVL 1. ONCE CAST, IF THE RECIPIENT OF THIS SPELL IS REDUCED TO 0 HP, THE SPELL TRIGGERS AND SAVES THEM FROM DEATH AND RESTORES A NUMBER OF HIT POINTS EQUAL TO THE CASTER'S LEVEL OF SKILL WITH THE SPELL.	GRIM BOLT - LEVEL 50 NECROMANCY CASTING TIME - 1 SECOND MANA COST - 25 POINTS DURATION - INSTANTANEOUS LVL 50. SHOOTS A BOLT OF MAGICAL DEATH UP TO 150FT. DEALING 12-72 POINTS OF NECROTIC DAMAGE. IF THE DAMAGE KILLS THE TARGET, THERE IS A 1% CHANCE THAT THE CREATURE BECOMES AN UNINTELLIGENT UNDEAD UNDER THE CASTER'S COMMAND.
RITUAL SPELLS	
DISPEL MAGIC ABJURATION CASTING TIME - 1 MINUTE MANA COST - VARIABLE DURATION - INSTANTANEOUS	FARSEER CONJURATION CASTING TIME - TEN MINUTES MANA COST - 150 POINTS

ALLOWS THE CASTER TO CANCEL ACTIVE MAGICAL EFFECTS WITHIN AN OBJECT OR CREATURE.	DURATION - CONCENTRATION ALLOWS THE CASTER TO CONTROL A FLOATING EYE. THE CASTER CAN SEE THROUGH THE EYE AS THOUGH IT WERE THEIR OWN BUT IS BLIND TO THEIR OWN SURROUNDINGS. THE CASTER CAN ALSO CONTROL THE MOVEMENT OF THE EYE WHICH MOVES AT 5 FOOT PER SECOND IN ANY DIRECTION.

He'd made gains in multiple spells and their related spell schools, had improved his Dodging, Meditation, Mind's Eye, Channelling and even his Arcana skills. Most excitingly, his Divination magic was approaching its first threshold and he was excited to find out the benefit he'd gain from breaking through it.

Both Bluzag and Libby had improved as well, Libby's bond reaching a new level, so that rodent had an upgrade point to spend. Unsurprisingly, it went into Intelligence, his familiar excited to find out her own threshold benefit.

But, it was in his Wight, that the most significant advancements had been made. Perhaps because he'd had the most potential for it, having had so few skills to begin with.

He'd even earned an extra two points in Endurance, in fact now that Ninetoes thought about it, they all had. It must have been the long days of travel.

Bluzag had improved all of his fighting skills and had passed the threshold into Poor for his weapons skills a couple of days ago, earning a new facet to the Skill. With a surge of excitement, Ninetoes realised that Bluzag's Blocking skill was only two levels away from the same threshold. With three points left to spend, the hobgoblin made a snap decision and spent them there and then, placing one into Charging Bull and the other two into Blocking.

As he did so, Ninetoes' day got off to a great start. Not only did Blocking gain its threshold benefit, but apparently level 8 in Charging Bull also added another bonus to the ability.

Undead name: Bluzag	Race: Half-ogre Wight (+1 Str, +1 End)
Bond Level: 12th	Bonded Wizard: Ninetoes
Hit points: 640/640	Mana points: None
Stamina points: 450/450	
Class: Warrior	Specialism:
Base stats: Strength - 52 (50) Agility - 19 (16) Endurance - 45 Intelligence - 10 Wisdom - 8 Charisma - 7	
Languages: Common - Basic Understanding Goblinoid - Basic Understanding Giant - Basic Understanding	Armour Class: Armour 15 + Shield 25 Total: 40
Racial Abilities	

TOUGH:
THE HALF-OGRE IS TOUGHER AND HARDIER THAN MOST CREATURES. +10% MORE HIT POINTS.

LEARNED ABILITIES

CHARGING BULL - LEVEL 8 COOL DOWN - 25 SECONDS LVL 1. AFTER TRAVELLING AT LEAST 15 FEET IN A STRAIGHT LINE, USER ADDS 50% DAMAGE TO THE NEXT ATTACK AND HAS A 10% CHANCE TO KNOCK OVER THE TARGET. LVL 8. CHANCE TO KNOCK TARGET PRONE INCREASES TO 20%.	WHIRLWIND STRIKE - LEVEL 6 COOL DOWN - 30 SECONDS LVL 1. CREATES AN ATTACK THAT SPINS 360 DEGREES THAT HITS ALL ENEMIES WITHIN 5 FEET FOR 50% DAMAGE. LVL 3. INCREASES DAMAGE TO 60%.
POWER STRIKE - LEVEL 5 COOL DOWN - 10 SECONDS LVL 1. ADDS 25% DAMAGE TO THE NEXT ATTACK.	

LEARNED SKILLS

ONE-HANDED BLUDGEONING WEAPONS: LEVEL 13 - POOR +13% DAMAGE. +13% CHANCE OF CRITICAL HIT. FIGHTING STANCE - YOUR FOOTWORK IS NOW MORE EFFICIENT, ALLOWING YOU TO SWING WITH MORE POWER, INCREASING DAMAGE BY 5%.	BLOCKING - LEVEL 10 COOL DOWN - NONE PREREQUISITES - A SHIELD LARGE ENOUGH TO COVER AT LEAST 30% OF BODY +8% CHANCE TO BLOCK -8% DAMAGE REDUCTION IMMOVABLE - WHEN SETTING YOUR FEET YOU CAN BECOME A BASTION OF DEFENCE, DOUBLING YOUR BLOCKING SKILL WHILE YOU REMAIN ON THE SPOT.

There was no question, Bluzag was becoming a powerhouse. Ninetoes' chest swelled with pride, his hard work was paying off. Soon they'd be back in Raveslan and he could finally complete his first Quest. From there, he'd head home to his village and re-join his people.

Master, warriors ahead. They are attempting to move stealthily but they are easy to notice.

His Familiar was becoming arrogant as her abilities improved, but as she sent him images his canines pierced his lips as he snarled; they were hobgoblins! This far into the Forests of Myr and in such numbers, they could not be Dakhec Druul, his people had not ranged this far for years.

And if these were not Dakhec Druul, nor of his village, they must be some other tribe of hobgoblins and, this far from any other territories, could mean only one thing, they were here to attack his people.

He pondered how to approach these invaders. If they were sneaking, then they already knew he was here, but that didn't necessarily mean they knew how many were in his party.

There was a benefit to surprise. It had undoubtedly saved his life in his battle with Bofar the wizard. With a whispered command, he sent Bluzag to hide behind a tree, asking Libby to cover the oaf with an illusion. She worked quickly and within moments, the tree seemed to have doubled in width. If he was honest, it would look weird and out of place, but only if you were looking for it.

Meanwhile, Ninetoes had continued his approach, casting Cloaking Shadows on himself... because it never hurt to be stealthy.

Not yet wanting to attack the warriors, he took a chance and focussed on his Mind's Eye skill. While he was still getting used to it, the Skill served its purpose and Ninetoes was able to see the smudged shapes of five hobgoblins in a semi-circle ahead of him, while five more were stalking behind him. They would completely encircle him within moments. Clearly Libby hadn't been quite as clever as she'd thought.

Still, there might still be more he could learn from these hobs before the fighting began. Staying in the shadows he called out.

"Hail friends, there is nothing to fear, I am one of you! I am—" he paused. He'd been about to announce his name, but then an uncomfortable feeling passed through his stomach as he remembered the reaction of the Krem when he'd given them a name the first time. His own people had nearly cut him down on the spot, just for having a name. Thinking quickly, he changed tack slightly, "—I am a Farn of our people."

A nearby bush rustled just slightly and through his arcane sight, he could see a taller and powerfully built hobgoblin hidden within it.

"Ha! You call us friend fool? Well then, let's be friends. You answer every question I ask you and we kill you quickly."

"Kill me? Why would we need to do that? Are we not hobgoblin brothers?" Even in his own head it had sounded weak, but he needed more information. Still, this dullard obviously thought he had the upper hand, and Ninetoes wasn't about to rob him of that notion. At least not just yet, he let them underestimate him until it was too late.

Carefully he focussed on the aura of the one that spoke to him and, as his eyes traced the outline of the warrior's weapons, he sucked in a sharp intake of breath and the slightly prickle of fear crept up his back. These were no mere warriors or scouts, their gear and arms spoke volumes.

These were ba'ardec; long-range scouts and veterans, picked from only the strongest and most skilled of the warriors to range ahead of an army. They were used to find and clear paths of monsters and enemies alike. Each one of them was an expert in the weapons they carried and their skills in stealth and tracking were unsurpassed. Apparently, underestimating one's foes was infectious.

As he stared aghast at the warrior around him, the leader whistled low and Ninetoes could hear the unmistakable sound of bow strings tightening from every one of the warriors.

Clearly confident of his kill, the hobgoblin in front of him stood up from his hiding spot and crossed his arms, an arrogant sneer splitting his bearded face.

Even the few short steps he'd taken had shown the feline grace and wiry strength that set these warriors apart and above their comrades.

"Ha! I'm glad I see you recognise just how fucked you are, but just to be clear, you are surrounded and a dozen arrows, laced with wyvern venom are pointed at your heart. If any one of those were to even scratch you, you'd be dead before you took a hundred paces. If you move a muscle, you'll be pinned to the spot." He poised in his monologue, waiting for Ninetoes to come out of his hiding spot and accept his fate.

Even as powerful as he'd become, Ninetoes had walked into this ambush without even drawing a weapon and he wasn't totally confident in the ability of his Wizard's Armour to absorb every strike; he needed time to make a plan and so he played along. Stepping out of his hiding place, he stepped forward slowly, hands raised and gaze cast towards the floor.

"Good. I told you these Dakhec Druul were dogs." He called out to the others and a whispered chorus of laughter followed his sneer. "So, first question; do the Dakhec Druul have patrols in these forests, or are you the best they have?" He asked. The remark was clearly intended to sting and the other warriors chuckled once again, a little louder this time.

Ninetoes considered the question for a moment. The ba'ardec would not have been sent out to roam the wilderness aimlessly, this hobgoblin almost certainly already knew the answer to his question, which meant that he'd asked it to gauge whether Ninetoes was likely to try and lie.

"I... i... indeed." Ninetoes stuttered, hoping that his enemy's arrogance would help make him seem more convincing. Meanwhile, he contacted Libby' *Little one, are you still close?*

Yes Master, to your rear and right, twenty paces?

"Excellent, thank you," responded the warrior, mockingly. "And, how far from the human village is their settlement?" This question was more probing, clearly he already had some idea, but nothing ironclad. Ninetoes still needed more time and so he chose to answer, keeping his response as vague as possible.

"Uh... um a couple of days, or m... m... maybe three, i... if...fff you walk slow." As he responded, he sent Libby instructions, hoping that Bluzag would follow her lead.

"Hmmmm, you wouldn't be trying to lie to me, now would you?" replied the hobgoblin, resting his hand on the pommel of his short sword. This was the weapon that set ba'ardec apart from other hobgoblins. While most warriors favoured the reach and weight of a longsword, the elite soldiers of the ba'ardec wielded the wide but short-bladed Waq, much like a falchion in shape but short and double-edge, able to be used to stab and cut. A vicious weapon to be sure. And when twinned with the Yorl, a serrated buckler, the ba'ardec could easily fulfil any role in infantry combat.

"No!" Ninetoes almost called out, his voice tremulous, "I... just don't really know," he stuttered.

"Ha! I can well believe it, the look of you. How did a skinny runt like you ever become a warrior? Or are you a porsht? Kicked out of your tribe for being so pathetic?" The warrior laughed aloud and Ninetoes could hear the other hobgoblins around him chuckling as well. *Keep laughing!*

He understood why. Amongst his people, his skinny arms and sallow skin made him appear weak and measly, a porsht was all these things and worse, it was the most hateful insult in their language. Ninetoes simply cowered, encouraging the warriors to laugh more, imbibing the offence and turning it into spite with which to strike out. Cowering lower to the ground, the laughter rose and some of the hobgoblins even stood up out of the hiding places, so sure of their dominance over such a weak specimen as he.

Time they regretted their actions I think. Libby now!

The chuckles caught in the throats of the warriors and their faces blanched with fear as they turned to stare open-mouthed at a new threat.

A troll lumbered out of the trees, crashing through branches and roaring with anger and bloodlust! Two nearby ba'ardec stumbled out of their hiding places, raising their bows to fire at the monster. Their sudden fear and surprise threw off their aim and their arrows whizzed ineffectively passed the creature.

The monster stepped forward and swung what appeared to be a massive branch at one of the hobgoblins, slamming into them and throwing their ragdoll-like body into a nearby tree.

"Hold you worms! Everyone direct fire on that beast!" shouted the warrior with whom Ninetoes had been talking. His voice was confident and commanding, setting him out as the clear leader. Ninetoes drew his cutlass and advanced on him.

The ba'ardec leader didn't even draw his blade, instead sneering contemptuously at the porsht charged.

SHINK!

He still wore the same stupid grin as Ninetoes removed his sword from the fool's spine. He'd been practicing on changing his orientation as well as his location when he 'stepped' with Arcane Step and he was grateful to the warrior for the opportunity to test it.

TRING!

An arrow deflected off of Ninetoes' Wizard Armour and he cast his gaze about for the archer. Although his allies' distraction had set his enemies onto the back foot, he needed to capitalise quickly or risk losing his advantage.

Noting the location of his attacker crouching in a nearby bush, he 'stepped' behind him and ran his blade into the back of the warrior's neck, the blade, already slick with blood slid in easily, the coppery taste filling his nostrils and, although he was loathe to admit it, the smell sent thrills through his body.

Looking across the clearing, he could see that the "troll" had dispatched another of the hobs, but the relentless hail of arrows from the other half dozen warriors was clearly wearing it down.

"Shield Bluzag! Libby, overwatch!"

Both his Familiar and his undead servant obeyed quickly, their recent training sessions meaning they understood his commands. Libby, he saw, glided to a tall tree and began sending him information about the battle-field, noting the locations of the other ba'ardec.

Bluzag meanwhile, having lost the cover of Libby's illusion, grabbed the shield from his back and rushed to stand in front of his Master.

As his party responded, Ninetoes was tipped off to the location of an-other foe by a movement nearby and he threw a Grim Bolt in the same direction. The bolt landed square in the warrior's back and threw him to the floor. Stepping closer to finish him off, but Ninetoes could see black magic racing through the hob's veins. By the sharp stink of the hob's evac-uated bowels, it was clear that he too was dead.

Nearby, two of his enemies took cover behind a large rock, peaking over to send missiles at Bluzag. Stepping up behind the half-ogre, Ninetoes rested a hand on the small of his servant's back and ordered, "Forward!"

Bluzag responded, marching towards the hobs. Even with as much progress as they'd all made recently, not a one of them was a match for a ba'ardec in a one on one melee. Ninetoes, however, hadn't even used half of his mana and so, as they neared the two warriors, he 'stepped' from behind his meatshield to appear directly behind them.

One of them was prepared for the move and spun around to release his arrow at point blank range and the missile punched into Ninetoes' shoulder, only missing his heart by the grace of his magical shield. Despite the shield absorbing the damage, physics was still at play and the blow throbbed a dull ache.

Ninetoes knew he couldn't waste any time and so cast Force Wave from his cloak, sending both his foes slamming into the rocks behind them. Both the warriors wheezed as the wave forced the air from their lungs and, although the magical wave wasn't enough to kill, it stunned both and Ninetoes was able to step forward and run through the one who'd shot him. Ninetoes' heart beat faster with the thrill of it and he went searching for his next victim.

Bluzag meanwhile, had closed the distance and, stepping around the boulder, swung his maul backhanded and mashed the other hob's face into the rock. Another of the ba'ardec watched the act in horror and his courage fled, the Wight hot on its heels.

Almost absentmindedly, Ninetoes tossed a Grim Bolt to splash against the fleeing enemy's neck, sending him tumbling ass over tit to crash into a tree, one more lifeless husk.

What that, only two enemies remained and, with Libby directing them and plenty of mana, the battle didn't last long.

Ninetoes was even able to take the last one alive by stunning him with a Shocking Strike and knocking him out cold with the hilt of his sword to the fool's temple.

This one he planned to question and so he removed his armour and most of his clothes, tying him securely to a tree.

***

Some time later, the hobgoblin prisoner woke up and struggled against the rope that Ninetoes had bound him with. Ninetoes had used the intervening time to loot the other corpses and had already learned enough to worry him. Checking over their gear confirmed his suspicions.

Each carried a hard leather pouch of poisons and venoms, the collection of which, Ninetoes knew, was part of their training. They also had quality longbows, crafted by using flexible wood of a yew tree, which was then hardened with magic to give the weapons incredible strength. It took a similar level of strength and suppleness to wield them, forming another pillar of the ba'ardec's training and Ninetoes breathed a sigh of relief that he hadn't had to face a flurry of the missiles all at once.

His shoulder still throbbed slightly from the missile that his magical armour had deflected, a keen reminder just how closely he'd come to being poisoned.

Bluzag had taken a couple of wounds, poisoned arrows having pierced his decaying skin. Being undead, however, had its benefits and the half-ogre Wight was clearly immune to the effects. Ninetoes knew that this wouldn't always be true, but the ba'ardec had clearly not been expecting an undead opponent.

His last find however, had been the most concerning. Each body had the same brand burned into the skin over their heart, the process of which was the final part of the relentless and brutal education of these elite warriors.

It was not the branding itself that worried Ninetoes, however, but the symbol the blemish held; two crossed and skyward pointing swords. To a hobgoblin and a member of the Dakhec Druul, that symbol was unmistakable, it was the mark of the Necht Sarm, the Swords of Nech and the villains who had once stood arm in arm with the Dakhec Druul, only to stab their brothers in the back, betraying his people and chasing them from their stronghold and into hiding here in the Forests of Myr.

Anger boiled up inside Ninetoes when he'd first seen the mark and he'd nearly torn out the surviving hob's throat. But his intellect cooled his emotions and he realised that he must discover more information. He couldn't let these fiends endanger his people.

That is why, when the fool awoke and his eyes connected with Ninetoes' own, only calm fury met the poor hob's gaze. Ninetoes could smell his prey's fear.

The boarder's eyes darted around the clearing, pausing briefly on the bodies of his comrades, the entire squad of highly trained and well-equipped warriors.

Ninetoes could imagine the thoughts passing through his prisoner's mind. Flashes of the battle, memories of this mage and the massive brute that had taken apart his squad in the barest blink of an eye.

Was it any wonder that this warrior, this ba'ardec was quivering at his feet, helpless before such power?

If the joy of battle had sent his pulse racing towards excitement, the fear in this fool's eyes was enough to make the hobgoblin wizard practically jubilant.

"Ha!" Ninetoes barked with an insane glint to his eyes. "The mighty ba'ardec quivers in the presence of a despicable porsht, such as me?" His voice was a whisper, but his victim heard every word, each syllable making him flinch.

Ninetoes could sense... no, he knew, that this hobgoblin was mere inches away from spewing out every secret he held, all Ninetoes had to do was push a little harder.

And he had the perfect tool.

Reaching across to his hip he drew his elven dagger, simultaneously igniting his eyes with Mind's Eye. He could see the black glow of the blade and beyond it the pulse of the hobgoblin's lifeforce within him, an array of bright and vibrant colours that the dagger's edge tugged towards it. He could hear his victim's breathing start to race but it was not enough, not quite, he wanted this pathetic creature to be completely under his control.

Using Minor Illusion, he projected an image of the blade's true edge onto the dagger, exactly as he saw it, even making it pulse. It was easy because he simply copied what he already saw, matching the movement. A thought at the back of his mind noted the slight swelling in his own chest of a Skill levelling, but Ninetoes only thoughts were for his victim.

The warrior's eyes widened further at the sight of the magical blade. Those without magic were often fearful of its power, and this poor fool was no different.

Ninetoes licked his lips.

***

Libby watched the exchange between her master and the hobgoblin warrior; if the mess of bones and skin could still be called such. The poor fool wet himself and her Master's smile had widened, turning his face into a leer. Libby blanched, she'd seen this behaviour in her Master before and it didn't bode well.

Master, I think you have him. He's petrified, he'll tell you anything. Please, just ask your questions. She suggested, almost begging.

Mmmm, what? Came back Ninetoes' distracted reply. But he continued with what he was doing, the blade glowing under the mage's magic.

Master! Master stop! She said, scratching her claws across his neck to articulate her point. Nothing. Her master reached his blade towards the hobgoblin.

***

Ninetoes absentmindedly shrugged off Libby's pleas and set about the task. This fool would tell him everything he knew. He was there, just on the brink, all Ninetoes had to do was push a tiny bit more. He moved the blade forward, enraptured by its pulsing black light.

The hobgoblin strained against his bonds, frantic with fear but this only increased the tempo of the energy throbbing off of him. Following the flow of light, Ninetoes roughly ripped the hob's jerkin to one side and found the source, or perhaps the outpouring of the energy as it swirled over his victim's heart; here the colours were mesmerizing.

While his Mind's Eye noted this, his mundane orbs saw the mark of Nech and his own anger pulsed inside him and he lanced the blade towards the spot.

He had meant to drive his dagger into the worm's heart, but something stayed his hand, perhaps even the blade itself and instead, the blade's magical edge caressed the flow of energy and as he watched, a thread of colour, a warm green light, flowed into the dagger and the hobgoblin screamed!

The sudden and wild noise startled Ninetoes from his stupor and he momentarily came back to himself. As the flow of energy ended, the hobgoblin breathed in through wracking coughs and pleaded.

On a hunch, Ninetoes cast Identify and a thrill shot through him as the green energy provided information.

ESSENCE OF ARCHERY
THIS ESSENCE WAS TAKEN FROM THE NECH SARM WARRIOR, EN'DE.
THE WARRIOR'S STRONGEST TRAIT WAS HIS SKILL WITH A LONGBOW.
EFFECT FROM ABSORPTION: +2 LEVELS TO YOUR LONGBOW SKILL

Wait, what? When the strange woman in the glade had told him that he could take other creatures' essence he had no idea she'd meant it this literally.

He considered the Essence of Archery information and how to absorb it. This was enough for the knife and the green energy spiralled out again, this time towards Ninetoes' own heart. The energy was warm as it passed into his chest and gave him the same feeling as when he levelled up a Skill. He didn't even need to check his Character Sheet to know. He'd just gained two levels in Longbow!

All of this had happened in the barest of moments and meanwhile, beneath him, his prisoner struggled in pain.

"Please… guh, please. I'll tell you anything."

Focussing on his Mind's Eye and carefully aiming the blade towards his victim's core and, he hoped, more essences, Ninetoes grinned, "I know you will."

CHAPTER 6
URGENCY

Ninetoes hadn't earned any more Essences from the hobgoblin, but his prisoner had told him everything he knew. As he'd stripped away more and more strands of the coloured light, the hobgoblin had begun to pale and his skin became achromic. By the end, his voice had become monotone and even his screams sounded mechanical. What he had told Ninetoes however, had left the apprentice wizard incredibly confused. The warrior had told him that the Necht Sarm were marching to war.

Apparently, a blight had overtaken their harvests and the tribe of Nech were starving and so they were striking out in search of more fertile land. The warrior had no reason to give Ninetoes as to why they'd chosen to invade the lands of the Dakhec Druul but to Ninetoes this mattered little and the apprentice wizard had nearly bolted to his peoples' village to warn them.

By this time however, his victim was spilling his secrets faster than Ninetoes could process them and so he'd stayed silent and listened.

It seemed that the approaching goblinoid army had needed to raid and ransack every settlement along their march just to feed themselves. Mostly this had been mere farmsteads, ranches and a couple of small farming hamlets. But just a couple of days ago the light company had come upon a larger human settlement with a palisade wall.

Based upon the hob's description, it could only have been Raveslan, the very place that Ninetoes was headed for. The Nechtsarm would reach the town in a little over a week.

His victim went on to explain that the light company's captain had decided to attack the town herself, confident that her men could infiltrate the settlement under cover of darkness and take control of the resources within, thus covering herself in glory. She'd sent the ba'ardec on to scout a route to the Dakhec Druul settlement while the rest of her band stayed behind to attack the town.

That was only a day ago and, had it ended there, Ninetoes' choice would still have been a simple one: to warn his people. But then, the hob had continued, perhaps hoping at this point that he could blunt the cruel-looking porsht's anger and had divulged one final piece of information.

"The Sarm, she's as clever as they come, she is," grinned the hobgoblin, a little of his fleeting emotion returning at the memory.

"She didn't attack right aways right? She waits and she watches and she sees lots of wagons and carts and people and such coming into the town. Most of us says, 'Let's go now, while there's lots of people going in and out.' But she says no, we wait and one of the Farns right, he argues with her, saying she's stupid. But the Sarm, she doesn't like that, oh no, she's had to claw and work for every inch; it's not often a woman gets to be a warrior, and a Sarm no less!" He added this last, his tone a mixture of disdain and admiration. Ninetoes allowed him to talk, desperate to hear any good news.

"Well the Sarm, she says, 'Go on then, what do you think we should do?'

"The Farn, he swaggers over to her and says 'We sneak in with these farmers and once we're inside, we slice their froats, simple.'

"The Sarm, she nods and smiles. 'Yeah,' she says, 'that's a good plan,' she says, 'except-' and she grabs him, spinning him around and places a knife to his throat!

"I'll tell ya, not a one of us saw where that blade come from.

"Anyway, she holds him there, arm around his throat and she points to the town with her dagger, '-except those. See those walls? Walls means soldiers.'

"'So?' Says the Farn, 'Ten human soldier ain't worth one of us.'"

The hobgoblin licked his lips, his mouth dry from talking so much. Ninetoes generously poured a little water into his victim's mouth from his waterskin.

"So, then the Sarm, she chuckles. Chuckles! Some of us, we'd seen her do this before, I trained alongside her, and that chuckle meant that she had him. So she says, 'Oh? Of course, you're right. Each of us is worth ten human fighters and there's what, thirty of us? Twenty once I've sent off the ba'ardec.'

"At this point she stops and turns the Farn to face us, and her voice is like one of the elders when she continues. 'So, how many human soldiers are there?' She asks the Farn and his face just looks gobsmacked.

"'Well, I dunno,' he says.

"'You don't know?' She asks, all polite like. And then she looks at all of us and she throws him to the floor.

"'Listen well, all of you. I would take any one of you into battle over ten human soldiers, but once we're inside, split up and divided and the humans close their gates, their doors will close and bolt, their soldiers will line the walls and their arrows will cut us down, one by one. We must be more careful.'

"'What then?' asks the Farn.

"'Look at them. Watch them. What are they doing?' she asked us.

"'Bringing in the harvest,' I says, I got a smile for that, but a nice one like.

"'Indeed Brev, indeed,' she says to me."

Ninetoes was surprised for some reason that the warrior had the same name as the Elder who had saved him from execution.

"'So what,' she continues, 'do humans do when they take in the harvest?' This time, she looked at the Farn for an answer, 'They has a gathering to celebrate,' he says.

"'Yes, good.' She says, her voice all honey sweet, like she was speaking to a child. I tell ya, I had a chuckle at that.

"'And at this party, the humans will eat and drink and, if we wait for the nighttime, they'll be drunk and our darkvision will mean that we can see and they cannot. They will be easy prey. This harvest festival will be on the eventide, tomorrow night.'"

Ninetoes blanched, the hobgoblins would attack Raveslan tonight. Hence Ninetoes' indecision about what to do next. He wanted nothing more than to race back to his village and help protect his people, but he was an Adventurer now and the people of Raveslan had been kind, he knew he must help them first.

***

With no more useful information to offer, the hob was worthless, so Ninetoes slit his throat, letting his blood nourish the soil. Ninetoes' anger had drain away and the action was perfunctory. As the torture had torn more and more of his victim's life essence away, the cold malice had left Ninetoes. As his knife bit into the course flesh of the jugular, they were both thankful that it was over.

Ninetoes looked up at the sun and noted its position, high in the sky. Midday.

He cast his gaze over the bodies of the fallen warriors and temporarily considered burning them, but reasoned that there wasn't time.

This meant that, even if he increased his pace to a quickmarch, he'd likely still only make it to Raveslan long after sundown; if the Necht Sarm attacked as planned, he would be too late. He could only hope that they would wait for the townsfolk to get nice and drunk.

Ha! Hoping's for fool's and priests. He thought generously. No, he needed to find a way of increasing his pace and with it the odds of reaching Raveslan in time to help.

Checking over his spells and his Character Sheet, he noted that the battle with the ba'ardec had gained him over ten thousand experience points and he was close to levelling again. This surprised him, he'd expected his growth to stunt after passing Level 10, as Master Foresto had told him it would.

Unfortunately, however, his spells held no solutions to his current predicament, and although he was sure that the ancient spellbooks he'd found in Kavralach would contain such answers, he didn't have the time to check.

Casting about, his eyes fell on Bluzag and, more importantly, the half-ogre's long legs. Despite his liberal use of Arcane Step as they'd travelled over the past few days, Bluzag had kept pace with him. Ninetoes was pretty sure that his Wight would have been able to outrun him easily, if he hadn't given the creature instructions to follow behind. What's more, as an undead, the Wight never tired unless he overexerted himself, like using one of his Abilities.

Catching a glimpse at the sun, Ninetoes made his decision.

"Bluzag, come here and kneel." He commanded.

Up until this point, he'd avoided commanding his ally as much as he could, maintaining a polite and respectful manner, but time was of the essence.

His gigantic servant stepped closer and knelt down. Ninetoes stepped behind him and, gripping the homemade satchel, he rested his foot on the half-ogre's belt and found that he couldn't really gain any purchase. He'd need to be more secure if he was to ride the giant all the way back to Raveslan.

What are you doing Master? Came a questing voice within his mind.

We need more speed if we're to make it back to Raveslan in time to save the town. I was planning to ride Bluzag.

Ride? Bluzag? He's not a horse Master, is that safe?

It doesn't matter, if I'm too late the few friends I've made will be dead. Libby didn't offer any further debate, but instead watched curiously as the hobgoblin set to work.

Reaching into his Bag of Holding, he pulled out a scrap of leather and with yet more use of the Mending spell, created a simple stirrup to stand on. He was quickly coming to realise that this low-level spell was one of his most useful.

As he completed his 'fix', he felt the tell-tale warmth of growth in the spell's ability. He made a mental note to check on the spell's growth later, but now was the time for haste.

Libby had already climbed onto her Master's shoulder as he worked, so that she could get a view of what he was doing.

For reference, I think this is a bad idea... Master? She added. Ninetoes, who was already well aware of the rodent's disapproval, ignored her.

Perhaps it was arrogant to believe that he alone could change the fate of the human settlement, but he'd be damned if he'd just stand by and allow people to die.

Responding to his lack of response, Libby spoke again. *Very well master. I'll ride down here.* She said and she scrambled down into his breastplate, her back end struggling to force its way in, until Ninetoes pushed gently on her derriere.

Testing his makeshift stirrup, Ninetoes hoisted himself up.

"Forward Bluzag!" Ninetoes cried, in an effort to get the journey underway.

The Wight lurched upright and began striding forward. Ninetoes found he was able to stay aboard and, adjusting his footing slightly, released his left hand to point over Bluzag's shoulder.

"We must make haste my friend. Run!... That way!" he added as Bluzag began bounding forward. For a moment, Ninetoes legs flew out from the stirrup and the hobgoblin was temporarily like a strange living scarf.

Having been prepared to fall, however, he'd wrapped his hand in the straps of the half-ogre's saddlebags. It was enough for him to reassert his centre of gravity and work his foot back into the stirrup.

Looking down, he could see his Familiar's head poking out from his armour and he grinned down at her, "You see my dear, it works!"

Bluzag's speed was impressive. Even at a full sprint, Ninetoes wouldn't be able to keep up and yet Bluzag seemed only to be jogging.

As he clung on for dear life, Ninetoes elected to do the maths to take his mind off of his discomfort. With a few false starts, due to his brain being bounced around, he estimated that they should make it to the human town shortly after sundown. Unsure if he would be able to hang on if the giant went any faster, Ninetoes accepted that this would have to be fast enough.

***

FORESTO

On the outskirts of Raveslan, Foresto muttered equations to himself as he worked on his current project, a magical construct known colloquially as a Golem. He'd made the automatons before of course, they were a Transmutor's bread and butter, but he'd designed this current model with a specific purpose in mind and it was proving to make for an interesting challenge.

When he'd last spoken to Bofar, the brutish evoker had been boasting over a great find of ancient knowledge. Foresto, like many of their colleagues, had been making their annual pilgrimage to Hilne for research. He was getting old and had used one of his precious teleportation scrolls to make the trip, doubting he'd be fit enough to make the trip on foot.

Bofar had seemed drunk when he'd spoken with him in one of the upscale bars, but the more the tiresome dwarf had boasted, the more information he'd spewed forth and the more it had intrigued Foresto.

Every scholar had heard of the ancient empire of Kavralar of course, but the subject had been deemed folklore and legend by most.

But then he'd mentioned a map and the location of something important in the forests of Myr. Foresto had always known that the forests near to Ravelan hid some magic of great power, it was why he'd chosen the town as his home so many years ago. That, and the fact that it was so far from the large cities and windbags like Bofar.

As the evening had worn on, Foresto had plied his 'colleague' with more drink and had gleaned enough tidbits of information to come to the realisation that Bofar must, at least in part, be correct.

He'd considered how best to use this information and decided to allow Bofar to have the initial 'find' and thus have to deal with whatever monsters inhabited the place and then head in himself to research the area.

But when the Ninetoes had come along wanting to be an Adventurer, the opportunity to have some earlier input was too good to miss. A thought in the back of his mind was concerned with how long the apprentice wizard had been gone, but the task should have been simple enough and the hobgoblin was exceptionally bright for his kind.

Since he'd returned from Hilne, he'd been working on his current project, building a golem to help him with his research. What's more, since Ninetoes had arrived in his small town, monsters had been sighted nearby. While most people assumed this was poor luck, Foresto recognised the signs.

The monsters had been encouraged into the area by the appearance of an Adventurer. Without the hobgoblin consciously meaning to, Ninetoes' very presence incited challenge from the creatures nearby. The monsters could not choose to ignore the call that they could choose to stop breathing.

Foresto was a powerful mage, but his talents and spells did not lie in destruction, but creation. He would build something that could achieve both these aims: protect the town and further his research.

Unsure exactly what Bofar's stumblings might uncover, Foresto had quickly realised that he'd need to find a means of taking all of his vast library with him to be sure that he didn't require him to make subsequent trips and so his first idea had been to create a sort of walking Bag of Holding, only much, much larger, in terms of its dimensional space. But this really wouldn't be good enough. He'd need to remember, by name, the tome he wanted to call it forth and would then need to re-read it to find the information he wanted. This would be too slow. Worse still, if the construct was destroyed, then so too would be his entire library and anything else he'd chosen to store within. It also wouldn't be strong enough to fight.

Next, he'd considered creating two constructs, one would be static, remaining in place here in Raveslan and thus a constant defence, while the other, built to be more like a normal golem, would travel with and guard him. The two constructs however would be linked magically and would open a 'door' or 'pathway' between themselves and thus allow him to move to and fro in an instant. Alas, this idea however, was probably beyond his capabilities with Conjuration magic. Furthermore, once he left the roaming golem to return to his home, he'd have no control over it and, while he could make the construct tough, he'd have no guarantees of its returning. It also held the same problem of needing to read any texts he needed and thus would slow down his research.

It had taken him another few days of pondering the problem before he'd come up with the initial ideas for his masterpiece, the Droidus Eruditus! He admitted that name needed a little work but the solution was perfect and, he'd realised, exactly what his own favoured school of wizardry was intended for.

The basic idea was simple enough: to create a golem that could hold all of his library's accumulated knowledge. The solution was also straightforward, if difficult and expensive to create. Wizard's and other magic users had been making Knowledge Crystals for centuries and he'd made plenty of them himself. Mages used them to hold masses of information and would normally sell them to people, often Adventurers, to grant them new knowledge, abilities or skills in the blink of an eye. He could store his library onto a collection of such stones and make them part of the construct.

But really, the golem needed to do more than that, it needed to be able to understand enough about the information it held so that it would be able to search through these knowledge banks and call forth the information he sought. He'd needed to find a way of granting the construct awareness and intelligence, consciousness even. This would also help in its ability to fight. He could load it with knowledge about tactics and fighting skills.

This then created his next problem. He could of course, build something with a certain degree of intelligence, enough to perform simple tasks for example, but providing it with real intelligence had bested even his centuries-deep expertise.

That was, until meeting Ninetoes and, more importantly, the young wizard's Familiar, had triggered a useful memory. He'd been surprised by how strong the pair's bond already was and that the hobgoblin had been able to cast the spell without any training. It reminded the old wizard that Find Familiar was more than just a spell, it was a deep and personal connection, a Promise, to another being and one that should never be taken lightly.

Foresto hadn't had a Familiar in over a century, when his own Familiar and dearest friend, Abria had died. Badgers, even magically-enhanced Familiars, simply didn't have the lifespan of a gnome.

He had long ago come to terms with her loss, but he'd never taken another creature as his Familiar and as such, had forgotten one of the most important aspects of the magical bond: that these magical companions grew more powerful and aware through their link with their master.

Before she died, Abria had been intelligent enough to converse with the wizard about magic and matters far beyond the normal abilities of a mere beast. He remembered her fondly and the long and peaceful years the two had spent in contented research and learning. His own level of the Find Familiar spell was ranked Practitioner and he'd earned a number of benefits along the way, thus any creature he bonded with would quickly become a powerful ally.

All he'd needed was to find a way to bond with a construct and his knowledge had quickly provided the answer, a Soul Stone. He remembered being so excited that he'd literally tripped over himself in his haste to locate one of the rare magical objects and he'd spent two days straight working to install the artefact into the construct.

Now as he rubbed sleep from his eyes, he promised himself a rest, just as soon as he'd finished this, perhaps the most important, step in his creation.

Reaching forward he placed the stone into the golem's chest. As soon as he did he felt the familiar warmth in his chest of a skill upgrade and he knew he was on the right path. The thin, glowing gem rested within the golem, in the housing he'd built in the construct's left breast. He concentrated his will on closing the cavity, his magic temporarily turning the metal breast plate into liquid, that he willed into place over the construct's… 'heart'.

He'd nearly lost his focus as his Transmutation magic had improved again. Skill gains of the Grand Master rank would normally take decades to achieve. Two skill gains in one minute!

The construct's inner workings whirled into motion and the golem lifted its head to look at its master. And there he could see it, even if the Skill gain hadn't been evidence enough, the golem's eyes shone with awareness only seen in 'living' creatures.

With the tiniest fraction of his mana pool, he cast Find Familiar and immediately felt a small part of himself *connect* with the golem.

Master? The voice in his mind was both unknown and yet familiar to him.

Hello my friend. How do you feel? This was perhaps the most important question he'd asked in all his long years and his heart paused in anticipation of a response.

Confused Master and… hungry?

"Hungry?" he muttered confusedly.

BOOM!!

***

Ninetoes was stiff and sore by the time the sun hid itself behind the distant hills to the west, but the silence of the forest was enough for him to hear the bustle and chatter of voices on the wind and he realised that Raveslan was nearby. Directing his "steed" onwards, they crested one final hillock and there before them was the town.

With a word he commanded Bluzag to stop and he climbed gingerly down from the half-ogre's back, his thigh muscles protesting the treatment. With little time to spare, Ninetoes stalked to the top of the hill and crouched down, scanning the scene below.

Much of it was in darkness, but a group of large bonfires in the town square marked out where the festivities were taking place and, as he strained his eyes, he could see figures on the palisades, although it was uncertain if they were friend or whether his foe had already breached the defence.

BOOM!!

An explosion shocked the entire valley, scaring beasts from their nests to scatter into the undergrowth and when the thunderous sound died away, the noises coming from the settlement had changed to screams and shouts of alarm. He was too late; the attack had already begun!

"Bluzag, with me!" He called, taking off down the hill, hoping his Agility score would keep him upright as he barrelled downwards into the darkness of the walls. Within three strides he could feel the rhythmic thump of his ally and servant just a step behind him.

As he hurtled down the hillside, he could see a fire billowing out of a tithe barn inside the protective walls of the town. The Necht Sarm must have set the fire as a distraction. He'd need to clear the walls and head for the fire.

As he ran, his goblin eyes penetrated the inky blackness, showing that the figures on the walls were both friend and foe and, while the human guards looked inwards, the hobgoblins were using the shadows to conceal their faces and were stalking right up to the soldiers.

Before he could reach them, two hobgoblin warriors stepped up to the watchmen and drove daggers into their throats. Quickly they began tying off ropes and slinging them over the walls to a squad of hobgoblins waiting below.

As he closed the distance, Ninetoes slowed to a trot, exchanging speed for stealth. He also cast Cloaking Shadow upon himself. For a moment

110

he considered casting it upon Bluzag, but the brute simply wasn't built for subterfuge and he decided not to waste the mana.

The hobs hadn't seen him coming and the two on the walls were watching inwards. His recent trials had taught him that while rushing into battle was foolish, taking the initiative could make all the difference between life and death and so he shouted, "Charge!"

As he shouted he sidestepped, allowing the half-ogre to surge forward and as the hobgoblins' turned, their eyes widened, locking onto Bluzag. Ninetoes was invisible in the hulking monster's presence and as the half-ogre crashed into the warriors waiting at the base of the wall, Ninetoes 'stepped' onto the palisade, adjusting his angle so that he continued his charge along the wall's catwalk and barged into the nearest warrior, pitching him off of the wall to crunch onto the rocks below.

Libby meanwhile leapt from her Master's shoulder to land on the parapet. Scurrying along its top, she took off towards the scene of the battle raging within the square.

The other hobgoblin however, already had her longsword drawn and she slashed it at Ninetoes. His momentum was too great for him to stop and he didn't have enough space to dodge, so Ninetoes simply sped up, accepting the dull pain of the sword's pommel on his shoulder blade and lost a few hit points. As the hobgoblin tried to draw back her blade to thrust again, Ninetoes wrapped his fingers around her arm and held it down at her side. The warrior grinned, clearly confident that she could win a contest of strength with such a pathetic excuse for a hobgoblin.

In a confusing moment, Ninetoes realised caught a whiff of the hob's scent and the olfactory sensation made him momentarily think of home and he smiled.

This drove the warrior into a rage, and in her distaste to even be touched by something so weak, she shouted. "How did one such as you ever earn that weapon at your hip?" She punched Ninetoes hard in the face, planning to dislodge his arms and run him through. The blow staggered Ninetoes backwards and his grip on her arm, but the damage was already done and the hobgoblin grinned back.

"No matter, I will take it from your corpse," she said. Her arrogance made her miss the signs and, as she attempted to lift her blade to point its tip at her assailant's heart, she found she didn't have the strength to do so.

Confused, she looked down at her arm and, in the firelight, could see that the colour, size and definition had left her limbs. As realisation dawned on her, her adrenalin-fuelled anger abated and she collapsed to her knees.

Still concentrating on his spell, Ninetoes stepped up to his helpless foe and drained the rest of her life from her with Grim Void, repairing the damage caused by her punch and dropping her unceremoniously to the floor once drained of worth. For a second, the feeling of absorbing another creature's lifeforce enveloped Ninetoes like a drug. But then the coppery scent of blood wafted into the wizard's nostrils and he came to.

Stepping up to the wall's edge, Ninetoes looked down to find that Bluzag had dispatched two of the hobs, but the other three had surrounded the half-ogre and were now co-ordinating their attacks to chip away at the Wight's hit points.

Clearly, he couldn't let this happen. It seemed that so far, his presence had gone unnoticed. He could have taken all three of the warriors from the wall with ranged spells, but he didn't know how long he'd need to be fighting and so he carefully climbed down one of the ropes while continuing his concentration of his Grim Void spell.

Keeping to the shadows, he drew his cutlass and waited for one of the warriors to pass near to him. As they did, he stepped forward and slashed his blade down across the hob's ankle, who collapsed with the audible pop of her hamstring snapping.

Stepping past this first enemy, Ninetoes stepped up to another of the warriors and, for a moment the music of battle rang out on their blades, until, strong as the hobgoblin was, his skill was outmatched by Ninetoes' own and he fell all too quickly.

With Ninetoes entrance into the melee and elimination of the first combatant, Bluzag had seized the opportunity and had quickly made mincemeat out of his own foe. As Ninetoes dragged his sword from the belly of his enemy, Bluzag stepped up and raised his maul over the disabled hobgoblin, who was currently trying to crawl away.

"Wait." Ninetoes commanded, his tone even. "I have a purpose for him."

Canting his blade, he shook off the majority of the blood to splatter onto the grass.

Stepping up to the fallen warrior, Ninetoes kicked away the hob's sword and crouched close enough to touch his face, his own rough hands almost tender on his enemy's face.

"Here Bluzag, take my hand." The lifeforce drained out of the hobgoblin and, passing through Ninetoes, was passed onwards to repair some of the damage that Bluzag had sustained. The act took barely seconds, so competent had Ninetoes become with Necromancy.

He took the moment of respite to count the numbers of hobgoblins. Five, plus two more on the walls. This, he knew, was not the whole of the light company. Unless, that was, his victim had been lying to him but something told him that he wasn't. So, there was likely to be more groups like this one.

Finally giving up his concentration of Grim Void, Ninetoes set to climbing the rope, ordering Bluzag to follow him. Going up was definitely much more difficult than down and he missed the bonuses that his Guardsman's Bracers had provided to Strength. Fortunately, no one was about to witness the uncomfortable mess he made of climbing over the wall.

Once on the catwalk, he took a minute to scan the town. The screaming had died down somewhat and the clash of metal and wood told him there was a battle somewhere in the square. He knew the safe thing to do was to circle the top of the walls and take care of any other groups, but by then the battle in the centre of town could well be over, with scores of townsfolk dead. No, the Adventurer thing to do was to forge ahead and protect as many people as possible.

As this thought occurred to him, Libby returned, gliding from a nearby rooftop to land on the catwalk next to her Master.

The worst of the fighting appears to be in the town square Master. The townsfolk appear to be surrounded.

Good work Little One. That cinched it. He couldn't wait.

As Bluzag made it onto the wall, Ninetoes streaked off towards a ladder leading down, and called back an instruction to follow.

Ninetoes had stayed in the town for about a week during his first visit but he hadn't explored much of the human settlement, so busy was he with his training. So, it was only by following the instructions of his Familiar that he was able to navigate the higgledy-piggledy streets to the town square.

For the festivities the townsfolk had erected three large bonfires in a roughly triangular fashion with maybe twenty or so feet gap between each bonfire. As he approached he could see the townsfolk huddled within the centre of the bonfires with a smattering of guards standing between them and the tightening bands of Necht Sarm warriors.

Even a cursory glance told him there were far more than the twenty his victim had told him there would be. His teeth ground with frustration at being duped, but a small part of him was impressed with the hobgoblin's fortitude and he made a note never to underestimate the resilience of the ba'ardec again.

The female Sarm his prisoner had described was easy to spot in the line of tightly packed warriors. She wore no helmet and rich black hair streamed behind her, reflecting the blaze of fire and death around her.

Ninetoes was taken aback, he'd expected a gnarled and grizzled beast of a creature to have succeeded in becoming a warrior, but the Sarm was none of those things. She was neither tall nor particularly short, standing shoulder to shoulder with her men, but somehow she seemed to stand out above them. Her movements were lithe but efficient, conserving energy but deadly in their accuracy.

She wore simple armour of studded leather and carried a shield emblazoned with her tribe's symbol. In her other hand, she carried a longsword of no particular note. If not that she was the one shouting out orders, she could have blended in with her men.

That is, except for her face. This too made her stand out. While not beautiful, her face was striking and fascinating and as she smiled with the thrill battle. The firelit glow in her eyes and they promised a glorious death to any who stood before her. It was, in its way, inviting.

What shall we do Master? There are too many of them?

Libby's question shook him from his reverie and he continued to slowly scan the rest of the battle. His Familiar was right, there were many hobgoblins and they were getting the best of the battle. The square was already littered with fallen humans, dwarves and halflings. But this wasn't what gave Ninetoes pause, but rather how thickly mixed the hobs were with the town's own defenders. Any ranged attack he made would risk hitting them, or worse the non-combatant townsfolk.

Time was of the essence however, as most of the town's guards were only partially equipped and many of them showed signs of fatigue or heavy drinking.

CRASH!

Every head turned at the sound of splintering wood as a massive figure pulled the wheel and axle from a fishmonger's cart and flung it into the ranks of Necht Sarm, only barely missing the town's militia.

"Sorry! My fault! Now, use the barrels my dear."

Ninetoes recognised the voice of his mentor, Foresto. Following the sound of the voice, spotted him ducked behind the tavern, gesturing towards a pile of barrels stacked beside the pub. The gigantic figure stepped into the firelight to pick up a barrel and Ninetoes could see that it was some sort of mechanical, headless man. It must have stood ten feet tall and as he watched, the creature tossed the barrel as though it was an apple. *Woah! This thing is strong!*

115

But, as the barrel smashed apart against a building far behind the line of hobgoblins, it was clear that the mechanical creature was not very accurate and just as likely to hit the defenders as the hobs. Even still, the hobgoblins were now ducked behind their shields and had drawn back their line, providing the townsfolk a much-needed respite.

As Ninetoes watched, the Sarm was quickly dishing out orders and he could see two hobgoblins pulling rope from their packs. Ninetoes wasn't sure what they planned to do, but it couldn't be good. It was time to act.

"Bluzag, shield!" He shouted and tucked himself behind the half-ogre. "Forward."

Bluzag's feet stamped towards the line of Necht Sarm. Following closely behind him, Ninetoes quickly ran through his spells and selected his new favourite.

Poking his head out from behind his meat shield Ninetoes sent two Grim Bolts into the hobgoblin's shield wall. He'd aimed low, hoping to catch their ankles, but even still one of the bolts splashed ineffectually against the iron rim of a shield. A yelp of pain told him that his other attack had hit, however.

When nothing fired back at him, Ninetoes signed in relief. His Cloaking Shadow must still be concealing him from his foe.

Through the dimly lit space, Ninetoes heard the melodic voice of the Sarm shouting an order for archers and so, as Ninetoes stepped back behind Bluzag he ordered the Wight to stand still and activate his Immovable skill. A moment later the sounds of arrows punching and screeching past his servant's shield told Ninetoes that they'd succeeded in drawing the hobs' attention. *Good.*

Checking over Bluzag, he could also tell that his Wight had unfortunately not gone unscathed. Ninetoes poked his head out long enough to fire off another bolt of necrotic energy at the hobgoblins, but all too soon he heard another barrage of missiles slam into Bluzag.

While the Wight felt no pain from the assault, physics still had an effect on the massive undead, and the force of the barrage was enough to stagger the Wight slightly.

Ninetoes knew he couldn't just stay here and use his towering servant as his meatshield. Even Bluzag's undead nature didn't make him immune to damage.

Ninetoes nearly 'stepped' away to begin tearing into the hobgoblin's flanks, but he'd be outnumbered and outmatched in terms of martial skill. But more than that, recognised that he must start thinking like a Wizard and so instead, he looked about the battlefield for an alternative.

The alternative came in the guise of another missile sent hurtling into the ranks of Necht Sarm, this one a clay jar filled with a viscous, clear liquid that splashed all over the ranks of hobgoblins as it crashed near to them. Two more pots quickly followed, one missing completely but the other smashing into a warrior's centre mass and throwing him bodily into a comrade. The pots seemed a little more accurate, but not particularly dangerous.

That was until Ninetoes noticed a burning log rise from one of the bonfires of its own accord and whizz off towards the hobs.

Turning he could see his mentor wearing the same mischievous grin the devilish little gnome always displayed when torturing Ninetoes with his 'lessons'.

Turning back, Ninetoes watched as the incendiary crashed into a hobgoblin shield which glistened with whatever the liquid was. It immediately set aflame and the gnome's plan became clear.

WHOOSH! Flames engulfed the hobgoblin who screams piercing the night. The hob twisted in pain and ignited the shield of the warrior to his left, who was also coated in what was clearly oil.

For a few moments of painful squealing, it seemed the plan would work, but the Sarm's control of her men was like iron and she leapt forward, kicking the shield from one of the two hobs and throwing the other to the floor.

In the confusion an arrow took one of the shieldless warriors in the chest, but then the Sarm barked an order and the shield wall closed ranks, sealing the breach. Behind the wall of steel Ninetoes could see the hobgoblin rolling in the dirt and quenching the flames.

Worse still, now that her enemy seemed to be out of tricks, the Sarm sent out clipped and clear orders and three columns formed from the ranks of warrior hobs.

Each one began marching towards a different foe. One squad bared down on the townsfolk, another marched on Foresto and the last one was aimed at him.

***

VORTIGA

Vortiga didn't really have friends, not even as a young pup. She'd never really felt the need. No one had ever stood up for her and so she'd learned to never need them to. At least, not since the first time she'd tasted blood.

It was her own that time. She lay on the ground, her lip bloodied and swollen from the beating a brutish older boy had given her. She couldn't remember his name, it hadn't ever seemed important enough. But she had learned two important lessons that day. She didn't need anyone else and she would need brains more than brawn to survive.

That poor boy had been her first victim too. She'd tricked him into stepping too close to the worg cages and he'd lost an arm. It was a shame, he'd have grown to become a capable warrior, but an example had needed to be set.

Since then her cunning and ruthlessness has been tested too many times to count, but Vortiga's malice always won out. The Curn has seen that and given her this command. At first, she'd bulked at the thought of leading the 'Light' Company, assuming it was just one more slight against the "upstart wench".

But the Curn was as cunning as she was and she'd quickly learned what a gift and honour he'd given her.

The Light Company didn't often march with the rest of the brigade, instead ranging far ahead, where they would be the first into battle and so more likely to cover themselves in glory and claim loot.

But it was more than that. Away from prying eyes and the stuffy old traditions of the other commanders, Vortiga could craft her company into the weapon **she** wanted. What's more, the Curn had placed a squad of ba'ardec under her command and she'd fashioned them into the diamond-hard tip of her spear.

Still, not a day went by when one of her 'men' didn't challenge her. She welcomed this as a part of command. It was the nature of the world that only the strongest survived and only the ruthless should lead. A principle she'd used to sharpen her company, promoting only those who were both strong and clever. She was still left with a few officers left over from the previous Sarm of course, but she always sent them into the most dangerous of engagements. They'd learn to fight smarter or they'd die, either consequence suited her plans.

She'd known that assaulting this human settlement was a risk, there were just too many unknowns, too much she couldn't account for. But her men were hungry for battle and tired of living off the land and so she must feed their lusts.

More than that, however, promotion required glory and what more glory could be found than taking this settlement before their army even arrived? She would stand atop the battlements and welcome the Curn and his vanguard through the open gates; then none could deny her valour and skill.

And now, with her shield wall tightening the noose around the foolish and drunken town guards, she could taste her next victory.

CRASH!

Whipping her head around, Vortiga caught sight of the towering automaton, gears within its body whirling as it wound up to throw a cart at her men.

"SHIELDS!" She shouted and her men responded as one, raising their shields and bracing their back feet. The debris smashed into her line and knocked back her men but they absorbed the majority of the damage.

While the golem was unexpected, she'd seen such things before and knew this new foe would pose no problem. "You two, ropes, we'll bind the bastard up and trip it over."

As she gave out her orders another voice rose above the din.

"Forward," it shouted as one of her men went down. Searching the darkness, Vortiga noted another new threat, a huge warrior clad in piecemeal armour.

"Rear rank, bows!" she called. "Bring that beast down. Aim for the eyes!" One of her Farn took over, directing his men into a steady barrage of arrows. *Ha! Was this all they had?*

More missiles, thrown by the golem, smashed into her ranks, splashing something all over the front rank.

As soon as Vortiga got a whiff of rotten eggs, she was moving and as the faggot of burning wood bounced against one of her men she acted without thought, she could not let her men lose cohesion for a second.

"Drop!" she commanded as she kicked the burning shield from one of her men and wrestled another to the floor.

Behind her she heard the choking sound of one of her men dying but she couldn't worry about that and instead dragged the soldier she held back to his feet and shoved him back into line.

"Close ranks!" shouted another of her Farn, this one a female like her. She'd never been more proud of them. Her enemies had spent themselves attacking her column and failed, now she would roll over them.

"Dosh!" she called, directed at the female Farn. "Take your men and kill that Wizard," she commanded, pointing towards the automaton.

"Sir!" came the clipped response.

"Dalar! You keep at these fools." She gestured towards the town's crumbling defences.

"Sir!" Her heart swelled with pride for her men.

"Front rank, up!" And after the barest of moment's pause as they responded to her command. "Forward!"

As she marched in step with her men, she stepped over the corpse of one of her warriors and as she looked down she noticed his skin was a spider web of blackened veins. "Magic!" She spat in disgust.

"Keep your wits about you men, there's a second mage about."

She hated magic users, as did all of her tribe. Then she spotted it, the strange patch of shadow moving behind the behemoth ahead.

All too late she realised its significance as one of her men was blasted from his feet by a ball of black energy. "The mage is behind that brute! Front rank charge! Second rank, loose!"

***

Shit!

The Sarm has spotted him somehow and now an entire squad had been unleashed, each of them seconds from crashing into Ninetoes and Bluzag.

Meanwhile the town's defenders were quickly losing cohesion and were being steadily forced back towards the press of townsfolk. The scene wasn't much better for Foresto as the last band moved to encircle his golem, two pairs of hobgoblins carrying ropes between them, their plan now clear.

An arrow crashed into Ninetoes' head. Most of the blow was absorbed by his magical armour, but the force of the blow knocked him down and rang his bell, disorienting him for a moment.

Another pot smashed into the approaching ranks of Necht Sarm and Ninetoes' attention was jerked back. What could he do? He couldn't fight so many!

Set them on fire boy! Shouted a voice in his mind. He recognised the voice immediately, Foresto! *But, what?* His addled mind hadn't caught up and the voice shouting within it wasn't helping.

Fire boy! Fire. His tone had become the same exasperated voice it did when Ninetoes was being particularly dim.

Apologies master, the battle is confu-

Shut up boy and burn them!

Oh right. Stepping from behind Bluzag he could see that the hobgoblins were almost upon him. Lacing his thumbs together, he shouted, "Burning hands!"

A gout of flames shot out of his palms and splashed over the charging ranks of hobgoblins.

FWWOOOOMMMM!

As the spray of fire lit the oil heat blazed over Ninetoes' face, singing the tips of his facial hair. The explosion sent the entire front into a screaming and tangled mess and their charge was shocked into disarray.

It wasn't enough to blunt their assault altogether however. And, although he could no longer see her through the smoke and ash, Ninetoes could hear the Sarm martialling her forces once again.

Ergh! What do I have to do to shake this woman's calm?

Master! On your left!

Libby's warning made him turn his head. Charging towards him, some remaining Necht Sarm rallied and streaked towards the young Wizard. Ninetoes dove back behind Bluzag and the half-ogre activated Immovable, setting his feet.

Thanks. He called out as he caught a glimpse of Libby gliding over the battlefield. He could even see the tell-tale signs of her casting magic and was, once again grateful for his incredible Familiar.

A second later the wave of enemies crashed into the towering wall of flesh and metal. Bluzag accepted their charge and stood strong, then stomped forward a step.

Brushing his shield to one side and thrusting his maul out to the other he broke their charge.

His shield swept aside two hobgoblins with it and his maul punched into the chest of third, the crunch of bones deciding the fate of this one long before his broken body hit the floor. Stamping down, the behemoth crushed the skull of another, but the last of them managed to roll out of the way of the lumbering giant.

The awful smell of blood, shit and piss filled the air to be mixed with the strange and salivating scent of pork.

Around the bulwark of lifeless flesh surged yet more Necht Sarm. Every one had murder in their eyes and something else.

Ninetoes recognised it immediately; the bloodlust of battle and the desire for glory. Mere weeks ago, Ninetoes would have quailed if faced with such cold animosity, but his recent travels had hardened him and instead of backtracking, Ninetoes stepped forward **into** their charge.

Clearly this was not what they had expected from a measly porsht because all four warriors stumbled to a halt. Alas their surprise was short lived and, while Bluzag dealt with his own smaller group of enemies, these four surrounded Ninetoes. *Damn it!* He must start thinking like a Wizard.

As it always seemed to do, the chaos of battle chilled Ninetoes' mind into a kind of crystal clarity and he quickly considered and discarded a dozen plans. Suddenly one of his foes lanced forward and the battle was joined.

Ninetoes didn't consciously remember drawing his sword but there it was, a firm reminder of his battle focus. Parry, thrust, block. A lightning blur of movement, testing his skill to its limit and yet he'd only just managed to turn his attacker's strikes, the ache in his wrists telling him this warrior was **much** stronger.

All too late he realised the whole assault had been a feint to test his skill and they'd found him wanting.

This Sarm had trained her men well. Twice he'd fought them and twice they'd surrounded him. He must do better!

Two quick jabs sparked the armour on his flank and he felt his mana drain as the magic tapped it for energy. He could feel their grins. They had him!

Ninetoes caught the next lunge on his blade and cast Shocking Strike as he did so, sending a spark of light leaping back up his attacker's sword to leave him momentarily stunned. He used the chance to ram his blade hilt-deep into the hob's neck, but as he did so, another strike lanced across his back and penetrated his shield, drawing blood for the first time. He jerked with the pain and with a sucking squelch, his cutlass was pulled from his hand, the body of his victim dragging his weapon to the ground.

The warriors were too fast again and a quick series of attacks drove him away from his sword. He must fight like a wizard, but without his sword—

CRUNCH!

Pain seared through his body. This time the blow had smashed into the unprotected shoulder of his shield arm, strong enough to break his collarbone. Somewhat fortunately, the blow hadn't been meant to kill but rather to wound; these arseholes were toying with him!

In his anger he lashed out with a Grim Bolt, but his aim was thrown off by pain and the hobgoblin dodged lazily, sneering back at Ninetoes' feeble attack.

Rather than killing him outright, the Swords of Nech slashed and poked, chipping away at his health pool. Ninetoes' anger grew; how could he be so foolish as to cross blades with these brutes? He was a Wizard! If he could only draw them in, but they knew they had him! Their lips curled in arrogant sneers.

"Ha! Look at the porsht, of course he would resort to magic. Too weak to become a Warrior eh?" one of them mocked. They were right of course, he must resort to magic.

Ninetoes wasn't too proud to use the same duplicitous tactic twice. Clearly these fools took him to be a weak porsht, like the ba'ardec had. Well, he'd turn that arrogance against them.

He slumped into himself, trying to look as meek as possible. This wasn't difficult as pain lanced through his shoulder with every movement. The hobs took the bait and tightened their circle around him. Closing in for the kill.

Taking a deep breath to concentrate through the pain, Ninetoes rotated on the spot, trying and failing to keep them all where he could see them and the attack he knew was coming. The attack that would finally end their sport and with it his life.

Sweat beaded on his back and trailed down his spine. He was tired from his fraught journey to reach the town. He couldn't maintain fighting them for too much longer, he needed to end the fight. But to do that, he needed patience. He needed them to make the first move.

He felt more than saw the attack and in that same instant triggered Force Wave, sending all three assailants flying backwards as a wall of sheer energy blasted out from him in every direction. One had been much closer than he'd realised and this one took the worst of it, thrown fifteen feet away and landing awkwardly on his neck: a snapping sound marked the hob's end.

The other two were knocked prone and had probably lost some hit points but not enough to take them out of the fight. But that hadn't been Ninetoes' plan and instead, gritting his teeth through the pain of his own broken body, he stumbled over to the closest warrior, grabbing out at whatever he could reach. The hob tried to dodge and Ninetoes caught only his ear, but it was enough. He cast Grim Void.

Cool, healing energy flowed into Ninetoes, stolen from his victim. His wounds quickly began to heal. He nearly collapsed from the shock of his bones realigning themselves but he dug his nails into the soft flesh behind the hob's lobe to help him cling on through the screaming pain, his own mixing with those of his foe.

As the energy flow ceased from his enemy, he dropped his gaze and saw that the ear was only attached by a single strand of bloody flesh. He dropped it in disgust.

A few yards away, the other warrior was scrabbling around on the floor towards his weapon and Ninetoes knew he must be quick.

Still concentrating on his favourite spell, he stumbled across the intervening space and fell upon the warrior, kicking him hard in the jaw and then straddling his back. He couldn't let the hobgoblin gain any purchase and so he slid himself up his body, pinning his arms to the floor with his knees. Next, he reached down to throttle him.

He couldn't beat the Warrior in a fair test of Strength; but then in Ninetoes' opinion, only fools would fight fair.

125

As the hob struggled he managed to release one of his arms and slap Ninetoes in the face. By then, however, Grim Void had already done its macabre work and the paltry damage was quickly healed by the fool's own life force. The hob continued to struggle for long seconds, for which Ninetoes was grateful, as he absorbed every ounce of strength, power and malice his foe had for him.

Eventually the struggling beneath him ceased and Ninetoes reached out to place the hob's sword into his palm. With the last of the Warrior's strength his fingers wrapped around the hilt, only a moment before the light left his eyes. "May Sarm take you brother." He offered his enemy.

Ninetoes' body finally felt whole once more. He realised that he'd taken enough damage to require both hobgoblins' health points to replenish his own.

Standing up and Ninetoes took a deep breath. He could feel that his health pool was nearly topped off, but with his Wizard Armour gone, he felt more vulnerable than he had done in weeks and he cursed himself for once again acting like a spellsword instead of fighting like a Wizard.

Quickly he checked his Character Sheet and noted that he still had more than a hundred mana points left and so recast his base level Wizard Armour spell, while retrieving his sword. His magical shielding wouldn't stand up to much punishment, but it still made him feel safer.

He quickly cast his gaze about the battlefield. Bluzag was finishing his own fight and, by the signs of it, he'd suffered much as Ninetoes had.

Foresto's own immolation magic had been far more successful than Ninetoes' had however, and the band of hobs sent to deal with him had halved in size. His golem was now wading amongst them, batting the warriors every which way, their bodies smashing into the dirt and lying in still crumpled forms.

Even the town's defenders seemed to be holding the line as the people threw everything they had to hand at the hobs. Literally, Ninetoes realised, as he saw the innkeeper lobbing potatoes into the ranks of Necht Sarm.

126

For a moment one could be fooled into believing that the defenders had the best of it, but not Ninetoes, he could sense the ebb and flow of the battle and knew that the tide was only moments from turning. But what could he do? One against so many.

He could have attempted using his Necromancy magic to raise a squad of undead to balance the odds, but this would be time-consuming and worse, would reveal his new Specialism to the people of Raveslan.

Then it hit him. For all their attempts at breaking the wall of Necht Sarm shields, one thing has held them together, the fiery female Sarm. Her will had kept the hobgoblins fighting as one cohesive unit throughout and thus Ninetoes knew what he must do.

"Bluzag, hold this position. Stay behind your shield and only counter-attack."

Libby, where are you?

Above Master. I can see the whole battle from here. She didn't only send him this message, but also images of what she saw and what she'd been doing. Since he'd seen her last Libby had been soaring through the smoke-filled sky above the battle, creating illusions to distract the hobgoblins. Her actions had led to nearly a half-dozen kills.

Good work Little One. Where is the Sarm? He didn't need to give her any more detail, their thoughts now able to convey more than words.

To your left Master and, I think she's hunting you.

Good. Let's use one from our own playbook. Find somewhere good and project an image of me. Do you think you can make it move?

Of course, Master. I could make it dance, if I'd ever seen you so lively.

Ha! That won't be necessary, just a quick distraction will do.

As they'd talked he'd drained his Gem of Power, boosting his mana back past the two hundred mark and used some of the energy to strengthen his Wizard Armour, breathing a sigh of relief as he did so. No amount of magical armour would matter of course, if he couldn't deal with the Sarm and end this conflict decisively.

Although a lot had happened, barely a few minutes had passed since he'd reached the city, so Ninetoes' casting of Cloak of Shadows was still fresh and his plan was simple enough; use Libby's illusion to get the drop on the Sarm.

Having seen her fight he knew that being so close was a risk so he'd have to use Grim Bolt to kill her.

Quickly, he dashed into hiding and waited for the Sarm. With the constant feed of images from his Familiar, he knew the hobgoblin warrior was close, stalking this way in search of her quarry. He also knew exactly where to look for his illusory doppelgänger.

Libby had outdone herself and his copy was poorly hidden and right in the Sarm's path. Facing away from the Sarm, it was the perfect illusion of the perfect prey.

Libby even had it 'casting' a spell! She had made it so the hobgoblin couldn't resist their ruse; his Familiar was swiftly becoming a mastermind.

The Sarm spotted the copy and, without a moment of pause, charged for it, shield held before her with her sword resting on its iron-bound edge, tip pointed straight for the copy's spine.

As the Sarm took off, Ninetoes began casting his spell and sent the bolt cutting through the darkness.

Ahead of him his prey smashed into and through the illusion, stumbling forward and for the barest of moments she faltered in confusion, her stumble also threw off his attack and the bolt of black death sailed uselessly over her head.

It did not, however, escape the Sarm's notice and in an instant she had not only turned to find him but had taken three steps. And in those three long steps, she had somehow closed the distance and was on him.

With barely a moment to choose between fight or flight, Ninetoes chose the former and stepped forward, reaching for her neck and casting his most deadly spell, Grim Bolt.

His grip on her neck wasn't strong but he knew that it didn't matter. Because of his spell it didn't need to be and within moments she'd be like a ragdoll, held up only by his strength. He heard the clatter of her weapons as they dropped to the ground and he knew she was done for.

Only, she wasn't. And as he watched her face, expecting the light to go out of her eyes, he instead saw them regain focus and a look of anger and hatred stare back at him.

THWACK!

Her fist drove into Ninetoes' gut, driving the wind from him and forcing him to double over. As he did so, her knee rammed up and into his face. He felt a crack as his face exploded in pain.

He stumbled backwards, still more surprised than hurt; why hadn't his spell worked?

As his vision cleared a little, he looked up and saw a look of such passionate murder in her eyes that he quailed. The Sarm charged forward, snatching up her sword from the ground and driving her shoulder into his solar plexus, sending them both tumbling onto the floor, but where Ninetoes fell backwards and bashed his head, the warrior controlled her fall with a roll, grabbing her sword as she landed on top of him, straddling him with her knees pinning his arms to his sides, much as he'd done to one of her men.

His vision was all blurry stars but he could feel the hatred buffet off of her in waves and he felt genuine fear for the first time. Reaching up for her, he tried and failed to cast a spell, but the pain made his words falter and the casting died on his lips. Was this his end?

But, even as this cowardly thought occurred to him, his resolve hardened. He was Dakhec Druul, he would watch his doom approach head on and so he opened his streaming eyes and looked straight into hers as she raised her sword, the tip aimed straight at his heart. As she stared back she grinned a curious grin and whispered to him.

"May Starm take you brother."

Then punctuated her final word by driving the blade down into Ninetoes' chest... or at least she tried to.

As Ninetoes watched the sword spear down towards him, a large black mass crashed into her side, kicking Ninetoes in the temple as it did.

As a small part of him questioned, *What the fuck?* the blow sent Ninetoes into the welcome oblivion of darkness and peace.

CHAPTER 7
IMPAIRED

Ninetoes awoke some time later, a blinding sun directly above telling him that he'd been out for a goodly few hours. "He's awake," called a male voice off to his right.

Sitting up Ninetoes winced as stiffness made his muscles spasm. Looking about he could see that he was still where he'd fallen and before him stood Bluzag, his back to Ninetoes. Nearby sat a human wearing the livery of a Raveslan guard, the very one whom Ninetoes had met the first time he'd visited town. He was seated on a pile of lumber eating an apple and wore a grin that suggested the battle had gone their way. He nodded at Ninetoes, his bandaged head making the move a little comical.

"Alrigh'?" he asked.

"Err... yes. Yes, I think so," responded the hobgoblin. As he cast his gaze wider, Ninetoes could see that many of the townsfolk were around, cleaning up or repairing damage or sat having a wound or injury tended to. The nearby buildings were fire damaged, some extensively, a few even having burned down to the foundations and all those he could see showed signs of burn damage.

At least the absence of hobgoblins meant that they must have won the battle, he doubted he'd have woken up at all. Still a little confused, Ninetoes had to find out what had happened and tell Foresto what about the approaching goblinoid army.

"Do you think you could ask ya man to stand down?" said the guard, gesturing towards Bluzag. Directing his attention to the Wight, Ninetoes realised that his ally had his shield raised and his weapon held ready to strike.

"He's not let no one near ya all night, else we'd have moved you with the other wounded an' seen to ya injuries."

"Bluzag, stand down," Ninetoes commanded, too tired to ask politely. The undead immediately dropped his arms to his sides and stepped back to stand at Ninetoes left flank. The hobgoblin stood himself up, his knees creaking with atrophy.

Still a little confused, it didn't escape Ninetoes' notice that his last instruction to the Wight had been to hold his position, so his current behaviour was odd.

"Ah Ninetoes, excellent. Quite the er... manservant you have there." Foresto approached from behind a nearby ruin, his towering construct stood nearby holding up a massive beam aloft as though it were a twig. Beneath it townsfolk searched through the rubble of a collapsed building.

"Master Foresto, hello. Yes, my er... friend here is very protective of me. I hope he didn't hurt anyone?" he questioned.

"No, no. He simply would not allow anyone to approach you and, with so many injured and the town ablaze, we elected to leave you where you were until you woke up or we could find a way to help you. Your Adventurer's blood seems to have healed the majority of the damage, although I think your nose seems to be a little... ur, wonky?"

Ninetoes reached up and touched his face tenderly. True enough, his nose seemed to kink in the middle. It must have been broken in the combat and, without healing magic or being properly set, had healed crooked. *Huh, no matter.* He'd never been considered handsome even with a straight nose.

"Would you like me to try and fix it my friend?" asked his mentor. It was the word 'try' that held Ninetoes' attention most.

"Um, no. No thank you master," he replied, cringing as his teacher huffed at his use of the honorific.

"So, he lives eh? Good, now he can be bound and jailed with the other one." A squat barrel-chested man had strode purposefully over as they'd talked and now stood staring down his nose at Ninetoes, despite being a few inches shorter.

"As we have discussed Kenwyn, there is no evidence that Ninetoes was working with the hobgoblins and in fact, as I have stated numerous times, he was fighting against them!" Foresto's voice was tired. It seemed that this was a well-trodden path and by the end of his response he was wagging his finger. Ninetoes had seen the diminutive wizard make such a gesture before and had seen larger men quail in its presence, so he was surprised when the stumpy man stood his ground.

"And as I have pointed out, the bandits were upon us without any alarm raised, meaning they must have had help. Who better than your own pet goblin?" he growled back. Amongst non-goblinoids, the distinction between the honourable hobgoblin and their fallen brethren tended to be a moot point and they tarnished all of his kin with the same brush. To him, being called a goblin was the equivalent of being spat in the face. The insulting term stung Ninetoes all the more however, because he had grown used to not hearing such language within the town.

"Had help? They didn't need help, most of your militia were drunk! And as for Ninetoes," Foresto was nearly shouting by this point, "he and his companion here killed more of the attackers than your men managed to!"

"Or so it would seem," responded Kenwyn, a smile slapped across his face, as though this statement had earned him a great victory.

"ERRRAGH! You are a fool Kenwyn, just like your father! If not for Ninetoes dealing with their leader, we'd likely have lost the battle and our homes!"

"Ha! His mountain of a man was the one to take the wench out of the fight and it was the militia who drove them back. Your goblin shaman here just burned down half the town! Explain that you silly old fool!"

Bluzag stopped the Sarm? But how? Ninetoes' nearly lost himself to that confusing piece of information, but then the man's final words registered and his heart sank.

Looking again at the damage surrounding them he felt so ashamed. Had he really been the cause of all this destruction?

"Yet another point that we have already discussed, you pompous twat! The fire was my idea and was the only reason your militia weren't surrounded! And, and…" The gnome's usual patience was clearly wearing thin and he seemed almost lost for words. "And thus they were able to drive back the hobgoblins!" Ninetoes noticed that purple energy crackled over the wizard's hands, warning of arcane retribution, but the human didn't seem to notice, or care.

As Kenwyn wound up for a fiery retort Borris, the town's master blacksmith, hastily approached.

"Enough of this. Both of ye. Kenwyn, Foresto is correct, there's no evidence ter link the Adventurer te the attack, and Foresto, rather than allowing your temper te get the better of ye, perhaps ye could have yer golem help me at me shop; I's 'oping most of the forge is salvageable."

Both Kenwyn and Foresto seethed, glaring daggers at one another. But Ninetoes saw the opportunity presented to him and chose to take it.

"My friend Bluzag here is very, very strong, we would be happy to help you master dwarf. Bluzag, with me." Not giving anyone a chance to argue he quickly headed towards the ruined blacksmiths. He'd find Foresto later when the human wasn't around. Borris jogged to catch up to the pair.

"Pay no mind te Kenwyn, he's an ass. If ye friend be as strong as ye make out, then ye have me thanks." Borris smiled.

"And if it means aught te ya, I saw ya both fightin' and ah know that many more woulda died without ya. Ya alrigh' ba me." The dwarf offered his hand as he stepped in front of Ninetoes, stalling his escape. A smile creased the dwarf's white beard and Ninetoes reached out, clasping the old smith's wrist.

"What happened? After I was knocked out I mean," Ninetoes asked.

"Well, I didna' see ya fall mind, but the fire tha' yoo and the ol' wizard started caught hold of the buildings te the west o' the square, behind the hobs. When ya man there knocked out their leader they lost focus and

Foresto's golem smashed their lines. By then, the militia had rallied and pushed 'em back. Wi' the fire at their backs and spears before 'em, they broke, and threw themselves onto the militia's blades, most didna even try to defend 'emselves, it was like hogs to slaughter. I'll tell ye, it were a chillin' thing te be'old." His last statement jogged Ninetoes' memory.

"Well, there's worse to follow. Their whole army is on the way here and they can't be more than a week away," Ninetoes stated.

"Wha'?" Borris looked dumbfounded.

"On my way here I was attacked by some of their scouts. I took one prisoner and he told me everything," Ninetoes explained.

"Well, then ma' forge will have te wait fa now. Ye need to speak to the Council." Borris adjusted his course and made for the Greenhill Inn. Ninetoes could see that it was now the centre of activity. It had always been the largest building in town, but now it was one of the only buildings in the square left standing.

"You boy, run and fetch the other council members and be quick about it," Borris commanded a young lad who was carrying a bucket of water in one hand and a ladle in the other, offering the wounded something to drink. But, at the tone of the stout dwarf's voice, he took off like a shot, heading firstly towards where Foresto and Kenwyn still argued. Borris led Ninetoes inside the inn.

"Here my friend, ye must be hungry." Borris handed Ninetoes and Bluzag a hunk of bread and set about cutting them each large helpings of cheese from a nearby wheel. Ninetoes could feel the light tug of tiny claws on his neckerchief as his familiar roused herself for her favourite meal.

Cheese?

Here little one. He gave her half his own helping. *Stay with me and help with any details I miss.*

Of course, Master. Is… is this all there is? She queried, the huge chunk of cheese having already disappeared. Having not even started his own, Ninetoes handed over the second half. Even as he watched however, Bluzag's hand raised to his shoulder and his own chunk to Libby. *What? Libby*

134

did you...? But before he could finish the thought the Kenwyn stormed into the taproom.

"What is all this Borris?" he blustered. "I thought we'd dealt with the goblin for now," he added, glaring at Ninetoes.

"I find myself agreeing with master Kenwyn, there is more important work to be done." This came from a tall, grey haired woman who had to stoop as she stepped under the lintel. Ninetoes had never met her, but he knew that she ran the general goods store and was well respected by the folk of Raveslan.

"And you're righ' o' course mistress Emblyn, the matter o' the Adventurer," he leaned into the term, looking significantly at Kenwyn as he did so, "has been dealt with. This is another matter that we need te discuss," the dwarf explained.

"Very well Borris, but why does the... he, need to be here?" Asked Kenwyn, gesturing towards Ninetoes. "Such meetings should be private."

"Cos it's 'im that's got summut to tell us. Ahh, ye tell 'em lad." By this time, Foresto and the last member of the Council members had entered the inn, this one a halfling woman of middling years, whom Ninetoes didn't recognise.

Seeing Ninetoes looking a little nervous, Foresto spoke up. "Ninetoes, these goodly folk and myself make up the town Council. This is mistresses Emblyn, proprietor of the Golden Spindal and Ffion, head of the Bevin household and the owner of Raveslan Ranch. Borris you know of course and Kenwyn you've just met," he finished quickly, mumbling the portly human's introduction.

"Hah! I am the Lord Baron of Raveslan, Foresto, and don't you forget it," steamed Kenwyn.

"We don't have a lord or baron anymore Kenwyn, as well you know." Emblyn stepped in before Foresto could respond. "But your family name is well respected, of course. Shall we begin?"

"Ar... yes, of course my dear." Foresto, clearly about to argue with Kenwyn, relented.

"The Adventurer here tells me he fought a bunch o' the goblins on his way here and that one o' them gave up some information, reckon we need ta hear it. Go on lad." Borris gestured open-handed towards Ninetoes, whose stomach was currently doing flips with nerves. Ninetoes wasn't much of a public speaker and he'd apart from Foresto and the innkeeper, he'd never spoken to any of these people. For a moment he wished he could simply be battling worgs.

"Master Borris is correct. I was on my way here, having completed my Quest." He looked to Foresto at this point who smiled and nodded. "Well as you know, my people, the Dakhec Druul, inhabit a settlement not far from here hidden by the forests, so when I saw more hobgoblins I was wary of them.

"Only, these were not my kin and not of the Dakhec Druul. They attacked me, but not until they'd attempted to force me to tell them where my people are hidden. You see these hobgoblins were Necht Sarm and they hate my folk. Worse still, these were ba'ardec, elite warriors."

"So? Goblins killing goblins! What does any of this have to do with us?" interrupted Kenwyn.

"He's getting to that, so shuddup and let him speak," Borris responded.

"Please Adventurer, continue," said Emblyn, smiling at Ninetoes.

"Thank you, mistress. As I was saying, I was able to defeat them and what's more I took a prisoner. I... interrogated him and he revealed that they were just one troop. The rest of their army is marching here to Raveslan."

"Well? So what? We saw off this... army, not that it was much of one." Kenwyn interrupted again. This time Ninetoes responded quickly himself, he needed to show this fool what he was made of.

"No, you're wrong. Those warriors were only the Light Company and even that was incomplete because the troop of ba'ardec had been sent ahead to search for my home. The whole army will be hundreds strong and will be marching from the east, what's more they could be here within

136

the Tenday." All of the councillors' faces paled slightly, silenced by the news. Emblyn was the first to speak and her words were a whisper.

"But why here? What do they want with us?"

"You they will take into slavery, but it's not really your people they want, it's your resources. An army marches on its stomach and this one has little food. But it's not really **your** town they want at all. They are marching to finish what they started a lifetime ago; they seek to destroy my people."

"But why do they seek your people at all my friend?" asked Foresto.

"My people are many things and sadly one of them is vengeful. Amongst the hobgoblins there are stories that it was the Dakhec Druul who betrayed the other tribes, rather than the other way around. This is enough for them to seek our complete destruction."

Kenwyn growled at this. "So they only attack us simply because we are on their way! I told you the attack was his fault! Goblins are all the same: filthy beasts! They know only how to destroy and now we will pay the price for their bloodlust." He paused mid-diatribe to catch his breath, his chest heavy as he wiped sweat off of his jowly face before continuing. "I say we open our gates, offer them food, as much as they want and then send them on their way. We could even send one of the huntsmen to show them his village!" Kenwyn spat out. Ninetoes blanched, ready to offer a rebuttal, but he was beaten to the punch.

"You are a fool Kenwyn. If we open our gates they'll slaughter the men and carry off the women and children, I've seen it before." This was the first time the halfling woman had spoken, but everyone paid attention when she did, even Kenwyn.

"What then? Flee? Leave our town to the likes of him?" Kenwyn's voice was beginning to betray his fear, cracking as he pointed at Ninetoes.

"We may have to. We barely stood up to three dozen of their warriors. If what the goblin says is true and this army is made up of hundreds, there's no way we can defend ourselves." Ffion responded again and it didn't slip Ninetoes' notice that she called him goblin.

"But of course, that's it isn't it?" Kenwyn's voice was becoming shrill as he strode towards Ninetoes, pointing his finger in his face. "This isn't true is it? You just wanted to scare us into leaving? I told you he was with them!"

"Enough of this Kenwyn! The Adventurer fought with us last night. I'd even go so far as to say that his actions saved us. No, I believe him, but then we **must** flee. If we tell people straight away, we could make it to Pamor or even Ffestyn within the week. It would be hard starting out again but-"

"No, no Emblyn. We will not flee." Foresto spoke up for the first time since Ninetoes had given his news, his voice confident.

"Then what Foresto, surely you of all people believe your apprentice's story?"

"Oh, I believe him. What I'm saying is that we must not flee, but stay. Stay and fight." Everyone stared aghast at the gnome and Ninetoes could understand why. Their walls might deter the beasts and monsters of the forest, but they'd barely survived the hobgoblins' first attack, they'd be slaughtered if they stayed.

Ninetoes, along with most of those present opened their mouths to argue. Rather than face any more arguments, Foresto continued. "We send someone to Pamor to beseech the city Council for mercenaries or even better, Adventurers."

The room went silent as the group considered his words. Ninetoes could tell, as the silence stretched on, that they were considering Foresto's suggestion. But not him, he knew that it was fruitless to stay. Again, it was Emblyn who broke the silence.

"But the Council owes us no responsibility and we cannot fund an army ourselves, a company maybe, but it would bankrupt the town; what good would that do?"

"You're right my dear, of course mercenaries may not be the answer. Adventurers are cheaper, a full party should do I think."

"Wha'? A single party of Adventurers? They'll do even less good than a company o' soldiers," Borris scoffed.

"Hmmm, I forget sometimes that most of you have never left this small part of the world." Foresto chuckled to himself. "I have heard stories of parties of Adventurers that carved their way through entire hordes of monsters, and things much worse than hobgoblins. Adventurers can hold such power as to make them like the gods! A single party of Adventurers of a high enough level would have no trouble keeping us safe." Foresto explained.

"Is this true my old friend; that such people exist?" Emblyn asked.

"Oh yes my dear. I once met an Adventurer, a wizard nonetheless, who was powerful enough to make his castle fly!"

"It's true. I have also seen the power that Adventurers wield and while I do not like to leave my fate in the hands of such creatures, they may well be our only hope." It was Ffion who spoke and again those present listened closely to what she said.

"No!" Ninetoes hadn't meant to speak out but what they said was utter madness. "The Necht Sarm destroyed my people, casting us out of our stronghold and hunting across the Sweetsea. My people once numbered in the tens of thousands, now we barely fill a village!" His voice became soft and bitter with his last words.

"I do not take this threat lightly my friend but I don't think you yet understand the incredible powers Adventurers can hold." Foresto stood in front of Ninetoes, holding the hobgoblin's gaze as if they were both of a similar height. "Barely more than a week ago you were yourself little more powerful than these good folk and now you are ten times as powerful. Gods, by your own admission, you single-handedly destroyed a troop of elite soldiers and I daresay, it wasn't particularly difficult?"

Ninetoes mouth had been opened, about to respond, but it snapped closed as he considered this.

His battle with the ba'ardec had been fierce but he'd never really feared for his own safety. Certainly, he hadn't fought alone, as Foresto had suggested but weren't Bluzag and Libby proof of his own growing power? In response to Foresto's question, he simply nodded.

"Very well, then I suggest we put it to a vote." Emblyn's voice was formal as she said this.

"Seconded," rejoined Borris.

"All those in favour of sending someone to Pamor to find a party of Adventurers, say 'Aye'."

"Aye." All but Kenwyn raised their voices in agreement.

"All those against?"

"Me and I think you're all fools," stated Kenwyn petulantly.

Ninetoes chose to speak up. "I agree with Kenwyn, I'm not so sure this is a good idea. What happens if this fails or is too slow?"

"He's not wrong." Borris chipped in.

"Foresto, didn't you tell me you have a spell that allows you to communicate over long distances? We'll start making plans to evacuate the town if we receive no word." Emblyn spoke in clipped and even words. The next discussion will be who goes. Any volunteers?" Emblyn seemed to have taken a lead now and her tone remained formal.

"I suggest Foresto. He's a wizard and, as he's just pointed out, the only one of us to have travelled extensively. He can take his pet goblin." Kenwyn's tone was dripping in smarm and by the looks on the other councillors faces, Ninetoes could see that they were all too familiar with such antics.

"Foresto canny go, his magic and his golem are our best defence," Borris argued. Ninetoes didn't want to point out that he also thought Foresto was too old for such a journey.

"I agree with Kenwyn. Mostly." Foresto's comment surprised them all, "Ninetoes and his comrade are the perfect choice. They are Adventurers and more than capable of making the journey." *Wait what?* This conversation was quickly getting out of hand, Ninetoes didn't want to go to Pamor, he needed to get back to his people and warn them. He must speak up.

"Master Foresto I'm proud that you think I'm capable but I cannot go. I'm sorry, but I must warn my people of the danger approaching." He explained. Bluzag stared at the crowd but offered no support or argument.

Clearly, he wasn't about to offer any of his own words of discouragement for this mad plan.

"Please Adventurers, the roads are dangerous these days, our people are farmers and craftsmen, they are not built for such endeavours," Emblyn pleaded.

"Of course they will go Emblyn my dear," Foresto asserted and at Ninetoes' look of concern he turned to the hobgoblin, "and I will warn your people Ninetoes. Emblyn is correct, I have a spell that is a much more efficient means of contacting Brev. What say you?"

Ninetoes considered this for a moment. He wanted to see that his people were safe, but he couldn't leave Raveslan to be destroyed. Worse still, if Raveslan fell then his people stood even less chance of holding back the tide of enemies. No, his people would be better served by Ninetoes helping to stop the Necht Sarm here. Looking Foresto in the eyes he nodded.

"Wait wait wait. We haven't even voted, who's to say that this gobbo is the best choice. I still think he's in league with the others." The other councillors were clearly tired of Kenwyn's argument as not one of them even wasted the breath to argue.

"While I don't completely agree with Kenwyn, I'm also not sure it would be safe to trust all our lives to a couple of... Adventurers. Perhaps we should send someone else along too, someone we know better," suggested Ffion, her use of the honorific had been different from the others and her disdain was obvious in the way her face cringed as she used it.

"Hmm, Ffion makes sense, this venture is more likely to succeed with greater numbers. Borris, didn't you tell me yesterday that your apprentice needs to make the journey to Pamor to formally take her Tools with the Guild?" Emblyn said.

"Aye and Bes's strong and handy with a mace. Reckon she'd go if I asked 'er," Borris confirmed.

"Excellent. It's settled then. The Adventurer will safeguard young Elizabeth on the road to Pamor. She will engage the services of a band of Adventurers to protect the town. I will provide resources for the journey,

Borris will provide Elizabeth with weapons and armour, and of course any services you require Adventurers. Ffion, can you provide horses and tack for the party?" Emblyn had truly taken charge now that the decision had been made.

"Aye, I will offer what assistance I can," the halfling confirmed.

"And I will supply healing potions and a few other useful items," added Foresto. He smiled at Ninetoes, but his eyes said something else. Ninetoes couldn't place it but the look gave him a feeling of growing apprehension.

"Finally then, the question of payment. The party will need to have the means to employ these Adventurers, I suggest we send them with a small portion as down payment. Foresto, what do you think would be a reasonable sum?"

"Hmmm, a reasonable sum would be two thousand gold pieces." An audible gasp could be heard from Borris, Kenwyn and Emblyn as Foresto casually noted the fee.

"Wha... bu... we cannot possibly... Foresto what nonsense is this? Such an amount is enough to bankrupt the entire town!" Kenwyn spluttered. "This entire endeavour is doomed before it is even begun!"

"I will put up a thousand gold." Ffion said calmly. The comment was missed by Kenwyn as he continued to bluster.

"Not even during my father's reign could the town have provided such a sum!"

"An' I can add a magical weapon to the pot, Adventurers love those. They sell for one 'undred gold or more in Pamor," added Borris.

"I can scrape together, hmmm... maybe a hundred gold of my own. Kenwyn? Kenwyn! What can the town's coffers afford?" Emblyn asked. Kenwyn stared aghast for a moment and then attempted a different tact.

"The town coffers? Hmmm, perhaps fifty gold," he suggested, looking a little meek.

"Fifty gold?" exclaimed the tall and severe-looking woman. Stepping up to Kenwyn, she arched herself over the rotund fool. "At our last meeting, you told this council that the town's treasury was looking healthy with more than two hundred gold! 'More than enough to see us through a harsh winter', you said. Where is that money now Kenwyn?"

"Uh... I er, it's... it is all there. But the mansion is in need of repairs and it is up to the town to maintain its civic buildings," he answered quietly. "It's in the by-laws," he added half-heartedly.

"Civic building? It's your house!"

"Ha! Repairs? Yet another extension more like. What is it this time, a wine cellar?" Ffion guessed, but at the sheepish and surprised look on Kenwyn's face, it appeared to be more than random conjecture.

"Very well, the town will add two hundred gold. That still leaves us six hundred short," summarised Emblyn.

"Then it will not be enough. Adventurers are greedy, selfish creatures. They'll sack the town themselves if we promise more than we can pay," commented Ffion.

"Then I will add an offer to sweeten the pot. For each member of this band of Adventurers, I will produce a magical item of Uncommon quality, made to order. This is worth far more than the gold we're missing and will be too tempting an incentive for a group of Adventurers."

"A generous offer to be sure Master Foresto. Let us hope that Bes and the Adventurer can convince the Council of Pamor to send aid, otherwise I fear that the cost of these Adventurers will cripple us. Even if we do survive the attack, the town will struggle to feed itself," added Emblyn.

"I will provide Bess with a purse of two hundred gold to take as a down payment," confirmed Ffion. It didn't escape Ninetoes' notice that the halfling did not trust him with the money.

"And so to the matter of Ninetoes' payment," Foresto interjected before Emblyn could move on.

"He'll just take his pay from the fortune we're paying the Adventurers," huffed Kenwyn.

"No, the Adventurer should be paid for delivering the message and Bess safely to Pamor," Ffion argued and Ninetoes thought for a moment perhaps he had the halfling wrong. "As I've said, Adventurers are dangerous and should always be paid in full. I will pay him twenty-five more gold, up front for this minor Quest. Do you accept?" she asked. Her voice shook with a strange magical tone.

"Ah..." Ninetoes had wanted time to speak with Foresto, to seek answers before being sent off on another Quest, but it seemed he was not to be so fortunate. "...I agree." A feeling like a lock being slammed into place made his chest tighten.

"Very good. Well, if there are no other items to discuss, we all have plenty to be-" Emblyn started.

"Ah, actually I have one more suggestion," interjected Foresto. "I think the prisoner should also travel with the party."

"Wha'? Ar ye' cracked ol' man?" barked Borris.

"I hasten to agree with Master Smith here, Foresto, what possible reason could there be for us to give her up? Should it come to it, she could be useful for information or even as a bargaining chip," stated Ffion.

"All good points lady, of course, but please hear me out." Foresto paused, waiting for a signal to continue. Emblyn gestured open handed to the gnome and he went on. "You are correct that she likely has much information that could be useful, but she is extremely unlikely to tell us any of it. As for a bargaining chip, holding her here would mean that the hobgoblins are honour bound to assault our town and attempt to retrieve her, they will not bargain. Am I correct Ninetoes?"

"Indeed, Foresto is correct. Hobgoblins do not bargain with enemies, they would rather see her die in the fighting. If you hold her hostage they will only attack sooner and with more brutality," he answered.

"Thank you my friend. There is more to consider besides. Firstly, we have nowhere to keep her here and she will only try to escape, meaning we waste resources trying to keep her confined. Then, if she does escape, she'll re-join her army and tell them all she has learned, such as our inability to defend Raveslan from a single company of their soldiers.

In Pamor they have facilities to hold prisoners. Furthermore, her presence is proof of our claims and may sway the Pamorian council into helping. She is proof that an army marches close to their lands, which may be enough to force them to act." Foresto waited, clearly preparing to counter any arguments that came.

"How is one hobgoblin proof of an army?" Ffion asked, her voice more intrigued than argumentative.

"The Pamorian Council have Diviner's amongst them, they will be able to read her mind."

"Then why no' simply demand tha' they read Bes' mind or tha' o' the Adventurer?" Borris asked.

"Because, as mistress Ffion already pointed out, the prisoner would be a wealth of information. She has seen this army, not merely heard about its existence."

"But on the road, it will be much easier for her to escape master Foresto," Ninetoes chimed in, not particularly happy that they wanted to heap another problem onto his plate. Worse still, if the prisoner was who he thought it was, the last time he'd seen her she was trying to kill him.

"Aye. I dislike agreeing with the goblin, but he's right," Kenwyn added.

"This may be true, but this army travels from the east, whereas Ninetoes and Bes will be headed westwards. Each day they will take her further away from her allies, reducing the damage her escape could cause."

"Hmmm, there may be something to this idea," admitted Ffion.

"Thank you my dear, but there is one more reason." His voice quietened to a whisper. "Our people are still reeling from the battle, but within the day they'll come to realise that we have one of those who killed their kin held captive in the town. If she stays here, I'm afraid our people will do something that they'll regret."

"Maybe we should let them." Surprising everyone, Ffion's voice spoke with a calm and confident timbre but hatred burned in her eyes.

"I don't say this for the hobgoblin Ffion, but for our people. The **act** of murder is easy, but living with its stain on ones' conscience is not." Foresto's eyes stared straight into Ffion's clearly searching them for something. The silence stretched on until it became uncomfortable. Finally, her voice cracking slightly, Emblyn spoke up.

"You have made some interesting points Foresto. I motion that we take a vote," she said.

"Seconded," said Kenwyn, the usual sneer absent from his voice.

"Very well. All those in favour of sending the prisoner to Pamor with the party, please say 'Aye'."

"Aye."

"Right, the motion is carried unanimously."

Ninetoes was surprised. When Foresto had first suggested it, he'd thought him mad, but even Kenwyn had been won over by his arguments.

"I call this meeting to a close. Thank you all for your time." Emblyn rose as she spoke, heading for the door.

"Righ', back to it then," Borris said. "Will ye man to come help me?" He asked Ninetoes, eying up Bluzag. Ninetoes had almost forgotten his Wight was there, so still did he stand.

"Yes, of course. Bluzag, please go with Borris and help him in whatever way he needs? I'll be along shortly."

"Ya'll be leavin' teday then?"

"I see no reason to postpone." The Quest wasn't one he'd have chosen for himself and now, with the addition of the prisoner he'd be taking, it had become even more difficult to accomplish. Nonetheless, it met with his goals in the long run. Stopping the Necht Sarm and protecting his people were all he cared about and if he needed to the help of other Adventurers to do so, then by the gods he'd get them. With the decision made, he saw no reason to postpone.

"Aye, well I'll have Bes ready ta go as soon as she's equipped," Borris said over his shoulder as he left.

"I'll ready some things for you," Emblyn added.

Ffion had already disappeared but Ninetoes would visit her as well, they'd never make the journey in time without horses. The other council members left the taproom, but Ninetoes stopped Foresto, waiting for the room to clear before speaking up.

"Master Foresto, there is much I'd like to discuss with you, but I must make haste. I do have one question before I do though."

146

"Stop with the Master nonsense, you know how I feel about it. Well done for completing first successful Quest. While I'm sure there's quite the story to tell, it'll have to wait. But you can ask your question."

"Why send the prisoner?" Foresto's arguments might have swayed the council members, but Ninetoes knew that the hobgoblin army would attack just as hard whether the town had a prisoner or not. He also wasn't loving the idea of fighting monsters with a murderous warrior at his back.

"Because my friend, when the people of this town come looking for someone to string up, and they will, do you really think they'll be content with just her? There is already plenty of suspicion surrounding your part in the attack. Staying will only worsen the situation." The argument stalled Ninetoes and considered this. He'd only ever helped the town, surely they would not harm him.

But he knew deep down that it wasn't enough. He'd already felt the sting of their prejudice and, if he was honest, he was glad for a reason to escape it. *Peace.* Said a voice. *Not all feel this way.*

Ninetoes smiled at the warmth of that feeling. "You're right Foresto."

"Of course I'm right! Now, go prepare yourself for the journey and come see me before you leave."

CHAPTER 8

TIT FOR CAT

Something had been bothering Ninetoes ever since he'd woken up, but he'd been immediately distracted by the town guardian from there, his morning had disappeared.

A feeling niggled at the back of his mind and now that he had a moment of peace he decided to concentrate on it.

Bluzag had been standing over him when he'd woken, but he clearly remembered telling... no, commanding the Wight to stay put, to hold his ground and *only* to counter attack. So how had it been that he'd charged in to save Ninetoes? Was he able to disobey Ninetoes? The thought made the hobgoblin Wizard shudder, he had assumed that Bluzag would follow his every command to the letter. Perhaps Ninetoes had placed too many points into the half-ogre's Intelligence score.

Reaching what was left of Borris' smithy, Ninetoes found Bluzag holding a large section of collapsed masonry, the Smith was crawling beneath it, collecting items into a wooden box. Ninetoes had known that the Wight's Strength score was high, but the ease with which he was keeping the stonework aloft showed just how prodigious it really was.

"Hail Borris, I trust Bluzag is being useful?"

"Ha! Ah dinnae kno' anyone else tha' cannae lift a wall, aye he's right handy te have around alrigh'. It's just a shame both ye Adventurers will be leaving tagether." This was the second time that Bluzag had been mistaken for an Adventurer and, due to the truth of his origins, Ninetoes chose not to correct the old Smith. The Wight was proof of his new statue as a Necromancer and, despite the obvious power that it held, he wasn't sure he wanted people to know about it, especially considering the prejudices they had already shown him because of his race. He really needed to talk to Foresto, he at least might understand.

"I'm only glad to have Bes along, I fear the Council of Pamor will not hear the words of a hobgoblin, Adventurer or no."

"Aye, ye may have the righ' o' it there. The humans cannae be righ' backward in their thinking o' the other races."

Ha! That's quite the understatement. Although once again, Ninetoes chose not to share his thoughts.

"Alas Master Smith, there doesn't seem much here to salvage." Ninetoes gestured around them and it was true, most of the building was a collapsed mess. Only one wall, the one attached to the forge, was still standing. But worse, the fire had turned most of Borris' goods into slag.

"Aye, 'tis true. Luckily Bes had been making a shirt of chainmail for herself, to offer as proof o' her Tools to the Guild, so she'll be well protected, an' ah'v salvaged a mace for her to carry. Ah also found this-" he held up a soot-blackened pot helm for the hobgoblin to see, "ah can clean this up afore ya go, should fit her olrigh'."

Ninetoes was glad, he'd been concerned for Bes's safety, especially as it was now his responsibility.

"But ah'm afraid I got naught for ya man here! Well, nothin' big enough!" he said, arching his neck back as he looked up at the half-ogre.

"No worry, I... we'll replace some of his gear with the smiths in Pamor." Ninetoes responded.

"Aye. Well, then ye'll wannae visit ma cousin, Adrik. He runs a shop in the north ward, Bes knows the way," Borris offered.

"My thanks. I'll return here for Bluzag and Bes once I've finished sorting our gear and mounts," Ninetoes promised. Stepping out of the ruined building, he made a beeline for the Golden Spindle, Emblyn's shop.

Hoisting his pack, Ninetoes noted the absence of his Familiar's weight on his shoulder. Come to think of it, he hadn't noted her presence since the meeting had broken up.

Little One? Where are you? He sent out.

Nowhere Master. She replied cryptically. Ninetoes had become used to such responses from his Familiar, normally when she was hunting for a prize to fill her belly.

Two score footsteps later and the apprentice Wizard had reached the general traders, currently surrounded by a line of people, queuing to receive a bowl of stew and a hunk of bread. Emblyn stood off to one side, directing her staff, and as she noticed Ninetoes she nodded and made her way over to him.

"Are you hungry? You'd do well to leave for such a journey on a full stomach," she offered, gesturing to the large pot of steaming stew.

"Thank you, but I ate already," Ninetoes replied, keen to make a start.

"Very well. I have already prepared everything you'll need," she said as she led him within the shop. Once inside, Ninetoes could see that far from being a shop, the Golden Spindle was more like a barn or warehouse, with rows of shelves lining its length, each one stretching high above the ground. Leading him to a long counter near the door, she gestured at the goods laid across it.

"Four Bedrolls, four weeks' worth of rations, two lamps and oil, four mess kits, a hatchet for firewood, four water skins, a tinder box, fifty feet of hempen rope with a grappling hook, two tents and four backpacks to carry it all," she listed the items as she pointed to each one in turn.

It was a goodly amount of gear and too much to reasonably carry for the party, unless Ninetoes used his Bag of Holding. This, he was loath to do, or even to reveal the presence of such a prize.

"This is too much Mistress, far too much and most of it is completely unnecessary," Ninetoes replied.

"What? This is the standard equipment that Adventurers buy when they visit my shop, normally they want much more. Including-" she said, hefting a long ash pole, at least ten foot long, and a bag of flour onto the counter "...these, although I'll admit, I have no idea what use they could ever have for such things."

150

Ninetoes chuckled. "I'll agree I can't fathom it either. But for those of us carrying the weight of such items, we'll need only these." As he spoke he moved three of the backpacks, two bedrolls and two water skins to one side. He also collected a folded piece of tarp from a nearby shelf. Then, on a second pass added the rope and hook to the pile as well.

"We'll need the rations as well of course. I'll return with the horses shortly and collect it all then. And thank you Mistress, I know these goods don't come cheap."

"Cheaper than seeing my shop ransacked by angry goblins... no offence," she chuckled morbidly.

"None taken. Could you point me in the direction of Mistress Ffion's ranch?"

"Of course, hers is the large, walled building out of town, on the sou—"

YYYYYEEEEEEEEEOOOOOOOWWWWW!

A feline screech sliced through everyone's ears, making most of them wince. But Ninetoes had heard something else, only this was the mind-speak he shared with his Familiar.

Ya ha ha ha! Run pussy, run!

Dashing outside, Ninetoes could see a ruckus beginning over by the Inn. "I'll return soon Mistress," he called over his shoulder as he began walking quickly towards the disturbance.

His long legs brought him swiftly to the crowd gathering nearby and, as he jostled and excused his way to the front, he looked for the cause of all the trouble.

An ugly ginger cat stood atop an upright barrel, its back arched and heckles up as it spat and hissed at two large and rabid-looking dogs that were barking and growling beneath it. The poor feline was trapped by the deranged looking animals and was out of its wits with fear.

But it wasn't this scene that held Ninetoes attention, but the gleeful laughter filling his mind.

Ha he he he! Now who's afraid? Oh, ha ha ha!

His Familiar's laughter suddenly became demented and as Ninetoes checked again on the cat, could see a small puddle of urine forming on the barrel's top.

It was then that Ninetoes finally recognised the poor creature as the cat that had attacked Libby on their first visit to the Inn.

His Familiar had been petrified of the beastly feline and had never again left his side when they were outside the Inn. But now his Familiar returned as a warrior-mage!

I think that's enough Little One, although I'll note I'm impressed that you can now manage two illusions at once. Ninetoes had to wait a long moment for the squirrel's mirth to subside, but she'd dropped her illusion as soon as he'd suggested it.

Thank you Master, although if you had looked closely, you'd have seen that they were the same dog, only mirrored to appear as two. She explained.

Still quite the feat Little One, your powers grow strong. Now, hop down and come with me, we have much to do before we leave and more important business than your entertainment.

He didn't know exactly where she was, as she was concealing herself with Cloaking Shadows, but he'd started to get a sense of a lofty location as he'd neared the disturbance.

Moreover, he'd done the maths and realised that Libby should have been a little short of the one hundred and twenty-five mana that it would have cost to cast both spells together.

How did you manage to cast both spells? He didn't need to offer more detail to his question, his thoughts conveying the specifics.

Um… I just did Master. I knew what I wanted to do and I did it. Her reply was nonplussed.

Curious, Ninetoes retrieved her Character Sheet from his pack as she glided down onto his shoulder.

FAMILIAR NAME: LIBBY	RACE: SQUIRREL (+1 AGI) PER LEVEL

LEVEL: 13TH	BONDED WIZARD: NINETOES
HIT POINTS: 13/13	MANA POINTS: 19/130
STAMINA POINTS: 156/156	

BASE STATS: STRENGTH - 1 AGILITY - 43 ENDURANCE - 3 INTELLIGENCE - 26 WISDOM -13 CHARISMA - 14	ARMOUR: NONE

RACIAL ABILITIES

CLIMB: CAN CLIMB ANY ROUGH SUR-FACE AT NORMAL MOVEMENT SPEED.	GLIDE: THE SQUIRREL IS ABLE TO LEAP AND GLIDE SHORT DISTANCES.

LEARNED ABILITIES

CUTE: THE SQUIRREL'S NATURAL APPEAL GIVES IT AN ADVANTAGE WHEN CASTING ENCHANTMENT SPELLS THAT ATTEMPT TO 'CHARM' A CREATURE.	SNEAK AND HIDE: THE SQUIRREL'S SIZE AND DEX-TERITY MAKE IT EASIER WHEN TRYING TO CONCEAL ITSELF.
SPELL CHANNELLING: THE FA-MILIAR CAN CHANNEL MAGICAL ENERGY TO AND FROM ITSELF INTO ITS BONDED WIZARD, RANGE LIMITED TO 10 FEET.	STEAL: THE SQUIRREL'S SIZE AND DEXTERITY MAKE IT A NATURAL THIEF.

SURVIVAL INSTINCT: THE SQUIRREL'S NATURAL INSTINCT PROVIDES IT WITH THE WISDOM TO RUN, 25% RESISTANCE AGAINST 'FEAR' ATTACKS.	**ZIPPY:** THE SQUIRREL'S SIZE AND DEXTERITY MAKE IT DIFFICULT TO ATTACK BY LARGER CREATURES. **QUICK WITTED:** ONCE PER DAY, THE SQUIRREL CAN CREATE AN ILLUSORY COPY OF ITSELF TO DISTRACT AN ENEMY.
SPELL CASTING AFFINITIES	
ENCHANTMENT - 75% SPELLS KNOWN - CHARISMA	**ILLUSION*** - 75% SPELLS KNOWN - MINOR ILLUSION*, CLOAKING SHADOW

Unspent upgrade points - 0

Sure enough, Libby seemed to have increased her level by two since his last check, presumably in response to their recent battles. But more than that, she seemed to have already spent her Upgrade Points, both of them on Intelligence.

While this explained her increased Mana Pool, there was still something off, as she still had nineteen mana left over. With a Wisdom score of thirteen, there was no way that she'd regenerated fourteen mana in the moments since the encounter with her feline adversary.

Then Ninetoes noticed the small star next to both Libby's Illusion Affinity and her Minor Illusion spell.

At first this confused him, but then the knowledge, as it had been doing lately, appeared in his mind, as if from... elsewhere. The star meant that something had changed about his bond with Libby and that the answer could be found on his own Character Sheet.

As his feet walked him through the gates and out towards Ffion's Ranch, Ninetoes considered another issue he'd been noting recently. His Character Sheet was becoming so full of Skills and Spells and other information that it was so long as to be a nuisance, certainly not something he could quickly get out in the middle of a battle.

As he held the parchment and internally berated the document, it suddenly shrunk to perhaps half its length and as he checked it over, he could see that much of the information had disappeared. Now, rather than having descriptions of all of his Skills, there were instead simply listed with their level.

More worryingly, however, all of his Spells had been wiped from the parchment completely.

Character name: Ninetoes	**Race:** Hobgoblin (+1 End, +1 Int)
Level: 12th	**Experience points:** 84,565/88,000
Class: Wizard	**Specialism:** Necromancer
Hit points: 240/240	**Mana points:** 380/380
Stamina points: 200/200	
Base stats: Strength - 13 (9) Agility - 20 Endurance - 27 Intelligence - 38 (33) Wisdom - 24 Charisma - 12 (7)	**Varied stats:** Fitness - 20 Will - 25

ARMOUR CLASS: 27

SKILLS

ARCANA 13
BASIC FIRST AID 5
CHANNELLING 14
DODGING 7
LIGHT ARMOUR 12
LONGBOW 15
MEDIUM ARMOUR 13
ONE-HANDED BLADES 13
RITUAL CASTING 2
SKINNING AND BUTCHERING 3
SNEAK AND HIDE 7
TRAP BUILDING 4

SPELL SCHOOLS

ABJURATION 14
CONJURATION 7
DIVINATION 9
ENCHANTMENT 2
EVOCATION 10
ILLUSION 6 (15)
NECROMANCY 50
TRANSMUTATION 5

His concern brought him to a standstill as he turned the paper over and over in his hands, seeking an answer. It didn't matter how he did so, however, his Spells were gone.

Slumping to the floor his heart raced at the thought that he'd lost his magic, he reached into his Bag of Holding for his Spellbook.

At first, he didn't recognise the tome and nearly returned it to his bag, but something about it made him look more closely.

When Foresto had given it to him, it had been a simple leather-bound book with nothing of any interest on the cover and only the first few pages filled with spells, many of them blank.

Now, the book had swelled to twice its original size and the cover, while still wrapped in leather, had changed to a deep blue colour, so dark that at first he'd considered it to be black. The tome also had a simple ivory clasp holding it shut, but at a touch from Ninetoes, it unlatched with a comfortable *Click!*

Within, the pages had changed as well. Where previously the spells had been written in the steady and flat Common alphabet, they had been transformed into the flowing letters of the goblinoid language.

The penmanship was awful, the letters leaning precariously into one another, making them difficult to read and follow.

Ewe! Who's writing is that? Is that supposed to be 'Arcane'? Exclaimed his Familiar, perched on his shoulder, studying his Spellbook.

I'm not sure Little One, but it is difficult to read. This wasn't completely true, and Ninetoes had a sneaking suspicion that, although he'd never consciously put quill to parchment, the handwriting was all too familiar to him.

Wait, can you read it?

The sudden silence from Libby spoke volumes. *I have been able to for a while.* She said carefully. *Ever since my Intelligence reached 20.*

He considered this for a moment. As a warrior of the Dakhec Druul he'd never been able to read, he'd never really needed to. But then, when he'd become an Adventurer he'd just... sort of... known how to. He'd even found that he loved to do so. He wondered once again at the magic of his world that simply allowed people to know stuff just because.

Then why not tell me? He asked curiously, thrilled at the potential that this offered.

Um... well, I've been... trying to learn some other spells. She finished in a rush, clearly hoping he'd miss exactly what she said.

Really? You sneaky little... But how have you been getting at my Spell-book? It's been safe inside my Bag of Holding.

157

Oh, that's easy. I can use your magic bag. She grinned at him mischievously. *I've been waiting until you're asleep and then retrieving stu-... your book.* She admitted. Reaching into his Bag of Holding, Ninetoes muttered "All the cheese."

An absence of any weight on his hand told the hobgoblin everything he needed to know and, removing it palm up, he found nothing but a few stale crumbs.

Libby climbed onto Ninetoes palm and he brought her closer to his face. *We will have to discuss your eating habits Little One, but for now, tell me, have you had any success?*

A little shamefaced, the little fungal thief looked up at her Master. *A little Master, but so far only with a couple of spells.*

Really? Which ones?

Reaper's Sorrow and Grim Void Master. As she said this, her Character Sheet, still held in the hobgoblin's other hand, glowed and changed. Looking it over, Ninetoes realised that a new Spell Casting Affinity had been added, Necromancy.

NECROMANCY - 50%
SPELLS KNOWN - GRIM VOID, REAPER'S SORROW

Studying these, his mind filled in the gaps.

He recognised that while Libby could cast these spells, she would suffer a penalty towards the costs of spells cast from a Spell School where her affinity was lower. For Necromancy, with an affinity of only 50%, casting would require 50% more mana to the cost, meaning that she must have tapped into his mana to cast Reaper's Sorrow.

Still he was surprised it hadn't occurred to him to cast it on her himself, he didn't know what he'd do if he ever lost her.

But what he didn't understand was, how she'd gained the affinity in the first place. Flicking through his Spellbook, he soon found the answer.

FIND FAMILIAR - LEVEL 13
CONJURATION
CASTING TIME - ONE MINUTE
MANA COST - 80 POINTS
DURATION - CONSTANT
RANGE - BOUNDLESS
LVL 1. CONJURES A SPIRIT FAMILIAR, BONDED
TO THE CASTER THROUGH AN EMPATHIC LINK.
LVL 3. ALLOWS THE CASTER TO EXPEND THEIR
OWN ENDURANCE POINTS TO ENHANCE THEIR
FAMILIAR'S.
LVL 4. LINK WITH BONDED CREATURE CAN
NOW ALLOW SIMPLE IMAGES TO BE COMMUNI-
CATED.
LVL 5. ENHANCED BOND - SEE FAMILIAR STATS.
LVL 12. FAMILIAR GAINS A BONUS TO SPELL
CASTING AFFINITY EQUAL TO THE BONDED
CASTER'S SPECIALISM LEVEL.

This was incredible! It meant that the more powerful that Ninetoes became as a Necromancer, the more powerful Libby would become as well. At the moment this would be costly for the cheese-weighted rodent, but over time she would become extremely powerful and...

Wait, can you control my undead servants?

I have only tried with Bluzag, but yes. When I saw that hobgoblin bitch about to kill you I sent him to help.

Amazing Little One! But how did you communicate with him? I have to speak to him directly, the hobgoblin queried.

Oh, that's easy. I just spoke into his mind, like I do with you.

Of course! The answer was simple, so simple in fact that Ninetoes realised he'd been missing a trick by speaking out loud to the Wight.

Have you tried to cast Created Undead?

Not yet. When I read the spell, I realised that the cost was too expensive unless I found something weak enough.

This was true of course, even a Level 1 creature would cost Libby nearly forty mana and she would only be able to afford a Level 3 without tapping into his own. He couldn't remember the last time he'd Identified something so weak, which was strange as he'd definitely passed by such creatures on his journey towards the ruined city.

What about Grim Bolt? You'd have plenty of mana to cast that? he asked.

I just haven't got to that. It took me a few nights to find something that I could cast and, to be honest Master, I left the Necromancy spells until last, they just seemed a little... gross.

Her answer saddened Ninetoes. While he'd shared her feelings about Necromancy originally, he'd come to realise that the spells themselves were just a means to an end. Moreover, since speaking with the mysterious elven woman in the glade, he'd come to think of his status as a Necromancer as making him somehow... special.

Well, you should get used to them Libby. These spells could save your life, and are far more deadly than an illusion of a rabid dog! His mental tone had been harsh and Libby shied away from him. Instantly he felt the sting of his words as their bond rebounded his own derision back at him.

I'm sorry, I meant no harm. But my point remains, these spells make you stronger, more able to defend yourself. She didn't come round immediately, but their bond shared much more than words and she quickly looked towards him again.

You are right, Master. With your help I'll learn as many of your spells as I am able.

All of this had distracted the aspiring Wizard from his original reason for checking his Character Sheet; how had Libby cast these spells at such a reduced cost?

Focusing on the magical parchment, Ninetoes noted that, when he concentrated on a Skill or Spell School, it expanded to provide more detail. A brief study of the document revealed an answer.

ILLUSION - LEVEL 6 (15) BEGINNER

+6 (+15)% DURATION OF ILLUSION SPELLS.

ILLUSION SAVANT I - ILLUSION SPELLS COST YOU 10% LESS TO CAST.

Yet again, his mind grabbed the necessary detail straight out of the ether. The blue words signified Libby's own ability with the school of Illusion. This only displayed because Libby's level outran Ninetoes' own, and because of it, she could cast these spells to greater effect than the hobgoblin wizard could.

With this new information in mind, he scanned his Spellbook for his Minor Illusion and Cloaking Shadow spells. Sure enough, he found the same blue writing, highlighting improvements and benefits that Libby had gained to the spells.

MINOR ILLUSION - LEVEL 6 (15)

ILLUSION

CASTING TIME - 10 SECONDS

MANA COST - 25 POINTS

DURATION - CONCENTRATION

LVL 1. CREATES AN ILLUSORY OBJECT OF THE CASTERS DESIGN. CAN BE NO LARGER THAN 1 FOOT BY 1 FOOT BY 1 FOOT.

LVL 5. INCREASES SIZE OF ILLUSION TO 5 FOOT BY FIVE FOOT BY FIVE FOOT.

LVL 8. CAN NOW ADD SIMPLE MOVEMENT TO AN ILLUSION.

LVL 11. CAN NOW ADD SIMPLE SOUND TO AN ILLUSION.

LVL 15. CAN NOW MIRROR AN ILLUSION TO CREATE A SECOND ILLUSION THAT COPIES THE FIRST IN ALL ASPECTS.

Clearly, Libby had become quite the Illusionist and, with access to more dangerous spells, she was quickly gaining the potential to become deadly in battle as well.

Currently, however, she lacked a large enough mana pool to last long in combat, what she really needed was a way to gain more mana and make her truly dangerous.

He also noted with a smile that his own Skill level with Cloaking Shadow had improved to 7 and that at level 8 he'd gain a benefit, he'd have to practice that as much as possible. His experience points had also shot up to nearly eighty-five thousand and he was only a few thousand away from Level 13. These thoughts carried Ninetoes to the Raveslan Ranch.

FFION

The ranch took up at least a few dozen acres of prime grazing land for the herd of cattle, horses, ponies, and even a few rarer magical creatures. In fact, cattle were in the minority, the Raveslan Ranch instead being famous for its stock of fine mounts.

It was actually the one reason that the town itself could be found on any maps and Ffion's family were famous across the Sweetsea region.

This was all the more impressive, as Ffion herself had arrived in Raveslan only fifty years ago when her hometown had been sacked and ravaged by a plague of hobgoblin raiders. The penniless, widowed refugee and her four boys had been lucky, finding safety and succour and, what's more, the town offered her work and the opportunity to start again.

Since then, she had worked tirelessly to build her business and, more importantly, to give back to this place that she now loved with a fierce passion.

But, she'd never forgotten her hatred and anger towards the filthy goblinoids. And now, her life and her home were once again threatened by the merciless creatures and, it seemed, the town's best hope was one of that same godless race.

Worse still, he was an Adventurer. She remembered their kind too from those same dark days. How they'd arrived all too late to save her town and yet revelled in the slaughter of the entire goblinoid army, before moving on, leaving the people of her settlement to starve.

She'd approached them as they sat eating, pulling haunches of meat and all manner of food from their magical bags.

Desperate she had asked them for food, just a little she'd begged, to feed her children.

They'd said there was enough food in their bags to feed every survivor for a week! And then they'd just laughed at her. She remembered their strange words, their oddness only lending salt to their sting, "Fucking en pee seas!" She'd ducked, fearing that these were magical words, before scurrying away.

But then, years later, their kind began arriving at her ranch, wanting to buy her horses and other mounts. She'd sold to them, of course, business was business. But she'd always made them bleed coin and now, as yet another of their kind approached, she'd make the hobgoblin bastard haemorrhage gold!

***

163

Ninetoes reached the wooden palisade that surrounded the main compound of Raveslan Ranch. The walls were thick and tall and looked like they were well-built and kept in excellent condition.

Over the gateway was a simple barbican; mostly just a raised platform, but two archers peered down at him, the sun glinting off their iron pot helms and the tips of the arrows already on strings.

"Oooo goes there?" shouted one.

"It is I, Ninetoes the Wizard! I have come to collect mounts for my journey to Pamor; surely the Lady Ffion told you to expect me?" he returned.

"*Lady* Ffion? Oooo la di da!" The guard laughed quizzically.

"He means Ma, ya dolt!" admonished the other. "Aye, she told us to expect an Adventurer. Didn't say nuffink about no gobbo though. Woss ta say yoos not 'ere to attack us?" He grinned at his companion as he finished his question.

"Attack? Wha-? You watched me walk here from the town!" Ninetoes replied. "I must make haste if I am to save your home!" he answered, learning into his final words.

"Is that a threat gobbo?" accused the first guard, drawing his arrow to his chin and aiming down its length to Ninetoes' chest. As he did, the other guard copied the action.

"Please! Calm yourselves. I am only here to purchase some horses and I have gold to pay," Ninetoes replied, drawing a handful of golden coins from his Bag of Holding while simultaneously pumping a little extra mana into his Wizard Armour.

For a moment the scene seemed to freeze; the two arrows quivering on their strings, the guards' eyes glinting with avarice and Ninetoes holding his breath and wondering what he should do next.

SHINK!

Ninetoes nearly 'stepped' atop the wall at the sharp sound of wood on wood. But, as the gates creaked open and a familiar voice rattled against the walls, Ninetoes breathed a sigh of relief.

"You two! Stop messing around with that goblin and get to polishing the leather!" Ffion's voice here in the open was like iron and the two young men snapped to attention.

As the gate opened far enough, Ninetoes could see into the courtyard beyond. Surprisingly Ffion stood clear across the space, at least a hundred yards away and yet her voice had sounded like she'd been next to him.

"Adventurer! This way," she instructed, turning and striding towards a tall barn, the doors of which were wide open.

Once inside, the hobgoblin could see half a dozen halfling men and a few humans at work, tending to dozens of animals, each one stabled in its own space. The barn must be at least two hundred feet long and fifty foot tall.

As he entered, his neck craned up and he could see that there was a second, mezzanine floor along both sides of the building filled with rows of stables, only these stables seemed different.

Some were larger, others smaller. Many were empty, but a few held creatures that Ninetoes had only ever heard of in stories. As he followed Ffion up a ramp to the second level, he could see two hippogriffs stabled side by side, their avian heads turning, as their sharp eyes tracked his movement. One of them flapped its wings and kicked its hooves in an aggressive display of challenge.

Directly opposite to these, Ninetoes could see some kind of gigantic insect, caged in walls of thick iron bars, that were bolted to the floor and continued all the way to the ceiling. As his curiosity took him a step closer, the monstrous creature thrust its head forward and a jet of thick, lurid, green liquid splashed into the bars!

A moment too slow, Ninetoes raised his hands and cast Barrier.

The heavy, viscous liquid however never left the cage and instead the blue light of a magical barrier flowed around the cage in response to the attack.

Ninetoes was grateful to magic as the acid sizzled and bubbled its way down the bars and onto the hay-strewn floor.

"Get away from there, those runes are expensive!" Ffion barked over her shoulder.

Ninetoes' longer strides caught him up to the halfling women shortly thereafter; as she stopped before a large pen at the back of the barn. The stall was full of stocky-looking wolves.

Except, as Ninetoes studied the canines closer he realised that they weren't even fully grown, but massively oversized wolf pups, each one bigger than a normal wolf.

"Dire wolves. You Adventurers seem to love them as mounts; I can't rear them quickly enough. These ones won't be ready for a month or so though." Ffion explained. As she did, the large doors behind her opened and three halfling men each led in a horse.

Ninetoes didn't know a great deal about such creatures, but he could recognise that each one had a fine, glistening coat and were obviously well fed and kept.

"I set these three aside. I will gift the mare to Bess. She's a good girl and she works hard for our little town." Saying so, she gestured towards a palomino of at least sixteen hands.

Ninetoes noted that despite being sent on a Quest to save the town, he was apparently being charged for the other two mounts. He also didn't fail to notice the look of surprise on the faces of the three halfling stable hands. Clearly 'the boss' wasn't normally one for such acts of generosity. Ffion obviously noticed as well, as she added a further admission.

"Besides, I'll take possession of any foals."

"And these two?" Ninetoes stepped up between the other two horses. One was a black stallion, a little shorter than the mare, but he looked swift and powerful.

The final horse was as massive as a draft horse, easily eighteen hands at the withers and coloured a dark bay. They all seemed strong and healthy, as much as Ninetoes could tell.

"I selected the bay for your talkative ally and the stallion for you. He's fast and can run all day. He will serve you well."

Ninetoes could only agree, the black was clearly the mount of an Adventurer, the type of beast that the bards sang of when they told tales of Heroes; yes, the stallion would do nicely.

However, he didn't know how to explain that Bluzag didn't need a mount; his undead nature allowed his Stamina to tire so slowly as to be almost inexhaustible. He nearly decided to save his money, but he reasoned that he needed something to carry the prisoner, and he could always sell the creature later.

"How much?"

"Straight to business, excellent. The stallion is thoroughbred and one of the finest animals I've ever reared, two hundred gold. One hundred for the bay and another twelve for saddles and tack."

Three hundred and twelve gold!

Ninetoes' face blanched, such an amount was enough to live a life of luxury. Even the cost of the saddles was incredible. Gods! He'd bought a magic sword for twenty-five!

"That seems... ah... a little steep. I am riding to save *your* town. Could we not arrange some sort of discount?"

Ninetoes had the money of course. The treasure he'd found in Kavralach made him a very wealthy hobgoblin, but he had plans to use that money to rescue his people from their isolation.

"Hmmm, you're correct, you are doing us a great service. I will only charge you for two of the saddles and tack. Call it three hundred and six."

Wha-? She was going to charge him for Bess' saddle? Ninetoes took a deep breath to calm the rising anger, he needed these horses and there was nowhere else nearby, clearly 'Lady' Ffion dealt with her competition with the same steely ruthlessness that she was now using to extort a king's ransom out of him.

"Very well, three hundred and six and you'll have the horses tacked, ready and waiting by the east gate within the hour." Ninetoes knew it was a paltry attempt to regain some ground but he had to at least put up a bit of a fight.

Ffion obviously knew it too, or so it seemed by the wolfish grin on her face. Perhaps he'd conveniently forget to include her ranch in his efforts to protect the town.

Hoping to gain a little awe and respect from the halfling harpy, Ninetoes held his hand into his Bag of Holding and clearly stated, "Thirty platinum pieces and six gold."

As the weight of the coins tugged at his arm, he removed his hand and held it out to the merchant. Ffion seemed unimpressed, and even a little disinterested. Instead of leaping forward and grabbing the treasure, as he'd hoped she would, Ffion simply nodded towards Ninetoes and one of the stable hands stepped forward and took the coins.

For the next few minutes, the halfling fastidiously inspected each and every coin.

By the way he concentrated, Ninetoes assumed he used some sort of Identify spell or a Skill perhaps. Once he'd scrutinized the final coin, he turned to Ffion and nodded. The stable hand handed Ninetoes back two platinum pieces and five gold.

"Very well. Here is the promised payment for the safe delivery of Bess to Pamor. The horses will be fed, saddled and waiting for you in one hour. I'll even have my men collect your goods from Emblyn en route. Don't be late, or they'll be brought back here and you'll be charged for stabling." With these words, she and the other ranchers dismissed Ninetoes and returned to their various chores.

Ninetoes suddenly felt invisible.

With a huff, he stamped off and when nobody opened the main gate, Ninetoes simply 'stepped' to the top of the wall and then again down to the road. *Argh!* He would be glad to be done with this accursed town!

FFION

Standing out on the walls, watching the retreating form of the Adventurer, Ffion's avarice warmed her heart. *What a fool!* He'd paid three times what those animals were worth.

Strangely, he hadn't tried to cheat her or even haggle. Which was refreshing really.

Despite being wealthy beyond wonder, Adventurers normally argued over every coin spent. Some would try to steal her mounts, others to intimidate her, once an Adventurer gave her a pile of illusory gold! They'd seemed so real. After that, she'd pestered Foresto to help her.

He'd taught her a single spell, Identify. He'd warned her that without practice, she could still be fooled by magic more powerful than her own ability with the spell and so she'd practiced daily. Now, her skill was in the Renowned Ranks and she had never been duped since.

She'd even paid the old wizard to teach all her boys too. Not-a-one could match her skill but they were all proficient enough to smell a rat. But this Adventurer… he'd just paid for the beasts, no questions asked.

Oh, they were fine animals, Ffion's reputation was too important to her to allow her stock to be considered poor quality, but the dark bay was better suited to fieldwork and, had she sold it locally, a farmer would pay her no more than thirty-five gold. As for the stallion… well, she'd never seen a beast more difficult to break. Strong and fast, sure. That horse was worth every coin… to someone who knew how to bring such a mustang to bridle. That poor Adventurer wouldn't stand a chance. He'd never walk straight again.

She made a mental note to instruct Jac to sedate the horse. She didn't want to endanger the mission and the stallion would certainly get them safely to Pamor, but within a couple of days, the Adventurer would wish he'd never sat in a saddle.

One thing was for sure. There was something… 'off' about that Adventurer. She only hoped that was a good thing.

CHAPTER 9
PRISONER

Making his way through the town, Ninetoes stopped briefly at the Golden Spindle, telling Mistress Emblyn that the ranchers would collect their gear.

While she seemed busy, she promised she'd see them loaded. From there, he headed for the house of a local washerwoman who, according to Emblyn, was 'looking after' the prisoner, although she didn't elucidate as to why.

He wanted to retrieve the prisoner and then make his way out of town to visit Foresto on the outskirts. He was also of the opinion that the sooner he could collect her, the safer the prisoner would be.

Approaching the building, Ninetoes could see that there was nothing unique about its single storey and thatched roof. He'd walked past it once already, so well did it blend into the dozen or so identical dwellings.

Knocking on the door, the hobgoblin waited. Only a moment later, the door opened to reveal, unsurprisingly, a middle aged, human washerwoman. Emblyn hadn't even bothered to provide a name and time was of the essence, so Ninetoes forestalled any conversation.

"I'm here for the prisoner."

"Aye, Emblyn said ya'd be by." So saying, the portly women stepped deeper into the room, gesturing Ninetoes to follow. Stepping into the small space, he instantly understood the reason for using this house as the impromptu jail.

"I normally keeps pups in it. Aye, I know what ye be thinking "Mistress Ffion's got all them magical beasts an' wotnot", but ev'ry 'ome needs a dog I always ses."

Across the space the far side of the room was taken up by a squat, wooden cage, four foot square and maybe three foot tall. Within it, her hands and feet bound, lay the hobgoblin Sarm.

When Ninetoes had last seen her, he'd thought she was to be his undoing. She'd seemed so powerful and dangerous then, but now, she seemed completely defeated. Her armour had been removed and her clothes were torn and filthy with grime and muck from the bottom of the cage. Moreover, the whole left side of her face was distended and blackened with bruises, the eye swollen shut.

"Ah'll be glad ta be rid of her, the pups are out back an' I ain't cleaned out the cage since afore she arrived," the women complained. A pang of guilt sliced through Ninetoes. This was no way for a Sarm to be treated, Nechtsarm or otherwise. Nonetheless, she was still a dangerous foe and he must not show any weakness in front of her. Not least because such an act would only further dishonour the Warrior.

"Yes well... let's have her out then," he commanded. The woman reached into her apron and removed a simple iron key, which she used to unlock the cage. Stepping back, she kicked out at the prisoner.

"Ge' up then. You're goin' ta Pamor. They'll execute ya there, sure as the Sun's risin'!" The hobgoblin woman crawled unsteadily out of the cage and rose shakily to her fall height.

Even stooped over as she was, she still towered over the washerwomen, who sensibly backed off as quickly as her waddling gait would allow.

Seizing the initiative, Ninetoes stepped between them and, staring straight into the hobgoblin's one good eye snapped out a quick threat.

"You're to come with me. We ride for Pamor and your incarceration. I'll take no trouble, or you'll feel the sting of my blade."

"Huh. I don't seem to recall it stinging all that much," she replied, her voice hoarse. Ninetoes realised that arguing with her would serve no purpose, so he grabbed the rope between her wrists and led her through the door.

As it was, she didn't resist and in fact, once they were outside, she stood up straighter and took a deep, shuddering breath.

For just a moment, while she stood there with her eyes closed, her face turned towards the sun. Ninetoes saw a glimpse of the wild and beautiful warrior he'd witnessed during the battle.

But then, as the clouds covered the sun, the hobgoblin opened her eyes and caught him staring and an ugly look slid over her face.

The moment passed and Ninetoes tugged the rope binding her arms. The jailor handed Ninetoes a key and he turned his back to the hobgoblin woman. Out of sight, before tucking it into his breast pocket.

Next, he stopped at the remains of Borris' forge and, retrieving Bluzag and Borris' promise to tell Bess to meet him later, Ninetoes relinquished the Sarm's leash over to his Wight and headed for the east gate.

Ninetoes urgently needed to speak with Foresto and ideally at length, but it appeared that circumstances were against him, so he'd have to cut the visit short, having barely an hour before he needed to meet Bess and the horses. He had no doubt that Ffion would make good her threat.

Foresto's little house was much as it had been, which he supposed wasn't all that surprising.

While he had grown and changed so much, barely a few weeks had gone by since he'd first arrived here.

He found the front door open and could hear the old gnome clattering around in his workroom.

Leaving Bluzag with orders to keep watch over the prisoner, Ninetoes ducked inside.

He'd never been beyond the comfy library-cum-study of the wizard before and had only ever caught glimpses of the laboratory workroom that lay beyond.

As he stepped across the threshold between the two rooms, he was awestruck by what he found beyond. He'd been impressed before by the magic that allowed Foresto's tiny home to hold a library of hundreds, if not thousands, of books. But the workroom took this magic to a whole other level and the space could only be described as bar-like.

The room was a massive, chaotic mess, that must have been at least a hundred foot square and was the epitome of the gnomish mage's habits and behaviours. The entire space was filled with work tables, forges, alchemist stations and cages filled with raw metals, stones and wood.

All of this fit inside what, from the outside, appeared to be nothing more than a coal shed.

At first, Ninetoes couldn't find the mage, but he followed the poetry of expletives that the gnome seemed to so pride himself upon and discovered the little wizard's rear end sticking out of an unlit forge.

The old coot didn't seem to have noticed Ninetoes yet and so, sensing an opportunity for some long-awaited payback, Ninetoes crept closer, until he was right next to the devil's delicate derriere.

Taking a deep breath, Ninetoes all but shouted.

"I'm here Master-" THUMP! "-as you requested." Ninetoes couldn't help but snigger as he heard the gnome's head bash the roof of the forge.

"What in the blue balls fuckity fuck?" yelled the wizard. "You made me hit my shit-sodding head!"

"Oh, I'm terribly sorry master."

As much as he tried, Ninetoes couldn't keep the mirth from his voice. Foresto wiggled his hindquarters out of the iron beast and whipped around to stare Ninetoes in the eyes.

With his face and hands covered in soot it made him seem all the more comical. As Ninetoes tried and failed to stop himself from laughing, the gnome's face, what of it that could be seen under the mess, grew redder and redder.

"You did that on purpose!" yelled the miniscule mage, but his voice rose with glee as it did in volume. "Ha! I owe you one goblin!" So saying, he barked laughter himself. "Well, enough of this, there is much we need to discuss my friend."

Casting a quick cleansing spell, Foresto made for his library as he did. Ninetoes quickly followed, remembering that he did indeed have much he wanted to ask the wizard and making a mental note to find such a useful spell for himself.

"So my friend, you completed your first Quest. Well done!" Ninetoes beamed a sharp-toothed grin at the praise.

"Indeed. Only, it was not as, er… simple, as you suggested that it would be. There was a whole army of goblins and bugbears and Bofar was in league with them. Correction: he was leading them and he was there to take control of an ancient machine that would turn them into undead, which he intended to use to conquer the whole of the Sweetsea region and-"

"Calm yourself my friend," Foresto said, his voice the level timbre of a teacher or parent, that also quavering with a touch of the arcane.

Once Ninetoes had begun speaking, all of the events of his recent weeks started to pour out in an uncontrollable deluge of words, but Foresto's voice and, he assumed, some subtle magic, was enough to calm his beating heart.

"Good. Now, again. This time more slowly and methodically." Foresto's eyes didn't leave Ninetoes' as he spoke and the hobgoblin couldn't have looked away even if he'd tried.

"Yes Master. Well, I left Raveslan in search of Bofar…"

***

A short time later, he'd finished reporting his adventure to the old gnome, leaving no detail out and, as he came upon them in the tale, removing the stack of books he'd gathered from his Bag of Holding and presenting them to his mentor.

It was however, the magical eraser, a simple gift that he'd picked up for Foresto, that the mage was most excited about.

For his part, Foresto sat and listened quietly, asking questions only when Ninetoes paused. For much of the story, Foresto seemed nonplussed, even when Ninetoes described Bofar's use of the machine. When Ninetoes queried his lack of surprise, Foresto explained in simple terms that, when Adventurers were involved, a Quest was never as straight forward or simple as it seemed. He did however ask to see Ninetoes' Character Sheet.

Ninetoes had been worried about this. Although his conversion into becoming a Necromancer had not been his own choice, now that he'd had the chance to experience some of the benefits, he was reluctant to undo it.

But, he was well aware that many people distrusted or even hated necromancy. Foresto himself hadn't even mentioned the school of magic when he'd trained Ninetoes, except to say that it was only used by dark wizards, to which the hobgoblin assumed he meant evil.

Ninetoes was afraid that his mentor would tell him to turn away from the magic, or worse, would attack him as an evil wizard!

Now, however, with little option but to acquiesce, Ninetoes handed over his Character Sheet. The old mage barely glanced at the page, before his eyes lasered their way back to Ninetoes face.

"A Necromancer eh? Few choose this Specialism, what made *you* choose it?" His tone was direct but his voice was almost a whisper and the now familiar coppery taste of magic in the air, told him that Foresto was weaving a spell of some kind. A definite aura of danger now surrounded the small wizard and, despite how far he'd come, Ninetoes had little doubt that the gnome could destroy him utterly in a moment.

"I... er, didn't. That is, I didn't choose Master," he added the honorific in the hopes of de-escalating.

"Explain." The single word was a command and Ninetoes' words left his mouth before he'd even had the chance to consider it, as if they were pulled from him by force.

"As I told you, the magical device, the Animator, was activated by Bofar and all I could think of was to grab my ally Bluzag and try to save hi-" he started.

"But that's not all is it. You touched the contact point and cast a spell didn't you." It wasn't a question, but an assertion. The gnome went on, but he wasn't really talking to Ninetoes, but rather to himself.

"Hmmm... must have absorbed the necrotic energy from hundreds, if not thousands of life forms, hmmm but the new spells, where did they come from? Ah, he must have been in contact with Bofar, absorbing some of his knowledge. But a choice... he must have made a Choice."

"Foresto? Foresto! Master! What do you mean a Choice?" Even spoken, the gnome had placed an emphasis on the word that was easy to detect. Ninetoes raised his voice in to forestall the gnome's mutterings.

"Hmmm, what?" The gnome, startled from his musings took in the hobgoblin, seemingly for the first time.

"What happened to me? Should I be worried? And what choice? I didn't choose this." Ninetoes asked, as worry edged into his voice.

"Choice? Of course you made a Choice, it's those around you that don't, or can't." But, at the look of shock and fear on the hobgoblin's face, Foresto went on.

"My apologies, let me explain." Foresto's tone softened and he offered his apprentice a smile.

"I'll start by saying that what happened to you is... unusual, to say the least. In fact, I have never heard of it happening before and so I can only posit what I believe to have happened and I do not have all the answers." Settling back into his armchair, Foresto took on the visage and tone of the educator.

"As we have already discussed, Adventurers are unique on Adrenon, in that they seem to be able to grow in power, quickly making them far stronger than the average person. But what really sets them apart, is that they have a Choice! They are far less attached to this world and as their power grows, they are able to choose *how* their power grows. Normally, when an Adventurer reaches a certain Class and Skill level, they are able to choose a Specialism and this then grants them certain further Abilities, Skills and or Spells, unique to this Specialism. In your case the events in which you found yourself meant that you were force to Choose. What's more, it is a Choice that very few people choose. Necromancers are often shunned by people because their magic is so related to death. That is not to say that it doesn't have its uses of course, and it's obviously very powerful, but the realm of the dead is not something to be taken lightly."

Ninetoes considered this. He didn't remember being offered any Choice during the battle with Bofar. There simply wasn't time. Bluzag had been dying, or perhaps already dead and the Animator was siphoning his life force and those of everything within… well miles maybe? All he remembered was grabbing the half-ogre and the machine and drawing some of that power off.

But you did Master.

I did what; Little One? Once again, the pair were able to share their thoughts in an instant.

You Chose Master. Don't you remember? That, that thing, that consciousness, it offered you power, enough to save yourself and us and you… you took it. She ended the thought quietly, as if even her thoughts tried to avoid it.

Yes. Yes you're right. And she was. Now that she'd said it, it was so clear. He had taken the offered power, a deluge of it. In fact it had nearly overwhelmed him. It would have, if not for her; his Familiar.

Foresto began speaking once again, drawing him from his thoughts.

"A part of me would suggest that you drop this Specialism and work on improving one of the other spell schools with the aim of becoming something other than a Necromancer. But another part of me is interested to see what you make of it. One thing is true Ninetoes, you are… a rarity."

"With respect, I do not want to change Specialism, Necromancy has saved my life many times already and helped to save this town!" Ninetoes' voice had become indignant, now that he knew Foresto wasn't about to blast him into dust and his racing heart had begun to settle.

"And neither should you let anyone make your choices for you my friend, that's my point." Foresto's smile waned.

177

"Very well. And I appreciate your advice. I have many other questions—"

"Hullo?" Bess's head followed her question through the door announcing her presence.

"Ah Bess my dear, please come in." Welcomed Foresto.

"If it's all the same Master Foresto, I won't," the tall, young woman answered.

"Ha! Not still scared that I'll turn you into a newt are you?" The old coot's usual mocking tone had returned and, to Ninetoes, it seemed the moment had passed.

Foresto reached into his own Bag of Holding and retrieved a number of small items that he placed on the end table between him and Ninetoes. "I have prepared you some Healing Potions and a Spell Scroll of Winnie's Voice. I'm afraid it only works once and the message must be short. It will also only contact me, or I'd have simply contacted someone in Pamor. It won't give us much time to evacuate; certainly we won't have time to take much with us, but we'll be able to escape with our lives. Well, unless we're eaten by something in the wilderness.

"Here is also the twenty-five gold I promised you for delivering Bofar's notes to me and thus completing your first Quest." Foresto gave Ninetoes a small pouch that clinked with coins. Ninetoes chose not to insult the mage by counting it, at least not in front of him.

"I also have this for you," said the gnome, proffering Ninetoes a book. It looked similar to a book on magic he'd given him when he'd first taken the hobgoblin on as his apprentice.

"This will take you on to Level Thirty in Arcana, you can return the other one I gave you."

At the sheepish look that his apprentice was now sporting, the shorter wizard continued. "Ah, I see, you haven't finished it yet? No matter, what is your current level in the Arcana Skill?" he asked.

"Well, um... Level Thirteen? I've been so busy and, well frankly I hadn't realised that just reading the book would increase my Arcana Skill," he apologised.

"Level Thirteen? You're lucky to be alive! Using magic is much more than just throwing lightning bolts, and no, 'just reading' it won't help. You must absorb the knowledge and understand it. For now, take them both and study them as often as you can."

Finally, he indicated a fine golden necklace that held a small blue crystal. "Bess, this is for you. It was to be a gift to congratulate you on becoming a journeyman and buff your skill, but instead I have enchanted it with magical protections, please wear it and stay safe."

As Ninetoes carried the necklace to the door, he cast Identify on it.

NECKLACE OF PROTECTION - MASTERWORK, VERY RARE

PROPERTIES: +30 TO ARMOUR CLASS. CASTS PROTECTION FROM POISON (LVL 50) PROVIDING 75% RESISTANCE TO POISON DAMAGE AND THE POISONED EFFECT. THESE EFFECTS LAST UNTIL THE ITEM IS REMOVED.

The item's magic was incredible! The necklace alone would mean Bess's AC would be higher than Ninetoes. With armour and a shield, it'd be like she was wearing a suit of walking plate mail, nothing would be able to touch her. Which was obviously the point.

Moreover, while Ninetoes had yet to come across any creatures that could poison something, he figured that being all but immune to those effects was pretty good, to say the least.

The workmanship of the metalwork was also exquisite and spoke of the gnome's many and varied talents.

"Oh, no… I can't accept this, it's too much," stuttered Bess, as Ninetoes crossed the room and held it out to her.

"Oh pisswash! This necklace was always meant for you, I and everyone in town is very proud of you. Now, stop being a drama queen and put it on, so that I can ensure it works properly," responded Foresto. Ninetoes didn't think the old wizard would ever give the young woman something he'd never tested, but it seemed like an expedient way to get her to wear it, so he didn't argue.

As Ninetoes watched the girl place the necklace around her neck, a thought occurred to him.

This strong and powerful woman was now more than an apprentice blacksmith, she was the best hope of convincing the Council of Pamor to help Raveslan.

Right then and there, he made a promise; he'd let no harm come to this woman and he'd help her reach Pamor. As the clasp clicked into place, Bess dropped her hair and the moment passed. Ninetoes' intent however, remained as strong as stone.

"Remember young Bess, follow the Tradeway road eastwards until you reach Caillic's Steading and then catch a boat heading southwards along the river. The barge will carry you straight to Pamor. Do you have gold to pay for it? Ah, no worry, here take this." So saying, Foresto thrust his own coin purse into the young woman's calloused hands.

"There's no need, I have gold to pay." Ninetoes argued.

"You must start thinking like an Adventurer Ninetoes. They will argue, persuade and bully every copper piece out of a transaction. The gold is part of your payment for the Quest, which, I might add, you did not bring up in the meeting. Very foolish, very foolish indeed!"

Ninetoes grimaced, Foresto was right, he hadn't even broached the issue of payment. Although, he'd been given little opportunity to discuss anything at all, so…

No, he mustn't think like that. He had made the Choice to act and his resolve to protect Bess hardened. He'd do more than protect her, he'd help her succeed and he'd save Raveslan.

"You can keep the pouch as well, it acts in a similar fashion to your Bag of Holding, only for coins, gems and small items. It's quite limited in space, but it'll serve for the few coins you have."

Ninetoes grinned his signature, toothy grin at this; he hadn't yet mentioned the mountain of treasure he'd taken from Bofar's camp.

"Finally, Ninetoes, what item do you request as your part of the reward for defending the town? You will be, after all, one of the Adventurers being contracted to protect Raveslan."

The hobgoblin considered this, but he didn't really need to think hard. Mages were nothing without mana to cast spells and he could use every bonus he could get.

"I would like an item that increases my mana pool," he responded.

"Good choice ma boy, good choice. Now, as time is of the essence, off with you all, you rapscallions! And Ninetoes?"

"Yes Mas- er... yes?"

"Safe journey and good fortune Adventurer."

***

Ten minutes later, having met the ranchers as planned, the party was saddled and ready to go. It had only taken so long, as Ninetoes had insisted that the prisoner be fixed in the saddle by tying her ankles together and thus, there'd be little chance that she could escape the horse. With Bluzag holding the reins, Ninetoes felt confident that she was as secure as they could make her for the journey.

As for himself, Ninetoes had never ridden a horse, or indeed any animal for that matter, so he waited for Bess to mount her own while he paid close attention and then attempted to copy her movements. He was successful, but he knew that it was mostly to do with his Agility score rather than any skill.

Now in the saddle, the rest of the party seemed to be awaiting his command to move out. He realised that he should, perhaps, say something heroic and set the journey off in high spirits but his mind was blank, so he settled for something simple.

"For Raveslan!" he called and then kicked his legs into the horse's flanks, as he'd seen people do.

But, rather than spur off into a dramatic canter as he'd hoped the stallion simply stayed exactly where it was and instead lowered its head to nip at the grass. The action was slow but strong enough to pull the reins out of the inexperienced hobgoblin's hands.

"Perhaps we should just leave," suggested Bess and leaning down, she grabbed the reins herself and kicked her horse into motion. The stallion responded to the tug and began walking along beside the mare.

Ninetoes, his face a shade of pink better described as magenta, simply elected to agree.

Kicking her own horse into a troy, Bess moved off and Bluzag jogged after her.

Ninetoes considered being angry, but in truth, he was rather grateful for the smith's presence.

CHAPTER 10

BUGS

The journey to Pamor should take three days, maybe a little less if they were lucky enough to find a barge waiting for them at Caillic's Steading. The Tradeway was a fine, paved road, built on the backs of orcish slaves by the city state of Ffestyn, to open up trade for their halfling merchants.

The return journey would take longer of course, as the barges had to travel upstream, adding perhaps another four or even five days to their total journey. That left them with only two days in Pamor to conduct their business. It would definitely be tight, but certainly possible and, even if they were unsuccessful in securing aid, with the use of the Spell Scroll Foresto had given them, the people of Raveslan should have time to escape the village and head for the safety of the port city themselves.

All of this hinged on the fact that they could trust the word of the ba'ardec he'd interrogated. For Ninetoes, this meant that time of the essence. As he had no intention of letting the town fall.

The first day of their journey had gone smoothly and by casting as often as possible, Ninetoes had managed to get his Cloaking Shadow spell to level 9 and Libby's had increased to 11. However, by the time they'd broken their journey to rest the horses at midday, Ninetoes' legs were sore and aching, and the prospect of remounting was an unpleasant one. His spirits had been raised however, when he'd checked his Character Sheet to find that he'd picked up a new Skill, Riding, which had already levelled up twice.

> RIDING: LEVEL 3 - BEGINNER
> +3% BETTER CONTROL OF MOUNT AND -3% STAMINA LOSS WHEN RIDING.

The Skill's use was obvious, but Ninetoes hadn't realised that his Stamina was being used up until he noticed the Skill's description. As he scanned up the parchment however, he could see that it had reduced slightly. He supposed that if they travelled faster or significantly farther, it might create a problem, but currently it seemed manageable enough.

Annoyingly, it seemed that the prisoner's own Riding Skill was reasonably high as she didn't appear to be suffering at all. As she caught him looking her way, the hobgoblin smirked at Ninetoes and a sudden urge to strike out and wipe the look off her face overcame him.

He'd even taken the first few heated steps towards her before he felt Libby's tail brush his neck and her calming voice enter his mind, *Be at peace Master.*

The sudden feeling of anger eased and Ninetoes diverted his march towards his own mount and pretended to check his saddle, not that he really knew what he was doing.

"Easy Ninetoes, you'll hurt him like that," corrected Bess, as she came over from her own mount and readjusted the straps. Eager to appear as if everything was normal, Ninetoes observed her movements closely and took note of what she did. It was clear that the young woman was not only Skilled but had an affinity with the animals. Which, he supposed, made sense, given her chosen career.

"Time to head out," he said the words with intent and Bluzag snapped to attention, tugging at the rope holding the prisoner and then lifting her into the saddle. Ninetoes reached beneath the horse to tie her in place when she spoke up for the first time.

"You should be ashamed of yourself porsht. These villagers are weak and are prime for the picking. Yet here you are scraping and bowing to their whims. I thought even Dakhec Druul had more honour and pride than this, but perhaps this is why your people live like cowards, hiding in the forest like anim-"

CRACK!

Her head whipped back as Ninetoes' fist made contact. The blow hadn't been hard, Ninetoes had struck out more in anger rather than with any plan of attack. But as she brought her head back around, he could see that her lip was bleeding.

Far from looking pained however, the Sarm was chuckling silently, her hazel eyes filled with glee and Ninetoes' anger boiled hotter. Without thinking his hand reached for his sword, drawing it and slicing towards her throat.

This time, Libby's scream of *Stop!* Went ignored as a bloody rage filled the hobgoblin Wizard. Then, at the last second, Ninetoes turned the blade and it whistled past the prisoner, and flew back to its scabbard.

It had not been his Familiar's warning that stayed his hand however, it had been the look of hunger and longing on the prisoner's face that. Even in his rage Ninetoes had noticed it.

As his blade had sped towards her, the women had even leaned forward, desperate almost for his blade to bite. Luckily, he'd realised her ploy before it was too late.

"You will ride with us all the way to the human city and there you'll tell their mind-wizards everything you know!" He growled through a jaw so clenched, it hurt. "Only then, once you are nothing but an empty and worthless shell might I grant you death." His voice was husky with anger and hatred, but his words carried and the smile was finally wiped off of her face.

I thought you were going to kill her Master, Libby said, a hint of surprised respect in her mental voice.

I was Little One, I was. She manifests such anger in me! I will be more careful from now on.

"Bluzag, gag her," he ordered the Wight, handing it a strip of cloth taken from his Bag of Holding.

Awkwardly mounting up, Ninetoes kicked his heels. He wasn't sure exactly why it did, but this time the horse obeyed his command and walked forwards.

***

PORTSMOUTH, 2017

"As you step into the smoky confines of the tavern you are assaulted by the smell of raw fish. Across the taproom, a busty wench tends-"

"Urgh, why is it always 'busty wenches'? It's so tropey and... barbaric." Complained Solveg.

"Perhaps it is tropey on purpose," suggested Bruce. "To keep things in line with expectations. It helps move the story along if people stay within such comfortable banality."

"Nah! It's just because Arthur Forsythe was a lonely old perv and making up buxom tarts was the only way he could get his dick wet!" interjected Tony helpfully. Solveg visibly grimaced at the remark, but Daphne snooted her horsey laugh, so Tony knew he'd hit the mark. *Man, he was a funny fucker!*

"Anyway," said Felix, "An'rik approaches the young... er... woman and asks, 'Do you know of any useful rumours of work for an Adventuring band such as ours?'"

"Oh, sorry luv. Not 'eard naught like tha,'" replied Bruce, in his one and only accent.

"Fer fuck sake Bruce! This is the third pub we bin in an' there's still no hint of a Quest?" moaned Tony.

"Not true, the Adventurer's Guild had a bounty for information on the location of Torgen's Tears."

"Yeah an' that Quest was for a party of Level Twelves! When're we gonna find a Quest mate?"

"You haven't quite asked the right questions of the right people," the GM explained.

Ergh! That pompous twat always stuck to the book, word for word. Why they couldn't just skip ahead was beyond Tony. He was bored of this talking bullshit, he wanted to hit something.

"Right! Let's head back to the Guild and question the leader," suggested Solveg.

***

STONEBARROW REGION, 2301 AC

Ninetoes held out his hands and cast Barrier, the mess of acid splattering against the shimmering blue shield. Then, rolling towards the monstrous insect he grabbed one of its legs and cast Grim Void.

Expecting the battle to be all but over with that, Ninetoes was extremely surprised to find himself flying through the air as the gigantic bug kicked its leg hard into his face.

Slamming into a nearby tree, Ninetoes felt his ribs crack as pain exploded through him. Stunned for a few seconds, all the Adventurer could do was hope that the monster didn't follow up its attack.

THWACK!

More pain blossomed through Ninetoes as someone kicked him in the kidneys. Looking up, he could see the prisoner standing over him, wrestling with her gag.

"…mwa mer… ah! I said get back in there and help the smith!"

Ninetoes didn't need to be told twice as he noticed that Bess was standing between himself as the giant bug.

Swinging her mace into the monster's abdomen, Ninetoes heard an audible crack. The young woman was nearly as tall as Bluzag and her body was covered in thick muscle. Ninetoes had thought that the hit would break the monstrous bug's armour, but he could tell from the creature's stance that it was more angry than injured and it's chitinous armour remained intact.

"And tell this brute to stop tugging me around the place!" the prisoner ordered.

Ninetoes took a moment to cast Identify, hoping for some good news.

ANKHEG - LEVEL 15
PRIME STAT - STRENGTH
PRIME TRAIT - ACID SPRAY
458/502 HP
2500XP

Nope. "Bluzag, smash that thing in the face and then activate Immovable!" Ninetoes wasn't of a mind to take orders from anyone, least of all the prisoner bitch, but they needed to surround this bug and overwhelm its defences, and Bluzag had the best chance of surviving its attacks.

The party had spent the last half an hour of their journey searching for a likely location to make camp. They'd come across this open space next to the road and, shortly after they'd dismounted, the monster had attacked, burrowing straight out of the ground and nearly disembowelling Ninetoes' stallion.

The poor animal had been shocked, but its survival instincts had kicked in and it had kicked out its powerful hind legs, which sent the monster crashing onto its side. This had given Ninetoes enough time to dive in between his mount and the monster, hoping that his magic would protect them.

"Bess, take the right flank and aim for the leg joints!" Out of the corner of his eye, Ninetoes could see the prisoner hurrying to take cover behind a tree, he tried to keep one eye on her and the other on the beast.

CRUNCH!

Bluzag's maul mashed into the thing's head and the sound alone suggested the creature was hurt.

It looked almost identical to the massive insect Ninetoes had seen in Ffion's ranch, only bigger. It closely resembled an ant, although so gigantic that Ninetoes could see how thick the exoskeleton was.

Assessing their situation quickly, Ninetoes realised that, by far the most dangerous attack they'd witnessed in the early stages of the battle was the acid attack, but it hadn't used the same ability since ineffectively spraying Ninetoes. Did this mean it couldn't use the same attack a second time?

But, as a similar gurgling sound burbled through the gargantuan insectoid, Ninetoes had little doubt that the monster's acid attack was just about to devastate his Wight. They had to kill the beast before it could finish recharging its acerbic vomit!

Drawing his cutlass, he assaulted the flank opposite to Bess. He was hoping to sever a leg at the joint. Opposite him Bess was merrily hammering down blows onto the creature's other flank. She'd managed to damage one of its legs, but it didn't seem to have done any lasting damage. Worse still, Ninetoes' own most powerful spell was unable to get through its armour. Instead he must find a way through its exoskeleton.

As he circled it, he sought out a weakness or chink in the armour but the bug's back was covered in thick, overlapping, chitinous plates and he couldn't find an opening large enough for his blade.

"Argh!"

On the far side of the monster, Bess was sent sailing into the air as one of the monster's powerful legs flicked the young smith in the chest, much as it had to Ninetoes only moments prior.

He watched in fear as the girl slammed into a tree, but her necklace glowed with warm blue magic and seemed to protect Bess from the worst of the damage. It did not however save her backpack and the article was ripped open, spilling its contents all over the floor.

For a moment Ninetoes considered retreating. Perhaps scattered they could outrun the thing? It wasn't perfect, but if worse came to worse, he could always sacrifice the Wight.

It would be a loss for certain, but in time he could replace the towering meat shield. But by the time he finished the defeatist thought, however, Bess had shrugged off her pack and re-joined the fight.

As the battle continued and as acid attack continued to build, he wracked his brain as his weapon furiously assaulted the beast. Then he noticed something.

Whenever he attacked low, the creature blocked the manoeuvre with one of its legs, even accepting damage to the limb, rather than the body. That's when it clicked, it was protecting its belly!

So then, was the armour of its undercarriage weaker? He didn't have time to question it, he must act.

But between the sharp legs and its frantic movements, Ninetoes would be lucky to slide an arm beneath it, let alone bring his sword to bear.

Then, a wonderful and stupid idea occurred to him. As equally suicidal as it was incredible! At least this time he'd have an audience for his epicness.

"Bess quick, come around here!" he ordered and the tall, powerfully-built woman did as he bid.

"Attack these two legs and be ready."

"Ready for what?" she asked, her voice showing signs of fear.

"You'll know it when you see it!" he shouted, his own voice high with excitement.

As Bess took his place, Ninetoes sheathed his sword and balanced on the balls of his feet, ready for his moment.

At the front of the monster, the horrible sound of churning liquid built to a crescendo and Ninetoes knew that he'd be too late, Bluzag would be drenched in burning acid.

SHHHHRRREEEEEKKKKKKK!

A hippogriff swooped down out of nowhere and the Ankheg turned to face the new threat and released its vomit of burning death at the winged creature. The cone of acid chundered towards the winged hybrid and… passed right through it?

190

The hippogriff was an illusion! Libby had given them the time he needed to get into position!

Libby great work!

"Now!" Ninetoes shouted and Bess swung her mace two-handed, swiping towards all three legs on one side. The monster responded by leaning away and lifting them away from the blow.

Ninetoes seized his opportunity, diving beneath the insect.

"Wha'?" Was all Bess had time to say, before the monster realized what the hobgoblin had done and attempted to slam its whole weight straight down onto the prone Adventurer.

As for Ninetoes, his plan had been simple enough; get the insect on its back. So, as he threw himself underneath the monstrous bug, he'd used two spells. Holding his palms to the floor he cast Barrier and with his cloak, he activated Force Wave.

The concussive force of the second spell smashed up into the insect's carapace.

The first shock wasn't enough, but as the wave of force rebounded off of Ninetoes' own barrier, a second wave blasted both the hobgoblin and the bug upwards. Ninetoes had planned well and instead of rocketing straight up, he'd angled his Barrier at a slight curve and his enemy was sent off at a shallow arc to land on its back.

Bess seized the opportunity and ran screaming towards the disabled creature and Ninetoes rolled out of the way. She swung her mace in a mighty two-handed attack straight down onto the weaker underside, causing the monster to squeal a horrible and unnatural scream and Ninetoes knew that his gamble had paid off.

Drawing his own weapon, Ninetoes plunged it into the monster's flank, igniting his attack with arcane lightning as he cast Shocking Strike. As he stood, grasping his sword and channelling magic into his spell, a mean, rictus grin played across his face, yet again his power and intellect had found his foe wanting!

That's when the bug swiped one of its legs and sent the hobgoblin rolling unceremoniously backwards onto his arse.

Despite the force of the blow, Ninetoes hit points only dropped by a few, the impetus of the attack lessened by his roll. But, for the monster at least, it was already too late.

Between Bess' massive, hammer-like blows and Ninetoes' own critical strike, enhanced by his magical damage, the monstrous insect was soon dead.

The smith's final blow turned into a wet smack as her mace finally cracked through the shell and exploded the organs it found within.

Quickly scanning the treeline, Ninetoes searched for any additional threats and then for the location of his prisoner. He didn't have to look far, she was still where she'd been since the beginning of the fight, although rather than watching the battle, her eyes were locked onto Bess' discarded pack. Noticing the mage's gaze, she turned to stare back and held her bound hands out in front of her, waiting politely to be taken back into custody.

Frankly, this behaviour made the hobgoblin wizard so nervous, he almost wished she'd tried to run.

"Well, not how I'd have done it, but it seems to have been effective." She quirked and Ninetoes felt his face twitch in annoyance.

"Woo! I was smackin' it and then it just- Whoosh! And then you were on it! And then the sparkling and crackling! Gods I feel alive!" trumpeted Bess, her arms flapping as she jumped up and down with excitement and adrenaline.

"It was pretty epic wasn't it?" The feeling was infectious and Ninetoes quickly forgot about his prisoner as he grinned back at Bess, whispering to her. "Best you secure the gold and pack it down deep, we don't want to draw any more attention to it."

"Of course you're right," she said, scurrying off.

Louder, for everyone to hear, Ninetoes addressed her again. "Now, while you make camp, Bluzag and I will check the perimeter for any more threats." So saying he looped a rope through the prisoner's bonds and then tossed it over a branch. Grabbing the other end, he dragged the rope down and the prisoner's arms jerked above her head. Finally, he lashed the rope around the tree and tied it off.

"Bluzag, the left flank." *Libby, go with him and alert me to anything suspicious.*

As she circled around to the right-hand treeline, Ninetoes considered the battle. Bluzag had performed well but would have been a smelly mess of flesh and bones, had it not been for his own quick wits and a little luck. His spells had kept him safe, but he'd have run out of mana if he'd had to fight it alone and apparently his Grim Void spell was extremely weak against creatures with thick armour. What he needed was something with a little more explosive power. He made a note to search Pamor for more spells to buy.

Why is it Master, that you give Bluzag verbal instructions? Libby entered his internal ramblings.

How do you mean Little One?

Well, we speak like this, in our minds. Would it not be more efficient and tactical to do the same with Bluzag? She questioned.

Ah yes, well… you're right of course, it's just that, his, er, intelligence is not up to such communication.

It's how I speak to him, she responded, a slight smirk evident in her mental voice. Ninetoes was a little taken aback. It had occurred to him, *of course*, but he'd been so busy, it'd slipped his mind.

More interesting however, was that this showed massive growth in Libby's own intellect. Only weeks before she'd been nothing more than a simple beast, not even able to comprehend language even the most rudimentary languages. Now she was able to communicate with her mind. She truly was a marvel.

Can you speak with others this way? he queried.

I don't think so. That, or everyone else is extremely rude. And, I couldn't speak to him before.

Before? he questioned, although he was pretty sure he could guess what she meant.

Before he, um, died, she replied, giving the mental equivalent of a shiver as she thought it.

Hmmm, it was certainly useful that both he and Libby could speak telepathically with his undead and they'd have to add it into their training regimen.

I meant that he could give instructions to his undead servants and that Libby, acting as a scout, could change or adapt those instructions. It also meant that he could fashion for her her very own undead defender!

His thoughts carried him around the camp and by the time his patrol was complete, he'd made a short list of the types of spells he would search for once they reached Pamor. It had also occurred to him, that now that he was Competent ranked in Necromancy, there may be some more spells that he could add to his repertoire from the spellbook he retrieved from Kavralach.

When he returned, he found that Bess had already cleared a space to camp and was building a fire.

For a time, they each went about their chores; Bess cooking a simple stew of dried meat and veg and Ninetoes erecting a shelter with the tarp and rope from his Bag of Holding. As the rich smell of grub filled his nostrils, Ninetoes looked towards Bess. The girl smiled and nodded towards the hobgoblin woman.

"Do we feed her?" Then, when she saw the look of surprise on Ninetoes' face. "I'll bet she wouldn't feed us if the tables were turned."

Ninetoes was taken aback by the question. His people could be brutal to their enemies and of course they took prisoners, normally to ransom back, but the Dakhec Druul were an honourable folk. They treated their prisoners with respect.

Still, Bess wasn't wrong. He'd been told tales of the Nechtsarm: that they were ruthless, evil murderers and slavers to boot; so should they treat her with more respect than that? He made his decision. He would be better.

"We feed her." And, taking a bowl and spoon from his pack, filled it with the bubbling stew. Then, stepping over to the prisoner, he knelt before her and released her from the bonds around her wrists.

"Bluzag, keep a close eye on her. If she does anything aggressive, break her arms," he instructed, keeping his eyes trained on hers as he did. She nodded back to him as she reached for the food.

"Thank you," she muttered, dropping her own eyes away from his.

"We have a long journey together, I would like to avoid any unpleasantness, despite our peoples' histories?" he commented while retrieving a second bowl and helping himself to some stew.

"Then you *are* Dakhec Druul," she stated simply.

"Indeed," he replied in the same monotone.

"What's that? Dakkec Drool?" asked Bess, stumbling over the unfamiliar words. Ninetoes looked in her direction and addressed the question.

"My people are the Dakhec Druul." Correcting her pronunciation.

"Oh, so is that your word for 'hobgoblin'?" she enquired further. Ninetoes grimaced at the girl's ignorance. He even caught the prisoner's eye and shared a brief exasperated look, as to say "humans".

But he wasn't really surprised. His village had always remained hidden from the humans, as well as from enemies amongst their own kind. So it was that they must seem a strange and barbarous race to the fairer folk. Such a feeling was surely exacerbated by the banditry that his people conducted along the trade routes. He knew that they only did so when times were hard but for the humans it must make them appear monstrous.

Ninetoes had been surprised by the greeting he'd received when he'd first arrived in Raveslan. The humans had been... well, nice! He'd even asked Foresto about it, who'd explained that it was one more benefit of being an Adventurer. He'd explained that to most people, Adventurers were either friend or foe and nothing in between, although he hadn't been able to explain further. Bess had shown him friendship however, so he chose not to hold it against her.

"No. My people, the Dakhec Druul, are but one tribe of hobgoblins in the Sweetsea region. We were once the most powerful too, and held the other tribe's allegiance. That is until her people," he nodded at the female hobgoblin, "betrayed us and drove us from our fortress, Vawshak Nye."

"And what are your people called?" Bess asked the prisoner.

"We are the Nechtsarm. The Swords of Nech. And we didn't betray the Dakhec Druul, they betrayed us! Betrayed all our people."

Ninetoes hand had nearly struck out, the move perfunctory. But in honesty, he wasn't sure if what she said wasn't true.

He caught Bess watching, giving him a questioning look.

"Honestly, neither of us can be sure which version of events is true. It happened a lifetime ago, and neither of us was there."

"You may not be sure porsht, but I know my words are true," she growled back.

"So… what they were saying is true? Your people are only attacking Raveslan because it's between them and his village?" Bess asked, a degree of anger tinting her tone.

"It is not the only reason, but yes, your town serves as a convenient staging ground before we move on to dig out the remaining Druul from their squalid little nest. There is much honour to be gained in destroying the last of the Wrapping Doom."

"You'll find my people more than a little difficult to 'dig out'." Ninetoes spoke back, although this time he managed to keep his tone level. In response she simply grinned back at him.

"So you'd slaughter a town full of people, simply to get past them to slaughter more people?" Bess's voice had broken with anger and she'd risen to her feet.

At first her questions had seemed innocent enough, but her mood had changed with her most recent words. She held her spoon towards the prisoner as though it were her mace. "You would kill women and children? What glory is there to be found in murdering innocent men fighting only to protect their families? What honour can be found in that? The people of Raveslan have done nothing to you or yours! And… and yet you'd cut them down as if they were only vines blocking your way! You speak of these Dakhec Druul as if they are vermin, but they have never attacked my home or slaughtered my friends!" she continued, her face had turned blood red with anger.

"I… uh…" The prisoner barely stumbled a response. Ninetoes was gobsmacked. Bess' angry tirade had left the hobgoblin prisoner speechless. "My people are starving, they… the blight it's-", she continued to stutter, but her words fell on deaf ears, Bess had stormed off.

***

There was no further conversation that night and, with Bluzag keeping watch, Bess quickly fell soundly asleep beneath the tarp.

Ninetoes, his mind still buzzing from the events of the day, studied the ancient Kavralach spellbook, hoping to find something to supplement his arcane ordinance, his own spellbook sat open and waiting for new spells.

It quickly became clear that, while Ninetoes' leap through the levels of his Necromancy skill had been meteoric, his growth with the other spell schools had been fairly average and so, while the spellbook was chock full of interesting Necromancy spells, most of them required not only Skill levels in his Specialism school, but also in Skill levels in at least one other spell school.

Instead, Ninetoes investigated the lower level spells from other schools that he could cast. He had the option of two new spells that he could learn; Madigar's Madness and Pick Lock. The latter of these was pretty straight forward, it allowed one to magically unlock stuff, he would definitely add it to his own repertoire.

```
PICK LOCK
PREREQUISITES - TRANSMUTATION BEGINNER.
CASTING TIME - 15 SECONDS
MANA COST - 25 POINTS
DURATION - INSTANTANEOUS
LVL 1. UNLOCKS ANY DAMAGED QUALITY
LOCK.
```

But it was Madigar's Madness that really caught his eye, mostly because it was an Illusion spell and thus Libby could cast it.

```
MADIGAR'S MADNESS
PREREQUISITES - ILLUSION BEGINNER.
CASTING TIME - 15 SECONDS
MANA COST - 50 POINTS
DURATION - CONCENTRATION
LVL 1. THE CASTER ATTEMPTS TO CREATE AN
ILLUSION WITHIN THE MIND OF A TARGET
WITHIN 100 FEET. IF THE TARGET FAILS TO
SAVE AGAINST THIS ILLUSION, IT CAUSES THEM
TO BELIEVE THAT THEY ARE ON FIRE, DEALING
2-12 PSYCHIC DAMAGE EVERY TEN SECONDS.
```

The spell was incredible. It would allow Libby to play a more effective role in combat, actually dealing damage! The cost in time and mana was arguably a little high, but she could concentrate on it and potentially take an enemy completely out of a fight.

Libby?

Way ahead of you Master. His Familiar was sitting nearby, focussing her attention onto a crow perched in a tree across from their camp. As he watched, the poor creature began to flap its wings furiously, squawking noisily into the gathering darkness.

It's working!

I can see that Little One but perhaps that eno-
SQUARK!

The crow collapsed, falling from the branch to plummet at the ground, its body landing heavily onto the floor. Within moments however, it shook off the worst of the effects and flew away.

Whoops. I hadn't meant for that to happen, even if the bastard thing had been eying me up for supper. Libby's voice was dry with insincerity.

Ninetoes wasn't surprised by Libby's tone. Amongst beasts, the squirrel had always been prey. Since becoming his Familiar she'd grown in strength and often took umbrage at what she considered "bullies".

What he was more surprised with was the ease and speed with which his Familiar had dealt with the creature. But, as he looked down at his Spellbook, still open on his lap, he noticed a page glowing and, thumbing to it, found Madigar's Madness filling the parchment. Only now, the spell had upgraded, the now familiar blue of his Familiar's Illusion skill showing some of the new abilities.

MADIGAR'S MADNESS - LEVEL 6 (15)

ILLUSION

CASTING TIME - 15 SECONDS

MANA COST - 50 POINTS

DURATION - CONCENTRATION

LVL 1. THE CASTER ATTEMPTS TO CREATE AN ILLUSION WITHIN THE MIND OF A TARGET WITHIN 100 FEET. IF THE TARGET FAILS TO SAVE AGAINST THIS ILLUSION, IT CAUSES THEM TO BELIEVE THAT THEY ARE ON FIRE, DEALING 2-12 PSYCHIC DAMAGE EVERY TEN SECONDS.

LVL 10. PSYCHIC DAMAGE INCREASES TO 3-18.

LVL 14. PSYCHIC DAMAGE INCREASES TO 4-24.

It certainly explained how she'd killed the crow without meaning to, the Level 14 buff having tripled the psychic damage! But it didn't explain **how** it had become so powerful.

Strange. The spell is already Level 15 for you.

Perhaps, when a new spell is learned, it does so at the caster's Skill level? Libby suggested, and the young apprentice Wizard was hard pushed to argue with her.

He'd never really checked before, but if she was correct, then it would mean that gaining new spells wouldn't be such a grind, instead, they'd start off at least as powerful as his Skill level.

Excited, he tested the theory and, sure enough, as the spell appeared in his own Spellbook, Pick Lock was already more powerful.

PICK LOCK - LEVEL 5

TRANSMUTATION

CASTING TIME - 15 SECONDS

MANA COST - 25 POINTS

DURATION - INSTANTANEOUS

LVL 1. UNLOCKS ANY DAMAGED QUALITY LOCK.

LVL 5. UNLOCKS ANY POOR-QUALITY LOCK.

Ninetoes was thrilled. He'd learned two useful new spells for himself and, perhaps more importantly, he'd found another way to strengthen his little Familiar.

Ninetoes replaced his spellbooks into his Bag of Holding and lay back on his bedroll. Feeling that his time had been well spent, he closed his eyes and was soon asleep.

***

In the morning they awoke to a light rain that must have moved in during the night and, as Ninetoes hefted his pack, his breath froze in front of him, the autumn was quickly becoming a cold one.

By the time they were ready to be off, each of them was damp and chilled and as Ninetoes carefully climbed into his saddle, his thighs reminded him of their distaste for long hours in the saddle.

Worse still, the docile horse of the previous day, had become a fiery rocket between his legs and, try as he might, he could barely stay upright in his saddle. More than once, it was only his high score in Agility that allowed him to keep his seat. Within minutes, Ninetoes was damp, tired and aching all over.

As the stallion pulled ahead of their column a third time, Ninetoes pulled back hard on the reins, only to have the stallion pull back even harder, while skidding to an abrupt halt. The hobgoblin wizard slid forwards and out of the saddle to crash face first into the muddy floor of the road.

Luckily enough his Wizard Armour absorbed most of the impact, but Ninetoes could still feel bumps and bruises all over. As he attempted to stand, his heel caught his cloak and the hobgoblin pitched forward a second time into a tangled heap.

By now, the prisoner was laughing heartily behind her gag and Ninetoes' embarrassment sored to previously unexpected heights. As he righted himself, he searched for his errant horse.

Instead, his emotions still bubbling away, Ninetoes strode over to his horse and grabbed the reins. The Wizard's sudden movement shocked the horse and it bolted away. Ninetoes had been ready for the move and held on tight but despite his best efforts, the stallion was simply too strong and it pulled him off of his feet and snapped the reins out of his hands.

By now, Bess had dismounted and was stepping carefully over to the horse, clicking her tongue and attempting to bait it with an apple, but the stallion was still skittish and continued to skip away.

"I can't understand it. Mistress Ffion's horses are the pride of the Raveslan, she'd never sell a horse that was so untame."

Thinking back to the grins and shifty looks the ranchers had given him, Ninetoes wasn't so sure, but he saw little point in arguing. Deciding to deal with the issue as a wizard, Ninetoes walked over to Bluzag and mentally explained his plan.

Using his Farstep spell while taking passengers was a quick way to drain his mana, but he hadn't cast any other spells today and so, with his hand of the small of the Wight's back, Ninetoes 'stepped' in front of the horse. As soon as they appeared in front of the beast, Bluzag grabbed the reins and, despite the stallion's wild thrashing, the giant's iron-like grip held the creature in place.

The horse pulled and strained angrily for long minutes, but Bluzag's undead endurance was more than up to the challenge of holding it in place. The only problem was, every time Ninetoes approached the fierce creature, the stallion would resume its thrashing; there was simply no way that Ninetoes would be able to ride it.

"That is a rare beast, but it has the rage of a tempest Ninetoes. There's no way you'll be riding him until he's broken and we don't have time for that," Bess commented.

"I fear you're right my friend, but walking will also be too slow."

"You'll have to share with her," the girl suggested. "I'd offer you a seat up here, but there's just no room."

Ninetoes had to agree. While there wasn't an ounce of fat on Bess, she was a mountainous young woman and she filled her saddle amply.

"Aye. I think you're right. Very well." So saying, Ninetoes 'stepped' into the saddle behind the prisoner. He wanted the sudden spell to surprise her and remind her of his power. Drawing his elven dagger, he held the blade out where she could see it.

"Now, I don't like this anymore than I imagine you do, but it is what it is, so let's make the best of it, eh?" The Warrior didn't say anything but a brief nod of her head told Ninetoes she understood.

"Very well then. Bluzag, lead the stallion and follow me." With that, he kicked his heels and they started off again. The draft horse was much more amiable and trotted along without any fuss. Perhaps he'd sell the stallion on, once they reached the Steading.

The rest of the damp and miserable day passed in a grey stupor until.

Hours later, as what little light there was, descended behind the western hills, a large and well-lit building appeared on the horizon. Ninetoes' party had reached Caillic's Steading.

CHAPTER 11
CAILLIC'S STEADING

"Oh, Caillic's a sweetie!" exclaimed Bess. "Her and Borris are old friends and whenever she travels through Raveslan, which she does at least once a year on her way to Ffestyn, she stays with the old smith. In fact, I sometimes think they're more than just friends, at least… well, Borris always wears his favourite red shirt the day after she stays." Bess added with a slight shudder. "Still to this day she makes candies to give away to her guests and she always smells of toffee," Bess added with a smile. "Ha! She always brings me a big enough bag to gum up my teeth for a week. I love the old bird, I just can't wait to see her and tell her my news! She also buys a few horses from Ffion when she passes through, so I'm sure you'll be able to trade in that stallion if you like; get something a little more your speed."

The young human girl had been buoyant ever since the party had caught its first glimpse of the Steading on the horizon and since then had talked non-stop about the place and its fabled proprietor. Ninetoes had even shared a rare grin with the prisoner as Bess had launched into her third minute of continuous chatter.

So far, the female hobgoblin had been no trouble and Ninetoes had even left her gag off after she'd remained silent throughout a roving luncheon. Her own Riding skill was clearly far in excess of his own and, after he'd got over his initial annoyance at this, he'd paid closer attention to her movements and had done his best to copy them. After a little practice, he'd found the ride subtly easier.

204

He'd also taken the time to check through his Character Sheet in an effort to forestall the damp monotony of the soaking ride. Ninetoes had earned a couple of thousand experience points and was now just spitting distance from Level 13. He had also discovered that some of his Skills had increased, Channelling to 15th, Riding to level 7 and both his Light and Medium Armour Skills had increased to level 14, presumably during the battle. *Apparently being kicked by a giant bug is good for you.*

Both Skills had also picked up a new ability as well and interestingly, it appeared to be basically the same for both armour skills.

LIGHT ARMOUR: LEVEL 14 - POOR	MEDIUM ARMOUR: LEVEL 14 - BEGINNER
14% DAMAGE REDUCTION WHILE WEARING LIGHT ARMOUR.	14% DAMAGE REDUCTION WHILE WEARING MEDIUM ARMOUR.
ROLL WITH IT - YOUR MOVEMENTS IN LIGHT ARMOUR HAVE GROWN MORE FLUID. WHEN KNOCKED OVER BY POWERFUL ATTACKS, YOU NOW REDUCE THE DAMAGE BY 5% BY ROLLING.	ROLL WITH IT - YOUR MOVEMENTS IN MEDIUM ARMOUR HAVE GROWN MORE FLUID. WHEN KNOCKED OVER BY POWERFUL ATTACKS, YOU NOW REDUCE THE DAMAGE BY 5% BY ROLLING.

The ability seemed to be in response to Ninetoes rolling when being hit by the Ankheg's flailing legs. He wondered if this meant that different Skill abilities could be gained, only if certain conditions were met. He asked this question aloud to Bess, but the look of confusion on the girl's face was answer enough. Instead it was the Sarm who answered.

"You can gain one additional Ability for each ten levels of a Skill. These Abilities differ based upon each person and can only be gained once certain prerequisites are met."

"Prerequisites?" he asked, before realising whom he was addressing. Despite it being odd that she'd responded at all, he figured he'd capitalise.

The look of surprise on her own face showed that she hadn't meant to answer and it must have been the monotony getting to her as well.

"Yes, certain conditions such as reaching certain milestones with a related stat or doing enough of a certain type of action. Can you tell me the Ability you have gained?"

For a moment Ninetoes considered ending the conversation there and then. He didn't really want to give his enemy any more information about his Skills and Abilities than necessary but ultimately decided that on this occasion the risk was outweighed by the reward. Moreover, she'd been polite enough to answer his query.

"I have gained an armour Ability called 'Roll with it.'" He stated.

"Indeed, I know of it. In fact, it's one we teach to the ba'ardec. It is one of the armour Abilities that can be gained after reaching the Poor rank with Light or Medium Armour and is gained once a person performs a number of successful rolls while wearing such equipment, the rolls need to have aided the person in reducing the amount of damage that they take." Ninetoes grimaced at her mention of the Skill's rank, it meant that she had a good idea of his own level in the Skill. He'd have to be more careful when discussing such matters in the future.

"I see, thank you." As he said it, the woman's body tensed slightly in surprise, and while he couldn't see her face, he reasoned that this must be due to the gratitude he'd shown and so Ninetoes decided to push his luck a little.

"What other types of Abilities should I look out for at the Apprentice ranks?" he asked, trying to keep his voice as nonchalant as possible. He while she paused, obviously considering ending the conversation before giving her enemy any more knowledge. Enough time passed however, that Ninetoes thought he'd hear no more from her. But they seemed to be in a contest of trying to out-surprise one another.

"Well seeing as I don't expect you'll live long enough to reach those ranks I see now harm in telling you."

For a moment, she turned in the saddle and sized him up with her eyes. He attempted to sit a little straighter under the scrutiny and she grinned mischievously at him.

"For someone of your… build and the odd style of fighting you attempt, I would suggest that you train yourself to learn the 'Unhindered' Ability. I'm betting that your Endurance is pretty low and so your Stamina pool is suffering. You probably get winded easily, as so many mages do. If you gain this ability it'll help reduce the amount of Stamina you use from fighting in armour. Running in your armour will help you gain it." *Useful indeed.* Ninetoes ignored the jibe and stored the information away.

"What if you accidentally gain a different Ability? Can you still learn others?"

"You can, but it's much more difficult." Ninetoes paused, waiting for more information, but apparently the Sarm had told him all she would.

"You have my thanks. Here." Ninetoes decided that the information warranted a sign of his appreciation and so he removed his old travelling cloak from his bag and wrapped it around her shoulders and then dismounted. "Use it to hide your bonds, there seems little purpose in arousing unwarranted concern or anger at the Steading."

As he laced the reins over the horse's head and began leading it the rest of the way, the hobgoblin woman's eyes followed the young mage, as she pulled the cloak tight against the cold.

With the last half mile or so of road, Bess continued her diffuse description of their destination. In the distance they could see the main structure, a three-storey stone and wooden tavern that rose above the encircling palisade walls. This ring of safety enclosed not only the main building but also a number of smaller buildings that combined with the tavern to create a small, fortress-like island in the ocean of wildness that seemed to reach almost up to the barrier.

Bess had already explained that the Steading also included a number of nearby smallholdings outside the walls, that kept the tavern and its occupants fed and watered. She'd described Caillic as if she were the local

Lord or Lady, mentioning stories of the old dwarven women exacting her own frontier justice onto outlaws and ne'er-do-wells.

She was currently explaining that, if the stories were true, Caillic had come across the abandoned tavern over a hundred years ago and had seized upon the opportunity to start her own business by cleaning it up herself and supplying simple food and lodging to travellers. As the Tradeway had opened up between the great city states to the east and west, Caillic's little inn had become more and more popular and she'd expanded several times. Nowadays the Steading boasted its own smiths, cartwright, horse trader and even a small apothecary, all housed within the thick stone walls and guarded by a troop of Pamorian cavalry, who patrolled the roads as far as a day east and west of the Steading, keeping the roads clear of monsters and bandits.

The Steading was also the mounting point for the ferry northwards to Pamor. The lands here abouts were thick with dangerous monsters and, after a number of failed attempts to build a road to the Steading and so the Tradeway, the Pamorian council financed a fleet of ferries that made a constant journey between the Steading and the rich port town. As the party closed in, they could see the small dockside of the barge port with a small warehouse nearby.

"That warehouse was only made this summer, Caillic told me about it when she passed through a few weeks past. She's very proud of it as..." Ninetoes tuned out the rest of Bess' prattle. Instead, he focussed on the squad of mounted soldiers riding towards them.

"Evening travellers, if you're making for the Steading I suggest you make haste, the gates will be closing soon and they open for no one, even me!" As he rode closer, Ninetoes could see that the speaker was a tall and handsome human wearing an eyepatch that had been festooned with a small green gem where the eye would have been. Each member of the troop wore short, rich green capes, lined with fur.

Noticing the sudden silence, Ninetoes turned to see Bess visibly swooning over the fellow, her cheeks rosy red.

"Hail and my thanks for the advice. Where then, may I ask, are **you** headed?" the mage queried.

"Monster hunting eh! Blighters are only out in the dark, but we'll keep ya safe, 'ey boys?" He slapped his thigh as he shouted the last and his squad rejoined with a hearty, "Woof!" before increasing to a gallop and disappearing into the night. Ninetoes actually heard Bess squeak as the man flashed her a charming smile as he passed by.

"Fools! Monsters should never be taken so lightly," muttered the hobgoblin Adventurer.

"Oh… oh worry not, that was Captain Hudson Savage, the leader of the Emerald Wolves!"

"Ha!" barked the prisoner and Ninetoes found himself once again grinning back at her. "He is a fool! The porsht is correct-"

She stopped herself mid-sentence and turned to face Ninetoes, her face a mixture of concern and confusion.

"Porsht? Is that the hobgoblin word for wizard?" chimed in Bess, ignoring the insult to her fancy and, perhaps, to head off the brewing violence.

"Not exactly, but it'll serve. In fact, it's rather growing on me," replied Ninetoes simply, before yanking hard on the reins and lengthening his stride to end the journey as quickly as possible.

After that, the last couple of minutes of travel to the Steading passed in a confusing silence, annoyance and distrust roiling through Ninetoes. As they reached the gateway a guard waved a welcoming "Hullo!" and guided the party into the compound.

Ninetoes was impressed. Their view until now hadn't done the Steading justice. The main tavern building was huge, each storey taller and grander than was necessary.

The ground floor level was built in huge and weather-aged stone blocks that looked too big to have ever been moved or worked by anything less than magic or giants. Above this, the second two storeys were made of wood, but to describe them as such simply didn't take the artistry with which they had been constructed into account. Every layer was of shaped and carved wood, worked into a series of beautiful friezes. What's more, it seemed that the images were moving, if only slightly.

"Each of the layers tells the story of a great Hero," commented the party's de facto tour guide. "I've only been here once before, but Caillic told me some of the stories. That one is the tale of Wrizer the Traitor, who slew the dragon Vercingetorix. And that one's Duke Cavalier, who saved Harken from the hill giants by seducing their chieftess."

"Wait! Seduced? As in…"

"Yep, if you go around to the right-hand side of the stables you can see when he had to climb up to-"

"Nope! No thank you."

"Nope! That's fine," both Ninetoes and the prisoner responded quickly.

As Ninetoes watched it was as if the images came alive, so incredible was their craftsmanship and Ninetoes could imagine the stories, even though he'd never heard them. The movement was subtle but created the sense of life.

"Oh and look, she's added one since I was here last!" Ninetoes looked up to a row of images a little way up into the third storey. The carvings were too high up for him to see any detail, but he could see a band of warriors carving through a plague of monsters.

"Wait, do you mean to tell me that Caillic sculpted those herself?" Ninetoes exclaimed, his voice displaying his admiration.

"Well, I mean she does it with magic, but yeah! She told me that she waits until she's heard the same story told by lots of bards before she chooses to place it on her walls."

"Ahem!" As they stood commending the impressive building an officious-looking halfling coughed into his hand. Turning to look at him, he quailed under the combined glare of both hobgoblins.

"You'll be wanting stabling for three horses and two rooms." This was said in a monotone that showed little interest and most certainly was not posed as a question.

"Stabling yes, but we'll just take the one room," he informed the man. Then, turning to Bess, he whispered his reasoning. "I want to keep an eye on the prisoner and she won't be needing a bed."

The young smith simply nodded and smiled at the halfling. "Where's Caillic?"

"Hmmm, I see. Very well, one room it is and I'm very sorry, but the mistress has left stern instructions not to be bothered by well-wishers." The man's tone hadn't changed one iota since he'd arrived. All except for when he said the word 'mistress', then his face had paled slightly.

"Well-wishers? Why would people be-" Bess trailed off as her own face dropped, but then hers displayed a sudden sadness. "Oh no!"

"What's the matter Bess?" Inquired Ninetoes.

"It's her birthday and I have nothing to give her!" The young woman hadn't shown herself to be a flighty and excitable young girl, but her reaction was way out of proportion as far as the hobgoblin was concerned.

Hobgoblins didn't celebrate the anniversary of their births, instead they celebrated actual achievements, such as when a cadre of young men completed their training to become warriors or when a fierce monster was slain. So, rather than say anything particularly useful, Ninetoes simply stared back at the girl, dumbstruck.

"Oh no, no no no! We were making her something, a piece of armour, but it must have been destroyed in the fires and, what with everything going on, he must have forgotten." This, it seemed to Ninetoes, was his 'in'.

"Of course he did and thus there is nothing to worry about. Once we have explained why we're here, this Caillic will understand, I'm sure."

"Understand? Of course she'll understand, but the damage will be done. No, it's you that doesn't understand! Caillic is our dearest friend and Borris and I always makes a massive effort for her birthdays. Oh, she'll say it's alright, but she'll be disappointed."

Ninetoes could feel his annoyance, close to the surface at the moment, threatening to spill over. "No, of course I don't understand, there is nothing **to** understand. This day is just like any other and we have more important things to do than worry about gifts for some elderly dwarven madam!"

Ninetoes words, loud as they were, were swallowed by the sudden wrapping silence.

"Oh, I do so look forward to havin' hobgoblin visitors. They're always so... forthright." The voice was old, much older than the attractive, yet slightly crinkled mouth from whence it came, had any right to be. Ninetoes felt so alone under that ice-cold stare that he visibly wilted.

He was, nonetheless, surrounded by many people who were urgently going about their business, each staring somewhere else. He could barely even meet the dwarven woman's eyes but a part of him told him that he must and so, with an effort of will, he raised his eyes to meet hers. A moment of time passed, but for Ninetoes it seemed to go on for an age. Until, finally, the woman smiled at him and winked.

"And if it isn't my little Bess? I thought I could hear your voice resounding through my halls."

"Caillic!" The girl shouted, lifting the diminutive doyen bodily off of her feet into a rib-cracking hug. The hug however continued, long past the time in which Caillic was still hugging back and, from where Ninetoes stood, he could see that Bess' face was buried into the dwarf's shoulder.

"Lass, lass wot's the problem? Is... is Borris alrigh'?" The mention of her master only made Bess cry all the more. "Now, that's enough! You put me *down* and tell me wos wot!" Ninetoes noticed that Caillic's voice reverberated with magic and power and wasn't at all surprised when Bess promptly and gently deposited Caillic onto the ground.

"Better and...?"

"I'm sorry Cai, I really am, but Raveslan was attacked and yer present was in the smithy when it burned down and-"

"Bess! That. Will. Do!" Again, her voice shook with power and Bess, who had still been rambling, simply stopped. "That's better. Now, tell me what happened. Slowly."

It didn't escape Ninetoes' notice how similar Caillic's actions were to Foresto's use of magic to calm his own ramblings. Could this dwarf cast spells of such power?

Bess paused for a moment and when she spoke her voice entered a dry and uniform tone that was so out of character for the energetic young woman that Ninetoes' worried something was very wrong. But for the next ten minutes she described to Caillic about everything that had happened to Raveslan, Borris and herself over the past few days. Her report was brief, efficient and informative. By the end of it, Caillic's eyebrows had risen into her hairline and she looked at Ninetoes and the prisoner with respect.

"...and this is Ninetoes and Bluzag, the Adventurers I spoke of and, er, well, I'm afraid I don't know her name." Bess finished, gesturing to the prisoner, her voice finally soundly more normal.

"It matters not what her-" Ninetoes began.

"Vortiga." The prisoner interrupted with a simple declaration.

"Very well. Osian, escort these people to my office and arrange for food, rooms and passage on tomorra's ferry. Also, see to their horses and, once she's finished, send Gwen to my office as well." All of this was said in the same commanding tone that Ninetoes had heard Ffion and Emblyn use, the same tone of voice he strove so hard to earn for himself.

"Of course, Mistress." The officious-looking halfling snapped to attention and began barking orders to the various stable hands, labourers and servants nearby.

"Please, follow me," Caillic added to the party in a softer, more welcoming tone. Despite the length of her legs, the dwarf's walking pace somehow meant that Ninetoes, the prisoner and even Bess were forced into a light jog to keep up and so Ninetoes was unable to pay close attention to many of the tavern's features as he was led to a long flagstone hallway that fed towards an ominously large wooden door.

As he neared it, Ninetoes could see that this door was fashioned similarly to the walls outside and was covered in a scene of might and magic, etched into the dark wood. It echoed the friezes outside but seemed to focus on a story all its own, but before he could interpret it further, Caillic swung the door open and ushered the party in.

"Welcome to my Steading. Please make yourselves at home." The dwarf gestured to a circle of old, but comfortable-looking leather chairs that surrounded a huge fireplace and, while Ninetoes, Bess and the prisoner took a seat, Caillic scooted around a massive desk to grab something from a drawer.

"Is your… colleague not sit- ah, I see." Caillic half-said gesturing towards Bluzag.

Both Bess and the prisoner wore looks of bemusement, but Ninetoes was more concerned by the knowing nod that the dwarven entrepreneur had offered him as she'd gestured towards his Wight. It spoke volumes of her knowledge and, he believed, power.

"So, you journey to Pamor in search of aid," she stated. Bess looked to Ninetoes for a lead.

"Indeed. We hope to implore the Council for help. If that fails, we plan to contract a group of Adventurers."

"I'm sorry ta say that I think your request will fall on deaf ears with the Council, they're a bunch of greedy old bastards that do nothing if there's nay profit in it. You'd collapse if I told ya how much gold my Steading brings into that city, but I've never been given so much as a goblin's cockfull of aid from those miserly arseholes."

"Hmmm. Still, we must try," offered Ninetoes. He was grateful for any help, but he was concerned that the clever dwarf showed abilities that spoke of a powerful mage. Ninetoes had only met two mages, Foresto and Bofar and the latter had been a villain. Until he knew better about Caillic, he'd keep cautious.

"As ya say, as ya say. Now, when them ol' goats turn ya away, go see Bod at the Guild, he's an ol' friend and he'll set ya right, an' tell him Caillic sent ya."

"Indeed. Well, I'm grateful for your advice but I think we should find some food and head to bed, we have an early start." Ninetoes aimed his last remarks towards Bess.

"Now, now. I've not seen Bess for near a year and there's food on its way." Caillic stalled Ninetoes' escape. "He's an impatient one in'ee?" Caillic chuckled to Bess.

"We have a long journey an-"

"Yes, yes. Calm ya cockles Adventurer. Ah, here's the food," she said in response to a knock at the door and, as she opened it, a human girl wheeled in a trolley filled to bursting with delectable-looking vittles: Roasted meats, pies, bowls of vegetables and warm freshly baked rolls filled the room with mouth-watering smells and Ninetoes' stomach grumbled.

It felt like an age since he'd cooked tomac pa in the Keep of Kavralach. They had to stay the night anyway; what harm in eating free food?

He sat back down with a whumph! "Perhaps we should stay for dinner."

Ninetoes wasn't gluttonous, he'd never been one for large portions and he managed to keep his wits about him. But it was the prisoner that really worried him. They'd left her gag off to allow her to eat but Ninetoes had sat next to her and eyed her carefully, ready to pounce if she spoke. She did not, however, say a word, nor did she eat very much, taking only a roasted chicken leg that she nibbled on slowly.

By the time they'd finished, Bess had convinced Caillic to tell a story and, as rich red wine was poured for the guests, Caillic stood before the fire and began to tell the tale of Duke Cavalier.

"Duke had never been much of a hero, his rapier was dull and he lacked any skill with a blade, but he survived not by the cut of his sword, but by sharpness of his tongue." She grinned, easing into the rhythmic lilt of the story-teller. But, while the woman was an attractive woman, this was not what held the audience's attention. No, instead it was focussed on the mantelpiece behind her.

On it rested a large piece of flat, polished darkwood, almost black but for a sheen of purple. Ninetoes had noted it when he'd first entered, but assumed it was just an idle curiosity that Caillic used to adorn the space.

Now, however, the smooth face of the wood was alive with motion and texture and, as Caillic spun her yarn, so the images on the wood followed her story, giving life to her words. A brief casting of Identify provided some interesting information.

> **THE BALLADEER'S SHADE** - MASTERWORK, VERY RARE
>
> PREREQUISITES: UNKNOWN
>
> PROPERTIES: PROJECTS THE USER'S WORDS INTO IMAGES.

His skill with Identify was clearly a little too low to learn all of the item's secrets. Nonetheless, the item was a wondrous thing and clearly worth a fortune. Just to be sat on Caillic's mantle like a piece of old driftwood, spoke volumes of her power and the control she wielded over this place.

The party sat transfixed, watching how a human man of, not inconsequential beauty, missed an overweight goblin with his rapier, nearly being run through for his troubles.

"By the time I first met Duke, he was already on the run, having let his tongue get the better of him he'd angered a lord of some petty fiefdom to the north, by wooing the man's wife. The same troubles had separated him from his most recent band of adventuring companions and the poor man was a haggard wreck, arriving at my Steading a penniless and dishevelled wastrel."

Behind her, Ninetoes could see Duke, just as she described. The wood even picked out details such as the tears in his once fine clothes and the limp and empty scabbard at his hip.

"Duke, I suppose, had thought he could hide out here, cheating coin from fools and talking his way into travellers' beds to get by and if not for that first night, bless him, he might have succeeded.

"How was he to know that I would be working the bar myself that night? Had he but asked a single person more acquainted with the Steading, he might have saved himself a whole mess of trouble."

She chuckled at the thought and sipped her wine.

"Alas, for poor Duke thought he'd try to lie his way through a game of cards. Now, I'm sure you met the lascivious Captain Savage on your way in tonight? Well, Hudson is a recent procurement and before him, I employed a brutish man called Argus. A blunt but effective tool was Argus, but not someone to take lightly, as Duke did that night."

She paused but the images behind her continued, showing a giant of a man roaring in anger as he overturned a table, spilling Duke and the cards to the floor. Reaching for a massive axe, the monster towered over the cowering wretch of a man.

"But I will not have blood spilled in my pub... it's a bugger to clean up and stains the wood. 'No!' I said, 'Kill him outside!' And that is when Duke showed his true power. Raising his hand, not in defence, but in welcome, he pulled back his collar and proffered his neck to Argus. 'Go ahead!' he cried.

"Well, this stalled Argus and I both and the bastard seized his opening salvo. 'Oh! How ashamed I am to attempt to trick the mighty Argus of Ffestyn! I am scum to think I could best one such as you, even in a game of chance!' Now, I weren't swayed one jot, but there was magic afoot and Argus was always a weak-minded fool. The giant, he smiles down at Duke and chuckles, 'Calm my friend,' he says 'I was just a little hot-tempered is all, my apologies!' A little hot-tempered? I once saw that man crush another's skull for calling him a bastard, it's why I hired him actually. But I'd never seen the man so calm as he did then, and I looked at Duke differently from then on. That, I said to myself, is a man I could use. So, I offered him a job!"

The scene on the wood changed, Duke now sat on the taproom's stage, telling tall tales to a room filled with revellers, all of them enraptured.

"But, as young men are wont to do, Duke became restless and bored of my comfortable little inn and, when rumours travelled through, of trouble in the West, Duke took up and off with a band of Adventurers and went to seek his fame and fortune." Caillic paused to wet her whistle and the group sat patiently, waiting for her to continue.

"The trouble, it would transpire, was a clan of hill giants, ransacking their way out of the western mountains and killing all they found. I suppose he thought that he could let the Adventurers do all the heavy lifting and then spin whatever tale took his fancy.

"He had power, that boy, of that, I've no doubt. By the time he left here, those poor boys were wrapped around his pinky finger, believing him to be their best hope for greatness.

"Only, as the tale goes, when this band of Adventurers met the giants in battle, all went ill for them. Oh, they slew a few of the giants, no doubt, but the chieftainess, she was too much for them, much too much and before Duke could blink, his party was paste!"

On the Shade, Ninetoes watched as the Adventurers were each crushed, splattered or torn apart by the giantess, until only Duke was left standing.

"Now Duke was always a little light on details or specifics about what happened next, but if you've ever seen a hill giant, female or otherwise, you'll understand lack of elucidation. They are disgusting, vile creatures that treat everything smaller than them as breakfast, lunch or dinner, the only difference being the time of day."

In the background, the giantess could be seen and she was an aggressively unattractive creature. And, that's not to say that she was unattractive and aggressive, but rather that her hideousness was such that it alone was an assault on the senses. Massively obese, covered in splodges of muck and viscera, her hair matted with filth, but it was her mouth that was truly terrifying. Unlike so many monsters that Ninetoes had come across that had long, sharp teeth, this creature looked almost human and her flat, brick-like molars promised a slow and painful death and they grinded you into pulp.

"Now, we've already discussed Duke's way with the fairer sex and his silken tongue, but there must have been powerful magic afoot indeed for him to convince such a beast to spare him.

"Duke admitted something to me once, when he was drunk and pliable, the secret of his success with women he said; 'They want only…' he said '…to be loved. Bedding them is as simple as listening to their problems and agreeing.' Now, I can't imagine what problems the giantess had to share, but share them she did and woo her did he and, well the rest as they say, is history…"

The magical carving cut off at that point, not showing the physics-defying and stomach-churning act that was to follow. A fact for which Ninetoes was only too grateful.

"And thus, having saved the town of Harken, Duke had finally become exactly what he wished to be, a Hero, whose tale was told far and wide. Not in small part by Duke himself.

"And when he returned here, he was a rich man, his stomach spilling over his breeches from too much celebration and enamoured with his own success, but a Hero nonetheless. His tale, of course, had preceded him and thus it was that he made his way onto my wall." Caillic finished, gesturing to the window, outside of which could be seen the magical carvings whose enchanted curves reflected the moonlight.

"Oh, thank you Cai, that's always been my favourite. I'm always so jealous that you've met so many famous people," Bess cut in as soon as the tale was finished.

"Hush now girl. You're still young and have adventures yet ahead of you. Now, off to bed with you." Standing, Bess hugged Caillic closely before grabbing her gear and heading out. Ninetoes thanked Caillic for her hospitality and followed closely, guiding the prisoner ahead of him.

The room set aside for the party was large and comfortable, clearly intended for wealthier travellers. Nonetheless it had only a single large bed and a long couch.

Unrolling his bedroll, Ninetoes elected to take the sofa and gestured for the prisoner to take the floor nearby. Bess, finally taking notice, looked at the large bed and grins, before flopping down into its warm comfort.

Stationing Bluzag in front of the door, Ninetoes set about removing his armour. Having not dared to do so while on the road, Ninetoes hadn't done so in over a week and, when the prisoner turned her nose up at the smell, Ninetoes couldn't really blame her. Mentally, Ninetoes noted that a cleaning spell really is a must on his wish list for Pamor.

***

VORTIGA

Vortiga had never been one for stories, although she had been temporarily impressed by the moving pictures. She was also very grateful for the distraction they had afforded her.

She'd have liked to have eaten more, not knowing when she'd get to eat again while on the road, but she needed all the time she could get to whittle the end of the chicken bone against the edge of her manacles to a point thin enough to fit in the lock.

When the old wench started her tale, she'd been able to work more vigorously, but even now, laying in the last of night's welcome darkness, attempting to pick her manacles, she wasn't sure it was going to be enough and she might have to resort to plan B before too much time passed.

She'd never actually learned to pick locks, so little use would a Warrior have for such a skill. But, as she quietly fiddled for what felt like the tenth hour straight, she thought she was getting the idea. She could feel her makeshift pick grating against something and almost turning it, but each time she tried, the 'pick' would slide off.

Frustration got the better of her and, temper flaring, she pushed too hard and heard a snapping sound as her hand came away with only half a bone. Worse still, the other piece was wedged into the lock.

Enraged, she nearly screamed, but she calmed herself. Losing control would not help her escape, but would see her fail, and Vortiga refused to fail. Breathing deeply to steady herself, she considered plan B.

There was definitely something unnatural about the gigantic Adventurer, Bluzag. He never seemed to sleep or eat, he never uttered a sound and he followed the porsht's orders exactly. Vortiga could only wish for such undying devotion from her men, but every one of them challenged her constantly. It did, however, pose her quite a problem, especially since he'd left the giant on guard while he slept.

It mattered little, of course, the giant just one more threat to manage, one more challenge to overcome and, while her second plan was riskier, it was also more fun.

Its usefulness as a pick now spent, Vortiga whipped the bone fragment across the room, aiming for the door to the jacks.

Her aim was true and a clatter drew the giant's attention for a moment, enough for her to sit up and grab the mage's dagger from its sheath. It didn't matter that the prost had kept it in his hand while he slept, she took it with ease.

As the blade whispered free, it shone in the morning light and reflected the sight of the giant approaching from behind. Gods, but he was quick, quicker than she'd given him credit for, but Vortiga was faster.

"Stop!" she commanded. "Or I'll slit his throat." The elven blade barely rested on his neck, but even that was enough to break the skin and a bead of crimson life seeped out of the porsht. She cringed at such weakness.

The hulk stopped as the room around her awoke.

"Whas goin'on?" asked a drowsy Bess. Surprisingly, the porsht remained silent, his eyes attempting to pierce her own.

"Nothing that won't be over in a moment if this fool releases me from my bonds and lets me walk away. And no magic porsht or I'll kill you, this blade seems hungry enough for it." She spoke confidently, secure that she had the mage exactly where she wanted him.

With one hand holding the knife, she sent the other into his pockets, searching for the key to her manacles. It took her longer than she'd have liked, but she found the article.

A ring on the porsht's pinky finger took her notice and with a grin, she grabbed as well, slipping it on her own pinky. She knew that she might well need some wealth soon enough. She considered trying to use the key to release herself, but there was no way she could do so without removing the blade from the mage's throat, so instead she decided to shame the porsht a little further.

"Here, unlock it," she said, thrusting the key and her wrist in Ninetoes' face. "And then shackle yourself to the bedpost," she added, glee making her chuckle.

Click. The manacle around her knife hand dropped free, but then the porsht fussed over the other. "There's something wedged into the locking mechanism, I cannot get the key to fit."

Fuck! No matter. She could release the other bond later, it wasn't ideal but she'd make do. Adaptability, that's what the Curn had always appreciated her for, she thought on her feet.

"Fine, girl, grab the rope and tie him and the giant to the bedpost."

Bess looked at the hobgoblin mage but he only nodded. He was such a fool, a weakling; how had he ever bested ten ba'ardec? Nevertheless, the girl's hands were deft and quick and within moments the two Adventurers, *pah!,* were tied together in a lover's embrace.

Stepping behind the smith, she struck out with the pommel and with a heavy thud, Bess collapsed unconscious to the floor. She certainly wouldn't be out for long, but Vortiga saw no need to murder the girl.

As she stepped to the door, she watched the porsht's eyes seethe with anger. She drank it all in, revelling in it. But then she was away, stalking quickly and quietly along the hallways. She'd been careful to make a note of every turning, staircase and exit as they'd been led here and she knew her escape route to the inch.

As she reached the taproom, Vortiga took a moment to scan the room for anything useful. Briefly she considered the strongbox behind the bar but quickly discarded it, the juice wasn't worth the squeeze. Across the room however, slumped over a table, was a fat dwarven merchant, clearly too inebriated to make it to his room and too heavy to be carried.

Vortiga dashed across the adjoining space and relieved the portly moron of his coin purse and, on second thought, his belt. The article was far too long to buckle around her own waist, so she just tied it there instead, tucking her purloined dagger into it. Finally, she pulled the hood of her cloak over her head and made for the door. Once outside, she could see that the dawn had just risen and so she quickened her pace.

As she saw it, she needed two things to make good her escape, speed and a means of exiting the compound gates unhindered. If the guards saw a manacled hobgoblin stalking through the courtyard towards them they'd just as likely shoot her. But, if they saw a message rider, heading out early, she might just manage it and so, instead of heading for the gate, Vortiga headed further into the Steading towards the stables.

As she approached, she noted that the stable doors were still shut and so, as she entered through the smaller door, she took the time to quietly lift the bar and swing it open. Then, stepping into the gloom, she began looking for a swift mount.

Vortiga's eyes adjusted to the darkness quickly and she realised that something was definitely 'off' about the room. A sharp tang assaulted her nose and looking around, she noticed that splashed across the floor was blood, not masses, but enough to raise the hackles on her neck. Even stranger, however, this blood was thicker than it should be and looked as though it was mixed with viscera and mucus.

Yet, as curious as this was, it wasn't information that helped her escape and so she continued on until she'd found the party's mounts.

Stepping into the stall with the stallion, she grinned. The fool had bought a horse that was far too much for him but for Vortiga, a much more accomplished rider, the stallion was perfect and so she set about saddling it properly.

While she knew that time was tight before the porsht was freed and the alarm raised she would be riding this animal for days and doing so without a saddle was a fool's game.

"Whacha doin' there?" The voice was female and light, with the slight twang of the halfling people. Turning around, Vortiga directed her eyes too low, as she took in the lithe, tall women before her. The... human? woman leaned nonchalantly against the wall of the stall, directly in the way of Vortiga's escape.

She wore leathers that kept her arms free and she looked fit and strong but curved as only a woman can be and for a moment, Vortiga's heart raced a little faster. Strangest about the woman however, was that one whole arm, all the way up to her shoulder, was covered in blood, gore and mess.

"I am... er, leaving early. I have messages to carry eastwards and there's a storm brewing they say." Vortiga's confidence grew in the lie as she told it, meanwhile keeping her hands busy on the buckles of the saddle. So many times had she done this, she needn't look anymore.

"Oh aye? Where's your messages? I don' see no bag." She chuckled as she spoke.

Shit! Thinking fast, Vortiga didn't miss a beat. "Indeed, I have only the one message and an important one for the... Elders of Ffestyn." The lie was thin, but she only needed moments more and then she could force her way out.

"Hmmm... only you messengers don' usually wear manacles an', well that ain't yer horse luv." The woman straightened as she said this and Vortiga realised that her paper-thin ruse had been torn.

She turned to look into the woman's piercing green eyes and took a moment to savour her beauty. She was sorry she'd have to kill her but she must escape and return to her Curn.

As she stepped forward, she drew the elven knife, brandishing it towards the woman, but rather than stepping back in fear, the woman grinned and, as she heard a low, menacing growl come from behind her, Vortiga realised this woman had known all along that she did not belong and had only been talking to stall her. Then, with two simple words, Vortiga's hopes of escape were dashed.

"Rufus attack!"

A solid weight smashed into Vortiga's back, throwing her to the ground and as she tried to bring her hands in front of her to stand, teeth clamped around her wrist, sinking into her flesh and tugging, making her yell out in pain.

In front of her, the woman stepped forward and kicked her other hand out from under her, sending the dagger skittering from away and causing Vortiga to fall face first into the dirt.

Next the woman leaned down and put her knee in the small of the hobgoblin's back, pinning her arm in place.

Vortiga tried to roll but it was no use, between the woman and her... wolf? there was little she could do and as she heard the slap of feet enter the stables, she realised her chance to escape was gone.

***

It had taken Ninetoes too long to realise, after briefly considering using Burning Hands to turn the ropes to ash, that he could simply tell Bluzag to rip the ropes apart. The half-ogre Wight's strength was truly prodigious and more than up to the task.

He cursed his own stupidity, *of course she'd run!* He'd known she'd try but had foolishly believed he was a match for her.

He'd already woken Libby and sent his dozy Familiar chasing after the prisoner. Bess, meanwhile, had come to with a splash of water to her face and had grabbed her mace. Ninetoes was grateful to Vortiga for not killing the girl. Together, all three trooped through the halls, searching for their lost charge.

It didn't take them long to find the main door of the taproom wide open and stepping out into the dewy cold of the morning, a note from his Familiar helped Ninetoes catch sight of the open stable doors and he recognised where Vortiga's plan had taken her.

His heart raced, as his mind berated its own stupidity and the Adventurer led his little band across the courtyard, only to find, as they entered the space, that the hobgoblin Sarm was disarmed and apprehended.

"Um... thank you!" Ninetoes said, crossing the stables and retrieving his knife from the floor. For a moment the woman looked as if she might argue but as he placed the dagger safely back in its sheath, she remained silent.

"She summit to do with you?" asked the woman. At first he'd taken her for a human, but as he got closer, he could see that there was something slightly... off.

"She is my prisoner. Bluzag, go take charge of her and reattach her manacles." Ninetoes answered.

"Oh aye? An' whas she done eh? Ex-wife? I've heard you goblins got funny ideas on women, reckon I'da let her go if I realised she was just trying to escape a nasty marriage." She seemed to say this half in jest, but the large wolf at her side growled low in its throat.

Stepping up to his side, Bess spoke up. "Gwen? Gwen! I'd hoped ta see you." Then, rushing forward wrapped the slighter woman in a deep embrace.

"Bess?" came the muffled response as she struggled with the younger woman's stocky weight.

"So, who's gonna explain to me why there's a ruckus in me barn and an angry merchant in my pub?" Caillic stood behind the party, two large men flanking her, each one dressed in breastplates and carrying naked blades and serious looks. The dwarf's voice was once again the low and threatening tone of a predator and every other creature in the barn shuddered to hear it. Even the massive wolf tucked its tail between its legs and back away behind its mistress.

"Ah, mistress Caillic. I grabbed this horse thief trying to steal the Adventurer's stallion," answered Gwen. "An' I'm sorry I didn't answer ya summons last night, but one o' the heifer had a difficult labour, I had ta stay an' help out. I musta fallen asleep here in the barn, until Rufus woke me up saying there was someone sniffing about the horses."

"Good work Gwen, a ten gold reward I think for such quick thinking, ain't that right Adventurer?" Caillic growled the last, clearly not meant as a suggestion. "But, what I wanna know is, why she was stealin' a horse in the first place; I thought she was a member of your party?" She said, directing her attention solely onto Ninetoes.

"My apologies mistress. This Warrior led the attack on Raveslan and is now my prisoner. We are taking her to Pamor to be imprisoned there." He answered.

"Then why not tell me? We coulda' locked her up in the jail." Her piercing eyes searched his face, making Ninetoes squirm under such scrutiny.

"My apologies. I sought to avoid trouble and feared that she would be at risk if word got out who she was and what she had done. I'd kill her myself if she weren't so important."

"You shoulda' trusted me, Bess woulda' told ya. Well, no harm done I 'spose. Now, you just pay up that reward and we'll say no more about it." As she said this, she sent her guards to relieve the prisoner of the items she'd stolen from the merchant.

Ninetoes' anger sparked. Who was this woman to give him orders? But the emotion was short-lived. This Gwen had done him a service and deserved to be rewarded. Reaching into his new coin pouch, he retrieved ten gold pieces and handed them to the woman.

"You have my thanks." As he did so, Caillic and her guards began moving off.

"Wait, what was it that you wanted me for mistress?" Gwen asked, stalling her employer's retreat.

"Ah, yes. This Adventurer it seems has a horse that's more'an he can handle. I was gonna ask if we had summit more appropriate?" Caillic said, stepping back into the room, while simultaneously dismissing her guards.

"Aye, we got some fine mounts in at-"

"Er, actually, I do not want to sell or trade this horse." Ninetoes responded, his tone a little brash at first, but at the look Caillic gave him, he measured his tone.

"Ah, that is, I was hoping the horse could be trained here?"

"But Ninetoes, we must be away to Pamor, we don't have the time to wait for the horse to be broken, that could take days, if not weeks." Bess argued.

"Aye, Bess is right. I can do it alright, make this beast as pliable as ya like, but it'll take at least a couple of days." Gwen threw in.

Ninetoes turned to the apprentice Smith. "You are correct my dear, but we won't need our horses from here on. The barge will take us straight into Pamor and back, which will hopefully grant Gwen the time she needs. If not, then I can trade the horse in then. Correct me if I'm wrong, but you'd likely have needed to finish training the horse to be able to sell it?" Ninetoes had thought about this while he'd drifted off to sleep the previous night.

He'd realised that Ffion had cheated him and that he'd likely lose out if he were to sell or trade the horse now.

"Aye, true enough. You'll have to pay for the training and the stabling mind." Gwen cautioned.

"Of course. How much for three days?" Ninetoes grinned, happy that he'd got his own way.

"Ten gold. Nine for the training and one more for the stabling." Ninetoes nearly lost the grin from his face at the price, but he handed over the gold and shook Gwen's hand.

"And thank you again for your assistance."

"Ah, thas' no trouble, Raveslan was my home once. I'da done it for free." Ninetoes finally lost his smile as Gwen stepped away, grabbing Bess around the shoulders and chatting away.

CHAPTER 12
TORGAN'S TEARS

Caillic graciously took the time to lead the party to her small dockside. Not least, it seemed, so that she could show off the construction work that she was having done to expand the Steading further.

"...and then all of the trade that passes through here will pay me for safe keeping. It may also be the case that a small settlement builds up." The dwarven woman finished, rubbing her hands with glee.

Honestly, Ninetoes hadn't been paying much attention to their tour guide.

Rather he had been considering the events of the morning. He'd been foolish to take the prisoner too lightly; she could easily have slit his throat while he slept. He nearly promised himself that he would never make such a mistake again but he realised that he was making too many such promises.

Instead, he decided that once he reached Pamor, he would spend some gold on buying magical protections for both himself and Libby.

"Thank you for your hospitality mistress Caillic and of course for your help with, well, everything." Ninetoes addressed their host.

"Aye, well anythin' fer ma little Bess." Replied Caillic, standing at barely waist level to the young Smith and yet somehow seeming to tower over her. "The ferry'll be leavin' within the hour, so I'll leave you now, Bess'll show yeh. Remember me warnins' lad, those buggers in Pamor'll be no help. Go see Bod."

As Bess reached down to lift Caillic into one more bearhug, Ninetoes shoved Vortiga and gestured to Bluzag as they made their exit. A moment later, Bess caught up to him.

"Mmmmm, it was good to see ol' Cai and I think we should follow her advice."

"I have been paid to see you safely to Pamor and seek aid for the town. We will speak with the Council before the Guild. We have to drop off the prisoner anyway. Hopefully the wizards of Pamor will be able to learn enough from her mind to force them to act," Ninetoes explained as they reached the dock.

Before them was a small fleet of barges and smaller vessels. The dockside was already a bustle of activity, with labourers loading the boats with goods, livestock and victuals.

Casting his gaze across the scene, Ninetoes took a deep breath. He wasn't agoraphobic, but he certainly wasn't a fan of so many people in one place and for a moment, he reconsidered his visit to the metropolis that was Pamor.

"That's the ferry over there," pointed out Bess.

Caillic had made sure their rations were topped off on their short walk down to the docks, so there was nothing more to do but head for the shallow-hulled vessel.

"Perhaps you should do the talking Bess. Folk take issue with my people," he said to the smith.

The young woman straightened at the show of confidence and strode forward to speak to a man who was obviously the bargemaster. He was a tall and skinny man, although he was still dwarfed by the strapping young smith. His clothes appeared good quality, if often repaired, but it was his eyes that stood out, as they cast an analytical gaze over first Ninetoes and then his prisoner as Bess spoke with him.

"I'll take no nonsense," he declared loudly, stepping up to the rest of the party.

"This is the captain of the Kerensa," offered Bess.

"Any funny business or antics-" he said with a particular distaste, "-an' I'll toss you off my ship in a second; an' there's nasty things in the water. Understand?"

Ninetoes, a little taken aback by the abrupt tone, rallied himself quickly and smiled, trying not to show his canines. "Of course, captain," he said, hoping the honorific would help.

"An' yer prisoner? I don't care how important she is, she's fish bait if she does anything stupid," the bargemaster said, staring hard into Vortiga's eyes.

Turning, Ninetoes caught the look of genuine fear that passed over his prisoner's face and Ninetoes was grateful to the man for his words. After a moment Vortiga's eyes dropped from the man's to stare aghast at the river. A moment later, she nodded one quick nod.

"Aye, very good. Name's Lowen. Ye can stow ye stuff aft, an' I'd lose the armour, else you'll sink quick as a turd." With that, the bargemaster turned around and left, heading towards a group of stevedores and began yelling orders that were so sprinkled with obscenities, Ninetoes expected a fight to ensue. Instead, the workmen grinned and yelled straight back.

"Well, um… let's get on board." Ninetoes addressed the party. Reaching out to grab Vortiga's chains, he missed as the hobgoblin woman dashed up the gangplank and made straight for the middle of the ship.

Ninetoes nearly shouted an alarm, afraid the troublesome Sarm was making a break for it again. Instead, however, the prisoner stopped at the mast, offering up her bonds. "This would be a good place to shackle me, don't you think?"

Ninetoes was taken aback. The woman had lost the normal sneering and angry tone she used and sounded almost pleading. Nonetheless, he took a moment to analyse the suggestion, trying to work out how she might turn this to her benefit.

Try as he might, he couldn't come up with anything and, in fact, he had been considering the same thing before she'd suggested it. So, with Bluzag on hand to keep her from making any sudden moves, Ninetoes released one wrist and looped the chain around the mast, before re-shackling her wrist. "Bluzag, keep an eye on her please," he said, as he moved to the aft of the boat.

The rear portion of the vessel had a small quarterdeck with two stairs leading up from the main deck, on either side of a door, currently ajar, that led into a dark room at the rear of the boat.

Atop the quarterdeck, sat a long rudder and a few barrels tied to the gunwales. The forward portion of the ship was also filled with boxes, barrels, and piles of sacks. Finally, a large hatch in the deck that was currently wide open, allowing the labourers to load more goods into the bowels of the craft.

The door led into a gloomy cabin, with yet more piles of goods, stacked high enough to cover what little light entered through the portholes. There was also a single hammock, a large, square table with four chairs and two large chests, bolted to the deck.

"One on the left is mine, if I catch ye near it I'll have yer hands off. Ye can use the one on the right, here's the key. It's the only one I got, so don't lose it," grumped Lowen as he entered the cabin behind Ninetoes and Bess, before grabbing a vicious-looking hook and exiting back onto the deck.

Stepping up to the right-side chest, Ninetoes tried the key and found that the chest was empty, but for a small puddle of water.

Turning around to address the girl, his words caught in his throat as he realised she was almost completely naked. Turning quickly, he decided the best thing to hide his embarrassment was to do the same and so he began unbuckling his breastplate.

A few minutes later, both of them had stored their armour, packs and Bluzag's heavy backpack in the chest. They both elected to keep their weapons upon their persons and Ninetoes kept his Bag of Holding and due to its size, nobody commented on it.

As they came back out on deck, there was a brief exchange where Lowen suggested that Bluzag remove his armour also but Ninetoes simply explained that the giant-like Adventurer was superstitious about taking it off. This, rather weak response, seemed to mollify the salty bargemaster and within minutes, the barge's sails were dropped by the only other person on board, a young human deckhand by the name of Deck. And with that they were away.

***

Ninetoes had never been on a boat. In fact, he couldn't even remember ever having been in a river, since before becoming an Adventurer, but he could swim, he knew that; he just didn't remember how he'd ever learned.

But, as the barge pulled away from the shore and began gliding downstream, the young hobgoblin took his first deep and relaxing breath in what felt like weeks. Ever since his strange transformation into an Adventurer, he'd barely had a moment to stop and think; at least about anything but his next move.

Leaving Bluzag to guard the prisoner, he and Libby climbed the short stairs onto the quarterdeck, pausing at the top of the steps to wait for Lowen's assent.

The bargemaster was leaning nonchalantly against the rudder and nodded amiably at the hobgoblin and, with a slight smile, offered Ninetoes a patch of deck to sit down on. His crotchety behaviour seemed to have been left behind at the dock and the man finally seemed to be acting as his name implied. "Ahhh!" he said simply, conveying his ease and contentment with a single noise.

Tossing down his satchel, Ninetoes eased himself down into a sitting position, his back against the gunwales. His furry companion dove into his bag and returned a moment later dragging half a wheel of cheese with a crusty bread roll balanced atop it. Quite how she'd achieved such a feat, Ninetoes was unsure, but wonders never ceased when it came to his crafty companion. So, rather than concern himself further, he instead reached forward and helped her extricate the prize.

And, though he'd never tell her, decided that due to her expanding waistline, that he'd help her finish it. At first he reached for his knife, intent to cut the cheese into equal parts but today he decided, was to be a day of rest and so instead he simply broke it into three pieces, giving a chunk his Familiar and then another piece for himself. Then, tearing the bread in two, handed Lowen a piece of both. The bargemaster took the offered meal, proffering a pleasant smile in thanks.

With the Steading drifting off behind them, the three sat in companionable silence while they ate. Once the cheese was gone, Libby dove back into the Bag of Holding and, for a moment, Ninetoes nearly stopped her from eating anymore. But when she dragged out the leftovers of the tomac pa, the apprentice wizard instead summoned two forks from within the magic satchel and shared in this luxury as well. At first, Lowen eyed the pie with suspicion but a single bite was all it took to cast his aspersions aside and dive in with gusto.

Once the food was gone, Ninetoes retrieved his books on magic and studied them until, at some point, his full belly and the calm, rhythmic flow of the river carried him off to sleep.

***

He awoke later to feel refreshed and rested. Returning to his studies, he found the concepts easy to grasp and by the time that the sun sank behind the treeline, he'd finished the first book Foresto had given him. More so, he found that he understood it all. Much of it, he realised, had been things that he'd noticed himself or discovered during his travels but had never stopped to consider. Even more exciting was that a glance at his Character Sheet told him that he'd reached Level 20 in his Arcana skill and had picked up not one but two new features, evidently having missed the first because of his lack of knowledge.

Clearly the increased reading speed would have been more useful to him in completing the first book and so, yet again, Ninetoes wished that he'd had the time to do things in the correct order. But, wishes were for djinns, as the old saying went, so instead, Ninetoes decided to pay closer attention to his studies. *Ha! I'll add that to the list!*

Standing up, the hobgoblin disturbed his Familiar, who gave him an angry squeak before bounding off towards the main deck and, his nose now told him, dinner.

"Reckon the girl's cooked up somethin' for everyone," commented Lowen. "Your book seemed interestin'? Leastways you was lost to the world."

"Indeed, I have been trying to finish it for a while. Your boat is… calm and peaceful, it made the task a simple and enjoyable one."

Stepping down onto the main deck, he found that Bess had indeed cooked and, what was more, had carried the square table and chairs from the aft cabin and had set it for dinner. Sat at the table already was Deck and, bizarrely Bluzag.

Stepping up to the table himself, Ninetoes nodded towards Bess as she ladled stew into a bowl and handed it to the young deckhand.

"Deck! Come take the rudder!" called Lowen from the quarterdeck. The young man looked annoyed but not particularly surprised and so, without any argument, grabbed a small hunk of bread and headed aft. Moments later, the group was joined by the bargemaster.

"I'm grateful to you for cooking Miss," Lowen's voice grated out, although his tone and expression were anything but polite. It appeared that he'd reapplied his grumpy visage of the morning. "By the gods yer giant friend here is gonna break me chair he's so large!" he growled towards Bluzag.

"Indeed, Bluzag will not be eating with us Bess," Ninetoes commented to the young hostess.

"But why? He's gotta eat, don't he? It seems to me that he never eats, which is queer enough."

"He, um… doesn't remove his armour, it's against his religion, thus he eats in private," Ninetoes fabricated quickly. "Bluzag, would prefer to take his meal into the cabin and eat it there." Ninetoes commented, while mentally following it up with a command to toss the stew off the ship once out of sight.

Ninetoes was a little surprised by the bargemaster's second U-turn of the day but he wasn't about to call him on it. As far as he was concerned, this was his boat and he could act however he pleased.

"Do you think… would it be alright to bring Vortiga to the table? Seeing as Bluzag will not be joining us," Bess stuttered, clearly concerned that Ninetoes or Lowen would argue.

"Seems fair," Lowen said simply. "Can't go nowhere but off the boat." He chuckled meanly to himself.

Ninetoes had indeed been about to say 'no' but in the face of the bargemaster's admission, it seemed petty to argue. "Very well." And, reaching into his pocket, retrieved the key and brought the hobgoblin woman to the table, reshackling her en route. Vortiga gripped tightly onto Ninetoes' arm and, looking back, he could see the whites of her eyes and she stared in open fear at the dark waters that trickled by the boat.

"Will we continue to sail through the night Master Lowen?" Bess asked, clearly attempting to spark a conversation.

"Not unless you want us to crash lass, or worse, be attacked by summut," he grumbled back.

"So, then we'll make camp somewhere?" she tried again.

"Obviously."

"And where will that be?"

"Hrumph, will you not shut up and let me eat in peace woman?" he growled. Then, when he saw her staring straight back, refusing to be intimidated by his bluster, he conceded. "Fine! We'd normally have stopped a few miles upstream but we caught a good wind and so I'm aiming for a further campsite by some ruins. They're still aways off mind and so we'll continue until after dark."

"Ooooh, ruins?"

"Argh! Enough girl. No more questions." Lowen, clearly having reached his limit of 'polite' conversation set to his meal, tearing his bread in two and dunking both pieces into his stew at once. As he finished, Bess looked likely to ask him more and so, after ladling more into his bowl and grabbing another hunk of bread, the bargemaster stormed off to the quarterdeck, sending a surprised Deck back to the table.

"Alright Miss, is there any more stew? We don't normally eat so well," he asked.

"Aye there's plenty more, but your normal fair must be downright awful if you're wanting seconds of my cooking."

"Ha! You've... got... no idea," he said between large mouthfuls. "Normally... just hardtack and... cheese."

Cheese? Perked up the small sylvan swindler.

"Argh! Where did you come from?" Deck yelled, holding his spoon threateningly towards Libby.

"Ah, worry not my friend, this is my Familiar, Libby. She has quite the taste for cheese."

So, there's no cheese? she grumped to Ninetoes, before scurrying back inside his breastplate.

"A Familiar?" Deck asked, tucking back into his grub.

"Indeed, she is my bonded companion, she and I can speak to one another using only our minds," Ninetoes boasted.

"Oh right. Master Lowen's got one o' them," Deck commented, completely ruining Ninetoes' showing off. Curiosity however, won out over his annoyance.

"Really? And what animal is he bonded to?"

"An owl, Kowann, he's the only reason Lowen'd risk travelling at night. Much more use than a little squirrel I reckon."

"More useful" Ha! What does he know?

For a moment, Ninetoes was jealous; an owl certainly sounded more useful than a squirrel. But then the feelings of annoyance from the little thief bled through and he instantly felt ashamed for thinking it. Keen to move on, Ninetoes selected a different, safer topic. "So, Deck, your name is an odd one, from where does that hail?"

"Ha! Deck ain't me name. Me name's actually Breock but Master Lowen never seemed too bothered to learn it, so he just called me Deckhand. But then, even that seemed like too much hard work and so now he jus' calls me Deck," the young man explained.

"Oh, but that's awful," exclaimed Bess. "You should set him straight."

"To what end Miss? Plus, you're no one to talk, calling yer hob friend here Ninetoes," Deck replied.

"But, what do you mean? Ninetoes is his name, I always assumed it was a goblinoid word." Bess looked genuinely confused. Vortiga's face meanwhile had a grin that grew wider the more the two said and, when Bess finished her admission, she audibly barked with laughter.

"Ha! Ninetoes is no word in our language."

"Then..." Bess began, turning to look directly at the hobgoblin Adventurer. "...do you have only nine toes?"

"I have the toes I have." Ninetoes replied, annoyed that the conversation seemed to have turned against him again. "It matters not. I am an Adventurer and a Wizard and people will come to know my name and fear it!" he said grandly.

But it was no use, the three table guests were all grinning widely and were on the precipice of unfaltering mirth. Ninetoes knew that he must do something now or risk ridicule for the rest of the journey. Wracking his brains, he searched his surroundings for inspiration and quickly found his solution. Between some barrels towards the aft lay the body of a rat, killed by the looks of it, by poison.

Sashaying across the deck, in as mystical a manner as he could manage, Ninetoes swept up the slightly stale body by its worm-like tail.

"See here that this rat is dead?" he questioned, almost shrieking the last word, in his excitement to amaze. At the table, the rest of the group sat half smirking and half grimacing, and they all nodded apprehensively.

"Then… watch closely," he said, this time in a staged whisper.

Reaching within himself for the pool of magic, Ninetoes muttered the incantation for a spell that he'd never knowingly cast before.

The groups' eyes followed the hobgoblin's own focus and all of them stared at the lifeless rodent and at first, nothing happened. Then slowly at first, the rat's claws began to twitch. In the half-light of the deck lanterns, it was hard to see the change. The first to notice was Bess, who gave out a startled cry.

Ninetoes had already begun to grin. He'd felt the spell take hold and create a tiny connection to his own mind. As Bess yelped, he laid the rat onto the deck and commanded it to roll itself over onto its paws. Then, as his audience stared transfixed at his creation, he coaxed it into stepping towards them, grinning mischievously, as they all took a collective step back.

"Have you brought it back to life?" asked Deck, in an astounded whisper, keeping his eyes locked on the rodent.

"In a manner of speaking, yes," Ninetoes answered, still running high on a combination of his own achievement and their amazement. Having the spell in his spellbook and seeing the spell take hold were two different things; it truly was incredible.

"In a manner of speaking?" The normally quiet hobgoblin woman spoke up. Her own eyes had shifted from the rodent to Ninetoes' own and were now a mixture of fear and… something else.

"I have reanimated it," Ninetoes clarified.

"What's that mean?" asked Deck.

"It means that creature is now Undead," Vortiga elucidated.

"Undead? Like a walking skeleton or summit?" The man shrieked, his concern turning into panic in a heartbeat.

"A zombie actually," Ninetoes offered, enjoying seeing the man's mockery replaced by fear.

On the table nearby, Libby crept to the edge for a better view and Ninetoes could feel her emotions still broiling with annoyance towards the 'foolish man'. With his consent, she took total control of the zombie rat and had its head snap towards Deck. As he yelped in fear, she stalked it forward, forcing the man backwards, towards the gunwale, all the while both Familiar and Master revelled in their own joke.

SPLAT!

Everyone had been watching so closely that no one had noticed Bess snatch up her mace, until she'd smashed the weapon down onto the re-animated rodent. "Erugh!" She screamed as she sent her mace splatting down a second time, this attack completely superfluous and only acted to send the vermin's viscera all over Deck and herself.

But Bess wasn't aware of where she'd hit, her attention by this point completely focussed on Ninetoes. "Why would you do that? Zombies are evil! Everyone knows that!"

Her angry rant had carried her over to within an inch of the hobgoblin and by its conclusion, she was all but screaming in his face. Casting his gaze about, Ninetoes finally noticed the looks on everyone's faces. Deck was visibly shaken, Lowen was standing atop the stairs, training a crossbow on his chest and Vortiga was staring at him with an even stranger look in her eyes.

"I… I am sorry," he whispered out. Unable to look the young, human woman in the eyes, he muttered the next words towards the hard, wooden deck. "To me, they are neither good or evil, they are simply tools. Like any other magic."

Her breathing still shaking with anger, Bess stepped away to kick the remains of the rat into the river. Then, with a last disgusted look at Ninetoes, she stomped off to the cabin. Ninetoes could only watch as one of his few friends left him feeling rotten.

"Here." Ninetoes was shaken from his stupor by Lowen, as the skinny bargemaster thrust a scrubbing brush and bucket into his hands. "Clean that up," he commanded, pointing towards the mess of blood and gore on the deck.

Taking the proffered items, Ninetoes set to work, grateful for the distraction. Deck went to the front of the boat and made himself busy and Vortiga, taking her bowl of stew to the mast, sat down to finish what was left of her supper.

As the blood seeped into the wood, it didn't take Ninetoes long to realise that he wasn't going to be scrubbing all of the stain away but after a few minutes, the worst of it was cleaned off and Ninetoes stepped to the edge of the ship to toss the reddened and filthy water away.

As he did so, the barge rounded a bend and before them stood an incredible sight. Off the starboard bow, another river fed into the River Menylynn that they sailed upon. This river it seemed, fled down from a lonely mountain that they could only just make out, far in the distance. Then, just before it reached this confluence, it crashed over a beautiful waterfall.

But that wasn't what was so incredible. Rather, it was the gigantic statue, carved into the rock of the cliff face, that the waterfall crashed down over and beside. The statue was that of a robed man who held a sword at his right-hand side, its tip piercing the ground. Most of his left-hand side was all but hidden by the cascading water. Only it's left hand could be seen, bent at the elbow and resting with its palm flat on its stomach.

It was its eyes however, that truly struck the observer, for they seemed to be so desperately unhappy as to hold tears enough for a city's worth of people.

While some of the face had eroded with time, the artisan, whoever they were, hadn't just instilled such sorrow into those eyes, but more had diverted a small tributary of river water to trickle from them to give the impression that it was indeed crying. The effect was immediate and transfixing.

"Torgen's Tears," Lowen called down from his place beside the rudder. "The resting place of a once great king. Last of his line, on account that his kingdom was destroyed. That's why he's crying, or so they say. It's also where we'll be spending the night. Deck, make ready to tie us off," he added as he steered the ship towards the shore.

"They say the waters here abouts can wash away any sin," Deck offered Ninetoes as he grabbed a rope nearby and leapt off the barge onto the shore nearby. Ninetoes wasn't sure what, if anything the deckhand was implying, but the ruins certainly warranted a closer inspection.

A bath wouldn't kill you either Master, his ever-faithful familiar commented. And in all honesty, Ninetoes couldn't disagree with her. So, with this in mind and keen to leave behind the glares of his companions, Ninetoes snatched up his Familiar. Leaving Bluzag with instructions to watch Vortiga and follow Bess' commands, he 'stepped' from the barge onto the shore, upstream from where Deck was tying off the mooring lines.

His long legs quickly carried him closer to the waterfall and the thunderous sounds of the water crashing into the pool beneath was enough to give him a feeling of solitude. He hadn't washed properly since his strange meeting with the elven woman, so he quickly shrugged off his clothes and left them in a heap nearby before diving into the splashpool and submerging himself in the freezing waters.

The shock of just how cold it was took him by surprise and he crested the surface in a mess of flapping and spluttering. Content that he was about as clean as he would be anytime soon, he splashed his way back to the shore and dove into his pile of clothes, keen to be dressed and warm as quickly as possible, even going so far as to wonder whether he could manipulate his Arcane Step into dressing himself instantaneously.

Sensing his Familiar nearby, he called out with his mind, *Better my dear?*

A little she offered. *It'd be better if you weren't redressing into the same smelly clothes.*

He considered this and realised that, with his Bag of Holding, there wasn't any good reason he could think not to have a second set of clothes and so added it to his ever-growing list of shopping.

You may be right Little One, or perhaps I should simply go naked like you do?

Ergh! Yuck! And have all your dangly bits flapping about all over the place? I think not Master she thought back, causing them both to chuckle.

Not yet ready to head back and face the rest of the group, Ninetoes elected to explore the waterfall and see if he couldn't climb the statue. As he stared at it from the bottom, there was definitely something... off, about it and he wanted to get a closer look.

Using Arcane Step, he leapt across a series of stepping stones that crossed the river and made it to the foot of the statue. Taking a moment to plan his pathway up the statue's body and for some mana to recharge, Ninetoes was struck by just how impressive a feat the colossus was.

It must be at least two hundred feet tall and, despite its location, seemed to have withstood the test of time, with little wear visible and no apparent signs of erosion or water damage apart from around the mouth.

And, not that Ninetoes was an expert, but the craftsmanship seemed flawless. That, even at this distance and angle, he could make out every stroke of detail provided by the artist's tool.

Once he was confident of his route, Ninetoes 'stepped' and then 'stepped' again and so on until, less than a minute later, he'd reached the flat of the statue's left wrist. Here he paused, long enough to plan the next part of his ascent.

Looking back out towards the barge, Ninetoes could see that the party was watching him climb. He realised with a degree of shame that this spell might have been a better choice to show off his talent and power than Create Undead had been. He'd known that people feared the Undead. It was after all why he'd kept Bluzag's nature a secret but in that moment it had seemed like such a wonderful idea. Now, it seemed, everyone hated him.

With this thought colouring his cheeks a deep maroon, he 'stepped' again, keen to be as far away from the others as possible. This time, he'd taken a slight risk and 'stepped' to the folds of the statues' robes and, as he materialised, he had to reach out and grab the rockface to avoid losing his balance and falling.

His Agility score almost certainly saved his life once again. But he didn't care and instead simply 'stepped' again, twice more onto the almost sheer face of the sculpture's chest. His spell would have allowed him to have 'stepped' further, but he could only 'step' to where he could see and so it took him a little while to reach the right-hand shoulder where he finally paused again.

He had meant to travel all the way to the crown of the colossus' head, but when he'd reached the shoulder, he'd realised that the area had been carved into a series of steps, cleverly hidden from below. Now that he was here, he could see that the steps led to a depression in the nape of the neck, that could be only one thing, a door!

Pulse quickening, he climbed down the steps. The door was made out of the same stone as the rest of the statue and was also concealed from a cursory glance by the talent of the sculptor and the weathering of time and nature.

Ninetoes could see that the door was fixed in place and as he put his shoulder into it, couldn't move it an inch. He spent a moment checking the seams, annoyed but unsurprised that the door hadn't yielded so easily and that was when he found something even more intriguing.

As he'd crouched down to allow his hands to follow the seam along the floor, his fingers brushed something papery.

Looking down, he could see a leaf of parchment, wedged under the door. The parchment definitely had writing on it, but with so little revealed, he couldn't make out anything.

Carefully, he took hold of the two corners he could see and began to gently tease at the parchment. Again, his high Agility score helped him and within a dozen seconds he'd managed to reveal some arcane formula and two words, *Tally's Pocket*. A spell scroll!

With excitement coursing through him, he began to pull at the parchment with even more haste. This of course, was his undoing, or rather the parchment's.

Rrrrrrippp!

The section of parchment that Ninetoes was holding came away in his hands, torn almost cleanly along a fold line. Annoyed, the hobgoblin wizard studied what he had, hoping that he had enough of the scroll to cast the spell but even a brief scan of the arcane words was enough to tell him he had nowhere near the whole spellform. Angrily stuffing the parchment into his pocket, Ninetoes huffed.

By this time, the cavity that he was in was dark and it was only his goblinoid eyes that allowed him to see anything. Looking up, he could see the last of the sun's rays retreating over the top of the colossal statue. Looking down, he could also see that unless he started making his way back down soon, he'd be doing so in almost total darkness.

His emotions still broiling around inside of him, Ninetoes began the process of descending to the barge.

By the time he'd reached the bottom of the cliff, his thoughts had managed to completely tangle themselves up and he was now totally confused. Then, by the time that he reached the barge itself, he'd worked himself up to a simmering anger. He was angry at himself for revealing his Specialism as a Necromancer, angry at the rest of the party for how they'd treated him, angry at Deck for starting the whole thing off and angry at Chance for ripping the spell scroll.

A crude campsite had been set up around a small campfire. Bedrolls had been laid out, and Deck was already fast asleep. So it was that the first person Ninetoes found awake was Vortiga.

Seeing the hobgoblin Sarm sat quietly watching the fire stoked an even greater anger in Ninetoes and he stormed over to her. "Why aren't you chained to something?"

"That's not really up to me, now is it?" she snarked. For Ninetoes this was just too much.

"Bluzag!" he shouted and Deck snorted, almost waking at the sudden sound but Ninetoes didn't care. "Bluzag!" This second, louder shout was enough to wake the sailor.

"What is going on?" Bess stepped to the top of the gangplank, which now led down to the camp. When she saw Ninetoes, she glared down at him. "Why are you making all this noise?"

"I want to know where Bluzag is and why the prisoner is sitting with only her wrists bound. She could run away at any moment."

"Had you been here, rather than off climbing giant statues, you'd know," Bess snapped. "The prisoner has given Lowen her Promise as a Warrior not to run away, she's even been helping with chores and Bluzag is up here. He fell into the river when he tried to disembark and I sent him inside to remove his clothes and armour to dry off."

A cold, sinking feeling flooded through Ninetoes at her words, his anger extinguished immediately and he forgot about the prisoner.

After their reaction earlier at a mere zombie rat, Ninetoes could only imagine what the party would do if they discovered Bluzag was a Wight.

In an attempt to calm himself down, Ninetoes took a deep breath and stepped closer to Bess.

"Ah… I'll, er that is, Bluzag's superstitious and only I should… yes perhaps I should, um, help him with his… um, yes I think that'd be best." So saying, he climbed past Bess and made for the cabin, shutting the door behind him and leaning against it.

Bluzag was sitting on a crate, his boots to one side and the straps of his chainmail unbuckled, but blessedly still in place. Ninetoes released a stuttered breath of relief.

"What's going on?" called Bess from without.

"Nothing. Bluzag is just, um, embarrassed. We'll be out in a moment." Ninetoes answered quickly, while dragging a crate in front of the door.

His anger forgotten, Ninetoes started to think. He was in a definite and dangerous bind. Bluzag's clothes were sodden and so he couldn't go back out in them or the others would simply ask more difficult questions, but at the same time, Ninetoes couldn't just remove the Wight's clothes or he'd reveal its undead nature.

He supposed he could leave Bluzag in the cabin and claim that the Adventurer was simply praying or something, but even to Ninetoes the lie seemed paper thin.

With no practical ideas, Ninetoes slumped against the chest with all their belongings and wondered if there was enough material to fashion some sort of clothing out of his bedroll, but immediately discarded the idea as absurd.

Nonetheless, he considered the contents of the chest and his Bag of Holding for a better solution but nothing offered itself up. Next, he flicked through his spellbook. While he was impressed with how far he had progressed in just a few short weeks, it offered him no answers. That was when he considered the ancient spellbook that he'd taken from the ruins of Kavralach and, retrieving it from his Bag of Holding, he began slowly thumbing through the pages, desperate for any solution.

The book was divided into the various spell schools and so he ignored the sections on Divination, Evocation and Necromancy and instead headed for the chapter on Transmutation.

Although there were a few spells that might have offered a solution however, his level of Skill with the spell school was woefully inadequate to the task.

Next, he tried the Illusion chapter and, for a while he and Libby attempted to create an Illusion of clean clothes around the Wight. Even with his Familiar's help and growing proficiency however, their level of skill fell short on producing anything convincing or anything that would last long enough at least.

Finally, then, he paged through the Conjuration chapter, hoping to find a way to simply conjure a set of clean clothes out of thin air and, while he didn't find quite that, he did find a solution to his problem and what's more, something that would please the sensitive nose of his Familiar. Moreover, it would finally tick something off of his wish list.

Ninetoes had read and discarded the spell on his first reading of the book as a waste of mana. It was also one of the spells that required skill levels in multiple spell schools and he couldn't really understand its purpose. He'd supposed that a wizard might learn such a spell to clean their potion making equipment or cauldrons and such, but it had never occurred to him that he could simply use it to clean his clothes. While the mana cost was still an issue, in his current situation it was definitely energy well spent.

He had Bluzag remove the rest of his armour and clothes and pile them on the floor, noting that the Wight was still wearing the torn and bloodied shirt he'd died in. Ninetoes silently promised the Wight he'd replace the article and then took his time to read the incantation carefully and practice the somatic components with his hands.

After a couple of minutes, Ninetoes quickly removed his own clothes and added them to the heap. Feeling a little concerned of what people would think if they came in now to find him and Bluzag stood in nothing but their smalls, he quickly cast the spell.

A rich amber magic swirled out of his hands and snaked over the pile of clothes. Wherever the magic touched, the material changed colour as the clothes were cleaned.

But, as he watched, he noticed that the strands of magic began to return to his outstretched hand, although of a darker hue than before. These strands began swirling into a ball that hovered above the centre of Ninetoes' open palm, darkening further as it gathered more dust and dirt.

As the magic cleansing finished the items on top, Ninetoes removed them and, moving his hand over the other articles, steadily cleaned everything. The sphere of muck and detritus hovering over his hand became larger and darker with each path it took.

And, as the last of the clothes were cleaned, the ball over his hand began to shine a bright red and to spin, faster and faster until...

POP!

The sphere briefly ignited into a fireball the size of an apple and disappeared. Ninetoes was once again amazed at the wonders of magic and smiled.

Lifting the clothes from the floor he found them to be better than just clean. They felt new and softer and were slightly warm. Better still, as he lifted Bluzag's trousers, found them to be bone dry!

Checking his spellbook he found that, sure enough, the spell was level 7 and its area of effect had expanded to six feet with a bonus obtained at level 5.

He dressed quickly and helped Bluzag to dress and then replaced the Wight's armour, which had also been scoured clean and also looked almost brand new.

As he cinched his sword belt in place he commanded Bluzag to remove the crate from in front of the door and then stepped proudly out on deck, the Wight following closely.

By this point of course, it was pitch black outside and no one was on board to notice his triumphal exit. That, he supposed, might be for the best.

CHAPTER 13
VORTIGA'S MALICE

Ninetoes gave Bluzag strict orders to wake him before dawn but then, seeing as he wasn't sure that Bluzag could understand such a task, he came up with another solution. After ensuring that the Wight could count and some quick maths, he told the undead servant to count to twenty-five thousand and then wake him. With his body and clothes properly clean for the first time in what felt like weeks, Ninetoes found himself able to settle down to sleep quickly.

***

VORTIGA

Vortiga's day on board the barge had been a harrowing experience. She'd always been deathly afraid of the water, although she had no idea why. Lucky enough for her, it had never been a requirement for those aspiring to become a Warrior in her tribe, otherwise she'd never have succeeded in becoming who she was.

Even walking near a river or crossing a bridge brought her out in a cold sweat. She could take a bath of course, she wasn't completely spineless but she was careful to make sure to never allow her troops to see her reaction to the deadly element; such weakness could not go overlooked and neither should it. Such frailty disgusted her!

If she was completely honest with herself, it's why she'd been so rash in her plans to escape, so afraid was she of the journey on the river. But she'd failed and once again proven her flaws.

No! She would not follow that reasoning. The Adventurer may appear to be a porsht but he was far from it. He was instead a capable and, it seemed, powerful creature and she should respect that strength if she was to overcome it. What's more, she'd escape and once again prove her worth.

And such an interesting power it was. Necromancy! She'd only heard tales, of course, but she knew that such wizards were feared by all of the peoples of Adrenon, including her own.

The power to animate the fallen to fight! Such spellcasters could make enemies and friends alike into their undead thralls. It almost seemed a shame that she must kill him but she'd already come to terms with that; his spellbook and what was obviously a Bag of Holding, would hold many secrets and would, perhaps, be enough of a prize to encourage leniency from the Curn; although it repulsed her to think of such halfling-like be-haviour.

All such things were currently beyond her grasp of course and for now she must make good her escape. This time she must not fail!

If she did, she would fall on her own sword.

These fools had thought they understood her, that they could trust her word! The bargemaster had actually sat her down to explain how dangerous the forests nearby were and that escape would lead only to a quick death.

She'd stared back, wide-eyed, as if petrified by his descriptions. He'd then asked her to make a Promise! Which she'd given of course, as if her honour would require her to abide by any agreement she made with a human! *Ha!*

Oh, she'd towed the line, even offering to help wash the giant's clothes, *Gods the stupidity and arrogance of humans!* She'd only done so to steal the key to her manacles!

251

She'd never thought she'd get away with it and yet now, sat within night's comforting darkness, she unlocked the bonds and lowered them gently to the floor.

The light of the campfire was dying and within just a few minutes would be nothing more than embers and she would make her escape. Until then, she must come up with a plan for overcoming the towering and silent Adventurer. Her distraction tactic had only barely succeeded in her last attempt and so she couldn't rely on such a gambit again. No, she needed something to distract him for longer.

As she pondered this problem she allowed her breathing to steady and cleared her mind. The stillness of the night made this easy, as did its silence.

Only, it wasn't silent in the camp, not completely, and neither was the Adventurer. He was muttering quietly to himself. No, he was… counting? Strange to be sure but she wasn't sure how it could help her.

As she paid closer attention to him, she almost felt sorry for him. His words were ponderous and were clearly taking him a no insignificant amount of effort. But she still didn't see how she could… *Hmmm, perhaps.*

"Five fousind, free hundred and twenny one. Five fousind, free hundred and twenny two. Five fousind…" He lumbered on.

"Three thousand, four hundred and fifty-five. Two thousand, two hundred and twenty-nine…" she whispered quietly, joining the rhythm of the giant's dirge.

"Five fousind, free hundred and for'y two. Five fousind, free hundred and for'y nine, er no for'y free. Five fousind, two hund… no um, free hundred and for'y… um, four?"

Vortiga grinned with an unpleasant smirk and continued to mutter nonsensical numbers under her breath. It took a while, she'd give the brute that, he was relentless in his attempt to continue unhindered but, after a couple of minutes he faltered and paused, looking around for the first time, as if looking for a solution elsewhere, here was her chance.

"Why don't you find something to count?" she whispered to the hulking idiot. His head snapped towards her and she stared back at the black, empty space behind the slits in his helmet. Had she miscalculated? Could the mask hide deep and intelligent eyes?

But, as the moment stretched into a minute and neither looked away, she took a risk. "Like, leaves perhaps. You could collect them as you count and then, if you lose your place, count them to find it."

The giant looked away... at the trees!

And then, his steps as ponderous as his counting, he walked over to them and began reaching up to pick the leaves.

"One. Two. Free. Four..." *Gods! How stupid could you really be?*

Wasting no time, Vortiga raised herself onto her haunches and then, crouching low, she stalked through the camp. She assumed she'd have only a few seconds to make a dash for the treeline and so disappear into the darkness, but now she had plenty of time and so instead, she set about collecting items to ensure her survival.

The hobgoblin wizard and the foolish human girl had locked their packs away, but the girl, Bess, had kept her mace and shield resting nearby and these Vortiga snatched up first. The halfwit was also using her cloak as a blanket. She still had the one the porsht had given her of course, but any resource she could steal was one less they had, so she grabbed that too and, laying it on the ground, filled it with what food she could find quickly and then rolled it up and tied it into a loop that she threw over her shoulder like a bandolier.

She stared across at the porsht's Bag of Holding. He had it within reach, the strap looped around his wrist. She could easily relieve him of it. Her analytical mind kicked in. It was a risk to be sure, and every moment she stood thinking about it was time wasted. But having the bag and its contents would give her a better chance at survival. More than that however, she wanted the porsht to know that she'd taken right from under him, how close she'd been to killing him.

Then, why wasn't she killing him? She could take his own blade and to grate across the course, tough skin of his neck. Or she could just bash his skull in with her new mace. So, why did she stay her hand? He was her enemy and one who had treated her as such.

Except, that wasn't completely true. He had shown himself to be honourable, treated her with the respect of a Warrior. Even the cloak about her shoulders, the very thing keeping Autumn's chill from her bones had been his. *Arghh! He is a foe. Kill him and be done with it!*

She was acting foolishly. Hefting her weapon, she stepped forward.

"Ah Sally, wos tha' you got in your bag? Ooooh you dirty gir- he he he!" Vortiga leapt clear out of her skin as the deckhand's dreamy muttering broke the stillness.

Shaken by the moment, she reconsidered. He might appear to be a porsht at first glance, but he had as much mettle as any of her men and a measure more than many. Carefully she unlaced the strap from his wrist, her movements as gentle as a lover.

Her prize in hand, she stepped away and once out of earshot, she bolted for the treeline and headed up stream, back the way they'd come.

The darkness welcomed her and she embraced the solitude it offered. Within a dozen steps, her body had settled into its normal rhythms and her powerful legs quickly whisked her away from her jailors.

At first, she was so surprised by her easy escape, Vortiga sprinted almost flat out, expecting that, at any moment the alarm would be sounded and she'd be hunted. But, as the minutes wore onwards and still she could sense no one following her, she eased her pace to a quickmarch, a pace she could maintain for hours if she needed to.

Only, as she'd feared it would, her luck ran out.

She had chosen her path carefully, following the line of the river, so that, by always keeping it on her right she would find her way back to the Steading and from there head westwards. Her path also, however, offered her the cover of the trees.

A hundred yards ahead, she could see that the line of the trees turned sharply inland and, it seemed, created a small clearing. Slowing her pace to a stealthy crawl, she angled herself to skirt around it.

But, as she reached the edge of the trees and began to do so, the moon's light flashed off of something in the clearing. Curiosity got the better of her and she turned to look more closely. What she found changed everything.

Just a dozen feet away from her in the clearing lay a longsword. It was grasped in the bloody hand of a soldier and as she took in more of the scene, she could see from his green, fur-lined cloak that it was one of the mercenaries hired to protect the Steading, the Emerald Wolves, and he was not alone.

Scattered across the clearing were at least half a dozen or maybe more, every one still grasping the hilt of a sword or the shaft of a bow, although it seemed that these weapons had done them no good, as she could smell the coppery scent of spilled blood from everywhere. Clearly the monster they had hunted had slaughtered them instead. *Fools!*

The bodies she could see all wore chainmail and had some satchels, probably containing rations and other useful items. Such a bounty of equipment and resources could not be passed up, even with the mage's bag, she still needed to eat, and so far her attempts at retrieving food from the magic item had been unsuccessful.

Vortiga was no fool however, and so she waited, scanning the treeline for threats. Perhaps some of the troop had survived or, more disconcertingly, perhaps the monster that had torn through this group was still nearby.

But, after a few minutes of silent observation, the hobgoblin warrior decided that the risk was worth the reward and so, careful to place every footfall to ensure she didn't snap an errant twig or slide on a stone, Vortiga made her way to the closest body.

She would not be greedy, she'd decided, and would take only what she needed: a sword to replace the unwieldy mace, any food she find and perhaps some armour. She'd leave the distinctive green cloak, it would only be a liability at the Steading.

As she reached the nearest body, she groaned inwardly, the body was that of a bear of a man and his armour would dwarf her. Instead, she cast her gaze about and noted another body nearer to her size and build, so she stalked further into the clearing's centre.

No predator had attacked her so far but she would take no chances. It took her another couple of minutes to creep across the space, every footstep carefully chosen, her muscles coiled and ready to bolt at the first sign of trouble; but she made it to the second body without anything breaking the stillness of the silence.

This body also seemed to be covered in blood; whatever did this was clearly a fierce creature. To have killed a whole squad of armoured soldiers, even fools such as these, was a feat unto itself.

Shaking the thought away, she reached out to retrieve the sword, still grasped in the corpse's hand. Only, rather than giving up the weapon, the hand clung on.

Surprised that rigor mortis had already set in, Vortiga moved her hand to prise the fingers open but, instead of doing so, the hand clenched and, as she looked up, she noticed the eyes were locked on her!

"Oi, what're you doin'?" a voice whispered, emanating from the body. This fool was still alive and, as she wrestled with him for control of the sword, clearly still strong.

"Jenks! What in the Nine Hells is going on?" Another, harsher whisper asked from nearby. Only, she recognised this voice; it was the arrogant leader of the band… Captain Savage!

At the sound of his Captain's voice, the man before her intensified his struggle for his weapon. "Will. You. Gerroff?" he exclaimed, finally pulling the sword away from her hand.

"Dammit Jenks, who're are you talkin' to? That thing could be here any-"

"Mmmmmm, such tasting looking things. And already laying down, ready to be munched and crunched!" drawled a stomach-turning voice from above the clearing.

Vortiga whipped her head around to locate the speaker, but all she could see was the silhouette of a huge winged monster, hovering above them, its wings stirring the undergrowth near them.

"SHIT! To arms lads. Horn, Coop and Helder, fire! The rest of you, you know what to do."

From all around the clearing, Vortiga heard the twang of bowstrings.

Still looking at the monster, she could see the missiles thumping into it and, more importantly, the ropes leading back from them. Quickly following one, she found another warrior, this one so covered in mud and leaves that she realised that she must have stumbled into an ambush meant for the monster! Perhaps this Savage wasn't such a nugwart after all.

Her mind, battle-trained to a razor sharpness, took in the rest of the scene in a flash. There were three bowmen in total, each one holding a crossbow and each one had fired a bolt attached to rope, the lengths of which were secured to a tree trunk. More than that, each crossbowman was dashing towards another tree that, now that she knew what to look for, she could see held other lengths of rope.

As she stood, mouth agape, she noticed that all of the "bodies" were rising. Some of them headed for the ropes and began to pull the monster down towards the ground, while the rest surrounded the creature with weapons drawn, ready to carve it into pieces once it reached the ground.

Begrudgingly, Vortiga had to admit that it was a good plan. Draw the beast in with a promise of an easy meal and then use the ropes to negate its most potent strength; its ability to fly.

Not that she really cared, however, because she wouldn't be here to see its conclusion and instead she bolted for the far treeline. With any luck the fight would slow down the porsht and his friends as well.

THUMP!

"And where d'ya think you're going?"

'Captain' Savage stood over her, having just slammed his shield into her chest, arresting her movement and sending her sprawling backwards onto the floor.

Argh! She didn't have time for this and she certainly wasn't going to be brought low by some human!

Spinning on the floor, she swept his leg out from under him... or at least she tried, but instead he simply stepped back and lifted his leading foot, having seen the move coming a mile off. Rather than press his attack however, he smiled and bowed slightly, while drawing his sword in a flourish and gesturing for her to stand.

The blade glowed faintly red in the moonlight and even in the darkness, she could see the curve of intricately worked hilt.

Anger tinged Vortiga's face purple as she stood and he was grateful that the night hid her embarrassment from this cur.

She tested the mace's weight in her hand. It was well-made but nonetheless wasn't a weapon that suited her. Still, it would be enough to bash in this cretin's skull and then she could take his pretty sword.

Swinging it in a wide arc the mace flew towards the man's head but he easily retreated from the attack. She followed this up with a short attack form. Normally meant for a swordsman, it served well enough to test her opponent's defences. She watched carefully as he dodged most of her attacks and only took one hit on his shield; as she'd expected.

While he was clearly adept with his sword and board combination, his shield was little more than a buckler and wouldn't stand up to repeated blows from her heavier weapon. With this information in mind, she was now confident that she could end the preened dullard quickly.

But, as she attempted to begin a second combination of strikes, this one aimed at battering down his defences, Savage changed his tact from defence to offence and started darting forward, attempting to clip his blade around her own defences.

Ha! Is that all you've got? His attacks came to an end and not a single strike had even come close!

All too late however, she realised that his assault hadn't been to hit her, but instead it had driven her back. Back into the centre of the clearing and—

SHINK!

The monster's claws raked her unprotected back, immediately drawing blood and a screech of pain from the hobgoblin Warrior. Worse, its follow up attack slammed her down and pinned her to the ground.

Vortiga could feel her clothes soaking with blood and knew the wound was fatal. Looking up, she could see the monster's strangely human-like face, encircled by a mane of lion's fur.

"Mmmmm, how kind. You have offered me a snack to whet my appetite! Thank you, thank you. Perhaps you think that this will satisfy me? But no, I think I'll eat you ALL!"

The monster's sickly-sweet, almost childlike voice, slithered out over its razor-sharp teeth, but as it reached its final words, it screamed a yell of pure power and slashed its pinning claws in a wide arc, tearing through at least half of the ropes holding it down.

The monster was free!

***

Ninetoes woke with a start and he reached up to wipe water off his face. *Water? Is it raining?* Asked a small, sleepy voice, before snuggling deeper into the crook of Ninetoes' arm.

Annoyed but accepting that if it was raining, he'd have to at least move, Ninetoes opened his eyes and looked about.

While it was dark, the moon's light cast enough radiance, for even a human to see the entire camp clearly. Which is why the scene was taken in and was instantly confusing.

"Bluzag, what are you doing?"

"Countin' Master." Came back the slow drawl of his undead servant.

"Yes, but why are pulling down-" *Wait! Where's the prisoner?* "Where's Vortiga? Where's the prisoner?" His mounting panic making his voice sound shrill. But Bluzag just kept counting. "Bluzag! Where. Is. The. Prisoner?" This time he focussed his will, silently commanding the Wight to obey.

Bluzag dropped his collection of leaves and lumbered around to face his master. But no answer was forthcoming. Not that it mattered, Ninetoes had a pretty good idea of what had happened and he couldn't

259

blame Bluzag. Somehow that witch had confused his Wight and made her escape.

"We must find her Bluzag! She could warn her people!" Ninetoes was definitely losing his control and was struggling to think straight. Questions hurtled through his mind and none of them could have good answers: *How long ago had she escaped? Which way would she go? How would they possibly find her? And where was his fucking Bag of fucking Holding? Ergh!*

"What's all this blasted noise?" grumbled Lowen from his bedroll. Ninetoes spun on the spot, realising that he'd been pacing up and down.

"The prisoner has escaped!" he said, his voice almost a shriek.

"Oh, is that all? Best go find her then I 'spose." His voice was no less coarse, but he seemed unbothered.

"Well, yes. That's what I'm doing."

"Really, looks to me like you're trying to dig a trench." Lowen was grinning, as if this was all some joke. This only added to Ninetoes' growing panic.

"I'm thinking!"

"Nought to think about is there. Let me get me bow and I'll be right along."

"But, we don't know where she's gone."

"Oh, I can find her right enough. She gave me and broke her word, I could track her through the Nine Hells and back," the bargemaster commented simply.

"What do you mean?" Ninetoes asked.

"I cast a spell, Quarrel's Truth. Simple enough but powerful, when she broke her promise it activated and now I can follow her for as long as it takes." And, sure enough, after grabbing his bag, quiver and crossbow from the locked chest on his barge, Lowen began heading straight for the edge of the camp.

"Aye. She's no woodcraft, that's sure enough," he said, before stepping into the treeline.

So surprised was Ninetoes, that it took him a moment before he followed. "Bluzag, stay here in camp and watch over Bess and be sure nothing harms her. Lib, up into the trees and follow close." Then, as his Familiar leapt from his shoulder, the hobgoblin followed Lowen.

Despite the age difference, it was Ninetoes who struggled to keep up. But more than that, the older man managed to move without making a sound, almost as if he was gliding through the forest. Ninetoes on the other hand made enough noise for the two of them, although he couldn't tell whether his passage through the woodland or the drumming of his heart was what made more noise.

If she escaped, she could return to the Nechtsarm army and hasten their pace. His own mission was already short on time; if the hobgoblins attacked early, all would be lost!

Just as these thoughts threatened to overwhelm Ninetoes, he suddenly realised that he was alone, Lowen was nowhere to be seen. Turning on the spot, Ninetoes strained his eyes to find the errant bargemaster.

"Stop. Down," whispered Lowen from nearby. Ninetoes did as he was commanded and ducked down behind a tree, while still scanning the undergrowth, but to no avail.

"There, look," the voice sounded again and Ninetoes turned in its direction. This time he found Lowen hiding within a bush, pointing deeper into the forest. Following his arm, the hobgoblin tried to make out what the human was showing him, but even his goblinoid eyes couldn't pick out anything of interest in the dark confines of the wood. "What is it?" he queried.

"A battle by the sounds of it." Even with this description, Ninetoes still couldn't see a damned thing! He was so angry, he could barely think straight. Instead of completing his own mission, he was stumbling through the undergrowth, searching for that witch of a Sarm. He paused and took a deep breath to steady the drumming of his heart.

Once it stopped hammering through his chest he forced his ears to listen to every sound. It took him a moment, but once he'd heard it, the sounds of fighting were unmistakable.

"We should get closer and investigate," he whispered. He didn't want to admit that he couldn't see anything, especially seeing as a human shouldn't be able to see more than a few feet in the blanketing darkness.

"Very well, but this time, could you at least *try* to be quiet?"

A part of Ninetoes balked at the reprimand but he could hardly argue with it. Still, knowing that he needed to stay hidden and being able to do so, were two very different things.

As the bargemaster moved off, Ninetoes paid closer attention and attempted to follow and place his feet in the same spots. Meanwhile he whispered the incantation to Cloaking Shadow and, as the spell took hold, he felt Libby do the same before gliding onwards through the canopy.

It took them a good minute or two to slowly reach the edge of a clearing, the sounds of the fighting intensified with every step. It was clear from the shrieks and moans that the battle went ill for one side.

Lowen led them on a circuitous route, for which Ninetoes was grateful and by the time they came within sight of the scene, he'd replenished roughly a third of his spent mana and had meanwhile used his Gem of Power to reclaim the rest.

The battle unfolding before them was a mess, with what little light was being cast by handheld torches warping the scene further.

This was not Ninetoes' first fight however and he quickly took in the pertinent information; the Emerald Wolves were fighting what appeared to be some sort of flying lion.

"Shit a manticore!" The fear in Lowen's harsh whisper was clear and Ninetoes took a second to cast Identify and analyse the monster.

MANTICORE - LEVEL 26
PRIME STATS - STRENGTH, ENDURANCE
PRIME TRAIT - TAIL SPIKES
980/1053 HP
5000XP

As he read through the information, he also felt the warm pleasantness of his spell increasing in level, which must mean his Divination skill had increased as well. Something strange happened as it did; however, the information displayed by his spell increased and now revealed a weakness of the creature; its Intelligence. He wasn't sure how useful it would be right now, but he filed the information away nonetheless.

This was, however, the only warm feeling he got. The monster was a powerhouse and was clearly a deadly foe. He was only glad that this wasn't his fight.

As he cast his analytical gaze over the forces arrayed against the monster he quickly realised that the battle was almost over; and the Wolves didn't stand a chance. As he continued to scan the ground near to the manticore, however, his spell picked up something both exciting and terrible all at once.

VORTIGA - LEVEL 10
PRIME STATS - STRENGTH, ENDURANCE
PRIME TRAIT - LEADERSHIP
CONDITIONS - SEVERE BLEEDING
16/280 HP
2500XP

Vortiga was dying! Worse still, he didn't risk 'stepping' her out of trouble for fear of how much damage it might do.

Ninetoes' heart was a maelstrom of emotions. Relief that he'd found her; concern that she'd die before he could deliver her to Pamor; anger that he wouldn't be the one to kill her!

But Ninetoes had been created by violence and honed by battle. It was the one time that he felt truly calm.

As that feeling of oneness spread over him he knew he must save her and he began to act. Subconsciously, he sent his plan to Libby in an instant. Time for the hobgoblin wizard seemed to slow down and, even as he began casting his first spell, he searched the battle zone for what he'd need. Finding it in short order he 'stepped' and, as he reappeared next to the manticore he used his cloak's special ability and used Force Wave to shove the monster aside. Then he knelt down and grabbed Vortiga's wrist.

Lowen, who was still scanning the battlefield was surprised when he noticed the hobgoblin appear within its centre and punt the monster aside. Seeing him there, he made his own decision to help, and fired a bolt at the monster's flank, drawing its attention away from the foolhardy wizard.

Ninetoes noted the bolt whizzing over his head and was grateful to the cranky old coot for his aid as he began dragging Vortiga closer to the body of another fallen soldier. A comforting weight alighted on his shoulder and Libby immediately began Channelling mana into him.

If it hadn't been the thick of battle, Ninetoes might have thought twice about what he did next, but he couldn't waste any time and, as he reached out to the man hand, he thrust the other onto the ribbons of flesh that had once been Vortiga's back and cast his second spell.

As he drained the last of the soldier's life from him the man's last breath rattled out of his lungs. Ninetoes focussed its healing power into the Sarm. There was no way that he could completely repair all of the damage done to her, the poor man had only so much life left to give, but Ninetoes concentrated what he did have into sealing the worst of the damage and managed to reduce the Severe Bleeding condition down to just Bleeding, giving them both a little more time.

While Ninetoes searched the clearing, the sounds of fighting rose and well. All he needed was another dying creature from whom he could steal the life that Vortiga would need, but his search came up empty and worse still, across the battlefield he caught Captain Savage watching him, a grim look on the mercenary's face, showing that he must have seen what the hobgoblin had done.

Those eyes promised retribution, but right now they were the least of Ninetoes' problems as, with a gleeful squeal, the manticore turned its attention back towards the pair of hobgoblins and as it wheeled through the air, whipped out its tail.

Three spikes shot out towards Ninetoes and Vortiga.

"Oh no, no, no! You'll not have my supper you naughty little magiker!"

Rolling onto his back, Ninetoes cast Barrier and caught two of the missiles, the third slamming into his shoulder and pinning him to the forest floor. As his shoulder shrieked with pain he realised that there was no way he'd be able to block many more of the monster's attacks.

As it circled above, the manticore recognised that its foe was injured and its cruel eyes became alight with murder. It trumpeted once and then swooped in for the kill.

Ninetoes' magic was far from spent, but he didn't yet have enough to finish his plan and he certainly couldn't waste anymore on a spell. He really must stop getting himself into these situations, he was a Wizard for gods' sake!

But he hadn't always been, and as the monster plunged towards him, he grabbed his sword and with little in the way of finesse or skill drove the tip straight at the manticore.

The beast's own weight and momentum impaled it onto the weapon and, with a shriek of pain, it wrapped its wings and barrelled to the side, wrenching Ninetoes' sword with it before taking flight once more. Ninetoes grinned as the smell of fresh blood entered his nostrils.

"Argh! You little- You stuck me! You, I shall eat from toe to chin, magicky one!"

Above him, the monster dodged and wove between the hastily fired bolts of the Emerald Wolves, its laughter mocking their attempts at hitting it, but Ninetoes could tell from its course that it was simply circling back around for another pass at him. Apparently, it really didn't like mages, or perhaps it was being stabbed it did like?

Master!

His Familiar's presence within his mind reminded him that there were more important things to worry about.

As the manticore reached its zenith, its eyes locked onto Ninetoes and it dove.

Well, he didn't have any more swords to stab it with, but the weapon had given him the time he needed and, reaching through the bond he shared with Libby, he took the mana she offered. "This is going to hurt." He promised Vortiga, grinning evilly at her.

And then, all three of them 'stepped'.

As they reappeared next to Lowen, the old bargemaster yelped in surprise, but he managed to maintain his aim and another of his bolts slammed into the manticore's shoulder. Lowen ducked back into the precarious cover offered by the bole of the tree.

"Well, that was stupid," the bargemaster muttered to the Adventurer, but the grin stretching from ear to ear told a slightly different story; the old coot was enjoying himself. "Now what?"

Ninetoes' eyes looked longingly towards his sword still stuck fast in the manticore's breast.

But in the end it didn't take long to decide; his head ached with mana depletion and a moment's focus told him he had barely two mana points left; both Libby and Vortiga were unconscious and he'd made not one, but two knew enemies this night, the manticore's spike still protruding from his own shoulder. "We run."

"Aye, I reckon you've the right of it. I hope these poor lads have the same sense, that monster won't follow them into the trees." Lowen said as he lifted Ninetoes to his feet, while his gaze watched the Emerald Wolves as they continued to battle the manticore.

Ninetoes meanwhile reached into his Bag of Holding and snatched up his last two potions of healing. Passing one to Lowen for Vortiga, held the other in the hand of his injured shoulder, while the other hand reached across and grabbed the shaft of the spike.

Closing his eyes and gritting his teeth, he pulled. The pain was immense and it took an effort of will not to scream out, but the spike didn't budge.

"We'll deal with it on the barge, we must leave," said Lowen from the ground, as he poured the other potion into Vortiga's mouth. They watched as the worst of her wound sealed and her eyes fluttered open. She was still a little delirious, but she pulled her legs under her and Lowen helped her to her feet.

"We must leave lad," he said and Ninetoes nodded.

"Indeed."

***

The journey back to the campsite was not a pleasant one.

With Vortiga balanced between them, Lowen and Ninetoes dragged themselves through the forest. Behind them, the sounds of men dying could be heard for what felt like far too long and, not for the first time, Ninetoes questioned his right to be an Adventurer.

The pain in his shoulder dulled to a persistent, throbbing ache that twinged with every step, but neither of them slowed; fearful looks searching the skies for the monster's pursuit every few steps. By the time they reached the camp, it was the darkest part of the night and their last half mile had been an exhausted tumble through the bracken, before falling out of the treeline and collapsing to the floor near to the campfire that someone had taken the time to reignite.

Bess and Deck were awake by now and they stared in shock at the state of their companions; the young woman rushed over to help Ninetoes, as Deck took over the burden of carrying Vortiga.

"Oh! Your shoulder! What's that?" she called as she helped him to sit on a log.

"A manticore spike, it's stuck fast, do you have anything to help remove it?" Ninetoes said through gritted teeth.

"A, a what? Er, um…" she cast her gaze about before snapping her fingers "…my tools!" So saying, she dashed up the gangplank and aboard the boat returning seconds later carrying her pack.

A short search later and she pulled out a pair of tongs, normally used for taking red-hot metal from the furnace, it would serve. Passing the hobgoblin a roll of leather straps, she clamped the tool onto the shaft of the spike.

As Ninetoes bit down on the leather, Bess wrenched the tongs backward and, in one efficient jerk, pulled the manticore's missile from his shoulder.

With the last of his strength, Ninetoes thumbed off the cork from his healing potion and drained the bottle, before slumping to the floor and crawling to his bedroll.

***

Vortiga came in and out of consciousness during the flight from the battle in the clearing. But unconscious or not, the same memory kept swimming through her mind.

She'd been dead, there was no question in her mind. The monster had sliced her open and she'd felt her lifeblood draining onto the floor. She'd used the last of her strength to reach out and grasp the handle of her stolen mace, hoping that this weapon would act as enough of a replacement for her sword on her journey onwards to meet Nech in his endless halls. Then she'd closed her eyes and had given in.

But then… him! And shocking pain in her back as something had pressed down into her torn and mutilated flesh. It had been enough to bring her to and, as she'd opened her eyes, there he was, the porsht, standing tall before that monster and worse, saving her life!

The shame of it; to owe her life to such a craven being!

She tried once or twice to pull away from their grasp as they'd fled through the woods, hoping that perhaps they would leave her to die, but to no avail. Instead, she'd fallen into a painless and welcome oblivion.

Now she was awake again and could hear the humans muttering around her.

"Good gods, look at her back. How in all Adrenon did she survive?" Her back swelled with fresh pain as someone prodded at her ruined flesh.

"The Adventurer. He got to her somehow, far across the clearing in a heartbeat and then, well I dunno, used magic to stop her bleeding? And then swoosh, appeared right next to me, carrying the girl. I'll tell ya, it all happened so quick, I barely had time to fire three shots at the thing!" This voice she recognised as the captain of the boat they sailed upon.

"Will she live, do you think? Is there anything we can do for her? Or for him?" This was the voice of the smith, Bess. "And... hey, is that my mace? How in the Nine Hells did she hold on to it?" So saying, the owner of the voice came closer and wrestled the weapon sharply from her grip. "Bloomin' thief."

"The Adventurer will be fine. His wounds'll close, thanks to the potion he took, he'll just need rest. But her... that might be a different story.

The worst of the damage is healed, the Adventurer's magic and the potion saw to that, but a manticore's a filthy beast and it don't care what it eats or rakes its claws through."

"I don' understand." Queried the other human male's voice. Vortiga hadn't bothered to learn *their* names.

"Well, if she's unlucky, that wound'll get infected and then only expensive healing magic'll set her right. Not much we can do mind, just keep an eye on her. If she makes it through the night she'll probably be fine."

No! She couldn't die that way, she must try to escape.

But, as darkness took her once again, Vortiga's efforts to fight the creeping oblivion were in vain and she knew that her fate was now in the hands of the gods. With the last of her consciousness, she whispered a prayer, "Lord Nech, please don't let me die, I'll promise you-".

CHAPTER 14
THE COUNCIL OF PAMOR

Sometime later Ninetoes awoke. Stiff as a board and covered in aches and pains, he was nonetheless whole and, it appeared, safely aboard the barge and drifting downstream. Standing up, Ninetoes scanned the river's edge and found that the trees that had seemed so thick and impenetrable the night before, were now thinning and the river itself was widening and, as he continued to survey the scene, he noted a strange sight on the horizon.

"That'd be the Stormtops, the tower of Pamor's mages." Lowen spoke from atop the quarterdeck.

Ninetoes had never seen a structure so tall, even in Kavralach; the ancient city that he'd ventured to only a week ago. To his isolationist eyes, such a building simply shouldn't be able to exist.

From this distance he couldn't see the city proper, so far away was it, but the monument, for that was the only word he had for such an edifice, was tall enough to pierce clouds and be seen from so far away. But more than that, it was so thin! Atop the bole the tower widened to a disk shape with, what appeared to be, buildings on top. It simply beggared belief that the thing wasn't swaying in the breeze.

"Aye, it's quite the eyesore, ain't it?" Ninetoes couldn't disagree more with the sour boatmaster. To his eyes, it was incredible and definitely somewhere he planned to visit. "Now that you're awake, you can take over from Deck, I pay 'im to work the boat, not look after your prisoners and I'll be chargin' you extra for that, you mark my words." The barge-master seemed to be a confusion of grumpiness and affability, equal parts helpful and awkward, it made him impossible to read. Ninetoes thought this made him neat, and if he had more time, he'd have taken notes.

While he considered this, he searched the deck. Finding no one else, he made his way to the aft cabin. Inside he found the rest of the party. Bess was sleeping soundly nearby, encouraging the hobgoblin to whisper as he approached the deckhand.

"Did she survive?" The question was posed without emotion. As far as he was concerned, the hobgoblin woman was clearly more trouble than she was worth, but she was an asset and must be brought safely to Pamor. With the city on the horizon, this seemed like a foregone conclusion.

"She survived the night and the wound don't seem to 'ave festered as Lowen reckoned it might."

"Very good, I'll take over here, your boss wants you on deck."

"Aye. That one's a slave driver and no mistake." Then, as he opened the door and looked out, he turned back to Ninetoes. "I reckon we're about an hour or so from the docks, so you might wanna get ready to disembark, ol' Lowen's meaner than a striped snake when we're in port."

Ninetoes chuckled quietly as he crouched down beside Vortiga, wondering how in the world the bargemaster could be considered meaner still.

The prisoner's hands were once again bound, this time to a bracket set into the floor that was normally used for securing goods. She was lying on her side with her back left naked to the elements, the rest of her shirt having been removed for the bloody rags it was and her front was now covered by a blanket.

Ninetoes was no voyeur, but he couldn't help but be attracted to the fine, lithe figure of the woman and, while she was sleeping, she was almost handsome. *Ergh!* He shook the thought away. She was his enemy and a thorn in his damn side! Nonetheless, he was grateful for the thoughtfulness of the blanket. His people were... careful, with their nakedness.

She is not without a certain comeliness. Commented a voice within his mind. Looking around, he spotted his Familiar happily mopping up the contents of a bowl that lay beside Bluzag, who stood on guard next to the door.

271

It appeared Bess had attempted to feed the Wight again. No matter, clearly the food would never go to waste with his wily compatriot on hand to tidy things up.

She is our enemy and a brute, there is nothing attractive about her.

Come now Master, you forget that I can feel your thoughts towards her, you can't lie to me.

Well, er... she is a member of my race, I simply feel... homesick.

Uh huh!

Argh! Leave me alone.

The brief and silent exchange had gone unnoticed by the room at large, but beside him, Vortiga stirred and for a moment, he thought she'd heard. A second later, her eyes blinked open and she smiled dreamily for the briefest of moments as she looked up at Ninetoes.

The instance of pleasantness broke however, when she moved and pain crossed her face, forcing her eyes closed. Once it had passed and she reopened them, they held only disgust.

"You're alive. Good," he said monosyllabically.

"Indeed. Just long enough for you to deliver me to the human city and my execution," she snapped back at him.

"Ha! You don't think to make me feel guilty?" he asked incredulously. *The cheek of it.* "You attacked the humans, not the other way around."

"I simply ask that you give me a sword and let me die on my feet!" she growled back. Only this time with a note of something else in her voice, petition perhaps. "But of course a human lapdog like you wouldn't understand the way of a Warrior."

Ninetoes almost responded, but thought better of it. This was just one final and pathetic attempt to anger him into attacking her. Instead, he decided to get straight to business.

Stepping up to the chest holding their gear, Ninetoes set about reequipping his armour and adjusting his weapons. As he did so, he noticed some areas of rust and signs of wear on the leatherwork. He made a note to have his armour checked over once they reached port. The empty sheathe at his hip would also need addressing.

Next, as he removed a length of rope from his Bag of Holding he directed Bluzag to draw his weapon and step closer to Vortiga. Then he commanded the Wight to remove her manacles and stand her up. All of this he did without talking, to give the impression that Bluzag acted of his own accord.

As she stood, Vortiga readjusted the blanket to cover her modesty.

"I have a second shirt she can wear." Bess stood nearby, obviously woken by all the nearby movement. She handed Vortiga the article of clothing and held the blanket while the hobgoblin dressed. The prisoner remained silent, clearly done talking and so Bess set about her own preparations.

As she finished dressing, Ninetoes snorted out a laugh.

"It's a little big but—"

"A *little* big?" Hobgoblins were generally taller than humans, but Bess's broad shoulders and thickly muscled arms made her a giant in comparison to the Vortiga's slighter and more lithe form. Thus, the shirt seemed a dozen sizes too large for the hobgoblin woman and she'd had to stuff most of the excess into her trousers, creating a large bulge around her waist.

"It'll serve." Bess cut him off. She was right. They had more important things to concern themselves with.

Bluzag, keep your weapon ready and attack if she does anything aggressive.

Ninetoes' command preceded the hobgoblin as he stepped up to Vortiga and used the rope to completely bind her arms behind her back. Once he was content that she couldn't move her arms, he took the manacles from Bluzag and bound her legs together.

Finally, retrieving the shredded remains of her shirt from nearby, Ninetoes gagged his prisoner. She wouldn't be his problem for much longer, but while she was, he'd save himself from her forked tongue.

Turning to Bess, he noted that she seemed ready as well. "There's some stew left in the pot, want me to heat it up for you?" she asked.

"Please. I must speak with Master Lowen." So saying, he had Bluzag lead the prisoner out on deck to stand guard of her. Meanwhile, Ninetoes climbed the steps to the quarterdeck.

"I come to thank you for your aid last night," Ninetoes started. "And to find out when you return south to the Steading."

"It'll take the day to unload and then load goods to go south once again, so if the weather's with us, we'll be ready by tomorrow morning, but I promised the lad that he could visit his woman, so we'll probably stay for another night. Why, you looking for transport back?"

"Indeed. Successful or not, I intend to head back as soon as possible; our business should be done within the day, any longer we risk being too late."

"Aye, well the journey upriver's a day slower, that's for sure. But you'll find none swifter than the Kerensa." As he said this, an owl swooped down and landed on his shoulder. Ninetoes realised that, since Deck had mentioned it, he hadn't actually seen the bargemaster's Familiar.

Ninetoes was certainly no expert, but since he'd been an Adventurer, he was the only person he knew with a Familiar, although Foresto definitely knew the spell. It seemed incredible to him that someone as, well, ordinary Lowen should have one. Now that he thought about it of course, he realised how absurd that was. This was after all a magical world, why should the surly bargemaster have a little of his own. He also recognised that it explained a thing or two about their hunt through the forest.

"You'll take us back then?" Ninetoes asked, a little surprised with the ease to which Lowen seemed to be acquiescing. He'd imagined, after the events of the previous night, the bargemaster would want nothing more to do with them.

"Of course, me wife was from Raveslan, gods keep her. Deck will have to get his dick wet some other time. Find me at Tally's Troll on the dock front tonight. But keep me waiting and I'll have yer guts for garters. Now, bugger off, I've work to do."

With that dismissal, Ninetoes stepped down to the main deck, once again taken aback by the bargemaster's ability to be so kind and so salty, all in one sentence.

By now, Bess was waiting with a bowl of food. She smiled briefly as she passed it to him but then her face changed to a sombre expression.

"Quite the journey we've had," Ninetoes commented as he took a mouthful. The stew was still tasty and it warmed him against the growing chill. The young woman didn't seem to notice his words however.

Ahead, the city became clearer as they neared their destination. Ninetoes was equal parts impressed and impressively underwhelmed by the gargantuan mess that was the city of Pamor. He'd once heard somewhere that anything could be bought in Pamor, and now that he saw the place, he could well believe it.

As the barge meandered downstream, the city spilled out into the Sweetsea beyond, every inch covered in man-made structures.

The city rose atop three hills. The two further away created a shallow valley that ran into the sea. The third rose the highest and steepest, before dropping off completely into a cliff that tapered away from the sea. Atop this stood a squat castle.

At the base of the valley, the buildings were drab, monochromatic, slightly drunken dwellings that from this distance looked to be made of flotsam and scrap. But as his eyes climbed the hill, the buildings became grander and more colourful. Those at the hill's summit were incredible. Each one a colourful work of art and architecture that caught the sunlight and reflected it back in a rainbow of shades. The most impressive of these was, of course, the Stormtops, which rose out of the second tallest and furthest hill. The buildings at its base were so close that they seemed desperate to reach out and touch it.

The docks rested within the shadow of the tallest hill and the precariously balanced castle. Without really noticing, the silence of the wilderness that they'd left had become the constant hum and rattle of a city. But all this flavour and excitement played second fiddle to the smell. Even before he could see the buildings and people in detail, the wind brought their reek to his nostrils. Even from miles away they smelt of piss, sweat and desperation.

From the dock ward, a wide street snaked the tallest hill up to the castle built upon its summit. That, Lowen had mentioned, was where the Council could be found, meeting once a day at midday.

"You shouldn't have done that…" Bess spoke quietly but firmly. Unsure what she was talking about, Ninetoes took a bite and left the space open for her to provide more detail. "…brought that rat back I mean." She paused again and Ninetoes could see her hesitation, clearly she had more to say. "Lots of people, especially people in the countryside, are afraid of magic altogether, but not in Raveslan because we've got Foresto… but, but necromancy is just plain evil, everyone knows it."

Ninetoes waited a little longer, but the girl seemed to have said her piece. "I am sorry if you found it startling…" He looked at her face, she wasn't looking back at him, but she seemed to be listening. "… but to me, necromancy is just another magic, another tool and, well, it's one I'm rather good at. I don't consider it evil or good, it's just a mechanism for my magic. And one that allows me to do incredible things."

Bess cringed. "But it's vile. A person or creature shouldn't be puppeted back to life like that, it's disgusting."

"There's nothing vile about it, any more than using magic to lift something heavy or to light a fire. necromancy just does it differently. Surely you recognise there are things that would be impossible without magic."

"No! A life is sacred, we're not just meatbag tools when we die!"

Ninetoes was struggling to make himself understood. To him, the undead were, admittedly smelly, but they weren't evil. No more than a sword was evil.

"No, you see you're wrong-" As soon as the words left his mouth he regretted them.

"Wrong? The undead are an abomination, they're not gadgets that you can animate to do your bidding because… because if you're willing to use a body as a tool or a weapon, what else would you use a person for?" So saying, she stomped off to the prow where she stood, palpable waves of anger pulsing from her.

Ninetoes was growing annoyed. She just didn't want to consider things his way. "You just don't understand," he mumbled quietly to himself. What was it with people? Why couldn't they see that what he was saying was true? They ate animal meat and made tools from the bones, what was the difference? The strange elven woman was right, they were just afraid!

These thoughts and others carried the barge the rest of the way downstream to the docks and, without any further ado, Ninetoes and his party made their farewells, paid up their bill and headed into town.

The area around the dock was a combination of taverns, inns and warehouses, so they didn't hang around longer than it took to locate Tally's Troll and agree to meet there if they were split up, then they headed uphill towards the castle.

Bess, as the only member of the party to have visited the city before, was their de facto guide, but this didn't mean she needed to talk to Ninetoes and instead, she kept her strides long and maintained a short gap between herself and the Adventurers, uttering not a word. To all intents and purposes she could be just another traveller, someone who had nothing to do with the strange band of goblinoids.

A half an hour later they reached the main gate through the castle's curtain walls and into the outer bailey. Their journey had taken them through mostly residential districts, but Ninetoes had taken note of the market square they passed through and how to get back to it.

The hobgoblin's eyes had been on stalks, he simply couldn't take in the wonders that surrounded him quickly enough to compute and, by the time they'd reached the castle, his mind was exhausted. Of course, he did his best not to allow any of this to show on his face, he didn't want anyone to consider him a bumpkin.

The castle itself was a little lacklustre to Ninetoes' eyes. The castle in Kavralach had been far larger, although he hadn't taken the opportunity to explore more than just the keep. But this castle also showed signs of wear and unrepaired damage that the ancient keep simply didn't have, even after sitting unused for untold centuries.

He didn't know much about the human city, except that rather than having a single ruler or leader, they had a Council who made their decisions, much like the Krem of his own people did. The difference here however, seemed to be that rather than the meritocracy that guided his people, Pamor's leaders were chosen by popular vote, a system that Bess had told him was desperately corrupt and, by the state of their castle, he could well imagine it to be true. Nonetheless, this was to be their first stop. He wouldn't fail his Quest because he refused to ask the Council for help.

The boorish and dirty walls of the castle disappeared off in both directions before a circular tower rounded at each end stopped the castle before it fell of the cliff.

Ahead a large gate broke up the monotonous wall. It was shut, but a small door within the gate itself was wide open and was flanked by two grizzly-looking guards who, in opposition to the state of their surroundings, looked capable and dangerous. Both of them were humans and wore half plate armour that shone in the morning light. They held wide-bladed spears and shields and wore shortswords at their hips. All of this equipment also gave a slight gleam of magic. The only difference between the two was the contrast in ages, the one on the right clearly outdated the other by at least a couple of decades.

"Hold. State your business," the one on the left commanded.

As had become the norm, Ninetoes expected Bess to allow him to take the lead, but instead she stepped forward and spoke in a slightly wavering voice. "We are from Raveslan. Our town is threatened by an army of goblins and we come seeking aid from the Council of Pamor."

"Raveslan? That don't fall within our lands," the guard on the right answered.

"Nonetheless, we seek entrance to the castle and the chance to speak with the Council."

"As you say luv. Head on in to the left, enter the green door and speak to the Seneschal, he'll put you on the docket for today-"

"If you're lucky," chipped in Lefty.

"—aye, if you're lucky, and he'll give you a signal stone. Don't lose it mind, or you'll have to start all over."

"Thank you. We go left, you say?" Bess checked, clearly still nervous.

"Er, just you miss. Your-um, bodyguards will have to stay out here," Righty said, eyeing up Bluzag cautiously. Bess, for the first time since their argument, looked at Ninetoes. Concern written across her face.

"It's fine Bess, just be sure to include all we know and, well, you'll need to take the prisoner." Bess' face flushed bright red and her mouth began to open and close without words coming out. Recognising the smith was out of her element, Ninetoes stepped in.

"My good man?" He addressed the guard on the right.

"Aye." The guard's response was much more gruff when responding to the hobgoblin.

"This woman is our prisoner. She was taken in the goblins' first attack." He chose, much as Bess had clearly done, not to mention the fact that it was a *hob*-goblin army, but the presence of Vortiga was clearly enough for the two men to put the pieces together, if the looks on their faces were anything to go on.

"Oh aye and what're you? Her jailor?"

"Of a sort. I am Ninetoes, a wizard and Adventurer. I was given the Quest to escort this young woman," he gestured towards Bess, "and to deliver this prisoner to the Council. The prisoner is to be interrogated, she may know much about the enemy's plans."

"Oh aye." Was the guard's only response.

But by now, Bess had regained her composure. "We have brought the prisoner to be locked up and as proof of what we say."

"Harrumph, reckon you best go with her Todds. Go see the Seneschal and then take this one down to the dungeons." Righty commander the other guard, who then stepped forward to take the rope tied to Vortiga's manacles. Ninetoes mentally commanded Bluzag to pass it over and sighed quietly in relief. At least that part of the ordeal was over.

The younger guard led Vortiga and Bess into the castle walls and then disappeared. "Reckon they'll be a while. You'd best step back so that other people can get passed," stated the guard.

Ninetoes, having been about to question the guard on what he thought the likelihood was that the Council would agree to help, was momentarily confused about what to do and, when he didn't immediately comply, Righty raised his shield and said, in a far more commanding tone, "Step back please." Although the courtesy was nothing more than perfunctory.

Ninetoes quickly retreated, commanding Bluzag to do the same and, with nothing better to do, made his way over to a vendor standing on a nearby street corner.

The salesman had a small, canopied cart with a stuck pig turning above roasting coals. Beneath the coals was a long, iron oven, from within which the hobgoblin could smell baking bread. The smells were mind-alteringly good and so Ninetoes hastily joined a short queue of customers.

The vendor would remove a still piping hot bread roll from the oven in a thickly gloved hand and expertly slice it along its length, before stuffing it full of roasted pork that dripped with fat and gravy. On a small counter to the side were pots of sauces and shoppers were spreading copious amounts of them onto their food before moving off.

Once it was his turn, Ninetoes requested one for himself, his mouth already watering in anticipation. The vendor politely asked, "What about yer friend? He not hungry?"

At first Ninetoes considered an excuse, but the food smelled so good that he decided he'd treat himself, without anyone needing to know he'd been a glutton. "Yes of course, another please."

After slathering apple sauce generously over both, he took his two sandwiches and retreated to a small grassy area nearby and sat beneath a tree eating his first and, when he was pretty sure no one was looking, the second sandwich as well. They were utterly delicious and he made a mental note to return again before they left the city.

Just as he finished his second, an outraged thought entered his mind from his previously sleeping Familiar, *Why didn't you wake me?*

You seemed so peaceful my dear.

Well, you'll just have to go and buy another then won't you? I can't not eat one now that I can feel how much you enjoyed them; it wouldn't be fair. The last part of this she offered in a mewing tone, that was most unbecoming for his little rodent warrioress, but he couldn't deny her. And another thought occurred to him and thus he returned to the vendor and ordered two more.

Sitting back on the grass, he laid Libby's sandwich on the floor next to her, but kept the other well out of the rodent's reach.

A little while later, Bess and the guard returned through the same doorway. The young woman looked a little weary and seemed grateful for his simple gift, chowing down on the sandwich and demolishing it almost as quickly as his Familiar had hers.

Once she'd finished, she spoke up. "The Seneschal promised me that we'd be heard later today and he gave me this." She held out a small, polished crystal. "He said it would light up and vibrate when they were ready for us and that we should be ready to come back to the castle when it did."

Ninetoes considered the item and a quick casting of Identify revealed little more than the young woman had reported.

SIGNAL STONE - WORN, COMMON
PROPERTIES: THIS SIGNAL STONE IS MAGICALLY CONNECTED TO A SIGNAL GRID, WHEN THE GRID IS ACTIVATED, IT WILL CAUSE THE STONE TO GIVE OFF A FAINT BLUE LIGHT AND VIBRATE GENTLY.

Still, it was interesting for Ninetoes to see that such an item was so commonplace amongst the humans that they would literally give them away. Amongst his people only Elder Brev had anything magical. At least as far as Ninetoes was aware.

"Very well, in that case, what do you want to do until we are summoned?" he asked.

"I'd like to go to the Guildhouse to Take my Tools, but I think that will take longer than we might have and, once it begins, the testing cannot stop."

"Hmmm, well Bluzag and I have a need to repair and upgrade some of our gear and the market district isn't far from here, perhaps we should go shopping?"

"Mmmm, I had been wanting to find something to wear other than my leathers, let's do it." Bess seemed to have perked up and, since he hadn't had to apologise to change her mood, Ninetoes counted it as a win.

"Excellent!" With that they began marching off towards the market square that they'd passed through on their way to the castle.

Despite the threadbare and piecemeal quality of his clothes and gear, Ninetoes was in fact an extremely wealthy hobgoblin, having secured a King's ransom in gold, jewellery and coin from the ruins of the goblinoid camp that encircled Kavralach. He had an idea for most of the treasure however, he planned to present it to his people before leading them triumphantly back to the ruins of Kavralach and giving his kin a new home and, more importantly a new fortress to keep them safe. All the more important now that they were under threat once again.

But that, of course, didn't mean that he couldn't spend some on himself. He did, after all, have to survive and succeed in his current Quest or his village wouldn't survive for him to return to. He would see the Nechtsarm army destroyed and keep his people safe. Thus, as the party neared the shopping district, Ninetoes mentally made a list of things he'd like to find.

Now, what Ninetoes would have liked to do first was buy some more spells to add to his Spellbook or magical items to enhance his growing powers. But what he really needed to buy first was some new clothes. His own, while freshly cleaned, were becoming worn and damaged from his new life as an Adventurer. Bluzag's were even worse. The clothes had been rags *before* Bofar burned a large hole through his chest. Worse still, the undead body itself had begun to rot which only worsened the whole situation.

With an undisclosed amount of time before they'd be called back to the Council Ninetoes figured that clothes shopping would be the safest and most appropriate choice.

It didn't take the small party long to find a large store that advertised, amongst other assorted items, racks of clothes that catered for all sizes and races. Honestly, it seemed a little convenient to Ninetoes, especially when he didn't even recognise some of the races mentioned by the sign, but it served his purposes so he didn't question it for long.

Instead, after agreeing to meet Bess at the door in half an hour, Ninetoes led his Wight into the depths of the clothing racks in search of the 'Big and Tall' section. Within a dozen minutes, Bluzag's beefy arms were holding a pile with two shirts, two pairs of trousers, a cloak and a new pair of boots, all appropriately sized for the half-ogre's towering frame.

For himself, Ninetoes decided he'd replace his entire wardrobe and selected some hard-wearing trousers and dark-coloured shirts. All of this was cheaply priced as he had never been particularly bothered about his appearance. That was, however, until he'd spotted a dark green, crushed velvet waistcoat displayed on a mannequin. Checking the price tag he noted that it was ten gold. The single piece was ten times more expensive than all the other clothing he'd selected! It was an outrageous sum.

But he bought it anyway.

The weather had been getting colder and wetter of late and so Ninetoes prepared for the winter ahead and so also bought pairs of thick socks and two pairs of long johns. Finally, he bought a long, waxed coat. While it was unattractive and held none of the potent magic of his Sorcerer's Travel Cloak, it would keep him dry.

As he paid, he questioned the clerk about where he might be able to repair the damage his cloak had suffered. The young halfling girl apologised, saying that they were unable to repair magical items but to seek out the magical item shop across the square.

Ninetoes still had a little time left until he was due to meet Bess, so he headed back into the store and changed into his new attire. Having Bluzag do the same simply wasn't possible as there was too much likelihood that someone would notice his undead nature, so the hobgoblin stowed the rest of their goods in his bag of holding and made for the exit.

Bluzag was definitely starting to smell, but thankfully the city's own stink covered this up for the most part. Ninetoes would certainly need to find a way to remedy this in the future, but he had more important things to worry about for the time being.

He didn't have long to wait before a now smartly dressed Bess made her way to him, a smile plastered across her face. She was positively striking in her new clothing. She still wore trousers and a shirt but they were no longer the hand-me-downs she'd worn up until now, rather they were form fitting and accentuated her toned and powerful physique.

"I also bought a dress, but I'll likely never get to use it, the boys in Raveslan don't like being towered over." Her face was flushed and her cheeks rosy and her excited pleasure brought a smile to the Adventurer's face. Revelling in her delight Ninetoes stood tall and proffered his arm.

"Mi'lady," he added. Bess giggled and slipped her arm through the crook of his elbow.

"Where shall we dine my dear?" She asked in a posh and snooty voice.

"A good question." Ninetoes attempted a similar intonation but he wasn't sure he pulled it off. He also didn't know anything about Pamor. Instead he scanned the square for somewhere nearby, his eyes alighting on a small tavern of some kind a little ways off and he steered Bess towards it. "Here looks acceptable my de-", but before he could finish the thought, he felt a slight vibration coming from Bess' pocket and as he looked down he could see that the pocket was pulsing with blue light.

"Alas, it looks as though we've been called by the Council," she said, as she disentangled her arm from his and removed the glowing stone from her pocket. "We'd best make our way to the Castle."

Their moment of play had passed and they were snapped unceremoniously back to the Quest at hand.

A short walk brought them back to the same gate and the same two guards. "Back so soon miss?" asked Lefty. In response Bess simply opened her hand to reveal the flashing stone that sat in the palm of her hand. "Very good miss, please follow me. I'm afraid your bodyguards will have to remain here again though."

This time Bess was prepared for the guards and she straightened her shoulders and replied. "They are not my bodyguards. Well, not only my bodyguards. They are the Adventurers who helped to defend Raveslan and we are on a Quest to seek aid. It is perhaps even more essential that they speak to the Council than I do."

The two guards exchanged a brief look, then Righty nodded. "You'll have to leave your weapons here with us," he said, pointing to a weapon rack that sat beyond the doorway.

Ninetoes saw no reason to argue and so Bess and Bluzag left their weapons and shields. Without his cutlass, Ninetoes didn't bother. His dagger however, was a powerful magical item, and he would not so easily leave it lying around for someone to pinch. Instead, while the guards stored the other weapons, Ninetoes stowed the knife in his Bag of Holding. Luckily, the items seemed rare enough that neither guard took notice of it.

A few minutes later, the party found themselves sitting on a row of wooden benches in a waiting area. Two large doors stood closed, flanked by another two guards. These doors, Ninetoes assumed, led to the Council chambers. Indeed, he could hear the murmur of raised voices beyond.

Despite the haste with which they'd responded to the Signal Stone's summons, they still sat waiting for another hour before one of the doors opened and a boy in Castle livery read Bess' name from a scroll of parchment and hailed them onwards.

The room beyond was long and richly furnished. It was dominated by a large table that ran along its very centre. The piece was polished to a high sheen and despite being somewhat covered by books, piles of parchment and a scattering of food plates, it still shone with a faint magical light.

Around the table sat nine people. A plump, balding halfling sat alone at the far end, the seat of which had been built to accommodate his absent height.

Along each side of the table sat four more people. The left side held four humans, a younger woman and three greying men, while the right-hand side was made up of a male and female dwarf, another aging halfling man and... well, Ninetoes wasn't quite sure what the last man was. He was slimmer and taller than the dwarves and gnomes, but clearly shorter than the humans across the table. He had long black hair that was brushed behind two pointed ears. He'd only seen one of their kind before, but he reckoned that this man was an elf.

Every person around the table was dressed in fine clothes and had a pampered look to them, but those on the right-hand side of the table displayed their wealth openly with thick golden necklaces or bejewelled rings. All accept the elf, who wore simple but richly made attire.

Without pausing, the page led them from the door to the closest end of the table. This end had no chairs and so the party was left to stand, as the page darted off along the left flank of the table before seating himself at a small writing table on the balding halfling's right.

At a nod from the halfling, the boy cleared his voice and spoke up. "Miss Elizabeth Tailor of Raveslan seeks an audience with the esteemed Council of Pamor to request aid for their town. She is joined by the Adventurers Bluzag and... Ninetoes?" he finished, making a face at the hobgoblin's moniker.

"Very well," responded the halfling in a voice that conveyed his wealth and boredom all in merely two words. "Well, go on then," he added in a bark, when Bess didn't speak.

"Oh, er, sorry," she stuttered out. "Yer see, Raveslan's under attack... from hobgoblins," she added after a short pause.

"Yes. And?" Ninetoes was swiftly forming a less than positive opinion of this tiny oaf. He didn't look at Bess as he said this, instead his attention was focussed on his nails as he polished them.

"And, well we'd like Pamor's help."

"Obviously. This much we learned from the page. Don't you have anything else to say girl?" This time it was the dwarven woman who spoke. Her face was a crumpled mess of age and too much colour. Hobgoblin woman didn't colour their faces, but Ninetoes had noticed the practice since arriving in town. This dwarf apparently thought she could hide her wrinkles behind a thick layer of paint.

Ninetoes looked over to Bess. The poor girl's cheeks were burning red with embarrassment and so, despite not having been invited to, he chose to speak up. "A force of hundreds of Nechtsarm hobgoblins are marching eastwards through the lands to the south. Their Light Company has already reached and assaulted Raveslan, some four days ago and, despite turning back the initial assault, captive hobgoblins have confirmed that the main force will reach and intends to attack the town within six days, perhaps less."

"Oh ho ho. And it's a hobgoblin that brings us this news is it? I smell a rat." This time it was one of the humans who spoke up, this one with a strange triple scar running the length of his left cheek. Despite this feature, he was a handsome and fit-looking man in fine robes.

"But hobgoblin or no, he is an Adventurer Lord Pascoe, surely we can trust his word?" the younger woman asked. She was a plain looking woman with slightly buck teeth, but she spoke with the elocution of the affluent. Certainly, her dress alone was of a finery that spoke only of the most superfluous wealth.

The table of councillors meanwhile were laughing uproariously at the perceived joke. Ninetoes boiled slightly at the insult but then noticed the blush creeping up the woman's cheeks and realised that she hadn't intended the comment in mockery. He took note of this, perhaps she could be an ally.

"Ninetoes is not with the other hobgoblins. In fact, he fought against them at the first battle. What's more, he brought us word of the larger, impending attack."

As soon as she said it, Bess went quiet, clearly realising her mistake. The Council had already shown that they distrusted the hobgoblin and now, she'd all but confirmed that he had insider knowledge of their whereabouts and plans.

"Ah and there we have it. Evidently this goblin is a plant. Probably sent to scare these poor plebs into leaving the safety of their town and thus this goblinoid rabble, if indeed it actually exists, can stroll straight in and take the town without a fight. Such a gambit of course couldn't hope to work against Pamor, but for these bumkins, it has clearly proved effective," the same human, Lord Pascoe, verbalised Ninetoes' fear and, by the nods of agreement from many of those present, it seemed that things were quickly worsening.

"No! The prisoner," called out Bess hastily. "She can confirm everything we've said and hopefully provide more detail."

Many of those present chose that moment to study a parchment before them or look out the window. All except the elven man and the human woman, who both turned to look at the balding halfling at the head of the table. When he didn't respond to the unsaid request, the elf spoke up. "Master Gruffudd. The page made no mention of a prisoner."

A look of annoyance crossed the halfling's face and he stared back at the elf, a look of innocence painted onto his pudgy face. "Ah. Yes, I can see it here in the seneschal's notes, my apologies, it has been a busy morning thus far," he simpered. Turning on the page, however, his tone became a cold wrath. "If you ever want to be anything more than a messenger, you'd better remember to detail everything you're told boy!"

"But you said-" uttered the boy, looking up from his note-taking.

"Never mind what I said. What I'm telling you now is to instruct the Guard to bring us the prisoner that was brought in this morning by Miss Tailor here-"

"And perhaps we should have Master Aseir summoned as well," suggested the elf.

"—eh? Yes yes. Summon the mage as well boy. Well, hop to it!"

The boy snapped to attention and bolted off through another door further up the room.

"Now, while we wait, are there any of those honeyed pastries left; I'm famished?"

Ninetoes was of the opinion that Master Gruffudd had never been famished in his life. He chose not to air this point of view, however. Instead he waited in silence as the time they needed to save Raveslan and his home slipped steadily away.

CHAPTER 15
OF GREED AND FOOLS

PORTSMOUTH, 2017

"…and the monstrous things are eating all my grain, all I need is for some brave Adventurers to-"

"Ergh! Let me stop you there Bruce. We're not doing another crappy giant rats Quest. We're bored of this shit. Give us summut better to do," demanded Tony.

"It's dire rats actually and I'm sorry but at your level the module has only these low-level Quests available. If we had more players we could perhaps—"

"No! We're fine with the four of us, right gang?" Tony didn't wait for a response. He didn't want to have to share the loot or experience points with any more weirdos. "But come on Bruce, you're the GM, can't you just jump ahead a little bit? Or make something up?" This was part of the reason that Tony preferred tabletop gaming to playing video games, there weren't the same constraints or limitations.

"I'm sorry, the book is quite clear, the player characters must reach level-"

"Argh! Who cares what the book says? Just let us at it, I'll bet it'll be a cakewalk for us," he challenged, gesturing towards the other players for support.

The rest of the group had been quiet to this point. This wasn't the first time Tony had made this particular argument. But finally, Solveg spoke up. "Bruce, we understand that you're trying to run the module as written and we really appreciate all the hard work and time you spend preparing, don't we Tony?" she asked, staring daggers at him.

"Wha? Oh yeah. Thanks Bruce," he answered with a disingenuous smile and a double thumbs up for extra zest.

"Anyway. What if we went back to the Pamorian Adventurer's Guild; surely they have more difficult Quests advertised?" Solveg asked in a much more reasonable tone than Tony had.

"Wellllll, yes I suppose that's true. But those Quests are also level-locked."

"But within the context of Adrenon, the people aren't going to be so fixed in their understanding. Perhaps we could try to persuade Commander Swiftaxe to give us something more challenging?"

"I suppose." Solveg grinned and Bruce visibly blushed. "But it would be a difficult Persuasion check."

"Oh of course, of course, but my character has a massive boost to Persuasion and he can cast Charisma," Tony boasted.

"Excellent, then it's all on you then Ton, and if you fail we'll just come back to the brewer's to kill dire rats," Solveg said. Placing the glory onto Tony. Of course, it didn't occur to the arrogant and foolish brute that this also meant that any failure was all his as well.

***

Master Aseir, it turned out, was a human of Island descent. At least as far as Ninetoes could tell. He'd only ever met the fair-skinned humans of Raveslan and they all had the same blond and red hair. But this man was taller and slimmer, his skin was a rich mahogany and his hair was jet black. Above his lip, which was currently curled into an impatient sneer, was a thin moustache of the same colour.

He wore long, heavy-looking robes and carried a staff with a crystal affixed to its top and, while Ninetoes couldn't find a spellbook anywhere upon the man's person, he noted that spiralling the length of the staff's shaft were hundreds of runes carved right into the wood. Could he be a Wizard then? Perhaps the diviner that Foresto spoke of.

"So, what need do you have of me Gruffudd?" The man's visage might have marked him as a foreigner, but his use of the common tongue was impeccable and revealed that he must have lived within the Sweetsea region for a long time.

"*Master* Gruffudd," reminded the pouting halfling. "And we have a need for your magical services. Ah, here is the prisoner now." So saying, he gestured as the double doors opened behind the party and a pair of guards guided Vortiga into the room.

The Sarm was now chained at both wrist and ankle, with another chain linking the pairs of manacles. "If these people are to be believed, this goblin holds important information about an attack on our lands. You are instructed to search her mind for the truth of it." Then, at the raised eyebrows of the dark-skinned mage, added. "Please."

"Of course," acknowledged Aseir. "While I prepare, perhaps your page could arrange some chairs."

Nodding at the young lad, the halfling silently instructed the boy into action. The boy, who had clearly done so before, quickly pulled two chairs from the side of the room and placed them so that they faced one another, a few inches of space between them.

"Guards, seat the prisoner here," Aseir commanded, taking the other seat and then, once Vortiga was seated opposite him spoke quietly to the hobgoblin. "I warn you, this will hurt only if you resist. The outcome however, will be the same, whether you do so or not." From his tone, it didn't seem that this was meant as a threat, rather a simple statement of fact.

Holding his stave upright in his left hand, he reached out his right to Vortiga's temple, touching her gently with only the very tips of his fingers. Bound as she was, Vortiga could do nothing to stop him.

Under his breath he muttered the words of an incantation, which from its length alone, Ninetoes could tell was a powerful spell indeed.

Meanwhile, certain runes on his staff lit up with a bright white light. At a hunch, Ninetoes engaged his Mind's Eye skill and, sure enough, strands of light curled up from the staff, through Aseir's arm until they entered at the nape of his neck and exited again from the mage's eyes. From here, the strands leaped across to enter Vortiga's orbs. She didn't appear to be in pain, but a short struggle played across her face before Aseir spoke up again, this time his voice deep and monotonic. "The Adventurer tells the truth. At least as far as this woman believes. An army of five hundred hobgoblin Warriors marches from the west and are raiding their way eastward. This one was the commander of the skirmishers and took the risk of attacking the town of Raveslan in the hopes of winning glory and securing resources for her people. Although, hmmm… while the town is certainly a target, it is not their final destination. Rather their forces are struggling to find enough food and so seek to use the town as a staging ground for a much richer target."

This was news to Ninetoes. Destroying his village could be an important goal for the Nechtsarm, but it was by no means a *richer* target than the human settlement. His torture of the ba'ardec soldier had been brief, but he'd believed what the hob had said to be true. Could Vortiga be fooling the mage somehow? And if she was, why? But the look of surprise and confusion that briefly fled across Vortiga's face made it clear she wasn't trying to mislead anyone. The mage had access to all her secrets.

That was when Ninetoes caught it however, a short-lived exchange that passed between the mage's eyes and those of the elven man sat at the end of the table. Ninetoes didn't know what it meant, but he'd keep his wits about him and reached for his blade to keep it loose in its- *Argh! I must replace my sword!*

As Ninetoes scanned the Council's members however, the effect of the mage's words was much more significant and almost instantaneous. Faces across the table blanched as the blood drained. Ninetoes recognised the cold hard look of fear as it washed over much of the Council.

With a sneer, he also noticed that all those on the right-hand side of the table, save for the elf, reached up to a neck adorned with a necklace, or tucked a hand decorated with precious stones beneath the table. It was clear that, although the mage hadn't said the words, every person at the table had assumed the same thing; the 'richer target' must mean Pamor.

Was this mage bending the meaning of Vortiga's thoughts? If he was, then Ninetoes chose to keep quiet. The mage may or may not be trying to help, but he hoped that his odd choice of words might help their cause.

"Gods. Five hundred you say? We have barely two hundred men at arms!" Finally, the silence was broken, the ancient-looking man to Gruffud's right speaking up, his voice parchment thin and wavering as he began panicking.

"And the harvest is being transported into the City as we speak. If we're besieged we'll be unable to sell it on, we'll lose hundreds of gold in profit." This came from the weaselly-sounding voice of the other halfling.

"Now now, my friends, we shouldn't be hasty. This could still be a ru-" Lord Pascoe started, only to be interrupted by the other elderly human.

"What? A 'ruse' Jory? Aseir's magic has already verified the truth of the matter. We must close the city gates and turn out the militia. Run these vermin down I say. Kill them all!" Each councillor's fear seemed to charge on the next until the table's polished surface reflected only the pale white faces of horror and alarm.

All except the female dwarf, who's face, while showing signs of concern, also held eyes that schemed as she spoke up. "Aye! I agree with Lord Chenoweth, we should equip the militia and have them on the walls as soon as—"

"Ha! Of course you'd say that Adaira, it's your forges that'll turn out the spearheads and helms and your pockets that'll be filled," the other dwarf cut her off.

"Oh! An' ah suppose you'll not offer to feed this army eh?" she countered, avarice playing across her face.

The halfling, sensing an opportunity also chipped in. "Well, of course if such an army is to be equipped, Daffyd's Goods and Chattels will supply the-"

"How can you all think of profit at a time like this?" Her voice was quiet but clear and, despite being edged in fear, it grabbed the attention of all present. "People will die. They might already be dying in Raveslan and the only action you people can conceive of is to turn it to your benefit?" The young woman's face showed only open disgust. "House Fawkner will not support any course of action that is simply about lining your grubby little pockets. I propose we raise an army from the standing men at arms or hire an army of Adventurers and send them to wipe out this scourge. House Fawkner can raise a Fifty alone."

"Adventurers?" Replied the halfling incredulously. This Ninetoes assumed, was Daffyd. "It would be cheaper to let these goblins sack the city!"

"Aye and ye cannae bet it won't be our *noble* houses footin' the bill neither," chipped in the dwarven man, heavily emphasizing the word 'noble'.

"The city is wealthy, perhaps the richest on the Sweetsea, surely the treasury can afford to raise an army?" the lady responded incredulously.

"An' where d'ya think all that wealth comes from *Lady* Fawkner? It ain't them that live in the Castle Ward, I can tell ye, it's us wot's had te work for it!" This from the female dwarf, Adaira, was met by a chorus of agreement from the others sitting on the table's right side.

Ninetoes however, had been watching the elf and the silent conversation that he seemed to be holding with the mage. At a nod from Adeir, the elf spoke up.

"I think we can all agree that while such an undertaking would be costly, a siege would be far more damaging to our interests in the long run. Better to strike first no? While these hobgoblins are hungry and without a proper base." For a moment this quietened the councillors.

That perhaps, was why Gruffud, who, much like Ninetoes, had been silently studying those present, chose that moment to enter the debate. "Of course you are correct Rael my boy and, were your mother still here I'm sure it would warm her heart to hear you speak with such sense and clarity, never a shrewder woman have I met than the lovely Elin, she was

295

our father's pride and joy." He smiled at the young man whose racial origins Ninetoes could now only guess at. "And I agree with Mera as well, we must of course raise every soldier, household guard and scrapper the city has to offer. All of the noble houses I am sure would be willing to empty their barracks to protect our great city and of course every merchant company would be happy to spend their gold to see it equipped and resourced."

Rather than the rush of agreement that Ninetoes had hoped for, the table was instead quiet and looks of growing concern were replaced by ones of tacit contemplation. Looking down the length of the table, Ninetoes could see a greedy smile splitting Gruffud's plumpish face.

"Wait. 'Empty our barracks'? But-" Stuttered Lord Pascoe.

"Of course, Lord Pascoe. There is nothing to be gained from sending a force too small to be effective. We must send every fighter we can, guards and dockworkers, swine herders and smiths, every man that can carry a spear should be sent."

"Swine Herders?" questioned the dwarven man. "But surely some should be exempt. I mean this army would need to be fed."

"Certainly, it must be every man. Who would be left to feed if this army should fail?"

"But... who? That is to say, surely we should leave a force to defend the city. I would be honoured for my own household troops to perform such a duty," offered Lord Pascoe.

"A generous offer, your lordship," said Gruffud, his face now a mask of concern and gratitude. "Very well, then I propose a vote."

"Seconded," said Lady Fawkner eagerly. But Ninetoes, who saw the look of defeat on Rael's strangely fey-like face, realised that the vote would not go as she or he hoped.

"Very good. All those in favour of raising an army of *all the able-bodied* men and, I suppose women-" Gruffud added, looking directly at Adaira, "-please say raise your hands."

Lady Fawkner and, unsurprisingly, Rael raised their hands. Then, a moment later, Gruffud himself raised his own. "All those against." The rest of the Council raised their chubby, frail or gaudy hands above their heads.

"Hmmm, a surprise of course, but the Council has voted, Pamor will not raise an army to assault the hobgoblins. May I suggest instead that we send a commission to Raveslan to offer them refuge here in the city?"

Damnit! It was exactly how Caillic had said it would be. They'd have to head to the Adventurer's Guild.

"A Commission?" stuttered out Bess. "But...what good could that possibly do? If you don't help, there will not be anyone left to accept your offer."

"The girl is correct. My people will sack the town. They will murder everyone capable of holding a sword and make the rest into slaves." To everyone's surprise it was Vortiga who offered this insight.

While Ninetoes recognised that this wasn't completely true, and that he could use Foresto's communication scroll to evacuate the town, it was still a massive blow. The hobgoblins would leave nothing of value behind. For the people of Raveslan, it would be like starting all over again. They'd be ruined.

"A dire situation indeed," responded Gruffud solemnly. "But one that could have been avoided of course, had Raveslan accepted our generous offer of patronage and protection two harvests ago," he finished, to an assembly of nodding heads on both sides of the table.

"Generous?" Bess' voice was reed thin with shock. "You demanded fifty per cent from everything we sent to market." Tears filled her eyes as she spoke. "You are all cowards," she finished quietly.

Most of the councillors looked away from the unseemly display. All except Lady Fawkner and Rael who both had the good grace to look extremely uncomfortable and ashamed and Gruffud who stared back at the young woman, daring her to go on.

"You need not return Miss Tailor. You could find work here, perhaps take service in one of the noble houses or perhaps work at the docks."

Her cheeks, which had turned pink with embarrassment, now lost all colour as she stared back at the rotund little man. "No. I will return home.

And I'll fight alongside my friends and, if it's my fate, I'll die beside them." Her voice grew in confidence as she spoke, until she was all but growling as she finished. Her eyes never left Gruffud's.

"You will not return alone my dear. I will lead the Commission and fight beside you," spoke up Lady Fawkner, her voice quavering with passion.

"Mera no! It's too-" But whatever it was or was not, Rael never got the chance to finish saying before he was interrupted.

"The motion is raised for Lady Mera Fawkner to lead the Commission to Raveslan, do I hear it seconded?" Gruffud spoke smoothly and quickly, looking at Lord Pascoe as he did so.

"Seconded," barked up the scarred noble.

"Very well, all those in favour?" Every hand but Rael's flew into the air.

"Against?" The man's arm barely passed his shoulders, despite how slumped they were.

"The motion is carried. Lady Fawkner will journey back to Raveslan with Miss Elizabeth Tailor to offer refuge to any survivors. Are you getting all this down boy?"

"Yes Master," the page replied as he hurriedly finished his notes.

"Word for word?"

"Of course, Master."

"Good. After your mistake earlier I am seriously considering some lashes," Gruffud warned.

"Yes Master," said the crestfallen young man.

"There's no need for that Master Gruffud. I am honoured to travel to Raveslan," offered Lady Fawkner.

"Very well. I think that's enough business for now. Jory, will you join me for lunch?" And with that, the Councillors stood and began heading for one of the far doors. Already their conversations had moved on, Raveslan's plight all but forgotten.

While Caillic had warned Ninetoes that this would happen, the experience left him feeling hollowed out nonetheless. Monsters and danger, he knew what he was doing, but in this arena, he'd been woefully unprepared. He wasn't sure exactly how it had happened, but the Council of Pamor had just signed Raveslan's execution order and they'd done it with a smile. Ninetoes could only hope that their back up plan of hiring Adventurers would pay off.

As he turned to collect Bess and leave, however, his eyes locked with Vortiga's. The Sarm wore an expression similar to his own; disgust. She and her people might be the sworn enemy of his own, but at least they treated each other with respect and honour.

In that moment, Ninetoes felt rancid. He'd consigned Vortiga to a coward's death. Whatever else she might be, she was a Warrior. What's more, she'd had his life in her hands twice. Twice she'd been able to kill him in his sleep but she hadn't taken that choice.

Maybe, a stray thought said, she just didn't have the chance, or perhaps she just doesn't consider you a threat. But Ninetoes knew that wasn't it. Vortiga was cunning enough to recognise Ninetoes as a problem she needed to tackle, but she hadn't taken the easy option. No, she'd treated him as a Warrior.

And now? What could he do for her? He could cut her down, he supposed. But that was no better a death than being hanged. Could he challenge her to a duel or something? The Council would probably enjoy such a spectacle! And it would only serve to confirm that prejudices.

But no, he didn't have any time to spare and if he was honest, he probably couldn't win a fight without his magic. She'd die with a blade in her hand perhaps but it would be a false death, there could be no such honour in it. For her or him.

The guards brought Vortiga to her feet and began heading for the door. His chance to do anything would soon be gone. Could he? Could he give her a chance to escape? Even were she to fail, wouldn't there be some honour in dying trying to escape?

"Come on you," said one of the guards, tugging at Vortiga's chains.

But how? What could he even do? Ninetoes' hand rested, slipped into his bag and a stray thought summoned his elven dagger. It was a fine weapon, although too slender for a true Warrior's hand. He'd often considered it to have been made for a woman's hand.

"Hold a moment." Ninetoes stepped forward.

"Yeah? Wot?" The guards paused.

"This… filth. She's getting off too easy for my tastes. You mind if I give her something to remember me by?"

Charisma wasn't a spell that he'd ever had cause to cast before, but he felt the warm feeling in his chest of a Skill level earned as he did, so he reckoned it had taken. At the same time, he'd offered his hand to the guards, upon which sat two fat gold coins.

The right-hand guard barely even looked him in the eye as he snatched up the treasure and guided his fellow guard off to one side, showing their backs to the hobgoblins. "One minute and don't make a mess."

Pleased with his success, Ninetoes was temporarily taken aback by the look of revulsion he found waiting on Vortiga's face. "Ergh! A porsht after all. I should've slit your throat when I had the chance."

With little time to waste, Ninetoes stepped straight up into her space and headbutted her in the face.

CRACK! *Gods that felt good.*

Vortiga's head snapped back, but she wasn't stunned for long. It didn't matter however, it was all the time he needed. Stepping in as close as a lover, Ninetoes grabbed the waistline of her trousers with one hand and stuffed in the knife with the other. He finished the move by pulling the oversized shirt down to cover the bulge.

The Sarm stared back at Ninetoes and for the first time, seemed genuinely astonished by what she'd witnessed. He enjoyed her amazement. It would make the next bit easier. "Porsht, hmm. I'm growing to like that name" he said out loud. "This will help you hide it." He leaned in to whisper. The smile that followed reached up to his eyes.

Stepping forward again, he slammed his fist into Vortiga's gut. The hobgoblin's legs buckled from beneath her and she slumped to the floor, although it was unclear if he'd actually hurt her or if she was in on the gambit.

"Tha's enough." The guards had turned back and were grinning at the state of their prisoner. Stepping over, each lifted Vortiga under an armpit and dragged her towards the door. Neither seemed any the wiser of his ruse.

Ninetoes' eyes tracked his enemy as she passed out of the room and was sure he caught a tiniest hint of a toothy smile.

**

"What was that?" Bess blustered at Ninetoes.

"Nothing more than she deserved," he responded, attempting and failing to hide his own smile.

"What's the matter with you? Why're you smiling?" Bess had already been in tears and Ninetoes' attitude seemed likely to tip her over the edge.

"You're right, I'm sorry. It's just-"

"Adventurers. Miss Tailor. Please let me introduce myself, I am Lady Meraud Fawkner, but please just call me Mera." The young woman couldn't have been much older than Bess and she must have been a couple of feet shorter, but nonetheless her very presence demanded attention.

"Lady Fawkner, this is Bess, my companion Bluzag and I am Ninetoes." He responded as formally as he could.

"So that wasn't a joke, that is actually your name? Does it have something to do with your feet?" she asked, a playful grin creasing her face.

"Er-".

"Yes, it really is, but he's a little sensitive about it." Bess, who seemed to have brightened somewhat, filled in where the apprentice wizard had failed. Lady Fawkner snorted like a mule in response. Added to the slightly horsey shape of her face, it was all Ninetoes could do, not to laugh. But for Bess, whose day had already held so much sadness, it broke a dam and she barked with laughter at the woman's equine guffaw, only to instantly catch herself.

301

"Oh, my Lady, I'm so sorry, I didn't mean to laugh at you, I mean that is I-" she stared aghast and tears once again threatened to fall down her cheeks.

"Ah ha, he he. Elizabeth, think nothing of it. Alas wealth brings many advantages and sadly one of those is a house filled with all too many mirrors! I know what it looks like when I laugh. Even my father, gods rest his soul, used to call me his Little Nag. Although I'll never know if it was my face or how I used to harass him so. *He'd* never have let those cowards leave your people undefended and the Council is a poorer place in his absence."

"No my Lady, you tried to stand up to them. You are not a coward like them," Bess offered weakly.

"Ha! And look at the good it's done. I'll be honest with you my dear, this Commission will be of little help; if what the hobgoblins said was true?" This finally seemed to direct the conversation back to Ninetoes, so he chose to step in.

"Indeed it is my Lady. Many Hobgoblins consider everything spoils of war, including taking slaves. Although, adversely, few hobgoblins keep slaves. Unless you count goblins, and believe me, my people do not," he answered, before asking his own question. "My Lady, if as you say your Commission is unlikely to help; why risk the journey? The way is dangerous and I cannot promise you your safety," he ended brutally, hoping at least to dissuade the noble woman to join his Quest. He already needed to keep Bess safe and she knew how to fight! Having just got rid of Vortiga, the last thing he wanted was another problem.

"Worry not Adventurer, I will protect myself," she answered, a little steel present in her voice. "But instead, perhaps you could explain why you smuggled a knife onto the prisoner?"

Ninetoes was stunned. He'd thought himself so clever and that he'd covered himself well enough to go unnoticed. For her part Bess simply stared in horror at the hobgoblin.

"I, er... it's a matter of honour, um..."

302

"You mean it's true! Why would you do such a thing?" Truly the Lady Fawkner was adept with subtle and dangerous weapons after all and, as his constant companion Anger boiled up inside him, he found his voice once more.

"What of it could you possibly understand Bess? Or she, a Lady of Pamor? Have you ever gone without? Had to fight for anything *my Lady*?"

"Ninetoes! You can't speak to the Lady that way."

"No Bess, he's right." The use of her nickname gave Bess pause and she stared back at Lady Fawkner. "And I don't mean it to accuse you of anything Adventurer. I simply mean the question I asked, I'm interested in why you did it. She was, is, your enemy, is she not? Then why give her a weapon?"

Ninetoes, who had been allowing his anger to take control, ready to defend himself and argue with this foolish rich-girl, was once again disarmed.

Nonetheless, they were still within the Castle walls and so he chose his words carefully. "She is my enemy," he answered, but before speaking again, he turned to lock eyes with Bess. "But she is also a hobgoblin and a Warrior. Amongst my people this is no simple name or title. Not just everyone can pick up a weapon and fight. The training and trials take years and only a few are rewarded with the honour of becoming a Warrior. To become a Sarm," and at their look of confusion he added, "a Sword, er... Captain, to become a Sarm, Vortiga must have proven herself above all others. Moreover, for a woman to achieve this? Vortiga must be truly exceptional."

"So, you respect her? What's that got to do with giving her a weapon?" Bess' tone was equal parts outrage and genuine curiosity.

"The greatest glory for a Warrior is to die in battle. My people have a saying when Warriors go off to battle, 'Come back with your shield, or on it' do you understand?"

"Yeah sure, you're all so hyped up on bloodlust that you'd rather die in a glorious battle than live to see your children grow up?" Bess answered hotly.

"No Bess. It means that, for a Warrior, the safety of our people is worth more to us than our own lives. That, if you're not willing to give everything to protect them, then what was the point in fighting in the first place?" he answered.

"The Ffestynians believe the same thing you know. It's why they're such a powerful fighting force. But that doesn't totally answer my question Ninetoes; why give her a dagger?"

Ninetoes sighed. "Because for a Warrior, for Vortiga, losing her life to the hangman's noose is as bad as returning without her shield. Instead she... I, would rather die giving my all. That's why I gave her the dagger, to-"

"Let her slit her own throat?"

"No. Never that. To give her a chance at dying as a Warrior, with a blade in her hand."

"And if she kills the guards instead?" The balance in Bess' voice was gone, now it held only disdain and anger.

"Then they too will have the honour of reaching Starm's Halls," he said quietly.

"Argh!" Bess screamed and tore away from Ninetoes, storming through the Castle gates and with her went any hopes Ninetoes had of repairing their already damaged friendship.

Mentally commanding Bluzag to follow Bess and keep her safe, Ninetoes rounded on Lady Fawkner. "I assume you intend to turn me over to the Castle Guard?"

"You will watch your tone Adventurer," she said harshly, her polite and friendly tone had vanished with Bess. Now there was only a dangerous edge to her voice. "I will make the Guard aware that the hobgoblin is armed but won't mention you. Despite the Council's spineless response, I would not see Raveslan fall because of your honour," she finished. Ninetoes, feeling like a naughty child, chose not to respond.

"Well then, it seems we are to travel together. What plans have you made for your return trip?" Plain she might be, but her face held two intelligent eyes that sparkled with cunning. Clearly Mera Fawkner was more than she appeared at first glance.

"We meet the bargeman at Tally's Troll tonight and we sail tomorrow morning. Hopefully by then we'll have found someone to help," he added bitterly.

"And your next step?" she enquired, the edge now absent from her tone.

"I plan to speak with the Adventurers' Guild. Raveslan had expected the Council to offer no help and sent us with the means to contract a band of Adventurers. Once I have my bearings I will head that way." The snark was weak and barely hit the mark, but Mera showed a brief look of shame.

"Very well, then we'll take my carriage." Then, when Ninetoes looked ready to argue, added, "You've already admitted to not knowing the way and my carriage will be much faster than walking. Plus, the support of a noble will give your contract added weight." She said all this as she walked towards a trim-looking carriage, manned by two liveried guards, both of whom looked grizzled and more than ready to tear Ninetoes a new arsehole if the Lady ordered it.

While the Lady wrote and handed a note to a nearby Guard, Ninetoes seriously considered ignoring her command. What did he care what she thought?

But in the end, he thought better of it. Lady Mera Fawkner had already proven herself to be a difficult opponent, he would not give her reason to cause him more problems.

Plus, his Familiar pointed out, *she's right!*

CHAPTER 16
THE GUILD OF ADVENTURERS

The ride across town was a silent one. Lady Fawkner sat across from Ninetoes, staring out of the window and refusing, or so it seemed to him, to look his way. It was, however, also blessedly short and within the span of a handful of minutes, they'd arrived.

Surprisingly, the Guild was not in the richer part of town, but nearer to the docks. The carriage pulled up in a busy street, but the Lady's guards acted as bulwarks and the flow of traffic curved around their impressively wide frames, providing a clear path to a large gateway through a tall, stone wall. No guards watched the entrance, but there was nonetheless a sense of grandeur and menace about the place that spoke to its significance.

Passing through the thick walls, brought Ninetoes and the Lady into a large courtyard and training ground. To the left stood a goodly sized stable that climbed to three storeys. From his current vantage, he could see that the ground floor held only horses, whereas the second floor, if the sounds were anything to go by, housed wolves. The third floor was too high up for Ninetoes to make out very much detail, but it held a balcony or perhaps, a landing platform and he assumed it was for flying creatures, like the Griffons Ffion sold in Raveslan.

Perhaps, instead of keeping his stallion, he would buy himself to a flying beast. He could just imagine the looks of wonder on the faces of his people as he returned to them a powerful Adventurer, nay a Hero, astride a mighty griffon!

"Perhaps if you're finished gawking we could make our way inside Adventurer?" Lady Fawkner cut into his daydream with her barb. Ninetoes chose not to answer and instead fell into step as they crossed the space.

The rest of the courtyard was made up of target ranges, training dummies and a few shallow pits filled with sand, each occupied by pairs of fighters sparring or practicing.

"The Guild also offers training in many areas of combat and magic, for a cost of course."

"Oh?" Ninetoes offered.

"Indeed. Hail Gustav!" she called out and a tall elf who stood nonchalantly with a longbow turned her way, offering a broad and handsome smile.

"Mera! It's good to see you," he called back, before turning and using his bow to slap the legs of the young man he was standing with. "Widen your stance! How many times?"

"The Guild itself is more of a compound. It offers lodging, food and learning as well as providing Quests to Adventurers. It also doubles as a fortress in times of siege. Of course not all Adventurers use the Guild, but most start out here," Lady Fawkner offered. Ninetoes, who had been ignorant of the Guild until just a few days ago, listened carefully.

"And so the Guild is where people can come to hire Adventurers?" he asked.

"Not exactly." She paused for a moment, as if considering how best to answer. "Say you have a problem, in your case this army of hobgoblins, you bring this information to the Guild and offer a reward for aid. The Guild will then decide what Tier of Quest it is and so what Level of Adventuring party is needed and how much it is likely to cost. You do realise, that for an Adventurer to travel alone or in too small a group, he must be either extremely powerful or incredibly stupid?" Ninetoes ground his teeth at the implied insult, but he still wanted to know more and so he chose to ignore it and move on.

"Indeed, have you ever provided a Quest to the Guild?"

"I have not, but my father did it often though, normally as the Chairman of the Council on behalf of Pamor and he would often bring me with him." A warm smile crossed her face at the mention of her father.

"I see, could you then suggest what Tier of Quest Raveslan's problem should require?" he asked and, it seemed by the look on her face, that her Ladyship considered this to be a sensible question.

"Hmmm, it is hard to tell. While the number of monsters involved, in this case hobgoblins, is high, the risk from losing only a frontier town is relatively low," she pondered allowed and Ninetoes was stunned with how insulting it all sounded. But Mera's tone wasn't one of derision, rather she simply sounded analytical, like it was a difficult maths problem. "I would guess a Tier Two, perhaps a Tier One."

"And, what is the real difference between these Tiers? Would it be better to have a Tier Two?"

"Another good question," she offered and, despite himself, Ninetoes smiled at the praise. "Well, a Tier Two would ensure that it is offered to more powerful Adventurers only. Adventurers I think, that would be more likely to succeed in wiping out the entire goblinoid army, but this would then make it extremely expensive and thus, I would imagine, out of Raveslan's price range. Adversely, a Tier One Quest could be taken by a larger range of Adventurers, really of any power and skill level but the weakest of initiates.

Due to the lower price of this of course, you're less likely to attract Adventurers that are powerful enough to succeed. Of course, there's nothing to stop someone from offering a smaller reward for a Tier Four for example, but doing so would just be foolish.

Adventuring is an expensive business and so Adventurers won't waste their time for too little pay." Lady Fawkner's answer carried the pair the rest of the way into the main Guildhouse; a well-kept four storey, brick building, adorned with brightly coloured flags.

For Ninetoes however, the Lady's words had caused him no small amount of concern. What if no Adventurers would take on their mission? Not only would he have failed his own Quest, but the hobgoblins would roll over Raveslan and there would be little to stop them from destroying his own home.

The inside of the Guildhouse was a large, open space that surrounded a depressed fighting pit, only this one was at least five times the size of those outside. The sides of the pit were tiered seating that led down from ground level into a ten-foot-deep walled pit. The walls of the pit glowed with a faint aura of magic and a quick activation of Mind's Eye told Ninetoes that the magic held the bluish hue of Abjuration; clearly it was some sort of shielding magic to keep those in the stands safe from the combat that took place within.

Lady Fawkner caught note of where Ninetoes was looking and helped him fill in the blanks. "Adventurers use the Pit to duel, test their skills and even settle arguments. I'm told the Guild in Ffestyn has one large enough for Party combat, but this one allows only single or paired combat."

He nodded his thanks and nearly deactivated his Mind's Eye. Twice today however, the Skill had offered him useful insight and with such a small cost in mana, it seemed that he would do well to maintain it, so he left it active while he scanned the rest of the space.

Looking up there was a mezzanine level that jutted out from three sides of the space, with a staircase either side of the pair leading up to it.

Even from where they stood, Ninetoes could see a number of merchant's stalls selling weapons, armour, potions and other adventuring gear. This balconied area was also lined with more seating that overlooked the Pit and what looked like a tavern of sorts.

Ninetoes was in awe. If all the seats were filled he reckoned there must be space for at least a couple hundred people, but surely there couldn't be so many Adventurers in Pamor alone? And Ffestyn's pit was even bigger? "My Lady, do you know how many Adventurers the Guild holds?"

"Hmmm, the simple answer is that I don't know for sure, but I think you also misunderstand. The Pamorian Guild is just one of hundreds of such guildhouses, most of which offer the same services. In fact, I'm told that most of the guildhouses are all but identical. The Adventurers don't live here, not really.

Rather they move around, chasing Quests, fortune and glory. In all the years I visited here with my father I never saw it full however and there were never more than a few dozen Adventurers at any one time." Ninetoes was more and more glad that he'd chosen to come here with her ladyship; she was a fountain of knowledge.

"Where do we submit our Quest?" he asked, realising perhaps that as interesting as all this was, they had come with a purpose.

"At that booth over there. The attendant will take down all your details and the details of the Quest and then pass it on to the Commander for approval and a Tier rating." She pointed as she spoke. "Then, the Quest will be put onto that board and will be available to Adventurers. Don't worry though, Adventurers seem to have an innate ability to turn up just when they're needed, we shouldn't have to wait long."

As instructed, Ninetoes approached the booth, where an attractive gnomish woman stood making notes into a large ledger. "Excuse me, I am Ninetoes and I'm an Adventurer."

"Safe journey and good fortune Adventurer. Are you here to register with the Guild?" she asked and a wide and welcoming smile lit up her face.

"No, well not yet. Rather I am here seeking aid for the town of Raveslan."

"Ah, you have a Quest then, excellent. Please give me the particulars in as much detail as you can manage." She closed the ledger and opened another from a shelf beneath the counter as she spoke. Flipping to a page roughly halfway through the book, she looked up Ninetoes expectantly, her quill poised and ready to write.

For the next few minutes, Ninetoes described the situation with as many details as he could remember, including how much gold the town could pay and the nature of the magical item reward Foresto had offered. As he neared the end, Lady Fawkner added some details, including that House Fawkner officially endorsed the Quest. He wasn't sure exactly what this endorsement entailed, but the clerk took note of it, so he hoped it would have some positive effect.

"Very well. Is there anything else?" The gnome asked, turning the ledger so that Ninetoes could check what she'd written. Everything seemed in order, so he simply shook his head. "Excellent and the gold?"

This stumped Ninetoes a little as Bess had been carrying the gold but she was nowhere to be found. Rather than hold things up, he reached into his own magical coin pouch and drew out twenty pieces of platinum, handing them over to the woman.

"Thank you. The Guild will keep this money safe until we can assign a party of Adventurers to the Quest. Can I assume that you'll be joining them and taking a portion of the Quest rewards Adventurer?"

Good question. Ninetoes was still in two minds about whether to stay and fight for Raveslan or return to protect his people, in case the town should fall. That, however, was a decision for another day. "My companion and I will accompany them back to Raveslan, alongside her Ladyship here and one of the townsfolk."

"Alright, I'll just make a note of that. An escort component might raise the Quest's Tier rating." And putting quill to parchment she did just that. "It's a quiet day, so if you'd like to stay nearby Adventurer, I'll take this to the Commander right away."

Ninetoes didn't mind one bit. He was itching to explore the merchant's stalls he'd seen. "Of course. I'll be upstairs," he told her. She nodded and stepped away.

"Well, I have preparations of my own to make, so I'll leave you here and meet you at the Troll." So saying, Lady Fawkner left Ninetoes alone. Well, almost.

She was... interesting.

Indeed. Ninetoes thought back to his Familiar. Unsurprisingly the little rodent had mostly been asleep since their last meal outside the Castle gates, but he'd felt her stirring when they'd reached the Guildhouse. She'd stayed hidden, watching the strange human closely.

She was watching you, you know? And she has the eyes of a hawk, I'm sure she saw me, despite my casting Cloaking Shadows. But she only had eyes for you, I think she seemed... afraid of you.

311

Curious. Well, for now I'd like to do some shopping. I want to see what we can find to keep you safe. Libby nuzzled into Ninetoes neck.

Can we also buy some cheese?

***

Ninetoes couldn't remember ever having lots of money, until becoming an Adventurer. Well, that wasn't strictly true. He couldn't really remember very much at all about his life before he became an Adventurer, but he was pretty sure he'd never been wealthy. By the standards of his people, the Dakhec Druul, who eschewed money and really only bartered for the things they used, even the twenty-five gold reward for his first Quest would have made him a rich man. As he'd quickly discovered however, for an Adventurer the small pile of gold was nothing, barely enough to properly equip oneself.

The treasure hoard he'd discovered in the goblin camp outside of Kavralach, however, had made him stupendously rich even by the standards of his new life.

Most of the gold, of course, was for his people to give them a new home and to build or repair the defences to protect it. But that didn't mean he couldn't spend some of it on himself and he had an itch that he hadn't been able to shake since stepping onto the dock. He was however, also sensible not to flaunt such wealth as he recognised the risk that this would pose.

So it was that instead of immediately going on a spending spree, Ninetoes had decided to sell off some of the items that he had no use for. This of course would make him some gold and make it less suspicious when he started pulling platinum pieces out of his Bag of Holding.

Firstly, he visited a vendor selling magical clothing; robes and cloaks and such. He managed to make ten gold pieces for Bofar's blood-stained robes, which he realised in hindsight, perhaps he should have taken the time to wash. He also parted with five silver pieces to the same vendor in exchange for repairing his magic cloak, with a promise to collect it later that day.

Next, he visited a merchant who sold spell components and sold off the dire rat brain and hearts. These earned him only a handful of silver. Temporarily he considered selling off the Nechtsarm poisons he'd taken off of the ba'ardec. Ultimately however, he decided to keep them. Using poisons didn't really seem his style but you never knew what might happen. The merchant also didn't want the dire rat claws, instead pointing him towards a stall selling magical items. This was the stall that Ninetoes was most interested in visiting and had partly avoided it to increase his own sense of childlike excitement.

He was not, however, done selling and instead sought out a vendor selling jewellery. He wanted to sell off some of the treasure he had and turn it into coin. This also allowed him to maintain his ruse, rather than for any real need for more coinage. The only merchant, however, selling such was the magic item vendor so he took a deep breath in an attempt to calm himself.

Through his Mind's Eye the items on display sparkled with such mesmerizing colours that before he knew it, he found himself beside them, leaning in close to ogle their beauty.

Ooooooo, pretty.

Indeed, Little One. We must be sensible of course but-

What is that? And that? And what's that do? We must have one of those...

***

Some time later, Ninetoes and Libby sat slumped together at a small table drinking some tea. He'd never really had the drink before but as he'd stumbled, dazedly into the 'tea shop' a pleasantly plump dwarven woman had taken him by the arm and guided him into a large, comfortable armchair and said simply "Oh dear. I'll get you a pot of tea."

The last hour was a blur. Ninetoes vaguely remembered the hooked-nosed merchant at the magical item stall asking him if there was anything he could help him with and then… everything else was a daze of excitement, gold and wonder.

"Another pot dear? Or some cake perhaps?" The plump dwarf was back, offering him the same welcoming and motherly smile as before.

"Hmmm, um yes please. But what's cake?"

"What's cake? Oh dear, I think perhaps the Madness has jumbled your mind lad. I don't think I've ever seen it affect someone so." She looked down at him, concern written across her face. Leaning down, she placed the back of her hand to his forehead. "Aye. Some cake it is and yes, little one, I'll bring some for you too." At this, Ninetoes looked down to see his Familiar staring directly at the woman, clearly focussing all her will in projecting her telepathic voice, begging the woman to notice her. *Bring me some too.* Ninetoes doubted she could hear Libby, but the intensity of the rodent's eyes carried all the necessary meaning.

Shaking himself out of his stupor, Ninetoes looked up at the woman. "Excuse me, "madness"?" he questioned.

"Oh aye. I sees Adventurers get carried away with buying stuff all the time. Around here we calls it the 'Shopping Madness'. An Adventurer will come in and spend hundreds or even thousands of gold on magic rings and wands and whatnot and then forget to eat! Thas one o' the reasons I opened my little tea shop 'ere, to make sure they gets at least somethin' in their bellies," she said chuckling, as she retreated behind the counter and out into a small kitchen.

On the table before him, Ninetoes found a number of small packages and parcels. These, he realised were his purchases but he couldn't remember exactly what he'd bought or even how much he'd spent! He'd have to check his treasure hoard when he was somewhere safe, but for now, he wanted to check what he had.

Starting with the smallest parcel, Ninetoes found a bracelet. A quick cast of Identify reminded him of the details of what he'd procured.

```
BRACELET OF PROTECTION - FINE, RARE
PREREQUISITE: CANNOT BE WORN WITH AR-
MOUR.
PROPERTIES: +10 TO AC. ALLOWS THE WEARER
TO CAST BARRIER (LEVEL 10) ONCE PER DAY.
```

This had been a canny find. He'd been desperate to find something that would help protect Libby but all of the items on display were for Adventurers, not their Familiar's. In fact, the vendor had seemed surprised that Ninetoes had been so bothered about his squirrel, noting that most Adventurers didn't even seem to notice that the creatures were there until they wanted something.

When he'd picked up the bracelet however, he'd reckoned it might fit Libby around her waist. With the vendor's permission they tried it on and, while a little tight, it had fit! With the merchant's assurances that it would work as intended, Ninetoes hadn't even asked how much. He'd just bought it.

Next, in a larger box was an attractive, if simple, circlet made of a silvery metal and set with a single blue gem in the front.

```
CIRCLET OF INTELLIGENCE - FINE, UNCOM-
MON
PROPERTIES: +10 TO INTELLIGENCE.
```

This one's abilities were straightforward enough and powerful as was the wand he found in the next package.

```
WAND OF FIREBALLS - FINE, UNCOMMON

PROPERTIES: THIS WAND HAS 4 CHARGES.
EACH CHARGE CAN BE USED TO CAST FIREBALL
(LEVEL 20). ONCE A CHARGE IS SPENT THE
WAND WILL NEED TO BE RECHARGED (200
```

MANA PER CHARGE).

He'd been wanting more fire power and now he had it. Looking at it, he remembered asking the vendor about recharging it. The man had said that any spellcaster with enough mana could do so, if they knew how.

He'd said this with a smug grin, probably assuming the hobgoblin wouldn't have the Channelling skill. It was a prodigious amount of mana at his current level, so he wouldn't be recharging the wand during battle, but with his Meditation skill, he could easily manage it afterwards. *If I'm still alive.*

Concentrating on the idea of the Fireball spell, Ninetoes' Identify spell provided him detail.

FIREBALL - LEVEL 20 (ITEM)

EVOCATION

CASTING TIME - 5 SECONDS

DURATION - INSTANTANEOUS

LVL 20. SHOOTS A BALL OF FIRE TO EXPLODE IN A 20 FT RADIUS SPHERE FROM THE POINT OF IMPACT. DEALS 10-60 POINTS OF FIRE DAMAGE TO ANYTHING CAUGHT WITHIN THE AREA OF EFFECT.

Yep! That'll hit the spot. Pun intended. A small voice sighed within his head, but he ignored her.

Instead, he rubbed his hands with glee and eyed up the next parcel. This one was wrapped in brown paper and tied with string but his dexterous fingers released the item in no time. It was a candle.

> **AVERY'S RITUAL CANDLE** - FINE, VERY RARE
> PROPERTIES: ALLOWS THE CASTER TO PERFORM
> ONE RITUAL OF COMPETENT OR LOWER SKILL
> LEVEL WITHOUT THE NEED FOR COMPONENTS.

This one came back to him with the same note of inspiration he'd had upon finding it. He'd found it hiding behind all of the other more exciting objects. He'd asked the merchant why it was so obscured and the man admitted that he'd had it for years, having purchased it with a number of other items when he'd bought the contents of a dead Adventurer's will.

He also admitted to having never been able to sell it. Adventurers, he'd said, simply didn't use Rituals because they were generally ineffective in combat. At one hundred gold it cost a fortune, but Ninetoes had read about Rituals that could cost a hundred times that in components, so he'd snapped it up.

He was now more than halfway through his pile of goodies and the dwarven woman had returned with another pot of tea and two delicate-looking plates, each holding a large helping of what Ninetoes could only assume was some kind of dark brown bread, only it smelled incredibly sweet.

"Excuse me. What's this?"

"Oh yes, this is chocolate cake dearie, it's a type of dessert. Go ahead, you'll like it I promise." He had no idea what dessert was, but chocolate he'd heard of. It was made from cocoa beans, which were bitter and horrible. Nonetheless, he'd done far more risky things recently than taste 'dessert'.

With a sideways glance at Libby, who for once was hesitant to eat something, he took a bite. The most wonderful mixture of tastes filled his mouth and the sensation exploded out of him, blasting Libby with a bolt of euphoric feeling. Without any further hesitation, she dove in.

Within a minute both of them sat back, licking the last remnants from their lips and whiskers and wide grins playing across their faces. Sated, Ninetoes considered the rest of his purchases.

A small box held six potions, three of which were healing potions although these were a little more potent than those Foresto had given him.

> **POTION OF HEALING** - NORMAL, COMMON
> PROPERTIES: IF CONSUMED IT WILL HEAL THE USER FOR 50 POINTS OF DAMAGE. IF APPLIED DIRECTLY TO A WOUND IT WILL INSTEAD REPAIR ANY DAMAGED BONE OR TISSUE, REDUCING A BLEEDING OR BROKEN STATUS EFFECT BY ONE TIER.

But as he Identified the other potions a new thrill ran through him. At first, he'd bought two of the Potions of Haste as they'd seemed so useful. But, after he'd asked if Libby could use them as well and was assured that, not only could you use them, but that she'd only need a half dose, he'd bought a third.

> **POTION OF HASTE** - POOR, COMMON
> PROPERTIES: INCREASES USER'S MOVEMENT SPEED BY 10% FOR ONE HOUR.

The merchant had sold Normal and Fine quality potions as well that increased the bonus to 25% and 50% but they were incredibly expensive and so he'd stuck with these.

As he unwrapped his last purchase however, he grew even more excited and he was once again blown away by how useful it could be and how, at last, he had something that could get both him and Libby out of a tight spot. It was a small stone cube with runes covering every face and would have looked like a simple six-sided dice had it not been for the way it shone with bright turquoise light under his Mind's Eye.

> **DOMINIC'S PORTABLE PROTECTION FIELD -**
> **EXCELLENT, RARE**
>
> **PROPERTIES: ONCE PER DAY THE WIELDER CAN**
> **PROJECT A FIELD OF FORCE IN A 10 FT RADIUS**
> **DOME AROUND ITSELF. THE DOME IS IMPENE-**
> **TRABLE TO EVERYTHING BUT WHAT THE**
> **WIELDER CHOOSES AND WILL LAST FOR 1 MI-**
> **NUTE OR UNTIL IT HAS SUFFERED 200 HIT**
> **POINTS OF DAMAGE OF ANY KIND.**

This was his trump card. His safety net. If shit got bad, he could pop this out and make a dash for it. It wasn't perfect of course but it was better than nothing and well worth the gold; all one hundred pieces of it. He'd keep this close, he decided, for emergencies. And he slipped it in his waistcoat pocket.

BWEEERP!

"Ha! Yer little squirrel likes my cake then? She can really pack it away can't she?" The dwarf was back again with another pot of tea. Ninetoes' bladder, however, told him that two pots were its limit.

"No more for me. How much do I owe you? And, is there any chance of buying some chocolate to take with me?"

"Five silver dearie and yes, five copper a bar." So saying, she shuffled off to the kitchen and returned with three bars. "And do come back luvy, Forbia always has a kettle on the boil and fresh cakes made up." Ninetoes was grateful for the old woman's hospitality, so he didn't quibble over the price. Instead, he paid up and placed each of his new items into his Bag of Holding for safe keeping, all except the chocolate, that he slipped into his Adventurer's backpack.

"Oh, oh good... I thought I'd... missed you." A short, slim man came barrelling into the tea shop, before skidding to a halt in front of the hobgoblin. He was clearly flustered and almost out of breath.

Ninetoes looked him up and down while the man took deep, steadying breaths.

He had short reddish-blond hair that was so bright it looked like spun copper and, just like Rael, the Counsellor who had voted in favour of aiding Raveslan, he had ever-so-slightly pointed ears.

"Indeed. And why were you looking for me?" Ninetoes responded when an idea struck him. "Has the Commander finished making his decision? Do you know what Tier he's chosen?"

"What? Who? No sorry, I'm not with the Guild, I'm a crafter and I make magic items. But no one ever seems to buy them. And, well the merchant mentioned that you'd bought lots of his and that you'd asked about stuff for Familiar and Companion animals and I thought you-"

"Woah! Slow down. Which merchant?" The man seemed a jumble of excitement but the hobgoblin was currently more concerned that people were talking about him buying lots of magical items.

"Which merchant? Er, that one," the man said, pointing. As Ninetoes followed his finger, he found the vendor he'd visited earlier at the end of it. Alright, that wasn't so bad. At least it was just two of them.

"Alright. Please slow down and start again. Or, better still, is there somewhere more private we can talk. I'd prefer as few people as possible know that I'm carrying expensive magical items."

"Oh, er... why don't we go into Forbia's Tea Shop, she bakes the most wonderful cakes and-"

"No, no more cake." He felt Libby deflate at the declaration, but quickly ignored the feeling as it originated from his fattening Familiar. "Don't you have a shop?"

"I do. Well, that is, not really but..." The man looked a little shame-faced. He was quickly beginning to get on Ninetoes' last nerve.

"Well, do you or don't you?"

"No, no I don't. But what I have to say won't take long." He stared at Ninetoes sincerely.

"Very well."

"Right, thank you. I'll start again. My name is Gideon and I'm a crafter." He spoke slowly and with purpose. *Now we're getting somewhere.*

"Hello Gideon, I am Ninetoes and it's a pleasure to make your acquaintance."

"Thank you. So, I normally work for my brother and help him to Identify and sell goods to Adventurers, but I also craft goods when I have the time. I'd like to run my own shop one day but I need gold for that. After he met you the merchant came to speak with me. He's been a family friend since forever and he told me that you'd been asking for magical items for Familiars." Ninetoes nodded at this and smiled hopefully.

Did he say Familiars?

He did my dear, now let me listen.

"Well, I make items just for Familiars and Companion animals. Rael, my brother, tells me it's a waste of my talents and that no one will buy them, and if I'm honest, he'd normally be correct."

"Not this time he ain't." Ninetoes, momentarily forgetting himself, gave his toothiest grin and the poor man shrank back. "What have you got?" he asked greedily.

"Is this your Familiar here?" Gideon asked, gesturing up to Ninetoes' shoulder, where Libby was now sitting carefully and eagerly watching the young man.

"Indeed. This is-"

"Libby, yes she just told me." Gideon said to Ninetoes' shock and surprise. Then, with a grin on his face, he removed a small clip from one of his ear lobes and showed it to the hobgoblin. Small as it was, Ninetoes could make out tiny runes etched into the small, metal cylinder and it shone under his magical eyes. "I call this a Familiar's Tongue. I realise the name could use a little work, but it works well." Ninetoes eyed it closely and cast Identify.

FAMILIAR'S TONGUE - NORMAL, UNCOMMON
PROPERTIES: ALLOWS THE WEARER TO SPEAK
TELEPATHICALLY WITH A WIZARD'S FAMILIAR
WITHIN 15 FEET.

"Fascinating. And yet you say that no one wishes to buy your items?"

"No, they don't seem to have any use for them."

Adventurers. Libby said in exasperation and both Ninetoes and Gideon nodded.

Strange, we both heard you that time my dear.

That's because I spoke 'out loud' that time, she answered, somewhat cryptically.

You mean, you can choose?

Of course.

"She can choose to talk to you, me or us both. But only while I wear this of course." Gideon answered the obvious question.

"Remarkable and you have more such items?" Ninetoes asked eagerly.

"I do but first I must offer my apologies and then ask you for a small boon. You see, it's generally considered rude to speak to one's Familiar or Companion without first seeking permission and so I ask your forgiveness for this." He paused.

"Of course, think nothing of it. If she hadn't wanted to speak to you, she'd have let you know herself."

"Hmmm, thank you. If I may say, you are a remarkable pair. I don't think I've ever met anyone quite like you." He stared intently at Ninetoes for a moment, before shaking his head as if to clear it and carrying on. "As for the boon. Might I ask Libby what it is that she desires?"

"Aye. Be careful though. She's like to tell you." He grinned and set Libby down on a nearby bench.

For a couple of minutes, Gideon sat beside the Familiar and talked with her at length before standing back up and addressing the hobgoblin once again. "Libby has made her request and I think I can accommodate her, but I'll need the rest of the day to work on it. She tells me you're staying at Tally's Troll?" Ninetoes nodded in confirmation. "Then I'll meet you in the taproom? Tonight?"

"Very good. What did she ask you for?"

"She, um asked me not to tell you." Gideon admitted, a little embarrassed. Libby meanwhile was grooming herself nonchalantly. A little too nonchalantly.

Libby?

Worry not Master, it won't be too expensive and you want me to be safe don't you? She looked at him with innocent eyes.

Argh!

Gideon sidled in to whisper. "She also tells me that you're a Necromancer."

An icy feeling flooded through Ninetoes and his hand instinctively reached for his absent sword.

Calm Master. He is different from the others. He's like Foresto, he seems more... aware. We can trust him, I think.

Ninetoes wasn't so sure, but if he couldn't trust Libby then he was screwed.

"Indeed, and what of it?" he whispered back.

"Well, my brother gets in items from time to time that he can't sell. Normally things that Adventurers bring back from a Quest that they don't want or can't use because they are related to the darker arts."

Intrigued, Ninetoes tilted his head. "Go on."

"Well, it just so happens that I have an item that might be of some use to you. I can give you a good price because my brother is unlikely to be able to sell it and will probably end up destroying it for the components."

"Hmmm, please, show me." Ninetoes' heart thumped loudly in his chest. Since Foresto had warned him that Necromancy was considered evil, he'd never thought to find items for his spell school and was too afraid to ask.

Gideon reached into a small satchel, but the way his hand disappeared, it was obviously a Bag of Holding much like Ninetoes' own.

Removing his hand, he held out a simple silver ring, unadorned with gems or stones. Within the band ran a strange runic writing too small to read with the naked eye, but Ninetoes recognised its curved letters, it was ancient Kavralian, the language of the city his treasure came from. He filed that piece of information away and focussed on the ring's abilities. With his Identify spell still in effect, he leaned in for a closer look.

> **RING OF EXANIMATE AUTHORITY** - EXCELLENT, RARE
> PROPERTIES: THIS RING ALLOWS THE WEARER TO INCREASE THE LEVEL OF UNDEAD THEY CAN CREATE AND CONTROL BY 2 LEVELS PER NECROMANCY SKILL RANK.

This ring was incredible!

One of the drawbacks to his Create Undead spell was that he could only animate a creature of certain levels. For each level of the creature the spell cost fifty mana and even with his Necromancy buff this was still nearly forty mana. That meant, with his current mana pool of three hundred and eighty he could only reanimate or assert his control over a creature that was level 9.

As it was, he wasn't even sure how he was able to maintain control of Bluzag who was a level 12. Come to think of it, he'd never needed to cast Create Undead to reassert his control over the Wight. Nonetheless, this ring would allow him to control a creature that was ten levels higher and, as he raised his rank with Necromancy, this would rise as well. He must have it.

"How much?"

"Well, it's of Excellent quality and is Rare-"

"But you've already said that your brother can't sell it."

"Indeed, so let's say two hundred gold." But as he said it, Ninetoes caught the briefest hesitation in his voice. Rather than haggle, he just waited, staring back at Gideon with glowing amber eyes.

"Hmmm, you're right, it will be difficult to sell to anyone else; one hundred fifty?"

Libby leapt onto Ninetoes' shoulder and her eyes joined her Master's boring into the merchant.

"Ah, of course as my first customers I'd like to offer you a discount, shall we say one hundred, but I really can't take a copper le-"

"Deal." Ninetoes grabbed Gideon's hand and shook it with one hand, while thrusting the other into his bag and removing enough platinum pieces, before shoving them into Gideon's palm. "You have my thanks."

So saying, he retracted his hand, palming the ring as he did and slipping it onto his middle finger. There was no rush of power as he'd hoped. Instead, he felt just a little more confident and the faint tether that held Bluzag's consciousness to his own thickened the tiniest fraction.

"Ah, there you are. Oh, hello Gideon. The Commander awaits your presence, he's made his decision."

CHAPTER 17
THE RED CREW

The young gnomish attendant had stepped up on the pair unnoticed as they'd concluded their deal and both men flinched in surprise as she interrupted them. Ninetoes recovered first and turned to her.

"Thank you, I'll be along shortly." Then, turning to Gideon. "I will see you tonight then. If your work is good, I'll owe you a pint." So saying, he turned and followed the retreating gnome.

The gnome led Ninetoes back downstairs, to a door to the right and slightly behind the booth she worked. "Please wait here. The Commander is just finishing another meeting but he will not be long."

Ninetoes stood to one side and took the opportunity to check his Character Sheet while he waited.

CHARACTER NAME: NINETOES	**RACE:** HOBGOBLIN (+1 END, +1 INT)
LEVEL: 12TH	**EXPERIENCE POINTS:** 84,565/88,000
CLASS: WIZARD	**SPECIALISM:** NECROMANCER
HIT POINTS: 240/240	**MANA POINTS:** 380/380
STAMINA POINTS: 200/200	

BASE STATS:	VARIED STATS:
STRENGTH - 13 (9)	
AGILITY - 20	FITNESS - 20
ENDURANCE - 27	
INTELLIGENCE - 38 (33)	WILL - 25
WISDOM - 24	
CHARISMA - 12 (7)	

ARMOUR CLASS: 27

SKILLS

ARCANA 20
BASIC FIRST AID 5
CHANNELLING 16
DODGING 7
LIGHT ARMOUR 15
LONGBOW 15
MEDIUM ARMOUR 15
MEDITATION 7
MIND'S EYE 8
ONE-HANDED BLADES 13
RIDING 7
RITUAL CASTING 2
SKINNING AND BUTCHERING 3
SNEAK AND HIDE 9
TRAP BUILDING 4

SPELL SCHOOLS

ABJURATION 14
CONJURATION 8
DIVINATION 10
ENCHANTMENT 3
EVOCATION 10
ILLUSION 6 (15)

He was, once again, pleased with his progress. He'd made improvements in a number of areas. Some he assumed were from the short, but brutal battle with the Manticore, while others had been through practice, the most notable of these being Mind's Eye.

This ability had skyrocketed since he'd arrived in Pamor and he vowed he'd keep it up whenever possible. It was also only two levels away from a potential Rank bonus, as was Conjuration. He made a note to focus some attention on those areas in the short term.

Checking his Spells, he also noted improvements in some of these and, more excitingly, bonus features in both Barrier and Reaper's Sorrow.

BARRIER - LEVEL 6

ABJURATION

CASTING TIME - 1 SECOND

MANA COST - 50 POINTS

DURATION - 5 SECONDS

LVL 1. CREATES A MAGICAL SHIELD THAT ABSORBS 100 POINTS OF DAMAGE.

LVL 6. MAGICAL SHIELDS CAN BE EXPANDED TO COVER A GREATER AREA FOR A COST OF 25 MANA PER 5FT SQUARE NOTE: THE SHIELD ABSORBS THE SAME AMOUNT OF DAMAGE.

REAPER'S SORROW - LEVEL 17

NECROMANCY

CASTING TIME - 1 MINUTE

MANA COST - 250 POINTS

DURATION - 24 HOURS

LVL 1. ONCE CAST, IF THE RECIPIENT OF THIS

SPELL IS REDUCED TO 0 HP, THE SPELL TRIG-
GERS AND SAVES THEM FROM DEATH AND RE-
STORES A NUMBER OF HIT POINTS EQUAL TO
THE CASTER'S LEVEL OF SKILL WITH THE SPELL.

LVL 16. THE NUMBER OF HIT POINTS RE-
STORED INCREASES BY 10% (ROUNDED UP).

The bonus to Reaper's Sorrow was low at only 10% meaning only an extra couple of hit points, but such things made all the difference. Most useful perhaps, was the fact that he could now use his Barrier spell to shield his allies. He must find a way to practice with these spells or at least find a means of learning more about them. Perhaps he'd have time once he'd finished with the Commander.

"Wooo! Nat 20 guys!" A silky, male voice leaped through the oaken door of the Commander's office, making Ninetoes stand a little straighter and put away his Spellbook. But, when no one came out he quickly grew bored.

To stave off the boredom, Ninetoes retrieved his new Circlet of Intellect from his bag. Watching the Character Sheet as he did so, he placed it over his hair to sit snuggly behind his dagger-shaped ears.

At first nothing happened. Then, a couple of seconds later, the numbers on his Sheet began to change. First his Intelligence shot up to 48, quickly followed by his Will stat, which rose to 28. Best of all however, his mana pool's maximum also leaped to four hundred and eighty, his mana then began steadily filling his enlarged pool.

He spent the next thirty seconds or so adjusting and readjusting his hair over the circlet until only the very front of the headband could be seen across his forehead.

While he was still fiddling, the Commander's office door opened and four Adventurers stepped out.

"Brilliant! And he said we each get rewarded with a magical item of our choice! All for killin' a bunch of gobbos." This came from a tall and heavily armoured human man who led the group. He had the sheer and haughty features of a noble, but his voice was the drawl of a commoner.

Next came another human, this one a woman and, from her attire, Ninetoes took her to be a mage of some sort. She was ugly as a stuck pig, made uglier by the coy smile she wore while staring wantonly at the armoured man.

Uncomfortable to look at this display any longer, Ninetoes directed his attention to the other two members of the little band. One was a strange looking creature.

Although it stood on two legs and walked upright, it was covered in brown scales and had a pulled, reptilian face. Dragged behind it, slithered a long, serrated tail that sawed along the wooden floor. Adrenon was truly a large and wondrous place.

This lizard-man hybrid wore only odd pieces of armour but he was so heavily armed with a variety of weapons, that it seemed that not a patch of scaly skin was on show.

The last member of the group was also wearing armour, only it appeared to be thick, hardened leather that left her legs and most of her arms free. At her hip hung a long, thin sword that Ninetoes immediately recognised as Elven-made and off of the opposite shoulder hung an unstrung longbow and quiver. She was, Ninetoes guessed, an Elf, but he'd already been wrong about the significance of the pointed ears once today, so he'd wait and see.

Like Gideon, her hair was golden blonde and hung loose but to her shoulders. She was little she was female, but androgynous enough in her armour that she could have been mistaken for a man from behind.

All of them looked competent enough, but their gear looked worn and cheap, nothing like his own, despite some of his having been found in an ancient city.

"What's more, with the coins he gave us, we can get some upgrades now." The party moved off, mostly ignoring Ninetoes as the man shared out a handful of platinum coins. "Daph, get as many spell scrolls as you can, you can add them to your spell book on the journey. An'rik you should buy some healing scrolls and Sar-"

"Yeah, I'm good thanks Tarqy. An'rik and I will go do our own thing. We'll meet you once we're done."

Ninetoes had a sinking suspicion that he knew where those coins had come from and he wasn't sure he was happy about it.

"Ninetoes is it?" Through the open door, another human sat behind a heavy oak desk. "Hurry up and come in then, I've not got all day." Ninetoes hopped to it and stepped into a small office.

The man watched him come in and despite his greying beard and hair he looked strong and healthy and his hazel eyes didn't seem to miss a thing. When Ninetoes politely waited by a chair, the man nodded and the hobgoblin seated himself and waited.

For a long moment the two men simply stared at each other, a contest of wills clearly in play that neither had consciously engaged in.

"So, you were the Adventurer that brought news of Raveslan's troubles eh. Caillic always did have a sense of humour." It was a statement, not a question, so Ninetoes kept silent. "What power Level are you?"

"Twelve," Ninetoes answered simply.

"Class?"

"Wizard."

His stern face brooked no argument, he clearly expected Ninetoes to answer with more detail.

"Necromancer." Ninetoes relaxed his muscles as he said the word, ready to bolt if things turned ugly.

"And you made the journey here alone?"

"No, I travelled with a... companion, a prisoner and a member of the town."

"I see. But you're the only Adventurer in the party?"

"Indeed." Ninetoes wasn't sure he liked where these questions were going, so he chose his next words in an attempt to change course. "Have you decided the Quest's Tier?"

"How many Quests have you already completed?" the Commander asked, ignoring Ninetoes' deflection. "And were you in a party for those Quests?"

"Er, one. And no. It was just me for most of it."

"One Quest? And you're already Level Twelve? But how? You must have been grinding mobs for years." His tone had become one of doubt, mixed with awe.

"No. When I became an Adventurer a few weeks ago-"

"Weeks?"

"Indeed. When I became an Adventurer, I travelled to Raveslan where I received my first Quest. The Quest was more difficult than had been presumed and—"

"I'll bet."

"—and by its completion, I had reached Level Twelve. Although I'll admit, I have not levelled up since then."

"Hmmm, this may succeed after all." This was said quietly, almost absentmindedly by the Commander, his eyes shone with a strange look, greed perhaps? It passed in an instant however, and he reached his hand across the desk and offered it to Ninetoes. "Safe journey and good fortune Adventurer. My name is Commander Bodrin Swiftaxe, but everyone just calls me Bod."

Ninetoes shook the man's hand. "Ninetoes, of the Dakhec Druul. It is a pleasure to meet you Commander. Now, the Quest? Raveslan is in dire need of help."

"Of course. The Quest has been set at Tier Two, but I'm afraid that due to the small reward on offer, you will struggle to find a party that would take it. Or, at least, that would normally be the case." Ninetoes' head began to hang, his skin mottled with shame. But then the Commander's last words registered and he looked up. "Really?"

"Indeed. That group who just left The-" He looked down at a ledger in front of him. "The Red Crew. Ergh, these stupid names. This party agreed to take your Quest."

"They're Tier Two Adventurers then?"

332

"Er… well, not exactly," he admitted. "But they are a balanced party and seem to know what they're about. They have convinced me that they'll be able to handle these Nechtsarm. I would, however, strongly encourage you to accompany them and help them defend the town."

"I see."

"Here is your share of the up front reward." He handed Ninetoes four platinum pieces. Four platinum pieces stamped with the face of Corvatch the 3rd, the very same coins he'd exchanged for a promise of help not two hours before. Once again, he found himself being drawn back to the fight. "I gave the rest of the party their money early as well, it seemed they'd need every coin they could get." He smiled wanly.

"And, that's it?" Ninetoes asked, a little surprised that the first part of his mission was over with so little affair.

"Aye. I've told them to meet you in Tally's Troll come sundown. That should give you a couple of hours. Why don't I introduce you to some of our trainers; I reckon that after only a couple of weeks of adventuring you've got some gaps in your Skills and knowledge?"

Ninetoes smiled back and nodded. "I would be most grateful."

"If you sign on with the Guild, I can offer you half price for your training costs?" His tone seemed a little too eager, putting Ninetoes on edge. But his manner had warmed significantly since the hobgoblin had first stepped into his office and he seemed unconcerned that the hobgoblin had admitted to being a "dark" wizard. Nevertheless, Ninetoes didn't know enough about the Guild and, as money wasn't really an issue, he chose not to join just yet.

"Thank you, Commander, I'll think on it."

"Bod, please. Follow me." So saying, he rose from his chair and ushered Ninetoes out of the office. "Now, do you have an area of study in mind? Any particular Skills or Spell Schools you'd like a boost in? I'm afraid we've no trainers for your Specialism."

This momentarily stumped Ninetoes. He definitely had areas that he needed help with but he couldn't expect to increase them all in such a short time. Rather, he needed to choose those areas that would be of most benefit in the coming fight.

As it stood, his Necromancy spells gave him both a strong ranged and melee offense, but his Abjuration skill was comparatively low. It was, however, not his weakest area and he'd just received a buff to his Barrier spell. What he really needed was a way to buff Bluzag to provide him with more protection. His Conjuration skill was also close enough to his first Rank bonus.

As they walked, he discussed what he wanted with Bod and by the time they'd reached the third floor, the Commander had convinced the hobgoblin that his best bet was to visit the Conjuration and Transmutation trainers, in that order. While he was no expert, he explained that far from just mending peoples' clothes, the school of Transmutation had spells that could make a person larger or smaller, make them stronger or weaker, it could weave and harden twigs into plate armour or turn a person into vapour. He'd pointed out, however, that at Ninetoes' current Skill level, the spells available would likely be too weak to be of much use, hence heading to the Conjuration trainer first.

Thus, Ninetoes found himself standing outside a medium-sized room covered in all sorts of a seemingly random assortment of everyday items and furniture. The whole space was then divided by a variety of different screens, each one made of a different material; one was wood, another a yellowish metal, another made from what appeared to be coal.

The reason Ninetoes was waiting outside the room was that the trainer already had a student, the same mage he'd seen downstairs and apparently a member of the Red Crew. Bod had assured the hobgoblin that he wouldn't have long to wait however, so he'd chosen to stay and watch, rather than go searching for the Transmutation trainer by himself.

"And that's how one rematerialises solids, understand?"

"Yeah, yeah. Is that it then?" The bored-looking Adventurer responded with barely any emotion on her face.

"Well um, yes. If you have any further-"

"No ta. Bye." And without further ado, she left, not even seeming to notice Ninetoes' presence.

"Hmmm, Adventurers," the Trainer said.

Ninetoes was at a loss to decide what race the trainer was. She was either a tall, slim dwarf, or a short human. Coming to Pamor had definitely opened the hobgoblin's eyes to the varieties and differences of people out there.

"Hello? I'm Ninetoes." Ninetoes presented himself, knocking gently on the door.

"Ah, I actually get a name this time eh?" she said, as she turned towards him and then waved him over.

"Commander Swiftaxe suggested that I seek out your tutelage," he added, in spite of her strange comment.

"Oh and full sentences too, this will be a treat," she said, sarcastically. She wasn't dressed as a mage; indeed, her outfit more closely resembled his own attire; a mixture of armour and robes and she carried a long, thin sword at her hip.

"Excuse me if this is a rude question, but are you a wizard? Or some other kind of mage?"

The woman's middle-aged face widened in a look of mild surprise.

"Huh. Most Adventurers don't even seem to notice that I'm a woman, let alone what clothes I'm wearing. But no, to answer your question, I am no wizard. I am what you Adventurers call a Spellsword," she answered.

"A what?" Ninetoes particularly hated it when people spoke about things as if he should know what they meant.

"A Spellsword. I weave magic into my fighting style to incorporate the benefits of both the blade and the arcane. It is a difficult balance but can be deadly in the right hands. By the empty scabbard at your hip and mismatched armour, I had taken you to be one. Or at least attempting to be one."

Ninetoes looked down at his empty scabbard and once again made a note to replace his sword. For the time being however, he unbuckled the sheathe and put it in his Bag of Holding.

"I seek to be a wizard, but when I became an Adventurer I was already proficient with a blade, habit has made me keep one to hand, until I lost it of course."

"Very well. I assume you've come for training in the Conjuration spell school, but I am also one of the Sword trainers."

"Aye, I've come for Conjuration training. I'm currently at Skill Level Eight and I'd like to reach Poor rank and learn the bonus ability. Can you help with that?"

"Level Eight eh? Yeah, I'm sure we can manage that. What Rank bonus would you like to earn?"

"You mean I can choose?"

"Of course, as a trainer I hold the Renowned rank and can teach you any of the abilities that can be gained."

"Wonderful, can I learn them all?" Ninetoes asked excitedly.

"I'm afraid you can only gain one per rank and you'll earn more choices at the next rank. The other abilities can of course be learned in other ways, but that's a much longer process. At the Poor rank, you could learn Conjuror's Choice, Knowledge Arcane One or Conjuror's Gambit One. Can I suggest Conjuror's Gambit One?"

"Hmmm, I apologise, I don't know what any of those do." Internally, Ninetoes had to once again smother his anger at the presumption that he knew stuff he didn't.

Rather than seem annoyed however, the trainer simply smiled. "No need to apologise, I am here to teach. Can you show me your Character Sheet?"

Ninetoes simply nodded and dug the scroll out of his bag, before handing it to her. After a moment's study, she turned it back to him. "Here I can see you've already chosen Abjuror's Choice when you ranked that Skill up to Poor, increasing Wizard's Armour to Level Ten. Conjuror's Choice is similar, allowing you to choose a Conjuration spell that you already know and increasing it to the Poor rank. With only three Conjuration spells in your list however, and with arguably the most useful, Arcane Step, being only two Levels away, I would suggest that this is

336

a waste. I'll admit to being a little curious about where you found that spell though. I've never heard of it."

Ninetoes didn't want anyone else to know about the store of loot and lost knowledge that he'd found in Kavralach, so he decided to ignore the question and move on. "Hmmm, mmm. And what about Knowledge Arcane One?"

A brief look of annoyance crossed the woman's face, but she evidently chose not to push the issue. "Knowledge Arcane One is again similar to the rank bonus you received in Necromancy, an interesting choice by the way, in that you can choose one spell of Poor ranking. Given your build, I'd expect you to get a choice between Tally's Short Step, which is a short-range teleportation spell, weaker and more mana-expensive than Arcane Step; Find Familiar which you already have; and Grease, which is a great spell, but then you could just pick that up from me for twenty gold."

"I'd meant to ask someone about that. Why is it that my Find Familiar spell is a higher Level than my Conjuration skill?"

"Ah, interestingly enough, I have only hypotheses for you there. To be honest, no one's really sure. It's clear that Find Familiar is no simple spell and, normally, once it's cast, it need not be cast again for a long time. Often with Adventurers, however, who see their Familiar's as particularly expendable, they never increase the spell beyond their own ability with the Skill. One thing that all Conjurors are certain of is that a good Familiar can be the difference between a life worth living and something much worse."

This certainly gave Ninetoes much to think about. "And all this explains why you suggest Conjuror's Gambit I assume."

"Absolutely. Conjuror's Gambit I, as the name implies, can be Ranked up again to be more powerful. It is, however, only offered if a caster already has a teleportation spell. Many casters don't gain access to those until they're more powerful and thus they miss out on the highest tiers of the ability."

"But what does it do?" Ninetoes was a little short with his question he knew, but time was definitely against him.

337

"Conjuror's Gambit allows a caster to adapt their teleportation spell slightly to swap places with another creature. At the first rank it only has a five percent change of course, but that's why it's so important to take it the first chance you get."

"I don't understand, why would swapping places with someone be useful to me?"

"Think about it. Why would you normally teleport in battle?" She asked with a knowing smile.

"To get out of dange- ah!"

"Yep. Your Arcane Step is already wicked good, but just imagine that while you're 'stepping' out of danger, you force an enemy to 'step' straight back into it!"

Ninetoes could definitely see the utility of such an ability. "You're right, it's the perfect choice. Where do we start?"

As ever, once his mind was made up, Ninetoes' will was iron and he was keen to move on.

"Excellent. So, what do you understand about what happens to you when you de-materialise?"

***

Sometime later, Ninetoes stepped out of the Conjuration Classroom. The Trainer's instruction, *Hmmm, I never thought to ask her name,* had been interesting and thorough. Not only had Ninetoes quickly gained both levels needed to reach the Poor rank and had gained Conjuror's Gambit I, he'd also learned a great deal more about how the Spell School worked and how it differed from its sisters.

He'd also purchase the Grease spell from her and had already added it to his Spellbook.

> **GREASE** - LEVEL 10
>
> CONJURATION
>
> CASTING TIME - ONE SECOND
>
> MANA COST - 50 POINTS
>
> DURATION - 1 MINUTE
>
> RANGE - 30 FEET
>
> LVL 1. COMPLETELY COVERS A TEN-FOOT SQUARE WITH SLICK GREASE, MAKING IT DIFFICULT FOR CREATURES TO PASS THROUGH.
>
> LVL 8. INCREASES AREA OF EFFECT TO TWELVE FT SQUARE.

Not a particularly powerful spell, but Ninetoes had already seen a few occasions where it could be useful and he intended to try it out as soon as possible. All in all, the training and the spell had cost him a little less than forty gold, which seemed a fair price.

With that done, however, he made his way along the corridor, following the Conjuration Trainer's directions to the Transmutation Classroom. Once he found it he stuck his head through the door to have a nose around, before announcing himself.

Like the Conjuration room, this one was filled with a menagerie of assorted items from lutes to potted plants. What made this scene odd however, was that many of the items present were completely unidentifiable as things and rather resembled heaps of slag or mounds of multicoloured dirt.

"Ah, Bod said you'd be along. Here to learn some Transmutation spells eh?" The speaker was a human man, bald and obscenely overweight and stretched out on a long couch, aggressively tearing meat from a chicken leg. Even this effort appeared to be too much for him, as he paused for breath between bites.

In front of him was a pile of cogs which he gestured the chicken leg at and said, "Please, take a seat."

As Ninetoes crossed the room he searched for an alternative seating arrangement. The man, who'd been eying the hobgoblin, carefully grinned. "Of course, if you'd rather not sit on metal then perhaps-" and with a flourish he cast a spell and the cogs morphed into silk cushions, each one a riot of offensive colours.

Honestly, Ninetoes would have preferred the cogs. "Er, thank you."

The man's face turned to one of annoyance. Clearly this trick was normally more of a cloud pleaser. "So, what Skill Level are you currently at?" he asked, his tone monotonic and bored as he went back to ravaging the roasted poultry.

"I am Level Five in Transmutation and I was hoping to reach level Ten and earn the Rank bonus."

"Ha! Bod said you were here for today only, and it's already late in the day."

Ninetoes looked out the window and reckoned it was only two o'clock, but whatever. "Well, then I'll take as much help as you can offer. Please."

"Woah now, I didn't say I couldn't do it lad, it'll just be more expensive is all." He rubbed the grease onto his robes, leaving new smears on top of older stains.

"Now, I can't teach you five levels in just a few hours, no one can." The Trainer said, pausing to take a breath. Ninetoes wasn't sure that this was completely true, but it was certainly the case that gaining the tenth level of Conjuration had taken longer than the ninth. "But, I am prepared to sell you one of these." So saying, he attempted to pull something from a pocket in his robes. His girth however, tangled the material and turned his big reveal into a one-sided wrestling contest that the Transmuter seemed incapable of winning.

An uncomfortable minute later however, he pulled a small crystal from the pocket. As it glowed with magical energy it grasped Ninetoes' attention. A flick of his will was all it took to ignite his eyes with Mind's Eye and he could see a mixture of white, green and blue waves pulse from the stone.

340

"What is it exactly?"

"I'm glad you asked."

I'll bet he is. It gives him a chance to catch his breath.

Ninetoes chuckled at Libby's jibe. But, at the look of annoyance from the Trainer, replaced his smirk with a more serious face.

"It is a Skill Stone. It is a means of transmitting knowledge from a Master of any Skill into someone without any. They are extremely rare however, because one must know how to create the crystals as well as the knowledge they wish to impart. As a Master of Transmutation I, of course, have the requisite knowledge of both."

"Interesting. So, within that stone is all of your knowledge about Transmutation?"

"Ha! Far from it. No, sealed securely within, is the knowledge of the first twenty Levels, it could take someone with no knowledge of the Spell School all the way straight to the beginning of the Apprentice Rank, teaching them both rank bonuses as well." As Ninetoes' eyes widen with avarice, the Trainer finishes baiting his hook. "It also holds knowledge of two useful spells from the School."

By now, Ninetoes was unconsciously licking his lips. Dry mouthed, his voice is barely a whisper. "How much?"

"Four hundred gold pieces." And then came his masterstroke. "But, with the Guild discount, that would only be two hundred." *Argh!* Commander Switfaxe had clearly planned this all along as a means to manipulate Ninetoes into joining the Guild.

Ninetoes hated being handled in this way. But he also really wanted that stone and four hundred gold was more than he'd already spent on all the magical items he'd bought.

Meanwhile, the Trainer's mouth slipped into a shit-eating grin. Clearly, he believed the apprentice Adventurer was easy prey. Believing perhaps that by amazing the young hobgoblin with the extent of the Guild's power and wealth, he could dupe him into joining their ranks. But Ninetoes would not so easily be taken advantage of.

Instead, Ninetoes reached into his Bag of Holding, while simultaneously holding the man's gaze and clearly enunciated the words "Forty platinum pieces." The man's jowly grin dropped as Ninetoes held the coins out to him. Then, when the man didn't reach out to take them, he reached forward and took hold of the other man's hand and pulled it forward, pulling the stone from it and depositing the coins onto the greasy couch.

Standing, Ninetoes turned his back on the Trainer and made for the door, but the man's wafer-thin voice caught him before he reached the door. "I, I, have more, if you're of a mind to-"

"No." He wasn't about to drain any more of his hard-won wealth on this flabby fool.

Instead, he left the man to stare in wonder after the young Adventurer. Having got what he'd come for, Ninetoes was ready to leave the Guild and find his friends. If, indeed, he could still count Bess as such.

Stopping briefly to retrieve his cloak, before making his way quickly downstairs and out across the courtyard, he suddenly paused. He never asked the Trainer how to use the Skill Stone. *Blast!* He'd look like a fool going back and the bastard would probably charge him for the information. No. He'd figure it out himself.

Walking out of the gateway onto the street the people bustled around him and, once again, he considered his time in the City of Pamor. It had been beneficial to be sure but he'd be glad to leave.

Climbing to his shoulder, Libby rubbed her face against his cheek and he smiled.

Time to head to the Inn I think Little One.

Yes Master. Hopefully we'll be in time for dinner but perhaps we should find somewhere to buy some cheese on the way there.

"Ha!" Truly his Familiar was a wonder. *I don't know where I'd be without you Little One.*

As the thought left his mind, Libby stood a little straighter and glowed a soft, warming orange and the part of him that was linked to her felt the change as well.

342

Awweh, what was that? It felt amazing. Libby's body shuddered from nose to tail and she smiled brightly at her Master.

I'm not sure my dear, perhaps your Character Sheet will tell us. He retrieved the parchment from his bag and the two companions investigated it as they wandered downhill towards the dock ward.

FAMILIAR NAME: LIBBY	**RACE:** SQUIRREL (+1 AGI) PER LEVEL
LEVEL: 15TH*	**BONDED WIZARD:** NINETOES
HIT POINTS: 15/15	**MANA POINTS:** 130/130
STAMINA POINTS: 163/163	
BASE STATS: STRENGTH - 1 AGILITY - 45 ENDURANCE - 3 INTELLIGENCE - 26 WISDOM -13 CHARISMA - 14	**ARMOUR:** NONE
RACIAL ABILITIES	
CLIMB: CAN CLIMB ANY ROUGH SURFACE AT NORMAL MOVEMENT SPEED.	**IMPROVED GLIDE:** THE SQUIRREL IS ABLE TO LEAP AND GLIDE MEDIUM DISTANCES.
LEARNED ABILITIES	
CUTE: THE SQUIRREL'S NATURAL APPEAL GIVES IT AN ADVANTAGE WHEN CASTING ENCHANTMENT	**SNEAK AND HIDE:** THE SQUIRREL'S SIZE AND DEXTERITY MAKE IT EASIER

SPELLS THAT ATTEMPT TO 'CHARM' A CREATURE.	WHEN TRYING TO CONCEAL ITSELF.
SPELL CHANNELLING: THE FAMILIAR CAN CHANNEL MAGICAL ENERGY TO AND FROM ITSELF INTO ITS BONDED WIZARD, RANGE LIMITED TO 20 FEET.	**STEAL:** THE SQUIRREL'S SIZE AND DEXTERITY MAKE IT A NATURAL THIEF.
SURVIVAL INSTINCT: THE SQUIRREL'S NATURAL INSTINCT PROVIDES IT WITH THE WISDOM TO RUN, 25% RESISTANCE AGAINST 'FEAR' ATTACKS.	**ZIPPY:** THE SQUIRREL'S SIZE AND DEXTERITY MAKE IT DIFFICULT TO ATTACK BY LARGER CREATURES. **QUICK WITTED:** ONCE PER DAY, THE SQUIRREL CAN CREATE AN ILLUSORY COPY OF ITSELF TO DISTRACT AN ENEMY.

SPELL CASTING AFFINITIES	
ABJURATION - 50% SPELLS KNOWN - WIZARD'S ARMOUR	ENCHANTMENT - 75% SPELLS KNOWN - CHARISMA
ILLUSION* - 75% SPELLS KNOWN - MINOR ILLUSION*, CLOAKING SHADOW, MADIGAR'S MADNESS	NECROMANCY - 10% SPELLS KNOWN - GRIM VOID

Unspent upgrade points - 2

At first glance, little seemed to have changed. Sure, Libby had gained two levels and so had two more Upgrade points to spend, but it didn't explain the glowing energy that still pulsed from her.

Studying the document closer, however, he noted that one of her Racial Abilities, Glide had become Improved Glide, increasing the distance from short to medium but that still didn't provide answers.

That was when he noticed the small asterisk next to her Level and, when he focussed on it, information filled their shared thoughts.

*The Familiar Choice - Choose from Path of Harmony I, Path of the Chain I or Path of the Maverick I.

What in all the Nine Hells are Paths? He hadn't meant to 'verbalise' the thought, but Libby heard him nonetheless.

I do not know Master but we mustn't be hasty. They must be important. Perhaps Gideon will know? She suggested.

Of course, my dear, you're right. If anyone would, he seems the most likely. Let's hold on choosing until we've spoken to him.

Agreed.

Short as their conversation was, it had carried them all the way to the docks and it was only a short walk until they found a large, slightly sloping Inn with the carving of a large, monstrous green head, hanging above the doorway.

CHAPTER 18
TALLY'S TROLL

Ninetoes wasn't the first to arrive at the Inn. A short scan located Bluzag, Bess and Lowen at a large table on the far side of the taproom. Each of them had a large plate of roasted meat and vegetables before them, Lowen and Bess having nearly finished theirs while Bluzag's sat untouched.

The bargemaster waved to Ninetoes and he headed across the bar, pausing long enough to order a pint of cider from a passing waitress, along the way.

"Hail. I trust everyone's days have been industrious." He was perhaps laying it on a little thick, but the look on Bess' face told him that she hadn't forgotten or forgiven what he'd done at the Castle.

"Aye, the barge is loaded. You might need to apologise to young Deck, he's none too pleased that he won't get to bread his crumpet for as long as he'd hoped, but we're ready to sail with the dawn. Bess tells me we've got some other passengers, they'll want paying for o' course, but there's room enough." He stared demandingly at Ninetoes and the hobgoblin huffed but he handed over some gold coins.

"I'll want a receipt this time," he grouched, but Lowen just nodded back as he tested the coins with his teeth. "Bess, did you manage to complete your testing at the Smithing Guild?"

"Aye." Was the only response he got.

"More'an that, she passed and, way you was telling it a moment ago, you done things with metal that no one had ever seen before," Lowen prompted, clearly sensing the frosty atmosphere.

"That's wonderful news Bes."

Just then, Ninetoes' eyes noticed something different about Bluzag. He now wore a breastplate, bracers and greaves, all of it a rich, dark, red metal and handsome to behold. "Did-, do you make this for Bluzag?"

Bess' mouth creased into a smile and her youthful buoyancy finally broke through. "Aye. I didn't have to make the whole suit, but once I arrived with Bluzag, the Masters assumed I'd brought him as a model and, well he needed some new gear and seeing as you weren't there and he didn't seem to have any of his own gold, it just seemed right."

Now that he looked more closely, he could see that the metal was clearly designed to fit not only the half-ogre's enormous figure but that it also worked well with his fighting style. The bracers were thickly plated on the outside where they would cover those areas not protected by the Wight's shield. The breastplate gave freedom of movement for Bluzag's massive biceps and the greaves reached over the knee joint without hindering movement and wrapped around to cover the ankle so that he couldn't be hamstrung by a rogue's blade. It was perfect.

"It looks excellent Bess, thank you."

"I'll make him a shield as well, once we're back in Raveslan and now that I'm a Journeyman I can take on my own commissions."

"Of course, I'm sorry, how much did all this cost?" Ninetoes said, reaching for his coin pouch.

"Oh, no… that's not what I meant. The materials are part of the trial, and Boris paid that months ago." Her voice showed her embarrassment.

"No. I insist. Good work deserves good pay. What would Boris charge for a suit like this?" he asked, opening the pouch.

"Er… well my works not as good at Boris' but, well I suppose… twenty-five gold?" She stammered.

Ninetoes had a feeling that she was trying to lowball him, but he didn't see any way of saying so without embarrassing her. So he simply counted out the coins and slid them across the table towards her.

"Fine craftsmanship, very fine indeed. You have my thanks Miss- ah, what is your name now?"

"Ha! I hadn't thought of that, I suppose I am now Miss Smith." Her smile shone out, lighting up the grim tavern and bringing smiles to the rest of the table's occupants.

For the next hour, the party sat and talked, comfortable in one another's presence and for that time, Ninetoes was able to forget how she'd looked at him that morning.

Then, as the sun dipped below the horizon and blanketed the City in a chilling darkness, the taproom's door opened and four Adventurers entered. Ninetoes recognised them immediately, but in an effort to hold on to the feeling of comfort for just a little while longer, he pretended not to notice.

It wasn't until the Red Crew spoke with the barman that they were sent over to the party's quiet little corner. The tall, handsome warrior stepped forward. "Alrigh, we're the Dread Crew, we've bee-"

"We agreed on the Red Crew." The armoured woman spoke up, interrupting the warrior's introduction.

"-n… Yeah, well I still say the Dread Crew sounds cooler."

"We took a vote," chipped in the mage.

"Alright! Alright, whatever. We're here to do the Quest, to save your town or whatever."

Ninetoes stood up. "Please join our table. This is Lowen, the bargemaster, my companion Bluzag and Bes Smith, newly appointed Journeyman blacksmith and Raveslan's representative." Finishing his introductions, he held out his hand in greeting.

The warrior however didn't even seem to notice, instead simply seating himself next to Bess and flagging down a waitress to order a drink. Without looking up, he simply said. "Right. I'm just gonna call you one, two, three and four." Pointing at each of the party members as he counted.

"Ergh, you're such a murderhobo! Ever heard of roleplay?" The elven warrior stepped up and shook Ninetoes hand. "I'm Sariel the Half-Elven Ranger, this is Daphne the Wizard, An'rik the Lizardfolk Cleric and that oaf is Tarquin, but he won't tell us what class he is." It seemed odd to

Ninetoes that anyone would introduce themselves by defining their race, but each to his own.

"It's Sir Tarquin and I told you, it's a secret because of me backstory. Huh, now who don't know how to roleplay?" The warrior, who was currently ogling Bess' cleavage, retorted.

"Er... excellent. Please join us for food and drink and we can fill you in on the details." Then, seating himself beside the other wizard, Ninetoes asked. "Do you mind telling me what Spell School you've specialised in?"

Completely deadpan, the mage stared back at the hobgoblin. "Oh, I don't roleplay." And she turned back to stare at the table.

Confused by her response, Ninetoes was struck dumb for a minute or so. Recovering in time to hear the end of Bess' summary of the Quest. "I will be joining you on the journey back to Raveslan."

"Oh god! We don't need a babysitter. How long you been questin' anyway?" Tarquin rudely barked.

"Um... I'm no babysitter and only a few weeks. There are dangerous monsters on the road and I seek your protection as much as I can offer you mine."

Tarquin looked about to argue, but the Cleric, An'rik, leaned in and whispered something to him. Tarquin's eyes widened and he grinned back at the lizardman and nodded. "Of course, 'never kick a gift horse in the mouth', I always say. We'll take all the help we can get."

An'rik and Sariel asked a few more questions about the Quest, which Ninetoes answered but Daphne seemed to be about as inanimate as Bluzag and Tarquin spent the time trying to persuade Bess to have a drinking competition. In the end, she was saved by the arrival of Lady Fawkner and Gideon.

"Ninetoes, I found this gentleman asking for you at the bar. Adventurers." She nodded to the other party members, but only the Ranger and Cleric offered her introductions. "Bess, perhaps you'd attend to me, I have had a room prepared for us ladies, apologies Adventurers I was unaware that we'd be joined by more women."

Bess didn't need to be asked twice and made her escape quickly, following the Lady upstairs.

Meanwhile, Gideon took the empty seat beside Ninetoes. "It's finished." And so saying, he held out a small, thick ring, sized it appeared, for a pinky finger.

It's beautiful, thank you Gideon. Ninetoes heard Libby's voice in his mind and, as he checked Gideon's ear, realised that the man could hear her as well.

Master, could you cast Identify and tell me what it says please?

Ninetoes quickly acquiesced and was not disappointed.

GIDEON'S RING OF THE TRICKSTER - NORMAL, VERY RARE

PROPERTIES: +5 TO THE WEARER'S ILLUSION SKILL LEVEL. ALLOWS THE WEARER TO CAST REFLECTION ONCE PER DAY.

Ninetoes had never heard of the Reflection spell before, but a brief manipulation of his will and the spell's details flooded into his mind and so into the link he shared with Libby.

REFLECTION - LEVEL 10 (ITEM)

ILLUSION

CASTING TIME - 1 SECOND

DURATION - 1 MINUTE

LVL 10. THE CASTER CREATES A DOUBLE OF ITSELF. THE DOUBLE WILL MOVE AND ACT AS IF A REFLECTION OF THE CASTER UNLESS GIVEN INSTRUCTION. IF THE CASTER CONCENTRATES HOWEVER, THE DOUBLE WILL MOVE AND ACT AS INSTRUCTED.

It's perfect Gideon, thank you. As she said this, Libby climbed into Ninetoes' outstretched palm and reached out her left foreclaw. Gideon carefully placed the ring over his wrist where it shrank slightly to sit as snuggly as a bracer. Libby's eyes glowed briefly with purple light and she smiled mischievously. *And thank you Master.*

Oh, it's no trou—

"It wasn't easy to make and it's unique, so I can't take less than fifty gold pi-"

Ninetoes held out his hand, a neat stack of seven platinum pieces sitting upon it. "Anything for my Libby," he said simultaneously with both his mind and verbally.

"This, this is too much. Please take some back." Gideon seemed uncomfortable with so much wealth on display and he tried to shove a couple of coins back towards the hobgoblin.

"No, keep it please. But in exchange, perhaps you could help us with some questions that we have. Surely you recognise that information can be just as valuable as your items?"

"Very well and thank you. What would you like to know? I fear I'm only really an expert in Familiars and Companions, although I know much about magic items."

"Excellent, then I think you're exactly the person we need." Ninetoes reached into his bag and brought out Libby's Character Sheet and showed it to Gideon.

By now, Tarquin and Daphne had made their way to the bar and An'rik was nowhere to be seen, but Sariel was staring closely at Ninetoes, clearly interested in what he and Gideon were talking about. Not seeing any particular reason that she shouldn't be included, Ninetoes gestured to Daphne's empty seat.

"Do you have some interest in Familiars Sariel?" he asked her as a means of bringing her into the conversation.

"Not exactly. It is difficult for a Ranger to get a Familiar, I was thinking of specialising in Beast Mastery and so I'd get a Companion animal though," she answered as she moved around the table to join them.

"Then I'd be happy to answer both your questions, Adventurers." Gideon smiled.

Placing the parchment down onto the table where everyone could see it. Ninetoes pointed to Libby's Level and the asterisk and then described the choice they'd been given. "Can you explain to me what these choices are?"

"Yes, yes I can." Gideon answered quickly and, for the first time since Ninetoes had bumped into him, his voice lost its usual quaver and he spoke confidently. "When a Familiar or Companion animal reaches certain levels, or to be more precise, when the bond they share with their Master reaches a certain level, the bonded pair are given a choice about how they want that connection to evolve. The first two choices you've been offered are the same given to every Familiar when it reaches Level Fifteen, but I've never even heard of the Path of the Maverick." This fact alone seemed to stall the young man for a moment.

He quickly regained his confidence however and smiled. "That can mean only one thing, Libby is truly special."

Tell me something I don't know.

The comment made both Gideon and Ninetoes grin but this only left Sariel confused. "It's just an 'in' joke." Ninetoes explained.

"But, seriously. I've studied every book in Pamor about Familiars and Companions and yet I've never even seen it mentioned." Gideon expanded.

"So then, you can't tell me what it is or does?"

"Er no. In fact, I'm rather excited to be able to expand my knowledge."

"How so? If you don't know what it is, then I won't risk Libby by testing it."

"Ah, no. You misunderstand. Here, it's probably easier if I just show you. Do you mind if I touch Libby's Character Sheet?" he asked politely.

"Please. Go ahead."

Gideon smoothed out the parchment and then touched his index finger to the asterisk. It briefly lit up and then the end of the paper extended slightly, filling it with more writing as it did. All four companions leaned forward to read the new information.

PATH OF HARMONY I

THE NATURE OF THE FAMILIAR MERGES TO BE-COME CLOSER TO ITS MASTER'S SO THAT THE TWO CAN WORK MORE CONGRUOUSLY. THE FOLLOWING CHANGES TAKE PLACE:

- THE MASTER CAN CHOOSE TO IN-CREASE EITHER ALL THE MENTAL STATS OR ALL THE PHYSICAL STATS BY +3.
- THE RANGE OF THE SPELL CHANNEL-LING ABILITY INCREASES TO 100 FEET AND INCREASES IN EFFICIENCY BY 25%.
- THE FAMILIAR GAINS A 25% INCREASE IN SPELL AFFINITY TO THEIR MASTER'S SPECIALISM BUT SUFFERS A -5% DE-CREASE IN AFFINITIES TO THE OTHER SCHOOLS.
- WHEN WITHIN 20 FEET OF ONE AN-OTHER A MASTER MAY USE THE FAMIL-IAR TO DUAL-CAST SPELLS TO INCREASE THEIR POTENCY BY 25%.

PATH OF THE CHAIN I

THE FAMILIAR BECOMES THE MASTER'S OBEDI-ENT AND UNQUESTIONING SERVANT. THE FOL-LOWING CHANGES TAKE PLACE:

- ALL THE FAMILIAR'S PHYSICAL STATS INCREASE BY +4, WHILE MENTAL STATS DECREASE BY -1.
- THE RANGE OF THE SPELL CHANNEL-LING ABILITY INCREASES TO 200* FEET BUT IT CAN ONLY TRAVEL FROM THE FAMILIAR TO THE MASTER.
- THE MASTER CAN CAST SPELLS THROUGH THEIR BOND WITH THE FA-MILIAR WITHIN THE DISTANCE OF THE

PATH OF THE MAVERICK I

THE FAMILIAR GAINS THE CONSCIOUSNESS AND INDEPENDENCE TO BECOME AN INDIVID-UAL. THE FOLLOWING CHANGES TAKE PLACE:

- THE FAMILIAR GAINS 10 UPGRADE POINTS TO SPEND HOWEVER THEY CHOOSE.
- THE RANGE OF THE SPELL CHANNEL-LING ABILITY INCREASES TO 100 FEET.
- THE FAMILIAR GAINS A 15% INCREASE IN ONE SPELL AFFINITY OF THEIR CHOICE.
- THE FAMILIAR GAINS 5 LEVELS IN THE SAME SPELL SCHOOL.
- FAMILIAR LEARNS ONE SPELL FROM THIS CHOSEN SPELL SCHOOL.

Woah! Er… what?

Ninetoes' thought and just in case he hadn't made her thoughts be 'out loud' he echoed the sentiment. "And, what does that mean?"

"Hang on a sec, I'm still reading," said Libby, staring daggers at Ninetoes. "What? I'm a slow reader."

When two creatures are bonded in the way that Ninetoes and Libby were, and when those two creatures were both impatient, short-tempered beings, those feelings of impatient will rebound against each other and cause a storm of irascible anger, the likes of which is only mentioned when describing an avenging god. So it was that by the time Libby finished, Ninetoes was fit to bursting.

"So?"

So?

Gideon actually shuddered at the combined verbal and mental assault, but the looks on both Master and Familiar's faces left him no room for levity and he hurried to answer.

"Of course, yes, right…" His stumbling did him no favours and Libby seriously considered casting Madigar's Madness to chivvy him a long a little. "Sigh. Right, here's what I know for sure. As I said, the Path of the Chain and the Path of Harmony are the normal choices provided and you probably noted that they both offer benefits to the caster but they also force the pair to work together in a certain manner." Ninetoes thought he understood, but he gestured for Gideon to go on.

"So, let's take the Path of the Chain. This is normally taken by casters who wish to have a servant or a sidekick in combat, a creature that will do their bidding without argument. They are in fact incapable of defying their Master's will. This can sound harsh, but if you consider that many Familiars are simply dumb beasts, *No offence Libby dear* then you realise that controlling exactly what they do can be appealing. This Choice also grants the Familiar physical enhancements, which can make them deadly in combat."

"And being able to cast a spell through them allows a caster to surprise an enemy, I like it." Plus, Ninetoes thought quietly to himself, not having Libby's nagging would be a boon. "What about the asterisk?"

"That is one of the drawbacks. While this Path offers the greatest Spell Channelling distance, that is also the limit of range that the Familiar can function without its Master."

"You mean the Familiar would just, what, stop at that range?"

"Not exactly, the bond between Master and Familiar ceases at that range, so the creature would simply revert back to its former bestial nature and the Master would have to cast the spell again. Some casters will regularly do this to change out their Familiar to suit their needs."

"Ha! Hear that? Remember that the next time I ask you if I need a bath."

All joking aside however, he could never shackle Libby in this way and she'd never be a close-quarters fighter anyway. He didn't even need to ask Libby her thoughts on the subject before he spoke. "This Choice is not for us, however, please go on."

"Certainly. Path of Harmony is often taken by straight spellcasters because it offers the opportunity to make your Familiar into a powerful caster in their own right and the bond also enhances the caster's own spell casting. Although they mostly choose it for the Dual-Casting ability. This can be incredibly powerful as it can enhance all spells cast, but for those within the Master's Specialism the effects are even more potent."

This definitely had potential. Ninetoes could imagine himself casting his spells enhanced by Libby's own capabilities. It would also grant her the ability to use more of his spells, this could mean Libby could create her own undead servants and bodyguards.

"What about this Path of the Maverick? What's your take on that?"

"As I've mentioned, I've never heard of, or even seen this Choice before but it's definitely interesting."

What could have given us a Choice such as this? Libby asked, beating Ninetoes to ask the same question.

"I apologise, but I really have no idea, but it would have to be something incredible, maybe even divine."

"Hmmm, interesting. What are your thoughts on this Path Gideon?"

"Er... well, if I may say so, it seems to reflect your bond perfectly." Ninetoes raised his eyebrows. "This Path may even be unique. It's almost to the point that it feels that this Path was made for you and Libby."

Ninetoes thought about this. For a moment, he occupied the space in his mind that Libby shared and the two of them debated the issue at length, all at the speed of thought. Then, as the two of them smiled at one another they joined their wills together and fixed them on their Choice. Libby's Character Sheet changed almost instantaneously.

FAMILIAR NAME: LIBBY THE MAVERICK	RACE: SQUIRREL (+1 AGI) PER LEVEL
LEVEL: 15TH	BONDED WIZARD: NINETOES

HIT POINTS: 15/15	MANA POINTS: 150/150
STAMINA POINTS: 163/163	

| BASE STATS:
STRENGTH - 1
AGILITY - 45
ENDURANCE - 3
INTELLIGENCE - 30
WISDOM -15
CHARISMA - 20 | ARMOUR: NONE |

RACIAL ABILITIES

CLIMB: CAN CLIMB ANY ROUGH SURFACE AT NORMAL MOVEMENT SPEED.	IMPROVED GLIDE: THE SQUIRREL IS ABLE TO LEAP AND GLIDE MEDIUM DISTANCES.

LEARNED ABILITIES

CUTE: THE SQUIRREL'S NATURAL APPEAL GIVES IT AN ADVANTAGE WHEN CASTING ENCHANTMENT SPELLS THAT ATTEMPT TO 'CHARM' A CREATURE.	SNEAK AND HIDE: THE SQUIRREL'S SIZE AND DEXTERITY MAKE IT EASIER WHEN TRYING TO CONCEAL ITSELF.
IMPROVED SPELL CHANNELLING: THE FAMILIAR CAN CHANNEL MAGICAL ENERGY TO AND FROM ITSELF INTO ITS BONDED WIZARD, RANGE LIMITED TO 100 FEET.	STEAL: THE SQUIRREL'S SIZE AND DEXTERITY MAKE IT A NATURAL THIEF.

SURVIVAL INSTINCT: THE SQUIRREL'S NATURAL INSTINCT PROVIDES IT WITH THE WISDOM TO RUN, 25% RESISTANCE AGAINST 'FEAR' ATTACKS.	**ZIPPY**: THE SQUIRREL'S SIZE AND DEXTERITY MAKE IT DIFFICULT TO ATTACK BY LARGER CREATURES. **QUICK WITTED**: ONCE PER DAY, THE SQUIRREL CAN CREATE AN ILLUSORY COPY OF ITSELF TO DISTRACT AN ENEMY.
STRONG WILLED: THE SQUIRREL'S CHARISMA AND PROPENSITY FOR BEING BOSSY MAKE IT MORE DIFFICULT TO CONTROL, GAINING 25% DEFENCE AGAINST THE EFFECTS OF ILLUSION AND ENCHANTMENT MAGICS.	

SPELL CASTING AFFINITIES

ABJURATION - 50% **SPELLS KNOWN** - WIZARD'S ARMOUR	**ENCHANTMENT** - 75% **SPELLS KNOWN** - CHARISMA
ILLUSION* - 90% **SPELLS KNOWN** - MINOR ILLUSION*, CLOAKING SHADOW, MADIGAR'S MADNESS	**NECROMANCY** - 10% **SPELLS KNOWN** - GRIM VOID
ILLUSION - LEVEL 25 (20) BEGINNER +25% DURATION OF ILLUSION SPELLS ILLUSION SAVANT I - ILLUSION SPELLS COST YOU 10% LESS TO CAST.	

KNOWLEDGE ARCANE I - ALLOWS THE CASTER TO CHOOSE ONE APPRENTICE RANKED SPELL.	

With the main choice made, the pair had also decided where to place the stat and affinity bonuses. Together they placed 2 points into Wisdom, 4 points into Intelligence, and 6 into Charisma. The choice to spend four points on Intelligence was easy; more mana and possibly an added bonus for reaching a milestone.

As Libby's eyes flicked across the Character Sheet at high speeds, it had obviously paid off with an increased reading speed. As for Wisdom, like Ninetoes, Libby had wanted to increase the pace that her mana regenerated. But Ninetoes had baulked at Libby's insistence of putting the other six points into Charisma. This was Ninetoes' lowest stat and for good reason, he'd never bothered to place any points into it. He'd never be handsome, so why bother?

Libby, of course, felt differently. She was convinced that the stat score had more significance and that it would help her improve her magic. Annoyingly, she'd been right and it seemed to have granted her a new ability, Strong Willed. Perhaps, Ninetoes admitted, he should place a few points into the stat himself.

The Affinity bonus of 15% and the extra Skill levels had of course gone into Illusion but they hadn't chosen the spell right away and their hunch had paid off.

Having seen that the Apprentice rank bonus for Necromancy was Knowledge Arcane I, they had bet that there was a good chance of getting a similar bonus for Illusion and they'd been right. That was why they were currently staring at a longer than normal list of spells from which they could choose two.

IRIDESCENT

PREREQUISITES - ILLUSION POOR

CASTING TIME - 1 SECOND

MANA COST - 50 POINTS

DURATION - 10 SECONDS

LVL 10. THE CASTER SHOOTS A BEAM OF BRIGHT RAINBOW-COLOURED LIGHT DIRECTLY INTO THE EYES OF A TARGET WITHIN 60 FEET. IF THE TARGET FAILS TO SAVE AGAINST THIS ILLUSION, THE DAZZLING LIGHT BLINDS THEM FOR THE DURATION.

MAGIC MOUTH

PREREQUISITES - ILLUSION POOR

CASTING TIME - 1 SECOND (+ LENGTH OF THE MESSAGE).

MANA COST - 100 POINTS

DURATION - UNTIL TRIGGERED

LVL 10. WHEN CAST ON A CREATURE OR OBJECT THE CASTER MAY LEAVE A MESSAGE THAT TRIGGERS WHEN THE CONDITIONS SPECIFIED BY THE CASTER ARE MET. THE MESSAGE CAN BE NO MORE THAN 25 WORDS BUT CAN BE IN ANY LANGUAGE OR VOICE THE CASTER KNOWS.

REFLECTION

PREREQUISITES - ILLUSION POOR

CASTING TIME - 1 SECOND

MANA COST - 100 POINTS

DURATION - 1 MINUTE

LVL 10. THE CASTER CREATES A DOUBLE OF ITSELF. THE DOUBLE WILL MOVE AND ACT AS IF A REFLECTION OF THE CASTER UNLESS GIVEN INSTRUCTION. IF THE CASTER CONCENTRATES HOWEVER, THE DOUBLE WILL MOVE AND ACT

AS INSTRUCTED.

INVISIBILITY

PREREQUISITES - ILLUSION APPRENTICE

CASTING TIME - 1 MINUTE

MANA COST - 150 POINTS

DURATION - 10 MINUTES

LVL 10. MAKES THE CASTER INVISIBLE TO THE NAKED EYE FOR THE DURATION. TAKING OR DEALING DAMAGE OR CASTING A SPELL WILL MAKE THE CASTER VISIBLE AGAIN.

SHADOW ARMOUR

PREREQUISITES - ILLUSION APPRENTICE

CASTING TIME - 1 MINUTE

MANA COST - 50 POINTS

DURATION - 5 HOURS

LVL 20. SHADOWS AROUND THE CASTER SOLIDIFY INTO WEIGHTLESS ARMOUR. PROVIDES AN ARMOUR CLASS OF 20.

```
TALLY'S TRAP
PREREQUISITES - ILLUSION APPRENTICE
CASTING TIME - 1 MINUTE
MANA COST - 100 POINTS
DURATION - UNTIL TRIGGERED
LVL 20. CREATES A 5-FOOT SPACE WITH A SIM-
PLE TRAP FROM THE CHOICES BELOW. TRIGGER
WHEN THE CONDITIONS DEFINED BY THE
CHOSEN TRAP ARE MET.
   •  SNARE - IF A CREATURE STEPS INTO
      THE SPACE AN ILLUSORY ROPE RE-
      TRAINS THEM.
   •  EXPLOSIVE - IF A CREATURE STEPS INTO
      THE SPACE AN EXPLOSIVE IS TRIG-
      GERED, DEALING 3-18 POINTS OF FIRE
      DAMAGE.
```

It was quite a list and certainly wouldn't be an easy choice. The spells were also listed in the two ranks, Poor and Apprentice, so Ninetoes was of the opinion that they'd have to choose one from each rank.

"Perhaps we should start with the tougher choice." Ninetoes said.

How do you mean? Libby asked.

"Well, if we choose two Apprentice spells you like and try to select them both we can find out whether or not this is possible. If it's not, then we choose a Poor rank spell."

Makes sense I suppose. Maybe we should ask these two for advice.

For the first time in a few minutes, Ninetoes remembered that they had company. *Oh yeah.*

"My friends. What spells would you advise?"

"Ah, you remembered we were here did you? We thought you two had slipped into a coma or something the way you were just staring at one another like that. You realise that's a little rude right?" Sariel commented. "Then we noticed that Libby's sheet had changed and we understood what you'd been doing. Your big friend there however, is still staring into space; is he alright?"

"Yes and a bold decision it was too. I'd-er, be grateful if you'd visit me the next time you're in Pamor, I'd like to take notes on your experiences with the Path of the Maverick," Gideon added.

"Bluzag's fine, just… tired I expect. And yes Gideon, of course I will, but first we've got to survive the return journey to Raveslan and stop the Nechtsarm. To do that I'll need Libby's help."

"And the help of the Red Crew of course," Sariel snarked.

"Of course, of course. For now, I'd take your advice on what spells Libby should choose." He showed them the Character Sheet and pointed out the list of spell choices.

"Hmmm, I've seen some of these spells before, there are some good choices. Shadow Armour is a particularly good protection spell but being able to turn invisible is arguably more effective at keeping one safe in combat. Invisibility has one definite drawback however, as soon as Libby attacks, she'd be visible again. What role does she play in battle?"

"Ah, I see your point. Libby has been acting as a scout, getting somewhere high and feeding me information."

"So then being invisible would seem pretty perfect."

Ninetoes thought about this and discussed it with Libby, this time being as brief as possible so as not to be rude.

"Libby believes that Cloaking Shadow already serves this role and she'd like to be able to play a more significant role in combat."

"Playing overwatch is significant Libby but the choice is, apparently yours." It was odd to hear someone direct their words towards his Familiar and he liked it. Libby stood a little straighter at her words and he could feel the squirrel's feelings warming to the half-elf. "Also, what's Cloaking Shadow? I've never heard of that spell."

Dammit! "We er… found an old scroll and managed to copy the spell, it provides a minor buff to sneaking." He tried, unsuccessfully, to play it off as nothing, but their declaration that it acted like Invisibility was a bit of a give-away.

"What about Tally's Trap? And, is that the same Tally who owns this Inn?"

"Ah ha ha ha! You're not saying you've never heard of Tally?" Sariel exclaimed. Ninetoes' teeth ground against each other. He was so sick of not knowing stuff that people thought he should. Just as he was about to respond rudely, Gideon spoke up.

"I've never heard of this Tally, is he, she special?"

"She's only one of the most famous Adventurers in…" Sariel paused for a moment, as if searching for the right word, "um, Adrenon." When both Ninetoes and Gideon stared back nonplussed, Sariel went on. "She was a mage of some kind, I'm certainly no expert, but she's in lots of the stories and she's supposed to have created loads of the spells."

"And does she own this tavern?" Gideon asked.

"I doubt it, she's been dead for like hundreds of years, it's probably just named after her."

Ninetoes' anger had receded a little and he was keen to get on with picking Libby's spells. "Intriguing, thank you Sariel. What about this spell; Tally's Trap?"

"It's a good one, it's even one that I can learn as a Ranger. The traps at base level aren't going to be very effective against big monsters, but it could be useful in the coming battle I suppose."

I agree Master. I think my first choice would be Shadow Armour, but why don't we try selecting Tally's Trap as the second choice? Ninetoes sighed inwardly. He hadn't wanted to force the issue, but the most important factor for him was to protect Libby and armour seemed the best way to do that. He nodded in agreement and quickly relayed Libby's plan to the others.

Then, with a manipulation of her will, Libby chose her first spell. And nothing happened, apart from the three Apprentice Ranked spells disappearing from the list.

Oh. Do you 'know' how to cast it now Libby dearest? he asked.

No. Strange, perhaps it's in your spellbook, she suggested and they quickly flicked through to the Illusion section and sure enough, there it was. This was brilliant! It meant any spell she learned, Ninetoes would have access to, if only he could reach Level 20 in Illusion. Not likely any time soon. Sadly, they'd also got their answer on choosing spells; their second choice would have to come from the Poor ranks. Of course, if their theories held true, once Libby cast it, it should rank up to Level 20.

"Alright. Now a Poor level spell."

"There's no question, Reflection is a brilliant spell." Sariel's excitement was infectious and Libby hopped up and down before the woman.

"That's true but Libby's bracelet already ha—"

"Ah, yes. Let's just look at the other choices first shall we?" Gideon had been about to spill the beans on Libby's Ring of the Trickster. Ninetoes was warming to the Ranger, but he wasn't ready to share all of their secrets. "Surely Iridescent is also a good choice? A blind enemy is an easy target and less of a threat."

And Magic Mouth would give me a voice. Libby's 'out loud' voice held a different feeling that Ninetoes was coming to recognise.

"I agree Libby, giving you a voice would be useful, but perhaps not at the expense of these other two spells."

So then, it was between Reflection and Iridescent. Certainly, Ninetoes was intrigued to see what a Level 20 Reflection spell could do, but he was still leaning towards Iridescent. Ten seconds didn't sound like long, but in the heat of combat, it could feel like a lifeline. What's more, Ninetoes could feel Libby's opinion mirrored his own.

"Iridescent seems the best choice."

So saying, Libby 'chose' the spell and the last of the spells listed disappeared with Iridescent reappearing in his spellbook. "Now all you need to do is cast them."

"Jack won't 'ave no magic in the bar. You'd better go out on the wharf if yer gonna start slinging spells."

Ninetoes hadn't realised how close the waitress was, but her advice was sound.

"Would you like to join us?" he offered to Sariel and Gideon. Both of them nodded enthusiastically and Libby hopped onto Sariel's shoulder and they stood up from the table. If Ninetoes had a spell to change the colour of his skin, it would have become a mottled green.

Stepping outside, they found that the sun was long gone and the streets were now lit by tall lamps. Holding out his spellbook so that Libby could read the spell, he attempted to learn it himself, but it just didn't make enough sense to try and cast it. For Libby however, she scanned the matter twice and then nodded.

She'd decided to start with Shadow Armour and with a brief moment of concentration, Libby uttered a string of arcane words. All around wisps of shadow started to be pulled towards her. Wherever there was a contour on her body, the shadows began to coalesce. At first, the silhouettes seemed lumpy and random but as Libby looked over herself, she guided the shadows into sleek armour that covered her forearms and back, leaving her chest free. As the last of the shadows made their way to her, Libby moulded them into the shape of a barbute helmet with cheek and nose pieces, long and angled enough to cover her pointed nose.

"Wow Libby! That looks so cool!" Sariel offered her hand for Libby to stand on and then held her out for the group to admire. It truly was a striking suit of armour and Ninetoes was once again impressed by his Familiar's ingenuity.

After a minute or so of praise, Libby evidently grew bored and loudly announced. *I need a volunteer for my other spell.*

Clearly, as she couldn't hear the rodent's telepathic voice, this was not meant to include Sariel and so Ninetoes and Gideon simply stared at each other.

"Well, obviously I can't do it, I have no magical defences at all, if it should go wrong, I could be blinded for the rest of my life," Gideon was quick to point out. Ninetoes was about to retort that he was about to battle an army of hobgoblins to save a town, but a small, pleading voice forestalled him.

Master? Please. I'll be careful.

Why don't we try it on Bluzag?

We don't know how it will affect him? We can't even be sure that it will.

But… perhaps we could wait until we have an enemy for you to test it on?

And what if it goes wrong in the middle of battle? Ninetoes felt that his Familiar was perhaps a little too keen to shoot him in the face with a blinding ray of light but his mind was not quick enough to come up with a good argument.

Fine, but only once.

Of course Master, once should be enough. Now, please stand over there.

Ninetoes chose not to be a wimp about it and, passing his spellbook to the Ranger, promptly marched over to the spot the rodent had directed.

He waited patiently while she checked over the spell one last time. She took a deep breath and then pointed at Ninetoes' face and a beam of multicoloured light burst from her left foreclaw and splashed into Ninetoes eyes, filling his vision with bright lights. The shock of it made him stumble slightly, but he kept his balance and attempted to blink away the lights. Meanwhile, he counted in his head and as he reached eighteen his vision returned.

"Well, that was effective. It couldn't see a thing, in combat I'd have been helpless. I think you chose wisely Little One." Libby beamed at the praise and bounded over to him, before scurrying up his trouser leg and onto his shoulder.

And you're alright now? There are no lasting effects?

I'm fine dearest, he assured her. *I look forward to our next combat training, you will be a formidable foe.*

Libby simply nuzzled against his neck and sent him feelings of love.

"We should re-check the spellbook. I'm curious to see if your new spells have gained any benefits from levelling up."

Hearing this, Sariel held up Ninetoes' spellbook and the group walked back into the tavern. They ordered more drinks on their way back to the table and then huddled around Ninetoes' tome to read it more closely. Shadow Armour of course, hadn't really changed, having already been Level 20 and it seemed that Libby's Ring of the Trickster didn't inflate her spell's level as well. Iridescent however, had gained a benefit.

367

The buff was a good one and explained why the spell had affected Ninetoes for longer than expected.

"Hmmm, you were right after all Ninetoes, this spell does seem a better choice for Libby than Reflection."

"But Libby already—ah, ow!" Once again the crafter had been about to spill the beans but this time all Ninetoes could think to do was stamp on his foot. At the shocked and indignant look on Gideon's face, Ninetoes quickly sent a message through Libby explaining his actions. As the squirrel passed it on the man's eyes widened slightly and he gave a small and almost imperceptible nod to the hobgoblin.

"I think with that it's time we headed to bed, we have a long journey ahead of us and Lowen will not forgive us for being tardy." Ninetoes stood and knocked back the last of his ale. "Gideon, you have my thanks and my promise that I'll tell everyone that'll listen of your skills and knowledge. Sariel, I will see you in the morning. Good night."

So saying, he stepped away before anyone could speak. Libby stayed a moment before leaping into the air and soaring to her Master's shoulder. Together they climbed the stairs to find their room.

It was a simple enough space and held six beds. Lowen and An'rik already occupied two of them, but Tarquin was nowhere to be seen.

Ninetoes chose one and had Bluzag pretend to sleep in another, giving him strict instructions to protect him.

It had been quite a day. While they'd failed to gain the Council's support, they already had the Adventurers they'd need and had even found time to become stronger. Despite everything that had happened and the thoughts swirling through his mind, it took him no time at all to fall into a deep and welcome sleep.

CHAPTER 19
THUNDERCATS!

Ninetoes slept so well in fact, that he was the last one awake and then he only awoke because Lowen kicked the end of his bed. The hobgoblin hadn't bothered to undress, instead just removing his armour and stowing everything but his breastplate in his Bag of Holding.

Now, awoken to the disgruntled visage of the bargemaster, Ninetoes elected not to bother arming himself for the short journey to the barge, as he wouldn't be wearing it while aboard anyway.

Instead he grabbed his stuff and headed out the door. The Inn wasn't far from where the Kerensa was docked and so only a short walk brought the party to the barge.

Lady Fawkner immediately commandeered the aft-cabin for her own chambers and disappeared within, while her guards carried bags and crates aboard the vessel before leaving the boat for the dock. This surprised Ninetoes, as he'd expected them to stay to protect her ladyship, but at least one of the parcels they'd delivered to the ship looked distinctly like a longbow and quiver, so perhaps she really could look after herself.

Libby left her Master as he boarded the barge and went off in search of food. By now Ninetoes was an old hand at how Lowen liked things to run on his ship, so he headed for the bow of the ship where he found an empty space to sit down and be out of the way. It wasn't long after that two dock labourers untied the boat from its moorings. At an order from Lowen, Deck unfurled the sail and a cold breeze filled the canvas and they were away.

"A penny for your thoughts." Sariel stood on Ninetoes' flank, staring upriver.

"Sorry, what's a penny?"

"A copper piece. It's just a way of asking what's on your mind."

"Ah. Nothing really, I was just enjoying the silence," he answered absentmindedly.

"Oh, sorry. I'll leave you to—"

"No. No, that's not what I meant. Please, take a seat." He gestured to a space opposite to his own and Sariel seated herself. "In fact, you might be able to help me with something?"

"Oh?" She said, intrigue levelling her tone.

"I bought this yesterday but have no idea how to use it." Ninetoes opened his hand, revealing the small Skill Stone in the centre of his palm.

Sariel stared at the tiny object, her eyes widening with surprise and awe. "You 'bought' one of these? What Level are you; that you can afford a Skill Stone but do not know how to use it?"

"I am Level Twelve."

"What? But how? You said last night that you've only been adventuring for a couple of weeks," she asked, stunned.

"It's a long story. More importantly, do you know how this stone works?"

"Oh yeah. It's simple enough, you just concentrate on it and it'll tell you everything. Careful though, it's supposed to be painful."

"Hmmm, perhaps I should wait," he said.

"Can't see any reason to. We're not going anywhere for a while. Well, obviously we're going somewhere because the boat's moving but-"

"I understand your point. Does it take long?"

"Just a couple of minutes I think."

"Very well. Here goes." Settling himself into a comfortable seating arrangement by moving some sacks of grain to create an armchair of sorts, Ninetoes held the stone close to his eyes and focussed on it. It didn't take long for the normally placid, soft blue whirls upon the sides of the stone

371

to start churning and within he began to perceive secrets of arcane knowledge locked within the crystal.

The process began as a steady flow, a slight pressure on his temples, but the more he learned, the faster the knowledge flowed until a deluge of understanding, comprehension and realisation chased its way into his mind, battering his senses and taking all of his focus to control and then… it stopped!

Ninetoes slumped back onto the sacks, exhausted with a headache stomping through his brain.

"How was it?" Sariel's sweet voice was a balm and Ninetoes came too, the headache slowly easing to a dull throb.

"Wondrous and painful in equal measure."

"Cool. What did you learn from it?"

"Transmutation magic. Here, look." He drew out his Character Sheet and showed the fair-haired girl every secret he held. The moment he realised what he'd done, he stared at Sariel and she stared back at him. His head throbbed harder and he cursed his own pain-addled foolishness.

"A Necromancer, cool," was all she said. Then went back to studying the parchment. Ninetoes could only stare, dumbfounded at the strange woman, until decency reminded him that doing so was rude and instead he turned to interpret the document himself.

TRANSMUTATION - LEVEL 20 APPRENTICE

+20% DURATION FOR TRANSMUTATION SPELLS

TRANSMUTATION SAVANT I - TRANSMUTATION SPELLS COST YOU 10% LESS TO CAST.

TRANSMUTOR'S ALTERNATIVE I - WHEN CASTING A TRANSMUTATION SPELL TO REPAIR, THE CASTER MAY EXCHANGE ONE MATERIAL FOR ANOTHER SIMILAR MATERIAL.

The Transmutation Trainer had mentioned that he'd gain the rank bonuses, but not what they were and Ninetoes was a little underwhelmed.

"I don't understand the purpose of Transmutor's Alternative, why would I need to change the material I'm using?"

"That's easy. Say you're trying to repair a hole in your breastplate, you'd normally need more steel, right?"

"Er, does it? I thought it was just doing so with, ya know, magic?"

"Oh no. You're using nearby materials to make repairs; haven't you ever noticed that?"

"Let's assume I have not, please proceed."

"Ok, so with this ability you could use wood or a different metal and your spell would transmute it into the steel needed to complete the repair."

"Mmmm, useful indeed."

"Oh, it gets better, at Transmutor's Alternative two you can do so when crafting stuff and at three you can exchange two of the materials."

"Ah, interesting. But, how is it that you know so much about Transmutation magic; I'd have thought it only the purview of Wizards?"

"Oh, my last character was a- ah, never mind." Strange response aside, the woman seemed a fountain of useful knowledge.

"I also learned two spells, Arcane Weapon and Leap." As he said it, he pulled his spellbook out of his bag and flicked through to the first spell and read it quickly.

ARCANE WEAPON - LEVEL 10

EVOCATION

CASTING TIME - 1 SECOND

MANA COST - 50 POINTS

DURATION - 30 SECONDS

LVL 1. ADD 1-6 EXTRA FORCE DAMAGE TO AN ATTACK.

LVL 7. CASTER MAY CHOOSE TO CHANGE THE DAMAGE TYPE TO EITHER FIRE OR COLD DAMAGE UPON CASTING.

"Alas, it's a shame about those spells, Arcane Weapon's ok, but Leap is hardly lifesaving, especially at your Level, you can probably fly by now, right?"

"Hmm, I do not know how to fly, no." A little peeved once again at peoples' assumption of his abilities and knowledge, Ninetoes nonetheless scanned the second spell.

LEAP - LEVEL 5

TRANSMUTATION

CASTING TIME - 1 SECOND

MANA COST - 50 POINTS

DURATION - 1 MINUTE

LVL 1. TRIPLES THE CASTER'S NORMAL JUMP-ING HEIGHT AND LENGTH.

At only Level 5 and Level 10 Ninetoes' two new spells were indeed a little lacklustre, but all knowledge was useful and he was sure he'd find a use for them eventually. He could definitely use Arcane Weapon to boost Bluzag's damage output.

Libby, alerted by the chatter and evidently recognising the half-elf's voice, gave up her hunting and climbed onto the Ranger's knee, clearly thinking she'd have more luck with Sariel.

Correctly gauging the squirrel's intentions, Sariel brought a brick of hardtack from her satchel and broke off a finger's worth and offered it to the Familiar. Libby stared at the morsel and then directly into Sariel's eyes. When she had the woman's complete attention, she dashed forward as quick as a flash and grabbed the larger remains of the tack and then leaped off her lap to glide to the top a large crate.

"Wha-?" Sariel cried out in surprise and then looked to Ninetoes for help. The Adventurer simply shrugged.

"She has quite the appetite." Ninetoes chuckled.

"I can see that. But you can tell her from me she'll need more than shadows to protect her if she steals my breakfast again." So saying Sariel hurled a tossed the remaining morsel at Libby. Her aim was perfect and it donked the little thief on the head. Libby stumbled, dazed at the edge of the edge of the crate and teetered off onto a sack of grain below with a soft thump.

Both Ninetoes and Sariel tittered at the sight. But when she resurfaced Libby was still holding her prize, shaking it at Sariel and chittering in indignation. Climbing back aboard the crate she turned her back on the pair and continued with her meal.

"Ahhh, I needed that." As he grinned at the half-elf, something occurred to him, a question that had been bugging him all the previous day. "Perhaps you could answer me this; why is it that the elven people in Pamor look so different from one another? They all seem to have different shaped ears and different coloured hair."

"Like who?" she asked curiously.

"Well, Gideon for one and he has a brother Rael, but they both look different from one another and you look different again."

"Oh, I see. That's because we're all different races."

"But, how can that be? You're all half-elves are you not?"

"To be sure, but what other half is just as important. For example, I'm half-elf sure but I'm also half-human. Gideon is half-elven and half-dwarven, it's probably why he's so good with his hands, it also explains his red hair. I'm sorry, I've never met Rael, what's he look like?"

"He's about the same height but slighter than Gideon and his ears were slightly more pointed."

"Hmmm, I can't be sure, maybe a half-gnome or half-halfling. Good lord that's a mouthful, you can imagine why people just say half-elf."

"Huh. Thank you. Do you mind my asking who your parents were?"

"Not at all. My mother was a wood elf from the Forests of Rend and my father was a human Adventurer."

"Interesting, your father must be proud of your choice to follow in his footsteps."

"My father's dead, a Nechtsarm mercenary killed him."

"So then you're here for vengeance?"

"Aye, it was fate that steered my path to Pamor and so to Raveslan and if he's there, I will avenge my father. I'm sorry if it offends you to hear me talking of murdering your kin."

"The Nechtsarm seek to finish what they began a lifetime ago and destroy my people, you'll hear no complaints from me."

***

PORTSMOUTH, 2017

Solveg rolls a dice and continues her boring little conversation with Bruce. It wasn't even important to the Quest, it was just dull! Tony needs to find a way to derail it so that they can get on with bopping some monsters and earning XP.

"Er, Bruce? I'd like to speak with the girl, wos-her-name?"

"Bess?"

"Yeah. That is, if you've finished talking to the hob Solly?" He watches as she cringes at the nickname. *Stuck up bitch.* She'd ignored his attempts at flattery and, when he'd tried being more direct at the end of the last session the prick-tease had slapped him! Well, guys like Tony didn't let stuff like that go.

"Urm, well I suppose so."

"Excellent. Er, so. Sir Tarquin sidles up to the girl with the big-" Tony holds his cupped hands in front of his chest, grinning wolfishly at Solveg, "-and sez 'Alright luv. What do ya think of me new cloak? It's got a bonus to Charisma.'"

"She seems unimpressed," comments Bruce dryly.

"Ergh, whatever. 'It's nice to see your friend the goblin's getting so close with Sariel, ain't it?'"

"'Yes, I suppose,' she responds. Er Tony, where are you going with this? I thought you wanted to move on." Bruce attempts. But Tony wasn't going to have any of that, if they wanted roleplay, he'd give 'em roleplay.

"'I mean, you wouldn't normally see an elf and a hobgoblin speaking to each other, except to exchange insults, their races hate each other,' Tarquin says."

"Okay, um... 'Yes, it's true but Ninetoes is different, he's not brutish like other hobgoblins.'"

"'Really? I 'spose you don't really hear about many hob mages, shamans and the like, but never wizards. Does he have a Specialism?' And I'll make a Persuasion roll to get her to tell me." He'd found this was the best way with Bruce; don't ask, tell. "Right, that's a twelve, plus me bonus.... Dirty Twenty. That's enough right?" Again, it wasn't really a question.

"Yes, that'll do. 'Now, you mustn't judge him for this, he's had quite the time of it recently,' she stutters."

"Yeah, yeah Bruce, get on with it."

"'He's a Necromancer,' she says. Her face shows fear as she whispers the name."

"Oh ho ho. 'So, he's Evil then,'" Tony states, his grin now reaching almost to his ears.

"'Oh no! At least, not the way he told me. He just uses Necromancy like any other type of spell, as a tool,' she says, but you can tell that she's a little uncertain herself."

"Bruce, I'd like Sariel to walk over and-" Solveg attempts.

"Oh no, hang on now, we didn't interrupt your conversation, now did we?"

"Well, actually you int-"

"Shut up Daph." Seriously, from his own woman.

"Perhaps... let's just let him finish Solveg. The book does mention this, so they evidently want the players to investigate."

"Hurumph. Fine." *Ha! And the horse you rode in on luv!*

"Now, where was I? Oh yeah. 'He ah, he tol'ja that did he. Cos the only Necromancers I've ever heard of is the big bad evil guy. I reckon we should keep an eye on him, make sure he don' try to turn us all inta zombies or summit.' And I'd like to cast Cacia's Counsel as I say this."

"Very well and she has to make a-?"

"Charisma save."

"Oh, Natural One. Bess stares back at you in horror. 'Really? Shouldn't we do something? T…, to stop him,' she stutters."

"'Nah, don't worry little lady, I'll protect ya.' And Tarquin puts his arm around her to comfort her."

"Ton, stop chatting up Bruce, I'm right here!" exclaims Daphne.

Twice in one session! She'd definitely be hearing about this later.

***

Ninetoes watched, with no small amount of consternation, as 'Sir' Tarquin led Bess aft. He wasn't sure what had happened but she'd seemed extremely distressed. Perhaps he should go and speak to her.

That would be ill-advised Master.

Why?

You were too busy talking to your new best friend to notice but it was you they were speaking of Master.

Me? What could I hav- Oh. Of course, he should expect Bess to be more comfortable with her own kind. And while he knew she'd taken poorly to his actions of the day before, he'd assumed the young Smith would get over them. Now, he wasn't so sure. Well, if it was that easy to find fault with him, then perhaps he was better off without her. He just didn't understand humans.

Ninetoes slumped grumpily back into his resting place. "Argh! Humans!"

Randomly removing one of the books from his bag, barely even noticing the title, *Corvash's Monograph on Animation*, before wrenching it open to a page somewhere in the middle and started reading.

The process was mechanical and fruitless, not of word of it sinking in. But Ninetoes didn't care, the tome served its purpose and shielded his emotions from the others.

"Right, I'll um, just go and speak to the bargemaster then," said Sariel. "Libby would you come with me; there's something I'd like to discuss?"

By now however, Ninetoes was actively tuning everything else out and so he didn't respond. At some point the act of dragging his eyes across the lines of text sent Ninetoes into a restless sleep.

***

DWUOOOOMM! Splash!

Ninetoes was startled awake with the sound of an explosion. His reflexes moved quicker than his body could keep up and although he tried to roll onto his knees and stand, instead he just flopped onto his side and did a passable impression of a landed fish.

With a sigh and a deep, steadying breath, he gave it another go. This time he found his feet and moved out from behind the cover of the crates. The scene before him was one of chaos, but worse than that, the normally comforting presence of his Familiar was missing from her normal perch on his shoulder or snuggled closely within his breastplate. *Libby?* He shouted mentally.

Master, I'm safe but Tarquin and Deck went overboard.

On the middle of the deck, beyond the mast, was some sort of massive cat with hazel-coloured fur and what appeared to be spikes trailing its spine. Ninetoes couldn't make out its face but more concerning was that the deck beneath its paws was a spider web of cracks and fractures that weaved out reaching as far at the gunwale where a three-foot section of the railing was missing.

Beyond the beast Sariel, Daphne and, somewhat surprisingly, Lady Fawkner were atop the quarterdeck, shooting missiles and spells at the creature, while An'rik and Bess stood in front of them, their shields overlapping.

379

Rather than leaping up the short staircase to attack them or even defending itself from their missiles however, the monster just stood there, a strange and rhythmic thumping sound coming from it.

"Help! I can't swim!"

Ninetoes turned in the direction of the terrified voice and found Tarquin, still dressed in full armour, splashing ineffectively in the centre of the river. Remembering her words, Ninetoes quickly scanned the water for Deck and found the sailor swimming for the portside shoreline. One of them at least was relatively safe.

There was little question that if no one helped Tarquin then the stupid Adventurer would drown, but whatever the monster was doing couldn't be good. *Ah! What should I do?*

Save Tarquin Master, we'll handle the giant cat.

Huh! At least one of them was turning up for work. *Alright, I'll be back as soon as possible.*

Just go!

Casting his eyes around, Ninetoes searched for a rope or something he could throw to Tarquin, but even as he did, he could see out of the corner of his eye the man's head disappear below the surface; he was out of time. *Ergh, fine!*

Ninetoes cast Arcane Step but for the first time attempted to use its new ability, Conjuror's Gambit, to swap places with Tarquin. The spell took hold, but as he appeared within the water, he was batted on the head by a gauntleted hand; the Gambit had failed this time.

The other Adventurer was flailing his arms around in a terrified and ultimately worthless attempt to stay afloat and Ninetoes couldn't get close enough to try to drag the fool above the surface, so he did the next best thing and grabbed the damned fool's sodden cloak and 'Stepped' back aboard the barge.

Tarquin, who had been almost perpendicular in the water flopped wetly to the deck, but Ninetoes managed to land on his feet.

He felt the drain of three-quarters of his mana disappearing in the blink of an eye but this time it didn't knock him out, he was definitely missing the buff from his Guardmage's Pauldron though. It did however leave him with far fewer options for dealing with the monstrous feline. Reaching into his Bag of Holding he summoned his Gem of Power and absorbed fifty or so points of mana as quickly as he could.

By now, the strange sound was no longer a thumping but had built to a fast-paced whipping sound and had grown noticeably in volume. Also, orange and blue lightning was surging around the thing's forepaws. Whatever it had been doing, the monster was clearly ready.

While barely seconds had passed, the rest of the party had not been idle and the gigantic cat was riddled with arrows and bolts, but was standing strong.

Ninetoes' knew that closing with the creature was dangerous, especially as he was a Wizard. He hadn't even managed to replace his sword and he'd given his dagger away.

His most deadly spell however, remained Grim Void. As the monster rose up on its hind legs, Ninetoes dashed across the deck and grabbed the cat's tail, casting his spell through the appendage.

This move would quickly prove foolhardy as lots of things happened simultaneously.

At first his spell took hold and not only did he feel the creature's life force drain into him, he also caught a glimpse of a strange scene of a waterfall and catching fish in his mouth.

But then the beast slammed its forward paws onto the deck of the boat and released the energy it had collected, unleashing it in a thunderous boom that crashed out in a wave of force.

Some of the cracks in the deck became fissures and water sprang up in several locations.

Ninetoes meanwhile clung on for dear life, but it was no use, the wave of energy was simply too strong and flung him out into the river for his second dipping.

This time, the impetus of the attack sent Ninetoes spinning deep beneath the surface of the water and, for a few heart racing moments, he was so disoriented that he couldn't tell which way was up.

Thankfully the attack's force was enough to send the hobgoblin crashing into the riverbed, the blow making the last of his air expel from his lungs.

As his body screamed for a fresh supply of oxygen, Ninetoes looked up through the murk, and saw the surface was too far away.

In that moment of fear, Ninetoes' mind cleared for the first time today and the same battle calm that had saved his life too many times to count, washed over him.

Tucking his feet beneath him he cast Leap, hoping that the spell would function even though his voice was incomprehensible underwater. Feeling the muscles in his legs coil like a spring he pushed off hard from the shingle floor and rocketed upwards to the surface and the promise of fresh, lifegiving air.

His head crested the surface and then, so did the rest of him and for a few glorious seconds he was completely airborne.

Gravity once again reasserted its control over him and he splashed back down into the river. This time however, his head only barely broke the surface before his head was free and he coughed up a mouthful of water, while his arms flapped around attempting to keep him afloat.

Looking about he could see the barge heading away from him both upstream but also towards the shore. He could also hear the sounds of shouting and battle. Despite already feeling wrung out, he began swimming for the shore.

The current was strong and Ninetoes' clothes weighed him down and so the short swim felt like it took forever but he made it safely and started jogging upriver to where the boat was now beached.

Before he even made it halfway, the sounds of fighting ended and Sariel's head appeared above the bow of the barge.

Waving, she called out. "Are you ok?" Exhausted, he simply nodded and she looked back to the deck and called. "He's alright."

Within his mind his Familiar had a different message. *I thought you'd died you dick! Hurry up and get back here!*

Ah, always good to hear your voice Little One.

Humph! It still surprised Ninetoes that his Familiar verbalised these sounds of disgruntled annoyance. Now that he could see the battle was over, he slowed to a walk but it didn't take him long to reach the barge.

By then, Lowen and An'rik had lowered the gangplank to the shore and the bargemaster and Deck were surveying the damage. Looking beyond the beached craft, Ninetoes could make out the waterfall that marked Torgan's Tears not too far away and he realised that he must have slept away all of the morning and much of the afternoon.

"Ah Adventurer, you survived, good," commented Lady Fawkner dryly.

"And you're well my lady?"

"I'm fine, Bess and the lizardman kept us safe," she commented pointedly.

Reaching the party, he sidled up to Lowen. "How severe is the damage?"

"Not so bad, thanks to you lad," he answered as he removed his hat and scratched his head.

"Thanks to him? I killed the beast," boasted Tarquin.

"Ha! Only because we'd injured the thing so much and only because Ninetoes saved you from drowning," Sariel put in.

"Sir Tarquin would never have drowned, he'd have found a way to survive," countered Bess, smiling doe-eyed at the tall man. Ninetoes felt bile rise in his throat at the sycophantic display.

"Of course I would." Tarquin assured her. "And while I'm grateful for all your help, I dealt the killing blow, stopping the beast from another thunderous attack and thus sinking the ship."

"Boat," asserted Lowen. "And if it hadn't been for Ninetoes grabbing its tail and distracting it, the second attack would surely have cracked the hull. It's how the monsters fight, sinking ships and then diving in to kill those thrown overboard."

"But it's a cat isn't it? I thought cats hated water," commented Daphne.

383

"Aye, that may be true of little ones, but these beasts love te swim," answered Deck.

"Strange, I've never heard of such a beast."

"That's because Forsythe got in trouble in the Eighties because of the name."

"What? Who's Forsythe and what name? What're these things called?" Asked Ninetoes.

"They're Thunder-"

"Don't," commanded Tarquin.

"Thunder-" An'rik persevered.

"Don't do it," Sariel reiterated.

"Thundercats!" As he finished Sariel shoved the lizardman and he tumbled into the shoals. "Hoh!"

"Thundercats? I've never heard of anything so silly," commented Ninetoes. "Although 'if it barks like a dog' eh?" He laughed at his own joke. No one else did.

CHAPTER 20
BETRAYAL!

The barge would sail but required plenty of minor repairs. With Ninetoes' and, it turned out, Daphne's Mending spells, these could be made before sundown but their current location was a poor campsite and offered little defence against another attack from the thunderous felines.

Ultimately, the party decided that it was worth sailing the short distance upstream to Torgan's Tears and the relatively safe harbour the river mouth offered.

Nonetheless, while the two Wizards and Lowen set to work on repairs, the rest of the party made the climb to the top of the waterfall and made their camp there. The cats, it seemed, were powerful swimmers and would leap from beneath the water to attack. The shallower water above the waterfall offered them less places to hide. Lowen had described how he'd witnessed the aftermath of such attacks before and had suffered a couple himself, even having lost the Kerensa's predecessor to the monsters.

"Normally Kowann would see 'em before they can attack and I'd steer for the shallows, they don't tend to attack if it looks too much like hard work." The bargemaster's Familiar was currently circling above the camp, keeping an eye out for trouble. The owl, apparently as crotchety as his master, had even allowed Libby to sit on his back and add a second pair of eyes to the task.

"Do you mind my asking what Level your bond with Kowann is?" Ninetoes asked as he ran his hands over an inch-wide fracture in the hull, his magic knitting the wound closed. Daphne was taking a break to meditate and help her mana to recharge quicker. She'd bottomed out first and had to take a short rest before Ninetoes' own mana had been depleted but in the hours of work they'd put in they'd both had drained their spellpower multiple times. Ninetoes had also gained six Levels with the spell, picking up another bonus at level 10.

MENDING - LEVEL 11

TRANSMUTATION

CASTING TIME - 15 SECONDS

MANA COST - 5 POINTS

LVL 1. REPAIRS MINOR, NON-MAGICAL DAMAGE OR SHARPENS NON-MAGICAL ITEMS.

LVL 2. ALLOWS CASTER TO REPAIR/SHARPEN TWO SIMILAR ITEMS WITHIN THE DURATION OF THE CASTING.

LVL 5. ALLOWS CASTER TO CRAFT SIMPLE OBJECTS FROM RAW MATERIALS.

LVL 10. INCREASES THE LVL 2 BONUS BY ONE ADDITIONAL ITEM.

It was not, as Sariel would have put it, a lifesaving ability, but it had certainly helped to speed up repairs and that might well mean the difference between saving Raveslan and failure, so he'd take it.

"I don' mind ye askin' but I ain't gonna tell ye," came back the surly response to Ninetoes' question about the bargemaster's Familiar.

"Very well, very well. Keep your secrets."

"Aye, I think I will and you should think about doin' the same lad," Lowen warned.

"I, er, don't know what you mean," Ninetoes stuttered.

"Oh aye, I saw ye showing that half-elven girl your spellbook and whatnots."

"We were just, um, exchanging notes."

"Oh right, as ye say. But ye should listen to me and keep your mouth shut more often, you ain't like them other Adventurers," the boatman expounded.

Ninetoes didn't say so, but he had to agree. He didn't understand why, but he just felt *unconnected* to the other Adventurers and not only because he was obviously more powerful than they were.

It was more than that. They just seemed to know so much more about their abilities and yet they seemed so... unshackled most of the time, as though their minds were elsewhere. Daphne had stood beside him repairing the ship for hours in total silence, for most of it she may simply have been a zombie. She didn't even seem to recognise that he was there much of the time. Perhaps she'd just tuned out for the duration of the boring and repetitive task.

A task that was now... "Finished." Ninetoes grinned at Lowen.

"Aye, you've done well and I'm grateful. Tomorrow you can finish up."

"Wait, what? But we've repaired all the damage from the monster's thunder attacks."

"True, true. But there's plenty more needs fixin' and there'll be no idleness on my boat for the rest of this journey, it's not a pleasure cruise."

"Ha! What gratitude," Ninetoes grumped.

"Gratitude? Reckon you owe me one or two more favours after the last voyage. You think I make a habit of fighting manticores?"

"Hmm, I guess not." He definitely had a point. "My apologies Lowen, of course I'd be happy to help out, whatever you need."

"Well, right now I need some dinner, let's hope Bess has made more of that stew eh?" Lowen's aging knees cracked loudly as he stood from where he'd been working and he groaned quietly to himself. For her part, when the pair made to leave, Daphne wordlessly followed them up the short trail to the waterfall's summit and on to their campsite.

"Hail the camp," called Ninetoes as they crested the hill. Sariel was taking first watch and he didn't fancy an arrow in his neck.

"Fear not hobgoblin, Libby told me you were coming," replied the half-elf from her perch, halfway up a pine tree just off the trail.

The confused look on the hobgoblin's face must have been visible in the growing half-light, because she tapped her earlobe and Ninetoes could just make out the glint of metal reflecting the campfire. Quickly the pieces slotted together. "Ah, you bought a Familiar's Tongue from Gideon?"

"I did. It seemed an efficient way to communicate silently and telepathically through Libby, plus this way she can direct us both as needed in battle." Ninetoes couldn't argue with her logic, but he believed there was more to it than that. He'd noticed how curious Sariel had seemed of his Familiar.

"You know, it's considered bad form to speak to one's Familiar without permission."

"Ha! Why don't you try telling Libby that?"

Tell Libby what? Kowann landed on Lowen's shoulder as Libby came gliding onto Sariel's.

Nothing Little One, just that Sariel should perhaps have asked me before communicating with you.

Oh really, why? It was said innocently enough, but by now Ninetoes had come to recognise the tone Libby was invoking for the trap for what it was. He wouldn't be fooled this time. He'd use direct and blatant honesty.

Because, Little Maverick, we have a bond I am jealous to share with anyone else.

Libby's eyes flashed with mischief but his forthright words had undone her ploy and, instead of countering with cheek, she leapt from Sariel onto her Master's shoulder and leaned in to nuzzle against his neck. *What we share is ours and ours alone Master.*

It was a simple and yet powerful promise. The same promise that had brought him back from the brink of madness on the roof of Kavralach Keep, when the Animator had promised him power beyond measure. *I love you Little One.*

And I you Master. Now, get a move on, Bess has indeed cooked her stew again.

The meal was a strange one, for the Adventurers were once again oddly silent. They ate their food, but only Sariel, who came for food after An'rik took her watch, spoke a word.

As the sun set, Tarquin joined the lizardman's watch, taking up a position facing upstream, while the cleric watched down. Bluzag of course would take his watch all night, surveying the treeline.

Lady Fawkner had apparently eaten her own rations and retired for the evening long before Ninetoes had arrived. Indeed, a large tent had been erected just for the noblewoman, and of course her ladyship wouldn't be taking a shift watching over the camp.

Lowen, Deck, and Ninetoes, however, shared their meal and an animated conversation about the battle with the Thundercat. Bess was unusually silent, but she wasn't glaring at him anymore, so he took it as a win. The day's events however, quickly caught up to each of them and they soon picked their spots and brushed away the worst of the stones and twigs to make as comfortable a bed as possible.

Shortly thereafter the rest of the party was soundly sleeping, and Ninetoes, exhausted from long hours of repairing the barge, was quick to follow them.

***

Ninetoes had drawn the short straw and would be taking the middle watch with Daphne and so it was that he grumpily shrugged off An'rik as the lizardman shook him awake.

A short distance away, Tarquin attempted to coax some life into the embers of the campfire to provide warmth against the night's autumnal chill, while An'rik woke Daphne. The man's handsome face was blemished by purple bruising around his eye.

Ninetoes couldn't remember seeing it happen, but Tarquin must have taken a heavy hit during the fight on the barge. Ninetoes still hadn't replaced his breastplate or other pieces of armour and given how tired he was, he considered not bothering. But his paranoia got the better of him and he bent over the article to strap it on.

As he leaned in however, he found Libby snuggled in his cloak, nestled in the bowl of his breastplate. He must have left it that way to keep it from getting dirty and his Familiar had found the perfect squirrel-sized bed. She looked so peaceful he knew he wouldn't risk waking her, so he left the armour and cloak where they were.

Instead, he snatched up his bedroll and wrapped it about his shoulders as he took An'rik's place, sitting on a blanket upon a rock, looking out over the waterfall far below. It was thoughtful of the lizardman to leave the seat warm.

He could hear the others moving around the camp behind him. He wasn't alone anymore and they'd handled the thundercat well enough, even without his help. Perhaps he should start depending on his fellow Adventurers for protection.

***

PORTSMOUTH, 2017

"Ok, everyone remember the plan?" Tony looked each of the other players in the eyes. All except Solveg, the stuck-up bitch would be sitting this one out.

"I cast a dispel magic spell," droned Daphne.

"Then I shank him," said Felix. Tony didn't really like the way he licked his lips as he said it, but at least he was enthusiastic.

"And then, if he's still alive we beat the shit out of him," Tony finished the plan. It was simple yet effective.

"And there's really nothing I'd have noticed? No way I can try to talk them out of it?" beseeched Solveg, her eyes pleading with Bruce.

"I'm sorry, the rest of the group made this plan without Sariel's, or my, knowledge." The GM replied, clearly not pleased with the events playing out. But Tony didn't care, this was his game.

"Anyway, that rich Lady said she'd pay us a hundred gold to kill him and then there's all his stuff. Plus, he's a Necromancer, Bruce was probably gonna have him turn on us in the middle of the final battle or somethin' tropey like that," Tony explained, once again, to these wimps.

The only problem he had with the plan was that he wouldn't get to be the one who killed the gob. But even with how well he'd managed to max his stats and attacks, a single Sneak Attack Felix's shadow cleric was clearly the best choice.

"Alright Daphne, when you're ready."

This was the most important part of the plan. Daphne, still only Level 3 like the rest of them, only had access to the Dispel Magic Ritual. Most new players didn't bother with ritual spells, including Tony, because they were simply not effective in combat unless you had time to plan your attack.

But Tony had been playing since he was a kid and he understood their value, **if** they could be used right. They'd had to conceal the ritual circle on the front of the rock and hope that two things happened: that the gob would sit on the rock and that he didn't see it.

Without even looking up from her phone, Daphne uttered "I cast Dispel Magic."

***

Ninetoes' thoughts were caught by a small flash of blue light that lit up the blanket Ninetoes was sitting on. But it was gone as soon as he'd noticed it. Reaching down he lifted up the edge of the blanket to get a look at the rock beneath.

At first he saw nothing, the darkness too enveloping, but then the clouds parted and the moonlight reflected off of a chalk-drawn shape. No, not a shape a ritual cir-

SHHHIIINK!

Pain lanced through Ninetoes' back and his body instinctively pulled away from the foreign object stuck in his back. This was a bad move as he could feel his clothes soak in his own blood. As he attempted to stand a booted foot stamped on his fingers and then kneed him in the face, knocking him flat on his back.

"Phew, he's still alive."

Pain blurred Ninetoes' vision but he could make out that Tarquin stood above him, sword drawn.

"We're under attack," he managed to wheeze out.

"Huh, still not cottoned on eh?" said Tarquin, a cruel grin plastered across his face. Tarquin raised his leg back and punted Ninetoes' kidneys right where he'd been stabbed.

The pain was immense and for a few seconds he collapsed in on himself, attempting to hide from it. He almost gave up at that moment as well. But he'd faced pain like this before and had overcome it. Wincing, he rolled sideways, trying to trip Tarquin, but man simply stepped aside and the pain-filled effort was in vain.

Worse still, as he looked up again, he saw that Tarquin had turned his sword to point down and was about to drive it through Ninetoes' chest. He struggled to roll away but pain overcame him as Tarquin stamped down on his crotch, holding him in place.

"Wait!" Relief washed through him as he heard Bess's voice. She might be no match for the Adventurers, but with Bluzag's help she could at least hold them off long enough for him to recover and join the fight. "Perhaps we don't need to kill him. Can't we just send him away?"

"Argh! We've been through this." Tarquin raged and Bess shrank away from the man.

An'rik held something aloft to show Ninetoes. It took him a moment, but then the grizzly object slowly turned as the lizardman held it by a tuft of hair. Ninetoes stared in disbelief, while Bluzag's empty eyes stared back, half his face missing in a mess of blood and core.

Tarquin took a deep breath, clearly trying to control his anger. "Look at what he's done! Bluzag's nothin' more than a zombie! He probably killed the poor creature to force it into his service," he explained, pointing his sword at Ninetoes as he spoke. "That's why he's gotta die, he's too dangerous to be left alive. I mean, you wouldn't want him turning you into one of them, would you?" Tarquin's voice echoed with magical power and a brief glint passed over Bess's eyes.

Eyes that hardened at Tarquin's suggestion and when she turned them on Ninetoes they held no mercy, only hatred. "You're right. He must die, just like the rest of his filthy kind."

What? Even Bess had turned on him, but why? It mattered not, even without Bess he had allies who could never be turned against him.

It took all of his willpower to concentrate, especially as An'rik roughly pulled his Bag of Holding over his shoulder, but he managed it. *Libby! To me! The Adventurers have betrayed us. Kill them.*

Master! Libby's telepathic voice screamed in terror.

Opening his eyes, Ninetoes looked for his Familiar only to be met with the cruel eyes of Tarquin. Searching desperately, he finally found her. Daphne held a hessian sack that shook and contorted as the thing inside it struggled to get free.

What's happening? Bluzag is gone! I can't feel him! Master!
THWACK!

Daphne smashed the sack with her quarterstaff and for the first time in weeks, Ninetoes felt truly alone. *Libby?* Nothing answered and now that he sought it, his connections to both his Wight and his Familiar were gone.

Stepping over to him Daphne removed his circlet, cramming it onto her own head. "Mine," she said to the others.

"Time to end this I think. But don't worry, we'll be sure to finish your little Quest. Wanna get paid don' we gang?" The other Adventurers chuckled and then stepped closer, raising his sword higher and then drove it down.

Pain erupted through Ninetoes chest but his death was blissfully quick and, as Tarquin pulled his blade from the hobgoblin's chest, darkness filled his vision and his heart pumped the last of his blood in a spray of sanguine eruption, before everything went black.

"Huh, tough bugger." Commented Tarquin.

Only, he wasn't dead. As Tarquin removed the blade, the most important spell he had, the one he cast every morning, kicked in.

Reaper's Sorrow wasn't pleasant, and neither did it really heal the damage, it just brought him back from the brink.

Despite the pain, and the worry for Libby, Ninetoes knew his own hope was to escape. Frantically he cast his gaze about looking for any means of reaching safety, but from his position on the ground he could see almost nothing but the faces of his assailants. The pain and the thunderous sounds of the waterfall crashing far below clouded his mind and he couldn't come up with a plan.

The waterfall!

But he couldn't 'step' to a location he couldn't see and he didn't remember it well enough to- except that he could. It wasn't his memory, but there it was, as clear as if he was looking right at it.

Ninetoes closed his eyes, not out of fear but to help him concentrate on his spell. It was a good thing he did. Had he opened his eyes he'd certainly have been distracted by the hessian sack swinging from Daphne's hand.

But Ninetoes didn't see any of that, he just 'stepped'.

***

PORTSMOUTH, 2017

"You what?"

"He teleported away," answered Bruce, a small smile hidden mostly by his thick beard, played across his face.

394

"That's bullshit! He was dead! How'd he-" Countered Tony, clearly angry that his kill had been snatched from him.

Bruce seized the initiative. "You don't know. But a splashing sound can be heard in the pool beneath the waterfall."

"Daph, get to the edge and shoot him." Tony demanded.

"I go to the cliff edge and shoot the hobgoblin with Arcane Bolt," says Daphne.

"Roll your attack please."

"Er... two, plus my bonus, that's-"

"Don't bother, it's not enough. He ducks under the water and heads for the falls."

"Shit! Shoot him again!"

"No point, Arcane Bolt ain't getting through water is it?"

"Wait, didn't that merchant say he'd sold his last Wand of Fireballs just before we arrived?" Asked Felix.

"So?"

"So, maybe it was him tha-" Tony caught on before Felix finished.

"Bruce, I open the Bag of Holding and say Wand of Fireballs."

Cringing, Bruce looks at Tony. "The wand appears in Tarquin's hand."

"Tarquin drops the bag, while dashing for the edge. 'Let's see him dodge this,' he says and points the wand."

***

The bolt of magic splashed into the river behind him and Ninetoes dove beneath the surface.

"Shit! Shoot him again!" came Tarquin's angry shout.

Adrenaline kicked in and he ignored the lancing pains in his sides as he swam with all his might for the waterfall. The current was too strong and he'd likely have struggled even at his best.

He quickly ran through his options and remembered that one spell he had that definitely worked underwater. He cast Leap as he reached the riverbed and then fired himself into the waterfall, landing hard on a shelf of rock, hidden behind it.

A second later the pool he'd been swimming in exploded in a fountain of water and fire, the cascade of falling water filled the space in barely a second but there was little doubt that he'd have been done for if he was still there or if they fired again.

If they could do that much damage to a waterfall, there was nothing he had that could- *Wait, my trump card.*

He stuffed his hand in his pocket and drew out Dominic's Portable Protection Field and without a second's hesitation, activated its field.

FA-DOOM!

The fireball temporarily paused the waterfall as the explosion shook the cliffside and flames rushed towards the hobgoblin, only to wrap harmlessly around the dome of energy that surrounded him.

FA-DOOOM!

Another fireball hit the waterfall, this one even closer to the ledge where he sat. The shield waivered but held. He'd survived! *Wait! Did that Wand have three or four charges?*

FAAA-DOOOOMM!

***

"Huh! Reckon that's got 'im," Tarquin turns, tossing the wand to Daphne.

"What the fuck is all that noise?" Lowen came striding aggressively up to the Adventurers, Deck a step behind.

"Shit, we forgot about him," An'rik whispers to Tarquin.

"Don' worry, I got this. You two go check for a body and finish him off if he's still alive," replies the man, placing his hand on the hilt of his sword.

The lizardman grabs his forearm and stops him drawing. "No, we need him and the other one to sail the ship," his whisper is hurried and harsh.

"Fine." Tarquin whispers back, before directing his next words to Lowen. "Not to worry, there was a monster attack. Sorry to say it got the hobgoblin but we saw it off with some well-placed Fireballs."

Lowen eyed the man closely, searching for something but ultimately coming up with nothing. "Fine, a loss to be sure, he was a brave lad. What was it?"

"A, er-". Tarquin stumbles.

"Manticore," adds Bess helpfully.

Lowen's face peels back into one of fear. "Right, in that case we'll have to risk it. Bess, wake her highness, if you'd be so kind and you lot, start breaking camp, we leave as soon as possible."

"Phew, that was close. I thought we was gonna have to kill 'em both and work out how to sail a ship," Daphne commented as she stooped to pick up the sack holding the squirrel. She was surprised, however, to find it lighter than before. Sticking her hand in, she called out. "'ere, this sack's empty, the squirrel got away."

"Ah, who cares, now that the gob's dead, she'll go back to being a plain old harmless squirrel. More importantly, we did it. I cannot wait to see what's in this Bag of Holding," Tarquin responded.

***

PORTSMOUTH, 2017

"With everyone's help the party has broken camp and boarded the Kerensa within half an hour. It is still dark, but with Kowann flying above, they meet no more trouble, imagined or otherwise," Bruce summarises. "Good session guys. Solveg, have you got a minute?"

Boasting amongst themselves, Tony and Felix grab their stuff and head outside, Daphne trailing behind, still surgically attached to her phone.

Closing and locking the door behind them, Bruce comes back into the room. Seeing Solveg, he sidles up behind her and kisses her neck.

Truth be told, he was still a little nervous about their relationship, he'd never had much luck with women, but Solveg simply twisted in his arms and kissed him full on the lips, sending thrills running through him.

"Are you ok? I know you were bonding with the hobgoblin, but they just sprang it on me and, it was a good plan and the book even says that Lady Fawkner will pay for-"

"Chill, it's ok. It's just a game, right?" Solveg answers, but it's clear from her tone that she's a little upset. "Thank you for letting me rescue Libby though, I think I'd have left if Daphne had gotten to take her as a Familiar."

Leave the game? Bruce blanched at her words. Now that they were an item, he didn't want to lose her over something so small. "Well, I had a plan for her to escape, but when you slipped me that note, it seemed like an even better solution." That wasn't strictly true. The squirrel was powerful, even for a Familiar, but he'd been shit out of ideas, until Solveg had passed him a note asking if she could snatch up the sack containing the squirrel.

"I'm only sorry I couldn't do more, Ninetoes seemed like a really interesting character."

"Yeah, he was."

"So he really is dead then?" She asked, her voice a whisper as she kissed the curve of his chin.

"Er... he—wait. You can't seduce me into revealing my story plans," he said. Although, in all honesty, she definitely could.

"Well, a girl can certainly try."

CHAPTER 21
KHULGAST'S TEAR

TARQUIN

The winds were with them and, despite travelling upstream, the journey was proving quicker than expected. They hadn't stopped all day and with any luck the Kerensa would reach Caillic's Steading in by the following lunchtime.

Daphne and An'rik had found no sign of the hobgoblin's body and before long they'd had to give up their search. It hadn't taken them long to discover that, far apart from the items of magical wonder that Ninetoes had carried, his Bag of Holding was also filled to the brim with gold.

In fact, when Tarquin, Daphne and An'rik had stood at the prow of the ship and held the magical satchel upside down and uttered the words "Everything", they'd nearly been bowled into the river by the deluge of treasures that cascaded out onto the deck.

This had been potentially ruinous for them as the barge was tipped to one side by the sudden weight and they'd have lost it all overboard if not for the skill with which Lowen controlled the rudder. Sariel had refused to take part in the looting of the fallen hobgoblin and had instead kept to the quarterdeck where she spoke at length with the bargemaster.

Meanwhile, the rest of the Adventurers had divided out the spoils. An'rik and Tarquin had shared the armour, the Cleric taking the Pauldron and Bracers, while Tarquin took the breastplate and Guardman's

Bracers they'd found on the undead giant. The bonus protection was negligible but the buffs to Strength and Agility were brilliant. It was only a shame they hadn't got the Bracer he'd been wearing, to think that the hobgoblin had access to so many items that he'd given some to a zombie! An'rik also took the pouch of poisons and, as far as Tarquin was concerned, he was welcome to it, poisoning wasn't his style. Daphne took the Circlet of Intelligence of course, boosting her mana a good deal and they agreed simply to sell the candle.

They'd divided the potions between themselves and agreed to sell off the other minor items and jewellery when they returned to a city. They'd likely lost a couple of items that the hobgoblin had on him, but all in all it was an excellent haul.

The cherry on top was the Wand of Fireballs, which of course, Tarquin kept for himself. After he'd had Daphne recharge it of course. In the battle to come, it would be his tool of destruction.

He'd almost laughed out loud when the noblewoman, Lady Wots-her-name, quietly handed him a small purse with a terse nod. Now, the one hundred gold seemed a paltry amount, but every little helped. He really had no idea what her beef was with the gobbo, and frankly he didn't care.

Yes, they'd done extremely well and it was all thanks to him.

Of course, they'd still complete the Quest, it wasn't often that a personalised magic item came along, even as a reward and where better to become stronger than against a bunch of low-level mobs? All lining up to be killed.

They still needed to survive the coming battle, it was true, but they didn't need to save the town to do that. If things got hairy, they could just leave.

Lowen had actually asked the Adventurers for help with the ship, but Tarquin had simply cast Cacia's Counsel and convinced the old man he didn't need to help. It certainly hadn't stopped the old windbag from press-ganging Daph and An'rik into service, but that wasn't Tarquin's problem.

Instead, Tarquin would spend the day practicing with his sword, gaining himself a level or two. What the party really needed of course, was some monster fights, nothing dangerous, just something to gain them enough XP to Level up before they reached this shitball town they were headed for.

Hmmm, perhaps my patron can help with that.

Tarquin had chosen his patron based upon which one made him the strongest in the shortest amount of time. That is why he was beholden to the power of a demon, a powerful one of course, little point shackling oneself to a pushover.

And so far, the bond had been both rich and fruitful. He'd gained an initial bump to his Charisma score and his Skill Levels with a sword. But recently, he'd also felt the fiend's influence guiding some of his actions, most importantly the party's decision to join this Quest.

He'd even felt this effecting what he'd said to convince Commander Swiftaxe to allow them access to it. Yes, the demon had been a sound choice and what worry did he have of such a creature, he wasn't truly of this world.

Now, how to make it send them some monsters? *Er... master? I, um beseech you for aid.*

There was no answering voice in his head as he'd thought there might be but he certainly felt a weight upon his mind, like a presence, so he guessed he was on the right track.

My party and I must grow stronger before the coming battle and to do so we need to fight and kill monsters. Is there any way you could send us some weaker creatures to farm for power?

Again, there was no response and the presence disappeared. Annoyed, he slouched across some sacks, sulking.

All at once the mental load returned, but this time it felt like his mind was at the bottom of the ocean and the pressure bearing down on it was enough to make his skull implode. He'd have cried out but he didn't have the capacity for such luxuries. Without thought, his body screwed itself into a foetal position and his bowels evacuated. At both ends.

Then, as suddenly as it had started, it ceased and Tarquin was left a stinky, ruined mess on the deck. It took him long minutes to come back to himself and he was grateful the rest of the crew was too busy to have found him like that because he wouldn't want anyone to find him so weak.

Luckily enough, nearby was a bucket, tied to a length of rope, used for hauling water onto the ship and with weak and shaky movements Tarquin managed to wash off the worst of the filth, although his clothes were ruined. He could have washed them of course, but that was women's work and why should he bother? He was rich now. He'd have to replace them when they stopped, perhaps there was a tailor's at the Steading?

None of that mattered however, because the pain hadn't been a punishment, but rather a gift; one of knowledge. Unrolling his Character Sheet, Tarquin studied his Master's largesse.

KHULGAST'S TEAR

CONJURATION

CASTING TIME - 1 MINUTE

MANA COST - 1000 POINTS

DURATION - THE DEMON RETURNS TO THE INFERNAL REALM FROM WHENCE IT CAME ONCE DESTROYED OR AFTER 10 MINUTES.

RANGE - 30 FEET

THE CASTER OPENS A TEAR INTO THE INFERNAL REALMS DRAWING FORTH A SINGLE POWERFUL DEMON OR 1-10 WEAKER DEMONS.

His patron had provided him with the perfect gift. Clearly the mana cost was far too much for a 3rd Level Warlock like Tarquin but his backer's power would grant him one free casting per day. He could use this ability to draw out a small number of weak demons for his party to dispatch and so gain experience from. He wouldn't tell the others about this ability of course, for fear that they might think him evil or worse try to gain his sponsor's patronage as well.

No, but if his band was to gain as much as possible from this gift, they'd need to start right away. As fate would have it, the Kerensa started to drift towards the shore and up ahead, Tarquin could just about make out a clearing, next to a short wooden dock.

Grabbing his gear, he stepped eagerly to the ship's edge and as soon as they were in range, he leaped down. "I'll gather firewood and check the perimeter." He shouted back to those onboard, before heading for the secrecy of the woods.

At first, he actually collected dried sticks and small logs, until he remembered that he wouldn't actually be bringing them back to camp. Once he was a few hundred yards back and well out of sight from the clearing, he searched for an open space to cast his spell. It didn't take him long before he found what he was looking for.

A large, old tree had collapsed, pulling up roots and creating a shallow pit. The remains of the tree hid the pit from the direction of the clearing and so offered even less chance of exposure. It was perfect.

Taking cover behind a nearby tree, Tarquin invoked his magic and began casting the spell. Almost from the first second a small bead of red light appeared in the centre of the ditch. As it grew, however, he could see that it wasn't light, but rather a tiny, shimmering window into another place, a realm of fire and ash. As the tear grew, Tarquin caught a whiff of sulphur and knew that the spell was working as planned.

As the rip grew to the height and width of a man, Tarquin felt it changed slightly and rather than continue to grow, the portal seemed to stabilise and ceased shimmering. He now had a clear view into the Infernal Realms and his pace quickened thinking about the power available to one brave enough to risk such a dangerous place. But this gateway was only meant for one-way travel, so that wasn't an option. Yet.

Beyond the doorway, Tarquin could see a small number of alien creatures moving about. It was hard to tell one from another as they all had too many of something; mouths with too many teeth, bodies with too many limbs or faces with too many eyes. One of them was much larger than the others however, and even as he watched the creature grabbed one of the smaller monsters and absentmindedly tore it in half like a hunk of bread, before stuffing the pieces into its two mouths. Meanwhile it's five eyes, all of which were different shapes, stared hungrily at the opening.

Tarquin didn't much like the idea of fighting any of them, but he certainly wasn't ready for that thing. Instead he cast out his intent and tried to call forth only the smaller demons. Within seconds a half dozen had spilled out onto the leafy floor where they dripped scum and ooze wherever they trod. It also didn't take long before one of them, a hideous creature with bat like wings and three snouts, began sniffing the air. It quickly registered Tarquin's scent, darting towards him and trumpeting its excitement.

Tarquin hadn't stopped to see any of this, however, having bolted for the campsite as soon as the first creature had stepped a clawed foot onto this plane. As soon as the nosey-demon had sounded the alarm all of the monsters had made to follow in whatever means they could.

All of them were quick, but the fliers held the greatest advantage of speed and Tarquin was a little worried that they might actually catch up to him before he reached the party so he quickly downed the Potion of Haste he'd taken from the hobgoblin and instantly felt his pace quicken. Nonetheless he called out a warning to the party as he neared the perimeter. "To arms, to arms, we're under attack!"

SARIEL

To say the half-elf was angry at the actions of her fellow Adventurers was a gross understatement. As far as she was concerned, such actions were the work of villains, not heroes.

It hadn't taken her long to discover the truth of the events of the previous night. While Tarquin's tale of a manticore attack had fooled Lowen and Deck, she could hear the faltering tone of a lie, even one told by an expert bullshitter such as 'Sir' Tarquin.

Her suspicions had led her to investigate the site of the battle. She'd found no evidence of a monster, at least not one with wings and claws. Rather, she found the blood and marks and footprints of a short but brutal fight of one against four. Later, she'd found the remains of Bluzag, decapitated and face down in a ditch; stripped of his armour and weapons. His wounds could only have been made with bladed weapons. Ninetoes had been betrayed and murdered by her party and she'd been too busy sleeping to try to save him!

Once Libby had awoken she'd confirmed all of Sariel's suspicions, after she'd finished bewitching the half-elf into believing that she was on fire. It had taken all her willpower to shake off the assault and then ten minutes to convince the squirrel that she'd played no part in the attack.

After that, Libby had explained that she'd awoken to find herself trussed up in a sack and, powerful as the Familiar was, all of her spells relied upon being able to see her target.

Despite all of this, Sariel still wasn't sure that they were wrong. What they'd done was despicable, but they'd done it with the best of intentions. At least, some of them had, hadn't they? Necromancers were known to be evil creatures and they always seemed to be the villain. But Ninetoes hadn't been like that; had he?

Certainly, Libby was a beacon of light. Sariel could detect no evil intent from the tiny rodent.

Since they'd broken camp and set sail, she'd kept the Familiar's presence a secret. It had been difficult at first. The squirrel was a firestorm of anger and vengeance but she was clearly no match for the Adventurers and neither did Sariel want to have to choose between her companions and the little beast.

For now, she'd keep her a secret and gather as much information as possible. It seemed clear enough from the events of the previous night that Bess was firmly part of the attack, but Lowen and Deck were innocent of any crime. That only left Lady Fawkner. If she was innocent as well, then perhaps she'd be able to use her power to bring the rogues to justice. It wasn't much of a plan, but for the time being, it was all she had.

She finished her chores and made her way to the aft-cabin that the noble had claimed for herself. Knocking, she didn't have to wait long for a reply.

"Enter," came a muffled response and the half-elf ducked inside, closing the door behind her.

"Ah, Adventurer welcome. Sariel, isn't it?" Her ladyship was sat on a chair, cross-stitching something onto a large piece of blue fabric.

The Ranger was surprised. She'd introduced herself the previous day but she hadn't really expected the noblewoman to remember her name. "Yes, er maam."

"Please, call me Mera. What can I do for you?" The Lady's tone was friendly and familiar, but Sariel could detect minute tones of discomfort in her voice.

"I wondered if you were alright? After the attack last night, I mean." It wasn't a particularly subtle way of starting her line of questioning, but speechcraft wasn't one of her strong suits.

"Hmmm, indeed it was shocking to hear that a monster could so easily make off with an Adventurer as powerful as the hobgoblin." The words didn't offer much in the way of information but Sariel couldn't help but notice the way Mera's mouth tightened as she said the word 'hobgoblin'.

"Quite. It was lucky we weren't all killed by such a monster."

"Oh, I don't think it was just luck my dear. The quick thinking and direct actions of your fellow Adventurers saved our lives. I have already provided your leader a reward for your heroic actions."

"Leader? Oh, you mean Tarqu-".

"**Sir** Tarquin my dear, he holds a title; does he not?"

"Well apparently bu-".

"Then it behoves you to use it; does it not?" Sariel was already getting tired of the rhetorical questions, but she nodded anyway. "Good, good. Now, if there's nothing else I have work to do."

This time the rhetorical question was clearly phrased as a dismissal, but Sariel wasn't to be so easily disregarded.

"Actually, I do have one question." And then, before the woman had time to argue, she continued on. "Don't you think it odd that only the most powerful member of the group was taken? Monsters that hunt tend to seek out the weak and lame, those easiest to dispatch."

Lady Fawkner's eyes widened slightly and a smiled curved the severe line of her lips. "An interesting observation, but I'm afraid I am no expert in the habits of monsters." Then she turned back to her stitching, once again dismissing the Ranger.

Giving up, Sariel turned to leave. Without looking at her and said almost as an afterthought, the noble spoke up once more. "Did you know he was a Necromancer?"

The question caught Sariel with such surprise that she actually stopped midstep. She dared not turn around, for fear the noblewoman would see the look of terror on her face. "I did my lady."

"Interesting isn't it? How their kind always turns out bad. And it's Mera, please."

Sariel didn't bother to answer, she recognised the third and final dismissal for what it was. The door clicked shut behind her and she stepped out into the cool light of early evening.

Well, did she know anything useful?

Sariel scanned the deck for Libby and found the squirrel hidden atop the crow's nest. *Not really, but I think she knew it was going to happen. But I'm not positive.*

No matter. She'll reveal herself when we start killing your companions. The Familiar had a way of conveying vengeance into her words, even through the telepathic link. Enough to send a shiver down Sariel's spine.

I've already told you I won't be attacking any members of my group unless we're sure that they attacked Ninetoes without cause.

Oh, they had cause. They wanted his stuff! Don't think I haven't seen them parading themselves around in his armour and clothing. I'll make everyone of them sorry!

Even Bess?

The question momentarily stalled Libby's viscous diatribe. Neither was sure about the Smith's allegiances. Certainly, when they'd first met, Bess had seemed indifferent to the onerous brute. But since the attack she was never out of his reach. Sariel was of the opinion that magic was involved.

She just doesn't seem the type and…

And I told you what she said! She was there!

And I've told you that I've seen Tarquin use magic to charm people before, I'm sure that's it.

Huh. You may be right. Regardless, the rest are dead!

You must calm yourself, they are no pushovers, even if you surprise them. For now, it appears we're docking for the evening. Stay aboard and I'll bring you food as soon as I can.

Fine, but if I see the opportunity to strike one of them down, I won't hesitate… and please save me some cheese.

LIBBY

She'd only ever experienced anger such as she felt now through the thoughts and feelings of her Master and then, powerful as it was, she had only ever been a spectator to it. But now, that anger and hatred was so all-consuming she could sympathise with her Master and even respect him for how well he controlled it.

Now she must learn to control it as well, and like her fallen Master, she would learn to sharpen it into a weapon with which to avenge herself on those who had killed him!

She ducked down once again. Kowann had noticed her presence in the crow's nest almost immediately, but he had left her alone. Well mostly. He seemed to take great pleasure in swooping down at her and performing a flyby every once in a while.

After their discussions with Gideon, Libby had been afraid that she would cease being **her** when her Master had died. That she would fall back into being as unconscious as her brethren, and that scared her, more than she was willing to admit. It was part of the reason she held onto her anger. While she felt that way, she knew she was still **her**.

Her stomach grumbled. *And now I have to sit and wait for Sariel to bring me something to eat!*

She hated being beholden to the half-elf for sustenance but for all her bluster, she knew it wasn't safe to leave her hiding spot.

And, she admitted to herself, she could probably stand to miss a meal or two.

"To arms, to arms, we're under attack!" Libby hopped to the edge of the platform and looked down towards the camp. While she couldn't see Tarquin, she recognised his arrogant, boyish voice and could trace that to movement in the trees below.

The campsite was held in a small clearing between the river's edge and the treeline. The Adventurers had already set up a small fire and were erecting the posh lady's tent. Into this, Tarquin skidded to a halt at the and barked out orders to the other Adventurers, all of whom, Libby was pleased to see, ignored him.

The strange lizardman suddenly became kind of blurry and more difficult to see and, with his dark green scales, he blended in almost perfectly with the foliage. The Wizard pointed her finger at something hidden from Libby's view and bolts of red light sprang into the trees, shortly followed by three wet smacks.

A group of creatures, each of them a strange mixture of different parts were flooding into the camp. The Adventurers had each taken cover behind a log or tree and were directing their attacks into the horde.

Libby didn't really care about the other Adventurers, except for the slight concern that if they were killed by whatever chased Tarquin that she wouldn't get to feel the satisfaction of murdering them herself. She did, however, scan the field for Sariel and what she found concerned her.

While the Adventurers focussed their attention on the main bulk of the force assaulting the camp, Libby could just about make out the fleeting image of something quick that was flanking the party. She only saw it herself because of her greater field of view and even then, it was the barest flashes of a dark-skinned, four-legged monster that moved with cat-like grace.

Worse still, Sariel, who stood loosing arrow after arrow, hadn't noticed that she would be the creature's first victim.

First, Libby tried alerting the Ranger telepathically, but she was clearly too far away. So, without much concern for her own safety, Libby sprang into action.

Libby had been systematically casting Cloaking Shadows every hour to help keep herself concealed from the Adventurers and luckily enough, her last casting was a while ago, so she had both the benefit of the spell but had recharged all her mana since then. Her Shadow Armour too, still had plenty of time left on it, so she was as protected as she could be without running away from the fight.

Leaping from the Crow's Nest, she glided down towards the clearing, but kept herself in line with the trees, searching for a good place to alight. Unfortunately, this still kept her out of telepathic range with Sariel.

She found a safe harbour quickly enough and landed on a branch to Sariel's flank. She wanted to help the half-elf, but she also didn't want to reveal herself to the others. As powerful as she'd become, she still only had enough mana to cast her most effective combat spell, Madigar's Madness, three times, so she needed to fight smart.

Now that she was beneath the canopy, she could see the skulking monster more clearly. Its movement did indeed resemble that of a feline, but that's where the similarities ended.

Rather than dark skin, as she'd first thought, the creature's body was a patchwork of tiny shimmering scales. As it passed by bushes and trees, its scales changed colour to match, making it blend into its surroundings. It was only because she knew it was there that she could follow it at all.

Because of this, it was difficult to see many details, but it definitely walked on all fours and had two tails that seemed to bulge at the end.

The monster had slowed, but stalked ever closer to Sariel. As she steadily emptied her quiver of arrows, every shot the half-elf took dealt massive damage to the other creatures and Libby could see their numbers were dwindling and that the battle was tipping in the Adventurers' favour.

Turning back to track the monster however, the situation was much more different. Now that it was so much closer, she realised that it was much bigger and more deadly than she'd thought. Perhaps she'd bitten off more than she could chew.

The beast had slowed down as it stalked Sariel. Growling low in its throat, it began coiling its hind legs beneath it. Libby recognised this for what it was and knew she had only moments to act.

On her short flight she'd considered her best choice of spells. Madigar's Madness was her only viable choice for killing the creature and it wouldn't necessarily alert the Adventurers to her presence, but they'd certainly think it odd if a monster just keeled over in the middle of a battle. She didn't need to kill the monster of course, she could just lead it away with her Reflection spell, but with only one casting a day, she'd rather keep that as a means of escape.

Finally, she'd decided that the best course of action wasn't to try to injure the beast, but rather to distract it long enough to alert Sariel of the danger and her best shot at that was Iridescent.

She hadn't used the spell since she'd tested it on her Master. At the thought a pang of sorrow shot through her, but she replaced it with anger and fired off her spell.

The monster's head snapped in her direction and although she couldn't see them, she felt the creature's eyes lock onto her and she felt, more than heard, its growl vibrate through her.

She stood stock still, rooted to the spot and unable to even think. The primal part of her mind took over and she bolted towards the bole of the tree and the protection offered by being in the higher branches.

Heart racing and her bowels threatening to empty in terror. What in the world had she been thinking? She was prey, she couldn't face such a powerful and deadly crea- *No!*

Her awakened mind fought with her primal one for control of her limbs. Libby made her Choice.

I am not PREY! Her consciousness transformed and she stopped bolting up the tree. She thought of her Master, standing tall in front of their enemies, protecting her with his very life. Could she really do any less; be any less?

I am not PREY! I will not run. I will fight.

She turned on the branch and took a step back, towards the fight. It felt like the hardest step she'd ever made. In that moment, she thanked her lucky stars she'd gained the Strong Willed ability. Without it, she'd have been gone. With this in mind, the next step was easier and so was the one after. Soon, she'd reached the branch's end and she leapt, gliding towards the monster. There wasn't time to climb back down, the monster, having disregarded her for weak and helpless prey, was almost upon Sariel. It was moments from pouncing!

It was too late for careful. She folded her legs against her body and plummeted like a stone towards the thing's head. She struck it hind-legs first with an audible clunk. It rattled her slightly but had the desired effect, and distracted the monster from attacking the half-elf. Scrabbling for purchase, her tiny claws grabbed a scale and she pulled herself and behind its head.

With a sickening crack, however, the monster's head rotated to stare two demonic eyes at her.

Momentarily mesmerised, she didn't notice a tail lashing out towards her.

Too late, she tried to dodge, but she could barely see it and it connected hard with her rump. Luckily for her, her shadowy armour absorbed the damage but the force of it knocked her off of the creature's back nonetheless.

The anticipated the follow up attack and was already in motion when it slammed into the ground where she'd stood. Diving for a bush, she tried to scurry into the creature's flank, but it simply turned to face her, its neck making the same unearthly noise as it clicked back into place.

Once again, she felt her muscles begin to tense in petrification and fear, but she would not give into it this time and instead she placed her forepaws firmly forwards. *Not this time fucker!*

Ah! So you are more than you appear. Good! But, consuming you will not be worth this one's while. Lay down now and this one will end it quickly. Fight and we will start at your belly and work out.

Libby was shocked. Of course, she'd known other creatures could speak with their minds, but she had thought this to be just a dumb brute.

She chided herself for her complacency, she'd never avenge her Master if she continued to be so foolish. That challenge awaited her still, but for now, she must focus her attention on this fool.

Ha! I offer you the same cur!

The sound that reverberated out of the monster was like nails on slate and had it not been for their telepathic link, she'd have thought the massive feline was about to cough up the mother of all furballs. Instead, it was laughing at her. And if she was honest, she couldn't blame it.

But the sound was loud enough that she wasn't the only one to hear it.

"There's another monster behind us. Shit I think they're demons!" shouted the female wizard.

Sariel turned to look into the gloom of the forest and finally saw it.

By now the Ranger had drawn a short sword and buckler and was dancing around two smaller monsters, both of whom it was clear were forcing her back towards the one Libby was facing. Fear filled her eyes as she realised the trap she was in and she started casting them about, looking for a means of escape.

That is delicious. You really think you pose this one any threat? We, who have slaughtered hundreds in our ascension. We, who were awarded the honour of coming through first by the Master! You think he'd have chosen a weakling? No, he chose the strongest to lead his assault. The creatures of this realm will flee before our ever-growing dread. We will fill its belly wi-

Oh, that's cute. Libby could feel the creature seethe with malice at being interrupted. *But you don't seem all that scary to me and I'm tiny.*

413

The demon's laugh reached a fevered pitch of excitement, bordering on arousal and it stalked in circles around Libby and spoke to her once again. *You may have overcome our mental assault while this one was camouflaged, but nothing has withstood our power when they've looked upon our true visage!*

So saying, the monster's appearance began to change. Starting at its head, the shimmering scales darkened and Libby could finally see the creature as it truly was. And it was absolutely horrifying.

Rather than scales, the monster seemed to be covered in plates of bone, in between which oozed a viscous, black phlegm. Rather than two tails, it had three and each one ended in a ball of sharp spines, two of which glistened with purple venom and the third seemingly ethereal.

But it was its face that was truly terrifying. In place of the eyes of a cat, flashed the many eyes of an arachnid, wrapping across its face, each one seemed to hold a different persona. These sat above a cruelly curved maw of fangs and a jaw that looked like it could crack rocks. Finally, the forked tongue of a serpent flicked out, licking its lips in anticipation for its meal.

Libby, however, chose not to take in these details, and was once again grateful for her newest ability. She was sure that looking at it would mean being petrified and helpless once again. Instead she enacted her plan.

She'd come up with it as soon as the monstrous fool had started talking. She'd grown to realise that her spells had a greater chance of success when she could see her target's eyes. She'd also known that this thing wanted her to be afraid, lusted after it, it seemed. And so she knew she could manipulate it.

As soon as it had started revealing itself she began casting. This time she must not fail. She finished her spell just as the monster finished throwing off its mirage.

Her biggest problem was which pair of eyes to choose, but in the end, she'd decided on all of them.

Her whole plan hinged on this. If the creature wasn't blinded, she was done for. Firing from the darkness of the bushes she sprayed the clustered orbs with rainbow-coloured light and the effect was immediate. The monster screamed in pain and frustration as its optical senses were flooded with too much light. Her spell had worked!

Without waiting and hoping against hope that her gambit continued to pay off, she summoned her mana and cast her second and probably final spell. The monster's screams increased in pitch and volume and all of those present were temporarily stunned by its dreadful potency.

Libby however, had been fleeing before its full effect took hold and leapt from knot to branch making her way up the nearest tree to the relative safety.

Magically, Libby was no slouch, but she definitely regretted all the extra helpings of cheese as she scrambled up the tree.

After the monster had ignored the effects of her first attempt at Iridescent, she'd realised that the creature must have some sort of resistance to her magic. Her new intellect had helped her realise that she'd have to find a means to tip the odds in her favour.

It's why she'd fired from the darkness, hoping that the buff would work in the half-light. The monster's obvious capacity for mental resilience was also why she'd blinded it before attempting to use her next spell. Just as she'd learned that a creature's eyes were a portal into their mind, so too had she innately understood that if the monster couldn't see that it wasn't in fact on fire, then it was more likely to fall foul of Madigar's Madness.

Looking at the thing's slimy body, she wasn't even convinced it could be hurt by fire. But of course, it didn't need to be, it only had to think it could!

Even with the buffs to her Illusion magic, however, Libby only had a tiny pool of mana remaining and she couldn't risk suffering from mana exhaustion in the middle of combat.

So it was that after only a handful of seconds she had to stop concentrating on her spell and the monster's screams lessened and then morphed into shrieks of anger.

Blinking its many eyes to clear them, its serpentine tongue tasted the air and found Libby's scent. With excited glee it began expounding its plans for her.

When I find you filth I will rip you apart! I will tear your limbs from your body one at a time and—

But whatever the demon would do to Libby's limbs, she never discovered. The lizardman Cleric had recognised the threat to his party and had used the monster's distraction to work his way into the demon's blind spot.

Libby watched with glee as the blurred aspect stalked up behind the demon and then ignited his blade with bright purple light. Just as the demon's eyes seemed to focus, the Cleric rammed his glowing blade into the spot behind the creature's ear.

The demon spasmed in pain but it still managed to lash out with its spiked tails. An'rik managed to catch two of the attacks on his shield but as his sword was still inside the monster, he was unable to block the third and it slammed into his ribs, the spikes puncturing his scaly hide.

Libby only had to wonder why the Cleric had left the blade lodge in the demon for a second more. The lizardman muttered a phrase in his own language and the hilt of his sword flashed with light and a quiet 'whoomph' sound emanated within the demon's head.

She'd had no idea how powerful the demon was, but it had suffered more psychic damage than she'd thought a creature could withstand. So why had the Cleric's attack been so powerful?

That's when something the wizard had said came flooding back. *Demons!* The Cleric's attack must have been anathema to the monstrous thing. If not for that, they might all have died!

The monster stopped moving and slid off of the Cleric's sword, slumping lifelessly to the floor. Then, as she stared at it in wonder, the body began to fizz. Within moments, the only thing left of the demon was an area of singed grassed.

"Yep, demons alright." An'rik said in the common tongue. Libby had been so transfixed on her own battle and the Cleric's timely intervention, she hadn't realised that the other Adventurers had dealt with their own enemies and, apart from the sizzling remains of a half-dozen other demons, the clearing was silent. "What I don't understand is why it was screaming; and why didn't it attack Sariel when it had the chance."

Libby was already carefully making her way back to the barge but the lizardman's question worried her. If they realised something else had been involved, they might search the area.

"I... er, I cast a spell on it." Sariel tried and Libby crossed her claws.

"Oh, what spell?" Tarquin asked suspiciously.

Clearly Sariel was at a loss. She'd told Libby on the first day of the journey that as a Ranger she knew a few spells, but most of them were just to buff her martial abilities. By now, Libby was within range of the half-elf and she offered her own insight, *Madigar's Madness. Tell them Ninetoes taught it to you.*

Sariel didn't make any outward indication that she'd heard her, but a moment later she spoke up. "I cast Madigar's Madness," she was clearly trying to sound nonchalant and bored.

"That's not a Ranger spell," spoke up the Wizard.

"No, not usually. Ni- the hobgoblin had a spell scroll, it was in his Bag of Holding, I snagged it when you emptied it."

Every member of the party looked stunned. But Tarquin's face quickly turned into an angry snarl. "That was party loot and you didn't even help-" he caught sight of Lowen nearby and stuttered for a moment, "er, help um, fight the manticore."

"You can dock it from my share of the reward when we get paid," said Sariel, locking cold eyes with Tarquin. A silent contest ensued and Libby's breath was held watching it take place. Clearly Tarquin couldn't risk arguing further for fear that the Ranger would spill the truth about what had happened to Ninetoes.

While Lowen and Deck were no match for the Adventurers, killing them would mean that the party was walking the rest of the way. Furthermore, Lady Fawkner was still an unknown quantity and killing her was more trouble than it was worth.

The moment stretched on, but eventually Tarquin seemed to reach the same conclusion. It wasn't worth the trouble. "Huh. Don't do it again, we share loot."

"Whatever," Sariel said rudely, before stepping over one of the spots of charred grass. "Not that there's anything to loot from these things."

"No. But my question is; where did these things come from in the first place? Demons shouldn't be able to leave their realm without help."

"There are many strange and nasty things roaming these woods. I suggest we sleep on the boat tonight," Lowen said, entering into the conversation.

"Aye, it's not a bad plan and it's only for one night," responded Tarquin.

So it was that the group began hauling their bedrolls back onto the ship. In the cramped conditions and with two people on watch, someone was always within line of sight of the mast, Sariel had no opportunity to deliver Libby anything to eat and so the squirrel went hungry.

CHAPTER 22
THE PATH OF THE MAVERICK

SARIEL

The half-elf was worried. She knew the squirrel wasn't about to starve, but with the party now sleeping on the barge, she'd had no opportunity to send up some food. She was concerned that the fledgling alliance she'd formed with Ninetoes' Familiar was already fragile enough, without adding problems to it.

If only she'd chosen to be a mage of some kind, she'd have a telekinesis spell by now and could just float some food up to the squirrel's hide in the crow's nest. Of course, if she'd chosen that then she'd never have considered buying the Familiar's Tongue from Gideon so that was a stupid line of reasoning.

No, she must find a solution to the problem with the tools she had. She briefly considered throwing something up or even tying food to an arrow and shooting it up, but these methods simply had too many ways they could go wrong.

She'd be dead if it wasn't for the little rodent. It may have been An'rik's Divine Strike that killed the demon but she knew that Libby had been the one to distract it long enough for the lizardman to make his attack.

She hadn't gotten a good look but the creature had clearly been much more of a threat than the other, smaller fiends and they'd caused the party enough trouble.

Still, the fight with the demons had given the party enough experience to level up and all of them had reached Level 4. She'd put her Ability Points into Dexterity of course and her Skill points into Longbow and Light Armour. This had been enough to rank up her Longbow skill and she'd gained the Apprentice rank bonus. She could now perform Sharp Shot I.

LONGBOW: LEVEL 20 - APPRENTICE

+20% DAMAGE.

+20% CHANCE OF CRITICAL HIT.

QUICK SHOT - CAN FIRE AT TWICE THE SPEED, LOSING 50% ACCURACY.

SHARP SHOT I - INCREASES THE DAMAGE OF A SHOT BY 50% BUT TAKES 5 SECONDS TO PREPARE. COSTS 50 STAMINA.

She knew from experience that if one worked at it, this could become Sharp Shot II and III and there was even rumoured to be a Sharp Shot Master, but she'd never met anyone that could do it. Or, at least, no one that was talking. She'd also gained a level in Spirit Knowledge, a spell that allowed her to analyse a creature and gain useful information. With the level, she'd gained a new ability.

SPIRIT KNOWLEDGE - LEVEL 8

ENCHANTMENT

CASTING TIME - 1 SECOND

MANA COST - 50 POINTS

DURATION - CONCENTRATION

LVL 1. REVEALS THE BASIC INFORMATION ABOUT CREATURES.

LVL 8. 5% CHANCE TO REVEAL A MONSTER'S WEAKNESS.

This was brilliant! Learning a monster's weakness could mean the difference between victory and defeat. None of this, however, helped her to get food up to the Maverick in the crow's nest.

That was a new one on her, she'd never heard of a Maverick Familiar, although the stubborn and wilful squirrel certainly fit the bill. Most Familiars that she'd encountered before were Path of the Chain and most Adventurers just wanted something to supplement their own martial prowess.

Often non-Adventurers would choose the Path of Harmony and, although she'd never asked him, that's what she'd bet Lowen's bond was with his owl. The owl!

She'd noticed the bird occasionally dive-bombing Libby during the day's journey but when she'd asked the squirrel about it, she'd answered that Kowann was just "being a dick" and didn't really say much. Certainly, if the owl was aware of the rodent's presence, then the bargemaster must also know about the stowaway.

If this was true; did he know Ninetoes had been murdered? It seemed like only one way to find out was to ask, but only Lady Fawkner had her own room, with everyone else sharing what little space was left on the deck, so the chance of having a private conversation was practically nil.

Or was it? Sariel searched the deck, scanning the railings until she found the owl perched on the wheel of the boat. It appeared to be asleep but she reckoned it was probably 'on watch' for his master.

She got up and climbed to the quarterdeck, ostensibly just to stretch her legs. She knew protocol decreed that it was bad manners to speak to a Familiar without permission from its master, but these were desperate times, so she risked the slap on the wrist.

Um, good evening Kowann, she tried. The bird ignored her, or remained asleep, it was hard to tell so she tried again. *Hello? Kowann are you awake?* Still the owl remained outwardly unresponsive.

I was in fact asleep, but this is hard to achieve when someone shouts directly into your mind. Did you know it's-

Yes, yes. I apologise for the intrusion but I need your help.

Kowann's head rotated slowly around to face her and his yellow eyes considered her intently. It must have known how unnerving the ability made her, because she caught a whiff of his amused thoughts. But he didn't say anything.

I need to speak with your master.

Indeed. He's the tall, skinny man down on the deck. You're welcome. And so saying he closed his eyes and turned his head back.

Wait!

Sigh Yes? The owl's tone had become bored.

I need to speak to him privately and I thought-

You thought to use me as a messenger, passing your words to him and vice versa. No thank you, I'd rather sleep.

Argh! This bloody bird! she hadn't meant to 'verbalise' the thought, but Kowann's head swerved around and his sharp eyes pierced into her hazel ones.

Cheek will get you nowhere dear, Lowen learned that the hard way. His mental reprimand was harsh, but at least she had his attention. Perhaps she could use that.

Oh, you're probably too stupid to pass my messages on accurately anyway, don't worry, she said, hoping to sound nonchalant.

"Too stupid"? Oh let me tell yo- Wait, I see what you're doing and such a gambit will not work on me half-human. Ha! The insult was a clever one and displayed how long the owl must have been around people to know that many half-elves preferred to lean into the elven lineage, as most considered the race superior to the humans. Frankly, Sariel didn't care, but Kowann didn't need to know that.

How dare you! I am of elven descent. We once used your kind to deliver messages across the Great Forest but we stopped bothering, now I can see why. That was probably total bullshit, but she hoped the owl wasn't quite that wise.

Ha! More than likely owls simply got bored and left. But, in honour of my folk's gloried past, I will grant you a single message. You're welcome.

Phew! Alright, she needed to be efficient with her words. *Please tell your master the following: Ninetoes was attacked by the other Adventurers, so be careful. His Familiar still lives and is hiding in the crow's nest.*

He already knows all of this, but a promise is a promise, replied the owl haughtily. He then swooped down to perch upon the gunwale next to his master. Sariel watched closely and noted that while the bargemaster feigned sleep, he nodded a few times and then the owl flew back.

Lowen bids you to be more careful, he is afraid that the other Adventurers may kill him and Deck if he causes any problems. He suggests you bide your time until we reach Caillic's and then part ways with them.

He may be right about that, but I need your help now.

Hmmm, but I have already ferried your message and, I might add, his response.

Please. Libby hasn't eaten anything all day. All I ask is that you fly up to the nest and drop her off this parcel of food.

I see. Well, the rodent is the most interesting individual onboard this tub. Indeed, she has some wonderful thoughts on you people. So then, what's in it for me?

Argh! *Look, all I have is this bread and cheese to give to Libby, but I can get you some meat if you give me a little time.*

Ha! And you think that I'll be so easily bought for a little meat?

Gods! What was it with this damned bird? *Fine, I'll get you... er, I dunno a whole chicken when we get to Caillic's. How's that?*

Very well, for a whole chicken, uncooked, I'll fly this package up to the crow's nest. Kowann actually offered her one of his clawed feet. She took and shook it carefully, trying not to imbalance him. She then handed him the little parcel of food she'd made and he flew out ahead of the boat, before circling back to the top of the mast.

But, instead of landing on the crow's nest, the owl alighted on the very top of the mast. She hoped this would be enough, for she needed all the help she could get.

LIBBY

The squirrel watched the exchange between the half-elf and the owl with great interest. She'd spent most of the evening moping in her little hideout, bemoaning her empty stomach and making ludicrous plans for how she'd avenge herself upon the Adventurers.

She'd just considered luring something nasty from the forest to do all the heavy lifting before finishing them off herself, but she discarded the plan as too dangerous. That's when she'd seen Sariel climb to the quarterdeck and stare intently at the owl for an uncomfortably long time.

Then the owl had glided down to the bargemaster before returning to the Ranger. Finally, the woman had passed the bird a parcel of something and Libby's heart had soared in much the same way as the owl had.

But, then he'd landed on the mast's top and, rather than drop the parcel down to her, he began clawing at the cloth that Sariel had wrapped it in. At first, she was just confused, but by the time she realised what he was up to, it was already too late.

Kowann pulled the packaging off of the parcel and let it drop into the crow's nest. Only then had he bent his head to look at her and those golden eyes stared into hers as he gobbled down her cheese!

Mother-

Now, now. Manners little rodent, or I'll eat 'your' dinner as well.

Eat my- you already did!

No no. That nice half-human down there sent up this lovely bread roll for you. So saying, he tore the roll into two and dropped half the morsel into the nest.

She almost didn't take it, but she was so hungry she couldn't stop herself from snatching it up. *Dick.* She thought 'out loud' but the owl's only response was to snigger telepathically.

As she ate, she looked down onto the deck once again and could see Sariel looking up anxiously her way. It wasn't the Ranger's fault the owl was an arsehole, so she waved down to the woman and watched as Sariel's face changed into one of glee.

Kowann had also given her another boon, without necessarily meaning to. The cloth that the food had been wrapped in lay nearby and, while it wasn't as comfortable as her cushion or as warm as the hide she made in Ninetoes' breastplate, it was a vast improvement on nothing.

Strange, she thought to herself, how much things had changed. She could remember being 'just' a squirrel and how, back then, curling up with only her bushy tail for warmth had been more than enough to make her content, but she'd become accustomed to the finer things.

She didn't really mind, but the thought certainly showed her how much her life had changed in only a few weeks.

Such thoughts and more carried her turmoiled mind into a much more peaceful sleep than the one she'd had the night before. The night her Master, her Ninetoes had been taken from her.

***

"Ho the dock!"

"Ho the boat!"

The twinned shouts roused Libby from her slumber and, blinking the sleep from her eyes, the tiny rodent looked about. The sun was already high in the sky and as she climbed to the nest's edge, she could see the burgeoning port only a couple of hundred yards away. She'd slept through the morning!

Stretching languorously she felt her tiny bones click and a thrill spread through her. Before doing anything else, she cast Cloaking Shadow and then Shadow Armour. Finally, she waited.

She could hear the rest of the crew moving about beneath her and after hiding for so long, she didn't want to give herself away now.

My Master bids you to wait until the Adventurers have disembarked and then come and speak with him. The owl flew above the mast and didn't bother to look at her, clearly maintaining the pretence that there was nothing in the crow's nest.

Of course, I am grateful for his help and yours, Kowann. The owl nodded and then glided over to the shore in search of breakfast.

Curious, what could the bargemaster want from her?

She didn't have long to wait to find out. Within minutes she felt the barge bump against the dock and then heard the gangplank being lowered and Lowen speaking with the Adventurers. She heard them clearly state that they intended to buy horses and then head out, so she wouldn't have long to spend talking to the bargemaster.

With that in mind, she didn't hesitate and jumped from the nest and plummeted towards the deck, only extending her 'wings' at the last moment to glide towards where the bargemaster stood speaking with a dockworker.

"—and if one of your lads damages my boat they'll be hell to pay!"

The dockworker rolled his eyes, but only after he turned his back on Lowen. The sight made Libby chuckle. She still wasn't keen to be seen and the dockside was a bustle of people, crates and churning mud. If she landed on the ground she'd never get herself properly clean.

Thus, she elected to alight on the rooftop of a partly built warehouse. There, she sent her mind outwards searching for Kowann's mind. It wasn't difficult to find as the owl had clearly watched her leave her hiding spot.

Please tell your Master I am here.

As you say. Libby watched Lowen closely and thought she could tell the moment Kowann had conveyed her message, because the bargemaster's brow furrowed and then he began searching the rooftops.

He found her quickly and strolled over to the warehouse she perched on. Once there, he reached into his pocket and removed an apple and then sat with his back against a crate and set about peeling the apple with a pocket knife.

Libby climbed down so that she sat only a couple of feet from his head, but kept herself concealed from a cursory glance.

"You were foolish to stay aboard little one. You should have fled when the half-elf freed you."

Please tell your master that I am no coward and that I seek to avenge my own Master, she sent to Kowann.

A moment later and Lowen chuckled. "Ha! They killed your Master handily enough, you would be no challenge for them."

Libby's emotions roiled with anger. The feeling only reminded her of her loss. *Size and strength are a simpleton's weapons, I will use subterfuge to fashion a far sharper blade and I WILL avenge Ninetoes.* Her voice was gruff, even within her own mind.

"And I'm sure you will become a deadly foe, even without your Master, but they outnumber you and have access to powers and skills you can only dream of. You have no hope of victory."

What's it to you old man? Leave me to my business. As soon as she'd thought it, she instantly regretted her words, but she was too angry to apologise.

"Old man is it? Why you stubborn little-" Lowen took a breath. "- listen, I'm here to offer you a place aboard my boat. It won't be the adventure a life with your hobgoblin promised you but I can guarantee you a full belly and what safety this life provides. It ain't much, but it's better than the quick death your current course will end in." As she finished his piece, he also finished peeling the apple. The peel was a single spiral of the reddish skin. For a moment Libby was mesmerised by the small but perfect feat of skill.

During that moment, and only during that moment, she seriously considered his offer. She could even imagine herself making a life on the Kerensa.

But the moment passed. Her path had been chosen already. She'd had this same choice once before, when the ettercap had Ninetoes pinned beneath the filthy water of its lair. She could have run then and there and lived her life as any other squirrel, but instead she chose the hobgoblin. Since then, there was no question, the two had become one.

And then? Then those bastard Adventurers had taken her Master from her. Tears threatened to overcome her, but instead she bared her teeth.

Thank you, but no. I am no longer prey. But the Adventurers will be mine. She didn't just say this to Kowann and the bargemaster, she made this promise to the very universe. She would grow stronger and vengeance would be hers.

Lowen stayed quiet for a little longer. Then, when he spoke up, his voice was gruff. "Very well. For reference, I think you're a fool. But... cantankerous old bastard he might be, but I can't say I'd do any less for Kowann."

Meanwhile, he removed something from his pocket, one of the vials of potion that Ninetoes had bought and a scroll of parchment. "And if you're intent upon it, you'd better take these. I took 'em out of that Tarquin-fucker's satchel, but I 'spose they're yours anyway."

While he spoke he fashioned a simple strap out of twine, his fingers a flurry of knot-making expertise that only a sailor could manage. "Here."

He held the vial out and Kowann swooped in to grab it before delivering it to Libby. The bundle was small, but bulbous-shaped, but the strap he'd made allowed her to carry it across her back or slung around her front if she wanted to glide.

Thank you. I know Ninetoes thought very highly of you Lowen, in what little time he knew you. And Kowann?

Yes little thief?

You're a dick.

Kowann chuckled but didn't respond. Libby smiled her own smile, and peeked inside the package, to find one of the potions of haste rested within. it wasn't much but her Master had turned such magical tools into deadly weapons, she would do the same.

With that thought she leapt off of the roof and began making her way towards the Steading proper. It took her a few minutes, what with so many people around, but once she was on the high walls of the compound she found moving around unseen much easier.

Libby made for the stables, hoping that the Adventurers hadn't left already.

Circling the main building, she found the Adventurers leaving the stables, each of them astride a horse. And Tarquin, the bastard, was on Ninetoes' horse! Was there no end to this arsehole's cheek? Argh! That prick seriously needed killing.

Libby? Is that you?

She caught Sariel's gaze and nodded. The half-elf pulled back on her reins. "Woah, er sorry guys, I don't think my saddle's on right, I'll catch up." And then she leapt down from her horse and began manipulating the straps.

"Argh, whatever, just hurry up," replied Tarquin as he kicked hard with his heels and spurred the stallion on, the rest of the party close behind.

"Yes sure, it won't take long," Sariel answered and then, telepathically. *Are you alright? And what have you got there?*

It's mine, Libby responded, too harshly.

Oh, of course it is, but do you want me to carry it? She sounded a little hurt. But Libby couldn't worry about that just now.

No. Thank you. It's one of Ni- it's one of my potions of haste.

Very well, do you want to ride with me? I could hide you in my satchel, there's plenty of food in there.

Libby thought about it. She was, once again, hungry and she didn't fancy walking all the way to Raveslan. But no, she had to grow stronger, she couldn't just become Sariel's companion, she must become more.

Thank you, but no. Surprise is my best chance of success. I will make my own way there. Then, as she considered the journey ahead, she added. *But if you could see your way to leaving me some food each night, I'd be obliged.*

Her stomach rumbled. But she couldn't follow it's one track mind anymore, she must evolve.

I appreciate your sense of independence, but if I may? I have a spell that can help.

What does it do?

It's called Endless Endurance, it'll stop your stamina from draining so quickly.

That definitely made sense. Libby was no slouch with one hundred and sixty-three points in her Stamina pool but her tiny size meant that she'd be using significantly more points just to keep up.

Yes, but please be quick.

Excellent, this won't take a sec. The Ranger muttered a short spell and green light surrounded Libby. She instantly felt stronger and quicker.

Thank you, now we must be away. And with those words she bounded for the corner of the wall. Springboarding from one side she tucked her feet and sprang to the opposite wall and then back again, until she'd reached the top. From there she leapt as high as she could before gliding westwards, following the treeline.

***

It was hard work and only a few days ago she'd have given up long before, but her anger drove her on. She'd glide as often as she could, but she couldn't fly and so eventually she had to come down and then she'd have to climb yet another tree to gain altitude. The bundle that Lowen had given her was a further burden but she'd endured, as she knew her Master would have.

In the end, she found it more efficient to leap and glide from one tree to the next and then she never had to climb far before she could jump and glide again. Nevertheless, by the time the sun had set and she'd caught up to the Adventurers, she was sore all over and utterly exhausted.

Worse still, if she remembered correctly, she had another day of travel before she reached Raveslan and she still hadn't come up with any sort of a plan for dealing with her adversaries.

True to her word, Sariel had parcelled up some food and tucked it into the nook of a tree branch. To anyone on the ground, it would have been almost impossible to spot, but from her vantage, finding it had been easy.

Tucking into the simple meal of cheese, *Ah cheese,* and apple filled her with a sense of accomplishment. In a strange way, she felt that she'd earned this meal, more so than any other she'd ever eaten.

She also realised that she was bored, so she took Lowen's bundle from her shoulder and carefully slid the parchment out. She already had an idea what it might be, but she hadn't had a moment to check since he'd given it to her.

Sure enough, once unrolled that light of the campfire below, lit up the familiar sight of her Character Sheet. A warm feeling ran through her, this was hers and, what's more, it was the only part of her bond with Ninetoes that still existed.

As she scanned the document, a thrill rushed through her. Some of her stats had changed!

HIT POINTS: 15/15	MANA POINTS: 150/150
STAMINA POINTS: 183/183	
BASE STATS: STRENGTH - 2 AGILITY - 46 ENDURANCE - 7 INTELLIGENCE - 30 WISDOM -15 CHARISMA - 20	ARMOUR: NONE ITEMS: BRACELET OF PROTECTION, GIDEON'S RING OF THE TRICKSTER
RACIAL ABILITIES	
CLIMB: CAN CLIMB ANY ROUGH SURFACE AT NORMAL MOVEMENT SPEED.	IMPROVED GLIDE: THE SQUIRREL IS ABLE TO LEAP AND GLIDE MEDIUM DISTANCES.
LEARNED ABILITIES	

CUTE: THE SQUIRREL'S NATURAL APPEAL GIVES IT AN ADVANTAGE WHEN CASTING ENCHANTMENT SPELLS THAT ATTEMPT TO 'CHARM' A CREATURE.	SNEAK AND HIDE: THE SQUIRREL'S SIZE AND DEXTERITY MAKE IT EASIER WHEN TRYING TO CONCEAL ITSELF.
IMPROVED SPELL CHANNELLING: THE FAMILIAR CAN CHANNEL MAGICAL ENERGY TO AND FROM ITSELF INTO ITS BONDED WIZARD, RANGE LIMITED TO 100 FEET.	STEAL: THE SQUIRREL'S SIZE AND DEXTERITY MAKE IT A NATURAL THIEF.
SURVIVAL INSTINCT: THE SQUIRREL'S NATURAL INSTINCT PROVIDES IT WITH THE WISDOM TO RUN, 25% RESISTANCE AGAINST 'FEAR' ATTACKS.	ZIPPY: THE SQUIRREL'S SIZE AND DEXTERITY MAKE IT DIFFICULT TO ATTACK BY LARGER CREATURES. QUICK WITTED: ONCE PER DAY, THE SQUIRREL CAN CREATE AN ILLUSORY COPY OF ITSELF TO DISTRACT AN ENEMY.
STRONG WILLED: THE SQUIRREL'S CHARISMA AND PROPENSITY FOR BEING BOSSY MAKE IT MORE DIFFICULT TO CONTROL, GAINING 25% DEFENCE AGAINST THE EFFECTS OF ILLUSION AND ENCHANTMENT MAGICS.	

SPELL CASTING AFFINITIES

ABJURATION - 50% SPELLS KNOWN - WIZARD'S ARMOUR	ENCHANTMENT - 75% SPELLS KNOWN - CHARISMA
ILLUSION* - 90% SPELLS KNOWN - MINOR ILLUSION*, CLOAKING SHADOW,	NECROMANCY - 10% SPELLS KNOWN - GRIM VOID

MADIGAR'S MADNESS, IRIDESCENT, SHADOW ARMOUR.	
ILLUSION - LEVEL 25 (20) BEGINNER +25% DURATION OF ILLUSION SPELLS ILLUSION SAVANT I - ILLUSION SPELLS COST YOU 10% LESS TO CAST. KNOWLEDGE ARCANE I - ALLOWS THE CASTER TO CHOOSE ONE APPRENTICE RANKED SPELL.	

Her Level hadn't changed, and she supposed it never would now that Ninetoes was gone. But she'd managed to increase Strength, Agility and Endurance, the latter by four points, more than doubling it. This had increased her Stamina points by twenty, for which she was grateful, but even better it proved that she could still develop on her own and she wouldn't be held back without a master.

She wondered if this would have been true had she and Ninetoes had chosen one of the other Paths.

But thinking about this made her sad, and she had no time for that. Without Sariel's endurance spell she would need plenty of sleep if she was to keep up the following day.

***

Sariel had tried to hang back again, but her companions had no patience and had spurred her on.

Libby had done her best but even with her increased stats, Libby had fallen behind by midday. She was angry at herself for her pace, but even they would struggle to keep up with horses.

She was surprised then, when she rounded a bend to find them standing around what was left of a battlefield, covered in yet more patches of singed grass. Keeping herself concealed and refreshing her Cloaking Shadow, she listened into their conversation.

"Another group of demons! I mean, what're the odds?" exclaimed An'rik.

"Aye, it's odd to be sure, but at least we're getting plenty of experience, right?" commented Tarquin.

"Huh, that would be *your* priority Tarquin. Aren't you worried what this could mean?" argued Sariel.

"Ah, you worry too much. This bunch was even easier than the second lot we killed yesterday."

They'd fought a second group the day before? That was news to Libby. But she'd been moving so fast trying to keep up, it was no wonder she'd missed it. She'd need to be more careful however, if there were such creatures roaming the forest.

"Besides, we'll be within the safety of Raveslan by sundown, so what's the problem?" added Tarquin.

"The problem, you ignorant dolt, is that Raveslan's not safe is it? It's under attack by a horde of hobgoblins. What if the demons attack the town and damage the defences? Or worse, what if the demons are working *with* the hobs?"

"Then we'll deal with them as well won't we? Seriously, these attacks have only been a good thing. One more encounter and we'll level up again! Personally, I'm hoping we get attacked at least once more before we reach the town!" Tarquin's statement met only concerned looks as the party broke away.

The rest of the party shared confused expressions and Libby could imagine why. Levelling was good of course, but each member of the party showed signs of injury and their armour was damaged.

For Libby, however, this had allowed her to catch up.

And, as Sariel made for the horses, clearly intent upon checking them over for wounds, the squirrel quickly made her way over to the half-elf and spoke telepathically.

I'm here, in the tree above. Are you alright?

Yes, I'm fine. But if I stay with this lot I'm liable to be dead sooner rather than later. You?

I'm fine, a little tired. Do you have any food?

Of course. Quickly hop down onto Goliath and I'll see what I have.

Goliath, it transpired, was Sariel's blood-red bay. By standing in between Libby and the others, Sariel was able to provide Libby with some much-needed sustenance without anyone being any the wiser. Sariel apologised, but she had too little mana left after the battle to cast her endurance spell again. But Libby didn't mind. She would succeed without it.

Do you have a plan for how you want to deal with the others? I was thinking that you could just wait for the battle with the hobs; they might do you a favour and kill them.

The same thought had crossed Libby's mind, but it lacked the satisfaction she sought.

No. But the chaos of the battle will certainly offer some excellent possibilities. Plus, there are allies I can call upon in Raveslan. Once you reach the town, make your excuses and find your way to the small house just outside of town, it belongs to the wizard Foresto, I'll meet you there.

Alright. But be careful, these woods seem to be crawling with demons and even someone as powerful and wily as you can't be expected to survive long against those odds.

I'll be fine. And Sariel?

Yes?

Safe journey and good fortune Adventurer. With that, Libby jumped into the branches and began her journey on. Now that they were so close, there was no need to plod along the road any longer. Libby could smell the town, its scent easy for her bestial nose to follow. Libby would outrun them!

By the time she reached Raveslan, Libby had increased her Endurance by another two points and had even managed to improve her Cloaking Shadow spell as well.

CHAPTER 23
RIVAL'S REFRAIN

In the space between a being observes. Not yet ready to cut a binding that so resonated with purpose and chaos, it chooses instead to effect its will.

Nearby other loops and hooks echoed its song but they are only pale reflections of the music, hollow and without resolve.

The observer had never been able to make music of its own but she so loved to listen. While she cannot cut and she cannot pull, she can gather, twist and strum. The music must play on.

VORTIGA

To say Vortiga had been surprised by the porsht's actions would have been a vast understatement and it only made her thoughts about the strange creature even more confused.

As a wielder of magic he was clearly adept and powerful but that made him a coward in the eyes of any hobgoblin. Magic users were always frail and weak and used the arcane arts because they were too infirm to wield a blade.

And yet? And yet Ninetoes showed no fear in combat. Certainly, in the battle at Raveslan he'd used the ogre for protection, but taking cover wasn't inherently cowardly, it just made tactical sense. But more than that, in the fight against the manticore she'd seen him risk his life engaging the monster and worse than that, he'd saved her life, *When I was too foolish to save myself.*

He may look like a porsht, but his actions were those of a Warrior. And amongst her kind, those of action were leaders. She had made up for her own slighter female body by learning to fight clever and dirty; was she really any different from Ninetoes?

Now of course, she had to deal with the fact that he'd given her a way out, if she was bold enough to take it. The dagger was a weapon in anyone's hands, but to Vortiga, it was also a tool. One that she could use either to help her escape or at least earn herself a Warrior's death. And Ninetoes must have known this. *Argh! What should she do?*

For now it was of little consequence, unless she could escape this cell and leave this stinking human cesspool. So, sitting on the floor, she closed her eyes and steadied her breathing, visualising the room she found herself in and those that lead away from it.

She was underground and the room was a simple box, ten feet to a side. In one wall was a large wooden door, within which was a small, head-height opening, criss-crossed with iron bars. Torch light spilled through the portal, but the only natural light came from a sloped opening, roughly a foot square, built into the edge where the ceiling met the rear wall. Access through this was blocked by three iron bars.

She'd looked through this when she'd arrived and it was obvious that while they were definitely underground, they were only one level down, so if she could remove the iron bars she could escape that way, but she'd still be in the Castle grounds. The same problem was true if she tried to dig out enough of the cobbled walls.

The biggest problem with these plans however, was that they took too much time. They had arrived in the city only that morning. And, since the cowards of the Council had chosen not to act, Ninetoes would be hastening his own plans. If she was going to make her way back to her Curn she needn't to escape now!

For the next few minutes, she considered and discarded a dozen more plans, each one more ridiculous than the last. A common theme ran through all of them, however, if she was to escape quickly, she would have to fight.

"—yeah, so her Ladyship reckons she'll deal with the other one, get some Adventurers to stab 'im up, she said. Wha ha ha ha!" A gruff male voice echoed down the corridor. Probably one of the guards and she almost ignored it for the banality it clearly was. But then, the voice said something that changed everything. "Right, so remember, 'er Ladyship said she's got a blade now, I keep the bow on her while you search her; right?"

"Right, but why have I gotta be the one to search her?"

"Cos I'm the one with the crossbow numbnuts."

This couldn't be a coincidence, they were coming for her and her best means of escape. Vortiga's eyes sprang open and she leapt to her feet, her body falling into the rhythms of battle that she'd trained for hundreds of hours to acquire.

It was like a splash of freezing cold water washed through her and the world seemed to slow down as she planned. If she kept the knife on her they'd find it and take it and with a crossbow trained on her, she couldn't risk using it. Or could she?

A crevice in the wall caught her eye. It stood at roughly chest height and was only a nook between two blocks but it should serve. Removing the dagger from its hiding place in her trousers, she flipped it so that the blade pointed towards her.

The footsteps of the approaching guards came closer and she knew she had only seconds to act. Thrusting forward, she jammed the handle of the weapon into the nook. Sliding off and discarding the sheath and leaving the blade protruding a few inches.

It was no sort of hiding place, but then, it wasn't supposed to be. Outside, the guards reached her cell and one of them placed the torch he was carrying into a bracket outside her door. "Back away from the door prisoner," he said. Vortiga seethed at being commanded by anyone less than her Curn, but she did as he bid.

The guard fumbled with a bunch of keys, trying two before he found the one for her door and unlocked it. Stepping back, he pulled the portal open and made space for the other guard to step in. This man was carrying a crossbow, which he had already trained on Vortiga. The bow was well-kept and each guard carried a heavy, polished truncheon on their hips. The manoeuvre was done quickly and efficiently and it spoke well of their training; this would be no easy fight.

"Right, we're gonna search you. If you move I shoot you, understand?" asked the guard holding the crossbow. Vortiga simply nodded and then raised her hands in supplication. "Good girl," he spoke with a gap-toothed grin.

Girl? Her blood boiled. She had killed men for a lesser insult. But she waited. Patience was a kingly virtue after all.

The other guard stepped forward, drawing his club with one hand and roughly searching her with the other.

He ran his hand all over her body. The feeling made her sick but she just stared at the crossbow, pretending to be scared.

"She ain't got nuffin Sarge," the guard said.

"Wot d'ya mean she ain't got nuffin?" the other asked incredulously.

"I means wot I says don' I? She ain't got nuffin hidden."

"Well then you're lookin' wrong ain't ya? That noblewoman said the other hob gave her a blade." Then, at the feigned look of surprise that Vortiga gave him, he added, "oh, don' worry luv, your boyfriend will get his as well, the Lady promised she'd take care of 'im!"

"Look, I'm tellin' ya, there's nuffin on her," insisted the first guard.

"Ha! Hidden it have we? It's probably in her cooch. Strip her," he commanded.

"Really?"

"Yeah, fuckin' really. Now get on with it!" Gap-tooth's voice was becoming hoarse and Vortiga could see his cheeks reddening with arousal.

The other guard stepped back from her and waved his club at her midsection. "Strip. Go on or I'll knock ya senseless and rip 'em off," he threatened, but unconvincingly. This was clearly more than he'd bargained for.

Vortiga reached down and pulled her shirt off over her head. Flicking her eyes up, she caught the horrid glimpse of Gap-tooth licking his lips.

Balancing on one leg, she started tugging at her trousers, only to stumble forwards a step closer to them. "Sorry." She muttered as she looked up at them. Gap-tooth's trigger hand left the crossbow to wipe the sweat off his brow. This was it.

Leaning forward as if to try again, Vortiga surged forward and rammed her shoulder into Gap-tooth's midsection and charged him into the wall. He was a short, paunchy man and rather than his chest, the dagger's blade was driven straight through his neck.

"Oi! Wha-". Spinning, Vortiga turned her momentum into a wild, haymaker.

CRACK!

If she was honest, she'd never expected it to connect and so it hurt her hand as she drove it into the man's face. She hadn't earned the title of Sarm without learning how to capitalise in a fight however, and a beat later, her other hand drove into the man's gut.

The blow drove all of the wind out of him and he collapsed forward. The combination was a simple one but effective and her knee was already in motion and once again the poor fool's head cracked as it met her attacks. She finished him by ramming her elbow down on the nape of her neck and he slumped unconsciously to the floor.

Turning around to check on Gap-tooth, she almost vomited at the sight. Rather than still being pinned to the wall, the corpse's weight had dragged it across the blade and nearly severed the head from its body. The blade must be incredibly sharp to perform such a feat.

Annoyingly, the open wound pumped bright crimson across the bodies, tarnishing any hopes she had of stealing their clothes to conceal her escape. Nonetheless, Vortiga was about her business quickly and efficiently.

She retrieved the dagger's scabbard and slid it onto the bizarrely clean blade. This was strange in and of itself. Having torn through a man's neck, it should have been coated in the sticky, coppery fluid. But the viscous liquid seemed unable to cling onto the blade.

She slid herself back into her shirt and then carefully, she eased the knife loose from the nook and stowed it back at her waist. Next, she checked over the two guards. This wasn't stealing, she promised herself, she just had a greater need for their stuff.

There wasn't much. Gap-tooth had a pouch containing a few coins and the crossbow and that only had one bolt. His pot helm had escaped the sanguine fountain so she grabbed that as well and stuffed it onto her head. As she moved onto the other guard he murmured and so she hastened her search. This one also had a few coins, which she added to the pouch and the bundle of keys but nothing else of use, so she rose and headed for the door.

She locked it behind her and then stalked off in the direction the guards had come from. Passing more cell doors on either side she heard the murmur of a few of the other prisoners. She considered releasing them and perhaps sowing a little chaos, but it was more likely that the alarm would be raised earlier and she'd never escape, so she carried on and made for the guard's common room at the end of the hall.

Even as they'd dragged her here, thinking her beaten and defeated, Vortiga had been aware of her surroundings and had noted the turnings and counted the steps between. She already knew the route out of the dungeons but she also knew that in her current state, she'd never escape without arousing suspicion. For that she'd need a disguise and the best place for that was her current destination.

Standing with her back against the wall she peeked around the corner to make sure that the room was empty.

Blessedly it was not only empty, but it also appeared that her jailors had been in the middle of their meal when they'd come for her.

She grabbed some food and shovelled it down her throat, barely chewing. She wasn't interested in taste, only the energy that the matter could provide. As she did so she scanned the room. A row of tall, wooden lockers stood against the wall. Each one had a simple padlock and, had she the time, she reckoned she could easily pick them. But time was the one thing she most certainly didn't have, so she turned away.

Only to turn back a second later. Perhaps, if the dagger could part flesh so easily, it was magical. It was worth a shot.

Drawing the dagger, she sliced at the padlock with a short, precise cut. A normal blade would have clanged off of the metal, blunting itself but Ninetoes dagger—No, *her dagger*, passed through the lock as if it wasn't even there.

Time was still running out however, so she wrenched the locker open and found exactly what she'd hoped for. The uniform of a Castle guard. Without any consideration of decency, she tore off her dirty clothing and replaced it with the slightly baggy garments. Sadly there was no armour, but the uniform offered her a better form of protection; anonymity.

The trousers came with a belt and so she affixed her dagger to it and stuffed her other belongings into a satchel she also found in the locker. Replacing the helmet completed the look.

She'd have preferred a different weapon but the prison guards only carried truncheons so she'd make do with the crossbow. The guard's frantic voice could be heard from the cells and her heart raced just a little more.

Taking a steadying breath, she was as ready as she was likely to be.

The route out of the Castle wasn't a long one, but she'd counted a dozen guards in between her and the gate. Even at her best she wouldn't be a match for so many all at once, so she needed to avoid raising any form of alarm.

So, before she left, she hastily scribbled a note on a piece of parchment, before rolling it up.

If she was stopped her plan was to say that she'd been given a message to deliver. She admitted that it was a little thin, but it was the best she had. She also knew that the most dangerous few seconds were those directly before her.

Once she was out in the courtyard she was probably home free, but the guards watching the entrance to the dungeons would be the most suspicious of anyone coming out. Once again Ninetoes' gift saved her life.

As she approached the stairs leading up and out of the dungeons she still held the dagger in her hand and its blade was so clean and unblemished it offered a mirrored surface. She used it to observe the two guards at the top of the stairs.

Once again patience was her most important tool and, as she watched the guards, she noticed that only one of them wasn't really paying attention. She'd have killed one of her men for such complacency, but today it might just save her life.

Watching carefully, she waited for him to start a particularly long yawn and then marched up the steps.

"Wake up man! You're supposed to be on watch!" Her voice was one that commanded men in battle and had been hardened by practice on the training grounds and in countless forays.

The guard snapped to attention, clopping his heels together and straightening his spear. "Yessir, sorry sir."

"Carry on," she said, already rounding the next bend.

Floating to her from the pair, the guard idly commented. "Strange, I didn't know we had any women officers." At these words, Vortiga quickened her pace.

Enough time had passed for the evening to completely settle in and Vortiga was grateful for the protection that the darkness offered.

For the next few minutes, Vortiga crept around another half dozen guards and made it out to the courtyard of the inner bailey. Her next and hopefully final hurdle was the pair of guards that watched the gateway between the outer to the inner bailey.

It had been perhaps five minutes since she'd escaped her cell and she couldn't hope for that little mess to go unnoticed indefinitely. She'd gotten this far as much from luck as from skill or judgement. She needed to get out, before Lady Luck ceased to find her amusing!

These guards were more heavily armed than those she'd fought in the prison. Both wore chainmail and carried spears and shields; short swords hung at their hips. She desperately wanted to relieve one of them of their weapon but she wouldn't start a fight if she didn't have to.

"You there, why aren't you at your post?" The speaker had just stepped out from a side door beneath the gateway. His helmet had a golden band around the crown and he also wore a breastplate and blue cape. It didn't take a genius to work out that this was an officer and probably of substantial rank.

She stepped over to him, getting as close as possible. "I've been sent into town to carry a message."

"Oh, to who? And why send you? That's what the squires are for." As he spoke, he gestured for her to follow and walked back through the doorway he'd stepped out of.

The room within was a small office with a wooden desk, chair and armour stand. The man closed the door behind her and then perched himself on the corner of the desk.

She'd known the lie was thin but she had one more gambit. "It's for Lord Pascoe and I didn't ask sir, it's never good to question your betters." She'd heard the name of the lord when she was taken before the Council and had made note of it for later.

"Saw an opportunity to get out of the Castle and waste some time more like. Who sent you on this errand?"

Vortiga was ready for this question and she had an answer prepared. "Master Aseir sent me sir." She grinned inwardly, this was too easy.

"Aseir?" The commander straightened as he said it and his voice took on a suspicious tone. "Who's your commanding officer?"

Shit. Clever as she was, she didn't have an answer to that and when she paused the man straightened up, making to step for the door, he even got as far as taking a breath to call out to the other guards.

But, as she drove her dagger into his throat, it turned out that the breath was to be his last. She took the weight of his body onto her shoulder and carried him to his chair as he gurgled his last words. "I am sorry. May Starm take you to his halls." So saying, she guided his hand down to the hilt of his sword.

445

Drawing his cloak up, she drew her blade out quickly and to the side, severing the artery in his neck. The blue of the cloak absorbed the blood and turned it a deep purple. For a moment she stood transfixed.

Now she was truly fucked. For killing a guard they'd hunt her through the Castle, for murdering their commander the Guard would stalk her to the deepest hell! She must escape as soon as possible.

Vortiga didn't panic, but she was on the very cusp of it. She took a breath, but rather than calm her, it shuddered out, almost wracking.

She scanned the room. She wanted the commander's sword, but she'd already killed the poor fool in cold blood; she wouldn't risk his place in Starm's Hall for her greed. Checking him over however, she found his coin purse and this one was filled with golden coins. Next, she checked his desk, but it held only ledgers and papers.

She turned to leave and stopped. Hanging on the back of the door was a brown cloak. She reached out and took it. It was plain but good quality and had a collar of wolf fur. Clearly the blue cape was part of his uniform.

Taking his sword was one thing, but he didn't need his cloak in the afterlife. She knew she couldn't wear it while in the Castle, one of the guards might recognise it, so she bundled it up and stuffed it under one arm.

With that, she stepped up to the door and placed her ear to it to listen. She could faintly hear the two guards chatting. This was her best chance. They'd seen her go in, if she came out and walked confidently towards the gate, they'd assume the commander had given her permission. It didn't really matter. She could hardly stay where she was.

Opening the door just enough to slide out, she quickly closed it behind her, adding a "Yessir" over her shoulder to sell the ruse further and then made for the gate.

The other guards didn't even look up. She was almost a little disappointed. Once she was through the first gate, the walk across the courtyard felt like a hundred miles. Even in the autumn chill she could feel sweat prickling the skin of her spine, but she kept her pace to a walk.

One of the guards at the gate looked up, but he didn't really seem to notice her. "Alrigh'?" he said amicably, but Vortiga's response was barely a croak. She marched passed him and she was out. She was free!

She was two streets away before she ducked into an alley and breathed a deep sigh of relief, her body shaking as the pent-up adrenalin released itself through her body.

She knew she couldn't stop now, she must keep going. One step after another she began to move again. She had no idea what the quickest way out of the city was, but she knew the docks would offer her a means of exiting, so she headed downhill.

Every minute that passed made her feel a little better and by the time she reached the market square she was feeling much more hopeful. It also finally dawned on her that now that she was free of the Castle, she'd need to come up with a plan of what to do next.

She needed to make her way back to her people and that meant finding a way upstream. Perhaps she could buy passage on another boat?

As the night crept on, Vortiga reached the docks and the wind off the river blew colder, so she threw the commander's cloak about her shoulders. Staying as far away from the water's edge as she could, she searched the boats, speaking with a few sailors and asking for a boat that was leaving north on the dawn tide.

A helpful halfling told her about a boat and pointed her on. When she found the vessel she laughed aloud. It was the Kerensa. The very same blasted barge that had carried her here.

Taking a moment, she knelt down and placed her hand on the cobbled street. She'd never been particularly religious. Like most of her men, she only really prayed to Starm and then only to ask him for strength in battle.

But on this occasion she prayed to Ryuna. Normally only gamblers and chancers prayed to the fickle and capricious Goddess of Luck, but Vortiga had no doubt that the Lady had been with her this night and she was grateful.

She had no desire to board any water bound vessel, least of all this one, but only fools ignored the will of the gods. Before she boarded however,

447

she needed to ensure she didn't starve along the way. The barge wasn't leaving until the morning so she had time to buy or steal what she needed.

The dockward didn't have many shops that were left open, but a general trader nearby still had its lights on, so she made her way within.

Fifteen minutes later, she was back beside the Kerensa, trying and failing to build up enough courage to board the boat.

At the traders she'd bought three waterskins, a week's worth of rations and a bedroll. Taking a few deep breaths, she finally dashed up the gangplank and onto the deck.

All that was left was finding somewhere to hide. It didn't take her long to spot the hatch into the bowels of the ship.

At least in the hold she couldn't see the water. Plus, during her first trip she could never remember the bargemaster checking the hold during the journey, so it seemed the perfect place to stow away.

The space was mostly filled with sacks of some sort of grain and so it was only the work of a few minutes to shift the bags and make herself a small cubbyhole. Once she was settled within it, she replaced the sacks, covering her entrance.

She laid her bedroll out onto the sacks and lay back. It didn't take sleep long to find her.

*****

Vortiga awoke with a start. The boat had rocked slightly and that was all it took. She wanted to sleep longer, for she had no desire to be awake for this journey if she could avoid it. But now that she was awake and could feel the rocking motion and hear the splash of waves against its hull, she was under no illusions about the prospect of getting any more rest.

Opening her eyes didn't really change anything, the hold was almost totally black. There was a tiny beam of light breaking through the deck above but it told her little except that it was now daytime.

Her ear, however, told her much more. She could hear voices, so the boat was populated now and, while most of them were unfamiliar to her,

448

she recognised one of the two that were closest to her position; it was the porsht.

With nothing else to do, she strained her ears to listen to their conversation. The deck's wood was thick, so she could hear little, but she quickly surmised that the other speaker was another Adventurer, a female one. Adventurers all had the same odd way of talking, using the wrong words in places to mean the opposite; well, all of them except Ninetoes, that was.

Getting to hear Adventurers talk was a rare opportunity. Vortiga's mind calculated all the secrets she could learn from them. Perhaps she'd be able to take these secrets back to her Curn and she wouldn't be executed.

She held her breath and strained her ears to their limit.

"Wha—?"

"...has quite..."

"...more than shadows to protect her...breakfast..." And then they started laughing. *Argh!* They were talking about nonsense! She was going to go mad cooped up in the hold!

Vortiga tried once again to sleep, tossing and turning to try to get more comfortable, but now that she could hear the porsht and the other voices, she couldn't **not** hear them. He enemy was so close and yet she could do nothing. She fumed at them, trying to force them to be quiet through sheer might of will. When that didn't work, she started promising them death and imagining the ways she'd kill them.

These thoughts and the gentle rhythmic motion of the boat sent her into a restless half-sleep, filled with waking dreams of blood and death.

At first her dreams were of the deaths of the porsht and his giant and then other imagined foes, her blade slick with their blood. But then they twisted into nightmares, an unseen monster raking her back with its claws, tearing her flesh open and draining her blood and her life. She turned on the foe and saw only Ninetoes, but the rage on his face was awful to behold and his hands were claws that dripped with blood.

Vortiga woke suddenly, but in the empty void she found herself it couldn't tell if she was still dreaming. Her heart raced and she felt or imagined the wound across her back. She screamed and called out, "Ninetoes!"

What? Why had she done that? But, before she had time to consider these strange, and muddled feelings the boat shuddered again, only this time it was much harder than a moment ago. Enough to tip it slightly on its axis and threw Vortiga hard into the wall, bashing her head hard.

She wobbled slightly on her knees and reached up to check her head for wounds. Her hand came away slick with what could only be blood. But there was definitely something wrong with that explanation. She didn't feel enough pain for a head wound and the liquid wasn't thick or sticky enough to be blood.

That's when she heard it. The hissing sound. The boat was sinking! Her stomach sank and she almost pissed herself in fear. She was going to drown!

Her panic took over then. Protecting her in its own way. It wrapped her in a bubble of stress and dread and would not let go. She was safe, it promised, if she just didn't move. If she stayed perfectly still and hid within herself.

Above her a battle raged, the Adventurers calling out, magic blasting and missiles flying. But Vortiga was inert to all of it. Her fear cocooned her.

DWUUUUOOOOMM! CRACK! Crack! Crack! Crack!

A second explosion rocked the barge and more cracks formed in the hull. Vortiga was quickly drenched from a half dozen tiny sprays.

She fell to the deck, wrapping herself up as small as she could. She screamed again, this time like a child might scream, screaming for it all to stop. But it didn't stop and nobody came to rescue her. Correction; nobody was coming to save her.

No! I do not need saving.

She asserted her will. She would not let her fear rule her. Not again.

I am Vortiga, daughter of Zuvrang!

450

Her muscles strained as she willed her fingers to untighten. Next, she set about straightening her legs. She couldn't stand in the tiny space, but she rolled onto her knees and got her feet under her. That felt better, but she needed to escape this watery prison.

She'd been shaken about so much, she had no idea where any of her stuff was so she used her hands to locate as many items as she could; it wasn't much. She found the crossbow and nearby her single bolt. She also managed to find her satchel as well, but it felt almost empty. She also had her bedroll and cloak, but if she needed to swim, she wouldn't risk being dragged down by the articles, so she left them where they were.

Turning onto her back, she kicked the sacks of grain aside and started crawling for the hatch that led up on deck. Luckily the design of the Kerensa had two hatches into the hold. One was in the centre of the deck, behind the mast, but the other was in the prow of the ship and it was always kept free of obstruction.

Making her way to this latter exit, she held her ear to it and listened for anyone in the immediate vicinity. It was clear from the change in sounds that the battle was over and the Adventurers seemed to have dealt with whatever had attacked the boat. Vortiga was also pretty sure no one was immediately above her, so she slowly lifted the hatch.

The sunlight that spilled into the hold blinded her. Had there been anyone waiting for her, she'd have been defenceless.

Once she could see again, she scanned around her and couldn't see anyone, so she pushed the hatch further and slid out onto the deck, easing the hatch closed behind her.

Now that she was outside the sounds changed. No longer muffled, she could hear a group of voices beyond the crates she hid behind. They were discussing the monster and beaching the barge to repair the damage. Looking to the shore, it was clear that they were heading for it and Vortiga whispered a prayer of thanks to Ryuna.

The boat quickly entered the shallows and she heard it grind against the rising riverbed. The last vestiges of the fear that had held her drifted away and she was once again able to analyse her situation.

It was clear that she couldn't just jump off of the boat onto the shore because that was the route the Adventurers would take. But, if she lowered herself off of the other side she might have enough cover. As the party lowered the gang plank and climbed ashore, Vortiga did just that.

Fear rose up in her throat again as she dangled herself from the side of the ship, but she swallowed it down and, telling herself that the water wasn't deep, she let go.

Dropping straight down, she tried to point her toes and make as little splash as possible. In reality, the fall had been barely two feet, into knee-deep water. To Vortiga, however, it was like falling from a mountain into a surging whirlpool.

From there, she crept along the side of the ship and watched the group of Adventurers. They didn't look like much, especially the porsht who looked more like a drowned rat than any sort of hero. She rather thought it suited him.

Shortly thereafter, the party boarded their ship. Vortiga now knew that their plan was to beach the boat a little further upstream at the waterfall that they'd camped at on the way south. The same camp that she'd escaped from. She shuddered involuntarily and the thought of the monstrous manticore.

As the barge sailed northwards, no one bothered to look down in the water and so Vortiga simply jogged into the treeline. Once hidden from view, she followed the course of the boat and then headed inland a little ways, so that she was more concealed from the Adventurers.

Now Vortiga had a choice. She knew that she should head north on foot, aiming to reach the human town in time to join the assault. But even if she succeeded, she had nothing to offer her Curn.

Perhaps, however, if she shadowed this party of Adventurers she'd have some insight or weakness to share with her people. Or perhaps she could find a way to poison their food or even- *Argh!*

She was grasping at straws and she knew it.

Worse still. If she was honest with herself, Vortiga knew where her hesitation really came from. That bastard porsht, argh how she hated him. But she owed him. He'd risked himself to save her life. Twice!

And now, the most recent of those choices was catching up to him. She didn't know exactly when the Adventurers would strike, but if it were her ambush, she'd do it here. She had to help him, her honour dictated it. She could no more ignore the impulse as she could stop herself from needing to breathe.

The question was how? If she revealed herself too soon, he was as likely to attack her as welcome her. She'd have to wait until the Adventurers made their move and then do what she could to help.

Skulking through the undergrowth, she followed the larger part of the party as they made camp atop the waterfall.

Once there, she took her time to dig herself a foxhole. Without tools the task was a difficult and tiresome one but she achieved it after an hour or so.

The sun had started to set as she cut some foliage from nearby bushes and used them to firstly line and then cover her hiding spot.

Then, ensuring that she could still make out the camp, she tucked herself within it. The fit was snug and if anyone came too close with a torchlight they'd be able to see her easily enough, but she knew the likelihood of that was low.

Most of her food had fallen out of her satchel when the monster had shaken the boat, but she found an apple and half a ration cake, so she ate those while she waited for the Adventurers to sleep.

***

For a long while, Vortiga watched the camp and the actions of the adventurers. The tall human was the laziest creature she'd ever seen, doing no work but instead insisting that Bess start cooking almost immediately.

The hobgoblin remembered the fiery young woman with respect; she'd been no Warrior but she'd shown spirit. But this! This fawning,

453

pathetic creature that seemed completely besotted with the lazy male showed none of the same fire. What had happened to her?

As the sun began to set, the group that were repairing the barge climbed the hill and she watched a short interplay between the porsht and the elf.

The elf seemed far more perceptive than the others, even turning at the tiniest sound she'd made. She'd have to be careful of that one.

As the smells of Bess' stew filled the air, Vortiga's stomach grumbled and she considered giving up her hiding place for something warm to eat. The thought was short-lived of course, the Sarm banishing such weakness with a disgusted thought.

She quickly grew bored, however, watching the fools chatter inanely and took the time to dig up some grubs near to her hiding place. They tasted revolting, but she needed the protein and she couldn't risk hunting in the darkness. As time wore on, the camp began bedding down, leaving only the tall human, the lizardman and Ninetoes' half-giant companion on watch.

The lizardman almost disappeared when he sat still, but the human may as well have been singing for all the noise he made; a blind orc could have found him in a storm!

She changed her hiding place as he did, using the noise to mask her movement and stretch her legs, placing herself midway between the human and the giant.

Vortiga felt her eyelids start to droop and so slapped herself hard. She must remain alert, or her opportunity to payback the porsht would slip by her. And that's when she noticed it, the slightest rustle in the bushes nearby.

Vortiga flattened herself to the ground. They couldn't have seen her, she was too well hidden in the darkness. She carefully drew her dagger, however, and watched carefully for movement. As the figure continued stalking nearby, she finally recognised the lizardman. But he wasn't sneaking towards her, but rather into the half-giant's blind spot.

"You, er... Bluzag, here come see this." It was the human, he'd also come nearer towards the porsht's companion, but he was directly in front of him, gesturing to something in the dirt. Bluzag stepped up to it and looked down, before looking back up and shrugging his shoulders at the human.

"No, look closer." Vortiga could see the ruse for what it was, but such thinking was obviously beyond the half-giant. She found herself rising and was almost upright before she checked herself. She owed the foolish brute nothing.

Bluzag knelt down to look at the spot the human had gestured to. And that's when the lizardman struck. Swinging a large mace straight down onto the giant's helmet. The metal collapsed like paper and the mace's head disappeared.

The monstrous warrior, however, was not so easily done for. He stood upright and turned on his heel to look his assailant in the eye, the move effortlessly wrenching the mace from the lizardman's hands. The human took the initiative then, chopping his longsword down onto the brute's weapon arm. It was a mighty blow, but not quite enough to sever the limb, which instead hung by an inch of muscles and flesh.

Bluzag looked dumbly down at his arm and then up at the man. The man stared back and a cruel smile spread across his face. Bluzag moved faster than Vortiga would have thought possible and wiped the grin straight off the man's too-perfect face, knocking him flat.

By now, the lizardman had drawn a short sword that we thrust into the giant's kidney, all the way up to the hilt. Normally a killing blow, Vortiga was stunned when the giant didn't collapse, but instead he just swung his only remaining arm and threw the other warrior to disappear into the undergrowth.

Turning back on the first, he attempted to stomp on the human, but an incantation spilled from the man's mouth and Bluzag froze midstep, paralysed with magic binding his body.

"I told you," the man exclaimed, "it's a zombie or something." And so saying, he reached up and wrestled the dented helmet off of the gigantic creature.

What they found beneath gave all present a moment of pause. The face was sunken and deathly pale, the skin blotchy and torn. The mace had destroyed one side of Bluzag's face and bone could be seen sticking out of flesh.

THUNK!

The lizardman had regained his feet and had yet another weapon in hand, this time a short warpick, that was now embedded in Bluzag's shoulder.

"Sorry," muttered the lizardman.

"Hurry up, I can't hold him much longer." Responded the human, one hand held out towards the giant, a thin chain of magic between it and Bluzag.

The other Adventurer wound himself up, bringing the pick in a mighty overhead blow, straight down onto Bluzag's crown, making a sound like a cracking egg and Bluzag's limbs, that had been straining against the human's spell, fell limp. "Phew," he muttered.

"About fucking time. Now quick, cut off its head to be sure." Answered the other.

Vortiga elected not to watch the grim scene, instead using the Adventurer's distraction to skulk back to her foxhole to be ready. If the Adventurers had attacked the giant, then there was no doubt that they'd make their move on Ninetoes tonight. She was worried that they might already have slit his throat while he slept.

Nonetheless, she watched the camp and a strange relief passed over her as she watched the porsht take his watch, sitting in the same place the lizardman had vacated. Perhaps he was safe for now.

But why hadn't they struck while he slept? There must be something else they needed to do. Then she remembered the fight against the ankheg and how the mage had protected himself with magical armour. Even as he slept, it would turn any blade long enough to wake him up.

456

As she watched, a tiny light flared beneath where Ninetoes sat. It could mean only one thing, the attack had started. She could see the other Adventurers moving about the camp, divided but moving in on the fool Ninetoes.

Vortiga began moving, but it was already too late. She watched in horror as the lizardman sank his blade into Ninetoes' unprotected back. She stood, paralysed with indecision. If she went now, she might be able to save him, but that was a big 'if', as three Adventurers were nothing to be taken lightly and all she had was a single bolt and a dagger.

But if she did nothing, he would surely die and her honour eternally besmirched.

She began climbing the hill, angling closer to the camp. She could hear the murmur of them talking, perhaps there was still time. Picking up her pace, Vortiga jogged towards the scene, hidden by the darkness.

And was just in time to watch the human warrior's blade thrust down and sink into Ninetoes' chest. She was too late, she'd failed again.

Just a few short days ago, everything had been different, everything had made sense. She'd been a Sarm, an officer in charge of her own unit of Warriors. They'd been so close to taking that stinking little human town and then- and then Ninetoes had entered her life!

Now she couldn't tell friend from foe anymore. Now she was angry over the death of a porsht?

"Let's see him dodge this." The words seemed to come from far away, but they shook something within her.

FA-DOOM!

For the second time that day, Vortiga was shocked by a loud explosion. *Damn it!*

Shaking herself out of her stupor, she cursed herself. She really didn't have the right to call herself a Warrior.

She blinked her eyes to help them clear the spots of light created by the flash of light that had preceded the explosion. But, as another explosion lit up the forest she wished she hadn't. One of the Adventurers was firing balls of magical fire into the splashpool; but why?

Then, as the third fireball hit, she saw him. The porsht was cowering behind the waterfall as the explosion detonated nearby. He was huddled against a ledge and was somehow still alive.

But, as the fourth ball of flames erupted within the wall of water, she saw him fly back away from the blast and slam into the rough wall of the cliff face behind the falls. Then the water, temporarily held back by the flames, reclaimed its course and obscured her view of Ninetoes.

Before she knew it, Vortiga was on her feet, sprinting for the pool. She replayed the scene in her mind. Her last glimpse of him, his limp body had been sliding down the wall and into the water. Within fifty yards she was at the water's edge and without a second thought for what she was doing, she dove into the pool. Fortunately for her, her hobgoblin darkvision functioned underwater and in no time, she'd collected up his broken body and re-surfaced.

She'd had the wherewithal to do so under the waterfall and so was shielded from view from the Adventurers above. She checked over his body and found it riddled with damage and open wounds, the worst of which was an open wound in his chest. Tearing her shirt sleeve and pressing it down, she staunched the wound as best she could but there was little more she could do for him while his betrayers were still nearby.

"You check that side, I'll check over here."

CHAPTER 24

ALLIANCE

Ninetoes awoke. And almost immediately wished he hadn't as his body reminded him of his recent troubles. *At least I'm alive. Sort of.*

He risked opening his eyes and then snapped them shut. Hoping that what he'd seen was a waking nightmare.

"I saw your eyes open. You are safe for the time being, but we must move quickly." Vortiga's voice was harsh with exhaustion. Ninetoes carefully reopened his eyes and stared up at his enemy. The two of them were treading water in a slash pool beneath the waterfall.

He pulled away from her embrace. At least, that's what he meant to happen, but as he clenched his muscles, his body protested with a violent wave of will-splitting pain and his head splashed back down.

"Where are we?" he asked, almost shouting over the din of crashing water.

"That is a stupid question Porsht, look around you."

He had to admit, it was a stupid question but he was at a loss for what else to say. "What happened? I remember the explosions and then my shield breaking and then... nothing."

"The Adventurers sought your death. When the fourth ball of fire hit, you were thrown against the cliff and knocked senseless. I scooped your body out of the pool and stopped you from bleeding out. But it may have doomed us both, however, two of them are searching the river for your body now, they will almost certainly find us, we must move or fight." Her hand gripped her... wait, his dagger, closely.

"I do have an alternative to fighting," he offered while he relaxed his muscles and considered how he could quickly explain his plan. Vortiga stared back at him, her eyes attempting to delve deeper into his thoughts.

"Proceed."

With that single word, a little of the tension gave way and Ninetoes released a sigh of relief. "This waterfall hides the tomb of an ancient king, there is a tunnel under the water. We could hide within until we're stronger."

"And how do you know this to be true? Adventurers would have raided such a treasure trove years ago if this was common knowledge," she argued. But her hand had fallen away from her blade.

"I... have seen it myself." This was not exactly true. The thundercat's memories were clear in his mind, he could see the tunnel entrance clear as day.

"Now I know this to be a falsehood. Our journey to Pamor was the first time you had been here."

He couldn't fault her logic but he knew that it was so and he also knew that the underwater passage led from the splashpool into the trove. He considered this for a moment, wondering just how much to tell her about his abilities.

Being able to absorb the memories of his foes was potentially one of his most powerful, he wouldn't give this information up easily. Gingerly the extricated himself and swam to the ledge.

Watching Vortiga, he could see her hand once again moving towards her dagger. "We fought a monster on the barge, er... yesterday. I absorbed some of its memories. The monster used the tomb as its home."

Vortiga's hand paused, halfway to her weapon. "And you trust this knowledge, stolen from a beast?"

The question was asked innocently enough, but Ninetoes could sense the threat.

"I don't know." He answered honestly. "But we stand no chance in a fight, especially while in the water." There was another reason that the tomb appealed to him, something else his vision had shown him, a pile of treasure.

As he spoke, he raised his hands in as non-threatening a manner as he could. "How else would you return to your Curn?" Ninetoes watched her closely and saw the look of shame that crossed her face at the mention of her warlord. Knowing that his next words were his most important and would decide if the two moved forward as allies or enemies, he chose them carefully. "Perhaps there is treasure to be found, perhaps even enough to make up for your failure."

Vortiga's hand flexed on the dagger and Ninetoes prepared himself to cast Barrier, but the move was involuntary and the Sarm didn't attack. Instead, her head hung in shame and she spoke quietly. "Very well. A temporary alliance."

Relief washed through Ninetoes. As powerful as he'd become, he stood no chance in a fight now. He grinned his toothy grin. "Excellent."

"So, how do we enter?"

"Ah, that will prove to be a difficult, but not insurmountable task." His grin stayed in place, but the mirth had left his eyes.

"Let's check by the falls, perhaps it's stuck on a rock," called a muffled female voice beyond the curtain of water.

"We will need to swim along the tunnel," he whispered urgently.

"Oh? And how far is that?" Ninetoes could see the fear in her eyes, despite the nonchalant manner with which she spoke. He remembered her behaviour on board the barge; how she'd grasped for the boat's mast. Worse still, Ninetoes didn't have a complete answer to this question. For the giant feline, the process had been a simple one and so its memories had never dwelt on the specifics. "Er… I don't know exactly, but not far."

"Typical," she growled.

"Typical of what?"

"Typical of a man to make a promise he cannot keep." Sounding unerringly like Libby. It also surprised Ninetoes that she considered him a man.

"We'll be fine," he promised. "But we must move, now."

"Very well. We'll go together, lest we get separated," she said. Once again, she tried and failed to mask her dread. Nonetheless, she dove beneath the water.

Ninetoes followed, thinking about what he was about to do and whether he had any spells that might help. If he'd had the components then his Farseer ritual would have been invaluable, at least in terms of gaining more information, but he couldn't wish the ingredients into existence, so that was a non-starter.

Leap had, of course, proved incredibly useful in escaping the water before, but he didn't see that it would offer much help in swimming along the tunnel. Arcane Step would be useful but he needed to be able to speak to cast it, so it offered little help here. Ninetoes resigned himself to making do with the strength in his arms and legs and swam deeper into the pool.

From the other side of the waterfall, the pool was heavily obscured, but from this side, Ninetoes could just about make out the dark shape that was the entrance to the tunnel. Taking a deep breath, he dove down.

Thankfully, what had seemed a long way down was an illusion and he only had to dive a half-dozen feet until he could make out that the tunnel's entrance was in fact the outlet of a pipe of some kind. It was covered in a thin metal grate, but something had wrenched a large hole through this impediment and so they were able to pass through easily enough.

What's more, as he poked in his head, he could just about make out dappled light up ahead, perhaps as little as fifty feet away.

Ninetoes watched as his enemy flapped her arms. A part of him suggested that now was the time to attack. She was weak in the water, it said, and her weapons would be next to useless.

But Ninetoes had given his word. For the time being, at least, they were allies and his ally needed help. He offered her his hand. Once again the stoic Warrior didn't meet his eyes, but she took his hand and together they entered the tunnel.

What Ninetoes lacked in strength, Vortiga lacked in practice and so neither one was any quicker or stronger in the water. After a few seconds they'd passed the grate and begun the long swim towards the solitary beam of light that marked their destination.

Every stroke was hard, painful work, his wounded body screamed in protest but there was no other choice, they were committed. After a few dozen yards, Ninetoes realised that there was a slight current in the water. Looking along the tunnel it seemed they hadn't made any real progress, their destination seemed no closer.

But none of that mattered. If he couldn't manage this paltry task, then he'd be best served by fleeing away from Raveslan and his friends. They must keep going. He pushed himself on and the pair continued on.

Ninetoes' arms started to burn and he could feel that his air was quickly depleting. Gazing along the tunnel he could see that they were much closer to their goal; another metal grate, this one, however, wasn't ripped open, but was still very much a barrier. Looking to Vortiga, he could see panic in her eyes.

Looking back, the situation wasn't any better, they'd have no chance of reaching the tunnel's outlet before they ran out of air!

Quickly, he cycled through his spell list, perhaps there was an answer there. But most of his spells required words to cast. Panicking now, he desperately considered plans of escape, but they were all fruitless. He had nothing, they were going to die!

Vortiga tugged at him and, when he didn't move, she let go of his hand and pushed off of the floor, launching herself at the grate. The fool was going to try ramming it.

Then he saw it, a flash of light off of the blade, as Vortiga slashed with his dagger, cutting a line through the grate.

Slash, slash.

She made two more cuts and he watched as the grate shifted. Vortiga grabbed the metal and started pulling, but it wouldn't budge. Even with the cuts she'd made, the thing was so old and rusted, that it was stuck.

Finally, Ninetoes' oxygen-deprived brain had a useful idea. Swimming to join her, he shooed Vortiga to one side and then swam back to the

463

floor. Once there, he activated his Sorcerer's Travel Cloak, aiming the wave at his feet.

Ninetoes shot straight up and blasted into the grate. His aim was mostly good and the section Vortiga had cut gave way and both he and the metal soared up into the room above. Before he reached the apex of his arc, Ninetoes slammed into the ceiling and then returned to the ground with a resounding thump.

He ignored the bruises riddling his body and gasped great lungfuls of stale, but glorious air. Next to him, Vortiga's head crested the water's surface and she did the same, before climbing out.

As they both lay on their backs greedily gulping down air, a horrible screech tore through the underground dungeon. Both Vortiga and Ninetoes rolled onto their fronts and prepared for battle, but nothing happened.

After a minute of fear-filled silence, Ninetoes offered Vortiga his hand. "See, I told you we'd be fine."

Vortiga punched him in the face.

***

Ninetoes held his nose and moaned. "Why did you hit me?"

"You'd already be dead if I meant you any real harm, so stop whining and use your magic to heal yourself," she told him.

"Everything hurts," he moaned. "And I don't have healing magic. Well, not exactly."

"Nonsense. You used magic to heal the wound dealt me by the manticore's talons," she corrected him.

Ninetoes was keen not to share too much, but he was in too much pain to argue. "I can only heal by stealing the life force of other creatures. Unless you're prepared to give me some of yours, I'm going to have t-"

"Are there any lasting effects?" she asked, cutting him off.

"Not if I only take a little. I would only nee-" he began to answer cautiously.

464

"Then go ahead," Vortiga interrupted. "But don't take too much."

"Really?" he asked, stunned.

"Of course. We are stuck here until you are healed; we stand no chance of escaping this place if you're injured."

Then, when Ninetoes looked about to argue, she forestalled him with a glare.

Now, while Ninetoes would happily kick this horse-faced gift in the mouth, he recognised that currently, he needed help. So, reaching into his pool of mana, he concentrated on his spell. It was more difficult than usual, but his Necromancy spells were so familiar to him, he succeeded.

Even without her trying to consciously resist his spell, Vortiga's natural defences kicked in and Ninetoes had to push a little harder than usual to make contact with her life force. While he could take a creature's energy in a torrent, on this occasion he was careful to take it in a slow and steady stream.

The effect on his tired and damaged body was instantaneous and his wounds began to heal. Many of these injuries were simply scratches and bruises, however, so with a conscious effort, he guided the healing energy away from these and focussed on the worse of his ailments; namely the massive wound in his chest that had been only partly sealed by Reaper's Sorrow and Vortiga's quick thinking. Slowly, the wound closed fully and he removed the sodden rag that Vortiga had used to staunch the bleeding.

By then, he'd tapped Vortiga for about a hundred hit points. Not knowing how much longer they'd be stuck together, he cut off his spell there.

"Thank you," he muttered and he attempted to sit up. There was still pain, but it wasn't anything he couldn't handle.

"I consider us to be even, by the way," she stated.

"Even?" Ninetoes asked, confused.

"You saved my life. Now I have done the same," she grated out.

"Saved your-? Strictly speaking, haven't I saved you twi-"

"Think carefully before you finish that thought Porsht, you are without weapons and are still injured," Vortiga warned.

"Fair enough. We're even. Now what?"

"Now we find our way out. After that I suggest you head northwards and create as much distance between yourself and the other Adventurers, they will not be so remiss when they kill you a second time."

"Oh, I'm not running away. I'll make each of those Adventurers regret they ever crossed me," Ninetoes said strongly. Despite herself, Vortiga smiled at that. "Where will you go?" he asked.

Vortiga considered this for a moment. "I must make my way back to my people. Your peoples' filth still mars the world. If I am swift, I can join the attack on the human settlement. If I cover myself in enough glory, perhaps I will be allowed to help destroy your tribe."

The effortless manner in which she idly described the destruction of his people, shook Ninetoes to his core. Even after saving his life, she still sought the annihilation of his kin.

"Then we are at odds. I cannot allow you to return to your people, if you still intend to destroy mine." He tried to say this in the same deadpan manner that she had spoken.

"Indeed. But if you fight me now you will die. Without your armour and weapons and in your current state, you will prove no challenge for me to kill. Help me escape this place and I will allow you to flee." Her hand rested on her dagger as she said it.

"Very well, but right now I need some time to rest."

"Huh, I only hope such weakness does not cost us both our lives."

***

Sometime later, after the pair had finished recovering, they stood up and took stock. "This is no does not look like a tomb Porsht."

"No, but this isn't where the monster had its lair. That must lay further along the tunnel. I suppose we could go back in and try to reach it?" the wizard suggested.

In response, Vortiga simply clenched her fists and Ninetoes sensibly shut up. "What do you take this room to be; some kind of storeroom?"

Ninetoes looked about. The room they were in was square and roughly twenty-five feet across. Their forced entry had spilled a fair amount of water across the tiled floor and he could see that there had once been an image or pattern in the tiles. Surrounding them were stacks of wooden crates, perhaps six feet long and a foot tall and deep.

"Perhaps. But what could be stacked so? Surely any gold or treasure would make such boxes too heavy; no?" posited Vortiga. The thought hadn't yet occurred to Ninetoes and he was impressed with how quickly she'd analysed the room.

"Well, why don't we open one and find out, it could be something useful," he suggested.

The pair stepped up to the side of a stack. The boxes were piled four high and so the stack was taller than they were. Carefully, they tried lifting the crate from the top of the pile, but halfway to the floor, the ancient wood began to crack and an awful smell escaped. Both hobgoblins shied away, losing their grip and, all at once the crate collapsed and the contents spilled out.

Both Ninetoes and Vortiga yelped in surprise and jumped backwards.

Noticing Vortiga and realising how foolish he'd sounded, Ninetoes controlled himself and stepped forward to get a better look at the wrecked contents. And there was no doubt about it, the box had been filled with the skeletal remains of a humanoid.

"Ergh, disgusting! Why would anyone show such a lack of respect to their dead as to stack them like, like dried goods?" Vortiga's normal calm and deadly veneer was starting to crack and Ninetoes could see the signs of fear creeping into her eyes. He couldn't let her lose control, it could mean both their lives.

That was why he kept quiet about what he'd just noticed. On the back of the plank of wood he held, the last remnants of the crate, were the claw marks of the poor soul who rested within. This creature had been put in the box alive.

Considering the past couple of days she had experienced, even the most hardened Warrior would be at the limit of their tether. His own was nerves were frayed and he was almost unstuck, but strangely the lifeless body gave him a little hope.

Looking around the room, there were five stacks of four boxes. Meaning, that if every box held a skeleton, there were twenty bodies here, plenty for him to work with.

In the short term, however, he needed a way to ease their nerves. There was also a door in the far wall, Ninetoes gestured to it. "Perhaps we should just leave this room and make our way onwards," he suggested. The other hobgoblin silently agreed and they headed to the door, which was blessedly unlocked.

The next room they found themselves in was another store room, with another door leading off to the left. The boxes in here weren't the same size or shape as those from the previous room, however. In fact, there were a variety of different shaped boxes, running from large crates to small chests.

Reasonably certain that these boxes were unlikely to be filled with bodies, the pair moved into the room and picked one each to open.

Ninetoes chose a cube-shaped crate, about two foot to a side. While he had nothing to open it with, the wood was so old it didn't take much force to open it.

Inside was a large, flat item, covered in leathers that were so old, they disintegrated as soon as he touched them. Beneath the covering, was a wooden shield.

Given the length of time it had been here, the shield should have been as fragile as the boxes, but the item seemed in excellent condition. Curious, Ninetoes activated Mind's Eye and could see the faint glow of green transmutation magic running through the shield. Casting Identify, Ninetoes sought more information.

FULL KITE SHIELD - FINE, COMMON
SKILL TYPE: BLOCKING
ARMOUR CLASS: 30

So the shield wasn't magical per se, but it would be useful nonetheless. Ninetoes smiled and looked over to Vortiga. "Here, see what I've found. This shield is still in good condition."

Vortiga didn't immediately respond, so the wizard turned to find his temporary ally. It looked like she'd already opened two boxes. The first had held maces and the box that Vortiga now knelt before held longswords.

The Sarm reached out cautiously, as though she feared that the weapons were illusions. Her fingers on one hand touched the hilt and then the other reached beneath to cradle the scabbard and she carefully lifted the sword from the box.

As she drew it closer to her, a wide smile spread across her face and once again Ninetoes recognised the striking beauty that her demeanour usually hid. Vortiga raised the sword to eye height and bowed her head to it.

Slowly, her fingers wrapped about the hilt and, in a sudden burst of movement, she drew the sword and the weapon whispered free for the first time in only the gods knew how long.

To Ninetoes, Vortiga changed in that moment, from the exhausted, slightly broken prisoner into the Warrior he'd witnessed across the battlefield. His breath caught in his throat to see something so perfectly deadly.

VORTIGA

Tears burned Vortiga's eyes as she held the sword, the leather-wrapped hilt of the weapon feeling so right in her hand.

There was a reason that a hobgoblin captain was called Sarm, it was because to earn the title, one must become an expert in the sword. The blade must become an extension of the body and soul. Oh, other weapons were fine for mere Warriors, but a Sarm must be something more!

Since waking after the battle in the human town Vortiga hadn't felt whole. She'd have carved her way into the deepest hell to retrieve her sword, her mark of honour and rank.

Everything that had happened to her could never have been so if only she'd had a sword. She raised the scabbarded weapon to touch her forehead and made it a silent promise.

Swift death to our enemies my friend.

Now, as she held the ancient blade, she could once again feel the blood coursing through her veins, she could feel the deadly intent that it promised. Closing her fist, she performed Devil's Tongue, drawing the blade and cutting to her side, all in one lightning movement.

The sword chased her movement, desperate it seemed, not to return to its confinement. She took that as acceptance of her promise and an uncontrollable smile split her serene face and a playful idea occurred to her.

Rocking back onto her feet, she performed Chase the Dragon, spinning on the spot while tucking the blade against her side so that it was hidden from an opponent. Then, as she locked eyes with Ninetoes, she thrust the blade's tip forward, lightning fast, until it stopped an inch from his throat.

"So, what have you found Porsht?"

NINETOES

He recognised the move as soon as she made it, he'd never seen it performed so perfectly and it moved too quickly for him to react. As the blade whistled towards his neck he had barely enough time to gasp.

"So, what have you found Porsht?"

Ninetoes caught the look of playful glee in her eyes and the smile hidden there. His mind realised that she'd been having some fun and his body unconsciously relaxed. Unfortunately for him, it started with his butt-cheeks and Ninetoes' backside let out a long, low trumpet of relief.

A smile of genuine mirth broke across Vortiga's face and she let the sword-point drop as she laughed heartily in his face.

Ninetoes didn't really think that this was the time for japery, but he couldn't hold his own laughter in check for long. A dam had been broken, and the two hobgoblins collapsed to the floor in hysterics.

"So, what did you find Po- Ninetoes?" Vortiga asked, after they'd both finished laughing. He showed her the sword and told her it had some magic within it.

"So, does that mean this sword is magical?" she asked.

Ninetoes ignited his eyes with mana once again. The sword gave off the same faint hint of transmutation magic. "Indeed, but I don't think that this would be considered a 'magic sword'," he said.

"You make no sense Porsht, you say it has magic within it, yet you say it is not magical. Explain," she commanded.

"Hmmm, I know it seems an odd turn of phrase. Let me put it this way, I think someone cast a spell on these items, likely something to protect them from degrading as these boxes have."

"Rather than fashioning them with magic?" she finished. Ninetoes nodded, once again impressed by her quick mind. "A shame that they're not magical but their presence is a boon nonetheless. Starm smiles on our endeavours." She re-sheathed the blade.

"We should find out whatever we can use from these boxes," Ninetoes said.

"Based upon what we've found here and the numbers of boxes and crates, I think I'm starting to understand the purpose of this place," Vortiga commented as she made her way to another set of crates.

"Oh?"

"There are boxes of weapons and shields and, I'd reckon-" she used a mace to bash open another crate, the weapon destroying the lid. From within she drew out a helmet. "-armour." She finished.

"Very well, but that doesn't explain why a person would take such care to keep these items in working order."

"There were ancient societies that would bury their rulers with all their wealth and treasures. Some of them even buried their servants with them too, so that they would be looked after and protected in their afterlife."

"And you think that's what we found next door? The servants of some ancient ruler?" He chose not to mention it, but it could explain why the poor people had been buried alive.

"Indeed, and this may just be the bounty that we've been searching for," she added.

"Really? I'll agree having these weapons and armour is useful, but none of it will be a replacement for what I've lost and there's barely enough here to equip a squad. Not that we have the bodies to fill them."

"But bodies are exactly what we have."

"What are you talking about Vortiga?" Ninetoes had thought the very same thing when he'd seen the body spill out of the box, but he wanted the idea to be hers.

"I thought you were a Necromancer, Porsht. I'd have thought the room next door was a treasure trove to a bottom-feeder like you."

Perfect. "You're right."

"Of course I'm right. Now, how many undead can you control?"

***

In the end, after some discussion and the gruesome work of opening the coffins of the ancient dead, the pair decided that given the tight quarters, Ninetoes would reanimate six undead.

The other crates were opened and Vortiga was able to dress herself in a full suit of chainmail with steel bracers and greaves. She also found a fine replacement for her guardsman helmet. Finally, she took a shield and a mace that she clipped to her belt.

They'd tried to equip the skeletons similarly but the armour simply wouldn't stay in place and the chainmail kept tripping them up. In the end, they'd settled for equipping three of them with swords and shields and three more with longbows and quivers.

Vortiga had expressed concern that the skeletons were unlikely to be able to fire the ranged weapons, but she was proven wrong when Ninetoes had all three fire shots into a pile of discarded armour, each one hitting their mark.

A liberal use of the Identify spell had told them that most of the items were of Fine quality and Common rarity, he was also pretty sure he'd felt his Skill with the spell increase, but without his Character Sheet he had no way of knowing for certain.

Nonetheless, the spell had shown them that one set of the items was different. Those items were now worn by Vortiga and were of Uncommon rarity. The armour was similar to the other suits but was a slightly different colour and the helmet was much grander; an officer's uniform.

HIGH STEEL HELM - FINE, UNCOMMON
SKILL TYPE: HEAVY ARMOUR
ARMOUR CLASS: 10

HIGH STEEL GREAVES - FINE, UNCOMMON
SKILL TYPE: HEAVY ARMOUR
ARMOUR CLASS: 6

HIGH STEEL BRACERS - FINE, UNCOMMON
SKILL TYPE: HEAVY ARMOUR
ARMOUR CLASS: 6

HIGH STEEL CHAINMAIL - FINE, UNCOMMON
SKILL TYPE: HEAVY ARMOUR
ARMOUR CLASS: 20

```
┌─────────────────────────────────────────────┐
│  HIGH STEEL LONGSWORD - FINE, UNCOM-          │
│  MON                                          │
│  SKILL TYPE: ONE-HANDED BLADES                │
│  DAMAGE: 10 -18 SLASHING                       │
└─────────────────────────────────────────────┘
```

Vortiga moved around in the suit and when Ninetoes told her the details she smiled once again. "Despite its age, this is the finest suit of armour I've ever worn," she admitted.

The skeleton's shield had the same statistics but their longswords were not High Steel and had a lower damage range of 7-13. None of them would put up much of a fight but they'd serve as a useful defence if whatever monster they'd heard screaming found them.

"I think we should go now." If had irked him somewhat that they'd found nothing for him, but he was a wizard and so would make do with his Wizard's Armour. As the thought occurred to him, he pumped a few extra mana into the spell.

With the skeletons taking point, the small group headed for the door. Ninetoes commanded one of the leading skeletons to open the door, while he and Vortiga stood back in case of trouble.

The skeleton opened the door and the hobgoblins peered into the next room. A short set of steps led down into a room that was longer than it was wide, although exactly how far the steps led down was uncertain as the floor was submerged beneath dark and murky water. At the far end of the room, another set of steps lead out of the water, to another door.

"Hmmm," commented Ninetoes. "I do not like the look of that, anything could be lurking under there."

Vortiga's eyes widened briefly in fear but she ground her teeth and stepped forwards. "There is little choice, we must proceed. But send a skeleton first."

"Indeed. You, cross to the far door and open it," Ninetoes commanded one of the skeletons.

He watched as the skeleton, devoid of any fear, followed his instructions. Or at least it tried to.

By the time it had climbed to the base of the steps, the skeleton was waist deep in water.

Reaching the far end it started climbing the steps, but then it stumbled as its lower leg crumbled to pieces. Unable to keep its balance, the skeleton fell back into the water.

For a moment, all they could see was the odd flash of ivory as the creature splashed about, trying to regain its feet. In the end, only the torso made it out of the water, with a single arm attached that dragged the ribcage out of the muck.

By now the entire thing was coated in some sort of goo that, even from this far away, Ninetoes could hear was sizzling as it ate through the bones. With a rattle the ribcage fell back into the water and vanished.

"Argh! This accursed place!" railed Vortiga. "If whatever is in that water can so easily eat bone we have little hope of crossing this room unscathed."

Ninetoes' mind was already considering how to overcome their current problem. The pool of water was at least a hundred feet long, so it was too far for Arcane Step. The skeleton didn't seem to struggle until the end of the room, so they might be able to wade that far and then 'step' but that was a big 'might'. Leap was out for the same reason, it just wouldn't take him far enough.

What they really needed right now was more information, so Ninetoes quickly cast Burning Hands, igniting one end of a strip of wood and creating a simple torch. Then, stepping to the last step before they became submerged, Ninetoes held out the torch and studied the water.

It took him a minute or so, but eventually the light of the torch shone off of a greenish substance on the stone floor. Once he'd found this first patch, he was able to trace its edge. Casting Identify, he learned more.

The Slime clearly wasn't a monster, because it didn't have any Stats or Traits, but it had hit points, so Ninetoes could kill it. The only question was, how?

"There seems to be some sort of slime on the floor, capable of devouring organic matter. The skeleton must have walked through some and it ate through the bones." He informed Vortiga, hoping that she might have some suggestions.

"Hmmm, as there's no way to simply avoid it?"

"It doesn't look like it crosses the entire room and for a significant distance. I'm a little surprised the skelly made it as far as it did."

"Indeed, and you have no magic that can destroy it?" There was a slight note of mockery in her voice, but Ninetoes chose to ignore it.

"If it was above the water I could probably just burn it away."

"Perhaps we could fashion shovels out of the debris in here and have the skeletons scoop it out of the way?"

It wasn't a terrible idea, but the skeletons were bound to be damaged in the process and Ninetoes didn't fancy digging through more of the coffins to find replacements. If only there was a way to keep the skeletons from getting covered in the slime, perhaps he could clear a path.

"I've got an idea," he said, smiling at Vortiga.

"What; why are you grinning at me like that?"

CHAPTER 25
TORGAN'S FALL

VORTIGA

Vortiga had no idea what it was that she'd done to anger the gods so much, but she cursed them now for ever allowing her to cross paths with the Porsht.

"This is madness. If I'm lucky the slime will only destroy my armour! Explain to me why you can't use one of the skeletons."

"I've already told you, I don't know what the magic will do to them, it could break my hold on them or worse, break the magic altogether and then we'd back to square one."

"And how is that worse than my dying?" she asked, exasperated.

"Oh, stop being a wimp. You'll be fine."

"That's what you said before the tunnel Porsht and we nearly died!"

"Do you know; that name is rather growing on me. Look, the spell will keep the slime from doing you or your gear any damage. All you have to do is walk in a straight line. Now, unless you have a better idea, I suggest we get on."

She was dealing with a madman, there was no other answer for it. But, if she were being completely honest, arguing with Ninetoes was the most fun she'd had in ages.

Oh, she loved the thrill of battle and there was nothing like watching her men follow her finely coordinated orders. But she constantly had to be on her guard, even around her own men.

Her Curn had always warned her that one mistake would be the only one she would ever make. That she'd lose everything if she slipped up. In this moment, however, she recognised that there could be a different life for her. She actually found herself grinning at the foolish wizard and despite her words, his plan sounded like it could work, it certainly offered the best chance of escaping this place quickly enough to reach her people.

"Very well. Let us begin."

"Excellent. Now, stand still while I cast and when I say, step into the water."

Vortiga did as he bid, holding the torch before her as she stood waiting on the steps. Ninetoes' spell took him a while to cast but she felt its effects as soon as he started his incantation. It felt as though a warm breeze passed over her skin, beneath her clothes.

"Excellent, it's taken hold. Step down into the water and step onto the slime."

Once again, she did as he said and stepped gingerly into the water. Each step took her deeper until she was waist deep. Before, even this much water would have been enough to set her heart racing with fear, but this time, she felt nothing.

She could, however, see something. The floor.

The water around her was crystal clear, although it definitely hadn't been when she'd stepped into it. Staring in amazement, she noticed that her clothes were also pristine. Stepping her foot forward, she carefully nudged the edge of a patch of slime with her boot. But rather than begin eating away at her boot, the slime vanished. She turned to speak to Ninetoes, but he wasn't watching.

Instead he was staring at an egg-sized ball of spinning fire that hovered over his hand. "It is working," she said to him, her voice conveying her wonder at the magical feat.

"Indeed, but it's draining my mana much more quickly than I'd like, it must be trying to clean everything that you come into contact with, we must make haste. Get moving."

Normally, she'd have reprimanded him for commanding her like that, but she could see the concentration on his face and recognised that while it might not seem like it, he was under a great deal of strain.

Vortiga moved, lifting her feet above the patch of slime before placing it squarely into the centre. The slime disappeared and left the flagstone floor and water perfectly clean. Bridging her foot slowly back to meet the other she cleared a path.

Steadily Vortiga curved a path through the slime. She'd quickly realised that it was more efficient when she shuffled her feet forward, clearing the way.

Once they were around three quarters of the way, she heard a grunt from behind her. Turning she found Ninetoes slumped over, almost double. In his hand was a small gem that glowed brightly as tiny wisps flowed from it to him. "What is wrong?"

"I'm running out of mana, I don't think I'll have enough to finish. We may have to turn back."

Part of her grumbled at this hold up, but she could hardly complain, without his magic they'd never have got this far.

"I think we should press on. If you run out we can use the skeletons to clear the last few feet." Ninetoes seemed like he wanted to argue, but while she kept moving forward he was beholden to keep his spell active, so she just kept going.

"Stop." His voice was barely a whisper, but Vortiga did as he bid. They must be no more than six feet from the steps.

"What's the problem?"

"I'm almost out of mana, if I keep it going any longer I'll collapse from mana depletion."

Urgh. "Very well, go back to the last room and rest," she commanded.

"What will you do?" he asked quizzically.

Vortiga had been stepping backwards as they'd talk, while judging the distance with her eyes. She could jump that. No problem.

"Wait you're not going to- Stop!"

Vortiga ignored his whining and dashed into a jump. Or at least she tried to. But the water pulled at her legs and what would normally have been an easy leap became impossible and she landed about two thirds of the way across the final patch of slime.

She didn't wait around to find out what happened when something ate through her boot however and simply jumped again, this time managing to land on the bottom step and then leaping another two steps up and out of the water.

She could already feel the burning sensation on the soul of her foot. Quickly, she used the step below to pry her boot off of her foot, but it was too slow and the sizzling sound changed as the slime reached her foot. In her panic to rid herself of the offending footwear, she kicked forward, flinging the boot spiralling off and into the water.

She sat down hard on the steps and surveyed her foot. There were burns and blisters along its length, but there was no slime.

"Are you mad? You could have lost your foot!"

"As you predicted, I am fine. Now can you make the same jump, or should I look for a bucket and start emptying out the water?"

"Make the same- but you didn't make it!"

"Of course I made it, I'm here on the steps aren't I?"

She grinned. The Porsht stared back at her in disbelief, which only made her grin widen all the more.

And that's when the tentacles grabbed her.

NINETOES

Ninetoes caught the tiniest of movements as he stared at Vortiga in disbelief. As he considered ways of wiping the smug look off her face he glanced towards it and was about to cry out in warning when the monster struck.

480

In the dungeon's darkness, its leathery green hide camouflaged it against the wall until the moment it launched its serpentine body at Vortiga and latched onto her with four tentacles that circled its beaked mouth.

Each tentacle ended in a viciously barbed claw and, while two of them slid off her armour, the other two found purchase and began dragging the hobgoblin Warrior towards its beaked mouth, which was already snapping in anticipation of its meal.

Ninetoes was so depleted of mana that he couldn't even risk using the tiny amount to cast Identify, not if he was going to be of any use in the battle. Vortiga meanwhile had managed to get her sword arm in between herself and the monster's beak, but she didn't have the reach to be able to draw her sword.

Ninetoes cast about for something useful to do, but he was just too far away and he couldn't get any closer without stepping into the slime. Worse still, since Vortiga had left the water the filth had begun moving back into the space she'd left and had obscured the water once more.

He didn't even have enough mana left for an Arcane Step.

It would have to be a ranged attack. Ninetoes called forward two of his archer skeletons, but as they got closer the monster manoeuvred itself to use Vortiga as its meatshield. His skeletons might be able to hit a pile of debris, but he couldn't risk their aim on such a tricky shot. He wasn't even sure he'd be able to make it.

But, maybe he didn't have to. One of the monster's clawed tentacles was latched onto Vortiga's sword arm. If he could break her arm free she'd be able to draw her sword. Vortiga cursed as the monster's beak clamped over her other bracer. He had no time to lose. He fired a Grim Bolt. And missed.

His head swelled with pain as it hungered for mana. What felt like fire lanced through his mind as he struggled to remain conscious. Ninetoes could hear the metal screech as the monster punctured Vortiga's armour. He had no choice. If the monster killed her, he'd follow soon enough.

He held out his hand, preparing a second bolt. Dizziness swept over him and his vision blurred. Shaking his head, Ninetoes gritted his teeth. Reaching up with the other arm, he steadied the first and fired.

VORTIGA

Dammit! If they survived this, the Porsht would never let her hear the end of this.

She struggled against the monster as it latched a third tentacle onto her flank and began to slowly but inexorably pull her towards its beak.

She'd already given up on her longsword, there was no way she'd draw it, so she attempted to reach for her dagger. But, as she did so the creature heaved her towards it and she had no choice but to ram her armoured wrist into its beak.

Within seconds, however, she realised her mistake as the monster's beak began piercing the steel and crushing her forearm. Something splashed against the wall but she had no time to check what it was.

Fighting with all her might, she tried in vain to break free. And then, all at once, the tentacle holding her arm weakened. Looking at the offending article, she watched as it shrivelled and blackened.

It was all she needed. She punched the monster in the side of its beak as she reached across herself and drew her sword, performing Devil's Tongue once again.

This time the blade met flesh and tore through the monster's midsection.

Blood pumped onto her face and she revelled. The monster's tentacles slackened slightly and she capitalised on its moment of weakness.

With her bracered arm pushing the thing's face backward, she rammed the tip of her blade straight up, piercing the thing's brain and out the top of its head.

The monster went immediately limp and now the only thing holding it upright was her. Wrenching her blade free, she used it to pry her arm out of its beak. Only then did she turn around to lambast the Porsht for his uselessness.

Only, he wasn't there. His skeletons stood waist deep in the water, but the hobgoblin wizard was nowhere to be seen.

"Where is your master?" She asked the skeletons stupidly. *What are they going to answer you with, fool? They have no tongues!* She scolded herself silently.

Scanning the room, she finally caught sight of his scarlet cloak floating in the water. *Shit!*

Without thinking she dove into the water, clearing most of the slimed area with her leap from the steps. Nonetheless she felt her face burn a little as some of the muck washed against it.

Beneath the water she could see nothing, but his cloak led Vortiga straight to Ninetoes and she lifted him out of the water and checked him over.

He was unconscious. *How did that happen?*

It didn't matter. Despite the progress they had made, she carried him back into the storeroom they'd left behind.

She also commanded the skeletons to come as well but neither one moved, so she reasoned they'd only follow Ninetoes' instructions.

As the adrenaline made its way out of her system, Vortiga laid the wizard onto the floor and then propped herself against a wall. She smiled. Gods she loved this.

NINETOES

Ninetoes awoke a little while later. Thankfully, while damp, he wasn't drowned, so someone must have scooped him out of the filthy water after he'd collapsed from severe mana depletion.

Sitting up he reached for his Bag of Holding to get some water and quench his thirst; only to remember that it was gone. *Argh!* He owed those bastards.

To avoid thinking about it, he searched the room for his companion. Vortiga sat nearby, stoking a small fire. "We survived then?" he called across to her.

"Aye. Although only just. I assume it was your magic that destroyed the beast's tentacle? I'd have been dead without your help, so it appears I owe you my life once again."

"Ha! And I suppose I pulled myself out of the water? We're good, my friend."

"Friend? Don't get ahead of yourself Porsht. We are allies, and temporary ones at that, nothing more."

"Huh, as you say. I don't suppose you have any food?" he asked as his stomach grumbled.

"I do not. I was running low when I reached your camp. If we don't find what we're looking for soon I suggest we cut our losses and leave the way we came in."

"You may be right, but if you'd seen the vision of treasure that I had, you would not be so hasty to leave."

"Aye, you may be right, but we can't eat gold."

An idea occurred to Ninetoes then. "What about the monster? Can we eat that?"

"What do you think I've been doing? But alas the answer is no. Once it was dead your spell continued to eat away at the monster. By the time I returned from rescuing you this is all I found." She gestured to the floor beside her to a lump of blackened flesh. Ninetoes hadn't really noticed it before because he'd taken it for more debris.

Now that he looked at it he was a little horrified. The monster's corpse was roughly half the size he'd remembered it being in life. As he approached her could see that it was drained of moisture and looked like it had laid in the sun for a month.

"Well, as you say, if we are unsuccessful we can always leave the way we came, at least the current travels downstream; going out should be easier than coming in."

Vortiga's only answer was to nod and then rise. She set about snatching up her weapons and shield and then headed for the door. "Come, we need to clear the rest of the slime to progress."

Ninetoes would have liked more time to rest. His mana was back to full but his Gem of Power was empty and he'd have felt more at ease if he could recharge it and then meditate to regain the mana spent, but Vortiga was right, they must keep moving.

Checking himself over he realised that his Wizard Armour had timed out. While the spell remained active even when the caster was unconscious, too much time had passed. Recasting the spell drained his dwindling pool of mana. Without his Guardmage's Pauldron or Circlet of Intelligence, Ninetoes had lost 13 points from his Intelligence and his mana pool had dropped by a massive 130 points, more than a quarter of what he'd had before. Now, with only 380 points, he had to be very careful with how he cast spells.

Wizard's Armour only cost 20 points to cast, but the hobgoblin would normally add to that by pumping in an extra 60 or 80 points to further strengthen his protection.

Without knowing what else they'd face, he couldn't risk spending much more. He settled on adding a further 60 points, buffing his AC by 3.

As prepared as he could be, Ninetoes headed for the room filled with water. There he found Vortiga, torch in one hand and sword in the other already standing in the murky water, roughly as far as they'd gotten before being attacked.

"What has taken you so long? I have been standing in this stinky pool for nearly a minute!"

"I needed to cast some protection spells. I am here now, so let's proceed." So saying, Ninetoes cast Deterge onto Vortiga once again.

By the time he'd finished the minute-long casting, there was already a space of cleaned water roughly an inch wide surrounding the hobgoblin Warrior. Looking down at this, Vortiga began the tiresome process of shuffling forwards, clearing a path through the remaining slime.

Even with Ninetoes' mana regeneration, the costly spell had left him with only 40 mana. A paltry amount and nowhere near enough for a battle. "I must rest and recover some mana, I suggest we stop here," he said, gesturing to the staircase.

"I will not sit on the stairs. Let us at least enter the next room?" Ninetoes considered this a poor idea, especially after being attacked only a short while ago, but he didn't have the energy to argue. Taking as long as possible to climb the steps, the pair reached a heavy, iron-bound door at the summit. Ninetoes could see a keyhole beneath the handle and a hope sparked within him that the door would be locked and he'd get the opportunity to rest.

Vortiga reached for the handle and pushed. "Shit, it's locked."

Ninetoes slumped down in gratitude and began arranging himself into the most comfortable seating position he could manage. "Annoying. I have a spell that'll unlock it but-"

"No bother, I'll just pick it," she replied.

"What?" he asked, a comically confused look across his face.

"Oh, I'm no expert but this thing can't be all that difficult." As she spoke, Vortiga retrieved two small slivers of metal from her pocket.

"Where did you get those?" Ninetoes asked.

"I found the metal amongst the debris while you were sleeping and hammered them flat with my mace. They are nothing special, but they should serve."

"And why do you know how to pick locks?"

"I had to make myself extremely useful to the Curn to even be considered for promotion, I have many skills."

Annoyingly, it didn't take Vortiga long to unlock the door and Ninetoes had barely recovered 30 mana. But, as the other hobgoblin opened the door and torchlight spilled into the room, all of that ceased to matter.

They'd found the thundercat's lair and the treasure of a once great king.

The vision Ninetoes had received from the monstrous feline simply hadn't done it justice. Clearly, the thundercat had never considered the mounds of loot to be of any interest, so its memories hadn't dwelled there.

When Ninetoes had opened Bofar's treasure chests and found them filled with coins, gems and jewellery he'd thought it a king's ransom. But that wealth paled in comparison to the mountains of treasure they now looked upon.

Vortiga took a step forward and Ninetoes suddenly came back to himself. "Stop!" he commanded.

"What?" she snapped back.

"I must rest. Let me take a short rest to recover some mana."

"As you say. I will check the perimeter of the room and see if I can find any traps." Vortiga started circling the room, eyes on stalks.

Ergh! Well, it's her funeral. Ninetoes settled himself into a comfortable sitting position and began to meditate.

At first, he simply concentrated on his breathing and brought it into a constant rhythm. Then, as his mana pool began to steadily refill he let his thoughts wander.

For a time he was able to avoid thinking about 'it'. About the thing he hadn't allowed himself to consider since waking up beneath the waterfall. Since then, he'd kept himself busy and kept his thoughts away from the dark corner of his mind where 'it' dwelt.

But now, with his mind unoccupied with other tasks his thoughts strayed towards 'it'. He tried not to, but that only made it more inevitable. *What happened to Libby? Was she alright? Or was she-* No, he mustn't even consider it. To think it would be to accept that it could be true.

And that's when he noticed it.

When meditating he always closed his eyes to save him from being too easily distracted. Normally this black space simply filled with visions of the things he was thinking of. But when he thought about Libby he didn't see her furry face, but instead was filled with those feelings of love that they shared. It was the bond that they shared.

Ordinarily, that bond was like a river of energy that flowed between them. When the wizard-bitch had hit Libby that bond had, for the first time, disappeared. Or, at least, he'd thought it had. Now, in his current state of semi-consciousness, he could feel the bond, if only faintly. It had never stopped, only become so weak as to be unnoticeable.

Now that he knew it was there, he reached out to it. His will sent a pulse seeking along it. At first, nothing happened and for long moments, Ninetoes thought the darkest of thoughts. *She's dead!*

But then a pulse returned. Weaker than his own but there nonetheless. It held no consciousness, no will of its own but the message was clear; Libby was alive.

He must get to her.

With renewed vigour, Ninetoes rolled onto his feet. His mana pool was almost completely topped off, but he'd rested long enough. "So? What have you found?"

His eyes scanned the mountains of gold before them, still not quite sure what to make of it all. There was just no way that it had stayed here untouched without defences.

"I am not sure. Do you have any spells useful for finding traps?" she replied quickly, clearly keen to be about their business.

Ninetoes didn't have any literal trap-finding spells but his Mind's Eye might offer some insight to any magical obstacles. With a mental flick, he ignited his eyes with mana. He also felt the warmth in his chest signalling a skill increase and once again he missed his Bag of Holding and, more importantly, his Character Sheet. Looking around the room, the only certainty was that they had no hope of carrying all this wealth away with them. But once they'd found a less dangerous way in and out, they could return to gather it up.

Just so long as they survived to do so.

His magical vision told him little of use on this occasion, however, as there was no magic coming from the floor, walls or ceiling, where he'd expected any traps to be located. While it was active though, Ninetoes cast his gaze over the piles of treasure and here his eyes lit up with a rainbow of magical light.

The room must have once been built for display as the columns and walls were painted with images of battle and scenes of journey. Much of it was worn or flaking with wear and natural damage, but it had obviously been an attractive sight once upon a time.

Around the space were chests but most of these held shattered locks and were tipped over and emptied, signalling that something had been in here since it was originally sealed. There were not, unfortunately, piles of bones to mark the location of any traps.

Light suddenly filled the space and Ninetoes quickly ducked behind a pillar. But when nothing attacked, he poked his head out from behind his cover.

"What are you doing Porsht?" Vortiga was standing next to an amphora that she'd just lit with her torch. Another was alight a few yards away.

"You startled me. Did it occur to you that those might be trapped?" he asked, gesturing towards the braziers.

"I smelt one first, besides we need more light." He couldn't really argue with the sentiment but their actions were growing hasty and impatient. It'd get them killed if they kept behaving this way.

"Perhaps you'd check with me next time, eh?" Vortiga only snorted in response, so Ninetoes turned back to the task at hand.

"We'll starve if we don't act soon. We must either take this wealth or leave, patience now will only cost us," she countered.

There were definitely a few magical items that he could see from his vantage, but most of them appeared to be magical weapons and so nothing that would help them in the short term. Finally, then, he allowed his mana-enhanced eyes to fall on the room's far end.

A stone table lay atop a dais of carved steps and something long and thin lay resting on top of it. Strangely, however, while whatever it was pulsed fiercely with magic, the energy wasn't coloured any of the eight he'd already learned about, but was instead grey or silver. It was hard to tell much more from this distance but if he had to bet, he'd reckon that this was the prized jewel of the collection.

Until they established whether there was any more danger, however, it would have to wait.

The room also had two other exits. An open passageway to the left that disappeared into darkness and another heavy, wooden door to the right.

By now, Vortiga had lit another four amphora and the room was bathed into the flickering light of the oil-fed braziers. She'd also edge around roughly half of the room to achieve this and now stood near the open passageway.

"What's next?" she asked. Ninetoes didn't want to admit it, but he was out of ideas. His best suggestion now was to throw something heavy at the floor and see if it set anything off. His hesitation must have been visible because Vortiga simply huffed and then took a standing leap into the room's centre.

Ninetoes' breath caught in his chest as he watched her as if in slow motion. She landed with a graceful patter as her naked feet slapped onto the cold stone of the floor. Despite her impatience, Ninetoes could see that Vortiga was coiled like a spring, ready to leap away at the first sign of trouble. But nothing happened.

"Well, this spot is safe at least," she said before leaping again, this time straight onto a pile of gold and, while she slipped and slid down it, nothing triggered. Reaching down she picked up a bejewelled sword. Through his Mind's Eye, Ninetoes could tell this wasn't magical but it looked to be worth a fortune in gems.

"Third time's the charm," and she made a massive leap, this time for the dais. The distance was too long, however, and her feet were slick with water and, so rather than landing as gracefully as she'd managed before, Vortiga slipped hard and bashed her knee.

Letting out a string of expletives, she dropped the sword and clutched at her wounded limb. But that, it appeared, was the worst that would happen, as no traps triggered and no monsters leapt out to grab her.

"Are you alright?" he called.

"Yes, only my pride is bruised. I think you should come see this." She was sitting beside the stone table, staring at the object atop it, rubbing her knee, she straightened and leaned closer.

"What is it?" Ninetoes called, curious.

"A staff for a mage I'd reckon," she called back.

He really didn't like the idea of stepping through the maze of treasure, even if she'd just done so. He was also confident enough in his own capabilities to recognise that he wouldn't be able to repeat the leaps that she took without magical assistance. He considered using Leap and following Vortiga's path. But it simply wasn't worth the risk and so instead he 'stepped', covering the distance to the dais in a moment.

As he touched down his eyes caught a wisp of orange light flicker through the grey energy that chased along the staff. For that was indeed what it was, a mage's staff! Ninetoes almost reached out to touch it, his avarice to own the thing was so great.

He remembered where he was, however, and reined in the compulsion. Instead, he cast Identify on it.

THE GREY STAFF - ARTEFACT, ARTEFACT
PREREQUISITES: UNKNOWN.
PROPERTIES: UNKNOWN.

Hmmm. Clearly the staff was something special, but his spell had told him little of practical use. He had, however, noticed that as he cast Identify another wisp of light flickered through the otherwise dull grey of the Staff's energy, although this one was white.

"Do not touch it!" commanded Vortiga in a harsh whisper.

"What the hell?" They were only on this dais because she'd risked their lives! That was it, he'd had it with this bossy, overbearing, old goat. Rounding on her he was about to give her a piece of his mind, but instead her mace connected with his face.

491

The blow smashed against his shield, which absorbed the damage, but it sent him crashing down the steps nonetheless. *What the fuck?* He'd been such a fool to trust her.

"It does not belong to you. It is mine."

Her feet slapped the stone as she rushed down the steps, but Ninetoes was ready for the second attack and rolled out of the way, before turning his dodge into an attack.

Spinning on the spot, he brought his hand to bare, an Arcane Bolt already formed and begging to launch. Lining up his shot, he triggered the spell and it whizzed towards Vortiga. Only to splash ineffectually on her shield.

Backing up, Ninetoes sent his undead against Vortiga. None of them was a match for the Warrior, even when they outnumbered her, but they were just a distraction.

He watched her closely and, the moment she smashed her mace through the skulls of one of his servants, he 'stepped' up behind her and grabbed her neck with Grim Void.

He'd learned his lesson when he'd fought her before and had already chosen his spot carefully, well out of reach of her weapons.

It didn't stop her swinging her shield in an attempt to bash him away, but Ninetoes had anticipated the move and when he'd 'stepped' he'd given his remaining skeletons the order to grab her and as she swung, a skeleton caught her shield and forced her to wrestle for control; she didn't stand a chance.

The rest of Ninetoes' wounds healed as he drained his short-term ally of her life. But then something strange happened. A vision crashed into him along with her lifeforce.

The memory filled his mind instantly, but it took him a second to make sense of it.

He watched himself as he stood upon the dais as he reached forward to cast a spell over the Staff. White light flashed through the Staff and his arms, no, Vortiga's arms drew back the mace to strike. Her lips formed words but they were not her own. "Do not touch it!"

Confusion washed through him, just as they had through her and the memory ended.

Ninetoes pulled his hand away and cancelled his spell and not a moment too soon. Vortiga's body was now suspended by his skeletons, as she appeared as little more than a skeleton herself, her skin hanging loose on her bones.

Although the memory was still confusing, one thing was clear, Vortiga hadn't attacked him, at least not of her own volition, something else had forced her to and it lurked nearby.

For now, however, he must save his ally.

His options were limited and he'd never tried it before, but he knew that in theory it could work. Reaching into himself, he drew out his own lifeforce and sent it into Vortiga. He did his best to send only what he'd taken but it was difficult to judge and the process made his head spin.

Vortiga rose, coughing up a little blood. "Ergh! There is something here, it was in my head, controlling m—"

"I know. We should escape for now, none of these treasures is worth our lives."

Vortiga didn't seem inclined to argue and, despite no obvious signs, the both began backing away from the darkened passageway to the left.

"Oh, you won't be leaving. Not since you've revealed yourself to me Necromancer." The voice seemed to come from all around them but it appeared to be a trick of the acoustics, rather than magic.

Ninetoes was on his feet in a moment, his hand alight with the crimson flame of his Arcane Bolt. It wasn't as efficient a use of mana as its necrotic counterpart, but he hadn't liked the lust with which the voice had said the word 'Necromancer'.

"You'd do well to lower your arms, you stand little chance of harming me, but I wish to learn from you. I promise it'll only hurt if you struggle."

Ninetoes and Vortiga circled, weapons drawn and back to back. With a thought, Ninetoes sent his skeletons into the darkened corners. Two of them clattered back, but the other vanished.

A second later there was a crunch and the ribcage and half the skull came clattering back out of the murk. Ninetoes' bolt flashed into the gloom and for a split second a serpentine form could be seen shooting further into the darkness.

"How dare you!" The voice screamed and a beam of thick, purple lightning shot from their flank and smashed into the floor between them. The pair were sent hurtling in opposite directions.

Ninetoes crashed noisily and painfully into a pile of coins, his body wracked with a stunning pain and for long moments he could barely move. He attempted to wriggle around to face the room's centre but what he found there offered nothing but trouble.

A gigantic snake was coiled around Vortiga and only her head was visible. The serpent's face was almost human-shaped. But the eyes betrayed its monstrous origins. Worse still, the thing's scales shimmered with the reds, yellows and oranges of magic.

"You would sssssstrike at me? I, who was there at Torgan'sss Fall! I, who have watched asss empiressss rossssse and fell? *You* think to best *me*? To steal *my* treasures? Foolissssh mage, I am immortal! Eternal! I cannot die." The diatribe had reached a feverish pitch, but it didn't escape Ninetoes' notice that the last three words were said in a sibilant whisper.

"Then you're just one more asshole I'll have to kill," Ninetoes tried, his head still rattling from the lightning bolt. The snake's eyes sharpened into slits and stared hatred back at him.

He heard Vortiga cry out and noticed a cracking sound coming from the serpent's body.

"Stop. I- apologies, we came here by mistake, now we seek only to escape."

"Do not lie to me ssslime. I read your thoughtsss as easssily as I controlled herssss," it boasted. Ninetoes wasn't sure how true that was, but he tried not to think directly of a plan, just in case.

"Then why aren't we dead? Why not kill us and be done with it?"

"Ha! And ruin all my fun? It has been some time ssssince I've had anyone to play with. I think perhapsss I'll have her tear off your sskin first and then we'll ssee where we go from there." As it said this, it loosened its tail and slithered into the dais, uncoiling itself from Vortiga as it did so.

Rather than collapse or run away from the monster, however, Vortiga drew her sword and began taking jerky steps towards Ninetoes. But he looked at Vortiga's eyes and saw genuine horror there.

The Warrior fought every step but, as she neared Ninetoes, it was clear that his ally was no longer in control.

"Or perhapss you'll kill her first. Was sshe your lover? Oh, please ssay it'ss so, it makes it so much more deliciouss when they're lovers."

"What? No…" Ninetoes wracked his brain for an answer. Then the monster's words came back to him. "… er, it must have been a long and boring life stuck down here, have you never considered lea-"

Another bolt of lightning shot at him, but he caught this one with Barrier. Or at least he tried to, but some of the tendrils licked around the shield and robbed him of his already limited hp.

"You don't think I've tried? With my power I could conquer king-doms, I could have been the eternal ruler of this land, nay thisss entire world." Vortiga meanwhile continued her puppet-like march towards Ninetoes.

"Then why don't you?" He watched the hatred course over the serpent as red magic charged up its scales. Ninetoes readied himself for another lightning bolt.

But when the monster fired, it wasn't at him, instead it fired at the Staff. "Because of that accurssed thing!" Rather than damage the Staff, however, the spikes of lightning just danced across the stone table. Had he not been watching closely, however, he'd have missed it this time, the wisp of red magic that played across the Staff.

An idea formed, but Ninetoes buried it deep, lest the monster see it and instead, he focussed on acting without conscious thought. Not giving the monster time to compute what it may learn.

It was a desperate and risky move, especially for someone who pre-ferred analysing before acting, but it was all he had.

"Then why not just destroy it? Or take it for your own?"

"Eeeeeesscehehheh! It already is mine, nothing that existsss here is anything but my possession. Even you goblin. There is nothing I cannot do! My magic comes from the time before."

"But you can't take it. Can you? Can't even touch it." He knew he was taking a risk, baiting the monster like this, but it was too powerful and they too weak to engage directly.

This time the lightning bolt did come for Ninetoes and his shielding spell was barely enough to keep himself from being torn apart. His Wizard's Armour was still active, but as the lightning's power forced him to the ground, he could feel his hit points draining away.

"I can take it for you!" He screamed out and the lightning instantly ceased.

Breathing heavily, he looked up at the monster. Its eyes bore into his own and he could feel it moving around inside his mind, attempting to read his thoughts. He avoided thinking and simply kept talking.

"I can, but only if you promise to let us both go."

A wicked smile curved the serpent's strangely human-shaped face. "I will allow you to try. But be warned, many have failed and they were far more powerful than you."

"I can do it," said Ninetoes, pretending a confidence he didn't feel. "But you must promise to let us both go. Make this promise and we will walk out of here of our own free will."

"Hmm, a clever one. Yes, I promise. Should you retrieve the Grey Staff from the Altar of Tears I will let you leave this place unharmed and of your own volition." For the first time, the monster's voice was level. But whether this meant that it could be trusted or not, Ninetoes had no clue. It was, however, clear he had little choice, so he stepped towards the dais.

Vortiga backed away, but her sword remained drawn. Climbing the steps, Ninetoes had to walk near to the serpent and it took all his will to remain so close to it.

Through his Mind's Eye he analysed the Staff. The energy that had been a dull grey was now an unattractive brown and for the first time since the monster had appeared, Ninetoes sighed in relief. His hunch appeared to be paying off. He cycled through the spells he thought he'd need and considered his mana pool. It might be enough, but he wasn't certain. He also didn't want to be collapsing with mana depletion in front of the monstrous serpent.

"Great one." He addressed the monster sycophantically, hoping to score some points. "I need to rest for just a little while, the spells I need require more mana that I have remaining."

The creature seemed to have calmed down a little, but its eyes became slits as it considered the hobgoblin. "And one such as you thought to best me? Ha! No, we will not wait, but I will gift you what you need."

A beam of rainbow light shot from the monster's brow into Ninetoes' own and he stumbled to the floor in pain. The sensation was similar to when Foresto used to recharge his mana but the serpent's mana felt like boiling acid.

"I do hope your entire plan isn't simply to try all of the different schools of magic, however, I tried that three centuries ago and it didn't work."

The burning sensation within Ninetoes was replaced by a feeling of being dumped to ice cold water. That was exactly his plan. In his shock, he nearly let that thought slip into his conscious mind, but he rallied.

"Of course not and I'm grateful for the mana Great One." His pool was now full, painfully so.

Without any further thought, he began casting spells. He started with Charisma. He knew it had no chance of making the monster any more friendly towards him, but it was the most costly spell he had and he wanted to give himself as much time as possible to recharge. Before him, a wisp of yellow peeled off of the Staff and the energy became a dark turquoise.

Next, he cast Minor Illusion and a purple wisp fled, leaving only green energy pulsing along the shaft. With his last spell prepared, Ninetoes flexed his muscles, ready to dodge should he need to. Then he cast Mending and the green energy became a wisp and lifted from the altar. The Staff still hummed quietly, but the energy that surrounded it was gone.

"Well? Now what? I have got this far before. I will create a particularly painful death for you, if you've wasted my time, mortal."

Ninetoes was of the opinion that if this creature really was immortal then it had nothing but time, but he refrained from pointing this out. Instead, he reached his hand forward and closed it around the shaft.

Everything around him slowed and then stopped. For Ninetoes, it was just him and the Staff. But there was something else, another presence. He couldn't see, or hear anyone but there was something close nonetheless. *Take it.* It said. *Only you can, it was meant for you.* It promised.

Who are you? He asked into the ether. Nothing came back. But he knew, just knew, that if he Chose it, he could take the Staff.

So he did.

CHAPTER 26
THE STAFF OF GREY

Power surged through Ninetoes' veins, electrifying his nerves and setting his body ablaze within a rainbow of light. Within a second the power reached his eyes and cascaded out in waves of force that knocked both Vortiga and the serpent off of the dais and sent a shower of golden coins flying in each and every direction.

"That's imposssssible!" Shrieked the serpent. "I have tried everything! Everything!" The monster coiled itself and then released itself to spring towards Ninetoes, teeth bared and death in its eyes. "Give it to me!"

Casting Barrier, Ninetoes barely felt his mana dip and, what's more, the serpent's movement was instantly arrested as it slammed into his shield.

This foe was no mere beast and instead of slamming into the floor, however, it coiled and redirected itself to Ninetoes' flank. From there it fired off a bolt of lightning.

Once again Ninetoes moved with a grace his battered body shouldn't have been able to achieve and created a second magical shield, bracing for the impact of the overspill of the monster's attack. Except, it didn't come. His Barrier had absorbed the entire lightning bolt.

Grinning his roguish smile, Ninetoes felt a confidence he didn't completely recognise. He felt like anything was possible. But it wasn't the overwhelming sense of arrogance that he'd felt as the Animator channelled magic through him. Or even the sureness that he could defeat the serpent. Rather he felt that, quite literally, *anything* could happen.

Right now, that meant he was certain that it was possible, however unlikely, to defeat this monster, what's more he felt he had a sense of how.

"Let us leave, Great One, as per our bargain, for which you gave your word." His voice wasn't that of a supplicant, as he'd roleplayed before, but rather the steady, even timber of someone speaking the truth.

"My word? Given to you, filth? No. No, you'll not be leaving. Weak as you are, there is clearly something different about you and I will find out what." As it spoke, its eyes strayed to Vortiga, showing annoyance. "Blast it, move!" it screamed at her.

Vortiga's eyes, however, no longer stared blankly but shone with purpose. As the monster noticed, she charged, a brightly glowing sword whipping out from behind her and moving at blinding speed towards the point at which the monster's body curved gracefully into its bulbous head.

Ninetoes was already in motion, heading for the serpent's other flank, meanwhile directing his last skeleton to attack. 'Stepping' he arrived as Vortiga's sword careened towards the monster and from his point of view could see the wicked smile on the serpent's strangely human lips.

There was nothing he could do as the monster created its own magical barrier in front of it. This one shimmered both blue and red and snapped with lightning. This could mean nothing good but Vortiga was committed.

Everything slowed down and Ninetoes watched helplessly as the monster's hungry grin seemed to welcome the Warrior's attack. But then the smile turned to a look of shock and surprise as Vortiga's attack crashed through the energy shield and sliced into the creature's neck.

Blood fountained from the wound as Vortiga tore the blade free with a wet squelch and twisted her hips to slice a second time.

While severely injured, the monster was far from done and as its head and neck turned away, its tail slapped Vortiga and the skeleton. The blow sent Vortiga careening across the chamber to smash into a far wall with bone-crunching force and shattered the undead servant into a thousand fragments.

All of this had happened in the blink of an eye, but it had been enough for Ninetoes to get into position.

Stamping his foot he activated Force Wave, attempting to angle it at the monster's serpentine base. A mighty spell it might be, but it moved the monster barely a foot backwards.

"He ha ha ha! Oh that was just lovely, what'll you do next, scratch me under the chin?" Its laugh was grating and high pitched and it clearly had no idea that Ninetoes hadn't been aiming to knock it back.

CRACK!

An inch-wide split opened in the floor near to a hole in the floor. The very hole used by the thundercat to get in and out of this chamber. In a heartbeat the tear chased its way towards where the massive serpent's weight was putting too much pressure onto it.

The look of surprise on the monstrous serpent's stupid face was something Ninetoes wished he could have captured for posterity. Pointing the Staff at the flagstones Ninetoes fired one, two, three Arcane Bolts, each one aimed at a different seam in the stonework.

The monster stared dumbly at the spots Ninetoes had blasted and then back at the hobgoblin wizard's face. The look he saw there was one few ever saw twice. A malicious look that said, "Got you motherfucker!"

And then the floor collapsed.

The serpent attempted to stop itself from falling but this was one time when a lack of actual limbs was a definite disadvantage and instead as its tail-end was caught by the current, the rest of it soon followed and the monster was whisked away.

Ninetoes' shoulders relaxed and he adjusted his grip on the Staff so that it stood upright, resting comfortably in his right hand, like a walking stick. For a moment he let the Staff bear some of his weight as he slouched into a deep breath, whispering his thanks to whichever gods had been watching over them.

Head up, Ninetoes scanned the chamber, searching for his ally. He found her atop a mound of coins and treasure, dazed and by the looks of her twisted arm, injured, but still alive. Gingerly stepping around the piles of gold, Ninetoes stepped over and helped her up.

One side of Vortiga's face was covered in blood and a dent in her helmet spoke of a head wound, so he cast Grim Void and shared a little of their dwindling health pool to repair the worst of the damage.

"Thank you," she muttered in response.

"I'm certain you don't want to hear this, but I don't think it's dead. We should leave as soon as possible and make for the forest."

"You'll hear no complaints from me but we should at least grab what we can carry, we might never get the chance to return."

"Very well. But we have only your satchel, so we should only take small, expensive looking items and let's not dally."

"Agreed."

For the next few minutes, the pair moved from pile to pile grabbing only the largest gems and most expensive-looking jewellery. For Ninetoes' part, he activated his Mind's Eye and took only items that sparkled with magical light, hoping that useful or not, the items would be worth more than simple gems.

With the time to consider it, Ninetoes realised that this strange but horrible dungeon might have been a real boon and that, if he was able to escape it, his new Staff and the, perhaps more importantly, the precarious alliance he had formed with Vortiga, might just make all the difference to the coming battle for Raveslan. He must tread carefully, lest he damage the trust he had garnered with the Sarm.

Vortiga, meanwhile, was replacing the High Steel sword for the glowing one she'd attacked the serpent with, as there was little doubt that it was magical. Certainly, it shone with wisps of blue and red light.

Ninetoes watched as she knelt down, sheathing the high steel sword and bowing to it reverently, before whispering something, as she laid it carefully in a place of honour, atop a mountain of treasure.

Snatching up the scabbard of her new sword, she attached this to her belt and in a move of incredible speed and skill, sheathed the blade.

Once the time had passed the pair looked out over the piles of gold, sighing with resignation. One day, they both silently promised and then headed for the wooden door. Once again they found that it didn't budge. For Ninetoes, who's mana pool had never felt so full, this posed no problem and he didn't even question using his Pick Lock spell to open the door.

That was why he was so surprised when the door still didn't move. *Hmmm.* "I think perhaps it's just stuck." He offered weakly to his companion. For her part, Vortiga gave Ninetoes her patented 'Men!' look and braced her shoulder against the door.

Between the two of them, they managed to force the heavy, wooden impediment open enough to see through. This revealed that the problem was apparently a foot or so deep of mud and silt that filled the next chamber. At about the same time, Ninetoes felt the strong warmth in his chest of a Level Up. He wasn't sure if it would work without direct access to his Character Sheet, but he mentally assigned his two Ability points, one each to Intelligence and Wisdom. He left his four Skill Points for later. He had a plan for them, but wasn't sure yet if it was the right course.

Another five minutes of sweating, cursing and arguing and they had the door open enough to squeeze through. The two of them were now bruised, scratched and thoroughly exhausted. Worse still, they hadn't eaten in nearly two days and were beginning to suffer.

Thankfully the room beyond was only filled with the silty mud for the ten-foot square space that made up the bottom of a set of stairs that carved up into the darkness above. Now that they were genuinely starting to worry about dying of hunger, the pair didn't even consider checking for traps as they squelched through the mud and onto the staircase.

The steps, it transpired, curved into a wide spiral staircase that even after five, long and leg-shaking minutes of climbing, they hadn't reached the top of and it was only after two breaks to catch their breath that they reached the top.

Here, Ninetoes finally found something to offer them hope that they had nearly found a way out, for in front of him Vortiga's torch lit up the desiccated remains of what he took to be a spellcaster of some kind.

But the reason for hope was that the spellcaster's right hand, that was trapped beneath what appeared to be a heavy, stone door, was gripping a piece of parchment.

Excitement and hunger made his movements shaking and imprecise, but as he knelt to check, he was able to confirm that the parchment seemed to be the other half of the spell scroll that he'd torn from the "secret" door he'd found in the crook of Torgan's neck atop the colossal statue. Carefully he retrieved it.

"What've you found? A piece of parchment? What use is that to us Por-"

"If I'm right, and I'm sure I am, this door will lead directly outside. This is our exit."

"Thank the gods. I was starting to wonder what you'd taste like."

Ninetoes chuckled cautiously, unsure whether the hobgoblin Sarm was kidding. "Well, now all we need to do is work out how to open this door."

"Well, it looks as if perhaps this poor fellow knew how, but was unable to reach. Look." And, kneeling down Vortiga picked up something from the ground near to the dead mage's other hand, retrieving what appeared to be a long, metal cylinder about the size and shape of a wand.

Which is exactly what Ninetoes thought she'd picked up until she held it under the torchlight.

Rather, it appeared to be some kind of hexagonal prism, covered in symbols. Stranger still, the symbols appeared to be on rotating tumblers.

Excitement coursed through Ninetoes as he realised that he recognised the shape of the symbols as the very same ancient language he'd discovered in Kavralach and a quick casting of Comprehend Languages and the hobgoblin mage could see that the symbols were letters. There were five tumblers and each had six symbols upon them. Obviously, one could rotate the symbols to spell out certain words or codes, but Ninetoes had no idea what the significance of this was.

"Look here." Vortiga said, gesturing towards a section of the wall above the corpse. Investigating it more closely, Ninetoes found scratch marks in the stone. It didn't take a genius to work out what Vortiga had plainly already put together and, tracing up from the marks, Ninetoes found a hexagonal hole that was, he was sure, a perfect fit for the 'wand'.

"It's a key." He voiced his conclusion, to which Vortiga nodded once.

"Well, aren't you going to use it?" She asked impatiently, staring daggers at Ninetoes. "What's the problem?"

Ninetoes who was mostly ignoring Vortiga's blustering, was instead focussed intently on the key and in particular at the second and third rows of symbols. But it wasn't the symbols themselves so much as the faint teeth marks that he'd discovered.

"Look at this." He held the 'key' out to Vortiga.

"So? It's some sort of code to unlock the door. Presumably this poor fool knew the code, he just couldn't reach the lock."

"If that was the case, why the teeth marks?"

"Hmmm, perhaps he needed to adjust those two to unlock it?" she suggested.

"Right, but then how do we know that he succeeded? Look at the arm under the door. That break would have sent the bone through the skin; what if he bled out while trying to open the door?"

"He might not have had time to set the code you think?"

"Indeed," Ninetoes replied, considering the conundrum again.

"What's it matter? If it's wrong, we just try again, give it here." Vortiga snatched the key from the mage and slotted it into the lock before Ninetoes could stop her.

"No!" He shouted, but it was too late. A clunk sounded as the floor beneath them became a short slide and they both slipped towards the heavy stone door. The 'door' meanwhile had raised just enough to send both them and the remains of the corpse clattering down into a trough beneath, before rushing back down towards them.

Reacting faster than should have been possible, Ninetoes grabbed Vortiga and 'stepped' outside and in a perfect world, that would have been it. But, as Ninetoes was quickly discovering, the world of Adrenon was far from perfect.

The angle from which he'd 'stepped' hadn't offered him much in the way of options and when the pair rematerialised they found themselves ten feet away from the nearest 'ground' and after the briefest of moments, their momentum arrested and gravity took over, sending the pair tumbling through empty space and crashing down into the splashpool far below.

Resurfacing and vomiting water from his lungs, Ninetoes dragged himself to the shore, to collapse next to Vortiga. "It might be trapped." He finished the thought.

CHAPTER 27

THE BEST-LAID PLANS OF SQUIRRELS AND GNOMES

Libby rested on the dusty ground around the back of Foresto's house. She could hear the old mage rattling around inside, but she didn't want to show up sweaty and disgusting. Instead she dove into the water butt around back.

If she'd had more time, she'd have cleaned herself properly but she wasn't sure how far behind the Adventurers were. She needed to tell Foresto all she knew and form a plan before they arrived.

Resurfacing and pulling her tired body out of the rainwater, Libby shook herself, clearing most of the water. Looking at her reflection in a window pane she realised that she was no longer smelly but she resembled a drowned rat. *Argh!* It didn't matter.

She scurried in through the open back door and into the massive workshop that was hidden in the tiny building. She quickly found Foresto standing at a short set of steps, leaning over the gigantic construct he'd built.

With a massive leap she landed on the thing's head and squeaked at the old gnome. After so much time being able to speak with her mind, it grated on her to use the primitive noise, but needs must.

"Oh, hello Libby, I had hoped to see you back today."

She waved her arms and tried to draw him over to a roll of parchment and pencil that lay nearby.

"I'm sorry little one, I don't have time for games. Where's Ninetoes?"

Argh! No, I can't talk to him. Just come over to the table you old fool!

"She requests your presence over by the drafting table Master," said a strange voice that seemed to originate from her derriere.

"The table? Whatever for?" Asked Foresto in a confused tone.

"She doesn't say Master. Please wait a moment." Then, directly into her mind. *Miss Libby, my Master wishes to know why you wish him to attend the drafting table?*

Wha- wait, can you talk telepathically? Libby asked, turning to look the machine-man in the 'eyes'.

Indeed, well to those of our kind at least.

Our kind? Libby really didn't think she shared many similarities with this thing.

Familiars.

Ohhhh. That made sense. Sort of. *So can you talk to Foresto for me?*

Yes. Is that why you wanted him to go over to the drafting table?

Yes, but don't worry about that now.

Very good. What would you like me to tell him?

For his part, Foresto had sat watching patiently as the two creatures conversed. But, as the golem began conveying Libby's story to him, his brow clouded over and energy started to crackle over his knuckles.

TARQUIN

The rest of the journey had been boring. Tarquin hadn't been able to summon more demons to fight and annoyingly they'd encountered no other monsters before reaching the little pisspot town, if you could even call it such.

This meant that, while they'd gained a goodly amount of experience, they hadn't managed to Level Up again. And now that they were here he wouldn't be able to summon any more demons because there were simply too many people around, someone was bound to see him. He'd have to make up a reason to head out of town.

"So, where to first? Speak with the town leader?" Sariel offered.

"Nah, I wanna go and meet this wizard and order our magic item. Bess where's he live?"

"Foresto lives this way," she answered. Now that they were here he'd probably let his spell slip from Bess. It'd been fun to use her as his servant, but he didn't really need her anymore anyway.

"Excellent, lead the way."

Bess skirted the town walls and headed for a tiny little hovel outside of the defensive walls. It was a classic trope. The old mage probably had a "bigger on the inside" thing going on in the little pigsty.

Bess reached the door and knelt down to be about the right height before rapping her knuckles on the blue wood.

A few moments later a gnome in long robes stepped out of the building. "Ah, you must be the Adventurers. I assume you're here for your magic items?"

"Huh, at least one of these NPCs is quick to do business. Er, yeah, we're here for the items; we get to choose them and you'll make them, right?"

"Indeed, if the town survives of course," he said firmly.

"Oh of course. But see, wouldn't it make more sense to make us more powerful *before* the battle?" He'd been thinking about this argument since leaving Pamor, but he cast Charisma as well, just to be sure.

"Hmmm, I suppose you're right. But I apologise, I will not be able to complete them all before the hobgoblins are likely to attack."

Annoying but not totally surprising. "So, how many do you think you could finish?"

"I suppose, depending on what you ask for; two, three in a pinch."

Hmm, not bad. "Alright, why don't we tell you what we want?"

"Very well."

"Right, well I want something to make me more powerful. Perhaps a ring with some nice stats bumps or something. Can you manage that?"

"Oh yes, certainly mister-?"

"Tarquin, Sir Tarquin."

He supposed the others probably asked for their items after that, but Tarquin had stopped listening.

SARIEL

Sariel watched Foresto closely for any sign that Libby had reached the town safely, but the old wizard betrayed no signs of having seen the squirrel.

I'm here.

The voice was quiet, even in her mind, but it gave her a focus and, looking past the gnome into the sitting room beyond, she could just make out Libby's shadowed form hiding on a bookshelf.

Did you reach him in time to tell him what happened?

I did and he's pissed so be careful. It's only because I explained that you Adventurers are still the town's best shot that he didn't start shooting off magical death.

Right. Have you formed a plan?

Not totally, but I've got the beginnings of one. Can you meet me here tonight?

I've got a better plan.

"- Sariel, Sariel? Wake up, it's your turn." Daphne waved her hand in front of the half-elf.

"Oh, er, sorry, I was daydreaming."

"Whatever. The gnome wants your order."

"Actually, I wanted to discuss it with him, which might take a while. Do you wanna wait?"

"Argh, if you're gonna take all day, I'm off." So saying, Tarquin and the others trooped off towards town.

Hmm, this'll work as well.

"Indeed, why don't you come inside my dear," said the gnome, gesturing for her to follow.

510

Sariel ducked down and climbed through the doorway only to suddenly feel foolish when the ceiling soared away from her and she realised she could stand easily once inside. *Cool.*

The gnome stepped to the door and shut it firmly, while watching the retreating Adventurers out the window. Once they'd turned towards the gateway into town, he turned and spoke. "Libby tells me that you're to be trusted; believe me when I say if you try to cross me girl, you'll learn to regret it."

"Of course, and please let me reassure you, I knew nothing of their plans and would have stood with Ninetoes had I known them," she said it fiercely, clenching her fists with helpless anger.

"Hmm, that remains to be seen, but for now, Libby has something of a plan, but it requires your help."

"You can count on me."

"Very well. Regardless, I have work to do. Let's take this discussion into my workroom and you can tell me what you want as your reward."

"Oh, oh no. I don't want anything, not after what they did."

"Nonsense. You're here to help protect the town, should we succeed you will require payment. Now, what do you want?"

"Oh, um. I really don't know what to ask for." Sariel had been so worried about what had happened and trying to make sure that Libby was safe, she'd had no time to think about it.

"Fine. You're an archer? A Ranger perhaps?" Foresto asked her.

"Yes, and I'd like to become a master of Beasts. But I don't know if that helps."

"Hmm, interesting. I haven't met a beastmaster in a long time, perhaps a- Hmmm, yes."

"You have something?"

"I do, but leave it with me. I wasn't lying when I told your companions that I can't make all the items quickly."

"That's fine, unless we do something about the other Adventurers, I might not last that long anyway."

"Ah well, that's just it, isn't it, but Libby has a plan to deal with them."

Indeed, but I need Foresto to finish the magic items, so let's leave him to work.

***

Sariel and Libby allowed the wizard to work, assisted by his golem. Meanwhile the two of them headed into the library and discussed the plan.

While Sariel was no tactician, she thought it had merit, but it certainly wasn't without its problems. Not least of all that they needed the Adventurers to see off the hobgoblin attack before they could initiate their plans.

The plan was straightforward enough. Foresto would make the Adventurer's their magic items, but would place a minor, but effective spell within each one. This spell could be triggered when the time was right and if everything went to plan, the spell would temporarily disable the Adventurers. Once disabled, Libby would deal with the rest.

Of course, if they disabled the Adventurers too soon, then the town would stand almost defenceless in the face of the Nechtsarm army, so choosing their moment was of the utmost importance.

With as many of the details worked out as they could, Sariel headed into town to meet up with the others, lest they grow suspicious. She needed them to trust her for the plan to work.

She found them a little while later in the tavern. They explained that they'd each been provided with a room to stay in and that they were expected to meet with the town's leaders later that evening to discuss plans for a defence.

She'd noted on her walk through the town that preparations were already underway. Much of the food had been harvested a little early and had already been brought inside the walls and it was clear that the town was full to bursting with people that would normally live outside the walls.

But there were also groups of men, young boys and old men really, being trained with the spear and she could hear the blacksmith's hammer working constantly.

Despite all this, it didn't seem like it would really account for much. Only the guards seemed to have any real armour and only a handful of these brave souls looked to have any actual skill with a weapon. Worse still, if what they'd been told was accurate then they'd be outnumbered by at least two to one, by battle-hardened and properly equipped hobgoblin soldiers.

The Adventurers were the town's one and only real hope and she didn't trust a single one of them.

"Oh, hello Sariel." She'd rounded a corner and almost knocked into Bess.

"Hi Bess. What're you doing out so late?"

"I'm helping Borris make arrowheads. He reckons the bow's the best chance most of these folks will have of killing any hobs."

"Huh, well I happen to agree. How're you feeling after you- er, travels?" Sariel wasn't sure, but she was pretty certain that Tarquin had been using some sort of charm spell on the poor girl. He'd stopped short of doing anything particularly unpleasant to her, mostly using her as a servant but he seemed to have grown bored of the smith since they'd reached town.

"I'm, um, fine I guess. It's just- oh, don't worry."

"No, please. Go on."

"Well, it's just… well I know that necromancy is evil and all that but I never saw Ninetoes do anything wrong and…" She faded off, her eyes filling with tears. "…I, I just don't know why I was so horrible to him. At the time it felt like it was the right thing to do. In fact, I've never been so certain of anything, but now…" The tears began to fall, thick and fast.

Sariel stood stock still. She'd never been one to hug people, it just wasn't who she was. But she also wasn't about to tell her to stop crying. She made her choice and took a chance.

"I think Tarquin was controlling you." Then, when Bess looked confused, she added. "With magic I mean. I think he was using some sort of enchantment to make you more susceptible to his words."

A look of genuine fear passed over Bess' face, followed closely by one of anger.

"No. Not Tarquin." She started hotly. "He is my-"

SLAP!

Sariel recognised the magically induced words as soon as Bess began spewing them and there was only one sure fire way to counter enchantment spells, taking damage. The slap wouldn't do much, probably only a single hp of damage, but it served.

"Tarquin is an asshole. And what's more you know it."

Bess held a hand to her cheek, already red with pain from Sariel's slap. For a second, she thought the well-built smith might thump her back. But instead a firm look crossed over her face and she roughly cuffed the tears from her eyes.

"I'm listening."

"Good. Now, Foresto has need of some more iron ingots, please deliver them to him."

A moment of hesitation passed over Bess and then comprehension dawned and she nodded.

"Very well." And Bess made to leave. As she reached the shadow of a nearby roof, however, she stopped and turned back to Sariel. "Safe journey and good fortune Adventurer."

***

After meeting with the town's leaders, the party divided up as best suited their skill set and Sariel spent most of the next day training teenage boys and girls to shoot a bow. Or at least that was the plan.

"No Peran, no don't-"

"Ow!"

"Gods, how many times kid?" For what felt like the fiftieth time that morning she showed the particularly dull-witted miller's son how to hold the bow to avoid the string slicing into his arm. Meanwhile she made a mental note to ask one of the leather workers if they could fashion a guard for the poor fools.

"Sorry mistress, I just can't seem to get it." *Argh. Now I feel like an asshole.*

"It's alright Peran, I'm sure you'll get it." But the truth was, there simply wasn't enough time for Peran or most of the others to become competent with the bow and if they were on the walls they were more likely to get killed. But Peran's nerves were not only because of his lack of skill with the bow.

Lady Fawkner, who also had some skill with the bow, had agreed to help Sariel and the woman's presence was clearly making the teens uncomfortable.

She wore leathers and a loose shirt, but despite her skill with the bow, there was no hiding the grace of her movements or the poise with which she held herself.

Everyone of them was born to the land and so brutishly strong and fit, so they had no trouble drawing the bows, they just couldn't hit anything. But the reality was, that the hobgoblins would probably be so many that actually aiming wasn't really an issue. Perhaps she'd been a bit too optimistic trying to teach them to hit the target at fifty yards. All they really needed to be able to do was draw and loose as quickly as possible. All she needed to do was find a way of teaching them to fire quickly and without carving their own arms open.

"Alright everyone, that's enough for a minute. Come over here and leave the bows behind."

The youths did as she bid and a few of them took the opportunity to chatter, as teenagers are wont to do. She needed to grab their attention before she lost it for good. "All of you, come sit over here."

"Yes miss." They intoned, probably thinking they were about to be told off for their failure. Mera Fawkner joined them, even going so far as to sit on the grass.

"Now, your problem. All of your problem." She added for Peran's sake as some of the boys started pointing and chuckling. "Is that you're treating the bow too harshly. The bow is an elegant weapon, unlike an axe or war-hammer, is it made for precision." They were listening now at least, so she forged on. "It takes strength to wield her well of course, but she doesn't want to be bullied or tugged around." She smiled. "She's a lady."

"A lady miss?" The boys looked utterly confused and about ready to start giggling like, well like teenage boys.

"Aye lads, a lady, like Lady Fawkner here. Now, when we approach a lady to ask her for a dance, we don't just stomp up and grunt at them, do we?"

Most of the boys shrugged but one of the girls grinned and spoke up. "You offer them your hand miss."

She'd clearly meant it like a challenge, wanting to see if the strange half-elf would actually offer the Lady her hand. And so, that's exactly what she did.

"You're right. I offer the Lady my hand." And so saying, leaned forward slightly and proffered her hand. A brief look of confusion crossed Mera's face, but she reached up and took it nonetheless.

"And then?" Sariel asked the group.

"Well, you gotsta help her up like," said the same girl.

As the girl spoke, Sariel pulled gently but firmly with her hand, guiding Mera's hand in a straight line upwards, while straightening her torso. The crowd gasped as they saw what she'd done. For her Ladyship, Mera Fawkner, was now standing before the half-elf with one hand on her left cheek and the other on the lady's shoulder.

For a moment it seemed that Mera would break away, but then comprehension dawned on her face. And, as Lady Fawkner stepped away, the teens could see that Sariel was in the perfect longbow pose, an imagined string pulled tight to her cheek. Mera smiled and she took over the lesson.

"You all see?" she asked them.

A chorus of silent confusion followed her words. So Mera stepped out of the strange pose, but Sariel stayed in exactly the same position. Sighs of recognition began trickling through the assembled teens, the girls at first but then the boys began to catch on.

Finally, Peran spotted it and couldn't help but exclaim. "She's standing like she's drawn a bow." A smack sounded and the poor lad whined.

"Gentlemen please stand." Now, when Sariel had asked them to move they'd done so only reluctantly. But when her Ladyship spoke, they shot to their feet as if her nobility were like magic. "Now, ask a lady to dance."

Even their trained response to obey their betters failed them at this. "Beggin yer pardon yer ladyship?" One of the braver ones asked.

"Just humour me lads. Now, find a partner and remember to be polite, manners cost nothing."

It was Peran who showed his courage first and stepped up to a pretty red-haired girl of about the same age. He bowed and then offered his hand. The girl smiled back, unbothered by the stares of her peers, and took his hand. In an almost perfect copy of Sariel's own move, Peran drew the girl up, placed her fingers on his cheek and held her shoulder.

"Excellent Peran, now again. And the rest of you, stop standing around staring and find a partner. That's it. And when you think you've got it, swap over and let the girls have a go."

Not to be outdone by Peran, the boys quickly headed for a partner. There were some scuffles as two boys went for the same girl and poor Merouda, the tanner's daughter had no one to practice with until Mera stepped in, but eventually the whole group was practicing the manoeuvre.

It wasn't perfect of course, but it was serving. Before long, she took them back to the bows and had them practice without arrows.

Finally, as they broke for lunch, the whole group was firing shot after shot into a heap of dung. It didn't matter that the target was massive and less than fifty feet away. Perhaps every fifth shot missed, and but every single teen was hitting it and there not a single one was injuring themselves. She called that a win.

"Alright everyone, go get some lunch in the square and meet back here within the hour." The teens walked away, once again dividing girls from boys.

"That was a clever idea." Mera stepped over, offering Sariel a ladle of water.

"Thank you, your ladyship."

"I only hope it's enough."

"As do I. They won't stand for long if the hobs get inside. Perhaps the others have had more luck."

Sariel was cautious of the woman. She still didn't know if she'd been part of the betrayal against Ninetoes, but for the time being at least, she was helping the town.

Some time ago, the townsfolk had begun work digging a trench around the outside of the walls, it had stalled during the harvest, but given the current situation had once again become a priority and the project was finished in record time.

At the Adventurers' bidding they'd started filling it with fire-hardened stakes. The work proceeded well but there was no hope that they could fill the entire trench before the hobgoblins were due to arrive.

The plan of battle was straight forward enough. Despite their superior numbers, the hobgoblins still stood the best chance of success if they focussed on one weak spot. That weak spot was the eastern gate. It was old and hadn't been repaired in years. Rather than replace it, the plan was to leave it as a tempting target and concentrate their defensive forces around the gate.

They had plenty of arrows and, with a little luck, the teens to fire them. What they lacked was strong fighters to hold the hobgoblins when the gate was inevitably breached. But that wasn't Sariel's problem, her job was to ensure that the archers were as ready as possible.

"Do you think we could get the carpenters to make crenellations?"

"A sound idea and a sensible precaution. I'll speak with Mistress Emblyn shortly, then I'll head to see Bess and the other smith, I have some ideas to share with him." With that Mera stepped away, leaving Sariel alone on the walls.

"Will it be enough, do you think Miss?" Sariel nearly leapt out of her skin, the girl had been so quiet. Turning towards the voice, she found the red-haired girl that Peran had chosen, Elewyn she remembered.

Sariel considered her answer carefully. She didn't want to scare the girl but she also didn't want to give her a foolish hope. She needed the girl to recognise that the risk was real so that she'd take it seriously enough to run if it came to it.

"The fighters are learning well and the defences are getting stronger with every moment that passes. But our enemy is strong, determined and experienced. The only certainty is that it will be a difficult fight."

"So you think we can win?" The girl was sharp and she hadn't let Sariel off the hook.

"I think it's unlikely but there is a chance."

"I'll take it." The young woman said simply. "And thank you Adventurer."

With that the girl slid down the ladder as if it were a slippery pole to land gracefully on the ground. Sariel was impressed. Her prime stat was Agility and she'd have struggled to make it look so easy.

I only hope that'll be enough to save her, she thought.

It might be but we'll make sure she won't only have to rely on her own grace to survive. Libby's voice filled her mind from close by.

How do Foresto's creations proceed? Sariel asked.

They are progressing, but he says he's struggling to make all of the enchantments fit on one item.

Then tell him not to bother with everything the Adventurers asked for.

I did, but he's concerned that they won't use them if they're not good enough.

Ha! That will not be a problem, we Adventurers are loot hounds, we can't resist its allure.

Hmm, that explains a few things. How does the training go?

Well enough but there's no way these villagers will be able to hold the hobs for long.

Then your companions will simply have to do their part. Although I have little faith in Tarquin there, I just passed him lounging out in front of the tavern. It is truly a wonder how he can be so blind to what is happening here. He is a brute. I look forward to killing him.

Sariel didn't like to hear Libby talk that way, but she couldn't argue with the sentiment. She'd also witnessed Tarquin's slothful behaviour. An'rik was helping to train the melee fighters and even Daphne was helping to prepare some arcane traps, but Tarquin only seemed interested in heading out into the forest to hunt monsters.

She couldn't argue with the notion that gaining experience and becoming stronger was important, of course, but he refused to help out in any other way. She was also concerned with how many demons they'd fought and that this was another threat they'd have to face, but she had to focus on one problem at a time.

In fact, if she didn't hurry she'd be late for training.

I have to go. I'll meet you at Foresto's after dinner.

Aye and be careful when you go on patrol. I hate seeing you risk yourself outside the walls.

I'll be fine and the four of us must get stronger.

Huh. That's what scares me.

LIBBY

Speaking with Sariel had finished her rounds. Honestly, she felt a little useless, having only messages to carry between Foresto and the others they trusted. Sure, the original plan had been hers but Foresto was the one with the knowledge to pull it off and it was Sariel and Bess that would be risking themselves in the thick of the fighting.

She could at least help there. Foresto had finished the item that Ninetoes had requested long before they'd arrived back and once he'd finished questioning her about her Master and everything that had happened, he'd given it to her.

It was a ring that fit her as a bracelet, but she had no idea what it did.

He'd seemed particularly interested in her description of the Path of the Maverick and had, at first, suggested that she was lying until she'd shown him her Character Sheet. Even this he'd thought was a hoax until she cast Charisma and the number for her mana pool had gone down.

He'd apologised profusely of course, but she'd managed to leverage the gnome's regret into a quick lesson in how to cast Identify.

Ninetoes had known how to cast it of course, but she'd never bothered to try it as she couldn't see the purpose with him around. But now she wanted to continue growing and she wanted to find out exactly what Foresto's gift did.

Try as she might, however, she just couldn't get Identify to work. Frustrated, she huffed at the gnome.

"Alas my dear, that problem I think is a simple one, but the solution is less so. You have very little affinity with Divination magic, so you're struggling to cast the spell."

So, what? I just can't cast it? she exclaimed and then waited impatiently as the golem conveyed the message to his Master.

"I'm afraid so. But there may be another solution," he offered.

Well what're we- Sigh. My apologies, what solution is that Master Foresto?

"No, I'll have none of that, you know my feelings on the honorifics. It works like this. While we consider the different schools of magic as different aspects of magic, the reality is that they're all part of the same flow of energy and the term magic is simply how to express its manipulation. With me so far?"

I think so. You're saying that spells are just a means of interpreting and changing mana.

"Hmmm, not exactly, but the analogy will serve. Now, Wizard's, Sorcerers and all other mages have found that certain flows of magic react more positively to certain tasks whereas others rail against being forced to do certain things."

Wait, you make it sound as if magic's alive!

"Of course it's alive my dear, how else would it do what it does?"

But- fine. Please proceed.

"Ha! Your Master would have got wrapped up in that one for an hour. So, let's take a simple example. The weave that we comprehend as Illusion magic, your chosen school, flows best when we set it to tasks that relate to stealth, hiding and manipulating a creature's mind. But in reality the same magic could perceivably be used to start a fire or heal a wound."

So, are you saying that I can use Illusion magic to cast any spell I want?

"Not any spell no. Some magic simply won't agree to be used to perform certain tasks. Illusion for example is the antithesis of Divination, the magic that would normally be used to cast the Identify spell. Thus your Illusion magic, which seeks to hide things, will be extremely unlikely to help you reveal something."

So how does that help me? she asked, a little frustration coming across in her mental voice. Thankfully, whenever the golem conveyed her words it, he?, only ever used the same monotonic voice.

"Ah, but you're not thinking laterally my dear. You have managed to learn spells from other schools have you not and, as your Character Sheet shows, you have a solid affinity with Enchantment. Well, it just so happens that Enchantment is only two steps away from Divination."

Two steps?

"My apologies. Consider for a moment, the eight spell schools as the points on a compass. Now place Abjuration at north, and Evocation south, then place Necromancy and Conjuration at east and west respectively. Then, proceeding clockwise from the top, add in Illusion, Enchantment, Divination and Transmutation in the spaces between."

As he spoke he drew the diagram on a scrap of parchment.

Once she could see his drawing, it was easy to see what he meant.

But then, how is it that Ninetoes is able to cast spells from each of the eight schools without any problems.

"Ah, this is just one of the ways that Wizards are the most superior breed of spellcasters. With study and practice, anything is possible. Even for you, if you took the time, weeks perhaps, you'd be able to cast Identify, but I assume you have more urgent problems to deal with."

Aye, I can think of a few Adventurers who need killin'.

"Just so. Thus, my solution. Because Enchantment is close enough to Divination, you should be able to convince its magic to change itself enough to perform an identification spell. It won't be as effective or elegant as Identify, but it should serve."

Looking at the diagram he'd drawn, she thought of another question.

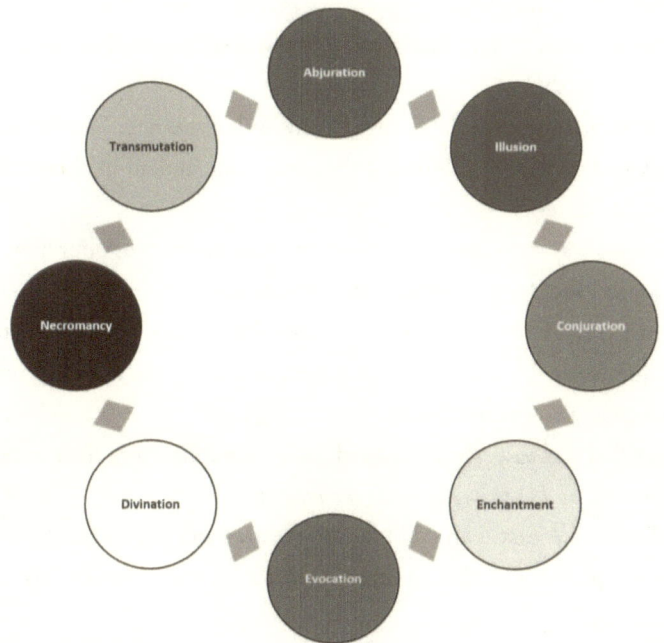

But if that's the case, why don't I just use Necromancy? That sits right next to Divination.

"You're right and it would work, but your affinity with that is only ten percent, barely any better than with Divination, you stand a much better chance with Enchantment."

Alright, so what do I do?

"Hmm, that's the tricky part."

How so?

"Um, well I don't know."

You mean you don't know why it's tricky?

"No, I mean I don't know how to do it. I've read about it but until I met Ninetoes and witnessed some of the miracles you two seem capable of, I never really believed it was possible."

Great. Thanks.

"I'm sorry Libby, but listen to me carefully. If there was anyone and I mean anyone in the world capable of this, it was Ninetoes. I believe that you hold that gift as well."

The mention of her Master stung. She was sure he could have done it; but what was she?

She wiped the negative thought away. What was she? She was a warrior. A spellcaster? No Illusionist. She was none and all of those things. She was a Maverick.

Foresto was right, she could do it. She just had to work out how.

Do you have any good ideas to start? she asked him.

"Just one, remember that you're asking the magic to do something unnatural to it. Consider how that feels and how you'd make yourself change your own nature."

But that was easy, she'd changed her own nature more than once.

But how do I even engage with the magic?

"That's the easy part. Think about how you feel when you cast. There's a part of you that the magic resides in, focus on that place and concentrate."

Alright, she could do that. Well, at least she'd thought she could.

Since she'd spoken to the wizard she'd been wrestling with the notion all day, but with no luck. It was part of why she'd agreed to carry the messages about town, to give her a distraction from her failure. But now, done with her mundane tasks, she found her mind drifting once again to the place that her magic resided.

She could feel it there. It was like a broiling mess of different tempos, sounds, tastes and feelings, all mixed in together and little of it made sense to her.

Just then, someone walked too close to her hiding place and she'd thought they were about to discover her and she ducked back to hide.

She noticed it then, the part of herself that wanted to hide, to stay safe and protected by the shadows. But it was more than just a part of her, it was alive in its own right.

Was that it, her Illusion magic? It was the least tangled, the most clear of the strands and, when she considered it closely and thought about it as an aspect of her need to hide, she could see that it pulsed in purple light.

Excited by her discovery, she considered the other strands. If she could identify her Enchantment magic, perhaps she could guide it into becoming something else. But they were just an amorphous interwoven mess. She couldn't tell one from another.

Then it clicked, she didn't need to. The strand would identify itself if she could remember how it felt to cast an Enchantment spell.

She thought quietly about this. She still only had one and she infrequently cast it, so why had she cast it when she did? Because she'd wanted something?

No, it was more than this and yet simpler... because she wanted to be liked! A strand lit up a dull yellow. *Yes! Now, how do I want you to identify this ring?*

And then it hit her. *I want this ring to like me, but I don't know what it is or what it does? Can you help it like me?*

The thought was too simplistic and was not enough to work. She drifted off for a time, lost in thought and experiments. But nothing she tried worked.

Nothing until, from far away, she felt a presence, his presence. A tiny strand of the bond they'd once held, but it was there and it held with it a simple truth, a promise. That wherever they both were they would find one another. So excited was she that she lost her train of thought.

Ninetoes was alive! He was lost but was on his way here.

Then there was only one thing for it, she must prepare for his arrival and to do that she needed to work this out. And that when it dawned on her, she already had.

I want to trust this ring and all it offers me, like I trust my Master. Can you help me to learn to trust it?

Within her mind information scrolled by in an instant and she knew. She'd created her first spell!

> **LIBBY'S LABELLING - LEVEL 1**
> ENCHANTMENT
> CASTING TIME - 1 SECOND
> MANA COST - 50 POINTS
> DURATION - CONCENTRATION
> LVL 1. REVEALS THE SIMPLE TRUTHS ABOUT
> UNCOMMON OBJECTS OR CREATURES OR THE
> UNCOMMON PROPERTIES OF AN OBJECT.

Ergh! The name could use some work but she was stunned nonetheless. She, a squirrel, had her very own, unique spell. She took a moment to calm herself down before investigating the magical ring that Foresto had given her, casting the spell upon it.

> **RING OF MANA - EXCELLENT, UNCOMMON**
> PROPERTIES: INCREASES THE WEARER'S MANA
> POOL BY A FACTOR OF 1.5.

Really? It just increases my mana? Foresto couldn't have just told me that?

She knew of course that Foresto had been trying to teach her something and it had worked.

She was already in motion before she realised where she was going and within moments she was gliding through the evening sky towards the old wizard's house to tell him the good news.

Beneath her the townsfolk were once again performing their evening rituals. Since the first attack and with so many more folk in town, the people had developed the habit of eating communally. Mistress Emblyn and a team of cooks spent all day cooking and preparing food for the entire community so that everyone could focus on the task at hand.

Now, in her own small way, Libby felt like she was contributing. It wasn't obvious and it might not save anyone's life, but she'd unlocked something powerful, she just knew it.

Catching an updraft, she floated higher and caught sight of the Adventurers exiting through the west gate. She still didn't trust the others, especially not Tarquin and so, rather than head straight to Foresto's she decided to follow the party and safeguard Sariel.

CHAPTER 28
CHOICES

Vortiga and Ninetoes left behind Torgan's Tears and made their way into the forest. Their first order of business was to hunt. They had to eat. Soon.

Conveniently the pair were already adept at hunting and due to the wild nature of the region, the woods were teeming with life and within an hour they had caught a pair of bunnies and already had them roasting on a magically produced fire.

Neither of them particularly wanted to stop long enough to cook the meat, but both of them were already feeling the effects of their hunger, so they decided to make the best of it and, while Vortiga watched over the food, Ninetoes Identified the weapons and items they'd taken from Torgan's tomb.

Wanting to save the best for last, he started with the sword Vortiga had used to smash through the serpent's magical shield.

> **MAGEBANE** - EXCELLENT, VERY RARE
> PROPERTIES: +5% STRENGTH AND ENDURANCE.
> CAPABLE OF PASSING THROUGH MAGICAL
> SHIELDS OF RESPECTED RANK OR LOWER.

Well, that certainly explained how Vortiga had managed to slice straight through the monster's magical protections. It had certainly been a stroke of good luck that, of all the magical swords present, the Warrior had chosen the one that would save them.

Ninetoes even commented on this to Vortiga.

"When you grabbed that staff, something happened to the serpent and it lost its control of me and what's more, it didn't seem aware. I had only seconds to grab something and attack and, I don't know, I just *knew* that this sword was the answer."

Ninetoes stared back, a little confused. He'd felt a similar surety and confidence in his actions after he'd taken the Staff. Was the Staff controlling them somehow? He'd heard of sentient magical items, but he didn't think that this was what the Staff was, at least, he didn't hear any voices inside his head.

"You realise Porsht that this sword is always the perfect weapon to kill *you* with, don't you?" Vortiga's wry tone and toothy grin shook Ninetoes out of his reveries. Her words were said with an innocent tone, but she had proven time and time again, what a deadly foe she was.

"Let me see what else we have and then we can decide how to divide the loot," he said, in a feeble attempt to change the topic.

When they'd ransacked the treasure hoard they'd had the time to grab a small selection of magical jewellery and a pair of magical boots. Ninetoes took them time to analyse each of these, sharing what he'd found with Vortiga.

BOOTS OF LEAPING - FINE, UNCOMMON
PROPERTIES: ALLOWS THE WEARER TO CAST
FOXALL'S SPRING THREE TIMES PER DAY.

RING OF LESSER MIND SHIELDING - FINE, UN-
COMMON
PROPERTIES: INCREASES THE WEARER'S RE-
SISTANCE TO MENTAL ATTACKS BY 25%.

"Well, all of those sound most useful to me, I suppose you could use the boots?" Vortiga offered magnanimously.

"Ha!" The cheek of it. If it hadn't been for him, they'd have never made it out of the tomb alive. But he couldn't really fault her logic, save on one point. While Charisma wasn't really an important stat for the mage, it did help to improve his Will score and, while he wasn't totally certain about how it functioned, he did want to improve it. "I think you need the boots more than I. The amulet however, is useful to me."

Vortiga just nodded and collected the other items, pulling the boots onto her bare and filthy feet. Ninetoes moved onto the scrap of parchment that he'd secured from the dead mage. Retrieving the other, screwed up and slightly sodden piece that was still in his pocket, he took a deep breath and cast Mending. To his sincere relief the spell took hold and the two pieces sealed themselves together. Ninetoes took a moment to study the spell scroll.

TALLY'S POCKET
CONJURATION
CASTING TIME - TEN MINUTES
MANA COST - 500 POINTS
DURATION - PERMANENT
ALLOWS THE CASTER TO CREATE A TINY
POCKET DIMENSION, LARGE ENOUGH FOR ONE
ITEM. AN ITEM STORED WITHIN CAN WEIGH

> NO MORE THAN 5 POUNDS AND CAN BE SUM-
> MONED DIRECTLY INTO THE CASTER'S HAND
> OR INTO AN UNOCCUPIED SPACE WITHIN 5
> FEET OF THEM.
>
> ONLY ONE ITEM CAN BE STORED IN THIS WAY
> AND A SUBSEQUENT CASTING OF THE SPELL
> WILL REPLACE THE ORIGINAL ITEM.

The spell seemed interesting, until its purpose became clear. The person casting this could hide an object in the space and retrieve it whenever they wanted. What's more, because it was a ritual spell he could cast it now without the need of his Spellbook. The spell also required only one component, the item that was being stored.

With a sure idea of exactly what he'd be casting the spell upon, Ninetoes finally cast Identify onto the Staff. This time more was revealed, but it was clear that it still held secrets to learn.

> **THE GREY STAFF** - ARTEFACT, ARTEFACT
>
> BOUND: NINETOES
>
> PREREQUISITES: SPELLCASTER WITH SKILL LEV-
> ELS IN ALL EIGHT SPELL SCHOOLS.
>
> PROPERTIES: INCREASES WIELDER'S MANA
> POOL BY A FACTOR OF 2.
>
> SIGNATURE SPELL 1: CHOOSE ONE SPELL (BAR-
> RIER), THIS SPELL IS NOW CAST AT A 75% DIS-
> COUNT WHILE HOLDING THE STAFF, AND AT A
> 20% ENHANCEMENT.
>
> *SOME PROPERTIES ARE STILL UNKNOWN.*

An Artefact indeed. Just the two properties he could identify made this one of the most powerful items he'd ever come into contact with. He was a little annoyed that the choice of Signature Spell seemed to have been already made for him, but seeing as it had probably saved his life, he wasn't complaining.

He also wasn't positive what being 'Bound' meant, but he had an idea that it meant it couldn't be forcefully taken from him.

While wielding the Staff he could cast Barrier for a little less than thirteen points of mana and with a pool that was twice as large! Even without the bonuses he'd lost when some of his magic items were stolen by Tarquin and the other Adventurers, Ninetoes now had a mana pool of seven hundred points!

Even as battered and bruised as the pair were, Ninetoes felt powerful and in that moment he resolved himself to his next course of action. While things were relatively quiet, Ninetoes cast Tally's Pocket onto the Staff.

The Staff disappeared but Ninetoes could still 'feel' the Staff in his hand. A thought was all it took to summon his newest toy to his hand.

For he knew must come next, he needed to at least to try and avoid a fight, so he willed the Staff into the 'pocket'.

Seating himself onto a log, Ninetoes took a moment to organise his thoughts and then addressed Vortiga. "I believe that we are at an impasse."

"Oh, how so?" The hobgoblin's words seemed mundane enough, but Ninetoes recognised the stiffness in her features.

"Now that we are free of the dungeon we must choose where we go next. I go to Raveslan to offer whatever help I can to the people there. If I am in time that means I'll be fighting your people. What do you plan to do?"

Vortiga looked up from the fire. "I also seek to reach my people and join the assault. Even if I am too late to sack the human town, I will be there when we find the enclave of the Dakhec Druul."

Ninetoes kept his features impassive. "So, you still intend to attack my people?" His fists clenched as he spoke and he watched Vortiga closely.

She didn't answer right away and he could see the conflicting emotions warring within for control of her face. "I do, but I do not seek your death and so I ask you to travel far away."

"Ha! If I were to do that I really would be the Porsht that you have named me. Thus we are at an impasse. I cannot allow you to return to your people and tell them everything you've learned and you cannot allow me to return and warn my people."

"This is so. What do you suggest?"

Ninetoes' shoulders slumped in resignation. "I suggest that we fight. At least the loser will gain a Warrior's death and a place in Starm's Halls. Furthermore, it serves neither of us to wait. This place is as good as any other." Slowly he rose to his feet, keeping his movements as smooth as possible.

Ninetoes truly didn't want this, but Vortiga had shown herself to be an immovable force. Despite everything that had happened, she was still set upon her original course, one that he couldn't allow her to complete.

VORTIGA

Mirroring Ninetoes' actions, Vortiga straightened from her position, kneeling before the fire. She didn't want this anymore than it appeared the Porsht did, but it seemed they had little choice. He was an Adventurer and a member of the Dakhec Druul and her people were their sworn enemies. The two tribes had been at war for more than a century, the fate of the Druul was written in the stars and she simply had no choice but to do as her people did.

Rolling some of the tension from her shoulders, Vortiga slowly drew her new sword, revelling for a moment in the feeling of strength and surety it offered. She'd watched the Porsht fight many times, however, and was not foolish enough to believe that he would be an easy kill.

Closing her eyes briefly she began a prayer to Starm but then checked herself.

Ryuna had seen her safely from the city of Pamor and perhaps the Lady of Luck would see her through this battle as well. While her eyes were closed she listened intently for any hint of an attack but when she opened them, Ninetoes was standing in the same place, although he now held the staff he'd taken from the tomb.

As if by an unsaid command both hobgoblins fell into fighting stances and began circling the fire. It occurred to her then that Ninetoes had chosen his position carefully. He knew as well as she, that he had the advantage at range, and that now, with her new sword, she would be devastating when she closed with him. She must be quick.

With a final breath to relax her muscles, Vortiga surged forward. Faster than a wildfire consuming dry grass, she leaped forward *through* the fire performing a perfect Leaping Salmon, the tip of her new sword cutting the air and aimed directly for Ninetoes' neck.

But the mage wasn't there. He'd clearly anticipated her attack and teleported away.

Reasserting her guard, she turned on the spot. He was still in the clearing and hadn't travelled far, but it was far enough.

Levelling his staff, he cast and a bolt of reddish-blue light leapt from its tip and shot towards her. The range was too far, however, and Vortiga had plenty of time to dodge. Leaping forwards at a forty-five-degree angle, she evaded the attack and charged forward.

If she could only close the distance and keep his attacks off her, perhaps she could wear down his mana pool.

He fired twice more as she dashed towards him. The first she avoided but the second splashed across her shoulder and nearly knocked her over. She expected to feel the horrid sensation of her body beginning to wilt from his life-draining magic, but it didn't come. For some reason he didn't seem to be using his most potent attacks.

But why? Perhaps he was simply trying to lull her into making a mistake. She would not be so easily undone.

As she closed this time she performed a scything cut. She didn't expect the attack to connect, but its momentum would allow her to turn more quickly and perhaps close the distance to wherever he teleported to next.

That's why she was so surprised when her sword met his staff with a thud.

Vortiga was an expert, however, and was ever the pragmatist, so with the barest flick of her wrists she tipped her blade back and struck for the opposite flank. The move was precise but Ninetoes managed to block it as she knew he would.

Placing a foot forward, she tucked it behind her opponent's and shoved with all her strength, sending Ninetoes tumbling backwards as she lanced her blade forwards.

The Porsht managed to turn his tumble into a roll and so her sword only managed to skewer and tear a line through his fancy cloak.

"Argh! What is it with things attacking my fucking cloak?" Ninetoes seemed strangely enraged by the damage and he leapt towards her, even though her blade still pointed towards him.

But, rather than impale himself on her sword, he teleported at the last moment and in the blink of an eye, she heard his foot land behind her. She began to perform Chase the Dragon, but something blasted into her back and the manoeuvre became a stumble. Once again she braced herself for his necromancy magic but once again it didn't come.

Vortiga righted herself and made another charge for him, only to slide on her first step as the ground beneath her became slick with a dark slime.

Try as she might, Vortiga couldn't right herself or reclaim her stance. But now, her hands as slippery as the rest of her, she lost the grip of her sword and it slid out of her reach.

In desperation she attempted to scoot along after it, but something arrested her movement and then her body contracted as lightning and pain shocked through her.

Panting heavily with exertion, she rolled over to see Ninetoes stood at the grease's edge, his staff pointed towards her and her sword resting at his feet. She was utterly at his mercy and yet still the killing blow didn't come.

She locked her eyes onto his face, expecting to see mockery there, but what she found was worse. His eyes looked at her piteously. "Stand down Vortiga, you've lost." His words were toneless. They both knew that she couldn't, her honour dictated a Warrior's death.

She didn't answer, an intense feeling of shame clouded her mind and she felt only anger; towards Ninetoes but even more so towards herself.

535

Fruitlessly she slipped and slid about on the ground attempting and failing to find purchase.

Finally, splashing her hands down she looked up at him. "Kill me then you coward! Do it!" she screamed at him.

"No Vortiga. No. Give me your word that you won't join the assault on my Raveslan or my people and I'll let you live."

"Never! Kill me porsht, kill me you fucking- you fucking-arrrrgghhhh!" she ended by screaming incoherently in anger and frustration. Tears burned her eyes and she didn't understand why. She desperately wanted to tear him apart, to rip through the human village and shit on the remnants of his people.

But then? Then she thought of Bess and Ninetoes and even Lowen. All of them had shown her a kindness of sorts and yet she'd offered none of them anything but hatred. *Argh!* Why was she so confused?

"Vortiga?" His voice was barely a whisper. "Let us end this."

Looking up she could see the sincerity of his words reflected in his eyes. He truly meant her no harm, she could end this now, the two of them still allies.

No. You are Nechtsarm.

The voice filled her mind. It sounded like hers but it wasn't. *Then was it?*

It didn't matter, it was right wherever it came from. She was Nechtsarm and he was her enemy, she could no more choose to let him live as she could choose to stop breathing, it was written in her very soul.

The Porsht leaned his staff forward slightly, perhaps to offer her aid and perhaps to strike the killing blow, it didn't matter, that extra inch was all she needed. Launching forward she grabbed the staff and yanked it towards her.

The mage yelled in surprise and alarm and took a step forward to balance himself, only to plant his foot onto the grease. He slid forward and Vortiga drew her dagger, preparing to ram it up into his throat as he fell upon it.

But something happened. Something that she had not foreseen and, based upon the look of surprise on his face, neither had Ninetoes. The Staff lit up with the same, strange, grey energy that it had been wrapped in when they'd found it in the tomb.

This time, however, the energy leaped from the Staff along her arm and along his. For the briefest of moments, the two of them were wrapped in the scintillating power of the Staff. For Vortiga, she saw everything Ninetoes was, everything he'd been, done and become.

And in that moment, she finally recognised that she had a *Choice*. She could choose what happened next. Choose whether she rammed her blade home and went to re-join her people and destroy his. Or she could choose to join him on his journey. Or, indeed, she could choose anything.

Vortiga had led a life of struggle. Everything she had, she'd earned. But she'd never had a Choice before. Always the way forward had always been defined for her.

Vortiga made her Choice.

CHAPTER 29
DEMONS!

Sariel went ahead. Not because Tarquin told her to, but because this was her job. She was the scout, the pathfinder. It was her job to alert the party to danger before it crept up on them.

She admitted, however, that with these demons that wasn't a difficult thing to do. While some of them were stealthy, like the giant cat that had nearly killed her, most of the demons were stupid, noisy little things. Deadly, there was no doubt, but only if you were foolish.

That's why she knew exactly where the main bunch were; roughly a hundred yards west, tearing some poor woodland animal to pieces and making a hell of a racket about it. But it was the other type that worried Sariel. Had it not been for Libby watching her back that stealthy demon would have had her.

What she'd give to have Libby with her now.

You called?

Libby? What are you doing here?

I saw you all leaving and decided to keep watch. I won't fight but I can feed you information and keep an eye on Tarquin.

Thank you but I'm not worried about him at the moment.

Well you should be, he's managed to flank all the way to the far side of the clearing.

What, how'd he get there? I only found this bunch of demons a minute ago. It was strange indeed, but it was good tactics, so she couldn't fault his logic. She was just surprised by how quickly and quietly he must be moving to make it so far without alerting the demons.

Well, I can't speak to that. But the others are about fifty yards to your rear.

Do you see any of those cat-like demons? she asked.

I do not and I've been keeping a close watch.

Well, it's getting dark so we'd better get this done. Keep watch for me?

That's why I'm here.

For the next couple of minutes, Sariel stalked closer to the group of demons. They weren't really eating the animal; a doe it turned out, rather they just seemed to be playing with it and she managed to sneak all the way up to the clearing's edge.

This time there was another, new demon type. A massive, brute of a beast with four thickly muscled arms and a monkey-like face. Its skin was the same oily black as many of the other demons they'd seen but when its muscles bulged she could see thick strands of red sinew as well.

This massive thug was also the only one eating the deer, ripping off huge chunks with its flat teeth and masticating slowly. It was clear from the way the other demons were acting that this monster was the alpha and so it became her primary target. She cast Spirit Knowledge to see if she could learn any weaknesses.

LESSER DEMON OF STRENGTH - LEVEL 10

PRIME STAT - STRENGTH

PRIME TRAITS - WRENCH, ENGORGE

300/200 HP

2500XP

Gods, this was only a Lesser Demon? And why were its hit points higher than its maximum? It must have something to do with one of its abilities. Honestly, she didn't like the sound of either of them and would certainly be keeping her distance.

She selected her favourite spell and prepared to cast it onto the big oaf. At the same time, she made the call of an owl, the signal to prepare for attack. A few seconds later, she heard three answering calls. But a couple of the smaller demons sat up straighter and at this the brutish demon took note, craning its head around, while slowly chewing.

Bashing one of the smaller demons aside, it got to its feet and sniffed the air. They were about to lose their surprise attack.

Sariel finished her casting and watched as motes of bright light landed on the biggest demon's head. The half-elf was already asking the lady to dance and, in one fluid motion brought the fletching to her cheek and calmly finished her count, "...four, five!"

Her missile flew fast and true and sank into the monster's eye, at least three inches of the shaft disappearing into the creature's skull. If it had been any normal beast that would have been enough, but this was a demon and instead it just roared with pain and anger and beat its chest, the sound igniting the other demons into a frenzy.

But Sariel had learned an important lesson from their first fight for these creatures and that's why, halfway through the brute's call to arms, a soft pop came from the beast's ear and the Lesser Demon of Strength collapsed to the floor.

The silence that followed was deafening. Each and every other demon was shrieking with excitement and anger one second, was struck dumb at the sight of their boss' collapse. Then, their own nature kicked in. Forgetting that they were under attack, the smaller demons set upon the corpse of the largest one.

By the time the Adventurers broke from cover and attacked the demons, there was little left of the massive one. Some of the smaller ones put up a bit of a fight and Tarquin took a nasty gash to the arm, but An'rik's magic healed it quickly enough and the Adventurers headed back to the safety of the town patting one another on the back and congratulating not only another victory but the warm feeling of having Levelled Up once again.

"What was that you used to kill the big one Sariel?" asked Anrik.

"Xynian's Message. It does extra damage, kind of like your Divine Strike, but less powerful." She showed An'rik her Character Sheet.

XYNIAN'S MESSAGE - LEVEL 5
DIVINATION
CASTING TIME - 1 SECOND
MANA COST - 50 POINTS
DURATION - 1 MINUTE
LVL 1. XYNIAN'S LIGHT HIGHLIGHTS THE TARGET AND DEALS AN ADDITIONAL 2-16 RADIANT DAMAGE PER HIT.

"But it also marked it right? I saw those little flecks of light fall on it before you fired."

"Yeah, they didn't serve much purpose in this battle because the attack killed it, but it would mark an enemy and make them easier to see. It also adds damage to each attack I make. I think I must have scored a critical to kill it outright."

"Indeed, you did well Sariel. But, perhaps next time we should have one of the heavier hitters make the first strike, like An'rik or myself," chimed in Tarquin, condescendingly.

Sariel just ignored him. She hadn't expected her attack to kill the demon but she wasn't going to tell them that.

LIBBY

From her perch in the trees she watched the Adventurers leave the clearing, as what little that remained of the demons evaporated into nothing.

She knew it was dangerous to stay out in the woods alone, especially at night, but during the battle she'd seen something very odd and wanted to check it out.

As she'd talked with Sariel before the fight, she'd watched as a couple more demons joined the group in the clearing. They'd come almost directly the same path as Tarquin.

While the warrior had improved his stealth certainly, she had still been able to see him easily enough, and she was curious how he could have come that way without the demons spotting him.

Now that the clearing was empty of threats, she glided from tree to tree in the direction they'd come from and before too long she found something. She heard it before she could see it, a strange sound like a clothesline flapping in the wind, then she saw it.

A strange window that appeared to be carved into the bole of a tree. But as she came closer she realised that it wasn't attached to the tree but instead it seemed to float just in front of it.

As she closed the distance to it, she realised that she could see figures moving around on the other side of the window and then, with a spark of energy something stepped through.

Libby's heart caught in her throat at the sight of it, as she'd thought it dead, but there was no mistaking the way it moved or the sharp glint of its eyes. It was the same demon that had nearly killed her and Sariel the first time they'd faced the demons.

She was concealed high up in the tree and the creature was moving away from her at a pace, so she risked casting her new spell, hoping to learn something of use.

LESSER DEMON OF STEALTH - LEVEL ???
PRIME STAT - DEXTERITY
PRIME TRAITS - CAMOUFLAGE, FEAR
300/300 HP
2500XP

Annoyingly the spell hadn't told her much she didn't know, but as this thought occurred to her, the words of the description changed.

```
ZAG'THONAR - LEVEL 20
PRIME STAT - DEXTERITY
PRIME TRAITS - CAMOUFLAGE, FEAR
375/400 HP
2500XP
```

As she tried to comprehend the meaning of the new information that had been revealed, the demon stopped, tilted its head and sniffed the air.

Ha! Strange that I should smell your scent again my plump little prey. Where are you now little on-

But Libby didn't hear what else the demon had to say. As soon as it had tilted its head she'd bolted. Her pudgy little belly was gone now, however, in its place was sleek and powerful muscle. Libby had also become far more adept at moving from tree to tree and she could now leap at least twice the distance she had before. Still, she didn't stop moving until she'd cleared the walls into Raveslan and only then to catch her breath.

From the wall's top she stared out into the dark forest, scanning the gloom for her foe, but she found nothing and after a few minutes of this silent vigil, she headed for Foresto's house.

She needed to warn him and to discuss what the strange window was and what it could mean.

As she soared towards the small house, she noted the old mage had left the window open for her. He'd explained of course that not just anything could fly through his windows, open or not and that the defences in place made the prospect a dangerous one, but the open portal was clearly an invitation to the errant Familiar.

Tucking in her legs, she took the risk and barrelled into the library, landing with a soft thump into one of the overstuffed chairs. From there she leapt once again onto the chair's back and on through the doorway into the workroom.

Foresto was once again working on his golem, this time he was adding heavily armoured plates to its chest but he looked up with a smile as she alighted on the workbench before him.

"Ah Libby dearest, but whatever's the matter?"

Demons, in the forest. Quickly tell him.

"Ah yes, Sariel mentioned yesterday. I may have to set the Adventurer's Guild a Quest to find the source if we survive the assault."

No, there's more. A… er, I don't know a hole or, um rip in the forest. Quickly, tell him. Her mind speech took on a more frantic tone at the wasted time that the golem spent relaying the message in its slow drawl.

"Wait, do you mean a tear? Like a window into another place, somewhere harsh looking?"

After she'd seen the cat-like demon, Libby hadn't really been paying attention to what was on the other side, but she guessed so. *Tell him yes. Also, tell him that I saw the same demon a second time, the one we killed the other day.*

"Oh, then this is worrying indeed. The was a portal to the demonic plane, although what caused such a thing to open is beyond me. Worse still, the tear will only grow until bigger, far more powerful demons are able to pass through it."

And what about the demon?

"Oh, you didn't kill it the first time, not really. Once a demon is destroyed in our realm it reforms in its own."

So, what should we do?

"Hmmm, nothing for now, but we should gather the Adventurers in the morning and close this tear."

They felt it before they heard it. The rhythmic beating of hundreds of feet marching in step. Then they heard the drums, beating the same rhythm and Foresto's face paled. "But, we're supposed to have another day."

"Quickly, head to the tavern and make sure the Adventurers are aware," Foresto commanded, his voice had changed subtly and it brooked no argument. Libby wrenched her tired body into action, dashing for the table's edge and into a shallow glide out through the door.

From there she climbed her way ever higher until she reached the crenellated top of the gatehouse and swooped into the town and on towards the Green Hill Inn where Sariel and the others were staying.

But she needn't have made the effort. As she climbed she could hear voices of alarm being raised and echoed throughout the town and, by the time she'd reached the Inn the sound of five hundred ironshod boots, marching in perfect step, had woken the entire town and the walls were lined with townsfolk.

Taking a perch on the tallest rooftop she could find, Libby looked out onto a sea of armoured goblinoids. Within the walls, the drowsy, half-dressed townsfolk, most of them unarmed seemed a paltry defence.

A trumpet split the night and every footstep stopped instantly. The sight caused a wave of silence to crash into the onlookers and fearful looks passed from one face to another.

In the hobgoblin ranks a disturbance could be seen. Responding to the barked orders of a select few, the army divided in half down the middle and then again until four squares had formed, each with its own flag hanging limply in the moonlight. But it was the precision with which all of this was achieved that was most frightening, the packed ranks moving as one.

The quick clip of hooves announced the arrival of a single rider, sat atop a brown destrier and bedecked in plate armour the colour of the darkest blood red. As he reached the front of the lines he pulled sharply on the reins and the horse stopped within a step.

The rider removed his helmet with one hand and drew his longsword with the other, pointing it to the sky. "To the people of this village I speak and to the gods above! I Ogren, Curn of the Nechtsarm, do give you my word. If you open your gates and lay down your arms I will let you live. I offer this only once."

The people of Raveslan stood, paralysed with fear and unable to answer. A murmur of concern and disagreement rippled through the townsfolk. "There are so many." "How can we stop such an army?" "We don't stand a chance." "Where are the Adventurers?"

Libby could tell that the people were about to break, someone needed to do something. She began dashing along the roof, quickly thinking of what she could do. Then someone spoke up from nearby. It was quiet at first but it grew in power and volume and, for the first and only time, she was happy to hear Tarquin's self-assured and arrogant voice.

"This town is not as defenceless as you might think." As he spoke, the faces of the townsfolk stopped looking like prey. "There are those here who stand against your tyranny and brutality, cur."

The people started to nod and a warm murmur began to pass through them.

"The Red Crew stand with the people of Raveslan and I call tomorrow a red day for you." A ripple of agreement began. "Who's with me?"

The crowd broke into a chorus of cheers and clapping. Those that had weapons bashed them on the wooden board or against shields, while those without stamped their feet. The noise quickly became deafening and easily a match for the marching the hobgoblins had made.

Below them Ogren turned his horse and trotted back to his lines and then off behind them, before disappearing into the treeline. The ranks of hobgoblins turned on the spot and began marching back the way they had come. They didn't go far, however, clearing intent upon setting up camp just outside the walls.

The Nechtsarm had finally arrived in Raveslan.

***

PORTSMOUTH, 2017

"If you don't mind Bruce, I've actually written a little summit for this bit," interrupted Tony as Solveg leaned forward to speak.

"Oh, um, of course. You don't mind, do you Solly?" Bruce asked, taken a little by surprise. Tony certainly knew how to play, but he'd never seemed particularly bothered about roleplaying. Still, he reasoned, perhaps the team was finally coming together.

"No, I don't mind," Solveg smiled and Bruce's stomach flipped.

He still couldn't believe it was going so well. Any relationship he'd had before would've fallen to pieces ages ago, but with Solly things were just… easy. It helped that they shared a love of board games and the two of them were putting in loads of extra time RPing the stuff with Libby, but even that came easy. His only current problem was Tony's obsession with having regular demon attacks. Ok, so it was a class ability, but did it mean he *had* to use it every day in game? It was seriously getting in the way of the story and worse still, he knew Solly had realised something was going on but he couldn't talk to her about it.

Still, if the party survived the battle he had loads of great twists and turns for them.

"…so can I roll or what?"

"Er, sorry?" Bruce had definitely been drifting off there while Tony had been talking.

"My speech, it was pretty good huh guys?"

"Oh, oh yeah, it was great and you, er, can have advantage on the roll," he fumbled a reply.

Tony rolled two d20s and everyone watched. "A nat one and a nat twenty, what're the odds?"

"Well, actually-"

"The townsfolk start, um, stamping their feet and clashing their weapons against their shields." He cut off Felix before he could do maths and ruin the vibe. "They start cheering and their calls drown out the noise of the hobgoblins marching. Nice work Tony. Well, that's probably a good place to leave it for tonight. Next time we'll do the battle for Raveslan. Can you guys get here a little early, it might take a while."

A chorus of agreement circled the table as the players stood up and started packing away their things. "Er, Solly could you hang back I've got some-"

"Oh, would you two give it a rest, we all know you're bangin'." Interrupted Tony.

"Er…"

"We were wondering how long it'd take you to work it out, we were going to tell you next week, after we've saved Raveslan. Right Bruce?"

"Ha! If that ain't a warnin' not to kill off her player next week, I don't know what is," quipped Felix.

"Yeah, well whatever, just so long as there's no favouritism. We all worked hard to get this far," Tony pointed out.

Bruce wasn't sure that was strictly true. Sure, the rest of the party had roleplayed their asses off and every combat he'd run had been well-played, even by Daph.

But Tony? If it wasn't combat, he may as well have not been present. Still, he didn't want anyone to think he was playing favourites, especially not Solveg.

"No problem guys. Please make sure you level up and come ready for a fight, this is gonna be some battle." And he wasn't kidding. On paper, there was just no way they could win, the hobs were simply too many. Even with the ideas he had to help, he wasn't sure it'd be enough.

"Alright guys, I'll be seeing you." Felix, never much for hanging around to chat, was always the first to go.

"Hey Felix, can we get a lift?" And goodbye Daph and Ton, always too lazy to walk.

"Yeah sure."

"Bye guys."

Solveg leaned into the door, clicking it shut. "So, the proverbial cat is out of the bag then."

"Yeah, sorry."

"Don't be. I'm not. Now I can proudly tell all the ladies that you're my man."

"'All the ladies'? Which ladies would those be?" He asked.

"My flatmates. They're curious why I keep coming home from game night all rosy-cheeked. Now I can tell them, it's because I've been having my wicked way with a gorgeous, dark-haired man."

"Gorgeous?"

"Damn right you're gorgeous. Now get upstairs before I tear your clothes off right here and make love to you all over your miniatures."

"Oh hell no. Those are expensive. But the vigorous love-making sounds great."

Bruce clicked the light off and chased the woman he was quickly falling in love with upstairs.

Left alone on the table, the dice that would decide the fate of Raveslan sat alone. Waiting.

CHAPTER 30
A FOOLISH PLAN

Ninetoes blinked. Vortiga blinked back at him. He'd seen the dagger coming and knew that he was probably done for. He'd never strengthened his Wizard Armour and she'd had him dead to rights.

And then she just dropped the dagger.

Ninetoes' own momentum had carried him into and over Vortiga and now the two hobgoblins lay next to one another on the grease, the Staff of Grey held between them. He had no idea what had happened, only that he hadn't consciously made the Staff ignite in grey fire.

"So?" he tried.

"So," she agreed.

"Now what?" he clarified.

"Now we get off the floor."

Ninetoes couldn't fault her logic and now that she'd dropped the dagger he was reasonably sure that he could cast another Shocking Strike onto her if she made to grab it, so he dropped his Grease spell and the two of them rolled onto their knees and stood, slowly to their feet.

"What did you do to me? Was it some kind of mind control?" she asked hesitantly.

Ninetoes stared at her, his own confusion written clearly across his face. "I have no idea. I'm also not sure that *I* did anything."

"What?"

"I think the Staff did it."

"But... how?"

"Honestly, I have no idea. I also have no clue what it did. In fact, the only thing that I'm sure of, is that it had very little to do with me." He shrugged. "What do you think happened?"

Vortiga stared at Ninetoes. Clearly, she had more questions of her own but she saw that Ninetoes had no answers, so she chose to answer him instead. "I am also uncertain, but I can tell you this. When I touched the staff, I realised that, despite who I am meant to be, I could choose to be someone else."

Ninetoes stared back, dumbfounded. "Er... what?"

"I think that all the staff did was make me understand that I didn't have to follow the path laid before me and, that if I chose to, I could follow a different path."

"Does that mean you're not going to try to attack my people?" he asked hesitantly.

"I don't know, maybe?" she offered, still plainly confused. "All I can say, is that before, when I considered that question, there was no doubt in my mind that I should... must, attack the Dakhec Druul. That because I am Nechtsarm, the only recourse for me was to stamp you out. But now, now I just don't know."

"So, what does that mean for us? Are we good?" Ninetoes asked, still cautious of being so close.

"We are." Then, when she saw his curious expression, she elaborated. "I realised that I could, indeed, choose not to kill you. Actually, I realised that I do not, in fact, hate you. And, while we're not about to become the best of friends, you have treated me with honour and shown me trust. How can I do any less?"

Ninetoes watched Vortiga closely. She'd made no move for either of her weapons and, he reasoned, she had already given up her best chance of killing him. Nonetheless, he needed to show her that he did, once again, trust her not to kill him.

Reaching down, he picked up the elven dagger. Holding it carefully by the back of the blade, he offered her the hilt.

Vortiga stared at the blade and smiled, perhaps the first and most genuine smile she'd ever given him and reached out for the knife, only to stop a few inches short of taking it.

"I'm grateful for the loan, but now that I have this sword, I no longer need it."

Ninetoes considered this. The blade was magical, the first magic weapon he'd ever owned, although he hadn't realised how powerful it was at the time. What's more, to him the dagger could be so much more.

Moreover, without his own sword, he was left with only the Staff and, while this was a powerful item, it wouldn't serve him well in close combat. Nodding to her, he sheathed the blade and returned her smile.

"So, will you come with me?"

"While I have no intention of fighting against my own people, I will travel with you and see if I can turn them away."

"Do you really think that really is possible?" he asked, still shocked at her change of heart.

"I do not. But then a few minutes ago I considered my own feelings on the matter impossible to change as well, so... well, frankly I have no idea. All I know for certain is that it is my Choice to go and find out," she concluded.

Ninetoes wasn't sure he completely believed her and was still concerned that this might all be some elaborate ruse, but a strange feeling had permeated her words and, with little other choice but to murder her, he decided to take her at her word.

"The only issue I see now, is that without transport, there is little hope that we can reach Raveslan in time to stop my people from sacking it."

Ninetoes grinned. "As it happens, I might just have an answer to that."

Vortiga stared back, cringing at the mage's signature smile. "What?"

"Well, it is, at best, a dangerously foolish plan."

"Oh gods. I've changed my mind. No, stop grinning at me like that."

"Oh, don't worry. I'm sure it'll be fine."

"Argh! Why must you always say that?"

***

Sometime later Ninetoes found himself hunkered down in a freshly un-covered foxhole. The simple hiding place had originally been dug by a member of the Emerald Wolves.

Finding the site of the Wolves' intended ambush hadn't been difficult and once there, they'd been able to reason that the area was clearly part of the manticore's hunting ground. Once they'd established that, they'd spent what was left of the day preparing the area.

Ninetoes had dug out a number of the foxholes to give him and Vor-tiga cover and somewhere to hide. Meanwhile Vortiga had hunted for enough small animals to entice the monster into the clearing, much as the Wolves had done before them.

Unfortunately, neither Vortiga or Ninetoes knew very much about the monstrous creatures, but they knew that they weren't particularly clever and that baiting the creature had worked once before, so they just had to hope that the manticore would be foolish enough for fall for the same gambit twice.

In the hopes of encouraging this further, Vortiga has cut open some of her catches and splayed their entrails all over the clearing.

They knew that the monster's most dangerous weapon, at least for them, was its ranged tail spike attack. These had already proven to be able to puncture armour, both mundane and magical. And so their greatest chance of success lay in remaining mobile, which is why Ninetoes had dug out as many of the holes as he could, so that the pair could bolt from cover to cover.

Beyond that their plan was pretty basic. They would use an illusion to bait the manticore into landing and hopefully trigger a large snare they'd made from the ropes left behind by the Wolves.

While trapped the pair would unload as much damage as they could onto the monster. Then, once it was dead they could start the difficult part.

With his enlarged mana pool, Ninetoes cast Cloaking Shadows on both of them and they were now hunkered down in separate foxholes on opposite sides of the clearing. Waiting.

And, as fate would have it, they didn't have long to wait before they heard the familiar sound of the monster's leathery wings. Ninetoes had been keeping a close eye and as soon as he saw the shadow of the manticore pass by, he cast his spell.

Now, while Ninetoes was no master illusionist like Libby and while no, he couldn't make it move, he still thought his deer looked pretty realistic.

"Ha! You think to trick me?" shrieked the sickly-sweet voice. "Come out little trickster. Come out now, and I'll eat you quickly." The eerie voice of the monster slithered across the clearing.

Ninetoes silently cursed, but they'd recognised that this could happen and had planned accordingly. And so he watched as, across the clearing, Vortiga stood up tall from her own hiding place. Gleaming in her ancient armour, she shouted. "No tricks then monster, come and meet my blade."

"Ewwww not another tin knight." It huffed. "Far toooo much work to get all the pieces out of the armours." And so saying, the monster banked and started to fly away.

Vortiga looked to Ninetoes for direction. Thinking quickly, Ninetoes made his choice and stepped out of his own hidey hole. "And what of me beast?"

The manticore turned towards him and he could see the monster fully for the first time.

Still piercing its chest was his cutlass, although the handle and grip were now mangled. Its lion-like head looked at Ninetoes and giggled.

"Ah, there you are little magiker, no more tricks now little dinners; I see your ropesies." *Shit, plan B then.*

But then a look of total recollection passed over the monster's face. "You! You stuck me with this nasty little thorn! You, you die first!" It shrieked, as its tail cracked like a whip and a flight of barbs shot across the clearing.

Luckily, they'd been aimed mostly for Ninetoes and so Vortiga barely had to dodge, but the wizard had no choice but to cast Barrier. The barbs stopped a few inches from Ninetoes' face and then fell to the ground, useless.

Ninetoes and Vortiga were already in motion, however. They'd discussed what they'd witnessed in the previous battle with the monster and had known that if they couldn't snare it, the monster would remain mobile until either it had won or had run out of tail spikes.

Thus, plan B.

Because of the Staff, Ninetoes had the best chance of blocking the manticore's attacks, while Vortiga's job was to distract it as much as she could and so, as the manticore lined itself up for a second barrage, the Warrior ducked behind a tree and snatched a rock from her pouch, winging it at the monster.

Her aim was good and, while it had dealt no damage, its timing distracted the brute and threw off the monster's aim and its second barrage of spikes were easily deflected by Ninetoes' spell.

Checking the creature's tail, Ninetoes could see that perhaps a half of the barbs were gone. Nodding to his ally, he dashed around the clearing's edge and prepared to use his blocking spell again. Once again the monster prepared to fire and Vortiga's rock disrupted the attack, causing the spikes to be all the more simple to stop.

By now, however, the manticore was wise to the tactic and so, instead of attacking Ninetoes, its next barrage went straight at Vortiga. The Warrior was crossing some open ground and, despite diving forwards, shield raised, three barbs punched into her flank.

Ninetoes stared in horror at Vortiga's unmoving form. He could see that while her armour had stopped one of the spikes, two more penetrated her torso and neck. "Ha! Got you tricksy little stone-thrower. Now for you, magicky dinner, oooohooooohoo, I loves the taste of magicks."

The manticore soared upwards to gain height and then loosed two barrages of barbs directly at the wizard, the second almost immediately after the first.

Ninetoes, who'd been running towards his fallen ally, raised his Staff and cast Barrier, but the second flight was too quick for him and, instead of blocking them, the second bombardment passed the immobile first and lanced into Ninetoes' chest with enough force to not only put him down, but also pinned him to the floor, only a few steps away from Vortiga.

"Yes! Ha ha! No more tricksy goblins, just nice sweet meats!" trumpeted the manticore as it looped in celebration and then dropped heavily to the ground.

Strutting over to its meal, the manticore preened itself, picking at its teeth with a clawed forepaw in preparation of such a delicacy. "Mmmmmm, hmmmm. Yes, the one without armours first I thinks, then the other one I'll saves. Yes."

The manticore stepped closer to the pair of foolish warriors, giggling in delight, before leaning forward to sniff at its meal. A disgustingly ecstatic sound emanated from the back of its throat and it nudged at Ninetoes' body.

That was all the prompting the Adventurer needed. Rolling onto his back, he triggered his Portable Projection Field, surrounding himself and the manticore.

Then, while the monster stared at him in surprise, Ninetoes used the monster's shock to let go of the cube and 'step' out of the field, leaving the manticore trapped inside its arcane walls.

The pair of hobgoblins had known from the beginning that they needed to find a way of negating the monster's ranged advantage but that the manticore would only come close enough for their trap to work if it thought they were already dead. And with the prodigious mana boost offered him by the Staff, Ninetoes had plenty of mana to cast Reaper's Sorrow onto both of them.

It had taken some work to convince Vortiga to let the manticore "kill" them, but in the end she hadn't been able to provide a better alternative and so here they were.

Pointing his Staff and with a quick inflection Ninetoes cast Grease beneath the monster's feet. A moment later, he reached out his freehand and cast Arcane Weapon on Vortiga's sword.

As the monster started slipping and sliding the pair took a deep breath. This was the moment of truth.

The way Ninetoes understood the function of the Portable Field was that, when he erected it, he could choose what could pass through it. When he'd done so this time, he'd allowed magic to enter or leave but not matter.

What they weren't sure about, however, as they hadn't been able to test it, was whether Vortiga's blade's special trait would enable it to bypass the shield. This was one reason they'd doubled up and cast Arcane Weapon, hoping that this would help to mask the sword's material components.

As soon as Ninetoes' spell finished chilling her blade with magical frost, Vortiga slashed in a short but precise arc, carving through the magical shield and across the manticore's face.

Ryuna must have been with them, as Ninetoes watched, breath held, as the blade passed through the forcefield and scored a bloody line of carnage and caused the manticore to screech in pain and anger.

"Ahhhh, curses you maggots!"

"Phew!" he muttered.

"Indeed," she responded, before launching into her next attack.

As slippery as the magical grease was, the manticore had four legs and a tail to help stabilise itself and it took barely three seconds for it to regain its balance and begin slashing at the shield.

They had only as long as it took the manticore to break free of its magical prison to deal enough damage to kill it and, as much as he might have wanted to, Ninetoes couldn't use his most potent damage dealing spells because they needed the body to be as functional as possible.

So, while Ninetoes sent bolt after bolt of arcane death into the dome, it was up to Vortiga to do the lion's share of the damage.

Ninetoes, not needing to aim, watched Vortiga work and she really was something to behold. She didn't just stand and hack at their imprisoned foe. Instead, she remained in constant motion, each slice gracefully flowing into the next cut or slash.

She also didn't stay in place and, while the manticore spent itself trying to batter through the same spot, she danced around the edge of the dome, always just outside the shield but close enough to score hit after hit on the monster.

In between blasts of Arcane Bolt, Ninetoes risked a second to cast Identify on the manticore.

Even as his spell triggered, the magical protection field shattered and the manticore surged forwards, death and hatred burning in its eyes.

Ninetoes didn't quail however, and did not retreat. Instead, he dove forward, grabbing what was left of his cutlass, putting all of his weight into driving it further into the monster's breast and tearing deeper into the monster's vital organs.

The manticore screamed in pain and arched its back, pulling the blade out of Ninetoes hands and prepared to leap forward and finish him.

This opening was all Vortiga needed, and she completed a perfect Chase the Dragon as the manticore surged forward from its hind legs, and she drove the tip of her frosted blade straight between the manticore's eyes.

Both the precision of her attack and the monster's momentum sent the blade screaming deep into its brain, killing it instantly. Even still the weight of the monster's inertia drove both the hobgoblins backwards and knocked them down.

Panting heavily, Ninetoes looked across at his enemy-made-ally. "See, I told you-"

"If you finish that sentence Porsht, I will invent a new method for you to breathe."

"- it'd be... er right, yes, now on to step two."

"And you're sure that you'll be able to control this thing once you bring it back?"

"I am," Ninetoes answered more confidently than he felt.

He knew that when he'd fought it previously the manticore was a Level 20 monster, but without the extra mana provided by the Staff of Grey, Ninetoes would have never even attempted what he was about to do.

At 50 mana points per casting Create Undead on the Manticore would cost 1000 mana, far more than Ninetoes had, even with the Staff. Even if he drained all 150 mana from his Gem of Power, he'd still be 150 points short. His Ring of Exanimate Authority, however, allowed him to create undead of up to five Levels higher, but what Ninetoes was unsure about was whether that meant the ring would negate some of the cost, or not.

Worse still, if the spell took all of his mana at once, he'd collapse from mana depletion long before he finished casting.

And, of course, all that was based upon the principle that monsters didn't gain Experience and Levels. If they did and the manticore's recent victory over the Emerald Wolves had been enough to gain a Level or two, this could all go horribly wrong.

As he completed his period of Meditation, he shook away such doubts and stood up straight. *This is going to work.*

Maintaining his seated position and staying in as meditative a state as he could. Ninetoes calmed his breathing and began focussing his will. Keeping his breathing even and his will focussed on the monster's corpse, he began casting his spell and, as arcane words spilled from his mouth, mana started to bleed out of him.

Thankfully, while it did so quickly it wasn't the torrent he'd feared it could be and he was able to channel the mana from his Gem to top himself up. Also, while it was only a little, due to the one-minute casting time, his mana regenerated enough to allow him to put roughly another 50 mana into the spell.

So focussed was he on the spell that he didn't notice as the body of the Manticore, now free of Vortiga's blade, began to move. Just a claw at first, but then a whole paw and eventually its head. In fact, it was not until the spell's casting time was complete – as the headache from severe mana depletion, pounded through Ninetoes mind – did he notice.

But, eyes blurred with pain and legs so wobbly he was only upright because he was leaning on his Staff, Ninetoes looked up at his creation. He'd done it!

Before him stood his newest undead! And, as this occurred to him, he felt the warm glow of multiple Skills and Spells increasing in levels.

The pounding in his head momentarily forgotten, he tested his control with something simple. Ninetoes willed the monstrous zombie to sit. Instantly the undead manticore planted its behind on the floor.

"Gods! It worked."

"You mean there was some doubt?" Vortiga growled.

"Well, not exactly but I wasn't sure-"

"I'd rather not know. Will it still fly?"

"I think so but I want to run some tests first."

"We have no time for tests, not if you want to reach Raveslan in time to stop my people."

She was right, but Ninetoes wasn't a fan of riding on a creature that'd been dead only moments before, at least not until he was certain it was safe. "Perhaps we could fashion a saddle or at least some reins."

"You are stalling, don't tell me you're afraid of heights, Porsht?"

"It's not the heights I'm worried about, it's crashing into the ground I'm afraid of."

"Come now, everything will, as you say, be fine."

Ninetoes could only grumble as his own words were used against him. Nonetheless, while Ninetoes gathered his things, Vortiga headed over to some of the rope left behind by the Emerald Wolves and cut off roughly ten feet of it with her dagger.

Returning to the monster's side, she asked Ninetoes to have it open its mouth and fed the rope through. Finally, she tied it into a loop and passed the 'reins' over the manticore's mane and handed them to Ninetoes who was now sitting in front of the creature's wings.

"It needs a name, this beast of yours," she commented.

"Really?" Ninetoes hadn't considered this, but he could see the use of a name. "Any ideas? How about Vengeance?"

"Hmmm…" She paused for thought. "I like it but it's a little on the nose." Then an idea struck her and she grinned. "It is not your vengeance, it is your Malice."

Ninetoes returned her grin. "Malice. Yes." Thrusting his hand out to her, he invited her aboard.

Vortiga then climbed up behind Ninetoes. There wasn't a lot of room between the manticore's head and its wings, but after a few moments of adjusting themselves, the pair were as comfortable as they were likely to be.

Having never flown, Ninetoes really wasn't sure how to guide the un-dead mount but he instructed it to fly and hoped that it was capable of doing the rest.

The manticore surged forward, heading directly for the trees and for a moment, Ninetoes was concerned he'd made a terrible mistake. But, as the monster unfurled its leathery wings and leapt into the air, Ninetoes released his breath. Banking left, the mount gained altitude and began to steadily flap its wings.

For the next few minutes, the three of them climbed into the sky and Ninetoes pretty much allowed the massive zombie to choose its own course.

As they'd hunted, fought and conquered the monstrous mount, night time had truly settled in and, above them the sky lit up with a glorious field of stars and innumerable as grains of sand. Looking up, the wizard searched for the Northstar. Resting at the tip of Starm's Sword, it wasn't difficult to find and Ninetoes took a moment to mutter a pray of thanks to the god of warriors.

Sat so close, Vortiga could help but hear his whispered words, and before he'd finished, the Sarm joined him in his devotion.

"I think perhaps we should offer our thanks to Ryuna as well. There is little doubt that the Lady of Luck has been watching over us lately." Vortiga commented.

Ninetoes simply nodded and listened intently as his ally made her prayer.

Once they were high enough up that he was fairly sure they wouldn't crash into anything, Ninetoes turned his mount south-eastwards and, wrapping his cloak about himself, he shut off his mind and let it wander.

They flew for some time and it wasn't until the sun broke out across the horizon before either of them spoke.

It was Vortiga who broke the silence. For a couple of minutes his companion had been fidgeting. Twisting, turning and looking downwards. "Wait, why do we travel so far east? Would it not be much quicker to fly above the river southwards and then follow the road to Raveslan?"

"It would, but we aren't going to Raveslan. At least, not straight away," he replied enigmatically.

CHAPTER 31

THE BATTLE FOR RAVESLAN

"A warm day greets the people of Raveslan. It would have been a good day to harvest, but such chores were beyond them, for today they would fight for their very survival.

The choice had been made for them by their leaders, but every one of them accepted it as their own decision because every one of them understood a simple truth. It didn't matter if you were noble-born or peasant, rich or poor, you'd die the same death on a raider's sword.

They could have left of course. Their leaders had told them what was about to happen, but this was their home and nothing would take it from them." The board is set, the pieces are moving."

Bruce was rather pleased with that little intro. It had taken him a while to write it but he wanted this session to be amazing.

"Ok, can you tell me where your characters are going to be during the assault please?" He looked out at the players as he said it. Each of their faces showed looks of concentration and not a little concern and he could well imagine why.

Normally he'd keep his monster minis behind his screen but for this battle, he'd actually had to borrow a bunch from another GM and there was simply no way he could hide them all, instead, they were arrayed behind him. He'd placed them in groups of ten on pieces of cereal box cardboard to make them easier to move around. He'd also spent most of his evening this week building and painting a cardboard replica of Raveslan's eastern walls. It wasn't perfect, but it was still pretty cool.

Catching Solly's eye, he grinned at her and she smiled warmly back, before turning back to the table and placing her mini of Sariel atop one of the taller buildings. Despite her efforts, she was one of only a handful of the defensive force's ranged fighters that could actually hit anything from such a range, but her job and that of Lady Fawkner, who shared the eyrie, was to watch for flanking manoeuvres and pick off the officers.

An'rik was already hidden within the treeline off to the southern flank. His job was to try and take out the hobgoblin Curn, in the hopes that it would cause the hobs to lose cohesion. The rest of the Adventurers and other fighters were centred around the eastern gate to deal as much damage as possible to the massed ranks of goblinoids.

Looking down at the stat block for Foresto and his golem, Bruce was once again surprised. The construct was incredibly powerful and the wizard was no slouch. What on earth such an NPC was doing in this frontier town normally made no literary sense, but it meant that Bruce could help out.

But everything else was in fate's fickle hands.

"Alright everyone, things will be a little different today, so this is how it'll work…"

RAVESLAN, SWEETSEA REGION, 2301 AC

Sariel let her eyes survey the ranks of hobgoblin warriors and mentally divided one of the four squares into half, and then quarters and only then, she began counting soldiers. She confirmed her original twenty-five on a second pass. Adding the pieces back together, the square she was counting from had a little more than a hundred men, a company then. And if each company was the same size, which they looked to be, then there must be roughly four hundred hobgoblins. Not as many as they'd feared, but certainly more than they could reasonably handle.

The hobs had spent the morning and much of the afternoon digging trenches and building a camp, giving the impression that they were here to stay. But if what Ninetoes had told them was true, then these hobs didn't have the food to wait it out. They would need to take the town in one bloody battle. And that's why the town's leaders kept its defenders on the walls all morning.

Before long, the lack of discipline started to tell and people started to wander off. At first it was for good reasons, like to help the carpenters or to use the jacks, but soon enough, those on the periphery just started to leave. Tarquin had tried to stop a group, but as the young lads pointed out, there wasn't anywhere they could go that was particularly far from the walls.

The Adventurers and the town's leaders had met briefly at that point to work out a rota and sent most of the people back to their chores. None of it had done anything to alleviate the oppressive atmosphere that permeated the town however.

Everyone felt it, like a weight bearing them down, making them walk more softly and never raise their voices. From her perch atop the Golden Spindle, the town could have been deserted; it was so quiet. Sariel had to keep checking over the sides to make sure that it was still populated and she wasn't alone.

As the sun began to fall, making its steady passage behind the western hill, Sariel adjusted her seating position for what felt like the hundredth time. It was currently her watch from the general trader's roof, the highest point in town, but she wasn't sure she'd be able to do anything else, even when she was relieved. *Ergh! Why don't they attack?* Of course, she knew the reason why.

These were trained, disciplined soldiers. Battle-hardened and immune to the boredom of war. As she'd watched them throughout the day, she could see that they were just going about their business as if nothing was going on. They could have been on a camping trip for all the trouble they made. Some had even been sleeping. In fact, now that she came to think about it, she was pretty sure that they'd slept in shifts.

But now, now they were on their feet and the speed and efficiency with which they'd formed ranks was eye-watering. Oh, the call had gone up and the town below her was a turmoil of people running around trying to strap on mismatched armour or string bows. A small scuffle even broke out at the base of a ladder leading onto the wall as peoples' tempers frayed.

Tarquin's words on the previous night might have emboldened the people of Raveslan to fight, but all it had taken was a single day of boredom to break down their discipline. The Nechtsarm's Curn was clearly a gifted and patient commander.

"What're they doing?" Mera Fawkner asked as she climbed through the hatch onto the roof. Apparently it was sundown and Sariel's relief had arrived.

"Nothing. It's like they're waiting for us to be ready. Which is generous of them, cos we definitely need all the help we can get."

Mera grinned at her. "I'll grant you the situation seems dire, but I've seen armies throw themselves at walls without ever stepping foot within them. They are a simple but incredibly effective method of defence."

"Huh, as long as we have people to hold them of course."

"The people will hold, because they must."

Mera may have been about to say more, but she stopped talking as something began taking shape within the ranks of the Nechtsarm.

The sound of a single drum began to beat, followed closely by a second and then a third and fourth. They were sounding out a march and as they did, the ranks of soldiers started moving forwards. They finally seemed to be about to make a move.

The people of Raveslan became silent as every eye watched the hobgoblins. Sariel couldn't see the faces of the townsfolk, but she could easily imagine the looks of fear, anxiety and concern.

"To arms." Came a solitary call from the gate house and the spell was broken as each defender set about whatever task they had, doing their best not to stare in horror at the army marching towards them.

But as she looked out over her archers, few of them seemed ready. What was she doing on this rooftop?

At first the drum's beat was slow and the soldiers' march with it, but as they reached the normal bow range of an archer, the drums' tempos increased and the soldiers began to jog forwards. There was collective breath held amongst the hobs, as they awaited the first missiles that would normally have fired into their faces.

But Sariel had been quite clear with her archers, wait until you can see the whites of their eyes. That saying had never really meant anything to her until she'd really thought about it, but as she'd instructed the teens of Raveslan in the use of the bow and in the rudiments of the tactics they'd use in the coming battle, it had finally become clear.

The best chance they had of making a dent in the massed goblinoids was for one, devastating punch, right into the front rank and for that, they needed to be close, unerringly so. That's why she'd used the phrase and, as she slid down the slate roof of the general traders to join her troops she shouted it again, as loud as she could. "The whites of their eyes, and not before!"

Sliding on her ass, she cast Jump. While her spell wasn't as powerful as the Leap spell Ninetoes had gained access to, it was more than enough to accomplish the task at hand and, as her heels hit the roof's edge, she pumped her legs down and leapt for the wall.

Luckily enough, her shout had alerted those nearby and a space was cleared for her as she landed softly and drew an arrow, all in one smooth motion.

"Let's invite these ladies to dance!" she bellowed and drew back her bow so that the fletching brushed her cheek. All about her the sound of more bow being pulled taut filled the air.

"Wait for it. Wait for it!"

She picked her target. A hobgoblin warrior in full chain, with a pot helm and full shield. They were good, these hobs. Even while charging they kept their shields high, covering their chests, with only their eyes unprotected.

But that's why she'd taught her archers to aim low. The fuckers couldn't charge if they could run!

For her own mark, however, she had a different plan.

It was a subtle difference, but the officers wore leather epaulettes, and with their shields up they were almost indistinguishable from the other soldiers. But her mother hadn't only taught her the bow, she'd also given Sariel her richly coloured, elven eyes.

"Loose!"

Fifty something missiles leapt from bows, staves and wands. In less than the blink of an eye they punched into the thickly packed ranks of hobgoblins, slamming back dozens of the soldiers. Her own arrow slammed into the eye of the hobgoblin Sarm she'd been aiming for and threw him back into the rank behind.

For a second the charge faltered and that was when they unleashed their most powerful weapon. A red and orange ball streaked out from atop the gate, slamming into the heart of the hobgoblin forces and exploding in showers of mud, limbs and death.

Three more, smaller explosions were triggered by the fireball; magical traps buried beneath the earth, and yet more goblinoids were thrown into the air, only to land as corpses.

"Again!" she screamed over the buzzing in her ears. And, while Tarquin couldn't hear her, it wasn't like he needed any encouragement. Pointing the wand, he fired the remaining three fireballs, spacing them out left to right and let the magic did its grim work, incinerating and shattering the bodies scores of hobgoblins.

A smattering of echoing explosions replied as more of the arcane traps that Daphne and Foresto had constructed detonated. Only one volley had been fired by the archers and yet before them the ranks of soldiers had been torn to pieces. A broken cheer went up from the defenders.

But even before the final fiery ball had smashed into the hobs, Sariel had felt her stomach churn as she realised something horrific. The rear ranks of soldiers were too far back from the bloody inferno that was the vanguard. They'd never charged. Instead, they'd watched, hollow faced, as their brothers died and the defenders wasted their best chance to survive.

As the townsfolk raised their arms in victory, the smoke began to clear and they could see what Sariel had already. The cheering collapsed and she could hear as a hush washed through the defenders.

Shakily, Sariel drew another arrow and fired, hoping to kill another officer, but her aim was wildly off. As the ranks of unblemished hobgoblin warriors stared back, pure hatred showed on their maroon faces and the faces of the defenders paled in response.

"Recharge it, quick," she heard Tarquin shout, as he thrust the wand into Daphne's hands. Sariel knew it would not be enough. If they had any hope of blunting the next attack, it was up to the archers.

"Archers, draw!" This time she didn't draw her own bow, instead she scanned the line to make sure that they were all doing as she commanded. They weren't. "All of you," she bellowed, her voice cracking under the strain. "Draw a fucking arrow and aim it at those hobs!" She moved along the line shoving those nearby out of their stupor. "Now!"

Finally, those nearby started to react to her words, but the hobgoblins' march had already drawn them even with the first devastating line and those still alive merged seamlessly with the ranks.

"Archers, draw!" This time she heard the promising sound of strings being pulled taut. "Same as last time motherfuckers, aim low and wait for my command." But, as soon as she finished, she realised the hobs were already charging. "Loose!" she screamed a moment later.

Once again, the carnage of the wave of arrows was devastating, but without the fireballs to support it, it barely bloodied the hobs' collective nose.

"Draw!" she commanded and this time, the archers moved without the need for anything more. "Loose!" The missiles clattered down into the hobgoblins, cutting down a dozen more, but they'd failed to stall the second charge. "Fire at will!"

A steady pattern of missiles began to rain down on the hobs, joined by the thump of rocks being dropped by those without ranged weapons. But Sariel watched as the goblinoids reached the walls and eastern gate and began to raise ladders.

That was when the cavalry arrived. Sariel and the other Adventurers had only been present for the very end of the final meeting of the town's leaders, but they'd understood that one of them owned a ranch of sorts, outside of the walls. Their plan was to launch a cavalry charge after the missiles had struck.

Sariel had not been confident of its success. Mounts they might have and presumably competent riders, but horses just won't charge a defensive line of soldiers without being trained to.

Staring at the battlefield now, however, she watched as a dozen halflings rode gigantic wolves into the ranks of hobgoblins, and she swallowed those reservations.

But when a piercing shriek drew her attention skywards, she finally felt like they might actually stand a chance.

Two female halflings sat astride what at first look appeared to be giant eagles, but then she noticed the horse-like rear legs and she realised the hippogriffs for what they were.

The monstrous beasts swooped low and grabbed hobgoblins, before flying up and dropping them, to land with a crunch in an unmoving heap.

For Sariel, however, there was nothing but more grim work to do. Nothing more to do now but draw and fire. Draw and fire.

LIBBY

When Sariel had described the Adventurers' battle plan, she hadn't really seen anywhere that she could help. At least not at first. But when she'd discussed it with Foresto, it became clear that the best way that she could help and at the same time gain the best possible opportunity to deal with one of the Adventurers, was to follow the strange cleric, An'rik.

After it became apparent that the hobgoblins weren't going to attack immediately, Libby had followed Foresto back to his workshop. It was clear that the wizard had a great deal to get done, but she hadn't stayed long, before she recognised that as far as she'd come, due to her lack of opposable thumbs, she wasn't going to be of much help.

Instead, she'd headed for the roof and kept watch to make sure the old gnome wasn't surprised by any hobgoblins. While she did so, she considered whether there were any other spells in Ninetoes' spellbook she might be able to create from Enchantment or, even better, Illusion magic.

Clearly her Master's most useful spell and the one he seemed to use for every situation was Arcane Step. It allowed him to reach places he wouldn't normally be able to and it gave him a lot more mobility in combat. But when she thought about it, these weren't areas that she lacked in. For this battle, what she really needed was something to give her an edge.

That's when she recalled one of Ninetoes' most recent acquisitions, the Grease spell. He'd never used it that she could remember, but she could certainly see how useful it could be in slowing down their foe. Perhaps Foresto knew the spell?

A short trip downstairs confirmed that the wizard did indeed know the spell and, what's more, he had an old spell scroll with it on that he gave her. The two also briefly discussed how it might be useful in the coming battle, and then Foresto went back to his work and Libby climbed back up to the roof.

For the next few minutes she had studied the Grease spell scroll, absorbing the details, but specifically not casting the spell.

GREASE - LEVEL 5

CONJURATION

CASTING TIME - ONE SECOND

MANA COST - 50 POINTS

DURATION - 1 MINUTE

RANGE - 30 FEET

LVL 1. COMPLETELY COVERS A TEN-FOOT SQUARE WITH SLICK GREASE, MAKING IT DIFFICULT FOR CREATURES TO PASS THROUGH.

Foresto had apologised that the spell was so low level, explaining that he'd bought it from a travelling salesman and had forgotten he had it, only to replace it with a more potent version later. But for the little squirrel, it was perfect.

Right, seems simple enough.

The spell conjured the grease into existence, essentially calling it forth from the plane of Earth. Now, Libby couldn't do that without any affinity to Conjuration magic, but perhaps she could find a way to make her own version.

Really, all the grease would do is make the area extremely slippery and make it difficult for a creature to pass through it at pace. So what if she could create the illusion of the grease. Certainly, if she could make a person hurt themselves by believing that they were on fire with Madigar's Madness, it would be even easier to make them believe that the floor was slippery. *Right?*

Well, it hadn't been easy, but after an hour or so of imagining different scenarios and focussing on her Illusion magic, she'd succeeded. She sat back on her haunches, scanning the lines of text that appeared when she concentrated on her Character Sheet.

LIBBY'S LUBRICANT - LEVEL 1

ILLUSION

CASTING TIME - ONE SECOND

MANA COST - 50 POINTS

DURATION - 1 MINUTE

RANGE - 30 FEET

LVL 1. COMPLETELY COVERS A TEN-FOOT SQUARE WITH THE ILLUSION OF SLICK GREASE. IF A CREATURE FAILS TO SAVE AGAINST THIS ILLUSION, THEY WILL BELIEVE IT TO BE REAL AND ACT ACCORDINGLY.

Sheesh, what was it with these spell names and all the heavy-handed alliteration?

It had worked and Libby had created her own version of another spell. It would also be more cost effective for her because of Illusion Savant I.

Now, however, she glided from treetop to treetop, shadowing the lizardman. His magic made it so that he'd been difficult to track. She managed mostly because she'd been watching him when he'd cast his spell and was able to recognise the tell-tale way the light curved around him.

The other Adventurers had equipped An'rik with the pouch of poisons that they'd found in Ninetoes' Bag of Holding and the Potion of Speed. She could also recognise he was wearing the magical amulet that Foresto had made for him. She hadn't been able to analyse it up close before the gnome had given it to him, but she knew that it was made to increase his damage with a critical strike.

Their plan was a good one. While the fighting took place on the walls, An'rik would sneak behind the enemy's lines and assassinate the hobgoblin Curn, their hope was that by cutting the head off the snake, the hob army would lose cohesion and they could hold against the hobs.

Libby and Foresto also believed that this was their best shot and that's why she'd decided to go along and ensure that it succeeded. And it was a good thing she had.

The hobs had sent patrols out into the forested areas, presumably as a counter to exactly this type of tactic and, if it hadn't been for Libby's quick use of Minor Illusion and even quicker thinking, the cleric would have been discovered twice already. And in fairness to the lizardman, it wasn't really his fault. The woods were thick with the goblinoids.

And not just hobgoblins, but their stealthier bugbear and goblin brethren. Ninetoes had once explained to her, that despite the passing resemblance, the three types of goblinoids never got on, but that as the most intelligent and militaristic, the hobgoblins would sometimes force the other goblinoids into slavery, using them as cannon fodder.

While the main force assaulted the town, it was groups of these 'lesser' goblinoids, led by a single hobgoblin, who stalked the forests and, even with her help, An'rik's progress had slowed to a crawl. The lizardman seemed clever enough and had used both the distractions she'd created to skulk past the earlier patrols, but at this rate, he'd arrive too late to have any impact on the outcome of the battle.

For her own part, Libby had no problems navigating past the goblins, but then she could fly. She also accepted that she wasn't likely to be much of an assassin, so she needed to help the cleric reach his destination.

What she needed was to create enough of a distraction, so as to draw multiple patrols at once and allow An'rik to penetrate their lines. But what would have such an effect?

These patrols were designed to ensure that nothing could pass through them and they wouldn't react unless they believed the threat was big enough. But what was a big enough threat to concern a whole army of goblinoids?

That's when it hit her and she set herself to her task.

Gliding to a lower branch to ensure that she had the range, Libby closed her eyes and concentrated on what it had looked like, the way its tails had moved and its body had seemed to absorb the light.

Once she had the image fully in her mind she opened her eyes and began casting, picking a spot for her illusion that was directly in the path of a group of goblins.

As soon as the first one saw it, the little green man yelped and sounded the alarm. "Monster!" he yelled.

Libby had the feline-like demon leap towards the group and the front two goblins fell back to the floor. Perfect! Seizing the opportunity, she guided her illusion of Zag'thonar towards a fallen gob, before slashing out with its claws.

The illusion passed through the goblin, but Libby cast Madigar's Madness as they did and the fool was dead before any of those present realised anything was amiss. By now the hobgoblin in charge of the patrol was barking orders at the other fighters and they circled the demon.

Libby smiled. She'd baited the hook, now all she had to do was reel them in. She watched carefully for the first to make their move, meanwhile having her illusion turning on the spot as though preparing to strike again. Then, as it turned its back on a bugbear, the warrior struck.

Now, there was nothing that Libby could do about the bugbear's mace passing straight through her illusion, but she could at least make it appear that the demon had allowed it to happen.

Shimmering as Libby had witnessed the real thing do when it dropped its camouflage, Libby's illusion made it appear as if it passed out of phase as the mace swung for it. Her timing was perfect and it looked realistic enough. Her biggest problem now was whether the goblins would realise the significance of what they believed they saw.

"Alarm! Demons! Second and Third squads, on me!" the hobgoblin officer called out in a clipped tone and from deeper into the woods, Libby heard the answering calls of two more hobgoblins.

She maintained the illusion for another minute or so, dodging the goblins' attacks and killing a bugbear with Madigar's Madness to continue to sell the fantasy.

An'rik meanwhile, was opportunistic enough and capitalised on the disruption to break through the enemy's lines. Once he was clear, Libby had the apparition bound off into the woods in the opposite direction and then she took off after the cleric.

So far so good.

While she followed, she climbed higher into the trees until she could leap from the uppermost branches and glide above the treetops. For a few seconds at a time she could glance at the battle that was unfolding before the town's walls.

What she saw was mostly a confusion of flashes of light, blurred motion and bodies. But one thing was clear, the hobs were at the walls and were making progress towards the top. An'rik had no time to spare.

***

As fate would have it, Libby's gambit had paid off and there were no more patrols between the cleric and the edge of the woods that met with the hobgoblin camp.

She watched the lizardman grow more and more confident as nothing appeared to stop him or get in his way and she worried that he'd make a wrong move and it would all be for nothing. There wasn't much she could do about that, however, so she just kept following, while keeping a weather eye on the path ahead.

Somehow, the cleric made it past the sentries and into the enemy camp unnoticed. He even took the time to stop off in the Curn's tent to loot. Meanwhile the people of Raveslan died on the goblinoid swords and all Libby could do was watch impatiently while the fool risked everything for a little gold!

By some miracle, he made it out unscathed and began searching for the Curn.

For Libby this was one more inconvenience. From her perch atop the tent, she could see the hobgoblin warlord sitting atop his big horse no more than two hundred feet away. But she was unable to communicate that to the idiot Adventurer, so she had to wait for him to work it out on his own.

Eventually he rounded a bend and spotted his target. The Curn was guarded by two more hobgoblins, both of whom wore a similar plate armour, only theirs was painted a dark blue. As strong as they'd become fighting demons, there was little doubt in Libby's mind that An'rik was no match for all three of the hobgoblin warriors. In fact, she wasn't sure he was a match for any of one them in a straight fight. But then, this wasn't meant to be a straight fight.

She watched anxiously as the cleric cast spell, after spell upon himself, presumably trying to 'buff' himself in preparation of his task. Meanwhile she heard the Curn shout for archers as two massive hippogriffs began flying over his army.

Once An'rik was finished, he just crouched down and began eating a ration cake. What in all the hells was he doing?

And that's when it hit her, he was waiting for his mana to recharge. Argh! How many people's lives would pay for his mana pool to be topped off? She knew it was risky, but she had to do something to spur him on.

She didn't want him to get too spooked and so run away, but she needed him to think that he needed to act now. She thought about it for a second and then once again cast her favourite spell.

PORTSMOUTH, 2017

"So, you're just going to sit there?" Sariel asked incredulously.

"For ten minutes, yes. That's how long it'll take me to replenish enough mana to continue, without any of my buff spells timing out," Felix explained, unphased by the looks of incredulity that faced him.

"But people are dying."

"And I just got hit, I need you to get back and start healing me," chipped in Tony.

"If I fail, it will cost many more lives than those being lost in the meantime," he replied, his tone still nonplussed.

"What's An'rik's passive perception Felix?" asked Bruce.

"Er... fifteen, why?" Replied Felix, a note of trepidation in his voice.

"Fifteen, ok. Yeah, An'rik can hear the voices of some goblins, he reasons that it's probably one of the patrols returning to camp." Bruce explained.

"So he's about to-"

"Miss his opportunity to strike? Yeah Felix, that's probably an accurate statement," said Bruce, grinning at Solveg.

"Very well. Then I shall have to make do. Bruce, An'rik draws an arrow from his quiver and carefully laces it in..."

LIBBY

The squirrel sighed with relief as she watched the cleric smear something on the broad-tip of an arrow and then string his bow. Her smile morphed into one of pleasure as the warm feeling of a Skill increase also slid through her chest.

So as not to ruin his shot with anxiety, she had the voices fade out, as if they were walking in the other direction. She watched as the cleric cast another spell, only this one was directly onto the arrow, which began glowing a dark purple.

Nocking the arrow, the lizardman adjusted his position a little. He was more out in the open, but he had a much clearer shot at the Curn. Drawing it back to his cheek, he angled the arrow upwards slightly, but the shot couldn't have been more than sixty feet.

Libby held her breath and watched, first the cleric and then the Curn. She heard the missile leave the bow and watched the Curn.

It was too fast to see it fly, but she witnessed it strike.

The Curn moved slightly at the last moment to seat himself more comfortably in the saddle. It wasn't much, but the tiny movement was enough to throw off the near perfect aim of the lizardman and, instead of sinking into the hob's neck, it shot past it, slicing through his neck and wounding him.

His hand went to the wound and in that instant chaos broke loose.

The Curn twisted in the saddle and his eyes locked onto An'rik. Pointing, he shouted a command, his words, however, were slurred and the two bodyguards stood for a moment confused, as their commander slipped from his saddle, crashing to the floor.

The soldier on the same side of the horse made to grab his leader while the other finally realised what the Curn had shouted and noticed An'rik.

The lizardman hadn't been idle of course, and was already weaving between guy ropes and tents and running as fast as he could for the safety of the treeline.

And that's when, with a wicked, toothy grin that her Master would have been proud of, Libby struck.

Holding the small green gem between her claws, she concentrated on the command phrase and activated its magic. The gem was a simple magical trigger. Or at least, that's how Foresto had described it when he'd given it to her, along with instructions on how to use it.

The gem, he'd explained, would trigger the spell hidden within the magic item that he'd paired it to. And the gem Libby held was paired to the gem within An'rik's amulet.

And while the spell was a weak one, it was incredibly potent when triggered around one's neck.

The lizardman screamed in pain and collapsed to the floor, his body spasming disturbingly in response to the Shocking Strike spell that Libby had just triggered.

She imagined that as the spell cascaded down through his spine that it might be quite painful, but she was pleasantly surprised when the Adventurer lost control of his bowels and shit himself as well.

By then the bodyguard had caught up and Libby expected that to be the end of An'rik the Cleric, but this was no brutish bugbear, this was a hobgoblin Warrior and a Curn's selected bodyguard to boot. His Curn's order hadn't been to kill, but to seize the lizardman, and so that's exactly what he'd done.

Libby didn't want to miss anything, so she leapt from to a better perch from where she could enjoy the show.

By the time An'rik's body stopped convulsing and he was able to move his limbs again, the hobgoblin had stripped him of his weapons and bound his hands. Exactly what they'd do to him once they realised that the lizardman's arrow had been laced with a deadly poison and so had murdered their Curn, Libby could only hope she'd get to witness. It wouldn't be quite the same as killing the Adventurer herself, but it would serve.

But as she settled in to watch she realised that the Curn was not in fact dead. He was still holding his neck but the worst of the bleeding had abated and when he spoke, his words were no longer slurred. Indeed, the

Curn seemed very much alive as he slammed his mailed fist into An'rik's long, serpentine jaw.

"How dare you sneak into my camp and attempt to kill me with our own poisons!" A bodyguard handed him a potion that he quickly knocked back before rounding on the cleric and smashing the glass vial into An'rik's eye socket.

The lizardman screamed out in pain, before collapsing. "Errrgh, you stink. What did you do to him Daas?"

"Nuffink Sir, I chased him and he just collapsed and then shit hisself," the hob explained. Libby didn't bother to suppress the feeling of joy.

"Arrgghh!!" An'rik screamed as the Curn ground his iron-shod boot into the lizardman's outstretched fingers.

"Obviously you know nothing of my people, or you'd have known that ba'ardec poisons have no effect on us. Even a lowly Farn is forced to develop immunities to our poisons to prove themselves, although only the strongest survive."

Libby watched the display, in two minds about what to do next. Part of her, the greater part of her, wanted nothing more than to witness the torture and murder of the cleric. It was little more than he deserved. But the other part of her recognised that while the Curn survived there was little hope of victory or survival for the people of Raveslan.

But what good could she really do anyway, the angry part of her asked. He is already dead; find another way. She knew that was bullshit of course. She couldn't hope to kill the Curn alone, but how to rescue An'rik?

Checking her mana pool, she found it topped off, meaning she had more than two hundred points to play with. She wasn't particularly concerned about escape. Her Cloaking Shadows were relatively fresh and there were plenty of things to leap off of and she could easily lose the hobs in the woods.

But even with a full pool of mana she just didn't have anything capable of dealing enough damage to kill all three hobgoblins.

What would Ninetoes do? He'd seek more information. She cast Libby's Labelling and looked at each of the assailants in turn.

```
HOBGOBLIN BODYGUARD - LEVEL 7
PRIME STATS - STRENGTH, ENDURANCE
PRIME TRAIT - DEFLECT
250/250 HP
1500XP
```

```
OGREN - LEVEL 13
PRIME STATS - STRENGTH, ENDURANCE
PRIME TRAIT - LEADERSHIP
CONDITIONS - MILD POISON
275/300 HP
3500XP
```

The Curn was, unsurprisingly, stronger than his fellows, but he was also suffering from a poisoned condition, despite what he'd told An'rik about being immune to the ba'ardec's poisons. Curious, she observed him more closely and watched as his hit points went down by fifteen points and then, ten seconds later, it did the same again.

As he raged at An'rik, kicking and thumping the helpless creature, his hit points continued to drop from the poison coursing through his veins. And, while he didn't seem particularly concerned Libby watched as he knocked back another healing potion and his hit points shot back up.

This was all great of course, but how could she use it to her benefit? Perhaps if she could find a way to stop him from getting more potions? They surely couldn't have an inexhaustible supply, but then, what if they did? She couldn't take that risk, she had to act. Now!

As much as she might come up with another plan, her best chance at success remained in freeing the cleric, so she started there and, acting totally against her nature, she climbed to the ground.

She needed to get the best possible angle of attack if she was to succeed and because of how the hobgoblins were all so intently staring down at the lizardman, she needed to be beneath them. It also meant she was less likely to inadvertently hit An'rik with her spell. She waited for the Curn to move over towards one of the bodyguards who was holding out a vial of potion and then she struck.

Casting Iridescent into the Curn's eyes, she watched as the beam blinded the hobgoblin warlord and then turned the focus onto the bodyguard that was facing him, blinding the second hobgoblin.

By then, however, she could hear the heavy footfalls of the other bodyguard heading her way.

Leaping up into the first bodyguard's hands she grabbed the vial and redirected her beam onto her final foe. This hob had the wherewithal to put a hand up in front of his face but she dazzled him enough to escape his attack and glided over to An'rik, dropping the potion on the ground before him.

She hoped that he'd get with the programme quickly enough to help out because she didn't have much hope of killing all three of them before they could see again. But just in case he wasn't, she focussed her attention on bringing down the Curn.

As she'd discovered the first time she'd encountered the demon Zag'thonar, if a creature couldn't see, if was far more likely to trust in its other senses and so believe it was actually on fire when she cast Madigar's Madness, and this was exactly what she was betting on once again as she cast the spell onto the Ogren.

The Curn screamed as one might when they were on fire and she mentally trumpeted her success, while she scrambled once again for the high ground. Even as she, did felt the now familiar feeling as another Skill increase warmed her breast.

Reaching the peak of a tent and looked back at the carnage she'd initiated. An'rik had indeed followed her lead and had retrieved one of his weapons from the pile nearby and now used the short sword to repeatedly stab the first bodyguard that Libby had blinded. Really, it didn't matter how big you were when something carves open your neck, you're still done for.

Phew! One down.

She sorely missed the information that Libby's Label fed her but she couldn't waste the mana on a second casting.

Thinking she was safe enough to contemplate such things was perhaps her first real mistake, as a meaty hand wrapped around her bushy tail and slammed her into a nearby tree; once, twice, three times.

Any normal squirrel would have been done for on the first attack, but Libby's shadow armour protected her and held for the first two attacks but she felt the full force of the third and final attack and hung limply in the bodyguard's hand as he squared off against An'rik, while keeping himself between his Curn and the cleric.

"I'm gonna finish carvin' you up and then I'm gonna cook up yer little rat," he ground out in his heavy voice. "You alright boss?" he added over his shoulder, as the Curn reclaimed his feet.

"Fine, fine. Well, seems you had a few more tricks after all eh? Well, we've had our fun, so it's time to finish it," said the Curn.

Libby's pain-addled mind was struggling somewhat to process everything that was happening, but one thing raged crystal clear into her mind. *These fuckers think the cleric did all this?*

Well, Libby must have been channelling some of Ninetoes' magic right then and there, because she saw red and her anger became a thing of its own and, before even she knew what she was doing, she was casting her Master's favourite spell.

The bodyguard suddenly seized up as though he was having a heart attack and collapsed to the ground. But, as the body is wont to do when it's under duress, the hobgoblin's muscles tensed and he kept hold of the tail in his hand and through it Libby drained every iota of his lifeforce, until he was nothing but a hollowed-out husk of dry skin, stretched too tightly over old bone.

Of course the Curn didn't see what had created this effect and once his bodyguard was no longer blocking his view of An'rik he stared in shock at the cleric. "You!" he said, pointing his sword at the lizardman, before charging the smaller man down.

An'rik, who had been just as astonished by the sudden exsanguination of the hobgoblin, was taken by surprise when the Curn attacked and so stumbled backwards, tripping and falling onto his rear. The Curn simply pressed the attack and chopped down with both hands driving his sword into An'rik's arm.

Blood splattered and An'rik screamed as his left hand and most of the forearm fell to the floor, severed cleanly from his body.

Still a little dazed and struggling to concentrate, Libby chose that moment to finish the fight. Leaping for Ogren's wrist, she sank her teeth in. But this wasn't her attack, just the vocal point for it.

And as An'rik clutched at the mess that had been his arm, trying fruitlessly to staunch the flow of blood, he watched in horror as the squirrel sucked the life out of the Curn of the Nechtsarm.

PORTSMOUTH, 2017

"Vampire Squirrels, seriously?"

"Yeah, come on dude, what?"

The party stared at Bruce, astounded by the description the GM had just given. Catching Solveg's grin, Bruce simply shrugged and continued reading details from his notes.

SARIEL

The half-elf breathed deeply with exhaustion and flexed her fingers. Looking down she could see that her bowstring was tinged with pink; her fingers bloodied from firing so many arrows. Looking out over the sea of bodies, she seriously began to despair. The hobgoblins just kept coming, an ever-turning tide. *They can't keep coming forever. Surely?*

"All we have to do is hold the line for a little longer, so just keep firing!"

An arrow thunked into the wooden merlon next to Sariel. With the day she'd been having this was par for the course, except for one defining feature; the arrow had come from behind her.

Combat reflexes kicked in and she twisted on the spot, sinking to one knee as she did and simultaneously drawing an arrow.

Without conscious thought, she aimed and fired, her arrow flying true and sinking into the chest of a lightly armoured hobgoblin warrior.

A hobgoblin warrior who was coming from the centre of the town square!

"Breach!" she shouted. "We've been flanked."

For trained soldiers that would have been enough, but for the youth of Raveslan, who were already having the worst day of their lives, her voice was just one more scream.

Sariel grabbed the two immediately beside her, but that was the best she could do.

A fusillade of arrows, each one fired by an expert, rained onto the defenders atop the walls, everyone hitting its mark, sending at least a dozen souls onwards.

Worse than that, there was something familiar about the gear and garb of these new hobgoblins. She couldn't place it at first, but then she paid closer attention to the curved shortsword each of them wore and the pieces slotted into place. *Fuck!*

"ba'ardec," she whispered in horror. "Archers on me!" she screamed, reaching into her quiver for an arrow; an arrow that wasn't there.

CHAPTER 32

NINETOES THE NECROMANCER

"And why in all the Nine Hells not? The battle is in Raveslan. If you hold out any hope of rescuing the town and thus your own people, we should make for the town with all haste."

Ninetoes grinned. "There is some… thing that we must collect before heading for the battle." He knew it wasn't necessary to play such guessing games, but he was a little bored.

"Indeed? A magical weapon perhaps? I'll agree that our new weapons are incredible tools, but neither will be sufficient to stop my people. It'll take an army to do that."

"Ha!" Ninetoes barked. But, as he heard the leather of Vortiga's gauntlet crease as her hand scrunched up into a fist, he reasoned he'd probably had about as much fun as he would get.

Nonetheless, he still held his tongue. Despite the distance they'd travelled and how much their relationship had changed, Ninetoes had only told Foresto the whole truth about the ancient city of Kavralach and what had happened there.

Vortiga might be his ally, but she was still a Nechtsarm and owed much to her people. Would the secrets and wonders held in the ancient human capital be enough to break their newfound alliance?

The apprentice wizard had already laid claim to the city, a place for his people to start again, to grow strong once more. How would Vortiga deal with this? She had agreed to help him try to end the fighting, but that didn't mean she'd want to see the Dakhec Druul grow powerful once more; or that she wouldn't try to seize the prize for her own people.

But, as they flew over the treetops, the first signs of the city began sprawling out into the valley before them. As massive as the metropolis was however, Ninetoes had a moment to decide whether or not he should turn back. Perhaps he could leave Vortiga here, at the city's border and proceed alone?

No. Such thoughts were not only impractical, they were also churlish and distrustful. Vortiga had already sacrificed much; could he really offer any less? Ninetoes made his decision.

He would stop questioning her loyalties and trust in the bond they had struck. "I discovered this city on my first Quest. It was human, I think, but it's ancient. What's more, it holds magical wonders and a strength to offer my... our people."

Vortiga was clearly stunned and it was obvious to imagine why. Even the ruins on the outskirts of the massive city were impressively built, but as the manticore carried them ever-closer to the city's heart, more and more of the ancient wonder's wealth, strength and power became evident.

Even to Ninetoes, who had been here before, he'd never seen the city from the sky. It was larger than he'd ever imagined it could be and there were buildings and structures that simply boggled the mind. His original estimation of what it could offer his people had been woefully incomplete; from here, the Dakhec Druul could become a power to be reckoned with, perhaps enough to rule the entire Sweetsea.

But, as he caught the strange look that Vortiga was giving him, he realised that her shock was more than just awe and wonder for the ancient city.

"You would share this with the Nechtsarm?" she asked, the disbelief clear in her voice.

Ninetoes took a moment to consider his response. When he'd come up with this plan, his only real intention had been to collect the army of undead that awaited him deep within the city.

His trials, injuries and exhaustion of the previous few days had only allowed him to see the next few steps and, in frank honestly, it hadn't occurred to him that it would require sharing this with her. But now that they were here, he a Warrior of the Dakhec Druul and she a Sarm of their oldest and most hated rivals, it had made him think; could this city be not only a safe haven for his people, but one for hers as well? For all of their people?

"Our people, the hobgoblins, have warred with each other for... I don't know, centuries? Millennia? This has always kept us weak. We've been so busy battling amongst ourselves, that the other races have come to think of us nothing more than pests." Then, at the look of indignation on Vortiga's face, he quickly justified his point. "Oh, an army of your people might be enough to scare a frontier town like Raveslan, but you saw the lack of concern in Pamor."

Vortiga spoke up then. "Are you saying that you plan to make this place a haven for all hobgoblins?"

"A haven? Yes, I suppose at first. But look at it. Really look at it. I've only just begun to unearth its wonders and yet I've quickly become powerful. With the strength and labour of our peoples, think of what we could find. And, if nothing else, there is fertile soil, readily built homes and enough cut stone to rebuild the inner wall in a matter of months.

"All of this, however, relies upon our peoples being able to occupy the same space without tearing each other's throats out. And that we're able to stop the attack on your home."

"Hmmm, you're not wrong, but look at how far we've come, you and I. If *we* can find a middle ground, perhaps our people can as well." Vortiga stared back, her eyes showing that she was still unconvinced, so Ninetoes continued. "Regardless of that, you're right that for the time being, we have more urgent matters; stopping your army."

As he said this, he sent his monstrous mount a command to land in the centre of the goblinoid camp that had just come into view. "But this, this is why we came here today." And so saying, Ninetoes cast an expansive hand out to gesture at the space below them.

"Are those goblins? And bugbears? Ergh! You think to use them as an army to fight my people? They won't stand a chance," Vortiga scoffed.

"This is an army, but not of goblinoids, not really," he countered.

"Explain," she answered shortly. This was, for Ninetoes, the Sarm's best feature. He appreciated brevity in conversation.

"They are undead. And they obey my will."

"All of them? If what you told me about your spell is true, it must have taken months to create so many and how in all Adrenon can you command such a number?"

"You are not wrong. Normally, creating so many undead would have taken weeks and would likely have been beyond my current capabilities. But, one of the wonders offered by this city is a machine that created this army and, by a strange twist of fate, placed them under my control."

This conversation had drawn them much closer to the camp and Ninetoes was now close enough to exert his will over the undead. As he did so, a large group within the middle of the army of skeletons and zombies turned to face him.

Vortiga flinched at the unnerving act and turned to show Ninetoes a look of shock. For his part, Ninetoes only grinned.

As the moment passed however, Vortiga studied the group and a look of understanding spread across her face.

"You can't control them all." The surety of her tone, showed that this was posed more as a statement of fact than as a question.

The grin on Ninetoes face faltered and he stared off into the middle distance. "Not all of them, no."

"No matter," Vortiga offered. "I'm sure we can find a way. It is an impressive sight. How many are there?"

Ninetoes, grateful for the praise, considered her query. "I don't know exactly, but I believe I can control perhaps as many as fifty, maybe fewer if I'm controlling Malice directly." With this statement, Ninetoes used the group under his control to clear a space for his manticore to land in. The monster landed gracefully and the pair climbed down onto tired and shaky legs.

"What do you mean control "directly"?" Vortiga asked.

"Well, I can simply give an undead a command and it will follow this to the best of its ability, this I consider to be "indirect" control. But, if I focus my will more intently, I can "directly" control their actions as if they were my own. Observe." As he finished, he took control of a nearby skeleton and had it perform the movements of a simple sword form with the rusted cutlass it held.

"And this "direct" control allows you to perform more intricate actions?"

"Correct. All of these undead are considered "unintelligent", all except Malice of course."

"Which means?"

"It means they are unable to perform any but the most rudimentary of tasks without "direct" control. Whereas Malice can, for example, fly. A far more complicated action."

"Hmmm, well fifty isn't an army, and if they're unable to even fight smart, then they won't help in the coming battle. Is there even enough time for them to reach Raveslan in time?"

"As for travelling, they're undead. They need neither rest, food or even air to survive. We could march them all day, every day for a year and they'd be able to fight at the end of it. But as for their numbers, I'm not sure. I was planning to move them in groups of fifty."

Vortiga's face became one of concentration. Ninetoes wasn't sure, but he knew that the Sarm was more than just a gifted Warrior, she was a tactician, one who'd nearly seized the town of Raveslan with a single company.

"I have it. Do you have any rope?"

Without saying anything, Ninetoes sent a zombie to collect some from the supplies of the goblinoid army. It returned within the minute and handed Vortiga fifty feet of hempen rope.

Taking it, she quickly tied the rope around the waist of the zombie that had brought it to her and then to around that of another zombie nearby.

"Ninetoes, give this one an order to walk over there."

Ninetoes had caught onto the simple idea and did as she bid. The first zombie stepped out of the ranks of undead and moved in the direction Ninetoes had commanded and, as the rope became taut, so too did the zombie tied to it.

"It works!"

For the next fifteen minutes the pair of hobgoblins tested the limits to their solution and discovered that a single zombie could pull along two more without the group simply stumbling into one another. Moreover, they realised that they had more than enough rope to tie all fifty of the zombies that Ninetoes could control to a further one hundred.

It was by no means perfect, and many of the trios of zombies fell over, or got themselves wedged into spaces. They discovered, however, that if the zombies were tied shoulder to shoulder, the primary zombie was able to guide the other two past most obstacles.

Ninetoes' knowledge of necromancy also filled in the final missing piece. That, while zombies won't usually attack without a command, if they are attacked, they would fight to defend themselves. So, as long as the primary zombie was close enough to engage, the other two were likely to join in.

Ninetoes hoped, however, that the undead wouldn't actually have to do much fighting and that rather, the threat they posed would be enough to forestall the need for violence.

Nonetheless, the pair spent the rest of the day selecting the most complete zombies and ones that were already wearing armour and carrying weapons and equipping those that didn't.

They briefly considered taking some of the worg zombies, but quickly realised that these creatures were ill-formed to lead other zombies and so agreed to leave them behind.

There weren't quite enough of the goblinoid zombies to completely fill their ranks, so they also brought along a number of ancient skeletons. They equipped these with weapons, but once again found that the armour simply hung off of their bodies. With the forest terrain they'd be passing through, it just seemed like a waste of time to equip them with gear the skeletons would probably lose along the way.

By midday, they had an army of one hundred and fifty undead, each one armed to the teeth and, thanks to Vortiga's skill and knowledge, divided into three groups.

The smallest group was made up of perhaps twenty skeletons and goblins that carried bows, these were to be their archers. Next was a group of roughly thirty. These were mostly bugbears but a few of the larger skeletons filled out the gaps. Each of these carried a shield and had been tied even more closely together. With practice, Ninetoes could form them into a cohesive shield wall.

Finally, all the leftover undead were given whatever weapons were left over. This group would make up the centre of Ninetoes' army. Their mass would add weight to the shield wall and provide cover for the archers.

If they'd had more time, they would have practiced moving the undead and performing more complicated manoeuvres, but time was definitely something they didn't have, so they settled for what they'd achieved and, before the sun set, they marched.

It took most of what was left of the day to leave the city behind. While the roads and streets would have helped a living army to move efficiently, the many obstacles simply slowed the undead down and Ninetoes found that he was constantly backtracking to unblock a group of zombies from a choke point.

Once they were in the forest however, their progress increased. While there were still plenty of obstacles, but his soldiers could spread out. Now, instead of a column, the undead became a line, perhaps six deep. And now, whenever a leader zombie approached an obstruction, they were able to go around it.

VORTIGA

By twilight, the army was deep into the forest. Vortiga had slept first, tied into the saddle. Ninetoes meanwhile, had directed his army, until the Sarm woke up and took the reins.

Malice didn't need any help in flying and, with a simple command the manticore could be controlled by the warrior. The undead were a little more taxing and while she could command them with a similar order from Ninetoes, there were still plenty of occasions when she'd have to wake him to take "direct" control of a zombie. Thus Ninetoes was only able to sleep in fits and bursts.

Despite these troubles however, with the dawn of a new day, the sun's light flooded over a deep, wide valley, divided by a road, and Vortiga's eyes recognised the location.

They were within a normal day's march of Raveslan. What's more, on a proper road, with little concern for obstacles, the undead could increase their constant, loping pace; they would reach the town within mere hours!

That thought excited Vortiga, but now that they were so close, she worried about exactly what they'd find. Even she wasn't sure that their efforts would be enough.

Trying to make sense of the last few days was nigh impossible, but one thing she was certain of; now that she'd made her choice to follow a different path, she hoped that she had the fortitude to see it through.

But so much... too much, rested upon fate and the will of the gods. What if the Nechtsarm had increased their pace and had reached Raveslan early? All of their efforts might be for naught. They might reach the human settlement to find it razed or occupied, the people slaughtered.

While she had no love for the townsfolk, Bess at least had shown her kindness of a type. But it was more than that. When Ninetoes had shown her the ancient city, she realised that the new path she had chosen had allowed this to happen and that, if she were brave, clever and bold enough, perhaps she could lead her own people to it as well.

Ninetoes' plans might seem crazy, but if they could bring them to fruition, it could mean a new age for hobgoblins.

A single question remained unanswered, however: what would she do when she reached Raveslan? There was no question that she would fight or kill her brethren, she couldn't betray them like that. But maybe, just maybe she could find a way to stop the fighting without more bloodshed.

She had to try. Didn't she?

This conundrum carried her through the next few hours of the tedium that was a long march. The undead made such a racket that most beasts simply fled from their path and any larger, more dangerous monsters chose not to engage such a large party.

They had spent the day travelling ever westwards, chasing the sun across the sky and hoping they would be in time. Then, as the sun's light began to disappear and the shadows began to chase the army of undead, the treeline on both sides of the road retreated and the town came into view.

What's more, the walls still held, and the eastern gate was closed and apparently secure. She could even make out the silhouettes of two guards standing atop the guardhouse.

Waking Ninetoes, she pointed. As he shook off the confusion of sleep, he followed her direction and gave his all-too-familiar toothy grin. For a second, she forgot herself and the sight made a matching grin crease her own face.

"It looks as though the town still stands."

This appeared to be true. But as they drew closer a sound drifted to them on the wind, one that neither of them could question, it was the sound of battle. Moreover, they could see the tell-tale signs of smoke and battle on the town's western side.

"Dammit, we're too late, the fighting has already begun. We must make haste and reinforce the defenders."

Even as Ninetoes made his statement, Vortiga's trained eyes picked out something new.

As they'd neared the town it was clear that the two guards standing atop the wall were indeed human defenders.

Nearby, however, stalking carefully along the base of the palisade, were hobgoblin soldiers. But this wasn't all. These hobs were too lightly armed and their movements too graceful.

To Vortiga, who had commanded a squad of these specialists, she recognised them immediately, they were ba'ardec.

Worse still, the pair were still too far away to warn the guards. That realisation stumped her for a moment. Would she have warned the humans if she could?

But, as Ninetoes guided Malice into a burst of speed, it didn't seem she'd need to answer that question.

"Ho the town! Ho the town! Malice, fly faster, straight for the gate." Ninetoes shouted.

The guards were alerted, but not to the imminent threat of the ba'ardec, but to the massive, flying monster that was bearing down on them. Vortiga couldn't make out what they said, but it was clear from their actions, they were about to shoot at the manticore.

"Ninetoes, be careful!" and as she said it, she pulled hard on the reins. Malice, confused by the contradicting commands, suddenly banked hard left.

A crossbow bolt slammed into the manticore's undercarriage, but the pair of hobgoblins were saved from the attack. The sudden movement, however, threw both of them from their seats and, as the manticore attempted to correct its course, the movement sent Vortiga spilling off of the beast.

She hit the ground hard and, for a few seconds, she was dazed and winded. Just for a moment, she promised herself, she'd stay right here.

Above her, however, she could hear Ninetoes shouting at the guards. His intention was clear, but either the guards had never met him before, or were so afraid of his monstrous mount, that they were unsure of his meaning.

Sitting up, Vortiga watched as Ninetoes finally gave up on explaining himself and instead, fired one of his black bolts, not at the guards, but at one of the ba'ardec climbing that were now climbing the walls.

One of the guards, confused at first, jeered at the wizard. Meanwhile, the other peered over the wall just in time to witness the first of the attackers reach the top of the wall.

Staring aghast, the guard raised his shield against his assailant, as the ba'ardec warrior brought his sword chopping down.

The guard wasn't quick enough and the hob's blade bit into his shoulder, missing his neck by a fraction. The guard, losing blood quickly, fell to his knees, while trying and failing to raise his own weapon to block the hobgoblin's follow up strike. He wasn't quick enough, but luckily for him, Ninetoes was.

Instead of carving into the guard's face, the hob's attack was stopped dead by Ninetoes staff. "Up." He commanded, while simultaneously whipping the head of his staff around and into his foe's chest.

The blow was a weak one, and for a second the ba'ardec sneered at the weakling porsht's attack. That smile however, along with the hobgoblin's lifeforce, drained out of him, as Ninetoes reached across to the now risen guard and he passed this healing energy into the human, closing his wound.

Standing straighter, the guard nodded. "My thanks, and my apologies, you must be Ninetoes."

All this happened in a matter of seconds, but that was more than enough time for a dozen or more of the highly trained hobgoblin scouts to make it over the wall and on into the town.

Vortiga, still on the ground beneath the town's walls couldn't see them, but she knew their training well enough and could guess their orders: regroup inside the town and assault the defenders' flank.

Whether or not Ninetoes understood this was unclear, but the wizard was currently distracted by the rest of the ba'ardec as they climbed the walls.

She watched as the Porsht, no… the Adventurer began firing more bolts of black magic at the hobgoblins, while shouting orders for his manticore to destroy their ladders.

Malice wasn't subtle about this and, plucking two of the hobs from rungs, spiralled up sixty feet before dropping them straight back down on the very same ladder. The simple tactic was effective and the hastily made wooden construct collapsed under the force of the meaty projectiles.

With Ninetoes' help, the two human guards had managed to grab and pull up another of the ladders, which now lay uselessly on the roof of a nearby house.

That left only one ladder. But Vortiga stood stock still, uncertainty worming its way through her.

Had it been simple warriors, she might have been able to command them to stop, or at least have slowed them down long enough for her to explain that there was an alternative. But the ba'ardec were relentless and would never have obeyed her over the orders of their Curn.

What's more, she just felt useless. She would not fight her own people but she couldn't turn on Ninetoes now. Instead she could only watch.

She watched Ninetoes work. Given his powerful magic, his flying monster and the fact that he held the wall, Ninetoes made short work of the final ladder. The ba'ardec might be well-trained, disciplined and perfectly equipped as pathfinders, scouts and infiltrators, but they were woefully under-prepared to fight the wizard and his manticore.

Even so, the ba'ardec didn't go down easily. When their last ladder was destroyed, they quickly formed a square with their shields, protecting a few archers in their centre. These archers peppered Malice with arrows.

Had the manticore been its normal living self, the poison-coated arrows might have been enough to bring the beast down. But as an undead the poisons were worthless, and the arrows simply made a mess of the brutish flier's feline hide.

Meanwhile, the ranks of undead moved ever closer to the town's gate and, when the hobgoblins saw the incoming zombies, they sensibly chose to give up their position.

Using their defensive formation, the ba'ardec made their way back to the treeline. Vortiga watched, once again impressed with their discipline as they disappeared back into the undergrowth.

Hand resting on the pommel of Magebane, Vortiga felt even more useless. She watched Ninetoes as he commanded Malice to land nearby, while simultaneously re-ordering his undead into combat ranks. He'd already sent one of the guards to mirror the ba'ardec, to ensure they didn't double back and was clearly preparing to march the undead to reinforce the townsfolk. With the fighting very much in motion and with little hope of a diplomatic outcome, there wasn't much for Vortiga to do.

As she watched the undead, however, she noticed something strange. The ground around a zombie's feet was cracking and bulging. Once she'd seen it, she noticed the same, strange phenomenon happening all over the area.

Checking at her own feet, she was relieved to see no signs of whatever it was. Returning her gaze towards the undead, however, she caught her first glimpse of whatever was causing it as a large, red and purple worm broke the surface of the ground.

The horrid thing must have been a foot in length, but its sinuous body, that was almost as thick as her arm, moved with monstrous efficiency towards the undead.

The nearest zombie, a bugbear, paid the strange creature no attention. This was, until the thing opened a three-part mouth, each section filled with rows of dagger-like teeth and launched itself at the zombie's chest.

At first the worm-like creature was stalled by the bugbear zombie's breastplate. Or at least, that's how it had seemed to Vortiga, until she heard the screech of metal being torn open. The undead bugbear watched, unperturbed as the vermicular creature burrowed not only through the breastplate, but into the zombie's chest.

Vortiga watched in alarm as seconds later, the bugbear dropped, inanimate as the sinuous horror tore its way free and slithered away. Worse still, Vortiga could see more than a dozen more of the undead falling to the worms.

She'd seen enough. Without orders the undead didn't recognise the worms as a threat until it was too late. If they didn't do something, Ninetoes' army of undead would be nothing but a pile of smelly corpses in no time.

Bursting into action, Vortiga sprang towards the first worm she'd seen. Two dozen, long and powerful strides brought her to within striking distance and, with a single, graceful spin, Vortiga drew Magebane and cleaved the worm in two the moment before it burrowed into another zombie. The two pieces plopped onto the floor, only to begin hissing and dissolving a moment later. Bizarre as this was, Vortiga had more important things to think about.

"Ninetoes!" She called, hoping to alert him to the danger and so command his zombies to defend themselves. But she received no reply and, looking up, she could see the wizard astride Malice, circling higher and, apparently, too far for her voice to reach clearly.

She shouted again, louder this time, and used her commanding voice to clearly enunciate. "Ninetoes, we're under attack!"

She wasn't sure he'd heard her, but then Malice banked, and the manticore changed course. The undead, meanwhile, began marching towards the town. Most of them at least.

Perhaps two dozen were now either inanimate meat sacks being dragged by their lead zombie or, in a few cases, simply stood stock still as a worm devoured their leader.

As the area cleared, Vortiga moved into their ranks and dispatched as many of the worms as she could, but as the last of the undead left the area, Vortiga realised that the worms she hadn't killed were now retreating.

Or, at least, that was her first thought. But, as her eyes tracked their movement, she realised that they all slithered to the same spot, before stopping and regurgitating the stinking waste of masticated zombie parts onto the ground, before circling back towards the ranks of undead.

Stunned and not a little confused, Vortiga nonetheless moved forward, intent upon finishing the grim work of dispatching the worms.

As soon as she stepped forward, however, a screech pierced the sky and a large shadow crossed over her.

NINETOES

Vortiga's shout brought a concerned look to Ninetoes face, as he realised that he'd left her at the foot of the walls. He'd been worried for her safety when she'd fallen, but he'd noted her regaining her feet and had reckoned she was mostly unharmed.

Now however, her voice was that of a Sarm, the commanding tone present that he had yet to manage for himself, demanding his attention.

He didn't catch what she'd said, but as he scanned below him, he could see a disturbance within his ranks of undead and, worst still, could see that some of them had already fallen to the attacks of an unknown assailant.

With a conscious and not inconsequential act of will, Ninetoes had the entire group of zombies he controlled march closer to the town. Meanwhile, he commanded Malice to circle back.

As the manticore banked, Ninetoes leaned out of his seat slightly and watched as Vortiga carved some sort of worm-like creature in half.

Now that he'd seen it, he spotted more of the sinuous monsters as they worked their way through his retreating ranks. As the area emptied of undead, Ninetoes could see the carnage already caused by the disgusting creatures. It was also quickly apparent that the worms were already retreating, perhaps because they'd finished their meal.

If he was honest, that seemed unlikely. The monstrous things had surprised his "army" and in a matter of moments had dispatched a score or more of his zombies. It was only Vortiga who had staved off a more serious result.

But what in the world were they? He needed more information, so he directed his mount towards Vortiga.

A shriek cut through the sky, somehow whiny and threatening all at once. In the corner of his eye, Ninetoes glimpsed a large creature as it launched itself from a treetop and shot towards Vortiga.

Ninetoes' gaze followed the creature, casting Identify to gather more information.

> **LESSER OFFAL DEMON** - LEVEL 12
> **PRIME STAT** - CONSTITUTION
> **PRIME TRAITS** - REND, COMMAND
> 250/250 HP
> 6500XP

The demon appeared to be some kind of massive bird that resembled a vulture, only two times as large and its head was covered in thick, grey scales. It surged towards Ninetoes' ally, its brown, feathered wings tucked close to its side and its curved beak clearly intent upon carving through her flesh.

Its shriek of rage, however, had been a mistake. Rather than run, or try to dodge, Vortiga stood calmly in the centre of the road, her sword held loosely by her side.

Briefly, Vortiga looked up at Ninetoes and nodded. "I'll deal with this, go save the town."

Her voice wasn't loud, but it was clear and confident and was coupled with the look of serenity on her face.

Ninetoes might still have tried to intervene, but he'd seen this face before. He'd stared into it too many times, and it was the demon he pitied in that moment. Instead, he guided Malice back towards the town, and left Vortiga to her work.

The Offal Demon meanwhile, streaked towards Vortiga clearly intent upon its kill.

But at the last and most perfect possible moment, as the demon stretched out its beak and claws towards her, Vortiga performed the simplest of moves.

Without moving her feet, she twisted on the spot and brought Magebane up and over her head to slice down onto the monster's neck.

And, had it been any other monster, that would have been enough, and the decapitated creature would have barrelled, lifelessly into the ground. But even Magebane's keen edge wasn't enough to cause more than minor damage to the demon's armoured head.

Vortiga stood aghast as the demon circled back, clearly intent upon attacking again. Graver still, the wormlike monsters had not been idle in the intervening moments.

Ninetoes' spell identified these as Minor Offal Demons and instantly recognised that they were using one of their Prime Traits to reform from a single creature into something much worse.

MINOR OFFAL DEMON - LEVEL 2
PRIME STAT - AGILITY
PRIME TRAITS - BORE, SWARM
20/20 HP
50XP

Perhaps triggered by the Lesser Offal demon's shriek, the worm-like Minor Demons had gathered together into a swarm. While their vulture-like commander had their enemy distracted, the swarm of other demons approached from Vortiga's blindspot.

Ninetoes knew that demons were particularly bad news, but little else of use. He also knew, however, that the people of Raveslan were fighting and, almost certainly dying, at the hands of the Nechtsarm. And yet, if he did nothing, his ally would surely die. Momentarily doubting his actions, Ninetoes wasted precious seconds debating what to do.

The certainty of one truth, however, forced him into motion: If he didn't act quickly, more people would die.

Vortiga had already shown herself to be a devastating warrior, but she was outnumbered and the larger demon had already shown itself immune to her weapons. He considered just shouting a warning but he knew this simply wouldn't be enough.

No, he wouldn't let another ally fall. He wouldn't let another friend be taken. Ninetoes made his choice.

Taking "direct" control of Malice, he turned the manticore towards the Lesser Demon, increasing his mount's speed and angling his descent so as to cut off the demon's line of attack.

It was a close-run thing. The Offal Demon was closer, but Malice was faster.

The manticore and its hobgoblin rider slammed full body into the side of the Offal Demon, ruining its attack and knocking it off to the ground, just off the road.

"They're demons!" Ninetoes shouted to Vortiga, pointing his staff behind her and firing off a Grim Bolt, before taking control of Malice and leaping the manticore towards his downed foe.

The Lesser Demon might have been thrown to the floor, but it was clearly made of sterner stuff, and before Malice could even reach it, it had found its feet and took off into the sky.

Confident that Vortiga could handle the swarm of worm demons, Ninetoes took off in pursuit.

VORTIGA

From out of the corner of her eye, Vortiga saw Malice's mass hurtling towards the vulture-like demon and sensibly, she stepped back.

With a crash of limbs the two large monsters bundled to the floor, but Malice stayed on its feet, while the demon rolled away.

"They're demons!" Ninetoes shouted, and leaning forward, he pointed his staff at Vortiga. The Porsht's words took a moment to register, but his actions were clear enough and instinctively she dove forward and rolled. That simple act probably saved her life.

As she rose back to her feet she turned on the spot, tracking the Porsht's movements as Malice took off and there, right where she'd been a moment before, was a swarm of demons, the writhing mass of worms undulated towards her at an incredible rate.

Gaining some distance, Vortiga took a moment to catch her breath and strategize. She'd already dispatched a half-dozen of these monsters without much trouble, but the swarm must have been made up of three score or more.

While the swarm moved quickly, she was easily able to outpace it. But to kill them, she'd need to get in close and, since she'd also seen them burrow straight through plate armour, she wasn't particularly keen to close with them.

If she had oil or tar, she could set them aflame. Perhaps she could make her way into the town?

No. Even if she found something, the worms would make short work of the remaining undead.

No, she had little choice but to do this herself, the hard way. And if she was honest, she preferred it that way.

After a moment to take in the terrain around her, Vortiga placed her feet carefully and raised Magebane before. As ready as she was ever likely to be, she moved towards the swarm.

Centred and calm, Vortiga's movement became flowing and rhythmic, like a dance. Her feet never left the floor, instead moving in tight, concentric circles and her arms moved Magebane into a complex and fluid sword form.

Her strategy was simple; don't get bitten. But that was most certainly easier said than done.

Vortiga's movements were, even in her own modest opinion, nearly perfect. Every time her blade moved out, it carved a worm in two and as it flowed back it blocked the strike of another.

For long moments, Vortiga was a blur of movement and the swarm shrank as more and more of the worms fell to the floor before sizzling into nothing.

But, with the swarm roughly two-thirds gone, Vortiga's arms started to tyre and, as her blade moved a fraction of a second too slow, a worm bypassed her guard and latched onto the fore of her sword arm.

Worse still, the demon seemed to have even less trouble with the chainmail armour than it had with the zombie's plate and, even as she sliced another in half, the Minor Demon's teeth found her flesh and made her scream with pain.

All at once, her calm, fluid movements stalled and Vortiga was at risk of being swamped. Leaping back, she barely missed another worm's teeth, and while she backpedalled quickly to create some space, Vortiga used her free arm to grab the worm that was latched onto her arm before it could burrow inside her skin.

A grim and painful wrestling match ensued, Vortiga screaming bloody murder as she simultaneously pulled and crushed the worm.

With a wet and excruciating slurp, she wrenched the demon from her arm, but its serrated teeth took with it large lumps of flesh and muscle and blood ran freely down her arm.

Dropping the worm to the ground, Vortiga stomped what little life the mangled demon had left and then continued to retreat.

The wound wasn't large, but it was deep and painful. Wobbling slightly from blood loss, Vortiga tore a length of cloth from her cloak and bound her arm as best she could, meanwhile considering her situation.

The swarm was now a tiny fraction of its original size, with barely a dozen left. Perhaps, she reasoned, she'd done enough? If Ninetoes returned in time, he could organise his undead into dispatching what was left of the worms.

Even as the thought occurred to her, however, Vortiga realised that her retreat had drawn her closer to the zombies and neither the Porsht, nor Malice were anywhere to be found. If she left the swarm to its own devices, it would set upon the zombies in no time, and all her efforts might have been for naught.

If she was completely truthful however, as she stepped back towards the swarm, it wasn't the thought of losing the undead that really bothered her, it was the thought of needing to rely upon anyone else to finish the job.

With her main sword arm out of commission, she couldn't perform the same sword form as before and moreover, she couldn't use the same tactic. But, with so few of the creatures left alive, perhaps she didn't have to.

This time, Vortiga closed within range of the worms, but only just, keeping at the very edge of what she judged to be the limit of their leaps and began slowly drawing the swarm away from the undead.

As carefully as possible, Vortiga chose her moment and stepped towards the worms and, the moment one leapt for her, she skipped backwards and sliced it apart. *One down.*

Within a few moments, Vortiga had repeated the process and claimed two more worms.

Despite being bound, however, her arm still dripped blood onto the floor and Vortiga's movements grew ever more sloppy. She knew that she couldn't keep up this tactic forever. Compounding the problem, the worms seemed to have grown wise to her tactics and, the next two times she stepped in, none of the worms attacked.

There were now so few left that Vortiga could count them. Only seven of the worms remained. Swaying on the spot, Vortiga decided that it was time to finish the fight.

Stepping towards the worms, as she had many times and, as expected, none of the demons attacked, but Vortiga was done retreating back and this time while they stayed still, Vortiga quickly skewered three worms.

The other four, however, finally sensed victory and leapt at Vortiga all at once. A single, sweeping arc of her blade was enough to end two of them, but the other two made it inside Vortiga's guard.

One made for the same hole that had already been torn through her chainmail, while the other latched onto her chest and made for her throat. Despite the obvious threat offered by the one on her arm, Vortiga sensibly dropped her sword and grabbed the one at her neck.

Kneeling, she bashed the worm onto the cobbled road until it stopped moving. But this was all the time the other needed and with a horrid slurping sound burrowed deep into her arm.

Fruitlessly, Vortiga grasped at what little was left of its tail, but she wasn't enough and the worm's sinuous body slid out of her blood-slick hand and disappeared inside her.

Screaming at the burning pain of something literally eating her arm from the inside out, Vortiga nearly didn't hear the guard as he rushed up to her side.

"What happened to the swarm?" he asked stupidly.

"Argh! My sword, my sword!" she screamed at him.

Looking round, confusedly, the guard spotted her blade nearby and picked it up, dumbly offering it to her.

"No! My arm, cut off my arm!" She cried out, holding her sword arm out to one side and gritting her sharp teeth.

"What I...? What?" The guard stared back, clearly way out of his depth.

For Vortiga, however, nothing was clearer. The worm was burrowing up her arm, ever closer to her heart, there was only one choice. "Do it!" She screamed, spraying bloody spittle onto his face.

Still a little stunned, the guard nonetheless rallied and, dropping his own mace to the ground, held Magebane with two hands.

With a gulp he raised the sword and cropped down.

Had the fool ever used a sword before that probably would have been enough, but despite the blade's magical nature and the burly muscles of the farhand-made-guard, the first cut didn't completely sever the limb.

With a force of will seen once in a lifetime, the guard watched in awe as Vortiga raised the limb once again. "Do. It. Fucking. Right!"

The second time, Magebane cut through cleanly and blood vomited out of the stump left below Vortiga's left bicep. For her part, Vortiga felt that this was a good opportunity to collapse.

CHAPTER 33

DESPAIR

The Offal Demon wasn't anywhere near as fast as Malice, but the manticore's turning circle was much less tight and the demon was easily able to outmanoeuvre Ninetoes' mount.

For his part, Ninetoes mostly just clung on, allowing his mount to do the flying while occasionally sending a Grim Bolt at the demon. Only one of these hit and to add insult to injury, the demon appeared to be immune to necrotic damage, and simply shrugged off the attack.

While the demon wasn't a danger, while it escaped Ninetoes' grasp, its presence wasted vital time for the wizard. Ninetoes knew that every second could cost another life; he must end this chase as quickly as possible. As quickly as possible, he needed to get his undead into the town, to engage the Nechtsarm.

His chase had already taken him near to the western gate on and he'd seen that not only were the defenders hard-pressed by the main body of the hobgoblin army, he'd witness the ba'ardec who had made it passed him stalking through the town and would be joining the fray at any moment, carving into the flank of the town's forces.

Quickly, he commanded Malice to change the angle of its chase, and Ninetoes forced the Offal Demon back towards the eastern gate and his undead army.

Once in range, Ninetoes concentrated for a moment and split the undead army into two halves, sending each group to wrap around the town and flank the main army of Nechtsarm from the west. Once the demon was dealt with, he'd deal with the ba'ardec within the walls.

Turning his attention back to the demon, he planned his attack. The demon was slighter than Malice and, despite its obvious tough hide, Ninetoes was confident that his manticore could tear the monster apart with his help.

What Ninetoes needed, however, was a means of closing the lead the demon had. Mentally he ran through his spells. But, despite how far he'd come in such a short time, he had no spells that could slow or paralyse the demon. The best idea he had was to cast Barrier to stop it in its tracks, but to do that, he'd need to be in front of it, which was exactly his problem.

The only other option he had was Arcane Step. He could, with a massive expenditure of mana, carry a second creature with him when he 'stepped', but with the ongoing battle he'd already spent a goodly amount of his pool.

Moreover, he didn't know if teleporting with such a large creature would cost him even more than usual. He'd also never 'stepped' while flying and had no way of knowing how it would affect Malice's ability to function.

A minor explosion sounded off in the distance and Ninetoes knew that somewhere in the town someone was dying and it was his fault. He couldn't waiver, or his people would be forfeit.

Draining his Gem of Power, Ninetoes topped himself off as much as possible and then took "direct" control of Malice. He needed to be as certain as possible that the manticore continued to fly once they'd stepped.

Steadying his breathing and tightening his grip on the reins, Ninetoes waited for his moment.

Tracking the demon's course, he held back until the demon was as close as possible and about to turn.

Focussing his will, Ninetoes cast Arcane Step.

SARIEL

Sariel's hand flapped about ineffectively for a good couple of seconds before her brain kicked in and informed her that she did not, in fact, have any arrows left.

Scanning the parapet, she located a handcart filled with bundles of arrows and immediately made for it. As she went she grabbed at as many of the archers she could that still hadn't realised that the greater threat was suddenly behind them.

The ba'ardec warriors were accurate marksmen, perhaps almost at her own level, so she had no idea how she was ever going to stop or even slow down their assault, but she had to find a way.

By the time she reached the handcart and refreshed her quiver, the archers had finally recognised the danger and at least a third of Raveslan's forces had started to engage the elite hobgoblin soldiers. This at least was forcing the ba'ardec to find cover and slowed down the pace at which they could fire; finally giving Sariel the time to consider a strategy for dealing with this new threat.

Casting her mind outwards, she called out to her allies for aid.

With a brief scan of the enemy, Sariel estimated there were perhaps a dozen ba'ardec, so not a full company, but that might also mean that there were more elsewhere. *Shit!*

Her plan would need to include checking the rest of the town, but that would have to wait. What she needed most was information, so with a burst of energy and a couple of mana-enhanced leaps, Sariel reached the eyrie at the top of the Golden Spindle.

There she found Mera Fawkner, unconscious and convulsing, with an arrow sticking out of her shoulder. Studying the Lady, Sariel could see that stemming from the arrow wound, the veins were black and swollen.

"Mera?" she asked stupidly, expecting the clearly injured and poisoned woman to answer her. For her part, Lady Fawkner simply started frothing at the mouth and pink spittle began staining her shirt.

Knowing that the ba'ardec were a possibility, Sariel had prepared a spell, Lesser Cure Poison, that should cure the poisons of the elite warriors.

Sariel hesitated, however. The spell was costly and would drain all of the mana she had left, but more, without knowing what the poison coursing through Mera's veins was, she wasn't sure if the spell would be powerful enough to save her. Moreover, she still didn't know what part Mera had played in the betrayal of Ninetoes. Could she really use all of her mana to possibly save her?

Sariel acted. She wanted to believe the best of the Lady and, whatever else she might have done, she'd received this wound in the defence of Raveslan. Sariel would figure out the rest later.

A rich, dark green energy flowed out of the half-elf's palms as she muttered the incantation. Starting at the extremities, Sariel's magic forced the poison out of Mera's veins the way it had gotten in and a nasty brown sludge began oozing out of the wound left by the arrow.

As her spell timed out most of Mera's veins appeared to have been scoured clean of infectant and Sariel slumped forward as a slight headache informed her that she was nearly completely depleted of mana.

With so little left, there was nothing magical she could do about the wound itself, so she grabbed a bandage from her pack and bound the injury as best she could.

As she finished, Mera awoke and screamed. "Goblins... breaching... east gate."

"It's alright." Sariel made the empty promise without thinking. "How do you feel?" she asked, handing Mera a waterskin.

Washing out her mouth, Mera looked up and finally focussed properly on the half-elf Ranger.

"I'm, ergh, awful. But I can fight. I think." As she said this, she eased herself up into firstly a sitting position and then onto her knees, before looking out over the town. "Fuck! They're already here. How long was I out?"

"I'm not sure, a couple of minutes maybe. If you're alright, I must leave and find a way to deal with the ba'ardec."

"ba'ardec?"

BOOM!

An explosion shook the nearby buildings and Sariel recognised the sound of a Fireball. Turning back to Mera she continued their conversation. "These new hobgoblins are their elite scouts. You're lucky I arrived when I did, or that poison would have surely killed you."

"Poison? Argh!" Mera exclaimed, looking down at her ruined shirt. "If you're going to kill them, then I'm coming too," she asserted.

"I don't think that would be best your ladyship, I-"

"No arguments. If I can't keep up, go on without me, but I'll have some vengeance before you kill them all."

"Ha! I appreciate your faith in my skills, but at best I think we might be able to distract them long enough for help to arrive."

"What help can you expect to arrive?"

"I don't know, but a girl can hope right?"

By now, the pair were moving along the rooftop, keeping themselves low to make it easier to maintain their centre of gravity. As they reached the edge they found a smaller battle raging between three burning buildings. Dozens of townsfolk were fighting the ba'ardec. Promisingly, three of the hobgoblin elite were already lying dead on the street and the rest were seemingly pinned down. Tarquin was single-handedly fighting two of the soldiers and was clearly having the best of it because of the advantage of reach afforded him by his longsword.

Nonetheless, the pair could see from their vantage point that a half-dozen of the ba'ardec had broken off from the main fight and were flanking around a building. In moments they'd take the townsfolk by surprise and the battle would quickly turn against the defenders.

"There." Leaving Mera behind, Sariel pointed and scraped the bottom of her mana barrel for enough mana to cast Jump one last time. Sariel sprung from the rooftop of the Spindle onto the building that the ba'ardec were flanking around and kept on running, allowing her adrenalin to burn off any suggestion of resting that her mana pool begged her for.

There was so much noise that she didn't even need to bother trying to be quiet as she dashed along the rooftop, only stopping once she'd reached the end. Looking down, she saw the last three of the ba'ardec as the party flanked around the building. *Dammit!*

She was too late to stop them altogether, but she'd still be able to turn their surprise attack into one of her own.

Before the three soldiers could round the corner, Sariel fired three rapid shots, each one into a different target, using her archery ability, Quick Shot. At only a dozen feet, she could hardly miss and each arrow cut into a hobgoblin's leg.

Even as the third arrow was in motion, Sariel was dropping to the ground and slitting the throats of these crippled soldiers.

Without even realising it, the flanking squad had lost half their number. But as the others turned at the death rattle of their comrades, they made for the ranger with grim and murderous looks.

Even still, the ba'ardec didn't immediately rush in and took the time to equip their odd, buckler-like, shields and fan out around the half-elf. "You're gonna pay for that girly," the one in the middle ground out.

Holding her longbow in one hand and a shortsword in the other, Sariel recognised that without the element of surprise, she was no match for the battle-hardened soldiers.

Of course, she didn't need to be.

TARQUIN

The Warlock was having fun. When he'd Levelled Up, his patron had given him a powerful new ability. Whenever he killed something, he reclaimed a little of its lifeforce, healing his wounds and helping to recharge his Stamina.

Stood atop the wooden walls, raining down Arcane Bolts and stabbing the occasional hobgoblin that managed to reach the top of a ladder simply hadn't been doing it for him.

When he'd heard Sariel's warning shout he'd found something far more his pace and he leapt down from the palisade and charged the new group of hobgoblins.

Daph had just finished recharging the Wand of Fireballs, so he whipped that out and aimed it at the space in front of the hobgoblins. In his excitement, however, his aim was a little off and instead of decimating their lines he only succeeded in killing three of them and setting some buildings on fire. *Ah well, a shame but no real loss there.*

He charged on and searched the ranks of hobgoblins for the easiest targets. He noted that two of the soldiers had been knocked back by the explosion, but had only received minor wounds. They would be meat soon enough.

Tarquin danced in between them, shouting a challenge as missiles flew overhead between the town's defenders and the other hobs. The two injured goblins were no match for his skill level and Tarquin took the time to kill them slowly and so earn as much Skill experience as he could.

As a shadow cast itself over him, the Warlock noted the Ranger leaping from one rooftop to another. Following her course, he noticed that some of the hobgoblins were attempting to flank around the building.

Not wanting to be caught between a rock and a hard place, Tarquin despatched his two current foes and stalked towards the back of the building.

Peering cautiously around the corner of the building, he saw three of the hobs making their way towards him. These were fresh and uninjured, so Tarquin ducked back, and began considering a path of retreat.

"You're gonna pay for that girly." Tarquin heard the gravelly voice and peeked around the corner once again. What he saw brought a smile to his face.

The goblin soldiers were not only facing the other way, they seemed to be completely intent upon the Ranger. Tarquin saw this as the perfect opportunity. Not only could he kill some more assholes but he could do it while appearing to be the hero. Still, he needed to play it safe.

As quietly as possible, he walked out into the space and pointed a hand at the middle goblin. As soon as they charged the Ranger, he fired an Arcane Bolt right into the soldier's back, injuring him and spilling him forward onto the cobbled ground.

Then, with a dozen quick and long strides, he was on the downed foe and driving his sword through the fool's neck.

Surprised, one of the hobgoblins hesitated and that was all the time Sariel needed to drop her sword and fire an arrow straight into his face from point blank range. The missile flew with enough force that it sprang out of the back of the goblin's head, dragging copious amounts of grey matter with it.

The last of their enemies didn't stand a chance and he soon fell to their blades, but not before he'd taken a slice out of the Ranger.

"Thank you," the Ranger said to Tarquin, as she held her side, clearly in pain.

"Of course," he nodded magnanimously.

"We should climb to the roof and find a way to flank them," she suggested.

"Indeed. Lead the way."

SARIEL

The pair dashed around the back of the building and made for the rear lines of the hobgoblins assaulting from within the town. But as they made it around the last corner, they found that everything had changed.

The ground was littered with the bodies of more townsfolk, one she noticed with sadness was Peran. A half dozen more buildings along the inside of the wall had caught on fire and the ba'ardec had managed to drag a couple of carts into the street, creating a defensive wall of their own.

That was when everything really went to hell.

She heard it before she noticed anything amiss. The creak of bending wood, followed by the shocking crack as it broke. Those in front of the gate were knocked aside and the goblins flooded in, their swords and spears dipped and rose, casting red shadows. Finally able to reach the defenders within the walls, all of their pent-up aggression spilled out and those few defenders left standing stood no hope of holding back the tide.

Searching across the melee, Sariel could see Foresto's golem, standing twice the height of the people around it. The towering construct's hands had been replaced with massive axe-blades, which were hacking through enemies to its left and right, but it wasn't enough and within moments the tide of goblinoids crashed into the creature, toppling it backwards into the melee.

Atop the gate, stood Foresto and Daphne, each of them raining arcane fire down on the attackers as quickly as they could but they simply couldn't keep up the pace and she watched as a stray arrow sliced into Daphne's neck and the wizard's body fell into the churning mass of bodies beneath.

Well, that's one fewer problem to deal with later.

The tempo of the battle changed in that moment. It was no longer a defence, now it was a rout. But the town's defenders were now stuck between a raging inferno, the goblinoid army smashing through the gate and the withering hail of the ba'ardec. Just as the hobgoblin Curn had promised, Raveslan was about to become a charnel house.

Looking around, panic played across her face as she turned to address Tarquin. "What should we d-"

But the other Adventurer was gone. One moment he'd been there and now he wasn't. She searched the battle, hoping to see him bravely carving through the hobgoblins, making his way towards the body of his fallen companion. Finally, she found him, far across town, making his cowardly way over the wall. The bastard was running.

Choosing to forget the craven warlock, Sariel cast her gaze about searching for a solution. An answer to how the fuck they were going to get out of this one!

But there was nothing. She had barely half her quiver of arrows left, she was at the bottom of her mana pool and her fellow Adventurers were either dead, lost or fleeing. She already witnessed one of the hippogriffs being cut down by archers, and the other was nowhere to be seen. Foresto was still fighting of course, but he couldn't prevail against so many. Powerful as he might be, he'd admitted to the Ranger that he had few combat spells and none that dealt a large area of damage.

The defenders had spent every trick and played every trump card they'd had and it hadn't been enough.

She scanned the scene one more time, hoping against hope that a solution would reveal itself. Finally, as she watched a townsman fall from the attack of a bugbear, she resigned herself to doing as much damage as possible before the end, and began firing arrows.

She aimed at the ba'ardec, trying her best to carve a hole in their defensive line so that the townsfolk might at least find an avenue of escape. But even that proved fruitless. A couple of the elite soldiers simply turned their bows on her, forcing her to take cover and keep her own head down.

Breathing deeply, about to give in to despair, the strange sound through the rumble and concussion of the fighting. Sariel looked about, panicking that it was one more problem that had no solution. Focussing, she realised that it was two distinctly different sounds. The first was an odd creaking, like hundreds of doors opening. The other sounded like wind rushing through a tunnel and was coming from above.

This, she decided, required more immediate attention and staring up, she struggled to make sense of what she was seeing and then, she simply refused to believe it.

At first she thought it was one of the hippogriffs, the one she'd just lost track of it in the confusion of battle. But, instead of an eagle's shriek the monstrous flyer let out the roar of a lion!

Banking, the monster whipped its tail and barbs shot towards the line of ba'ardec.

By this point, however, Sariel wasn't watching the flyer, but was staring in amazement at the mount's sharp-toothed rider. Whooping with joy, Sariel knew that they might just have a chance after all.

NINETOES

Guiding Malice low, Ninetoes took in the scene unfolding. They were late! The gate had been breached and the people of Raveslan were about to be overrun. His analytical mind quickly took in the details and could see that while the townsfolk were surrounded, they were hemmed in from the east by a group of ba'ardec. *Well, we can't have that now can we Malice?*

As he finished the thought, he directed the manticore lower still and then had the monster fire its tail barbs into the rear rank of soldiers, while simultaneously dropping the broken body of the Offal monster on two more.

Casting so many spells in quick succession, while directly controlling Malice had been no mean feat, but Raveslan's newest defender was more than up to the challenge.

His Arcane Step had carried both Ninetoes and Malice directly into the Offal Demon's path. A quick casting of Barrier and instantly arrested the demon's movement with a resounding crunch.

Still controlling Malice, Ninetoes had reached out the manticore's vicious claws and grabbed the dazed creature.

Even still it had required a casting of Arcane Weapon before the manticore's claws could penetrate the demon's hide and even then, the beastly creature had continued to kick and scratch at his mount's underbelly. Only Malice's undead nature meant that, while damage was being done, the zombified manticore simply couldn't feel pain and, as they'd whizzed back to the town, Malice had continued rending the beast into pieces.

As the body smashed into the ba'ardec beneath them, it finally died and began hissing its way into oblivion.

Now, Malice fired a half dozen more bolts, each one finding a mark, tearing through armour like a hot knife through butter and creating a gap in the defensive line of hobgoblin soldiers.

The people below shied away from the flying monster but nonetheless some of them noticed the gap and began fighting to widen it.

Ninetoes leaned out of his seat and fired an Arcane Bolt but the motion of his mount threw his aim off and it splashed uselessly onto a roof.

Reeling back for another pass, Ninetoes had Malice fire a barrage into the ba'ardec. The manticore was much more skilled at shooting while in flight and the missiles cut into the elite scouts, finally breaking their lines and giving the townsfolk a means of escape.

With the gate breached and the Nechtsarm hot on their heels, however, the people of Raveslan weren't really any safer.

Searching the field of battle, Ninetoes could already see that the town had suffered heavy losses and, while they outnumbered the hobgoblins, they were no match for them in terms of skill; the hobs would grind them into paste.

Considering and discarding plans, Ninetoes smiled with glee as the voice of his Familiar entered his mind and within an instant the tow had formed a plan.

With a flick of will, Ninetoes sent Malice to fly back towards the northern wall but he wouldn't be going. Instead he leapt from the manticore's back and plummeted towards the ground. But before he built up any velocity, however, he 'stepped'.

Learning to change orientation while 'stepping' had been difficult, but well worth it as he materialised into the thick of the fighting and shoulder-barged a heavily armoured hobgoblin in the back, sending her sprawling to the ground.

What the people of Raveslan desperately needed was space, so Ninetoes had teleported a few ranks back into the hobgoblin lines. After their initial shock, however, the Nechtsarm just grinned at the foolish wizard who now found himself surrounded by enemies.

This was, of course, exactly where Ninetoes wanted to be and, as the soldiers charged him, he activated his cloak and a surge of thunderous energy burst outwards from him, knocking the soldiers aside like so many wooden skittles.

Ninetoes was already in motion and casting his most deadly spell. Like the Reaper, he stepped amongst the Sword of Nech and dealt death, his touch a grim curse.

He managed to send a half dozen Nechtsarm to meet Starm. Not as many as he'd have liked, but for the first time in days all of his wounds, scratches, and bruises were healed and Ninetoes was at his maximum hit points.

Ready Master. Ninetoes smiled.

Staring at those around him his eyes broiled with malicious intent and his hands burned with black shadows. The soldiers about him quivered at the sight of this wraith-like creature that stared down a battalion of Warriors.

The roar shook them from their petrified reverie and they looked up just as a monster from nightmare landed to flank this reaper-made-flesh.

Many thought they'd seen this creature already, but they'd been mistaken. For now the monster blistered with the same dark energy as the mage. Its teeth seemed too many and its claws were as long and sharp as scythes. Blood dripped from a maw which promised a painful death. This was no mere manticore, but some sort of demon!

Ninetoes took a step towards the ranks of soldiers and each and every one took a step back. He took another and the monster leapt clear over him, whipping its tail, every grim bolt sent yet more soldiers clattering to the cobbled floor and one to Starm's Hall.

The front ranks of the Nechtsarm broke then.

Each hobgoblin crazed with fear, began trying to bully and force their way through the lines behind them. But just then, a second commotion started at the rear of the goblinoid forces and the clash of weapons sounded like a second battle taking place on that flank as well. Shouts arose of "Zombies!" and "Undead!"

621

Stepping forward, the people of Raveslan joined the fight then too.

Those still on the walls rained death down from above, and while those inside the town were too afraid to approach the monster, they threw or fired whatever they could to add to the cacophony of slaughter that was being enacted upon the army that had come to take their home.

For Ninetoes' part, once the soldiers before him broke, he 'stepped' to the top of the gatehouse to survey the battle from on high.

Wrapping Malice in an illusion had been Libby's idea and it had turned the tide. There was much he still had to learn, but he recognised the sheer, gut-churning power of her chosen spell school.

Like the name of his own people, the Dakhec Druul, his army of undead had managed to wrap around the Nechtsarm, sealing their doom.

Whilst two-thirds of the undead were effectively useless without instruction, once the Nechtsarm rear-guard had started attacking the uncontrolled zombies, all of the undead had joined the fight. Alongside the zombies, there were dozens of older undead, the skeletal victims of the Animator's only other use by Corvatch III. They had been Kavralach's original citizens. But these skeletons were so old and their bones so brittle with age, many and the hobgoblins made short work of them.

Ninetoes had to admit, while he didn't agree with his methods, Corvatch was certainly right that the undead were the perfect warriors. While the hobgoblins carved, bashed and stabbed the undead, the monstrous creatures didn't fall until massive damage had been done. The hobs meanwhile, were cut down one at a time.

Watching the slaughter, however, Ninetoes witnessed the worst aspect of battle. He watched as the anger of the people of Raveslan tore into the army of his people.

Watching it unfold, Ninetoes lost his taste for murder and, with the merest thought, he opened a gap in the ranks of undead and watched as the surviving Nechtsarm flooded out through it.

He couldn't stop all of the undead from fighting, but he had those under his control move backwards, dragging those they were tied to away from the hobgoblins. As the rear guard retreated, the pressure on those in the front rank eased and the goblins ran.

Injured, exhausted and missiles spent, it was all the people of Raveslan could do to watch their enemy as they fled into the woods.

A rough cheer rose from the townsfolk, but most were too tired or saddened by loss to take it up. Finally, those with any energy left closed what was left of the gate and used whatever they could find to bar it shut.

The battle for Raveslan was over.

EPILOGUE
A WOMAN SCORNED

Ffion hadn't liked the Adventurers from her first dealings with them and she trusted this group not at all, but there was something utterly and unexplainably despicable about the tall, handsome one that had arrived to "rescue" Raveslan.

Worse still, the fool had seemed completely unbothered by the situation that the town found themselves in. At least the others spent their time helping, but the human, Tarquin, did nothing but lounge around the tavern, somehow convincing people to bring him food.

But it had been Bess' behaviour that had concerned the halfling the most. She'd known the girl since she'd arrived as a teenager to apprentice to Borris. Being sent to a frontier town wasn't many young girls' first choice, especially not after having grown up in Pamor, but Bess had always held her head up high and worked hard to improve her craft.

She'd met the girl when she'd come with the old smith to shoe some horses, but soon after Bess had learned enough to do it herself. Ffion had been reluctant to allow the apprentice to work her animals at first, but Bes had stubbornly argued and demanded she be given the chance to prove herself and her master's confidence in her ability. This had impressed Ffion and, little though Bess had known it, Ffion and insisted that the girl be sent along from then on.

In all that time, while she'd noticed the girl's head turned once or twice by a boy, she'd never acted on it and had kept herself focussed on her work; something Ffion respected greatly.

So it was that watching the way Bess fawned over Tarquin, had driven Ffion to distraction.

Worse still, when the Adventurer had lost interest, the young woman had seemed to collapse in on herself and that, if possible, was worse. But it was also the first time that Bess had come to visit since she'd returned from her adventure to Pamor.

Within moments of her arrival the poor girl had broken down into tears. Not of sorrow, but of anger. She was angry at herself for the way she'd acted and the way she'd allowed herself to be treated. She'd even admitted to the part she'd played in the murder of the hobgoblin Adventurer and, while Ffion held no love for him, she had been able to see that he was different.

For Bess, this was a stain that she didn't know how to wash off and she'd been inconsolable. As her story unfolded, she'd told Ffion that the Adventurer Tarquin had controlled her with magic.

What's more, she'd told Ffion of a plan to exact revenge on the traitorous Adventurers.

That was why, when she spied Tarquin fleeing over the north wall from atop her hippogriff mount, she'd made her decision. The battle in her home town would not be decided by her actions, but she could stop the dastardly coward from escaping their vengeance.

She allowed him to cross the wall and head into the forest. Then, gliding soundlessly above, she chose the site of her ambush and flew ahead of the Adventurer, keeping out of his line of sight.

As Tarquin jogged into the clearing that she'd picked, a click of her tongue was all it took to command her well-trained mount into a dive. The swooping hippogriff tucked itself into a ball and plummeted towards her target, throwing out its wings at the last moment and giving the Adventurer all the warning he was going to get.

Tarquin stared back in horror at the monstrous hybrid. Even still, he was quick enough to roll forwards, attempting to get away. But it was too little, too late and the hippogriff's talons sank into the soft flesh of the human and bore him down to the ground with a scream.

With her knees Ffion guided her mount off of Tarquin and left him curled up on the floor, his legs a bloodied mess. "You are going nowhere Adventurer."

"Who the fuck are you?" he spat at her, even now his arrogance shone through.

"Me? Oh I'm no one but I'll deliver back to Bess nonetheless," she replied, hopping down from the saddle.

"Bess? The smith girl, what's her problem?"

Ha! Just like an Adventurer to see no issue with their actions. "I'll let her explain that, but for now you're coming with me."

"I don' fucking think so bitch." And as he said it he held his hand out to shoot magic at her.

For Ffion's part, she'd rather hoped he wouldn't come quietly; when Foresto had explained what the stone did, she had been desperate to test it out.

Anticipating the Adventurer's attack, she rolled to the side and activated the stone. Tarquin's body bowed backwards as pain streaked through it.

Foresto had crafted each of the items he'd made for the Adventurers so that they would sit somewhere close to the spine. In the case of the human, the tendrils of lightning sprang from a belt and lanced across his body to his extremities.

She was only sorry it lasted for so little time.

It was, however, time enough for her to take his weapons and set her own little magical item to work. She'd bought it years ago from a travelling merchant, having immediately seen the usefulness of such an item to one in her line of work.

As she sent it to wrap itself around Tarquin, her Identify spell, now so powerful that it was always active, kicked in and her eyes brushed over the information.

SELF-TYING ROPE - FINE, UNCOMMON

> PROPERTIES: WITH A SIMPLE COMMAND, THIS
> 50-FOOT LENGTH OF ROPE WILL WRAP ITSELF
> AROUND OR TIE ITSELF ONTO AN OBJECT, TY-
> ING A DEVILISHLY DIFFICULT KNOT.

When she'd still taken a more active role in the training of her mounts she'd used the item daily, but these days she mostly kept it around for sentimental reasons. When she'd dressed for battle today she'd thought to bring the item along.

It wasn't the only magical item she owned of course. Adventurers often had things to bargain with rather than coin, most of them she sold, but she'd kept a few, select items. She'd never let people know it but she could probably equip a whole party of Adventurers if she so chose.

Such considerations were for another time, however. Right now, she had a package to deliver and, remounting her hippogriff, she clicked her tongue and her command was instantly followed.

SARIEL

Even after everything she'd witnessed over the past few days, she was still amazed by the effect that Ninetoes' arrival had on the battle. She'd watched in awe as a fight that she had been convinced was lost, had suddenly become a rout.

As an adventurer, she recognised the power they could control, but she, like many others, had feared necromancy. And yet here, in their moment of despair, it had saved their lives.

Moreover, even after the way he'd been treated by the people he'd travelled with, he'd come.

But it was more than just winning. The behaviour of everyone, everything, involved had changed in that moment. The people of Raveslan had suddenly become more emboldened and the hobgoblins' morale had suffered the reverse.

Ninetoes' power was unmistakable and not a little bit frightening. For just a moment she considered running. Putting as much distance between herself and the incredible hobgoblin, but then, as she felt her own power grow as the experience from the battle flooded in, the feeling of fear passed and was replaced by one of reverence. She even joined the ragged cheer rising from the townsfolk but her eyes found the hobgoblin wizard and her chest swelled with wonderment.

"But... how?" Mera Fawkner stood nearby, wearing a stunned look that was mirrored on many of the other nearby faces the half-elf could see.

"I don't know," she answered honestly.

"It is the effect Adventurers have." The quiet voice of the gnomish mage surprised them both. "For good or ill, Adventurers shape the world around them."

"And what of him?" Mera asked quietly, nodding towards Ninetoes, who stood alone atop the gate, staring out after the retreating goblinoid army.

"That remains to be seen," he answered cryptically. "Sariel, if you have a moment, I'd like to give you your reward for helping to save Raveslan."

Sariel, whose arms hung at her side, feeling for all intents and purposes like two dead weights, just stared in surprise at the gnome. "Can't it wait?"

"Oh, you know what they say, "there's no time like the present", or do you have somewhere else to be?"

The Ranger, who's mind was even more tired than her body, couldn't muster an argument and so simply nodded and began climbing down the ladder to follow the gnome.

NINETOES

Little One! Libby bounded into his arms and he held her close to his chest. For long moments the two of them simply 'were'. Their minds exchanged the promise of enduring love. This was the first time in days that either of them had felt truly whole.

You're... you're so thin!

Ha! Oh Master, there is so much to tell you.

All of which can wait, Little One. Gods I don't know what I'd have done if I'd really lost you.

You have to tell me the story of how you killed that thing though Master. Libby said, gesturing to the manticore who sat nearby, staring vacantly in the freakish way that only the undead can.

Looking at the monster once more and then back at the people of Raveslan, he realised that much had changed since he'd left the town a week ago.

One thing hadn't changed, however, and that was, despite the part it had played in saving their home, the manticore would never be welcome in the town. And neither would certain other allies Ninetoes had recently made.

With a clarity that surprised even him, Ninetoes made a decision. *Ready for a quick flight, Little One?*

Really? I was kinda hoping just to sit and eat cheese for the rest of the day.

It won't take long.

And, so saying, he mounted Malice and within a quick command they were aloft. It didn't take long to find where he'd left Vortiga.

When he'd chased off the Offal Demon, he'd left Vortiga to deal with the swarm of minor ones, he was confident in her ability to deal death to the vicious little things, but he was glad to see her still alive as they landed near to the eastern gate.

It was with no small amount of concern, however, that he noticed her missing arm.

Is that the commander of the light company? Didn't we leave her in Pamor?

It's a long story Little One.

I'll bet.

"Hail Vortiga, what happened?"

The hobgoblin Warrior looked up but didn't speak straight away. She was clearly in pain and, by the pallor of her skin, it was clear she'd lost a lot of blood. Even more surprisingly, however, was that one of the town's guards stood next to her, binding what was left of her arm.

"This is Jenner, he saved my life."

"Hardly miss, you were just lucky they gave us a couple of potions to those of us on the eastern gate, else you'da bleed out."

Reaching into his reclaimed Bag of Holding, Ninetoes fished out a potion of healing and offered it to her. Vortiga didn't speak, instead simply offering a nod of thanks, before upending the vial and quaffing its contents. A little of the colour returned to Vortiga's cheeks and some of the pain left her face.

While Vortiga sat quietly, Ninetoes spoke up. "The battle is over. What's left of your people flee westwards."

"Hmmm, what's left of them?" The shame was evident in Vortiga's voice and Ninetoes could only pity her for the impossible choice she'd had to make.

"Perhaps a hundred escaped, but no one was in any fit state to count them." Vortiga didn't respond to that, so Ninetoes continued. "There's nothing I can do to ease your burden my friend, but perhaps I can offer you a means at least to catch up to your people or leave this place far behind." Ninetoes said, gesturing to the manticore.

Vortiga didn't speak at first and was clearly considering declining his offer. But then she straightened her shoulders and raised her chin.

Then, surprising everyone present, she grasped Ninetoes' wrist with her own and smiled. "Friend indeed."

Then, without any further discussion, Vortiga mounted Malice and the pair bounded away.

It was strange, he hadn't been sure if he could give total control of one of his undead to another creature. But then, as he'd considered it, he'd simply known that he could.

Ninetoes and Libby strolled back into town and, for once, the squirrel walked beside her Master, rather than atop his shoulder.

What do we do now Master?

Eat, sleep and then... who knows. I will tell you one thing though Little One, by the time we're done, Caillic would run out of wall before she ever finished telling our story.

Ninetoes will return in Rise of the Scourge Coven, Part Three of the Villain's Chronicle

ABOUT THE AUTHOR

Tim Andrews is a history teacher who has taught in various locations in the Midlands and South of England. Since becoming voluntarily incarcerated on the Isle of Wight ten years ago he has further immersed himself in the world of Fantasy Literature, board games and various role-playing genres.

Tim is happy to hear from readers and can be found on Facebook @peekay1982

Level Up publishing specialises in LitRPG and GameLit books. If you have enjoyed *Ninetoes 2: Reaper's Sorrow*, you might be interested in our other titles, which can be found at www.levelup.pub/books

To join our mailing list for news about forthcoming books and opportunities to be an ARC reader, just fill in the form on that page.

You can also find us on:
Facebook @LUPublishing
Twitter @LevelUpPub

... and by searching for Level Up WhatsApp group